The Tsar's Masquerade

A Novel

Raphael Mercikovsky

Raphael Mercikovsky AKA MFC

Copyright © 2009 by Raphael Mercikovsky

ISBN 978-0-7414-5273-3
Library of Congress Control Number: 2012942509

Printed in the United States of America

Published January 2013

INFINITY PUBLISHING
1094 New DeHaven Street, Suite 100
West Conshohocken, PA 19428-2713
Toll-free (877) BUY BOOK
Local Phone (610) 941-9999
Fax (610) 941-9959
Info@buybooksontheweb.com
www.buybooksontheweb.com

Author's Note

It seemed appropriate to collectively acknowledge the various contributions of the collaborators by joining them together under the pen name, *Raphael Mercikovsky*. They without exception, exhibited a fascination with this period of history and made every effort to make the events in this work of fiction reflect historical reality, or at least the possibility of it.

The authors conducted extensive telephone and internet interviews with knowledgeable individuals all over the world. As each new piece of information was developed it was analyzed for inclusion in the narrative. The project was exciting and rewarding and *The Tsar's Masquerade* is the result.

Titles and nicknames have been used interchangeably. For example the Empress Alexandra may be referred to as Alix, Sunny, Tsarina, Tsaritsa or Your Imperial Highness. To the children she was Mama or Mother.

The members of the Imperial family and their retainers, as well as other characters in this novel move about frequently, so each chapter is sub-headed with the approximate date and location wherein the events in the chapter begin. Chapter One introduces many of the characters who will play a role in the *Masquerade* and at first the various titles and positions at court may seem somewhat bewildering. However, the reader will quickly become familiar with the players as the story unfolds.

Raphael Mercikovsky

This work is not just about Nicholas and Alexandra, the last Tsar and Tsarina of Russia. The novel also lifts the Grand Duchesses out of the shadowy pages of history books, gives them personalities, and chronicles their development from children into mature young women. Alexei, the heir, is not overlooked nor are the heroes, Count Paul Benckendorff, and his stepson Valia. The readers will be introduced to everyone in the *Masquerade* and can then make their own judgments as to whether the Tsar was successful in his plan to save Russia.

The author has provided the reader a different look at the character of the Tsar and the mercurial behavior of his beloved wife. It is in essence a love story, plain and simple, but not the kind one would expect to find in a typical romance novel. It focuses rather on the overwhelming love Nicholas had for his family and his country and the measures he was willing to take to protect these two great loves. To delve into the character of the man it is necessary to understand the way in which mystical experiences affected his decisions and to accept the fact that the Tsar was a man of faith. Once he made up his mind on a course of action Nicholas became a driven man and no obstacle seemed too great to be overcome.

In March 1917 the first of two revolutions which occurred in Russia that year, led to the abdication of Tsar Nicholas II and the end of the three hundred year rule of the Romanov dynasty. In the vast body of literature which describes this collapse there is a tendency to portray Nicholas as a weak and vacillating individual who was easily influenced by his wife, the Empress Alexandra, and her spiritual advisor, the notorious Grigory Rasputin. The Tsar's indecisiveness and lack of concern, it is suggested, contributed directly to the overthrow of the monarchy and created the political climate that enabled the Bolsheviks to seize power later that year.

One might have assumed that, under the secretive Soviet government, any documents relating to the chaotic events following the takeover would be destroyed. Surprisingly, just the opposite is the case and numerous records, hidden away for decades, have begun to appear. The diaries, letters, notes, police reports, and a variety of other papers that relate to the period have encouraged a new round of examination, analysis and speculation. Conspiracy theories abound and there does not seem to be a consensus as to what really happened in the early days of the Soviet era. This story provides the answer to the dilemma.

Part One

Serafim's Letter

Prologue

July 1833 – Sarov. A message from the monastery had summoned Elena Motivilov to the bedside of the old priest, the man who had become her confessor, and subsequently her dear friend. Although the surroundings were familiar she approached the dying monk with some trepidation. In the nearly dark room she could barely make out his emaciated body as it lay on a wooden pallet, his long gray hair and beard matted and unkempt. She shivered from the cold dampness emanating from the floor and the aura of death in the air.

Father Serafim smiled up at her as she approached his resting place and the warm smile put her instantly at ease. He grasped her arm with one hand, gazed at her with tenderness, and with the other pressed a letter into her hands.

"My child I am entrusting you with a mission of great importance," he said. "You must deliver this letter to the Tsar when he visits Sarov. Elena, you will be an old woman before the opportunity presents its self so hide it well and tell no one. One day there will be a great celebration honoring me and this is how you will know the time is right. God be with you." Elena slid the letter into her dress, dropped to her knees, and pressed his hand to her cheek. Then she picked up the cross resting on his chest, kissed it and said, "Father Serafim, your trust is well placed. I will not fail you."

Aware that the exchange had fatigued the old priest the young girl made her way out of his cell and pushed through the throng of people filling the hallway. As she exited the monastery she was amazed at the size of the crowd that had gathered. People had traveled from all parts of Russia to beg Father Serafim for his prayers and his cures. Truly he is a great saint she thought to herself as she looked at the faces of the pilgrims, and it was evident from their grief that they all knew their saint was on his deathbed.

Once away from the crowd, she pulled out the letter and glanced at it. It was addressed *To the Tsar in whose reign I shall be glorified*, and was covered with five red seals. Pressed into the wax of four of the seals were the initials OTMA. Thankful that Father Serafim had taught her to read Elena went home and hid the letter. It would remain in its hiding place for seventy years.

Chapter 1

January 1903 - St. Petersburg. Stars twinkled brightly in the clear, cold night like thousands of diamonds strewn across the sky. In the frigid air the horses trotted briskly, their breath creating a foggy mist as they pulled sleighs carrying Imperial Russia's upper class to the Winter Ball. The coachmen slowed upon reaching Millionnaya Street and joined a long file of troikas that inched its way towards the Winter Palace. The occupants were unable to conceal their excitement and anticipation as they waited their turn to disembark. This ball was the most important social event of the St. Petersburg winter season and guests had prepared their costumes months in advance. Magnificent family jewels, furs, and fabrics were pulled from wardrobes and chests as members of the city's social elite vied among themselves to produce one of the most splendid spectacles ever seen at the Winter Palace.

In the White Drawing Room of the family quarters Tsar Nicholas II paced impatiently as he awaited the arrival of his wife, Tsarina Alexandra Feodorovna. Close friends and family members knew them as Nicky and Alix and most of the Imperial family members were known by one pet name or another. He heard a rustle behind him and turned towards the door. There stood his darling Sunny, a breathtaking vision in gold and silver.

"My darling, you look absolutely stunning," he said.

Alix smiled at the compliment. She usually hated these functions but tonight was different. This was her ball and she planned it down to the last exacting detail with all the meticulous creativity she was known for. Alix developed the theme for this historical masquerade ball from Nicky's frequently expressed admiration of the 17th century Tsar, Alexei. The director of the Hermitage Museum helped her achieve accuracy in her costume designs and to decorate the palace she had sent to the Crimea for trainloads of flowers that were unavailable in the harsh winter of the north. The flowers had arrived only yesterday so it had definitely been a stressful day, but now everything was in place. It should be an evening to remember.

Nicky extended his arm and they made their way to the Silver Drawing Room where the relatives awaited them. The family had gathered there to prepare for their entrance into the public rooms where the guests were eagerly anticipating their arrival. As usual Alix fumed inside as the Dowager Empress Marie Feodorovna, Nicky's mother, took her place by his side. Court tradition gave her precedence over Alix, and Minnie, as she was called, took full advantage of the opportunity to remind Alix of her proper place. There was no love lost between the two but they managed to remain civil with one another, especially in public. Nicky's brother Misha, the Grand Duke Mikhail Alexandrovich, and heir to the throne, turned to Alix, smiled at her, and offered his arm.

On signal the doors swung open and a voice began to intone the many titles of Nicholas, Tsar of Russia. Nicky and Minnie made their formal entrance into the ballroom followed by Alix and Misha. Behind them was arrayed the rest of the extended family, all in proper precedence, a multitude of Grand Dukes and Duchesses appropriately dressed in period costumes.

When the royal party entered the receiving area the room became very quiet as the guests took in the magnificence of the costumes worn by the Imperial couple. Although Nicky's short stature did not do justice to his costume, he still looked impressive. He was dressed as Tsar Alexei, in a robe of raspberry and white with gold embroidery. His headdress and staff were authentic items from the period. They had been brought from the Granovitaya Palace in Moscow for the occasion.

Alix had dressed as Marie, wife of Alexei and wore a recreation of a 17th century gown. It was made of gold brocade and embroidered with silver metallic thread. Diamonds, pearls and emeralds were sewn to the surface and formed a floral pattern. Strips of silver brocade and pearls trimmed the sleeves, hem and center of the gown. Her headdress was a scarf of fine white linen and atop the scarf a crown, crafted by Carl Faberge, adorned her head. He had also prepared a stunning necklace of old design with the center stone a magnificent 159-carat sapphire, an extravagant jewel, even by Romanov standards. Her earrings were so heavy that gold wire was used to attach them to her ears.

A signal was given and waiters began to circulate with trays of zakuski, a hors d'oeuvre, and an assortment of vodkas. The guests enjoyed the small repast before moving into the Hermitage Theater for the evening's entertainment. Seating was again dictated by protocol and servants were on hand to direct them to the six semi-circular rows of benches that descended to the stage. A balustrade separated the invited guests from the Imperial family's box.

Everyone remained standing until Nicky and the royal party was seated. Alix had selected tonight's program with care and she was sure everyone would enjoy the concert. The revered Feodor Chaliapin, a well-known opera star, was to sing a selection, accompanied by the St. Petersburg Symphony. Other noted musicians and the famed ballerina Anna Pavlova were also to perform. Soothing music soon filled the room and Alexandra felt herself begin to relax. She was uncomfortable at formal occasions such as this because she felt very awkward and as a result was extremely shy. Unfortunately this shyness was misinterpreted as arrogance and many, unfairly to be sure, thought the Tsarina to be haughty and unapproachable. Russian was really her third language and she often broke out in red blotches as she attempted to stammer through a conversation. The Russian court was extremely sophisticated, filled with intrigue, and had only reluctantly accepted the German princess as their Empress. Alix had grown up very simply and was not skilled in the perilous games played out of sight of the common people. Nicky was aware of the situation but could do very little to influence the court atmosphere. Alix had been in Russia for nine years and was still treated as a newcomer and she found it difficult to be around people who so obviously disliked her. However, she was not devoid of weapons and there was one card she could play which could never be trumped. Nicky loved her without reservation and as a result Alix could influence him, and more importantly, his decisions.

Once the concert ended everyone stood while the Tsar and his family arrayed themselves in front of the guests. The court photographer fussed about them, arranging and re-arranging, rushing back to the camera to check the framing, then back to the family until everything was to his satisfaction. After the official photographs were completed, many of the guests took advantage of the atmosphere to have individual snapshots taken.

The royal family and guests then adjourned to the large Skylight Room for dinner. The enormous room had been transformed into a garden by the skillful arrangement of the Crimean plants and flowers. Camellias, crepe myrtles, and roses of every hue adorned the hall in elaborate groupings while palms and other potted trees were scattered among the flowers to form a forest of color. A dome of greenery was made into a canopy over each of the round tables, which were covered with crisp white linen tablecloths embroidered with the Imperial monogram. The tables were set for ten and a selected few had places for eleven. Nicky liked to mingle and converse with his guests and at the end of each course he would join a new group throughout the meal. Alix hated being left at the head table without him so he always spent the first and last course with her.

Tonight's dinner was a true culinary masterpiece. Nicky and Alix enjoyed the meal with Minnie and Misha. Grand Duke Sandro and his wife Grand Duchess Xenia, Nicky's sister, were also at their table. The first course was rich, creamy oyster bisque.

"I wish this headpiece had arrived at the palace sooner," whispered Alix to Nicky. "I would have sent it back to have it altered."

"But you look radiant my precious, everyone says so,"

"You know they just say that because I am the Tsarina of all Russia. "

"You underestimate how marvelous you look this evening, Tsarina of all Russia."

Alix struggled to eat. She knew if she bent her head down the heavy Faberge crown would end up in her soup bowl. She tried not to attract attention but Nicky, always aware of her discomforts, noticed and laughed.

"This headpiece is so heavy I cannot put my head down to eat. I imagine I shall starve," she complained.

"Shall I feed you this bread, my dear?"

"No you may not. The Empress of all Russia cannot be fed like a child. "

Nicky chuckled and Alix responded with a laugh of her own. Nothing was going to spoil this wonderful occasion.

"I did not much care for the soup anyway" said Alix. "When you join Ella's table, you must let her tell you about her trip to Rome. It is quite interesting."

"Will you be all right without me, Sunny?"

"I shall try to manage," responded Alix with a smile.

The Tsar set his spoon down signaling the end of the course. Waiters clad in ceremonial red livery with white pantaloons and silk stockings began to remove the soup bowls and Nicky excused himself to join the next table.

"Good evening my friends," Nicholas said as everyone at the table rose to greet him. "Are you all enjoying yourselves?" A waiter placed a serving of Salmon Imperiale in front of him. The delicate fillets were wrapped in bacon and stuffed with truffles and covered with a white wine cream sauce dotted with sparkling beads of caviar.

"Her Imperial Highness has done a wonderful job. It is truly like a fairy tale," said Grand Duchess Marie Pavlovna. Everyone at the table nodded with agreement.

"I really enjoyed the ballet," continued Marie. "I noticed a new dancer."

"That is Anna Pavlova. I believe she just joined the Russian Imperial Ballet last year. Isn't she splendid?" asked The Emperor. Everyone agreed she was a wonderful addition to the company.

"She reminds me of that Kshessinskaya," added Grand Duke Nicolai Nicolaivitch, with a smile on his face. The Grand Duke was the Tsar's uncle and everyone referred to him as Nikolasha.

"Let us not go down that road again uncle," said Nicholas with a laugh. The ballerina Kshessinskaya had been an indiscretion of his youth. He had fond memories of her but no wish to rehash old times. He finished the course and was anxious to move on to the next table where the Grand Duke Sergei Alexandrovich and his wife Grand Duchess Elizaveta Fedorovna sat. He always enjoyed conversations with Sergei and Ella, as Elizaveta was familiarly called. Sergei was very witty and Ella, a famed beauty of the court, and Alix's sister, was also a wonderful conversationalist.

Again everyone rose when he reached the table. He greeted them and sat down. When the waiters brought the next course of Poularde with tarragon he realized Alix had spared no expense. The exquisite fattened chickens from France, with stuffed cucumbers and white tarragon sauce, were a very costly entrée and a rare delicacy. It was one of his favorites.

He could not wait to hear about Ella's trip and immediately brought up the subject. "The Empress said to be sure to tell me all about your trip to Rome."

"Oh yes, it was quite wonderful. You know Sergei had gone there as a child. We have become quite good friends with the Pope," Ella replied. "We were granted a private audience and he spent some time with us."

"He did not talk you into becoming a Catholic?" teased Nicky.

"No! He knows quite well we are strong in our Orthodox faith. However, we did have a long discussion about the differences between our two Churches," said Ella. "More importantly the Pope said he had a message for you and that I was to present it to you in front of many witnesses. He said that I should tell you in these words. *When the sun falls from the sky you will know the fate of Russia.*" There was an uncomfortable silence at the table and everyone looked quite puzzled.

"Sergei, did I quote the Pope accurately?" asked Ella.

"It is what he said, and I find it quite bizarre," added Sergei.

The Tsar knew that there was something very significant about that statement but he could see that Ella was very uneasy at burdening him with this now. He decided not to pursue the matter at this time and with a quick change of subject he said "certainly you have all heard about the canonization of the Holy Monk Serafim. I am overjoyed that it is coming to pass so soon. Alix has arranged for my self and several of the Grand Dukes to carry the relics from the monastery to the new shrine," said Nicholas.

"I know that the monk would never have guessed that one day he would be carried on the shoulders of his Imperial Highness, the Tsar of all Russia," said Sergei.

Nicky smiled and said, "I believe in my heart that he knew."

Nicky became ill at ease when he moved on to the next table. He knew the daughters of King Nicholas I of Montenegro, the Grand Duchesses Militsa and Stana, were seated there. Militsa was married to Grand Duke Peter Nikolaievitch, a cousin of the Tsar. Her sister Stana, however, was divorced and was involved in a rather discreet dalliance with Nikolasha. The Tsar ignored the affair and looked the other way because he admired the man and depended on him. The two sisters were known throughout St. Petersburg as the "Black Plague" because of their fascination with black magic, the supernatural and other forbidden forms of mysticism. The two were always trying to bring hypnotists and fortune tellers to court. Nicholas was opposed to it all but he appeased his wife by accompanying her to various meetings with the sisters. He knew that Alix would go with or without him so he attended to keep an eye on her, aware that she was easily influenced by new and exotic ideas. As he sat down, the sisters were already discussing a new form of the occult they had come across.

"It is quite amazing," said Militsa.

"Well, what does it do?" inquired one of the guests.

"It tells your fortune without having to pay a fortune teller," explained Militsa. "It is a board and you place your hands on it and it moves around and across these letters that will spell out all kinds of things." Nicky thought Militsa had provided a somewhat imprecise description of its powers but rather than get involved in the discussion he sat quietly eating his food. He knew from experience that this would be the only topic of conversation at the table and he ate quickly so he could bid farewell to the group. But before he could finish Stana intervened.

"Your majesty, you should think about getting one for the girls. They would have so much fun with it. I am sure her Imperial Highness would approve."

"I think my children are much too young for amusements such as that," said Nicky.

"Well, maybe not now but certainly when they get a little older," said Stana.

Here they go again, Nicky thought to himself. As if my wife is not enough for them, now they want my children. "We shall see ladies," said the Tsar, trying to maintain his equanimity. He looked down and realized that he had placed his silverware on his plate, the signal for the servants to clear the table for the next course and for him to leave. Perfect timing, he thought. The rest of the evening was a blur for Nicky. Course followed course and there was the usual chit chat as he moved from table to table. He had to admit that the beef tenderloin medallions garnished with slices of foie gras and asparagus were a standout. The meat was so tender that it melted in his mouth.

Nicky finally returned to Alix for the dessert course. He really did not desire anything else and was quite satiated from all the delicacies, but when he finished eating, the meal was officially ended, so he had the waiters serve him liberally from the trays of chocolates, cakes, and fresh fruits. He wanted to make sure his guests had ample time to enjoy the glorious end to this culinary delight. As he sipped his favorite French champagne he lovingly caressed Alix's hand under the table. "This will be the talk of St. Petersburg for sometime to come, my love. You have outdone yourself but I would have expected no less. Everyone is having a glorious evening."

"I am so pleased that our guests are having such a wonderful time," Alix said. "I just hope I can make it through the Polonaise. I can assure you that it will be the only time you will see me on the dance floor."

The Pavilion Hall was the setting for tonight's dancing and it was a truly breathtaking room. White marble columns formed arches that adorned the hall and supported a graceful upstairs gallery. Gilded stucco ornamented the room and the twenty-eight crystal chandeliers glittered and winked. The alcove leading to the staircase was decorated with four bubbling marble fountains surrounded by greenery and forming an oasis within the ballroom. The ball opened with the traditional polonaise and as the first chords of the composition were heard Nicky escorted Minnie and Misha led Alix out onto the floor. They promenaded around the room as they completed this obligatory ceremonial dance. Alix was about to pass out from the weight of her costume so when the dance ended she found her place quickly and sat out the rest of the ball. Nicky, always conscious of his duty, began to dance with the ladies of the court who vied for his attention. Waltzes and quadrilles were danced in rapid succession.

Suddenly the tempo of the music changed. Twenty young cavaliers began to beat time to the music with the soles of their boots and on signal, a like number of young girls, in the first blush of womanhood, rushed into their arms to begin the Russian Dance. The mazurka was a lively military and national dance requiring great skill. The couples rehearsed for months, all the mothers attending and even Alix had looked in on the rehearsals once or twice. As the music became more animated the couples flung themselves across the room. The orchestra finally reached a crescendo and the cavaliers fell on their knees in front of their nearly exhausted partners. The hall erupted in applause.

The dancing continued for hours and, as it progressed, famous Petersburg beauties flirted and intrigued behind their feathered fans. Grand old dames gossiped and reminisced about their youth and their experiences in this very hall. They made up for their faded beauty with opulent clothes and magnificent jewels. Dignified old men, who had served the Tsar's father, quietly discussed the issues of the day especially the worker's strikes, the various demonstrations, and the more and more frequent assassination attempts on members of the royal family and the government. The younger dandies, bored by any serious talk and conscious only of their own self-importance, competed for the attention of the ladies.

Alix was certainly one of the loveliest ladies present that evening but even her beauty paled in comparison to that of her sister Ella. The title of most lovely was a difficult choice between Ella and Princess Zenaide Yusupov. Zenaide was well known for her beauty and her slender build, dark hair and blue eyes were enhanced by her pale complexion. She was also one of the richest women in Russia and her jewels were stunning.

As the night slipped into the morning hours, Nicholas returned to Alexandra and signaled the formal ending of the ball by escorting her from the room. After what seemed an interminable walk, they finally reached their bedroom. Wishing for some privacy, they dismissed the waiting servants. Unlike most wealthy couples of the day, Nicky and

Alex shared a bedroom. Theirs was truly a love match and they cherished their private time with each other.

Alix sat down with a sigh, "Nicky release me from this torture," said Alix as she struggled with the crown on her head. I cannot take another minute of this agony."

Nicky struggled with the pins holding the crown in place and finally removed it from her head. "My poor dear, this weighs a ton. Let me ease your pain." Alix sighed with relief as he massaged her temples and neck.

"Wasn't it a glorious evening?" she asked.

"It was truly a stunning achievement, my darling and you were easily the most beautiful woman present."

"Thank you but I think Ella was truly lovely tonight," Alix said. "She certainly looked like a 17th century princess.

"Nicky will you pray with me?" she suddenly asked.

"Certainly my dear. What do you pray for?"

"You know, my dearest. I want a son and I pray that our trip to Father Serafim's canonization will be successful and our prayers for an heir will be answered." Nicky and Alix dropped to their knees in front of the icons on the wall and prayed together for their special intention.

After Alix drifted off, Nicky lay there staring at the canopy of the bed, unable to fall asleep. He kept thinking about the Pope's message, which Ella had passed on to him at the dinner table. It was quite troubling and very mysterious. Why did it have to be delivered in front of witnesses? And what of the prediction *"When the sun falls from the sky you will know the fate of Russia?"* The implication seemed clear enough. Russia was headed for some catastrophe, but when would it occur, what form would it take and why did the warning come from the Pope? He would have to discuss this message with Ella in more detail. Perhaps the context in which it was given would provide a clue to its meaning. Eternal optimist that he was, Nicky was sure everything would work out for the best. Comforted by this thought he finally fell asleep.

Chapter 2

July 1903 – Sarov. The weight of the young boy in the man's arms forced him to move carefully as he made his way down the dimly lit stairway. The woman followed with the four girls and though their faces were obscured in the dim light he was innately aware of the identity of each of them. As they entered the room at the bottom of the stairs a sense of foreboding overwhelmed him. Except for two chairs at the far end, the room was empty. Like a magnet he was inexorably drawn to one of the chairs and he sat in it without waking the boy who, by now, had fallen back asleep. The woman sat in the other chair and the girls stood behind. They waited patiently in the unnerving silence.

Eventually the sound of boots on the stairs could be heard and the door burst open to admit a group of unwashed, foul-smelling men who filed in and stood before them. The leader walked forward, bent over the man in the chair, whispered something to him in a gruff voice, and then strode back to join his men. At his command they produced revolvers from beneath their coats and opened fire on the small group at the far end of the room. In the enclosed space the sound of gunfire was deafening and smoke began to cloud the room. A heavy caliber bullet ripped through the boy and into the man in the chair and the intense pain caused him to loosen his grip and drop the boy to the floor. The hysterical cries of the girls slowly subsided as one by one they fell to the rough pavement, their youthful bodies torn and covered with blood. As the smoke began to clear he became aware that the leader was standing over him, brandishing a bayonet and preparing to finish the bloody task.

Nicholas Romanov, Tsar of all the Russias, awoke with a start, his body dripping with perspiration and shaking violently. He rolled out of the bed and slowly gained control of his emotions. It was the same dream he had experienced before but never had it been so vivid or seemed so very, very real.

Alix awoke a short time later in the Imperial bedroom at Alexander Palace to find Nicky agitated and pacing the floor. She had been so deeply asleep that his tossing and turning had failed to waken her.

"Was it the dream again?"

"Yes," he replied, "but much worse."

She could only imagine what he was going through. It was always difficult to understand the psychological trauma another person experienced in an inexplicable dream and Nicky's seemed to be recurring more frequently. She rose from the bed, knelt at her predieu, and began her morning prayers, drawing comfort from the many icons on the walls. The holy images, several of great age, kept her religious and spiritual heritage close at hand and they remained undisturbed even though Nicky thought the room looked like a funeral parlor. Nevertheless, the atmosphere in the smaller Alexander Palace in Tsarskoe Selo, outside of St. Petersburg, was more comfortable and less oppressive than that in the massive Catherine Palace a short distance away and was the main reason Alix had insisted on living there.

She tried to concentrate on her prayers, but was caught up in the excitement of the planned return to Sarov. Nearly a year ago she had made a pilgrimage to the town and visited the shrine of Serafim, a saintly monk, and hermit. In her heart she knew he was the answer to all her prayers and she believed, as only a person of great faith can, that Father Serafim would intercede with God, and that her prayers for a son would finally be heard.

Alix had been determined to see the holy man canonized and declared a saint and the Tsarina had steadfastly refused to be swayed by resistance from the Holy Synod. Everyone underestimated the relationship she had with the Tsar and she was able to influence the process despite the objections of the senior churchmen. She smiled as she recalled her response to the Orthodox Church's representatives. "Everything is within the Tsar's power," she had said at the time, "even to the making of saints." Although she had earned the enmity of some of the churchmen it was all worth it. In a few days time, Father Serafim of Sarov would be canonized a saint and declared Protector of the Tsar's family and God willing, she thought, my prayers will be answered and I will be granted a son. The church had ultimately relented and now, in the town of Sarov, the holy priest was to be declared a saint, in a ceremony that was drawing pilgrims from all over Russia.

ᘓᔒ

There was a palpable excitement in the air as Elena Motivilov made her way home, her body slowed by the arthritis that wracked her frail form. News had been received that the Tsar was definitely coming to the town of Sarov and Elena was in a mild state of shock. The previous year the Tsarina Alexandra had visited Sarov and Elena had been disappointed nearly to the point of despair when she learned that Tsar Nicholas would not be accompanying his wife. Now, with word of the Tsar's expected visit, she was filled with a feeling of exhilaration so intense that it nearly took her breath away. She finally reached the path to the weathered cottage that had been her home for so many years, made her way to the door, entered, and walked purposefully to a carved wooden box on the side board. Elena was ninety years old and had waited nearly seventy of those years to complete a task she had been entrusted with long ago. Now, at last, it appeared that the Tsar himself would actually be coming and she could fulfill a promise made so long ago. She ignored the clucking of the chickens calling to be fed and, in the dim light, unlocked the box with a key she always wore around her neck. The opened box revealed a yellowed letter given to her in 1833, when she was a young woman of twenty, and safeguarded these many years. Despite her physical infirmities Elena's mind was as sharp as it had ever been and she recalled the events surrounding her receipt of the letter as if they had happened yesterday. Now the time had finally come, and she looked at the letter with an overwhelming sense of relief. Elena returned the letter to its hiding place, locked the box, and placed it back on the shelf knowing that in the next few days she would finally complete the task Father Serafim had entrusted her with and that the burden of her secret would, at last, be lifted from her stooped and tired shoulders.

୯୫୭

The process of moving the Imperial household was a logistical nightmare but eventually everything was sorted out and Nicky, Alix and others of the family left Tsarskoe Selo to begin the long journey to Sarov. The duties of his office had prevented Nicky from accompanying Alix the previous year so this was to be his first trip to Sarov. Many of the family members were attending the ceremony at the urging of Alix but Sergei and Ella had their own special reason for making the long trip. Although Ella was an exquisitely beautiful woman there was an aura of sadness surrounding her that was attributed to her inability to bear children. Ella was going to Sarov to pray at the shrine and beg for a child just as Alix intended to do.

The closest stop to Sarov was located at Arzamas and the Imperial train pulled into the station at eleven o'clock on July 17, 1903 to an impressive welcome from a large crowd of fellow pilgrims. Nicholas and Alexandra climbed out on the platform and were greeted by the local nobility and town officials. The local women were clothed in dresses of brilliantly colored silks and elaborate brocades, their heads covered with gaily decorated scarves pinned under their chins. The men were quaintly dapper in their old-fashioned top hats and long coats worn, despite the heat, in honor of the day. The peasants were clothed in their best, in anticipation of the ceremonies to come. After a short ceremony, the royal party got into carriages and set off for Sarov. The other pilgrims would have to make the lengthy journey on foot.

It was a hot and dusty ride but everyone was in high spirits, even the thousands who faced the long walk in their thick clothes and heavy shoes. Sarov had grown in size in the seventy years since Father Serafim had gone to his eternal reward but even so the town would be overwhelmed by the sheer number of pilgrims arriving from all over the empire. There were literally thousands of peasants, some from as far away as Siberia, traveling on foot and hurrying to arrive in time for the glorification of the saintly Serafim. Whole families made their way through the dusty, brown film rising from the road, perspiring in the exhausting heat but holding icons high and singing religious songs.

Despite the heat, the countryside was beautiful and allowed the royal family a glimpse of a Russia they rarely saw in their isolation at the palace. The pomp and protocol of the court and the watchful eyes of the secret police normally kept them from contact with common people but today, with only a small Cossack escort to protect them, Nicky and the children reveled in the adulation of the crowds. At each village along the way they were greeted by the locals in their traditional dress and everyone stepped down from the open carriages to receive a blessing from the village priest. Adoring throngs of pilgrims surrounded them and cried out "Batushka" (Little Father) and struggled to kiss his hand or the hem of his clothes. Alexandra personally passed out holy cards with the image of St. Nicholas, as it was her custom to do, and the crowds pressed forward to receive these tokens.

As they returned to the carriage after one of the many stops, Nicky looked at Alix, gently placed her hand over his heart and whispered, "My darling, precious Sunny, on this most special blessed day I pray for you and not for myself. May all your hopes and prayers be answered."

"Oh Nicky, I have so many petitions but if only one is to be answered let it be that we are blessed with a son."

"Have faith my dearest. As the Angel Gabriel told Mary, nothing is impossible with God."

He winked at her and they both smiled. Nicky helped her back into the carriage, climbed in and waved one last time to the crowd before he sat back to continue the journey to Sarov.

It was after six o'clock in the evening before the entourage arrived at the monastery, where quarters had been prepared for the immediate family. Other members of the party were housed with local dignitaries and noblemen but most of the pilgrims would be forced to spend the nights in the open fields around the town. The ceremonies marking the glorification of Saint Serafim were expected to last for three days and Alix anticipated remaining for the entire period. After arriving in Sarov they immediately went into the monastery church to pray at the site of the shrine containing the relics of the beloved Serafim. Later Nicky and Alix joined Minnie and the rest of the family for dinner. Everyone was elated by the reception the Tsar had received but even more inspiring was the devotion and reverence they had seen manifested by the pilgrims flocking to Sarov. Conversation at the table was subdued as each one dwelt on the reason they had come. Later that evening, the Imperial couple made their confessions to one of the monks from the monastery in the very cell occupied by Serafim so many years ago. They went to bed feeling content and not at all tired by the long journey.

The next day was as hot and muggy as its predecessor but nothing could interfere with the sense of anticipation that infected the thousands of worshippers gathering in the area. Nicky and Alix spent the morning visiting churches and other sights in Sarov and as they walked the streets the crowds pressed in on them. At one point his officers had to hoist the Tsar onto their shoulders so everyone could see him, most for the first time. In the afternoon heat, Nicky, Sergei and the cousins set off for the hermitage on foot but since it was quite a distance Alix, Minnie and the other ladies went by carriage. The path to the hermit's caves meandered through the woods and the overhanging trees provided cooling relief from the hot sun. They stayed on late into the afternoon, glad of the respite from the dust and heat.

After the day of sightseeing and family visits, Nicky and Alix began their preparations for the evening's ceremony. Alix had spent much thought on her clothes for this evening. She wanted to look the regal empress but also the devout pilgrim so she finally decided on a simple dress of lilac cloth. She wore a hat trimmed with feathers and kept her jewelry simple with her trademark long strands of pearls and earrings of single, perfectly matched pearls. Nicky wore a uniform of summer whites, which accentuated his dark coloring and gave him a dashing look. However, he made the uniform as simple as possible by limiting the number of decorations on his tunic. After all, the ceremony was about Serafim and not the Tsar. As they departed for the abbey, Nicky repeated his comment of a day earlier.

"My prayer is that you find what you are searching for my dear. I hope all your prayers are answered."

The procession began with young altar boys dressed in red robes trimmed with gold and lined up two by two. Church leaders and the local priests followed with the icon of Father Serafim. The bones of the saint were in a solid silver reliquary, which Alix had commissioned. The reliquary was then placed in a highly polished mahogany coffin with hardware and clasps made of pure gold. The coffin sat on a platform covered with velvet and looped with ropes of red and gold. Alix had insisted the family have a role in the glorification ceremony. She looked on with pride as Nicky, Sergei and other family members, six to a side, shouldered the platform and joined the procession. Two long lines of monks followed behind. The procession made its way from the monastery church to the new shrine with its golden dome gleaming in the late afternoon sun. The magnificent chapel, located in the town, had been subscribed to by a number of Russian nobles and Nicky, with his great wealth had paid for the balance of the construction.

The route to the recently completed white church was lined with thousands of devout pilgrims. The peasants dropped bits of fabric and thread in front of the procession to be gathered up later as precious tokens of a holy saint. The crowd was generally silent but as the faithful recognized the Tsar helping to bear the relics they became enthusiastic and the procession took on a festive air despite the solemnity of the occasion.

The high Mass was celebrated with the utmost reverence by the Metropolitan Antony of St. Petersburg. The bishops of Kazan and Tambov and other prelates concelebrated, the intricate gold embroidery on their robes glittering in the candlelight. Incense filled the air and its smoky sweetness tickled the nose. The church was packed to capacity and the heat in the building was stifling. Because members of the Russian Orthodox Church did not sit during a service Nicky glanced at Alix, concerned that she might become faint. He need not have worried. Her face glowed in the soft candlelight and he had never seen her look so lovely. She turned to him and smiled, nearly overcome by emotion as the cathedral bells rang out and voices of the choir intoned the antiphon:

We magnify thee

Holy blessed Serafim,

We honor thy holy memory

And we ask thee to pray for us

To Christ, our God.

At one point during the long liturgy the crippled, the ill and those with emotional problems were invited forward to be blessed with relics of the saint. A number of miraculous cures took place, so many in fact, that Alix was encouraged to hope that her own petition would be granted by God through the intercession of St. Serafim.

When Nicky returned from the reception of Holy Communion to his place in the congregation he was distracted by movement in the crowd of worshippers. An elderly woman was painstakingly moving down the aisle, her face etched with determination. Something about her drew his attention and he was mesmerized and unable to turn away. As she approached him, she withdrew a letter from under her shawl and pressed it into his hands. He quickly tucked the letter into his jacket at the same time wondering at the impulse that caused him to hide it. When Nicky glanced up the woman had disappeared into the crowd.

As dusk faded to dark the ceremony of glorification finally reached its conclusion and Alix grasped his arm as they made their way from the church. He asked one of the attendees about the old woman. "It was Elena Motovilov," she replied. "She is one of a few still alive that knew our precious saint."

It was completely dark when they departed the shrine and as they emerged they gasped in amazement. The 300,000 pilgrims overflowed the grounds surrounding the shrine and stretched into the distance, each one holding a candle that flickered in the warm night breeze. Voices raised in song filled the air as if from heaven above. It was a profoundly moving experience and left a deep mark on all who were present. Nicky felt an enormous lift, both from the event itself and the extraordinary mood of the crowd.

Nicky and Alix awoke early the next morning. They had long planned to visit some of the inhabitants who had known Saint Serafim and Elena Motovilov had been mentioned as one of the few that remained. As they prepared to leave for her cottage Nicky remember the letter. He picked up his tunic, worn the night before, and withdrew the letter he had placed there. Caught up in the events of the previous evening he had totally forgotten it but now he examined the letter with some curiosity. It was yellow with age and the five red seals were dry and cracked but he could still make out the letters OTMA in four of them. The letter was addressed *"To the Tsar in whose reign I shall be glorified."* Realizing that this was no coincidence he opened the letter with trembling hands and began to read. When he had finished his face turned a ghostly white and he dropped the letter and began to weep. Alix retrieved the fallen letter, put her arms around the Tsar's shoulders and read it quickly. She too was overcome with emotion as she read the words Father Serafim had written seventy years earlier:

My son, give thanks to the Lord God who in his ineffable mercy has revealed to me that a great and calamitous evil shall befall Russia. War and famine will turn the people from God. Russia will be lost, drowning in sorrow in an abyss from which there seems no hope of rescue.

You, Nicholas, must sacrifice yourself and become a martyr. As the Lord said to his disciples, "If ye were of the world, the world would love its own, but because I chose you out of the world, therefore the world hateth you." My son be of good cheer, for from your royal line our Lord will bring forth a great saint. Through her intercession Russia will be saved.

At all costs you must protect your daughters. A great evil will hunt them to the ends of the earth and seek to destroy these instruments of God's grace and mercy. They and their descendants must remain hidden until a holy man ariseth. He wears white and travels the earth. The Lord God in his ineffable mercy bequeaths to your family a gift of fifteen years to prepare for these events. Remember this manifestation of God's kindness and use these years to plan well.

Serafim

She and Nicky embraced and held each other until they recovered. Nicky implored Alix to tell no one of the letter. "Sunny, it was meant for my eyes alone and I must decide what to do," he said. "Let us carry on today as if nothing is wrong." Alix silently nodded assent, surprised at Nicky's forcefulness. She was so used to her influence over him that his decisive, imperial manner confused her. Since they had previously invited Ella and Sergei to visit Elena Motovilov with them Nicky insisted to Alix that they all needed to go. He hoped the elderly woman could help them to a clearer understanding of the letter.

Nicky, Sergei and the two wives made their way down the fog shrouded path to Elena's cottage. They were accompanied by only two Cossack officers in the hope that a small escort, combined with the foggy conditions, would draw little attention.

Elena was expecting the Tsar and greeted the group at the entrance. She invited them into her home and offered each a hard wooden chair. The Cossacks took up their posts outside the only door of the rough cabin. She offered them tea, which they accepted, and then began to speak of the canonization. "I did not think I would live to see our blessed saint glorified. We must not waste time on inconsequential conversation as we have much to talk about." She cleared the tea table and placed a lit candle upon it. "Let us invoke St. Serafim to guide us in our endeavors." Nicky, Alix, Ella, and Sergei bowed their heads and prayed.

Elena rose and stood in front of Ella. She grasped her hands and shut her eyes and as if in a trance she spoke. "You will never bear any children but you will be mother to hundreds." When Sergei chuckled at this pronouncement Elena's eyes opened and she swung around, her finger pointed at him. "You there with the small head; you have little to laugh about because your head will go crack," she exclaimed as she smacked her hands together! Everyone looked up, startled by the sudden sound.

Nicky looked at Elena with worried eyes. She knelt before him and kissed his hands. "I press my lips not to the hands of the Tsar but to a martyr of holy Russia. I see a time of great hardship for the people. A rebellion will begin and innocent blood will flow like a river. A regal young girl, will float out of the abyss and spread God's mercy. Her light shines through all eternity."

At this point Alix cried, "I don't believe you, it cannot be!"

Elena was not distracted or upset at Alix's outburst. "Go tonight and bathe in the holy pool of Father Serafim. Later you will become pregnant and bear a son," she said. Elena left the room and returned with a piece of red material. "This is to make some trousers for your son and, when he is born, you will believe what I have been telling you."

Elena had no more to say so they rose and bid farewell to the elderly woman. Pale and shaken, they made their way back to their accommodations. The fact that Elena talked to the Tsar as an equal, when everyone else treated him with deference bordering on the ridiculous, added weight to their conversation. Her words troubled him but he knew they were true. She could not have known of his dream yet her description of their martyrdom contained many of the elements of his frequent nightmare.

As they walked Nicky asked them to tell no one of their encounter. Sergei laughed and said, "surely you do not take the words of a mad, old woman seriously. Clearly she is deranged. I give it no credibility." The others looked at him silently.

Ella, always the voice of reason and compromise, whispered, "time will tell the truth of her words." At any rate they all agreed to keep the substance of their meeting a secret.

Over the years Alix had become very high-strung and upon returning to their quarters she prepared to lie down on the bed. "I cannot face the rest of this day," she told Nicky.

"Woman you must pull yourself together. " We must act as if nothing were wrong."

Recognizing the deep-felt concern in his voice, Alix, for once, suppressed her own feelings of anxiety and they left together to continue with the remainder of the day's activities. At ten o'clock that night they made their way to the pool of Serafim, located near the hermitage. The moon had risen but it gave little light and the misty fog that rose from the surface of the water added to the eerie atmosphere. With only a small guard standing by, Nicky and Alix, in their simple bathing costumes, entered the frigid water, and with a curious lack of emotion, completed their ablutions. They dried off quickly and in the darkness returned to their quarters without being recognized.

The next day the royal family began the long journey by carriage back to Arzamas. Because of the festive nature of the past few days no one understood why Nicky and Alix were so somber. In deference to their mood, conversation was kept to a minimum during the long journey. Finally the party reached the Imperial train, shunted onto a siding at Arzamas, and after a quick meal, everyone retired for the evening. Nicky was unable to sleep and made his way to the parlor car. He was surprised to find Ella reclining on a sofa staring out the window. She seemed a million miles away and very troubled.

"Ella, are you all right?" asked Nicky with concern in his voice.

"No," answered Ella, "My head is full of conflicting emotions. I just do not understand what Elena Motivilov meant. It just does not make sense. Hundreds of children? What does that mean? And my beloved Sergei, his head will go crack? Oh I just cannot take it all in. And you Nicky? How can you be so calm?"

"Things are not always as they appear Ella. I must be strong for Alix. You know how she is."

"Do you believe everything the old woman said will come true?" asked Ella. She fervently hoped that Nicky would assure her that he did not believe Elena's predictions.

Nicky could see that she needed a comforting word. "I believe that the destiny of Russia, my own destiny, and that of my family are in the hands of the Lord. Be at peace my dearest sister. God's will has been manifested to us through this holy monk. We must accept our fate and trust in him who was sent to us by God. "

"Your faith is so strong Nicky. It must give you great comfort." With that Ella excused herself, disappointed that he was unable to provide a more comforting response.

Nicholas sat alone in the dark and thought about his conversation with Ella. For some reason he felt stronger and more capable of dealing with the events of the past few days. Yes, his faith did sustain him and he realized that St. Serafim had given him the strength to cope with an uncertain future, a future dominated by his recurring dream. But whereas before he despaired of ever interpreting his nightmare, he now realized that it did not matter, because an end point had been established. He had fifteen years to prepare for a future tragic event and though the dream would continue to plague him he took comfort in the knowledge that St. Serafim had, in a way, answered his prayers for guidance. Nicholas remained there in the parlor coach, deep in thought, through most of the night, as the train raced across Russia.

Chapter 3

August 1904 – Peterhof. It was a warm, summer day in Peterhof where the Imperial family had gone to escape the excessive heat of St. Petersburg. Nicholas had just returned from visiting the troops at the front and the news he brought back was of little comfort. The war with Japan was not going well and Russia was in the depths of a psychological depression. This national melancholy was brought on by the successful Japanese attack on the Pacific squadron at Port Arthur, in early February, and more recently, by a series of defeats along the Yalu River in Manchuria. The lines of communication were quite simply, too long, and it was hard to imagine a scenario that would lead to a Russian victory over the upstart Empire of Japan.

Nicky looked at the peacefully sleeping Alix and was glad to see she was getting some rest. Since their visit to Sarov, for the glorification of St. Serafim, a year earlier, Alix had become extremely nervous and high-strung. She had constant headaches and the slightest confrontation would send her weeping to her room for hours on end. She was often nauseous and mysterious aliments confined her to bed more often then not. He placed his hand on her swollen belly and worried about the life growing inside. The doctors assured him Alix was healthy and her ills were the normal result of pregnancy and a nervous disposition. Nicholas knew there was more to it than the doctors were saying and wished now that she had not seen the letter from Serafim.

Alix awoke and smiled at Nicky. "My dearest, please say it is not me who has put that furrow on your brow."

"Darling Sunny, you bring only happiness into my life."

"Go about your day. I think I shall lay here awhile longer. I promise to meet you for lunch," she said sleepily.

Later that morning, Alix arose and with the assistance of her maids began to dress for lunch. Suddenly the sound of a loud crash reverberated throughout the room as a large dressing mirror toppled to the floor. Glass shards flew everywhere and one embedded itself in the front of the heavy gown, which fortuitously, the Empress had just put on. Alix was not injured but she became quite agitated and looked at the glass sliver in consternation. She became very pale and her maids stood by helplessly, knowing the accident would send the Empress into one of her panic attacks.

"It's an omen," she cried out. "I shall die in childbirth!"

One of her maids ran out of the bedroom to find Dr. Ott, the Tsarina's physician, but Alix was an intelligent woman and when she realized the glass shard had not penetrated her dress she managed, with some difficulty, to gain control of herself. She removed the glass and then berated the maids for making such a commotion although no one would admit to knocking over the mirror. Alix had delivered four beautiful daughters and when she felt a sharp pain in her side she recognized it as the onset of labor. She motioned to the maids to help her undress and with their assistance she got back into bed. Sharp pains stabbed at her side as she waited impatiently for Dr. Ott to arrive and confirm that she was indeed, in labor.

News that Alix was in delivery spread throughout the palace and family members rushed in to gather outside the royal apartments. Nicholas was finally located and summoned to the palace. Alix's attendants took their place by her side to assist Dr. Ott in the birthing but as quickly as her labor began, induced by the trauma of the falling mirror, it was over. After a miraculously short struggle, and with a final push, Alix forced the baby from her body and into Dr. Ott's waiting hands. He lifted the child up for all in the room to see. Overcome with happiness, Alix cried out, "a son, I have a son."

Dr. Ott, handed the infant to the nurse, left the bedroom, and went to the study where the Tsar waited. Nicholas looked up expectantly at him. "Congratulations your Imperial Highness," said the doctor, "you have an heir." Nicky jumped up and rushed into Alix's room. His face flushed with joy, he took the bundle that was his son in his arms.

"We shall call you Alexei after Russia's great Tsar," he whispered to the baby. "Darling Sunny, there are not words enough to thank you properly for this wondrous gift." Alix smiled at him and drifted off to sleep, exhausted from her ordeal.

The children's nursery was filled with excitement and anticipation and when the four Grand Duchesses were informed they would not have lunch with their parents today their curiosity knew no bounds. They bombarded their governess with questions but she was very secretive and would not tell them the reason. They ate their lunch in silence, wondering what was happening. Olga at age nine, with dark blond hair and blue eyes was the oldest. She was naturally bossy and loved to order her sisters around. Tatiana, age seven, had gray eyes and dark brunette hair. Even at this young age she was referred to as "the little princess" for her regal bearing and manners. Maria was five, a chubby little girl with light brown hair and big blue eyes. She had a very friendly personality and loved to talk to people. The youngest, at age three, was Anastasia and until today the blue eyed, brown haired cherub had been the baby of the family and appropriately spoiled. The girls looked up from the table as their father entered.

"My darlings, I have wondrous news," he exclaimed.

"What is it Papa? What is it?" the young girls all shouted at once.

"I have something to show you. There is a new baby in the palace, and if you follow me we will sneak in to see him," their father said.

They walked down the hall from the children's wing and paused outside the door to the nursery that had been set up next to the Imperial bedroom. Nicholas could see the anticipation in their faces and it reminded him of Christmas when the children could hardly wait to open their presents. "Children we must be calm around the baby. We do not want to startle him," said Nicholas. "Do you understand?"

"Yes Papa, we understand," answered his daughters.

"Can we go in now?" asked Olga.

"Yes, my dears you may." Nicholas opened the door and before he could catch her Anastasia ran into the nursery. Quickly forgetting her father's admonition she shouted "where is my baby?"

"Shhh, my little one," said Nicholas. "We must be quiet." All the children gathered around the cradle to get a good look.

"Well, what is it Papa?" asked Tatiana.

"It is a baby, of course," stated Maria with a smug look.

The Tsar laughed. "That's right, it is a baby." Maria smiled. She was so proud to know something that her older sister apparently did not.

"Is it a boy or a girl?" asked Tatiana, as she frowned at her younger sister.

"It is a boy," stated the proud father. "His name is Alexei."

"Hooray," shouted the girls. The commotion woke the baby from his nap and he began to wail. The nurse jumped up to tend to her new charge.

"We should leave for now, girls," said their father. "We can visit him later." As he led the girls out of the nursery, Anastasia began to sob. "What is wrong, my little imp," he asked as he picked her up.

"I didn't see baby," cried Anastasia. She was too short to peer into the cradle and with all the excitement no one had noticed that she had not seen her new brother.

"Oh my poor angel," said Nicholas. He turned to the nurse who was holding the future Tsar. "Do you think it would be all right for Anastasia to give her brother a kiss?" asked Nicholas.

"I think that if the other children are very quiet and do not startle the baby again, it would be just fine," she answered. Anastasia stopped crying immediately. Her father put her down and she slowly walked over to the chair where the nurse was sitting. She bent down and ever so gently kissed the baby. Alexei stirred in the nurse's arms and let out a sigh. Anastasia looked up at her father. "He likes sister," she said. This was the first suggestion of the strong bond that would grow between the two youngest members of the Imperial family.

As soon as Alexei's birth was confirmed, a signal was sent to St. Petersburg. As the guns of the Fortress of Peter and Paul began to fire a salute, people gathered in the streets. When the cannonade neared one hundred guns, which indicated the birth of a girl, the crowd held its breath, counting impatiently. The gunfire continued past one hundred and a roar filled the air. Russia had a Tsarevich. People cheered, hats flew in the air and the cannon continued to reverberate as the exhausted gun crews at the fortress continued until three hundred rounds had been fired.

Back at the Peterhof Palace, Nicholas proudly showed Alexei to all the family gathered for the birth. Everyone was struck by how big and healthy looking he was. Minnie swore he looked just like his grandfather, Tsar Alexander III. "I am glad to retire as heir to the throne," announced Misha. "A huge burden is lifted from my shoulders." Until Alexei's birth Misha was Nicholas' designated successor.

CAED

The Baptismal ceremony was to take place a few weeks after the birth of the Tsarevich, and on the appointed day, when Nicky looked in on Alix, he found her still in bed. "Come my dear, you must get up. Today is Alexei's big day."

"I know darling," said Alix. "Look, I want to show you something." She picked up a pair of red trousers that were sitting on the table by the bed. "Aren't they precious? I did not want to make them until I was sure we had a son." Nicky looked at the tiny garment in dismay. "Oh, I am sorry," whispered Alix. In the excitement of Alexei's birth, she had forgotten the rest of the predictions made at Sarov. As the realization hit her, she sank back against the pillows.

"My dear, let us banish such thoughts from our heads. Today our dear little one will be baptized into our faith," Nicky reminded her. Alix gave him a wan smile.

"Darling, does Princess Marie really have to carry Alexei? I am a nervous wreck. She must be eighty years old. How will she ever manage?"

Nicky chuckled, "She's only seventy-nine and she will be fine. You know by now we cannot change any traditions. Princess Marie carried me for my christening and besides, we've taken every precaution. The cushion will be attached to her shoulders and the Grand Marshall will carry the baby's cape, but he is really there to prevent any accidents. So you see, there is no need to worry."

"I shall worry, have no doubt about that," Alix teased. "As a convert I still do not understand this custom which prevents us from attending our own child's baptism. Once again I will accept your traditions but this will be the fifth ceremony I shall miss. You have much to make up to me."

"Will this help?" Nicky asked as he pulled a long strand of perfectly matched pearls from his pocket. They were the size of raspberries and had a rosy pink hue."

"Oh Nicky, they are absolutely beautiful. Yes, you are in my good graces for the present," she said with a smile on her face.

Just then Olga and Tatiana barged in. "Mama, Papa, how do we look?" they chimed in together. Both girls were dressed in Sarafans, the traditional Russian costume, and the blue brocade brought out their coloring to perfection. With their long hair flowing down their backs, they were the picture of Romanov royalty.

"My precious ones you look lovely," said Nicky

"What is more important than how we look?" asked Alix as she frowned at Nicky.

"To be good, Mama," said the two girls.

Nicholas pushed the two girls towards the door. "Go on, let your mother dress in peace."

The August day was damp and wet but nothing could quell the anticipation of the crowd. The people waited in the drizzling rain hoping for a glimpse of their future emperor. Suddenly trumpets sounded and the procession from Peterhof made its way down the road to the church. Alexei was carried in a golden carriage escorted by a troop of cavalrymen in their elegant dress uniforms.

Royalty from all over Europe had gathered for the ceremony. Alexei's godparents came from the ranks of that royalty and included King Edward VII of Great Britain, Kaiser Wilhelm II of Germany, Grand Duke Ernest Ludwig of Hesse, and Dowager Empress Marie Feodorovna, his grandmother. To honor the Russian Army, the Tsar designated all the troops godparents as well. Sergei and Ella were also present with their wards, Dmitri and Marie. They had become guardians when the children's father, Grand Duke Paul was banished from Russia for disgracing the family.

Princess Marie, the Robes Mistress, carried Alexei up the aisle of the church. In spite of her gray hair and the wrinkles lining her face, she looked splendid in her court gown. She took the gold cushion that the baby lay on in her shaking arms. It was attached to her shoulders with a gold band to help her with the weight of the child. She also wore special shoes to avoid slipping on the highly polished floor. The Grand Marshal of the Court carried Alexei's cape, which was made of gold cloth and lined with ermine.

Olga and Tatiana were allowed to participate in the ceremony and followed in the procession with other young girls from the court. Onlookers were impressed at the sight of the two lovely girls, who though still very young, showed promise of the beauties they would become. Nicholas and Alexandra waited anxiously in a private room off the church.

Father Yanishev, who had taught Alix her catechism when she converted to the Orthodox faith, performed the ceremony. He held Alexei in the air and as the royal guests, the Grand Dukes and Duchesses and other officials watched, he immersed the child in the baptismal font and spoke the words of the sacrament. The Tsarevich let out a cry of protest as the chilly water closed about him and the crowd laughed at the antics of the young boy. He was a beautiful baby with blue gray eyes and the beginnings of blond curls on his head.

Later, after an elaborate buffet, Nicky received their guests as Alix reclined on a sofa nearby. The rain had passed on, the sun broke through the overcast and what had been a damp morning turned into a glorious afternoon. It was an opportunity for the royalty of Europe to get together without friction, and much satisfaction in the day's activities was expressed by their royal guests. With Alexei's birth, the continuity of the Romanov dynasty was assured.

As the afternoon progressed, Nicholas walked out onto the balcony to catch a breath of fresh air. All the excitement of the day had finally caught up with him and he felt weary and somewhat depressed despite the festive atmosphere of the ongoing party.

"Such a pensive mood you are in Nicky, for such a joyous occasion," remarked Ella as she walked out to join him.

"Oh, I was just catching some fresh air."

"I know it is more than that, Nicholas," said Ella.

Ella knew the time had come to broach the topic, which they had all tried to ignore since the visit to Elena Motivilov. She was aware, as well as he, that the birth of this son was a bitter sweet blessing because it was the first of the predictions to come true and now that it had been fulfilled, the rest of the prophesy was suddenly credible.

"I know what is bothering you," said Ella. "The birth of this child is the beginning, the first sign of things to come. Do not forget that Elena also predicted tragedy for Sergei and I. Sergei did not believe a word that old woman said but I was so sure that if you had a son, he would not be able to discount her forecast of danger any longer. Sergei has enemies and I am so worried about him especially now that it appears Elena was correct.

"Ella I am so sorry. I have been completely oblivious to your troubles. What will you do?" questioned Nicky.

"I will do nothing," responded Ella. "It is in God's hands."

"I will dispatch troops to your palace immediately," exclaimed Nicholas. "You must convince Sergei to stay out of sight for awhile. There is always a chance things will change."

"I remember our last talk," said Ella. "You were so comforting and I was so near to hysteria. Back then you were so resigned to our fate but now you seem ready to attempt to change it all. What has happened to you Nicky?" she asked.

"I have spent many sleepless nights pondering it all and I continue to wonder about something."

"What is it," asked Ella.

"If all of this is our fate, and it is unchangeable, then why were we told?" Would it not have been better to let us live our lives to the fullest without the knowledge of the certainty of our suffering? No! We were told for a reason and I believe it is so that somehow I could influence events and have an impact on the family's future, that in some way I could be the author of our history."

"You may be right and I pray that you are," said Ella. "My heart tells me that Sergei will die soon. Of that I feel certain. I feel so frightened for him because he has been given this time to prepare himself for his spiritual journey and yet he does nothing. He is so bold as to exit our carriage and spin around like a wild man and dare anyone to try and take his life. It is more than I can bear sometimes."

"Ella, you have done all that you can for my uncle," Nicky said in his most comforting voice. "They say that he has always been stubborn that way. If you have made peace with it then you need not worry about the rest."

"Thank you Nicky," said Ella tenderly. "You are such a dear."

"Well, as you said when you first came out, this is too joyous an occasion for moodiness. Let us try and put our minds at ease for now and enjoy my son's baptismal day. Despite what we know, he is a true blessing."

∞

A few weeks later, the Imperial family was enjoying a rare day with no official functions scheduled. Nicky took the children to church in the morning and then met Alix for a quiet lunch alone. They were unaware of the drama taking place in the nursery while they enjoyed their meal.

As the nurse drew the covers off the heir to the throne, she was surprised to find a speck of blood on his shirt. She carefully opened up the infant's small white shirt and saw blood oozing from his navel. From her experience she knew this was not normal for a baby several weeks old. She panicked for a moment, then calmed herself and called for the doctor. She sat next to the cradle but dared not pick up the child. Minutes seemed like hours as she nervously awaited the doctor's arrival. When he finally reached the nursery she breathed a sign of relief. "Have you called for the Tsar," he said as he began to examine the Tsarevich.

"No I did not want to alarm him," said the nurse. "It isn't serious is it?"

"Send someone to get the Tsar. If he is with the Empress tell him that one of the ministers needs to see him. We do not want to upset the Empress without cause," said the doctor. "And tell no one about this."

Nicky and Alix had moved to the sitting room after their lunch. He was sitting in his favorite chair while Alix reclined on the sofa. Suddenly a soft knock came at the door. The maid went to the door, partially opened it and had a conversation with the person on the other side. Nicholas could only faintly hear her talking but the tone of her voice was grave. "What is it?" asked Nicky.

"One of your ministers needs a moment of your time," said the maid.

Nicky turned to Alix, and said, "it appears I have not even a moment to spend with my wife, without interruption."

"The ministers need your counsel and you must give it to them," she replied.

"You know I would be lost without them," Nicky said. "There is just so much work."

"If you would only delegate more authority we might have more time together," sighed Alix.

"You know I would much rather stay and look at the beautiful face of my wife than the faces of those bearded old men," he explained.

Alix laughed as Nicky exited the room. When the door shut behind him, the servant explained that Alexei's doctor needed him immediately. A chill went down his spine as he made his way to the nursery and entered it. "What is going on?" Nicholas demanded.

"The Tsarevich is bleeding from the navel, your Highness," answered the doctor. "It is not normal for his age and he may be exhibiting signs of hemophilia. Of course, I will need to make some tests but I wanted you to be aware of the possibility."

A look of deep concern crossed the face of the Tsar and he was unable to voice his questions to the doctor. Terrible premonitions raced through his mind as he reacted to the news, but finally the Tsar took a deep breath and regained his composure. "When will you know what is wrong with my son," asked Nicholas.

"I must consult with specialists. Little is known of this condition," said the doctor, "but if the Tsarevich continues to bleed, it can be fatal."

"Please forgive my impatience. Consult with the other doctors but in the meantime I must inform the Empress of this disturbing development." Nicholas returned to the sitting room to find Alix happily knitting and he dreaded the thought of having to give her the news of Alexei's condition. However, he could not disguise the look on his face and it was evident that something was dreadfully wrong.

"Nicky, what is it? Did something happen with the ministers?" she asked. Nicholas did not reply as he stood silently and tried to find a way to break the news to her. He knew how delicate she was and how devastated she would be. "Nicky you are frightening me. What is the matter?" Alix demanded.

"It was not the ministers I had to see Alix," he said shaking his head, "but Alexei's doctor."

"What! Why was I not told immediately?" exclaimed Alexandra. "The impertinence of that woman trying to keep this from me." Alix quickly rose from the couch. "I must go to my baby, he needs me." As she rushed to the door, Nicholas grabbed her hand and pulled her into his arms. He held her tighter than ever before. He was afraid to look her in the face as he told her the news.

"Alix, wait. There is more," said Nicholas. "Alexei is bleeding from the navel. The doctors are with him now."

"What did you say," Alexandra cried out. She struggled to free herself but he would not release the hold he had on her.

"They are trying to stop the bleeding now. The doctor thinks he may be hemophilic," said Nicky.

"Oh those doctors know nothing," said Alix. "If we were told of his birth at Sarov, we would have certainly been told of this."

"Maybe we were told, in a way," said Nicky. "The material Elena gave us for the trousers was blood red."

"That is ridiculous. I won't hear another word of this. Now let me go, my son needs me," sobbed Alexandra. Nicky released her and she stormed from the room.

By noon the next day, Alexei's bleeding had stopped. He spent a peaceful day and hardly cried at all. Alexandra was reassured by his healthy appearance and would listen to no further suggestions that he might have hemophilia. Nicholas decided to let her be, for the present. He knew time would bring the truth to light and there was no need to worry Alix unnecessarily. He quietly conferred with the doctor and arranged for specialists to examine Alexei upon their return to Tsarskoe Selo.

Nicholas recalled the letter from St. Serafim and the predictions contained therein. The saint had promised them fifteen years. It appeared that the clock was already ticking.

Chapter 4

December 1904 - Tsarskoe Selo. The four young girls could barely conceal their excitement when the Imperial train jerked into motion, departed Peterhof and began the journey down to Tsarskoe Selo. As the royal coaches moved out of the station the Grand Duchesses dropped any effort to hide their youthful enthusiasm and their high spirited antics soon had the royal party in a totally relaxed and festive mood. The Tsar of Russia owned a large number of palatial homes but the destination of this trip, the Alexander Palace, was by far the favorite of the immediate family. When the locomotive pulled the cars onto the siding at Tsarskoe Selo it was running behind schedule but Nicky's daughters had kept everyone so entertained that it was a happy and somewhat boisterous group that disembarked. Nicholas and his entourage climbed into the waiting troikas and snuggled into the furs to keep warm. The drivers whipped up the horses and the sleighs sped through the town, down the tree lined boulevard, past the many mansions and on to their destination. The Grand Duchesses reacted with delight as the gates of the Imperial Park came into sight. Surrounded by a wrought iron fence, the park was an eight hundred acre oasis of trees, and landscaped grounds with a man-made lake and canals. Nestled among the trees, the golden Alexander Palace was a welcoming beacon inviting them in from the cold, crisp outdoors. Although it was just a short distance from St. Petersburg, capital of Tsarist Russia, the palace at Tsarskoe Selo, nevertheless, seemed a world away from the intrigue and gossip of the court. However, the murder of Nicky's grandfather Alexander II, on March 1, 1881 had a chilling effect on the Romanov family and many family members no longer lived in the capital for fear of assassination. Security at the park, therefore, was a continuing issue and the perimeter was regularly patrolled by mounted Cossacks in their bright red tunics and highly polished black boots.

Nicholas and Alexandra had chosen the Alexander Palace as their residence because it held many fond memories for them. Nicky, of course, was born and raised there and could recall numerous childhood experiences. During their courtship, Nicky had held a small, intimate ball for Alix there and they had danced the night away.

Consequently, of the many glittering palaces and retreats owned by the Tsar, the simple but elegant Alexander Palace was the favorite of the royal family and they spent the long Russian winters there. The mansion was a two story building with two wings attached by a center hall and yet, with only a hundred rooms, it was considered small and intimate by Imperial standards.

Once they chose it to be their home, Alix supervised a complete renovation of the family rooms. She designated one wing for the family, the center hall contained the public rooms and the other wing contained rooms for various members of the court and visiting family. Alexandra was a very inexperienced decorator and was heavily influenced by the style of her grandmother Queen Victoria. She wanted to create a warm and cozy environment for her family, an oasis where they could retreat from affairs of state and the public life. However, Alix proved to be a failure as an interior decorator and created rooms overflowing with chintz and with every inch of space covered with icons and knickknacks. Yet in Nicky's eyes she could do no wrong and the simple elegance of the exterior camouflaged the gaudy interior. Critics aside, Nicky and Alix loved their small retreat and in the end that was all that mattered.

The excitement of their homecoming in the winter of 1904 was somewhat dampened by the news that Alexei's condition was serious enough to cause concern. In the days that followed the return of the family, five of the finest specialists and physicians in Russia examined the Tsarevich. After additional tests and consultation they confirmed what Dr. Ott had initially suspected. The heir to the throne of Russia was born with hemophilia.

The shock of the diagnosis had a terrible effect on Alix's health and she spent the next seven days either in bed or dragging herself to a chaise lounge in her Mauve Boudoir. She had asked Miss Eagar, the children's nurse, to keep the girls away as she did not want them to see her in such a state. Her actions, of course, had the opposite effect and the children were very distraught because they were cut off from their mother, who was such an important part of their life. Nicky was very concerned about her but the court physician assured him that her depression was only temporary and that there was nothing physically wrong with her.

"Give her a few days and she will be fine," he told Nicholas.

The stalemate was finally broken when Alix received a little note from her oldest daughter Olga in which she wrote how much she missed her mother and wished she could see her today. How sad that my own daughters must write me letters when we reside in the same house, she thought, and vowed to get up and spend some time with the children. She resolved to surprise them when they finished morning lessons and were out for their exercise.

She dressed warmly for the occasion and, as she trudged through the snow; the sounds of laughter and merriment drew her to her destination. She came upon Nicholas and the girls sledding down a hill. The enjoyment in the faces of the girls immediately lifted her spirits and for a time, at least, she was able to put aside her melancholy. She hid behind a tree for a moment and marveled at the love and devotion on the face of her darling Nicky as he played on the slope with the girls. There was no doubt that these innocent young creatures were the most precious and important persons in her husband's life and that he would do anything to safeguard them. She savored the moment for a little longer and then stepped from behind the tree. At first the girls were confused when they saw a figure approaching but they finally recognized their mother, bundled up as she was, and met her with cries of joy. They began to run towards her but she held up her hand.

"Don't let me stop your fun," she told them.

The children ignored her suggestion. They had not seen her for a week and had no intention of missing the opportunity to shower her with hugs and kisses. Alix basked in the glow of their affection but eventually convinced them to continue their play.

Nicky stood with her and they watched the Grand Duchesses slip down the hill weaving their way between the trees. It was a glorious day and the girl's excited shouts echoed throughout the park. The sun, though not warm enough to melt the snow, was shining brightly and its rays produced a profusion of diamond sparkles. The atmosphere was so infectious that Alix, with a twinkle in her eye, turned to her husband and said, "I think I shall try it out."

"Sunny are you sure? It's been days since you've gotten out of bed, surely you are too weak," Nicky told her.

"I feel fine. Now give me a sled," she demanded.

Never one to back down from a challenge, especially one she had made, the Empress of Russia hurtled down the hill at breakneck speed to land at the bottom in a heap. Nicholas helped her up and brushed the snow off her clothes as the girls gathered around her laughing and teasing her about her sledding technique. Alix's face was flushed a delightful pink and Nicky caught his breath at her beauty. Lord, he loved her and in spite of her illnesses and prickly personality she was the one person in the world he was totally comfortable with. He caught her eye as she talked to the children and she smiled at him. It was wonderful to see her looking so happy and the afternoon turned into the most enjoyable family outing in many a day. The girls vied with each other and their parents to see who could make the longest sled run and the contest was finally won by Nicky just as the winter sun began to fade and the day drew to a close.

"Its time to call it a day," said Nicky. "Anyway, I think its time for some hot chocolate, girls. What do you say to that?" The smiles on the flushed faces of his wife and daughters was all the answer he needed so together they made their way back to the family quarters.

After they had chocolate Nicky excused himself. "I am sorry to put an end to our fun but I have an appointment I must not miss," Nicholas told his daughters.

Amid the sighs and complaints, Alix said, "Go to your appointment, dearest. I will stay with the girls for a while. We have some catching up to do."

Once seated in his study, he ordered the footman to send in Peter Carl Faberge, the court jeweler, who had requested the meeting. Faberge entered the room and bowed to the Tsar. He was a small, balding man with a neatly trimmed beard, flecked with gray. Nicholas' father, Alexander III had started the tradition of having Faberge make incredible jeweled Easter eggs for his wife Minnie. Nicky continued this tradition and every year he had Faberge make an egg for Alix and one for Minnie, the Empress Dowager. In his soft, almost effeminate hands, the hands of an artist, Faberge carried a package which he handed to the Tsar.

"I am surprised it is complete so soon. We usually don't see your workmanship until right before Easter", said Nicholas as he opened the box and took out the exquisite creation. He sat there in stunned silence for a few moments and then exclaimed, "You've outdone yourself this year. It is everything I hoped it would be."

"Your Imperial Highness, I was truly inspired by the occasion of your son's birth. An event of such magnitude needs a very special gift to mark it," said Faberge. "Once the inspiration struck me I could not stop working until it was completed and I wanted you to see it right away. The second egg will be ready at the usual time. I call this creation the Imperial Colonnade Egg."

It was a work so beautiful that words were scarcely adequate to describe it. Atop a base of pale green jade-like stone was placed a pink enameled pedestal. On the pedestal rested a Greek temple with six columns of the green stone, topped with gold ionic capitals. The temple was wound with a gold garland, and a similar garland, held by four silver cherubs, surrounded the base. In the center of the temple two platinum doves were intertwined. The pink enameled egg, set onto the roof of the temple, was a working clock with a rotating ring of rose colored diamond numerals. A diamond studded arrowhead mounted on the roof of the temple pointed to the time on the rotating ring. On top of the egg sat a plump silver cupid. Faberge explained the symbolism to the Tsar.

"The doves represent the love of your Imperial Highnesses, the four cherubs at the base your daughters and the garland is the rope that holds you together as a family and finally the cupid on top is the Tsarevich,"

"The Empress will be most impressed," Nicholas said. "This is truly a work of great beauty. Thank you so much." Long after Faberge left he continued to admire the egg and then he hid it away to wait for Easter.

The next day, after Olga and Tatiana had finished their lessons and the afternoon exercise period was over, the older girls went to the nursery to gather up their younger sisters Maria and Anastasia. They all went down the private staircase that connected their quarters to their parent's suite of rooms and entered the Mauve Boudoir where they were having tea together. Due to Alexandra's frequent headaches and bouts of depression this room had become the center of their family life and by necessity most activity took place around a specially constructed chaise lounge upon which Alix spent much of her time. It had a spring core, layers of plush padding and was covered with a rich silk fabric in a delicate lilac, with a unique sheen that glimmered in the light. A similar fabric was used on the walls and was said to have cost more than Mr. Faberge's Easter Eggs. Olga and Tatiana had asked their mother why there was so much mauve in the room.

"Ever since your father gave me a sprig of lilac when we were courting, I have loved the color. I treasured that flower and when we first moved in I ordered material to exactly match it. So now, long after that flower withered away, I can remember the day your father gave it to me whenever I look around this room," she had replied. The girls were entranced by her story and grew to love this room where so many happy gatherings would take place.

As the girls came into the room, they saw the familiar white-draped table set with a silver tea service and plates of hot bread, and butter for the children. They saw a plate of tiny vanilla flavored wafers as well, but knew better than to ask for a serving. As part of the disciplinary approach that Alix utilized, the children were forbidden to ask for anything from their parent's table.

Olga whispered to Tatiana, "they feed us like prisoners! Only bread and water."

"Well at least we can have tea," said Tatiana.

Life was anything but luxurious for the Grand Duchesses; the Empress would not allow them to be pampered. She raised them on the strict principles of the English nursery with Russian customs thrown in for good measure. The girls woke up to cold baths in the morning and took warm ones at night and in accord with a tradition of the Russian court slept on hard camp beds that went with them on all their travels. The maids were instructed to have the girls help clean their rooms and they dressed themselves. Their clothes were worn until they out grew them and then they were passed on to the younger girls.

"Girls, come and have tea," Alix said while pouring the cups. Nicholas had come in and promptly at five o'clock she began to serve. The Grand Duchesses were happy to see their Aunt Olga, Nicky's sister, join them today. She was one of the few relatives their mother allowed them to interact with and they enjoyed spending time with her.

The family was enjoying the simple repast when the unthinkable happened. Little Maria walked boldly up to her parent's table, snatched a wafer, and shoved it in her mouth. "There, I've eaten it all up, you can't eat it now," stated the little angel, defiance on her face. Gasps of shock from the other girls and then stunned silence resulted at this act of rebellion. She was normally so good and well behaved, that Olga and Tatiana, who were full of mischief themselves, had taken to calling her "stepsister," implying she could not possibly be an immediate relative. Alix sent for Miss Eagar, the younger girls nurse.

"What should we do about this?" demanded the Empress after explaining what had happened.

"Send her to bed," Miss Eagar's calmly stated with English practicality. "You must stop this misbehavior now, while she's young."

Alix agreed with Miss Eagar's pronouncement. "Maria, off to bed with you."

The Tsar watched all of this with an amused look on his face then put down his teacup and pleaded mercy for Maria. "I was always afraid that she might be growing angel's wings. I am glad to see she is after all just a child." Granted a reprieve, Maria remained and the family tea continued. There was a look of irritation on Nicholas' face as Miss Eagar left the room and Alix asked him what was wrong.

"What is that woman still doing here?" he demanded to know. "I thought I made my feelings quite clear that I wanted her dismissed. It was bad enough to discover that she was Irish not English, as we were led to believe, but then to have her teaching her papist ways to the children. It is too much."

"Nicky, I could not bear to send her away. It has been so hard to find a decent nurse and the children love her so. As I told you before, the girls were only playing with her rosary beads because they thought it was a pretty necklace," Alix replied.

"I will not have a Catholic instructing my children. You know how I dislike the papists. You must replace her immediately."

"I did not realize your suggestion was an order!" she said to him with some irritation. "I will take care of the situation tomorrow."

The exchange between Nicky and Alix, argumentative as it was, dampened the atmosphere and the older girls glared at Maria whose act of defiance had triggered the whole affair. In a valiant effort to change the subject Aunt Olga raised an issue that was even more upsetting.

"Nicky, Mama tells me that you and Alix are traveling to St. Petersburg for the Blessing of the Water ceremony? Do you think that is wise? There is a Father Gapon who is organizing the workers and I have heard that it is very dangerous in the city with the labor strikes going on."

"Olga, we cannot live in fear and I must fulfill my duties. I fully intend on participating in the ceremony."

"But what about an assassination attempt?"

"Please let us change the subject. I do not think this is an appropriate topic to discuss in front of the children. At any rate we are all in God's hands and He will protect us if He sees fit to do so."

When tea was completed Nicholas returned to his study to review the latest reports on the progress of what was now referred to as the Second Pacific Squadron. After a somewhat acrimonious debate among his ministers the Tsar had agreed to a bold but flawed plan to dispatch reinforcements to the relief of Port Arthur. These ships were borrowed from the Baltic fleet and had sailed from St. Petersburg for the Far East in early October. Because Great Britain was an ally of Japan and controlled the Suez Canal the Russian commander, Admiral Zinovy Rozhestvensky, was fearful that the British would attempt to block progress of the squadron. He decided, therefore, to send his newer and faster ships on the long journey around Africa while the older vessels proceeded through the Canal. The progress of the armada was hampered by one difficulty after another and by mid-December the main body of ships had sailed only as far as Angra Pequena in German Southwest Africa. Eventually all the elements of the fleet, including the follow-on Third Pacific Squadron, would rendezvous off the coast of Indochina and then sail northward toward Japan and their destiny.

Chapter 5

January 1905 - Tsarskoe Selo. Although the snow was fairly deep, the grounds keepers managed to maintain an open exercise path for use by everyone in the Imperial compound. Nicky had persuaded Alix and his sister Olga to take a vigorous walk in the crisp morning air and by midmorning they were well along the trail. The darkened, overcast sky, however, held promise of more snow and it appeared that this January would be a bitterly cold month. When the three royals turned back toward the palace the first flurries were beginning to fall and up ahead they could see a footman hurrying toward them. The man was quite winded by the time he arrived so, without speaking, he handed a telegram to the Tsar. Nicky opened it, quickly read the contents, and then shook his head in a gesture of resignation.

"What is it," Alix and Olga asked almost as one.

"The news is terrible," Nicky replied. "We have surrendered Port Arthur to the Japanese. The garrison Commander could not hold out any longer. What a blow to our nation."

Nicky had held onto a dim hope that Russia could retain possession of its only warm water port in the Far East. Because Japan had opened the conflict by surprise, without a declaration of war, there was an element of sympathy for Russia to be found among some governments of Europe, but this support did not initially translate to material assistance. Russia was forced to fight an aggressive enemy at the end of a five thousand mile supply line. By June 1904 the Japanese army had encircled and besieged Port Arthur and then launched desperate attacks to capture the port. The eighteen surviving ships of the Pacific squadron attempted to sortie to safety in Vladivostok but were turned back by the Japanese navy in a running action that became known as the Battle of the Yellow Sea. When news arrived that the Baltic fleet had sailed for Pacific waters the Russian defenders became even more stubborn and heroic in their attempt to keep open the naval base so the fleet could re-supply and prepare for battle. The Japanese, equally desperate to deny the port to the Russians, increased the ferocity of their attacks and finally the garrison was forced to surrender. The ships in the harbor were immediately scuttled to keep them out of Japanese hands.

Port Arthur had held out for nearly eight months but now it had fallen and the Baltic fleet, still enroute, would have to make its way to the naval base at Vladivostok. Nicky was crushed by the news and even his eternal optimism could not overcome the pain and grief which was almost more than he could bear. He rushed ahead to the palace to meet with his ministers and discuss how best to break this devastating news to the country.

❧

Against the advice of most his ministers, and despite the worry of his family, Nicholas, with the reluctant acquiescence of Alexandra, decided to leave the security and calm of Tsarskoe Selo and travel to St. Petersburg for the annual Blessing of the Waters. As expected, the news from Port Arthur had been received with dismay and outrage. Ever since the war with Japan had taken a turn for the worse, Russia had seen increasing unrest. Workers went on strike and terrorist activity increased. The Tsar's advisors continued to report on revolutionaries with bombs and various unsubstantiated assassination plots. Nicholas refused to be influenced by the reports. When the decision to attend the ceremony was finalized his sister Olga had made one last appeal to him to cancel the trip and remain at Alexander Palace.

"Olga," he had replied, "we cannot be held hostage by these rumors. Fear will paralyze us if we let it and then who would carry out our duties. As a leader of our Orthodox faith I must attend the ceremony." With that he left for the Winter Palace in St. Petersburg.

Nicky refused to believe that anyone would actually want to harm him. Every time he appeared in public the crowds were respectful and seemed pleased to see him. He was convinced of his subject's loyalty, especially the peasants and workers, and believed that they looked upon him as Father Tsar, a benevolent ruler who would take care of all their needs. Unbeknownst to him, the secret police staged many of these public outpourings of love and respect by organizing and encouraging the crowds to line the streets when he appeared. He truly had no idea as to the condition of his country when the New Year began.

That fateful January day in 1905 was cold and dreary, with low gray clouds in the sky. The streets of St. Petersburg were deceptively quiet in the early hours and the only break in the silence was the sound of hammers striking nails, as workmen put the finishing touches on a wooden platform for the dignitaries attending the Blessing of the Waters. Elaborate preparations were made for the ceremony. A gold canopy, adorned with blue stars, was erected over the opening cut in the frozen Neva River. A long red carpet stretched from the Winter Palace, down the stairs that accessed the river, and out onto the ice to the platform and canopy. The crowds of onlookers spread out on either side of the stairs. At mid-morning the Metropolitan of St. Petersburg, the clergy and invited guests readied themselves for the procession. The Tsar took his place among them and the ceremony began.

Alix and the Dowager Empress watched through their opera glasses from the windows of the Winter Palace, as Nicholas strode along the carpet, down the stairs and out onto the frozen river. He took his place under the canopy and looked into the hole cut in the ice. It was a black abyss and due to the frigid temperature a servant had to stir the slush every few minutes with a pole to keep the water from freezing over. Unlike many Russian Orthodox liturgies, this one was comparatively short, and blessedly so, because the icy wind blowing across the frozen river was chilling everyone to the bone. The Metropolitan of St. Petersburg dipped a cross into the water and intoned the blessing, while smoke from the incense wafted up into the wind and was quickly carried away.

At the appropriate moment in the ceremony the guns from the Fortress of Peter and Paul began to fire the traditional salute. These guns were regular artillery pieces but were normally served with blank ammunition during ceremonial occasions. Nothing seemed out of the ordinary until shortly after the sound of the fourth gun was heard a shell exploded out on the ice about thirty yards in front of the canopy and platform. Shell fragments and shattered chunks of ice were thrown in all directions and a policeman standing near the Tsar collapsed onto the ice, blood gushing from a terrible wound. No one who was there would ever forget the contrast of that bright red blood against the stark white of the ice. Pandemonium ensued as the crowd dispersed in panic but miraculously no one else was injured by the shell fire. Nicholas stood calmly, a dark silhouette against the bright ice as the guns of the fortress continued to deliver the required salute.

Alix looked on the scene in stunned horror. Nicky appeared so alone and abandoned, standing there on the ice, yet there was something resolute and courageous about his manner. The moment seemed suspended in time but the love she felt for him sustained her as she prepared to rush to his side. Suddenly, in the midst of the salute, another shell was fired from the fortress and this round impacted on the facade of the Winter Palace. It hit to the right and slightly below the window in which Alix and Minnie were standing. The concussion shattered the casement, knocked them back into the room and covered them with glass and crumbled marble.

Nicholas turned at the sound of the explosion, and was shocked to see the window where Alix stood disappear in a cloud of smoke and glass. In its place was a gaping hole and he could see no movement through the smoke drifting into the room. There was utter chaos around him as the police attempted to gain control of the crowd, but for Nicky there was only one concern. He dropped his prayer book and, forgetting his dignity, raced off the ice and across the courtyard toward the palace, shouting Alix's name as he ran. Amazingly, the salute continued to its conclusion but there were no more incidents. The smoke of the guns had drifted back towards the fortress, obscuring the scene and leaving the fortress commander blissfully unaware of the havoc he had created.

As Nicholas approached the palace his heart was pounding rapidly and, because of the damage, he feared the worst. The Tsar's personal guard came out and took up defensive positions while officers of the guard surrounded him and, after what seemed an eternity, escorted him inside to the family quarters. In a few moments he was at her side but in her confusion Alix did not recognize him.

The courtiers helped her to her feet and began brushing the debris from her gown. "Where is the Tsar?" cried Alix hysterically. "I saw blood, is he dead?" She struggled against the arms assisting her and tried to pull away, but she was light-headed and her legs felt as if they were going to collapse beneath her.

"Alexandra, calm yourself, you are making a spectacle," Minnie implored in a loud whisper.

"Do not tell me what to do!" cried Alix. "I must find my husband." With that she turned to run, but the skirts of her gown impeded her progress and she tripped, fell to the floor, and began to weep. Then she heard a familiar voice and through her tears she saw the object of her search, her beloved husband. He stood before her in his red uniform, flushed from his long run but full of life. Nicholas gently reached down, took her hands in his and kissed her palms while he helped her to her feet. She collapsed into his arms, holding him tightly and resting her head on his shoulder.

"Sunny, I am so relieved to see you are unharmed," he said. "My heart stopped when I saw your window shot out and I thought the light had gone out of my life forever."

Alix, oblivious to the courtiers and family present, remained in his arms. "My darling, you are my world. I died a thousand deaths seeing you so alone and vulnerable."

After assuring himself that his mother was uninjured Nicky led Alix away to their family quarters so they could regain their composure in private. Alix was understandably upset and wished to return immediately to Tsarskoe Selo. "It is the only place I feel safe," she told him. Not sure of the feasibility of secure travel at this time, the Tsar left her to confer with the head of his security detail and to arrange their departure as soon as possible.

CRBO

It was not until later that evening, when they were finally settled at Alexander Palace that the Tsar learned what had happened. Nicholas received the Chief of the Secret Police in his study and was provided with the results of the preliminary investigation. Nicholas read in stunned disbelief that two live rounds had been accidentally included with the blank ammunition laid out for the salute and had been fired in their turn during the ceremony. He looked up from the report and stared at the Chief.

"I cannot believe this was accidental when the two shots came so close to hitting their marks." The Chief assured him that he had interviewed all the key artillerymen at the fortress and he was convinced that it truly was an accident. He also informed the Tsar that the policeman who died was named Romanov, a fact which did little to dispel the feeling of unease that Nicholas was developing as a result of this tumultuous day.

Nevertheless Nicholas accepted the report, such as it was, because there was little else he could do. He was rapidly coming to the realization that many things were being kept from him and he wondered just how bad the situation in the country was. I must find someone I can trust, he thought, someone who will keep me informed. He remembered back to the time when his father, Alexander III, was suffering his final illness. They had many long talks as the Tsar attempted to prepare Nicky for the road ahead.

"There will be times where you will need someone of the utmost discretion to handle delicate situations for you," he told Nicky, "someone who is completely trustworthy. I recommend you keep Count Paul Benckendorff as a Marshall of the Court. He worked for your grandfather and for me and has proven his loyalty. I trust him implicitly."

Nicholas reflected on Count Benckendorff's service to their family. He had started out in the Corps des Pages and took part in the Russo-Turkish War of 1877. After the war, he became part of his grandfather Alexander's household and had served the Imperial family ever since. He now held the position of Grand Marshal of the Court and Nicky decided, after his meeting with the head of security that the Count was to have a new mission. He would become the eyes and ears of the Tsar, but funds for the Count's activities would have to come from the Tsar's private fortune to avoid compromising the Count's work.

Alix had gone to bed as soon as they came home. Today's ordeal had been too much for her delicate constitution. Nicky decided to peek in on the children before he turned in for the night. When he reached the children's quarters, he bumped into his sister Olga, who was going to her quarters after spending the evening with the children. Together they looked into the rooms of the sleeping children, precious girls who seemed like little angels as they slept, oblivious to the day's happenings.

As they left Olga inquired how he was. "I heard what happened today. How upset you must be."

"I just made the sign of the cross, what else could I do? If they were going to kill me, I was a dead man," he told her. "Anyway I have nothing to worry about until 1918."

"What do you mean by that?" asked Olga.

There was a short period of silence as Nicky realized that the stress of the day's events had taken its toll on him and he said something he should not have. "Oh, nothing really. I am just tired. I think I shall turn in for the night."

Olga knew that there was more to it than that but it was much too late in this eventful day to pursue a subject he so obviously did not wish to discuss.

ೞೱ

The troops stood in the square, nervously awaiting the protesters. Lined up one beside the other, they were ordered not to let anyone pass. The commander rode up and down the line forbidding anyone to fire until ordered to do so. In the distance faint sounds of singing could be heard, and, as the crowd came closer the soldiers could make out the words:

God Save the Tsar

Mighty and Powerful

Let Him Reign for Our Glory

For the Confusion of Our Enemies

The Orthodox Tsar

God Save the Tsar

Thousands of people poured into the square, hoisting banners high, and clutching holy icons and pictures of the Tsar. At the head of the mass of people strode Father George Gapon, Russia's foremost labor leader, carrying a petition to the Tsar demanding a constitutional government and assistance for the poor laborers. The soldiers were shocked to see women and children among the crowd and became uneasy. They had been led to believe that the petitioners were nothing more than an unruly rabble and they were surprised to find such an orderly and peaceful group. They would have been even more shocked to know that Father Gapon was thought to be an agent of the secret police because the priest never tried to conceal his connections with the authorities and attempted to work with them on other occasions. But a clash between the demonstrators and the troops seemed inevitable because of the sheer numbers of people involved. As those in the rear of the crowd pushed forward the citizens in front pressed in on the troops and the soldiers, untrained in crowd control, reacted in the only way they knew, by firing point-blank into the crowd. When the smoke cleared, bodies were strewn about the square, oozing crimson blood onto the contrasting white snow. In clashes throughout the city that "Bloody Sunday" two hundred died and another eight hundred were injured. Most of the demonstrators never realized that the Tsar was not even in the city and had no involvement in the massacre.

Nicholas was stunned when the news of the events of reached him at Alexander Palace. Only the day before his ministers had notified him all the factories in St. Petersburg were on strike and that the strikers numbered about 120,000. Nevertheless, he was assured that the city was calm and that the additional security measures taken were adequate for the situation. Now this devastating news. A terrible day, he thought. Lord, how painful and sad. My people only wanted to meet with me and now they are dead.

Word of the tragedy spread throughout the country and the world and the outrage was universal. The British press attacked the Tsar as a cold-blooded murderer. The Russian people, crushed by the events, reacted by crying out,"The Tsar has abandoned us, and we have no Tsar." Father Gapon prepared a letter that was posted throughout the city, calling for revolution. In it he wrote, "Nicholas Romanov, you are no longer our Tsar, but the murderer of Russia. The innocent blood of workers, women and children will forever stain your hands. The Russian people will never forget."

The tone of the letter made Nicky realize that he had lost his special relationship with the people and he reacted with great sadness. Later, at an emergency meeting of his advisors, he could only glare silently at them. Finally Sergei Witte, the Minister of Finance spoke up. "Your imperial highness, you must send word that the troops fired without orders and that it was a tragic accident."

"I will not allow the army to be blamed for this incident," Nicholas said. "After all they were only reacting to the provocation of the crowd. I intend to accept the blame. Now tell me why was I not informed the people wished to meet with me?"

"Your imperial highness it was too dangerous and we were concerned about your safety," said one of his ministers.

"I believe it was my decision to make. How dare you usurp my authority!" he stormed at them, and slammed his fist angrily on the conference table. "This did not have to happen. A peaceful demonstration has turned into a blood bath and now we must all live with these deaths on our hands."

"Your highness, you must not accept the blame. They are starting to call you "Bloody Nicholas," Witte informed him.

"Then arrange for a group of workers to come to the palace tomorrow. I will address them at that time and see what can be salvaged from this disaster." He dismissed his ministers and they left to do his bidding. Nicholas also departed, but he went in search of his closest advisor, his wife Alexandra.

As usual Alix was reclining on a sofa in her Mauve Boudoir. He spent a few minutes catching her up on the events of the last few days. "They are blaming me for what happened in Palace Square."

"It is not your fault. They were warned repeatedly to retreat and refused to listen. I admit the deaths were ghastly but if the soldiers had not fired perhaps there would have been even more. If only you had reliable ministers instead of that lot you inherited from your father. Quite an incompetent group, as far as I am concerned."

The logic of her reasoning completely escaped him so he merely repeated the sentiments he had expressed in the meeting.

"Lord, it is so painful and hard to think of the many killed and injured just because they wanted to see their Tsar."

Nicholas and Alexandra were both saddened by the deaths of so many innocents and were beginning to realize the implication of "Bloody Sunday." The Tsar was no longer looked on as a benevolent ruler but rather as a bloody despot. The events of January 9, 1905 lighted the fires of revolution that would eventually sweep away the Romanovs and plunge Russia into *an abyss from which there seems no hope of rescue.*

Nicholas left Alix lounging comfortably on her chaise and went off to continue his deliberations. Alexandra continued to work on items for an upcoming bazaar. During her first years in Russia the Tsarina had established the "Help Through Handiwork Guild" to make clothing for the poor and though the Russian nobility was generally reluctant to get involved, they could hardly ignore her efforts. Besides, she had the support of her husband and Nicky encouraged his household to become active in charity work. When the war with Japan broke out she changed the focus of her work and moved the guild to larger rooms in the Winter Palace where she and her helpers sewed bandages, and knitted warm clothes and socks for the soldiers. Her daily involvement ceased once her pregnancy with Alexei became more advanced and since his birth she had neglected the work totally. Alix had always been something of a hypochondriac but there was absolutely nothing imaginary about the terrible migraines that incapacitated her for days on end. "Well, at least I can sew," she thought, as she worked to fill the basket beside her with bandages. It was not too long after Nicky left her boudoir that she felt the familiar dull throb begin deep in her head. Alix did not know what triggered these episodes but the events of the last two weeks had created enough stress to weaken her resistance. She knew she would soon be prostrate from the pain so she called for her maid and had her dim the lights. Alexandra left orders that under no circumstances was she to be disturbed, because even the slightest sound increased her pain. She would not see the children or even Nicky when these attacks occurred. As the agony took hold of her she prayed that this latest episode would not last too long. Alix quickly put the finishing touches on a note to her daughter, Olga, and had her maid deliver it to the nursery. In the quiet lilac room that usually gave her so much comfort, she wept bitterly, knowing nothing she could do would mitigate her pain.

Olga accepted the message from the hand of the maidservant and quickly read through it.

My Sweet Child,

I kiss you tenderly and thank you for your little notes. I am sorry I could not see you alone but it's very difficult these days. Soon I shall be freer, and then you can tell us all, and everything that interests you. You see, I am generally very tired and therefore often do not keep you all for a very long time with us, and often very sad and do not want you to see my gloomy face. God bless you, Mama.

"Well Mama is ill again," said Olga as she read the note from her mother. "I just do not understand why she is always so sick. I think she could still see us."

"You must have patience with her. Her head aches so badly sometimes. Oh poor Mama. I can only imagine how bad she feels," Tatiana said sympathetically. "You know she loves us and will see us when she can." Alix would have been most distressed to hear her daughters speak so. She loved her children with all her heart and it devastated her not to be with them.

೦೪೭೦

Nicholas held the promised meeting with a carefully selected group of workers. "You were used as pawns by your leaders," he told them. "Strikes and disturbances will only compel the authorities to act with force. Unfortunately this force can result in innocent lives being lost. I know the life of a worker is difficult but much can be done to improve your condition. Have patience; revolts and anarchy are not the solution. Your acts on Sunday were criminal actions and that resulted in many deaths. I know your hearts are pure and I forgive you your indiscretions." For Nicky it was a heart felt speech but it did little to remove the hostility evident on the striker's faces or ameliorate the unrest when the substance of the meeting was reported to the various worker's councils.

The past week had left him shaken and confused and he seemed unable to cope with the speed at which the situation had developed. I did not expect things to deteriorate so rapidly, he thought. Nicholas sincerely believed he had the fifteen years St. Serafim promised him in the letter but the events of the last few days seemed to belie the prediction. He sat at his desk and mulled over a number of different options but could not come up with any satisfactory explanations. Finally, he took his true diary from its secret compartment in his desk and began to write his thoughts and feelings down in great detail. This second diary was a secret no one was aware of and he could thank his father for the good advice that led to the keeping of two separate journals. He left his primary diary on his desk and had caught Alix reading it more than once, and she even left him notes in it. The Tsar sensed there were spies in the palace so he was very particular with all his correspondence and that was one of the reasons he acted as his own secretary. The diary on his desk was a good medium to transmit information he wanted known. He was well aware that most of the court considered him to be dull and uninspired. Rather than be insulted by this attitude, Nicky encouraged it, realizing long ago that this perceived weakness in his character could work to his advantage. Nevertheless, he privately resented the patronizing attitude of the older Romanovs and refused to trust them in matters better kept close to the heart.

After finishing his work he went to check on Alix who was suffering from yet another of her migraines. As he walked down the hallway Nicky was surprised to hear the sounds of laughter coming from her boudoir. He entered the room to find Alix propped up on a sofa, with Anastasia on her lap, and a storybook open in front of them. Olga and Tatiana were applying themselves to their needlework and Maria was playing on the floor with Alexei. It was such a rare and tranquil domestic scene that the soft-hearted Nicky was nearly overcome with emotion. It warmed his heart to see Alix with their children. She loved them so much and suffered such guilt when she could not see them.

"Darling Sunny, I thought you were indisposed. You certainly look like you are feeling better."

"Mercifully the attack lasted only a few hours so I decided to spend some time with the children," she said.

The family enjoyed their evening together and the children were thrilled to see their mother. Alexandra had agreed to allow Olga and Tatiana to help with the efforts of the Handiwork Guild and the two older girls were hard at work on items for soldiers at the front. The two teased each other and tried to imagine the cavaliers who would wear their creations. The quiet interlude dispelled all thoughts of the turmoil outside the gates of the palace and in the contentment of a close-knit family it was easy to forget the horrors of "Bloody Sunday."

Chapter 6

February 1905 - Moscow. Ella watched from the window as the vehicle bearing her husband Sergei slowly moved away. Although the Grand Duchess could see the area directly in front of their palace she was concentrating on the carriage and was unaware of the inconspicuous figure lurking in the shadows across the street. Sergei had scoffed at the need for security and was alone except for the coachman. When the carriage moved nearer, the assassin saw his opportunity, raced out from his place of concealment and rushed unhindered toward the carriage. Sergei was defenseless and, as Ella looked on in horror, the terrorist hurled a bomb through the open window of the rig. It detonated almost immediately and the deafening explosion ripped the once splendid conveyance apart. It was a ghastly scene. Sergei was dismembered by the blast, one of the team was down, screaming as only a wounded horse does, and the coachman was seriously injured. Ivan Kalyaev, the assassin, was knocked nearly unconscious by the explosion but when he regained his senses he was amazed to find he was dazed but uninjured. He shook the cobwebs from his head, looked around and observed a strikingly attractive woman run out from the building across the way, screaming, "Sergei, Oh Sergei!"

Ella was followed from the palace by a number of servants, all in a state of shock as they took in the horrifying scene. Numbly Ella dropped to the ground and began to gather the bloody pieces of flesh and bone that were all that remained of her once strong, vibrant husband. With a handkerchief she took from her bodice she began mopping up his blood. Finally the task became too much for her so she directed the servants who had followed her to get a blanket and more cloths. While she waited she tended to Sergei's coachman, Andrei Rudinkin, who was very seriously injured. He feebly asked after the Grand Duke.

"He's alive and only slightly wounded," she lied, refusing to let him see her grief. After arranging for the coachman's care Ella gently began to gather Sergei's remains and place them on the soft blanket the servants brought to her. Despite their protestations she refused to leave until she recovered every possible bit of his flesh and blood. When her gruesome task was finally completed she allowed herself to be escorted back to the palace. Her composure finally left her and she broke down and began to sob bitterly.

❁

There was a flurry of activity at the Alexander Palace in Tsarskoe Selo as the final preparations were made for the formal dinner later that evening. Alix was busy conferring with her staff on last minute additions when Nicholas came into the drawing room. She looked up and knew instantly from the grave look on his face that something serious had occurred.

"I have terrible, terrible news," he announced.

Alix dismissed the servants and Nicky came and knelt in front of her sofa and placed his head in her lap. While she gently smoothed his hair he gave her the tragic news. "Alix! It's Sergei. He was killed this afternoon," he told her as gently as he could.

"Oh no! What happened?" Alix asked him, as she struggled to maintain her self-control.

"He was killed by a terrorist's bomb right outside his palace," he explained.

"Oh, poor Ella! How is she taking it?"

"Alix, I am so sorry. She saw the whole incident from the window and ran out of the palace to find that his body had been terribly mutilated."

"We must go to her. When can we leave?"

"My darling Sunny, we are not going anywhere and I must inform the family that they cannot attend the funeral. The police are convinced this is the beginning of a series of plots and we are all the targets."

"Nicky, she is my sister; I have to go to her. We cannot leave her all alone."

"Alix, you must obey me in this. Think of the children. Do you want to leave them without a mother?"

Nicky sat down beside her and took her into his arms. "I know this is difficult but I cannot make an exception for you. Our Russian family is the target of these attacks but your sisters and brother are German and will be able to safely join Ella, so she will have family present."

He fully expected Alix to object hysterically and then take to her bed, which seemed her usual response to any crisis of late, but this time she surprised him.

"There is much to do. I must cancel this dinner and send out condolences," she informed him, "so let me get started."

Nicholas left her to try to learn more about the situation in Moscow while Alix prepared a telegram to send to Ella. She called in her secretary and had him notify the family that tonight's dinner was canceled but she put off telling the children as long as possible so she would not break down in front of them. Finally she walked up the staircase to the children's floor. She waited in the Crimson Drawing Room while the nurse went to get the Grand Duchesses. As she sat on a sofa, she glanced around the room and her eyes came to rest on the portrait of Alice of Hesse, her mother and, of course, Ella's. The warmth of her mother's smile comforted her as she prepared to impart the sad news to her daughters. The nurse brought the girls in and Alix gathered them around her and gently told them of their uncle's death, leaving out the gruesome details. Olga and Tatiana cried and she hugged them both. Maria and Anastasia did not seem to understand the concept of death as they were still so young but when they saw their older sisters cry, they too began to weep. Alix hugged them all and told them, "it is very sad for us because we will miss Uncle Sergei, but he is happy among the angels in heaven and wishing we were not so sad."

It was only later when she remembered Elena Motovilov's predictions at Sarov and was able to reflect on them that she became very frightened. She lay awake waiting for Nicky to retire and when he finally came to bed she wrapped her arms around him and related her fears to him.

"Nicky I am so afraid that you are next. All of Elena's prophecies have come true and I cannot bear to live without you. I want us all to leave this ungrateful, godless country which murders its own rulers who are anointed by God."

"Sunny, whatever you think is best. We can discuss it tomorrow," he replied. Nicholas knew that for her peace of mind he needed to placate her, at least for the present. She finally fell asleep but the Emperor lay awake wrestling with the enormity of what she had suggested. I am the Tsar of Russia, how can I leave my country? I will not abandon my people. He recognized that his immediate family might have to leave for their safety but in his heart he knew he could never abandon his homeland, Mother Russia. He wondered if it might not be a bad idea to send them away for a little while, at least until the situation calms down. Alix will never agree to leave without me but I will not tell her until it is too late for her to object.

He reflected on St. Serafim's letter and remembered that it was quite specific as to the amount of time he would have to make preparations, but time passed so quickly and of the fifteen years nearly two were already gone. It was distressing to think of his own martyrdom but he refused to let fear control him and he knew that when the time arrived he would willingly die for Russia. It was not often he thought about his faith, which he tended to take for granted, but as he lay there he was humbled by the fact that God had sent a personal message and warning to him, through the saintly Serafim. In his humility he could not understand why he was chosen but the letter emphatically predicted that one of his daughters held the key to Russia's future. I will do everything in my power to protect them, he thought. Sergei's death only made it more evident to him how easily a life could be snuffed out and he was relieved he had increased the family's personal security. Alix would not be happy about it, as she disliked the lack of privacy, but like it or not, there would be police and soldiers guarding their every move from this point on.

CRBO

Kalyaev sat in one of the offices of the Moscow police station, his hands, and feet manacled to a chair, confused as to why he had been removed from his damp cell and brought to this well-lighted room. A guard stood in the corner watching his every move. A sound at the door caused him to look up and he observed a woman all in black, her head covered by a heavy veil, enter the room with a weary step and practically collapse into the chair next to his. He had no idea who she was until she whispered to him, "I am the wife of the man you assassinated," and lowering her head onto her hands she began to weep.

Kalyaev felt no sorrow for her. Grand Duke Sergei Alexandrovitch was a horrid, autocratic man who had to be removed. "Do not cry princess," he told her. "It had to be so." It amazed him that the Grand Duchess had come to speak to him. Last week they would have passed me on the streets without a second glance, yet it is only after I kill someone that they talk to me, he thought to himself.

"You must have suffered so to commit this murder," Ella told him.

In his agitated state Kalyaev tried to jump up but was restrained by the chains, so he shouted at her from his chair.

"Murder! Murder! It was not murder but the vengeance of a righteous people. I am their avenging angel attempting to heal their suffering; the suffering that a cruel government and a terrible war place upon them. Where was the Tsar when his people were shot down in the square, their only crime wanting to meet with him? Surely, you did not think that would go unpunished?"

"If you only repent of your actions, I will go to the Tsar and seek clemency for you and ask him to spare your life," Ella gently told him while trying to maintain her poise in the face of his anger. "I know your heart is pure, please try to see reason. My husband was a good man and he did not deserve to die."

"I do not want the Tsar's clemency. You and your kind are so high and mighty, sitting in your palaces while the people are murdered in the streets. Your days are numbered and the ones you trust the most with your safety will help to bring about your downfall," Kalyaev replied in a more subdued voice.

She rose to leave, realizing that her words would have no effect upon him. With true forgiveness in her heart, she handed him an icon. "I beg you to accept this icon in memory of my husband. I forgive you and will pray for you." Kalyaev refused to meet her eyes as she left. He was a hardened revolutionary but he had to admit she touched him with her kindness and spirituality.

Ella returned to her palace, her thoughts troubled as she reflected on Kalyaev's words. I must get word to the Tsar that we are living in a nest of vipers. The terrorist could have only meant that the secret police or the army is involved in a revolutionary plot to dispose of the Romanovs and usher in some new form of government. It must be the police, she speculated, the army has always seemed so loyal to the Tsar.

Ella's suspicion that the Okrana, the secret police, might be involved was not based solely on the ravings of an assassin. The notion that the police organization might harbor disloyal elements was not farfetched at all and many of the royals had long suspected the secret police of intrigue and manipulation. They were a power unto themselves, a complex organization with many faces and capable of almost any action, without restraint. They made effective use of a vast network of spies and informers and more than any other organization in Russia, the police had the pulse of the nation. There were those in the Okrana who wanted a return to the autocratic style of Alexander III, Nicky's father and wished to transform Nicholas II, generally recognized for his generosity and mercy, into a harsh, despotic ruler. It was not impossible that the events of "Bloody Sunday" had been orchestrated for this purpose. On the other hand there were those of a liberal bent who preferred a more democratic form of government such as a constitutional monarchy or the complete elimination of the monarchy altogether. If Ella was correct, it was this faction that had been responsible for her husband's murder, since Sergei was considered by most to be an unreformed autocrat. Corruption was rampant and rumor had it that even members of the extended royal family were funding some of the disruptive schemes. The revolutionary groups and even the secret police organization itself was riddled with double agents. Father Gapon was such an agent, hired by the police with the expectation that they could control the workers of St. Petersburg through him. Of course that effort was a total failure as Gapon appeared to have become a full-fledged revolutionary. An unfortunate side effect of the secret police's increased activity in safeguarding the Tsar was that more agents had access to the Imperial family's whereabouts and movements. The detailed records of their comings and goings, which the police compiled, had the effect of making the family more vulnerable rather than safer.

❀

Alix waited in anticipation for her caller, the Princess Maria Baria-tinskaya. Maria had been one of her maids of honor and a close friend during Alix's first years in Russia but a falling out had sent Maria to Rome. She had now returned to Russia at Alix's request to resume her post at the palace. Alix was relieved to have her back as the princess acted as an unofficial chief of staff for her. With her common sense and immense energy, she saw to it that the Empress's needs were met and solutions to various problems satisfactory to all.

Maria was ushered in and she nervously approached the Empress, who extended her hand. She kissed it and sat down at the request of Alix.

"Your Imperial Highness, I have something I must tell you at the very beginning and I hope you will not be too angered by it," she began. "I have become a Catholic."

Alix looked with consternation at her friend. "How could you have done such a thing and abandoned your faith?"

Maria carefully explained to Alix how she had become interested in Catholicism after an audience with his Holiness Pope Pius X. "There was such a sense of peace and calm about him and a total oneness with God. There was a yearning within me for that peace and I found it when I converted."

"This is difficult to accept but I will not keep you from your position at court," Alix replied.

"Your imperial Highness, I know I am not in a position to ask for special favors, especially under these circumstances but could something be done so I can practice my faith while I am in Russia. "I do not want to leave because of this."

Alix looked at her friend and knew that if she did not grant her this favor she would lose her services, something she was not willing to do. This is a small price to pay for her ability, she thought.

"I will speak with the Tsar. It will not happen immediately but I think by Easter we should have some progress," she told Maria. "But I must say I do not understand the hold this Pope seems to have over people. Ella spoke highly of his predecessor, Leo XIII, as well, and even seems to have developed a friendship with him."

"I can only say that he is a very holy man and if you met him you would understand. Thank you for your support in this. I know it may raise difficulties for you."

"Nonsense," Alix replied, as she dismissed her friend.

∞

The chill was beginning to dissipate and the first breaths of spring could be felt when Ella arrived from Moscow with her wards, Marie and Dmitri, to spend the Easter Holidays. Care was taken to ensure their rooms in the Catherine Palace were comfortable and they were invited to spend their days with the Imperial family at Alexander Palace. The Grand Duchesses, realizing their cousin's loss, went out of their way to be kind to Marie and Dmitri and let them use all their toys. The children spent much of their day in the huge playroom on the second floor since they were on holiday from lessons. Marie and Dmitri were amazed by the amount and variety of toys to play with. Alix was not one to spoil her children but Nicky was always pleased by the gifts given to the children by ambassadors and foreign leaders so she did not have the heart to limit the girl's collection.

Olga was happy to see her cousin Marie and remembering her mother's words to be kind, she brought out her most prized possession for her to play with. It was a soft, supple, leather trunk, which opened to reveal a doll with soft, bouncy curls and a complete wardrobe of stylish dresses, hats, and shoes. The French president had given it to her when she visited France with her parents. Marie was enchanted and found it hard to believe that Olga let her play with the doll. Dmitri meanwhile was enthralled with an Indian tepee and child-sized canoes. He had never seen anything like them. The girls informed him they were from the wild west of America. "America?" asked Dmitri. "Where is it? It must be very far away."

"Oh it is," said Olga. "Tatiana has some photographs of America."

Tatiana vied with Olga to show Marie the best toy and brought out her stereoscope, which gave the photographs a three dimensional look. She put in the images from America and the girls exclaimed over each picture while Dmitri clamored for his turn. "I'm not sure what this one is," said Marie. The scene showed an American family sitting on a blanket enjoying a repast from a wicker basket. "It looks like they are eating."

"Oh, that is a picnic," said Tatiana as she viewed the image.

"How do you know it is a picnic? Where are the tables and the servants to serve the meal?" said Marie.

"Turn the picture over. See it says "American Picnic". That is how they have picnics in America," Tatiana informed her.

"It looks like so much fun but of course a Grand Duchess would never eat off the ground," Olga said in a stuffy British accent, imitating their English governess. The girls all giggled and then continued enjoying the photographs from America.

Alix and Ella stood at the doorway where they had stopped to check in on the children. They looked at each other and smiled. "We should plan an American picnic for the children," they exclaimed at the same time. The two laughed as they walked arm in arm back to Alix's boudoir.

With the children happily occupied, Ella spent many quiet hours sewing and talking with Alix, who was full of sympathy and did her best to cheer her sister up. Ella told her of her spiritual longing and yearning for a simpler life since Sergei's death. In the late morning, Nicholas came in and asked Ella if she would like to go for a walk after lunch as the day was so lovely. A walk is just what I need and will give me a private moment to speak with Nicky, she thought.

"Alix, why don't you and Ella eat here? There is no need for you to be at today's lunch and this will give you both a chance to visit privately," Nicky suggested to the two sisters.

"That is a wonderful idea. Thank you darling," Alix replied.

"Ella, I will be in my study when you are finished and then we shall have our walk."

After Nicky left, Alix turned to her older sister with concern on her face. How could she possibly soothe her older sister's concerns when it was always Ella who assumed the role of family comforter?

"Ella, I am at such a loss for words," said Alix rather awkwardly. "It is still such a shock that Sergei is gone."

"Sergei was my whole world. What do I do now? My whole purpose in life is gone."

"You must think of Marie and Dmitri. You are like a mother to them and now they need you more than ever," replied Alix.

"The assassination was very traumatic for them and they are still having nightmares. It is good we are visiting for Easter; it will help take their minds off their troubles. It is so calm and peaceful here that it is like another world. You have truly made this an oasis away from the turmoil in the country," Ella observed.

"I try hard to keep it so for the children. They have no idea of the condition of our nation and what goes on outside these gates. It is so important to keep life as normal as possible for them, yet protected from events beyond the walls. That is why I try to shield them as much as possible from outsiders."

"It seems like just yesterday we were dancing at the Winter Palace. I never dreamed our world would be in such a state with the country at war, the Tsar almost killed, and now my husband dead."

"I try not to think about it too much or I will go mad. I hate to admit it but I am so high-strung. Yet with five children I must maintain my sanity. It is such a cross for Nicky to bear."

"You are right. We must not dwell on such things, especially on the eve of this great celebration. Now I must go and find Nicky before the rest of the day slips away."

Ella was ready to take leave of Alix. Although they had always been close she could see the unease her sister felt when talking to her and her own concerns made her impatient to be on her way. She excused herself and walked down the hall to the Tsar's study. Ella had looked forward to speaking privately with him for some time and she had so much to tell him. He had left the door open for her and she entered his private sanctuary. It was the one place in the palace that reflected Nicky's masculinity, unlike the other rooms which Alix had decorated. The walls and ceiling were paneled in a deep, rich mahogany, which gave the study certain warmth, but the natural darkness of the room was off set by the many glass and bronze chandeliers and the large window overlooking the grounds. His desk was shaped like an "L" and all the objects on it were meticulously arranged in a special pattern so that with a single glance he would know in an instant if his desk had been disturbed. His valet took no chances and kept a chart listing the placement of each item. Nicholas did not look up when she came in and seemed lost in thought as he sat in his green leather chair reading a letter.

"What are you working on so intently?" Ella asked him.

"It is a letter from Pope Pius X, one of several I have received. Since he came into power he seems determined to heal the schism between our two churches. Of course that will never happen while I have control but this latest request is harder to ignore."

"What is he asking for?"

"In the spirit of Christian unity, he requests that I allow the Catholics in Russia to freely practice their faith."

"It seems a small thing to ask. I do not see harm in granting his request."

"Actually I have wanted to discuss this with you. I have decided to issue an Edict of Religious Tolerance for the Catholics."

"What has brought you to this decision so suddenly?"

"In reality my reasoning is more practical than spiritual and I have considered this move for some time. Our church leaders will protest, of course, but you never know when we might need a special favor and this Pope Pius X appears to have great influence throughout the world. I am not promoting Catholicism but I have decided to let them practice their faith. Naturally they will do it in private and maybe this decision will give me a little peace."

"What do you mean by that?" she inquired.

"As you may well know Ella, my dear, one of Alix's Maids of Honor have embraced this faith and she has been urging me to do something for her. As a convert herself, though to the Orthodox faith she is much more tolerant than I am, but I think there is more to it than merely the possibility of losing her favorite helpmate. A number of influential members of the nobility are now Catholics so this Edict seems a good political maneuver. Yet I often wonder what would take them from their Russian faith and risk so much to embrace this religion."

"I think you will make a wise decision in publishing this Edict. It will not be something that you will regret later. Since Sergei's death I find myself more sympathetic to the plight of others. As you know I have been to Rome and the Catholics are really not so different from us," she replied.

"That reminds me Ella; I never got a chance to talk to you about that message from the Pope. The one you announced in front of all those people at the winter ball."

"Heavens Nicky, that must have been over two years ago. I don't remember what I told you. And why have you waited so long to ask me about it?"

"I just never seemed to remember to bring it up and since the night of the ball I have had so many other things to deal with. Issues that had to be handled immediately, including this disastrous war with Japan. When you mentioned your visit to Rome it refreshed my memory. The message you relayed from the Pope sounded as if it were a far off future event, something I could deal with later," explained Nicky. "But I remember exactly what you said. *'When the sun falls from the sky you will know the fate of Russia'."*

"Yes I remember now," said Ella. "I am sure you have many questions about that statement Nicky but I am afraid I have little insight into the reason behind Pope Leo's message."

"Certainly you asked him about it?"

"I did but he would not elaborate."

"How could someone make a profound statement such as that and not give some sort of explanation as to the meaning?"

"You did not seem to have a problem accepting the statements from Elena Motivilov when we were in Sarov, and they were just as vague," said Ella.

"But she was a woman of God and a protégé of Saint Serafim."

"And is not the Pope a man of God?"

"Yes, of course he is, but I give more weight to the prophecies of our own saints and holy ones," said Nicky.

"Evidently you attached a significant amount of weight to what the Pope said otherwise you would not have brought this up after so many months," replied Ella.

Nicky realized Ella had a remarkable insight into his psyche and sometimes seemed to know him better than he knew himself. He was grateful to have her as a confidante.

"You are right Ella, I have thought about it more than once," Nicky said, and a serious look came over his face. "I cannot make any sense of it. If it were true then it would seem the nation is headed for disaster, but does it refer to the war we are now engaged in or some future event? Saint Serafim promised fifteen years but the year 1918 seems so distant."

"Nicky I am sure that when the time comes you will look at all that has transpired and will know in your heart what it means. Now may we take that walk you promised me? The day is fading away."

Nicky and Ella strolled through the grounds of the landscaped park. The air was filled with a fresh scent, the first buds of spring were evident on the trees, and the sun gently warmed them. Ella spoke to Nicky of her meeting with Sergei's assassin and his prediction that those they most trusted to protect them would do them harm. Nicholas told her not to worry as he was quite aware of the danger surrounding them. "I appreciate your concern but I have my own agents and spies reporting to Count Benckendorff," he said. "I trust they will keep us informed. Now let us go back as it will be a long night and we must all rest."

When they returned, Ella gathered up Marie and Dmitri and went back to the Catherine Palace. Nicholas went to his study to do some final paper work and when he arrived there he found Count Benckendorff waiting for him. The Count was the Tsar's most trusted advisor and to find him at the palace at this time, when there was so many preparations to be made for the Easter celebration, was somewhat surprising.

"Your majesty, I have some alarming news," he began. "I have just received a communication from one of my agents. He informs me that there are credible rumors of a plan to assassinate you sometime during the Easter festivities. Unfortunately he has been unable to ferret out any of the details so we cannot take specific measures to foil the plot in advance."

Nicholas studied the Count's worried face for a few moments and then called in the head of his security force and had Benckendorff brief him concerning the suspected plot. The Tsar then ordered extra security to be put in place but made it quite clear to the two men that he wanted no disruption of the celebrations. Although he took the information seriously and did not down play its importance, Nicholas nevertheless felt no alarm at the news. The Imperial compound at Tsarskoe Selo was the one place in which he felt genuinely secure and he could not imagine anyone having the audacity to attack him here. After reviewing the arrangements one final time he dismissed the Count and Head of Security, completed his work, and then left to prepare for Easter. He had no intention of mentioning any of this to Alix.

Chapter 7

Easter 1905 - Tsarskoe Selo. The day before Easter was one of anticipation rather than festivity; a period of preparation instead of celebration. The entire nation was involved in readying itself for the most holy and important feast day of the liturgical calendar. The Resurrection of Christ would be celebrated with all the pomp and ceremony for which the Orthodox faith was so renowned. The traditional service would take place at midnight and would be followed by a day of feasting limited only by a household's means. The wonderful odors emanating from the kitchens of Russia were testament to the significance of the day and Alexander Palace was no different. While Ella walked with the Tsar, Alix had reviewed the final preparations with her staff. Now the rich smell of baking cakes and other pastries added to the excitement and anticipation of the children. Alix wished privately that the family had been able to travel to their palace at Livadia in the Crimea but Count Benckendorff advised against it and the Tsar had acquiesced. Anyway, Tsarskoe Selo was beautiful in its own way, just quite a bit cooler in the evenings during early spring. In late afternoon everyone had taken a nap and even Nicky, despite the threat on his life, was able to fall asleep.

Late in the evening, in the crisp night air, the faithful of Russia began to stream into cathedrals, churches and chapels all over the country and the Imperial family was no different. Easter bestowed a special equality on the people and rich or poor they joined together in joyful prayer to celebrate this holy occasion. Because the royal family was not traveling to the Crimea the family members would attend the Easter Vigil celebration in the magnificent church at Tsarskoe Selo, which was constructed in the eighteenth century for Catherine the Great. It was named St. Sophia after the truly majestic Byzantine masterpiece in Istanbul, the mother church of Orthodox Christians, which had fallen into the hands of the Turks when they captured the city in 1453.

Alix and Nicky stood with their two oldest daughters in the darkened church awaiting the start of the Easter service. As did all the members of the large congregation they too held lighted candles that softly illuminated the night and added to the sense of expectation. Alix had converted to this faith prior to her marriage, as was required by Russian law. Initially reluctant, she now embraced the new religion with great fervor and found tremendous comfort in its spiritual nature and the solemnity of its liturgies, which however, were sometimes painfully long and tiring. She bowed her head and prayed for the strength to endure the long service. If Christ could suffer on the cross I can surely stand in his house for a few hours, she thought.

Shortly before midnight the bells, announcing the coming Feast of the Resurrection, began to peal. The clergy, dressed in fine, gold brocade robes in honor of the day, filed out through the doors in the Iconostasis, the elaborately decorated partition between the sanctuary and the nave. The Metropolitan Antony of St. Petersburg, who, with his thick, graying beard and dark, penetrating eyes was an imposing figure, wore a magnificent gold headdress embellished with pearls, precious stones, and painted enamel medallions. He began the service by swinging the censor and soon incense began wafting upwards on a journey to fill the air with its sweet scent.

The procession, which symbolized the search for the risen Savior, Jesus, started at the steps of the altar platform. Following the Metropolitan were the priests, deacons, choir and then the Imperial family in order of rank. The entire congregation then joined the procession and the lighted candles they carried appeared as twinkling stars matching those in the bright, cloudless sky. Three times, they processed around the church until finally they came to a halt in front of St Sophia's magnificent facade. The choir moved up the stairs to the left and the Imperial family took its place at the head of the congregation. The crowd of worshipers was completely silent in anticipation of the coming event. At last Metropolitan Antony made his way up the stairs and peered into the darkened church as if he were looking into Christ's tomb. He then turned to the throng of people arrayed before him, and joyfully intoned the refrain, "Christ is risen! Christ is risen!" The congregation answered in turn, "Indeed he is risen."

Immediately the church bells rang out and on cue the choir broke into magnificent polyphony of such beauty that it seemed as if angels had been commissioned by God to fill the church with their heavenly voices. Unseen hands illuminated the inside of the church and the light shone through the door, spilled down the stairs, and brightened the faces of those standing in front. Nicholas turned to Alix and gave her the traditional three Easter kisses of blessing, welcome and joy.

At this point the worshippers proceeded to re-enter the church and the noise level rose as they made their way to their assigned places. In the ensuing commotion a man dressed in choir robes slipped away from the other vocalists and without hurrying made his way toward the Tsar. Nicholas caught the movement out of the corner of his eye and turned to look at the approaching stranger, somewhat confused at this unexpected break in protocol. Suddenly, when the man was but a few feet from the Tsar, he withdrew a knife from his robe and raising it over his head flung himself at Nicholas. His face contorted with rage, he shouted, "Death to the Tsar", and slashed at him. When Nicholas lurched back he tripped on the hem of Alexandra's gown and fell backwards causing the blade to miss him completely. Alix screamed hysterically but clearer heads prevailed and hands reached for the assassin and pulled him back. Two members of the secret police struggled with him as he fought in vain to complete his mission. After what seemed an eternity, they finally wrestled him to the ground, pulled his arms behind him and forced the knife from his hand. The police then shackled the assassin and rushed him from the church.

The Tsar stood up, miraculously unharmed, and the crowd breathed a collective sigh of relief. Nicholas motioned to the Metropolitan, who stood in stunned silence on the steps of the altar, to continue with the service. There was no question but that the liturgy would proceed. Historically the Tsars had shown an absolute dedication to their public responsibilities and no one had ever criticized them for neglecting their duties. Nevertheless when the choir began singing anew it was no surprise that the atmosphere had changed. What was only a short time ago a joyous celebration was now subdued and troubled. All eyes were on the Imperial couple and whereas Nicholas seemed outwardly calm his eyes were cold with barely concealed fury. Alexandra appeared on the verge of collapse, her pale skin streaked with the red blotches that appeared whenever she was extremely agitated. Aware that all eyes were on them she struggled to maintain her composure and was able, after a moment to get her emotions under control.

Due to the size of the congregation many of those in the church were unaware that an incident had taken place and were overwhelmed instead by the beauty of their surroundings. The interior of St. Sophia was truly breathtaking. Four huge columns of granite held up the center dome and created a sensation of tremendous height. Incredible works of religious art adorned the walls while tiers of icons decorated the Iconostasis. The gold leaf that covered much of the church reflected the dancing light of hundreds of candles. A large table was set in front of the altar and was overflowing with Kulich, Paskha, and other foods of the season, all awaiting the Easter Blessing. All the beauty of the holy site represented two centuries of dedication, devotion and sacrifice by the faithful, rich and poor alike.

Nicky and Alix stood quietly together in the front of church and the lengthy service continued with the canon, the hours and the remainder of the liturgy. Finally Metropolitan Antony gave the paschal blessing and the service drew to a close. The Easter celebration, however, was just beginning.

In spite of their inner turmoil Nicholas and Alexandra were determined to carry out their formal duties at the Alexander Palace. They stood on the Garden Terrace in a receiving line dispensing the three kisses of Easter and handing out Imperial Easter Eggs and holy cards depicting St. Seraphim. Legend held that on Easter morning Mary Magdalene carried a basket of eggs for her breakfast when she went to Jesus' tomb to anoint his body. When she discovered Christ had risen she uncovered her basket of white eggs and found they were tinted with all the colors of the rainbow. Eggs were given as gifts to symbolize the world resurrected in Christ. Nicholas and Alexandra carried on this tradition but instead of the painted eggs of the people their gifts were made of the finest porcelain, gold or silver and decorated with precious stones and miniature paintings. The value of the egg was based on the rank of the recipient. It took a considerable amount of time to properly greet all the members of the imperial family, the courtiers and retainers as well as other invited guests

The early morning light was reflected by the dew on the trees and grass and produced such a lovely effect that it encouraged the many guests to forget the unsettling events that had taken place just a few hours earlier. Instead they took a few minutes to enjoy the idyllic setting before moving into the Portrait Hall. Through the large windows, which overlooked the garden terrace and well tended grounds, visitors were able to make out the rapidly lightening sky to the east. The hall was filled with paintings of past Tsars whose life-sized portraits dominated the room. Large palm trees, shipped by train from the Crimea, were carefully spotted throughout the room to add a touch of greenery. A large arch, supported by columns opened off the room into the Semi-Circular Hall where servants were putting the final touches to the tables set for Easter breakfast. These two chambers, combined with the Marble Hall constituted the public rooms of the palace and provided a large area, ideal for entertaining.

Once all the guests were received, servants, in bright red livery, announced breakfast and the party adjourned to the Semi-circular Hall for a sumptuous Easter feast. The room was light and airy, and all the doors were opened wide to admit a gentle, though somewhat cool breeze, which provided a sense of alfresco dining. The tables were beautifully set with solid silver place settings, elegant hand painted porcelain plates, and delicate crystal glass, etched in gold leaf with the imperial double eagle. The traditional Easter breakfast consisted of Kulich, a fruit and nut cake, glazed with white icing and decorated with candied fruit which spelled the letters XB, meaning Christ is Risen. The Kulich was served with paskha, a sweet cream cheese carefully molded into a pyramid, also with the letters XB. When the cake and cheese were presented everyone broke their Lenten fast with great enthusiasm. Thick slices of kulich spread with paskha and hard-boiled eggs dipped in salt were washed down with iced vodka. Two servants were present for each diner to ensure the meal was completed in the forty-five minutes dictated by court protocol.

As the meal drew to a close, two footmen, each carrying an elaborately wrapped box on a silver tray, made their way to the Tsar's table. One was presented to Minnie and to Alix. Minnie opened her gift first and held up a beautiful Faberge egg for everyone to see. Then all eyes shifted to Alix and there was a gasp from the guests as she removed the stunning Imperial Colonnade Egg from its box. Her eyes glistened with tears as

Nicky explained the significance of each element of this egg to her. She was touched by the thought and care that had gone into her fabulous gift and she selfishly admitted to herself that her egg was all the more precious because it outshone the gift given to Minnie.

Finally, their endless public duties completed for a time, they retired to the family quarters and the exhausted Alix immediately went to her Mauve Boudoir to rest. The attack on Nicholas at the morning's Easter service had shaken her to the core but she had no wish to discuss it with him because he seemed so nonchalant about the whole affair. But she misjudged him badly because with his usual concern for her delicate condition he refused to let her see how unnerved he actually was. He walked to his study deep in thought, worried about the family's safety. Nicky focused on the fact that Count Benckendorff's spies were able to give him some information on the assassination plot but nothing concrete enough to act on. It seemed strange that the secret police denied specific knowledge of the plot but were conveniently placed to save his life at just the right moment. Another factor that he had not considered was the weapon used in the attempt. Certainly a revolver would have been a better choice and more effective in bringing him down without hurting anyone else in the crowd. It seemed very strange.

Ever since Nicky's grandfather, Alexander II, was assassinated, security for the Tsar had become a complex issue. A special Guards regiment was formed, by order of Nicky's father, to protect the Imperial family at Tsarskoe Selo. The regiment consisted of top men drawn from army units throughout Russia and was considered a prestigious assignment. His Majesty's personal escort was a unit of Cossacks dedicated to and responsible for the Tsar's safety. They accompanied him wherever he went in Russia and on his international travels as well and Nicholas trusted them implicitly. Most male members of the Imperial family commanded units of the Army and even the women served as honorary colonels of some regiments. Unlike the army, to which the family was attached through loyalty and service, the presence of the secret police was a constant irritant. Supposedly their mission at Tsarskoe Selo was the security of the Tsar but of late spying seemed to be their main accomplishment. Word of every movement or activity at the royal compound seemed to make its way to police headquarters in St. Petersburg. Every visitor was logged in and out, and their own comings and goings were carefully recorded. There was little privacy, even in the personal quarters, because it was not difficult to place an informant among the domestic staff. It was all quite frustrating especially in light of the day's events. Nicholas wondered how an assassin could so easily slip into the compound when security was supposedly so tight. Although he was unafraid for himself he feared that Alix and the children might be injured or killed in an attempt on his life. After all Alix, Olga and Tatiana had been standing right next to him when the incident occurred. What was it that St. Serafim had counseled him in the letter? *The Lord God in his marvelous mercy bequeaths to your family a gift of fifteen years to prepare for these events. Remember this manifestation of God's kindness and use these years to plan well.* The attempt on his life convinced him that now was the time to get started. His family's safety took precedence over any other consideration and so it was with little more thought that he sat down at his desk to draft a letter, a letter that would become the first in a series of actions to remove them from danger.

Of course, any effort to safeguard his family in the manner he was considering would take enormous amounts of capital. There were bribes to be paid, silence to be bought and the future to be provided for. Fortunately Nicholas did not lack for money and the letter, addressed to a trusted aide, directed that fifty tons of gold be placed in crates labeled arms and equipment and shipped to Vladivostok. When the gold reached the eastern port it was to be safeguarded until additional instructions were received. Nicky was convinced that strikes and riots made rail transport to the west a risky undertaking. Although he had not yet settled on the final destination of the treasure he was sure that the second stage of its journey should be by sea, preferably in a naval vessel.

Next he sent for his Chief of Police and Count Benckendorff to discuss immediate security measures needed to protect his family. The Tsar informed them he wished to move the family to Peterhof at once.

"Your Imperial Highness, I agree with the need to move to Peterhof but it is not possible right now. We cannot guarantee your safety," his Police chief informed him.

"Evidently you cannot guarantee my safety here"the Tsar said to him. "This was the one place I thought we were safe. Now even this sanctuary is denied us."

At this point Count Benckendorff added his endorsement. "Your Imperial Highness. The Chief is correct. St. Petersburg is seething with unrest. You must stay at Tsarskoe Selo until circumstances are more favorable for a move."

"We will continue this discussion later, but in the meantime start making preparations," the Tsar replied.

Nicholas dismissed the police chief but asked the Count to remain. He handed him the sealed letter.

"Please ensure this is safely delivered."

Benckendorff glanced at the address and looked up in surprise at Nicholas. He was one of the few trusted advisors who knew of the existence of the Tsar's private treasury, located in closely guarded but undisclosed locations east of the Ural Mountains. Russia was a barely tapped reservoir of immense mineral wealth and a portion of the gold from the mines in the Urals was sent periodically and with great secrecy to the Tsar's personal treasury. Each shipment was loaded into decrepit boxcars, connected to and disconnected from various locomotives, switched onto remote sidings, broken up at different stations and cars sent in one direction or another until the elaborate ruse achieved its purpose and all traces of the rich cargo vanished. Nearly fifty years of discreet transfer had resulted in an immense store of wealth and it was this accumulation that Nicky was about to tap for the capital to finance his plan. The few who had knowledge were loyal to the core and handsomely compensated to ensure their continued loyalty. Reports of the hoard of gold surfaced from time to time but without concrete evidence to support the rumors they generally faded away.

"I plan to send the Empress and my children to safety," Nicholas announced to the Count. "As soon as circumstances allow we will leave for Peterhof and from there I will send my family on our yacht to a safe refuge. I am still working on the details and the final destination but I want to be sure this matter is taken care of quickly. Have *Polar Star* ready to sail at a moments notice."

"Your Imperial highness, but what about your mother and the rest of your family?"

"They are safe. I am the target of these anarchists and my wife and children are in danger due to their proximity to me. As for the rest, they are not my concern. They have their own resources and can leave if they so wish."

"Your majesty, surely you are not thinking of staying. It must be obvious that your life is in danger."

"Have no fears for my safety. God must be protecting me. Over and over my life has been spared and I must believe that it is not yet my time."

Nicholas dismissed the Count, leaned back in his chair, and thought about his final words to Benckendorff. "It is not yet my time," he thought, "but the time is coming. I have thirteen years left to me; so many and yet so few." Like Damocles, the character from Greek mythology, he felt as if a sword was suspended over his head by a thin thread. He realized that power and wealth are frequently accompanied by heartache and turmoil. Although at times Nicky could hardly bear to think about these matters he was much stronger than people gave him credit for and he won the daily struggle to maintain a semblance of normality as he wrestled with the burdens imposed on him by his office. He found it amusing that he was seen as an unemotional, excessively calm, and stoic individual, who was somewhat naïve and lacking the understanding to deal with difficult situations. The truth, of course, was just the opposite but the Emperor was determined to keep up the external facade and hide the inner conflicts that tore at him on a regular basis.

Nicky continued working in his study for hours, refining the elements of his plan. He had been up for nearly thirty hours, was nearly murdered and was now faced with some unpleasant realities. He remained doggedly at work, consciously avoiding Alix and the troubling conversation that was sure to take place when he returned to their bed.

cs&so

Alix had awakened this morning to the sound of birds singing outside her window and was bursting with an energy so rare of late that she decided to go for a ride with her daughters and Princess Maria, her Lady-in-Waiting. It was a beautiful spring day when the open carriage, selected for its lack of adornment, departed Alexander Palace, passed through the gate of the compound, and set off for a delightful afternoon drive. She loathed the police presence at Tsarskoe Selo and studiously ignored the plain clothes policeman on duty near the gate. Alix hated their constant spying and knew that the time and date she left the palace would be in some report read by someone, somewhere, for some uncertain purpose. Once the carriage entered the woods the Empress directed the coachman to stop and ordered her Cossack guard to return to the palace. The officer in charge of the detail objected vigorously but Alexandra was adamant. "Do not think to follow us," she bid them, as they rode off. Then to the dismay of Princess Marie she took a nondescript brown coat from under the seat in the carriage and told the coachman to remove his imperial livery and put it on. "Now we are incognito," she told her laughing daughters as they set off on their adventure. More than once they had taken one of these "incognito" drives and they loved to look unobserved at the dwellings they passed, to see how ordinary people lived. Alix tried to instill in her daughters a sense of the responsibility that came with a life of privilege and wealth. It was good for her children to see that not everyone lived in a large palace behind carefully guarded walls.

Spirits were high and they all began to sing a silly song as the carriage turned down a narrow lane. The bright sun shone through the trees and embroidered a leafy pattern on the trail. The hoofs of the horses were muffled by fallen leaves and they were able to hear the chirping of the birds in the fresh clean air. It was truly a glorious day to enjoy the outdoors and everyone was having a marvelous time. Suddenly a fox darted from the roadside, ran in front of the team, and was nearly trampled. The horses spooked and reared backwards pushing the coach toward the edge of the road. The coachman struggled to maintain control but the carriage continued to roll backwards, sliding ever closer to the ditch alongside the road. Alix and Princess Marie held tightly to the four girls who did not appear to be overly worried. Despite the driver's skill the back wheel slipped and the conveyance overturned into the ditch, landing on its side. The occupants crawled out and although shaken up a bit, everyone seemed fine. The group peered down and saw that the coachman was pinned by the carriage.

Many thought of Alix as an invalid because of her hypochondria but no one could say she lacked courage. Always one to rise to the occasion, especially an emergency, she waded into the ditch and grabbed the reins, calming the struggling horses. The dirty water stained her dress and the flailing hoofs flung mud upon her face. Princess Marie directed the girls and together with the coachman, who finally managed to free himself, pushed and shoved the vehicle. It groaned and creaked as it inched its way upward and with a final strong push it bounced upright. They waded across the ditch and were now as filthy as their mother with their wet skirts and muddy faces.

Alix walked over to the coachman, who was very distraught. He was worried not only about the family but also about his job, especially since he was outside the compound without an escort. "Do not despair," she said to him. "It was not your driving that caused this. It was an unpreventable accident and since no one was harmed and the carriage is undamaged, I see no reason to inform anyone of this incident. Now take us back to the palace. We must not let anyone see us in such condition so drive us to the back entrance." The coachman assisted the Empress and her party into the carriage and they began their trek home.

On the ride back, Alix laughed at her daughters and teased them about their grubby appearance while she used her handkerchief to wipe the mud off of Anastasia's face. Maria appeared pensive and lost in her thoughts. She can be such a serious child, Alix thought, as she wiped her face as well. It is such a contrast to the exuberance she usually exhibits. Thank goodness she has Anastasia as a playmate to snap her out of her moods. "Well, children, we've made quite a muck of things, have we not? We must be careful and sneak in when we get home so your father does not see us."

When they arrived at the palace the coachman let them out at the back entrance and the whole, sodden group slunk into the private quarters, leaving a muddy trail behind. They almost made it undetected when Alix observed Nicky heading towards her rooms. She hurried her daughters along and they, with Princess Maria, scurried up the staircase to their rooms. Nicky came in and took in the sight of Alix, in all her muddy glory, as she stood before him with a guilty look upon her face. "What is the meaning of this mess?" he demanded. "You look an absolute disaster." There was no way around it so Alix explained what happened on their morning excursion. Nicholas exploded with anger.

"How could you be so irresponsible with your safety and that of our children? Did the events of Easter have no meaning for you? Alix, you of all people should understand the danger we are in and take the necessary precautions."

Alexandra had a stubborn streak but in this case she knew her husband was right. "Oh Nicky, I am so sorry to have worried you so. The police are so intrusive and I just cannot bear to be constantly spied upon. It was so wonderful to escape their scrutiny today and no one was harmed."

"That is not the point. We are in constant danger and must always be vigilant. I will not tolerate this disregard for security. Do not disobey me on this or I will forbid you to leave the palace."

"It is not necessary to take that tone with me! You have made your concerns quite clear. Now if I may take my leave, I need to change out of these wet clothes," Alix said to him. She then departed for her dressing room and a much needed bath and fresh clothing. I know he is right, she thought, but I hate when he talks to me as if I were a small child. He can be so dictatorial that sometimes I just have to leave the room. However, in her heart, she knew he was right.

Nicholas stood still, very disturbed by the exchange. He sympathized with his wife's desire to break free from the constraints of their virtual imprisonment but knew he had to stand firm when it came to their safety. It is good that I am sending them away, he thought, but it will be almost unbearable to live here in Russia without them, especially since I cannot predict the length of the separation. I will miss the children and my dearest Alix so much that I willingly accept this burden until it is safe for them to return. He wished he could share his thoughts with her but knew it was hopeless. She would never willingly agree to leave him, but he was convinced this was the only option open to them at this point. He had decided to explore Denmark as a possible destination and had been working on the logistics since Easter. It was his mother's homeland and there were no political obstacles that would prevent Alix and the children from staying there. She would not be happy about Denmark, given her feelings towards his mother, but in time he hoped she would understand and accept his decision. The idea that he was finally about to take concrete action helped calm his inner turmoil. Soon I will be at peace, he thought.

Chapter 8

April 1905 - Cam Ranh Bay, French Indochina. In mid-April the Second Pacific Squadron reached Cam Ranh Bay on the coast of French Indochina. For the next month Admiral Rozhestvensky loitered in the area, waiting for the rest of the squadron to join him. The Admiral was able to communicate with St. Petersburg and among the coded messages he received was a directive ordering him to immediately detach *Dmitri Donskoi* on a special mission. The old armored cruiser was to proceed independently to Vladivostok, taking every possible measure to remain undetected. Upon arrival the captain was to load a cargo of crates, labeled arms and equipment, take on as much fuel as possible and, when ready, get underway and retrace the voyage he had just completed. His final port of call would be signaled to him after he cleared the war zone.

Two weeks later, on a dark, foggy night, *Dmitri Donskoi* slipped through the Japanese picket destroyers patrolling the Korean Straits and made its way safely into the naval base at Vladivostok. There the ship was re-supplied, the secret cargo loaded, and coal bunkers filled. During the night of May 22 she slipped quietly back to sea and proceeded on a southerly course and was just in time to be caught up in the naval engagement known thereafter as the Battle of Tsushima. Few Russian vessels survived the onslaught of Admiral Togo Heihachiro's modern fleet and one by one units of the squadron were sent to the bottom or hammered into surrender. *Dmitri Donskoi* was the last to go. Her captain mortally wounded, the ship heavily damaged and unable to make any speed, the aged vessel was finally chased down and surrounded by six Japanese warships. The surviving senior officer, Commander Konstantine Blokhin, was determined to keep *Dmitri Donskoi* from falling into Japanese hands. Before ordering the crew to abandon ship he directed the sea cocks to be opened and the vessel scuttled. Slowly the battered but proud, old cruiser slipped beneath the calm waters of the Tsushima Straits, her flag still flying defiantly. With her went the dead and, of course, the secret of her cargo.

೦೪೮౦

Nicholas and Alexandra struggled to find normalcy in these trying days and were determined the children would not be affected by the turmoil sweeping across Russia. Fortunately the enclave at Tsarskoe Selo provided some insulation from the grim events taking place beyond the walls. To further lighten the atmosphere Nicky and Alix had decided that today was the day for an American style picnic. It was to be a surprise for the Grand Duchesses when they completed their morning lessons and instead of a formal lunch they were going to dine out doors. Alix canceled all their afternoon schooling so they could enjoy the rest of the day together, as a family. When the four young ladies completed their studies the tutor directed them to change into their play-clothes and they were, of course, quite surprised by this variation in their everyday routine. The girls put on their white sailor suits with crisp, navy blue ties and donned the requisite straw hats to protect their fair skin. Then, excited and filled with expectation, they made their way down the staircase to their mother's quarters. Alix looked up as her daughters came in and she smiled in anticipation of their delight when they realized what she had planned. They all gave her a kiss and asked her what was going on but she answered vaguely. "We must meet your father outside in the park and it is such a beautiful day I think we shall walk," she informed them.

Alix and her daughters set off along the groomed pathways but baby Alexei remained behind since he was too young for the day's activities. The afternoon was bright and sunny, the sky cloudless and the temperature mild. It was a perfect day for a picnic and Alix had worked very hard to ensure it was authentic. She had combed books from America, including Mrs. Beeton's Book of Household Management, which Nicky had given her. They had shared many a laugh over its suggestions. Mrs. Beeton stated that a proper picnic must have thirty-five dishes. It seemed to be a rather large number and Alix had questioned the American ambassador's wife about it at a reception for the diplomatic corps. Mrs. MacCormick replied that only a Vanderbilt would have so many and unaware that the Vanderbilt's were famous for their elaborate picnics Alix was not sure what she meant. At any rate she gratefully accepted the American woman's suggestions and gave all the recipes to her chef who had been outraged when asked to prepare what he called "peasant food." But Alix was adamant that this would be an authentic affair and the carefully packed wicker basket was waiting for them by the lake. She had decided to have the picnic there because the American ambassador's wife told her that they always held their picnics at a lakeside.

The groomed pathway meandered around the lake in Alexander Park and as they strolled around it the children's island, with its large playhouse, was in view on one side of the path while on the other was a wooded area with thick bushes. It was when they passed one such clump of bushes that they heard a loud rustling noise. Alix stopped, amused at her daughters' reaction. They clung together, debating who should see what was making the commotion.

"Olga, you look. You are the oldest," ordered Tatiana.

"No, I think you should look," she responded.

"Maria, you and Anastasia peer into the bush and see what it is," Alix suggested.

"I'm not going to do it. I am too afraid," Maria said.

Suddenly the branches and leaves began thrashing wildly about and the four girls leaped back with a squeal.

"Let us join hands and see," Olga said. "We will be safe if we stay together."

The four Grand Duchesses grasped hands and began advancing cautiously on the now still shrubbery. Just as they got close enough to peer through the leaves a large object hurled itself out with a roar. The girls turned and ran screaming up the path, not realizing they were being chased by their father. Finally out of breath, they stopped and turned to see their father, his face red with laughter, standing in the middle of the path.

"Papa, you frightened us," said Anastasia, her voice quivering while her sisters laughed at the trick he had played on them.

"I am sorry my dears but it was so much fun to give you such a fright," said Nicky. "Come let us get to our destination, your Mama and I have a surprise for you."

They rounded the bend in the path and a grassy area along side the lake came into view. Blankets were spread on the ground with a huge wicker basket atop and not a servant in sight. Badminton net was set up, as were other outdoor games including horseshoes, introduced from America and unfamiliar to the girls. The Grand Duchesses were astonished at the sight and looked at each other in bewilderment.

"Oh Mama, is it a picnic?" Olga and Tatiana exclaimed together.

"Yes my darlings. It is just like they have in America but the best part is that it is just for us, this afternoon," said Alix.

"I am sure Papa will be called away for some reason," said Olga, rather petulantly.

"Au contraire, I have given strict word that we are not to be disturbed this afternoon," her father responded.

"Olga, look! It is just like in our photograph," Tatiana excitedly pointed out to her sister. "Mama, what do we do first?"

"First we shall eat." Alix knelt down on the blanket and beckoned her daughters to join her. She opened the wicker basket, passed out plates and then began to remove the packed containers of food. The girls' eyes grew wide at the sight of all the delicious American foods. Normally they ate very simply so this meal was a special treat and their anticipation grew as more items were removed from the basket. There was fried chicken with its crisp, golden skin, potato salad all rich and creamy, baked beans, and thick slices of bread filled with meats and cheeses. Deviled eggs, slices of fresh vegetables with a tangy dip, and something very unusual called a potato chip, added to the variety. The desserts were creative and included freshly baked cookies of many varieties, cupcakes with sprinkles, an apple pie, and éclairs, a puff pastry filled with cream and topped with chocolate. The group on the blanket sampled each delicacy as it was offered and made a valiant effort to have a portion of each of the dishes. The American picnic food seemed so exotic and tasted so wonderful that their parents allowed the girls to eat as much as they wanted.

"My dear you have outdone yourself today. Surely this is far too many dishes," said Nicky.

"As you well know Mrs. Beeton says that you must have thirty-five items for a proper picnic," said Alix.

They smiled at each other and took total delight in their daughters' enjoyment of the picnic. With the lunch complete, they started to play the games set up for their enjoyment and with no servants present they were able to engage in some silliness. Nicholas put on quite a show with his badminton dance. Each time he hit the birdie he would twirl around or jump up and click his heels. The Grand Duchesses were surprised to see their sometimes stern father acting with such exuberance but they too soon joined in the fun and each vied with the other to come up with the funniest dance.

"I am surprised there is no security lurking about," Alix remarked.

"Believe me, it is there," said Nicky as he lay down on the blanket next to Alix to take a break from the games. "I would never endanger our family for a day of fun. I directed them to remain as unobtrusive as possible but if you look closely you will see them." Alix glanced around and the day dimmed a little for her as she realized those ever present eyes were upon them. Nevertheless she had to smile as she caught sight of little Anastasia attempting to throw a horseshoe. The poor dear had to use both hands and even then she could barely get it high enough to throw. With determination etched on her face she hurled her horseshoe and it landed with a thud only a few feet away. Tears welled in her eyes as her sisters laughed at her feeble toss.

"There, there, my little cherub," said Nicky. "I think we should all play hide and seek."

As they prepared to start the game, Nicholas observed Count Benckendorff walking towards him at a rapid pace. He knew it must be a serious matter that drew the Count to the picnic area because he had been quite explicit that he was not to be disturbed. "Olga, count to one hundred and everyone else hide. I shall be back in a short while and will join in when I return." The Grand Duchesses looked rather sadly at their father as he strode off to meet the Count.

"I knew he would not stay," Olga complained to her mother.

"Darlings, you know your father is the ruler of all Russia and chosen by God for his mission. We must respect this and remember that he has many responsibilities. I know that it is hard to share him, but we must."

"Yes, Mama," Olga replied and began to count dutifully to one hundred while Alix and the girls ran off to hide.

Normally it was difficult to read the expression on Count Bencken-dorff's face. He generally maintained his composure and was considered rather stoic, so Nicholas was surprised by his ashen pallor and knew that it could only mean bad news.

"Imperial Highness, we have just received an absolutely terrible communication from the Pacific. I felt that despite your desire for privacy today you would wish to be apprised of the situation immediately." Nicholas motioned to him to continue.

"The Japanese intercepted our fleet near the island of Tsushima and have succeeded in destroying or capturing nearly every ship in the squadron. There was great loss of life, nearly six thousand men, and many of the crews have been captured by the enemy. This is an unmitigated disaster."

The Tsar was not insensitive to the casualty figures but he needed more time to think things through. "Have a briefing prepared for me this evening. I will need all the details and how we stand in military strength at this point." He turned to walk back to the picnic but Count Benckendorff called to him.

"There is more. *Dmitri Donskoi* was caught up in the action, by chance it seems, and appears to have been sunk as well. Of course, you know what that means."

The Tsar was speechless at the news, so shocked that he did not know how to react. It was at times like this that he sought the comfort of his family and fortunately they were just down the pathway.

"Count Benckendorff, I must return to my children. We will discuss the situation later this evening."

Nicholas dismissed him, turned and walked slowly along the path to the lake, deep in thought. He struggled to accept the reality that his country had probably lost the war with Japan and he knew that when news of the defeat was made public there would be unrest and rebellion throughout the motherland. Equally troubling was the fact that a portion of the gold that had taken decades to amass now laid at the bottom of the Tsushima Straits. In retrospect the gold should have come across to St. Petersburg by rail. The situation was overwhelming but he was determined to rejoin the party and act as if nothing had happened. When he returned to the picnic area Alix rushed up to him and in a frantic voice announced, "Nicky, Maria is lost. The children were playing hide-and-go-seek and now we can't find her."

A frenzied search had begun for Maria and Nicholas joined the attempt to find the missing child. Olga and Tatiana had gone off to look for Maria before Nicky returned, after telling their mother "we think we know where she might be." The two girls started off at a slow walk following the path along the lake but once out of sight began to run. They knew where she probably was but did not want to divulge her secret hiding place to the others. There was a white tower on the grounds, which was usually kept locked, but the girls had found a secret entrance into it and on several occasions had sneaked away to play in the building. It offered an incredible view of the area and was such a fun place to play that they didn't want anyone to know about it. They slipped through the entrance and began to climb the many steps to the walk-around at the top. They were nearly out of breath when they finally reached the platform and saw Maria standing on tip toes, peering out over the railing. "Maria!" they both shouted at her but she ignored them and continued looking out over the countryside, seemingly unaware of their presence. Olga walked over to her with concern and gently touched her on the shoulder. Maria seemed startled by the presence of the older girls. She turned towards Olga, and thinking they were still playing hide-and-go seek asked, "oh, am I "it" now?"

Olga and Tatiana looked at her in amazement. "Haven't you heard us calling you? Everyone is frantically looking for you," said Tatiana.

"Whatever were you doing?" inquired Olga.

"I must have been day dreaming. I am so sorry that I worried you," she said in a very matter of fact voice. "Come let us go find Mama and Papa," and she started down the steps.

As the older sisters followed her down the staircase, Olga shook her head in amazement. "Whatever can she be thinking about that she loses all sense of her surroundings? It is as if she is in another world."

The girls returned to their parents and the search was called off. Maria was immediately contrite when she realized the fuss she had caused. Her sisters were sure she would be punished and they were quite surprised when Maria ran up to her father and gently took his hands into hers. She looked up at him with her brilliant blue eyes and said, "Do not worry so, Papa! Everything is fine."

Nicholas looked down at his precious daughter and wondered what she meant. She was only six years old and he thought she must have been speaking about her misdeed yet there was something more serious about her manner that he could not identify. It is almost as if she had looked into his soul and seen his worries. Could little Maria be clairvoyant? he wondered. At any rate, for some inexplicable reason, the blackness that filled his heart seemed to dissipate and he began to feel the slight stirrings of renewed optimism.

"Maria, you are correct, everything is fine. Unfortunately the hour is late so we must end our day and return to the palace. My darlings, let us thank your mother for a truly wonderful day." His daughters dutifully thanked their mother and the Imperial family began their stroll back to the palace. The Grand Duchesses ran ahead while Nicky and Alix walked hand in hand.

"Please tell me the news which has so distressed you," implored Alix.

"Our fleet has been totally destroyed by the Japanese. I fear this means the end of the war for us. We cannot continue suffering such devastating losses. If we end it now we may emerge from negotiations with a little pride intact."

"Oh Nicky, what a blow for our Russia."

Nicholas saw no reason to tell Alix about the gold shipment because he had kept the original arrangements from her and the loss had no bearing on his immediate plans. However, now seemed a good time to tell his wife exactly what he had in mind.

"Alix, I think we should leave for Peterhof. The situation in the country seems to have quieted down a little and I would like to be there before word of our defeat leaks out and fans the fires again."

"Are you sure it is safe to travel?"

"No, I am not but I am sure that it is not safe to remain here. I will make the arrangements but you must be prepared to leave within the next few days."

"Darling, that is hardly any time to pack. We have so much to do to get ready that I can hardly be expected to leave in less than a week."

"Alix, I am sure that you can manage it. Think how wonderful it will be at the seashore with the ocean breezes and fresh air. The change will do us all a world of good and it will be an opportunity to relax before we leave."

"Leave? Nicky what are you talking about?"

"If the situation does not improve in the country by the fall we are leaving Russia and going to Denmark. We will be safe there and I already made the necessary arrangements. I have purchased a small estate for us not far from Copenhagen and it has incredible views of the sea. We shall be very happy there while we wait out this unpleasantness," he informed her. He carefully avoided any suggestion that he would not remain with them.

"Darling I am stunned by this news. Why didn't you tell me sooner? How can we leave the country at a time like this? I know it is unsafe but can we abandon Russia when she most needs us?"

"Sunny, you must trust me and remember that we must protect our children at all costs."

For the next few days Alexander Palace was swept up in a whirlwind of activity as the family prepared to move to Peterhof for the summer. Nicky depended on Alix to handle all the domestic details but he did direct her to pack for the possible move to Denmark. It was a struggle to anticipate the needs for their extended trip without letting anyone know they were leaving the country.

Nicholas, on the other hand, closeted himself in his study, with Count Benckendorff, working on the plan for his family's departure. He also devoted himself to affairs of state and spent many hours meeting with his ministers. Despite the loss of the fleet the war with Japan continued and it needed the attention of Nicholas. The Tsar's head ached from the stress of dealing with all of this but he soldiered on and finally the Imperial family was able to leave for Peterhof.

Peterhof, the great Imperial enclave established by Peter the Great, was located on the southern shore of the Gulf of Finland not too far from St. Petersburg. The parks, fountains, and palaces were beautifully maintained and beckoned to the royals, who arrived in a festive mood. In wooded acres to the east of the great park was the Imperial family estate known as Alexandria Peterhof. It contained three unique homes, the Cottage, the Farm and the New Palace. Nicky's mother, the Dowager Empress, continued to call the Cottage her own so Nicky, Alix and the children resided in the New Palace. It was probably the most unique of their many residences with its mixture of styles. When Nicky was younger he and his brother used what was then the old telegraph tower as a bachelor home and a small villa had been added to the tower. After his marriage to Alexandra it had been expanded further and a covered walkway led from the second floor to the new addition. The New Palace held many fond memories for the royal couple among which were the births of their three youngest children. It was comparatively small and much more a home than a palace and was a place at which they were able to enjoy quiet family time away from duties of their public life. When there were social activities they took place at the larger Peterhof Palace located some distance across the park.

Alix quickly settled her children into the new section, which contained their bedrooms and playrooms. Her rooms were there as well and everything was decorated in the Art Nouveau style that she favored. It was all bright and airy with big windows that provided spectacular views of the sea. Nicky had a study in the old section and he spent most of his time there working in the walnut paneled room which was furnished with green morocco leather chairs and a walnut desk that matched the walls. It spite of the dark colors the room was bright and full of light. Nicky had a table placed on the balcony so he could enjoy the brisk sea air while he completed his reading. His desk faced a window, which gave him a breathtaking view of the Gulf of Finland and occasionally he glimpsed his children frolicking in the sea. Next to his study was an anteroom and throughout the summer it seemed as if one minister or another was always waiting there to see him.

The summer passed quickly in their idyllic retreat by the sea and the children continued their peaceful existence, blissfully unaware of anything that could influence the happiness they felt. Their days were a blur of lessons and official duties interspersed with swims in the sea and walks in the park. Alix immersed herself in needlework, preparing hand-crafted objects for sale in the bazaar she was sponsoring at the end of the summer.

Nicholas' time was anything but relaxing. Earlier President Theodore Roosevelt of the United States had offered to mediate the conflict between Russia and Japan and it was decided to send Sergei Witte, Russia's finest diplomat, to a peace conference which was to take place in Portsmouth, New Hampshire, later in the summer. Since Japan was winning the war militarily it came as somewhat of a surprise that the Japanese were willing to talk peace. However, the cost of the war had almost bankrupted the emerging Pacific power and the Japanese were willing to consider any reasonable suggestions for ending the war. Negotiations were not going well and Nicholas had received a telegram from President Roosevelt bluntly reminding him that Russia was losing the war and must make concessions. The Tsar wired Ambassador Witte to continue to fight for the best possible terms but in the end to do what was necessary to terminate the conflict.

Needing a rest from the stress of his office he decided to take Alix and his sister Olga with him for a few days when he went to visit several of the regiments garrisoned in the area. He planned to stop at Pskov to visit its famed monastery and he hoped the peace and calm it was known for would be a help and a comfort to Alix. She was very overwrought of late but he could hardly blame her. The events of the last few months were stressful and worrisome to say the least and she took the loss of the war with Japan to heart. Sometimes he thought she loved Russia more than he did. She had embraced her adopted country, its culture, and religion so completely and without reservation that he felt humbled by the depth of her devotion to it. It is such a pity, he thought, that people did not really understand her. If they did, they would love and respect her as I do.

୧୫

The week long trip went very well and Nicholas was surprised at the relative tranquility he found in the countryside. Although Pskov was less than a days journey from Peterhof, and relatively close to the capital there seemed to be none of the unrest and agitation that gripped the rest of the nation and there was an unexpected serenity throughout the region. They traveled on the Imperial train and Nicky loved the freedom it gave them. While passing through an area of exceptional scenery, he ordered the train stopped and went for a long walk through the woods with his sister Olga. Alix did not feel up to a walk and remained behind and since her moods were sometimes hard to deal with he was grateful for the respite. As the years passed he and Olga grew closer and she became one of Nicky's most trusted confidantes. She was the one member of his extended family he truly felt a kinship to. She was simple in her outlook, and money and power meant nothing to her. In many ways she reminded him of the peasants that he and Alix were so fond of. They enjoyed their walk together and though he wanted to tell her of his plan to send his family out of the country he decided against it. He did not want her to feel obligated to keep his secret from their mother whom he knew would be furious when she found out.

Alix had rested while they walked and greeted them cheerfully when they returned. They continued on their journey through the countryside and stopped later that day at a small village. The Tsarina reveled in the greetings of the people as they pulled into the station. Women from the town, dressed in brightly colored, traditional costumes, were thrilled to see her and handed her gifts of salt and bread, the traditional Russian gifts of hospitality and welcome. The womenfolk were surprisingly comfortable with the Empress and asked her all sorts of questions about her children. She loved nothing more than to talk about her family and, rested as she was, Alix was charming and responsive to the townspeople and quite at ease with them.

Once back on the train she lounged in one of the comfortable sofas, lost in thought. This trip is doing me a world of good. I so love seeing our people and they truly love and revere the Tsar. This is the true Russia and its heart is good. Yesterday they had visited some troops in the rain and she had been soaked and chilled to the bone when her new waterproof cape turned out to be not so waterproof. Days like today, however, made it all worthwhile. Tomorrow they were visiting the Pechorsky monastery with its 16th century fortress and caves. It was a spiritual center and a monument to Russian culture and military history. She glanced out of the window and enjoyed the view of the countryside as it went flying by. The land was flat but it was covered with lakes and wetlands, pine forests and meadows. The spring had made its impact and the air was fresh, the earth filled with color.

They spent the night on the train enjoying the comfortable sleeping compartments and in the morning were refreshed and looking forward to their visit to this holy and historic monastery. Nicky and Alix had a passion for Russian history and they loved visiting historical sites as well as archeological digs. They were both struck by the beauty of this medieval town, located a short distance from Pskov. The white walls of the monastery gleamed in the early morning light in sharp contrast to the green carpet of grass and the woods nearby. A guide was arranged for them and after his initial nervousness he settled down and gave them a wonderfully informative tour. "The Holy Virgin herself chose this spot in the valley and blessed it," Ivan, their guide, informed them. "Many dramatic events and military attacks have taken place here but not once did the pious monks interrupt their prayer or let the lamps before the holy icons go dark." They walked through the grounds and made visits to the eleven churches, three of which were dug out of the hillside and called cave churches. Alix was struck by the spiritual quality of it all. The monks were so devout and there was a sense of peace and safety that she had not felt in a long time.

Nicholas, on the other hand, was struck by the huge, stone walls with bastions which surrounded the monastery complex. They made it into a virtual fortress through which nothing could pass, and the many caves lent themselves to hiding places that no enemy could find. The entrance to the caves was through the Church of the Intercession and past the burial site of the monks. Their bodies lay on shelves one above the other and the skeletons appeared quite ghostly. It would take a strong constitution to explore further into these caves. He asked Ivan about the military history of the area and was informed by the guide that in over four hundred years the monastery had only been captured by the enemy one time. "Since that time Peter the Great fortified the fortress with earth walls, banks and ditches and now it is practically impenetrable." Nicky could not explain the feeling he had about the monastery, but he felt drawn to its atmosphere of safety and peace. Nicholas and Alexandra dreaded leaving the solitude of Pechorsky and returning to Peterhof. In the months of turmoil that lay ahead they would both look back and remember with fondness the few days they spent in this Russian oasis.

Chapter 9

September 1905 - The Gulf of Finland. A cheerful, somewhat boisterous group consisting of the Tsar and Tsarina, the children and a few retainers was on deck as the Imperial yacht *Polar Star* left Peterhof on a two week vacation cruise through the Gulf of Finland. Although this outing was starting later than usual, and rough seas could be a factor, Nicholas was unwilling to deny the family, what to them, was one of the highlights of the year and so far the weather in the Gulf was cooperating.

Their summer voyages were normally taken in July but the situation in the country prevented them from leaving sooner. Peace was finally negotiated with Japan and Nicholas was extremely encouraged with Ambassador Witte's success, so much so, that the Tsar had decided to grant Witte the title of Count. The settlement was much more than they had hoped for and Witte had achieved highly favorable terms, terms that included no indemnities and little loss of territory. Although Russia was still suffering internal strife, and strikes that paralyzed the country, with the Japanese issue settled, the Tsar resolved to enjoy this time with his family.

The group on board was much smaller than usual. There had been so much opposition from family and governmental officials to his leaving at this time that he decided to limit the guest list to his immediate family in order to avoid bickering and acrimonious debate. Alix allowed herself two ladies-in-waiting, one of whom was Anna Taneyeva, a new, young woman at the court. Everyone called her Anya.

Nicky's mother Minnie, the Dowager Empress, and her sons and daughters had come to see them off. They had great fun clowning around for the camera and Nicky looked forward to seeing the photograph of his brother Michael with him on his shoulders. The Tsarina remained below deck to avoid having to interact with his family. Of late the only one Alix seemed to tolerate was his sister Olga. Nicholas was sure some imagined slight had sent her below and he knew that her rudeness to his Mother was deliberate. It was a battle that would never end so he chose to avoid the controversy at all costs and maintain the peace as much as possible.

"Nicholas, where is Alix today?" asked Minnie rather pointedly.

"She is over tired from the preparations for our departure and has gone to her cabin to rest."

"Surely she would enjoy the fresh sea air. I find it invigorating."

Nicholas looked around for a way to avoid a conversation that would soon deteriorate into a defense of Alix's behavior. He caught his brother Michael's eye and realized he was laughing at the situation. It was then they started to clown around, much to their mother's annoyance. She disliked it when they acted with such lack of dignity and even more so when their silliness was captured on film. Watching her displeasure grow they finally settled down and then it was time for everyone to say their good-byes. Alix continued to remain below deck but all the children stood at the rail to wave at the launch as it ferried its royal passengers back to the dock.

"You can reach me by wireless or boat if necessary," he told them. "We won't be far away." Nicholas was ready to relax with his family and now felt as if he could.

The weather was still warm on that September day in the fall of 1905 but the wind blowing off the water created a chill in the air, a harbinger of the winter soon to come. It is a wonderful day, thought Nicky, as the ship set out through the gentle swells, and he found that the rolling motion of the deck relaxed him. His children waved their arms excitedly and he was amazed at how fast they were growing. The girls were all dressed alike, in crisp navy blue sailor suits piped with white trim along the collars and hems. Their outfits were topped with heavy pea coats with shiny brass buttons to ward off the chill in the air and each wore sensible black shoes with thick soles to prevent them from sliding on the deck. All were arrayed along the rail according to age from oldest to youngest and he was amused at how often that happened. Olga was now ten years old and becoming quite the little lady. She and Tatiana were inseparable while Maria and Anastasia were becoming closer as Anastasia got older. He was grateful they had each other to play with because Alix absolutely refused to allow the children any interaction with their Romanov cousins, except during official family functions. She felt that most of his relatives were lost souls and she had no desire for her precious children to be corrupted by them. Her attitude caused quite a lot of unwelcome tension within the extended imperial family but Alix was stubborn and headstrong and there was little likelihood that she would change.

As the shoreline receded in the distance, his children ran off to play, followed by five sailors. Each child was assigned a guardian for the duration of the voyage and except for Alexei they changed every cruise. Alexei on the other hand had a permanent protector, Seaman Andrey Derevenko and the muscular sailor went everywhere with the Tsarevich, hoping to prevent accidents which could trigger a fatal bleeding episode. It was a very stressful assignment, especially now that Alexei was walking but Derevenko, at least initially, was up to the task. Nicholas watched his children at play for a while and then went to see how Alix was feeling.

Dinner that first evening at sea was a lively affair. Anya, the new lady-in-waiting, was seated next to Nicholas and sensing the embarrassment she felt in finding herself in such close proximity to his Imperial Majesty, he set about putting her at ease. He knew that Alix was taken with her and seemed to truly enjoy her company yet he was surprised that she wanted to invite this rather dumpy girl, with little to offer in the way of stimulating conversation, on their cruise. He spoke to Anya about Alix and explained what a great help she had been to him during the war with Japan. "Without her, I could never have endured the strain," he remarked. When Anya replied, her words indicated an almost childlike adoration of the Empress and he began to understand Alix's insistence that she be included on the trip. Her cheeks flushed a pleasing pink and her eyes flashed with animation when she spoke and although she would never be considered beautiful her vivaciousness was quite attractive. Alix must really enjoy this hero worship, he thought, especially since it is such a contrast to the feelings of most of the women at court.

The days were getting shorter and the night's longer in these high latitudes so everyone slept late that first night. When they finally arose they were greeted by a brilliant sunrise which cast a bright orange hue on the water and created a panoply of color on the nearly calm seas. The royal yacht had steamed through the night and at first light dropped anchor in the secluded bay of a small island. It was a spot they had stopped at several times before and from the deck they could view the roughly hewn dock constructed from the tall pines that populated this isolated spit of land. It was a wonderful spot to stand and skip rocks into the water and the whole rocky shoreline demanded close examination by the exuberant children. With his daughters warmly dressed, Nicky set out in the launch for the day of exploration. The guardians were already ashore awaiting their arrival and the Grand Duchesses eagerly anticipated a day of play. The crew pulled vigorously and the boat reached the shore quickly and with a gentle thud slid on to the beach. One by one the girls were carried ashore by a sailor and placed on the sand so their feet would not get wet. Alix remained on *Polar Star* with her ladies-in-waiting and Alexei, who was not feeling well and was really too young for this excursion. This did not dampen her daughters' enthusiasm in the least as today they were to learn how to fish.

Olga, Tatiana, Maria, and Anastasia scampered off with the sailors from the ship who had prepared baited fishing poles for each of them. A crusty, old seaman named Khabalov assisted them and went over the finer points of casting a line and reeling in a fish. Five minutes passed and with the natural impatience of childhood the four girls began to complain loudly about the lack of fish. "Just give it time," said Khabalov. "Sometimes it can take awhile for the fish to bite. Patience. Have patience." Just then Anastasia's pole started jerking and bending and the line grew taut. Startled by the sudden pull on her line she screamed and dropped her pole which began to slide across the sand toward the water. With a calmness belying her years, Maria reached down and picked up the pole before it reached the water's edge and began to reel in the fish. Her older sisters looked on in envy as the fish came into view and they saw it was at least a foot long.

"Anastasia, come and see what you caught," said Maria, giving all the credit to her sister.

"You caught the fish," said Olga. "It is yours."

"No," insisted Maria. "It is Anastasia's fish. Anna go show Papa your glorious catch." Anastasia grasped the pole with her little hands, proudly turned around to show her father, and nearly whacked him in the head with the flailing fish. He chuckled as he admired her catch.

"I think it will make a fine dinner."

Tears welled up in her eyes as she said, "Oh no Papa, surely we cannot eat him."

Her tears softened his heart and he ruled that, "such a fine specimen deserves its freedom." They walked to the water's edge and he helped her set free the struggling fish. Fortunately she does not realize that much of the food she consumes was once a live animal or we would never get her to eat, he thought with amusement.

"Children, I think it is time for us to explore this island. Maybe we will find an old pirate's lair or buried treasure," said Nicholas. His daughters joined him and they trudged through the sand, and then carefully climbed over the rocks that framed the beach before reaching the pine forest. He encouraged athleticism in his daughters and they were lithe and limber with strong constitutions. They were able to walk for long distances without tiring and were not afraid to get dirty. They loved to collect bugs and mushrooms and pick flowers for their mother. He knew he would get an earful from Alix when they returned to *Polar Star* filthy from the day's adventures.

Alexandra was an indoor person and although she occasionally enjoyed outdoor activities she much preferred the genteel hobbies of a noblewoman such as needlework and flower arranging. While Nicky and the girls were enjoying the great outdoors, Alix spent more time with the young Anya. They both found to their great satisfaction a common love of music and spent the afternoon hours playing the piano in the salon. Alix introduced Anya to her dearly loved classics by Bach, Beethoven and Tchaikovsky and together their hands roamed the keyboard as they played duets. Both laughed when they struggled with a difficult section and they worked together until the piece flowed smoothly. "It's a masterpiece," exclaimed Anya while Alix smiled at her with genuine fondness. What a sweet girl she is and how I enjoy her company. It is so pleasant to just relax for a change, thought Alix.

Back on shore the day grew warmer and the girls removed their pea coats before they set off into the woods. They hiked for hours with their father, exploring all the hidden recesses of the island. They reveled in the sights and were thrilled when they discovered a patch of fragrant, fall blooming wildflowers, which they gathered to bring to their mother. The girls loved these jaunts with their father because a nurse was not along and they never heard "don't touch that", "watch your step," or "be careful." There were cuts, scrapes and small bruises to be sure, but never any major injuries and the girls grew up with a fearlessness rarely seen in children raised in such a secluded setting.

When they returned to the beach Nicholas ordered a roaring fire built and they all sat around in a circle and picked through the mushrooms they had gathered earlier. Nicholas gave each girl a metal cup to put their mushrooms in and then he liberally poured wine into each cup. His daughters used the sticks they had found and stirred the concoctions as they simmered and bubbled over the fire. Nicholas saw the pleasure in their eyes as they accomplished the simple task and his heart overflowed with love for each of them. He felt a sense of sorrow when he thought of little Alexei and how his activities would be limited because of his illness. He could not love the child more but when he anticipated having a son his expectation was of a masculine, rambunctious child, tearing about on horseback. The odds of Alexei living to adulthood were against him but Nicky vowed to let his son have as normal a life as possible. He did not want him to miss out on too many days like today.

With the sun beginning its slow arc towards sunset, they were rowed back to the yacht in time to dress for dinner. Alix gave him a disapproving look as she took in the disheveled state of her daughters, their hair askew and skirts clinging wetly to legs but she was totally disarmed when they presented her with the bundles of fresh, fragrant flowers. While the children were changing, Alix and Anya quickly arranged the fresh flowers for the table since they were having a special guest for dinner that evening.

The new Count, Sergei Witte, had arrived by boat to brief the Tsar on his diplomatic triumph and the older girls, having recently experienced an American picnic, looked forward to hearing about America. Witte had just returned from Portsmouth, in the state of New Hampshire, and Olga and Tatiana were convinced they would hear all about wild Indians and cowboys. At dinner he regaled them with an account of his trip to the United States and his triumph over the Japanese delegates. The girls were disappointed, of course, when the Count, filled with pride over his successful negotiations, kept the conversation centered on the diplomatic aspects of his trip. Witte was convinced that because the Japanese diplomats were secretive and unapproachable they had garnered little sympathy from the Americans. "They kept to themselves," he explained, 'but I made myself available to their press at every opportunity and as a result became quite popular. Although the Americans maintained their neutrality, they certainly leaned our way. The peace treaty that we negotiated was to Russia's advantage considering the number of defeats we suffered. However, I do not think we have heard the last of the Japanese. They certainly have ambitions in the Pacific." Nicholas congratulated him warmly for his role in the peace process but Alix remained tight lipped throughout the discussion. She had never liked Witte and even this success would not change her opinion of him.

After dinner that evening, in spite of his fatigue, Nicky reviewed a number of wires from his ministers. They unanimously agreed that the situation around the country was deteriorating rapidly and they urged Nicholas to return at once. The strikes had gone beyond annoyance and were now wreaking havoc throughout Russia. The banks, trains, bakeries, and newspapers were all shut down because there was no one to work. Food prices soared and in many cities there was no running water. Moscow appeared to be affected the most and its people suffered from the shortages but the unrest was not isolated to one major city. The epidemics created by poor water supplies and famine spread throughout the country and St. Petersburg, already a hotbed of conspiracy was becoming a source of major concern to the government. Nicholas was paralyzed by the news, unable to accept what was happening and incapable, in his present mood, of making any decisions or offering any solutions. He was Tsar of all Russia, God's anointed on this earth and he believed passionately in the love of the people for their ruler. This is the work of a few revolutionaries and not the will of the people, he thought. I am sure this unrest will all die down and anyway there is nothing I can do to alleviate the situation. He was determined to enjoy the rest of this vacation and not worry any further until the return to Peterhof.

The next day dawned bright and clear, a perfect day for sea travel, with a soothing breeze and only gentle swells in the Gulf. They were to spend the day aboard ship and the children were happily playing on deck, climbing on everything and "helping" the sailors with their chores. Alix lay contentedly on a pile of cushions she had ordered placed on deck, knitting away as the yacht proceeded through the calm seas. Nicky reclined next to her and they began to talk about the future. He told her about the current situation, and informed her that their trip abroad appeared imminent and could begin as early as the last week of October. When Nicky first broached the idea of a temporary exile in Denmark, Alix had reluctantly obeyed his order to prepare for the trip but after her initial resistance, she had become very comfortable with the idea and satisfied they would not have the everyday fear of assassination hanging over their heads. Although Denmark was Minnie's home, Alix had enjoyed their visits in the past and was quite sure they would be content there now. Her only real concern was the loss of the gold when *Dmitri Donskoi* sank, a fact that Nicholas had kept from her for a number of months. She now worried that Nicky would cancel their plans but he assured her that the loss would have no effect. He was still one of the wealthiest men in the world. The only complication was that shifting large sums of gold to overseas banks without alerting the rest of the Romanovs would require a delicate hand. Nicky was becoming adept at this and believed he could accomplish the transfers unobtrusively.

Satisfied that Alix understood the situation, Nicky left to work on his papers while she nestled back into the cushions, warmed by the sun and rocked by the swaying of the deck.

Anya came to join her and they had an enjoyable and somewhat intimate conversation. "I hope one day I can find someone who will love me the way the Emperor loves you," she told Alix.

"Ours is truly a love match," the Empress replied. "Many thought I was reluctant to marry the Tsar, but nothing could be further from the truth. I have loved him since I first met him and our love has only deepened over the years. My initial hesitation involved conversion to a new faith, but when my sister converted, and I was able to discuss the matter with her, my objections and concerns quickly evaporated. God called me to his true faith and I have been blessed accordingly." Alix was surprised to find herself opening up to Anya because she was usually very reserved with everyone but her husband. However, there was something about Anya that inspired the sharing of confidences and in the ensuing days Alix confided in her more and more. Once she began it was if the floodgates had opened and the Empress found it a great relief to unburden herself. She was able to share the frustrations and disappointments that had been bottled up within her for so long and which she had been unable to voice because of the restraints placed on her as Empress of Russia. Anya proved to be a good listener and a trusted confidante, one who Alix hoped would be discreet and close-mouthed about their conversations. Finally God has sent me a friend, rejoiced Alexandra.

During the next three days Nicholas received no news from the mainland and considering the early deluge of messages from his advisors he found this somewhat troubling. In the meantime the passengers and crew of *Polar Star* explored the many small islands off the coast of Finland. The family went ashore and the children continued to enjoy swims, hikes and picnics while Nicky occasionally did a little shooting. Game was scarce but he always found it a challenge to shoot a bird or two. It did not have the glamour of big game hunting but it did improve his skills. The days were very informal, lazy, and agreeable. Alix and Anya joined them on shore and took walks along the beach always engaged, it seemed, in serious conversation. Anya provided plenty of amusement for everyone with her habit of falling asleep in the middle of meals. She was unused to the physical activity the Imperial family enjoyed and found it exhausting. One night after she dropped off to sleep and almost fell out of her chair at dinner, Nicky presented her with a silver matchbox. "The matches are to prop your eyes open while we eat," he told her as she blushed in embarrassment.

Finally, after a three day interlude, a boat, dispatched from Peterhof, caught up with the Imperial yacht and Nicholas was given the news that the country was on the verge of revolution and he must return at once to resolve the crisis for the sake of Russia. Nicholas shared the news with his family, guests and the crew and with long faces they set sail for Peterhof. Alix, however, was surprisingly cheerful and everyone gave credit to her new friend Anya. Nicholas said to Anya, "You are to go with us every year after this."

They returned to Peterhof to face the growing crisis and the next few weeks were filled with uncertainty. Nicholas met with his ministers during the day but at night sought the counsel and advice of the Empress. She exerted a strong influence over him and it was not unusual for the Tsar to make a decision only to change his mind the next day after discussing the situation with Alix. Counts Benckendorff and Sergei Witte met with him daily and provided Nicholas with advice and potential solutions to the rebellion that was sweeping across Russia. Although Witte had developed into something of a hard-liner the two drastic courses of action he proposed were at opposite ends of the political spectrum. The first was to crush the revolution by force and appoint the Tsar's uncle, Grand Duke Nikolai Nikolaievich, as military dictator. The second option, even more controversial, was to submit to the revolutionaries' demands and allow the nation a constitution. The dispute about these plans went on for days and unless it was absolutely necessary, servants, family and friends alike, avoided Nicholas' study. Shouts of anger could be heard throughout the wing of the palace as Nicholas and his ministers "discussed" the situation.

"I will never, under any circumstances," shouted the Tsar, "agree to a representative form of government. I consider a surrender to the anarchists to be an act harmful to the people whom God has entrusted to my care."

"Your imperial highness, I beg you to reconsider granting a parliament and a constitution to the people. It is doubtful that our soldiers can crush this unrest without great loss of life and surely you do not want a repeat of 'Bloody Sunday.' Certainly you are aware that recent mutinies have destroyed morale in some units." Witte was treading on thin ice and he knew it from the expression on the Tsar's face.

"Our soldiers are loyal to the core, to their Tsar and to their country. They will follow orders," Nicholas told him furiously. "I maintain autocracy not for my own pleasure but because I am convinced that it is necessary for Russia. Now please leave me! I have much to consider."

Later that day he met with Nikolasha, as the Grand Duke was called, to discuss his role in the process. The Tsar had recently appointed him Commander of military forces around St. Petersburg and the first President of the Imperial Committee for National Defense. Nikolasha would assume these duties at the end of October. The Grand Duke was well loved by his troops and respected throughout Russia for his military skills. Nicky thought there could not be a better choice for a military dictator but try as he might he could not convince his uncle to accept the position. Over the next few weeks they would meet many times and although Nikolasha continued in his refusal Nicky knew he would comply, if ordered to do so.

That evening he spoke at great length with Alix and she agreed with him that a constitution was unacceptable. He arranged the next day for her to hear Witte's arguments but she was not to be swayed. Nicky was wracked by indecision, and Alix, realizing the decision was his alone, left him in peace to ponder the advice he had received. In the meantime she struggled to maintain a degree of normalcy in the family's daily routine. Everyday she tried to spend at least an hour in the workrooms she had established to provide clean linen and bandages for the wounded from the Russo-Japanese War. Unable to visit her hospitals at Tsarskoe Selo she had weekly reports sent to Peterhof to which she replied with detailed instructions. She also spent her time organizing and supervising her children's days. Her chief concern was their education, particularly the study of languages. One day her daughters would be married and she wanted them to be able to converse fluently in a variety of languages and not suffer the embarrassment she had at the hands of the Russian court. For that reason she had hired a new tutor who had come highly recommended to her by the Duke of Leuchtenberg, a cousin of Nicholas.

Pierre Gilliard was a cultured and gentle man and Alix had been moved by his deference to her. Today was to be his first as the girls' teacher and the Empress decided to sit in on the lesson. At the appointed hour she took Olga and Tatiana by the hand and escorted them to their small classroom on the second floor where Monsieur Gilliard was awaiting their arrival. Alix greeted him with a few pleasant words and directed him to sit opposite her while the girls sat at each end of the table. She did her best to set him at ease but he was obviously uncomfortable in her presence. To add to his discomfort, the lesson he had prepared for her daughters was too advanced for them so he had to improvise. She was pleased to see how well he handled the situation and it appeared that the glowing recommendation he had received from the Duke was, indeed, justified. Over the next few weeks she attended their lessons everyday, but she sat by the window as unobtrusively as possible. The young Frenchman seemed surprised by her interest and cheerfully gave her advice when she asked him the best method of teaching modern languages. Alix was satisfied with Monsieur Gilliard and her daughters liked him well enough. Although she could not know it now, this simple and dedicated young man would become a trusted helpmate and confidant to their family and would carry their greatest secret to his grave.

During this trying time, Alix tried to limit their social engagements to as few as possible but she always found time for her friends, Militsa and Stana, the Montenegrin princesses. She had been upset with them for a while when a doctor they had recommended inaccurately predicted Alix's fourth child would be a boy. The pregnancy had produced the adorable Anastasia and it was not until the birth of Alexei that the tension between them had been swept away. They came often for tea and she enjoyed the company of these two intriguing women. Although Alexandra was uncomfortable that Stana's affair with Nikolasha was becoming common knowledge she too disregarded it because she was unwilling to give up the relationship between herself and the two "mystics." Nicholas was unhappy with the influence they exerted on Alix but there was little he could do to prevent it. In the Romanov family the women generally were the most influential and assertive individuals.

As the days of September slipped past and October arrived, tension in the country grew at an ominous pace. Guards were placed at public buildings and mounted Cossacks patrolled the boulevards. The discontented workers began to organize into groups called Soviets and from one of these unions emerged a fiery orator, a man capable of whipping a crowd into a frenzy with his confrontational and dramatic speeches. Leon Trotsky was a dangerous man, an organizer who believed anarchy would lead to reform and reform to an elevated position of power for himself.

It was time for the Tsar to make a decision on the best course of action. But instead of firm leadership, the men who would be responsible for carrying out his orders were greeted at their next meeting with indecision. The nation was racing to full blown revolution but Nicholas could not bear the thought of giving in to the agitators. Consequently, despite the urging of his advisors, he did nothing.

ɔʒ৪ɔ

Grand Duke Nikolai Nikolaievich strode purposefully down the hall to the Tsar's study, a look of fierce determination etched on his bearded face. At six feet six inches in height, the Tsar's uncle was an imposing figure, and those waiting to see his Highness quickly made way as he brushed impatiently by them. He was one of the few individuals in Russia who did not need an appointment to see His Imperial Majesty. The Grand Duke was immaculately attired in a full dress uniform, every ribbon and award in its proper place and his mustaches neatly trimmed. To onlookers in the hallway his formal attire and ramrod stiff bearing bespoke the seriousness of the occasion. He barged into the study and stood there, his blue eyes blazing, as he waited with barely concealed impatience for the door to close behind him. At the sound of his entrance Nicholas stepped in from the balcony and started to greet him affectionately but was cut off when Nikolasha moved directly to the purpose of his visit.

"Nicholas, enough is enough! I will never agree to be a military dictator. You have procrastinated and delayed long enough. I will help you make the decision right now!" As Nicholas looked on in horror, Nikolasha drew his service revolver from its highly polished leather holster and with a steady hand, placed the barrel against his temple. As he stood before the Tsar a single bead of perspiration formed on his forehead and then slowly slid down his cheek

The scene was surreal and for a brief moment it was as if time had stopped. The two men stood silently, their eyes fixed on each other's face. The Emperor was not sure if the Grand Duke was bluffing but he knew he could not afford to lose this most respected member of the family. On the other hand, Nikolasha was humiliated that he had to threaten such a step in order to force the Emperor's hand. His sense of loyalty to the Tsar made what he was doing seem like mutiny but his love for Russia had won out over his love for Nicky. They stood at an impasse, the stubborn ruler, stiff and unbending, and the warrior with a pistol pressed to his head. Nothing had really changed. Nicholas was faced with the same two options he had been vacillating over for days. He could crush the rebellion with force of arms or he could sign a manifesto, which promised an elected assembly and a constitution. Finally, after what seemed like hours, Nicholas broke the stalemate.

"I will sign."

Nikolasha slowly lowered the pistol and let out a sign of relief. "Your Imperial Highness, I beg your forgiveness."

"You have won. Now please leave," ordered the Tsar.

☙❧

Nicholas sat at the breakfast table conversing quietly with Alix, Nikolasha, and Stana while awaiting the arrival of Count Sergei Witte. The day he so dreaded had arrived and though outwardly calm and relaxed, in reality he was torn by conflicting emotions of relief and humiliation. Relief that he had finally agreed to sign the detested document and humiliation that he was being forced to do so by the pressure his cousin and others had brought to bear. Although Nicky continued to hold Nikolasha in high regard, because of his ability and talent, the affection he felt for him was mitigated somewhat by the dramatic confrontation in the Tsar's study. Nicky was still shaken by Nikolasha's apparent willingness to take his own life if such a course of action would serve the motherland. In fairness to the Emperor it must be acknowledged that the Grand Duke had blatantly manipulated his sovereign because he knew the Tsar would never allow him to pull the trigger. On the other hand the incident re-enforced Nicky's belief that Nikolasha was completely loyal and went a long way to dispelling the rumors that he was plotting to overthrow Nicholas and seize the throne for himself, rumors that the Tsar had never believed anyway. He felt he could trust him with his life and with the fate of Russia.

And so, on this momentous morning in the autumn of 1905, the Emperor of Russia sat at breakfast awaiting the final draft of the manifesto which he and Witte had worked on for the past two days. The document to be signed on that seventeenth day of October granted the Russian people freedom of conscience, speech, association, and assembly and, most importantly, an elected parliament to be called the Duma. His weeks of indecision were finally over but he felt no peace. Alix was unhappy but resigned and not too concerned since Nicholas still intended to move the family to Denmark.

A footman informed the Tsar that Count Witte had arrived. Nicholas excused himself from the table and went to meet him in his study. Witte greeted him and said, "Your Imperial Highness, this is the only way. If we crushed the rebellion by force, in a few months we would have to do it all over again, rivers of blood would flow and in the end we would be back where we started."

"It is too early in the day to hear this all again. I have agreed to sign so let us get on with it," the Tsar wearily informed him. "Give me the manifesto!" Nicholas slowly reviewed the document and then, with total resignation, took up his pen and signed his name. With great care, he melted red wax, poured it on to the document, and pressed his seal into it. The October Manifesto was now official. The Imperial Double Eagle seemed to look accusingly up at him from the paper so he quickly handed the document to Witte. As soon as the Count had the manifesto in his hands, he put it in his briefcase, and took leave of the Tsar. He wanted to put as much distance between them as possible. Until he actually held the document in his hand, he had been fearful that the Tsar would change his mind and refuse to sign. Now the deed was done, and Witte had only to publish the contents of this fragile paper to ensure the political future of Russia.

Chapter 10

Late October 1905 – Peterhof. Nicholas sat alone in his study and pondered the events of the past few days. For the first time in months he felt an overwhelming weariness brought on by what he believed was the burden of leadership but in actuality was a sense of sadness and resignation. He knew his decision to avoid a confrontation would be treated by many as a sign of weakness but he now was convinced it was the only path open to him. At times like this he found consolation in his religious faith and was persuaded that his decision to release the Manifesto, despite a reluctance to do so, was the will of the Supreme Being. Nicholas was content to place the fate of the country in God's hands and wait for Him to lead Russia out of the intolerable chaos she has been in for nearly a year. He glanced out the window at the calm waters of the Gulf of Finland and sighed despondently. The few days of their family cruise had been so wonderful and relaxing that he bitterly regretted it had been cut so short. The Tsar particularly missed the freedom the family had when they were away and wished there was some way he could recapture what was rapidly becoming a faded memory.

He heard a slight noise behind him and glanced over towards the door. Alix stood there quietly, a vision in white, and truly she took his breath away. After all these years and five children, she remained a beautiful and elegant woman and he thanked God who had given him such a wonderful gift. Their eyes met as he stood up to greet her and no words were necessary to describe what they were both feeling at the moment. She walked over to him and carefully pierced his shirt with a new stickpin, fussing over it until she was satisfied it was just right. The jewelry was hand crafted of the purest gold and on the head of the pin was a swastika formed in perfect white diamonds. She gently stroked his arm and said, "My darling husband, I know the stress you have been under the past few weeks and I wanted to give you a small gift to show my love and understanding. This is a swastika and it is a source of motion and a symbol of purity and divinity." She then explained that the source was the point at which something springs into being and she wanted him to think of the stickpin as a reminder that they would soon start a new life together. Nicholas, touched by her thoughtfulness, embraced her, and kissed her tenderly. There had been few opportunities recently to show their sincere love and affection so they held each other tightly and cherished the fleeting moment.

Later that afternoon Alix was pleasantly surprised to learn that Olga, Nicky's sister, had arrived from St. Petersburg for a visit. "How did you ever get here?" inquired Alix. "We received word that the trains are not running because of the strikes."

"That is quite true, but you know how resourceful I am," Olga explained. "I came by boat and I must say it was quite the adventure. How are you holding up? We received word about the Manifesto and Mama is just beside herself."

"I am surprised you heard so soon, Nicky only signed it two days ago."

"Well you know Mama, she has her fingers on the pulse of everything," declared Olga.

Alix asked Olga to join her on one of her rare walks and had a carriage brought round to carry the two of them to Peterhof Park for a stroll through the manicured grounds. There were over one hundred fountains in the exquisitely landscaped park and all were operated by naturally generated water pressure without the use of pumps. The bubbly, gurgling sounds of the water as it gushed up in dramatic displays always relaxed Alexandra. They passed the Great Cascade with its marble statues and colonnades with water jets. A huge, water-spewing lion commemorated a great Russian victory and Alix's spirits picked up as she reflected on Russia's long and glorious past. She wondered what history would have to say about her reign as Empress.

"You are awfully quiet today Alix," said Olga with concern in her voice.

"I will miss Russia and feel sorrow at the thought of leaving her. Even though she is my adopted country I love her as if I was born here and her troubles are my troubles."

"What? Leaving? Where are you going?" Olga sputtered, stunned by her words.

Alix was dismayed when she realized that while lost in her thoughts she had let the secret of their departure slip out. Thank goodness it is Olga and not some court gossip, she thought.

"Watch your step, Olga," she reminded her as she stalled for time. "That stone will cause water to spurt out from the statue and you will get wet."

"Thank you for the warning. I had forgotten. When we were children, we would run through the park trying to find all the secret stones and benches that trigger the water. Now what about this trip? When are you leaving and where are you going?" demanded Olga.

Unwilling to lie to her, Alix confessed to their planned departure for Denmark. "Nicky has informed me that we leave on the first of November but you must not tell a soul. It is for our safety that we go and then only until we are free to return."

Olga was nearly speechless with shock. "Nicholas is going with you?" she asked.

"Yes, I would never agree to go without him," Alix replied.

The two women continued their stroll but there was no more conversation. Alix was ashamed of her carelessness and Olga, though she wanted to know all the details, realized she would get no more information from the Tsarina.

A few days after Olga's talk with Alexandra, Nicholas received an unexpected visit from his cousins, the Grand Dukes George and Alexander Mikhailovich. George and Sandro, as he was called, were his best friends from childhood. The three had been inseparable and shared many adolescent adventures as the young men reached their majority. They had spent many an evening together at Nicky's former mistress' house, playing billiards, carousing, and drinking late into the night. But that was years ago and all three men were married now and cognizant of their responsibilities. Nicky had taken an active part in convincing his father that Sandro was a suitable husband for his sister Xenia and the marriage that resulted produced seven children. George was married to Princess Marie of Greece.

"I am surprised to see you both. Is this a social visit? No one is traveling much these days, what with all the unrest," said Nicky.

"We came to warn you," replied Sandro. "The Dowager Empress seems to think that you and Alix are abandoning Russia and that is the reason why you signed the manifesto."

"I do not think I have ever seen her so angry," added George. "Are you really leaving the country?"

"No, I am not. What ever gave her that idea?" asked Nicky, with obvious irritation in his voice.

"I am not sure, but I think Olga may have let something slip out," said Sandro.

"I am not leaving the country but I plan to send my wife and the children to Denmark for their safety. Alix thinks I am leaving as well and I have not told her that I will be staying in Russia. She would never leave without me," he confided to his two friends. "It seems impossible to keep any secrets around here. What ever you think do not tell her or let this rumor spread any further.

"Well, if you think your mother was angry, wait until Alix finds out. I would not want to be present for that discussion," said George.

"Please join me for a game of billiards and let us talk of other matters," said the Tsar. "I could use a little relaxation today." Soon the three were sipping brandy, shooting billiards and reminiscing about their bachelor days.

"That is a very unusual pin you are wearing," remarked George when he noticed the new stick pin..

"Alix gave it to me. It is a symbol she is very fond of and is called a swastika," answered Nicky.

"I have seen it before," said Sandro. "Scholars have just started some archeological excavations at Ai Todor, our estate in the Crimea. They found an ancient Roman fortress and many interesting inscriptions among the ruins. One apparently told of the lost world of Atlantis, and that symbol you display is said to be a map of the four rivers that flow from it."

"I will have to share that with Alix and I am sure the next time we are in the Crimea we will visit this ancient fortress. It sounds fascinating," replied Nicholas while the three continued with their game. They would stay up until the wee hours of the morning enjoying each others easy camaraderie.

It seemed as if any member of the family who was tolerated by the Tsar picked that week to visit Peterhof. Although from Nicky's point of view the Montenegrin Princesses, Militsa and Stana hardly fit into that category Alix was so intrigued by them that they, as well as Nikolasha, joined the Imperial couple for dinner on a number of occasions. It was on one such night that Militsa chose to introduce a subject that would have unforeseen consequences for them all. A storm had rolled in from the coast, and the loud claps of thunder and flashes of lightning brought a surreal aura to the dinning room. With dark hair, smoky, brown eyes and full red lips, Militsa had the wild look of the gypsy about her and she enhanced this look with a selection of brightly colored clothes. She began to relate a story in a mesmerizing, almost hypnotic voice and quickly captured the rapt attention of the small audience gathered at the table. "There came to St. Petersburg a starets, a man of God, who has offered himself to us to relieve our suffering and turmoil. Father Grigory is his name and God has given him special powers. He predicted the destruction of our fleet by the Japanese and has shown on many occasions that he can see into the future." Just then a bright flash of lightning illuminated the room and briefly captured the look of spellbound fascination on the faces of everyone in the room. When a particularly deafening crack of thunder shook the room the entire group jumped in their chairs and then laughed nervously.

"He has wandered the country, but a poor peasant, yet gaining in holiness as he traveled from shrine to holy place throughout the country," Militsa continued, as the group settled back in their seats. Stana occasionally chimed in and together the two sisters told the story of this very unusual religious teacher. "Father Grigory has extraordinary gifts of prayer and healing and it is said he can bewitch the blood and control its flow from one part of the body to the other. He can even make a bleeding wound stop," she added. Before Militsa could continue, Alix interrupted." I must meet him as soon as possible," she announced. Alexandra felt in her heart that somehow this mysterious preacher was associated with relief and possibly a cure for her son, Alexei, and she would listen to anyone who might help the heir to the throne.

But Militsa was a crafty woman who loved the power she wielded at court as one who had the ear of the Empress. She was not about to let the starets out of her control and intended to become an active intermediary between Grigory and the Tsarina. "Father Grigory is a humble man and has no use for the richness and elegance of the court. I do not think he would consent to present himself to you and the Tsar," she replied evasively.

"Militsa, you know I must see him," implored Alix. "I do not want to impose on our friendship but you must arrange a meeting."

"Father Grigory has visited us at Sergeevka. Perhaps I can persuade him to make another call on us," she replied. Militsa knew Alix would want to interview Father Grigory as quickly as she could arrange it and by having her meet him at her home she hoped she could influence the situation. She was excited at the way things were working out and knew that if the Empress had to use her as a go-between her own prestige would grow immeasurably.

Nicholas had been exposed to a bevy of Militsa and Stana's starets, mad monks and holy fools and he was in no mood to meet a new one. He expressed his disbelief when Stana claimed that he came with the recommendation of the personal confessor of Nicky's own father. He still refused to agree to the meeting despite the entreaties of Alix, but then Nikolasha added his voice to those of the believers.

"Nicholas, I too was a skeptic but I saw him heal my dog," said Nikolasha.

"Certainly there can be no harm in meeting with the man."

Swayed by Nikolasha's arguments, and unable to resist Alix's pleading eyes, he reluctantly agreed to a meeting. Militsa and Stana would host the royal couple at tea at which time the starets would call and meet his sovereign.

The very next day a boat discharged a not unexpected passenger at the pier which served the palace complex. The Dowager Empress, like a ball of fire, stormed into Peterhof, so angry that she completely overlooked protocol and ignored the frightened footman who attempted to stay ahead of her. Minnie charged into the Tsar's study, waving a copy of the Manifesto. "Nicholas what is the meaning of this?" she demanded. "It is bad enough that you signed away your power with this vile document but now I learn you are planning to leave. It seems everyone knows your plans in advance except me. It is too much."

Nicholas was not surprised to see his mother especially since Sandro and George had warned him that the hammer was about to fall. He greeted her with a kiss on the cheek and told her of his plan to send the family away to Denmark. He shared all the details with her and laid out his reasoning behind the proposal. "Alix and the children are not leaving permanently but only until the Manifesto has its desired effect and the unrest in the country ends. I have purchased an estate by the sea for their residence in Denmark. They will be close, so you may visit when you wish to see the children."

To his surprise she was adamantly opposed to his plan. "Nicholas, how can you possibly consider sending your family away? It will look as if you are abandoning the country, like a coward, in this time of crisis," she told him.

"I am not abandoning my country, mother!"

"It does not matter. By sending your family away you are showing that you are weak and have no confidence in Russia or yourself. I raised you better than that! What if the people find out about your plan? It's bad enough that rumors about your flight are circulating at court. Certainly you are not going to go through with this hair-brained scheme?"

"My decision is made!"

Minnie's face turned red with anger, "Have you no respect for me. I am your mother!"

"And I Madam, am the Tsar."

On hearing the cold tone in his voice she knew she was beaten. Minnie's voice broke as she said, "well, I can see there is no changing your mind now that you have made your decision. Obviously my opinions mean nothing to you anymore, so go and live your life as you see fit." She walked sadly out of the room unable to believe that even her tears could not sway him. Minnie realized that her influence on her son was eroding and she unfairly blamed Alix for the current impasse, unaware that Alexandra had also argued against this self-imposed exile in Denmark.

The Tsar was distressed by the exchange with his mother and as he sat alone in his study he began to vacillate. Nicky was a loving and considerate individual and his generous nature often got him into trouble. Since he could not please everyone, all the time, he tended to favor his most recent contact and in this case, when Minnie departed, she was unaware that she had planted a seed of doubt in his mind. As for Nicholas, he hoped his mother would tell no one of their conversation, especially Alix, who still did not know that he was staying in Russia. He hoped to avoid a dreadful scene by holding this close until the last minute but was extremely frustrated that so many people had found out about his "secret plan." Nicholas was not a complex person but he was capable of complex thought and he vowed that any future efforts to safeguard the family would be developed more carefully and with greater secrecy.

CR&O

The odor emanating from the unwashed clothes and body of the vagabond, as he trudged along the road, was enough to make one gag. Long, greasy hair hung in oily tendrils about his face and bits of food clung to his gray flecked beard. He had dark piercing eyes and a large, bushy mustache, which barely concealed full, sensuous lips. He was dressed in a shabby cassock that was little more than an associated group of rags held together with patches. Passersby crossed the street to avoid contact with the ragged creature but one poor woman, in her haste to evade him, tripped and fell. When he paused to help her up she tried to pull away but was instantly mesmerized by his dark, piercing eyes. She felt him take her hand in his large, surprisingly warm one and, captivated by the aura surrounding him, she did not notice his odor or the dirty, cracked hand with its yellowed and blackened fingernails. He helped her to her feet, released her hand, and continued on down the street while she stood in wonder at the strange encounter. Despite the dirt and the torn clothes, Grigory Rasputin was a commanding figure, a man with a sense of purpose and an individual who would prove impossible to manipulate.

When he finally reached his destination, a large imposing palace in the coastal town of Sergeevka, he greeted his hostess's with a kiss. The two noble women seemed unconcerned with his appearance and welcomed him warmly in return. Militsa and Stana, the two Montenegrin Princesses, the infamous "black plague," were fascinated by their visitor. After arranging for his lodging they gathered for tea and from the moment he began to talk they were spellbound and hung on his every word. He conversed with them in the simple language of the peasant and spoke on a wide range of topics. For an itinerant preacher he was surprisingly well informed. Militsa and Stana looked at each other and smiled. They knew that the Empress would quickly accept Rasputin because of the mystic power he seemed to have. They naively believed they had cultivated him sufficiently and could now use the holy man to increase their influence with the Emperor and Empress. It was now time to arrange a meeting.

"Father Grigory, we wish you to call on the first of November. We have esteemed visitors who wish to make your acquaintance," said Militsa.

"I have told you before that I have no wish to socialize with the nobility and will not waste my talents on them," replied Rasputin.

"This is a request you cannot refuse. The Tsar himself extended this invitation to you," said Stana.

After thinking the matter over for several minutes he agreed to the meeting. "I will meet them but no others must be present for I have a private message for the Empress," he informed the two women. Militsa and Stana were not surprised at this because they were convinced he could foretell the future and they hoped somehow to be included in the private audience they had taken so much trouble to arrange.

A few days later, on the first day of November, the holy man returned to Sergeevka, and was welcomed into their home. Militsa and Stana were astonished by his appearance. Rasputin was dressed in clean garments with highly polished black boots, his normal body odor replaced by a sweet smelling scent. His freshly washed hair was neatly combed and gathered in a tie at the nape of his neck and his beard was carefully trimmed.

"Look at you all prim and proper to meet the Tsar. My have we gotten fancy," said Stana.

"You certainly seemed to have prepared well for your audience," added Militsa.

"Do not speak so to a man of God. It is none of your concern," Rasputin said as he reprimanded the two. Although he was impatient with the conniving women he knew that this initial contact with the royal family was dependent on them. Many thought him an illiterate peasant and he let the notion go unchallenged since it suited his purpose to have people think him uneducated.

He was a long way from the Siberia of his birth, physically, spiritually and intellectually. After a dissolute youth and an early "conversion experience" he had traveled Russia and spent many months in the libraries of various monasteries, immersed in holy writings. He had even walked over two thousand miles to the monastery at Mount Athos in Greece where he studied for two years. His time at the various holy places and shrines enabled him to study and learn, so that by the time he began his "public career" he was well versed in scripture and church traditions. The experience gained in these travels was reflected in his teachings which included the philosophy and theological approach of many different sects. Outwardly he maintained enough of the Russian Orthodox influence to gain him initial support from the church.

This was actually his second trip to the St. Petersburg area. His first was in 1903 and it was after that trip that he became determined to reach the pinnacle of Russian society. Thus, as it turned out, his protestation to the two sisters that he had "no wish to socialize with the nobility" was a blatant lie. His reputation for healing and prophesying having preceded him, he was received by one of Russia's most revered priests, Father John of Kronstadt, a saintly man who had been the confessor to Tsar Alexander III. For Rasputin to be accepted and blessed by this holy man was a huge first step in accomplishing his goal of penetrating the inner circle of court society. When he returned to the city in 1905, he was received by Archimandrite Theophan, the Empress Alexandra's former confessor. Rasputin had carefully prepared for his eventual meeting with the Tsar by talking to servants, socialites and churchmen alike, learning as much as he possibly could about the Tsar and his wife. He knew intimate details of their daily existence before they met and, through Militsa, was privy to all the court gossip. The informal audience was now at hand and was the culmination of much effort. Father Grigory was confident that once they met he would be able to manipulate them as he had so many others. Little do they realize how thoroughly I have readied myself for this moment, he thought, as he gingerly rubbed his still tender palm with his thumb.

"Now take me to your guests," he ordered the Montenegrin sisters.

Alix sat waiting impatiently, trying to concentrate as her emotions ran the gamut of hope, despair, and desperation. Would this holy man have a special message for her? Could it be true that God has given him special healing powers? she wondered. The door opened and Grigory Rasputin strode into the drawing room, his commanding presence instantly dominating the atmosphere. Alix could not keep her eyes off him and she felt a flutter of nervousness. The monk immediately approached Alix, ignoring the others in the room. The Empress was his goal and he knew if he won her over his future was secured. He knelt in front of her, took her hand and drew it to his lips, ever so carefully. Alix caught her breath as she glimpsed his palm and saw the familiar black lines of a swastika tattooed on his hand. Unable to understand how this could be she made the mistake of glancing up into his eyes and felt him look into her soul. For one brief moment she trembled in fear but then her anxiety vanished and she remained a captive of his penetrating eyes. At that moment Rasputin knew she was his.

"The captain does not abandon the ship and the wife stays by the captain's side," he whispered softly to her.

Nicholas looked on with annoyance as he saw Alix's reaction to the starets. He thought she was acting like a schoolgirl seeing her first love and he did not like the feelings of jealousy that stirred inside him.

"Rasputin is such an odd name for a man of God. Does that not mean a good-for-nothing, debauched person?" asked the Tsar in an effort to gain control of the conversation. Alix was irritated by Nicky's rudeness and Militsa and Stana looked at each other nervously while awaiting the monk's reply.

"Your Imperial Highness, I fully realize the derivation of my name but I retain it willingly and wear it as a badge of humility to remind me of my sinful beginnings. When I was a younger man I was a drunkard, a lout, and a thief, but God works in mysterious ways, and much like St. Paul in the Holy Scriptures, I experienced a roadside conversion which changed my life. I was given the gift of visions and one day I saw with my own eyes the image of the Lord. He showed me his Blessed Mother weeping for the sins of mankind and directed me to begin my wanderings and to cleanse the people of their sins. Since that time Our Savior has directed my travels and finally, after a very long journey, he has today led me to your side."

"So what message does he have for me?" the Tsar demanded skeptically.

The three women waited in breathless anticipation for the monk's reply. Rasputin moved to stand in front of the Tsar and hesitantly, as if in a trance, extended his arm to bless him. "Here is your message. Spit on your fears and rule as God has anointed you to do. Remember well these words, and heed them, and you will avoid misfortune." He spoke in a deep and soothing voice but Nicholas, nonetheless, was irritated at the peasant's informality. He started to reprimand him but for some inexplicable reason he held his tongue. Rasputin then bowed to the ladies and left the room ending the interview so abruptly that everyone was caught off guard. Nicholas and the women could only wonder about the significance of the brief interchange.

Militsa quickly followed the monk out of the drawing room, motioning him to wait for her.

"You must not try to meet with the Tsar and Tsarina alone, otherwise it will be the end of you. I must always escort you into their presence because the court is filled with intrigue and envy. There are also many temptations that would be dangerous to a simple peasant such as yourself. You need my guidance," she informed Rasputin. He stared at her with his dark, brooding eyes and she became quiet. He had no intention of following her advice, but did not inform her of this, and left her palace quite satisfied with the way the meeting had gone. His palm was still sore but the indelible mark was worth the price he paid in pain and he was sure that the figure had made a great impression on the Empress. When Rasputin dipped a needle into ink to create this crude tattoo of a swastika the sign, which in the past symbolized purity and divinity, was corrupted forever. Future generations would come to loathe the swastika and associate it with evil.

Father Grigory's thoughts turned to the Tsar and he recognized that Nicholas was much more complicated than he had anticipated and too preoccupied at this time to be easily manipulated. He knew that eventually he would be able to command influence through Alexandra and time was one commodity that he had a great amount of.

Rasputin returned immediately to St. Petersburg where he was staying at the home of a civil servant and his wife. His host was in charge of the roads at Tsarskoe Selo and, due to his position, privy to much palace gossip. Father Grigory had encouraged him to share the details of the royal family's daily life and through him learned much that would be of use. Of particular interest was the fact that the heir to the throne was ill and suffered from the bleeding disease. However, he chose not to disclose his knowledge of this information at his first meeting with the Imperial couple but held it as a trump card for later use. In the meantime he allowed rumors that he had power over the flow of blood to circulate and did nothing to dispel the atmosphere of intrigue that surrounded him. No one was aware that Rasputin would soon be leaving the city to travel to Siberia and his home in Pokrovskoe. Many months would pass before he met with the Emperor and Empress again, and the next time it would be on his terms.

Nicholas and Alexandra sat in silence for a few moments after the "holy man" left the room. Nicky still felt a flush of irritation at Rasputin's cavalier attitude and seeming lack of respect for his position. They visited for a little longer with Militsa and Stana who wisely avoided any discussion of the just completed meeting. Alix also sensed her husband's mood, and though barely able to contain her excitement, kept quiet on the subject as well. She naively believed that no one in the court knew about Alexei's illness and the worry she experienced as a result of it. Alix would try anything to alleviate the suffering of her son whereas Nicky tended to rely on the medical professionals. But this was different. Although there had been no mention of her son during the audience she believed God had brought this mystic to her and when she saw the symbol on the preacher's hand she viewed it as a sign of some supernatural power. When they departed the palace she felt the stirring of hope within her and a desperate need to discuss the day's events with her husband.

Alix could not contain her excitement and in the carriage on the way home to Peterhof, she brought up the meeting with Rasputin. "Oh Nicholas," she exclaimed, "this man is the answer to our prayers. Did you hear his message? We need not fear and must not leave Russia. Darling, I am so relieved that we can remain in our home."

Nicholas, of course, had been through this before and considered Father Grigory just one more in a long line of Stana and Militsa's eccentrics. At first he did not attach much significance to the audience but as he listened to Alix he had to admit that this simple peasant was not typical of the men and women the sisters usually cultivated. The man was very confident and much more subtle than Nicholas had expected and the effect he had on Alix and the Grand Duchesses was obvious. Still, although he was unwilling to attribute too much importance to Rasputin's words, he realized that properly managed the monk's predictions might provide a solution to the dilemma he faced. To Alix everything he said seemed prophetic but the Tsar knew the subject of his family's flight was the topic of much gossip and this monk could easily have manipulated the information to his advantage.

"Sunny, you seem so convinced this Rasputin is a man of holiness, but I am not so sure. How do we know his words were a message from God?" Nicky asked her.

"My darling Nicky, God gave me a sign when Father Grigory spoke to me. On his palm was the swastika, a sign of divinity. When I saw it on his hand, I knew he was sent to us by God, and when I looked into his eyes I was sure of it."

"I still am not convinced that he meant that we should cancel our plan to leave the country," he argued. "I still think it is necessary to safeguard the family."

"But Father Grigory said, 'rule as God anointed you to.' And I must agree with him. It is not the time to show fear," she replied.

Nicholas realized the time had come and gently took her hand in his. "My darling Sunny, there is no easy way to tell you, but I am not leaving Russia. You and the children must travel without me and remain away until it is safe to return. I did not share this with you earlier because I did not wish to distress you."

Alix was upset at the news and disappointed that he had not shared this aspect of the plan with her but instead of slipping into one her moods her spirits soared. "Nicky, can you not see? We are safe now. The captain's wife does not leave her husband and therefore I will remain here with you. Father Grigory has given me hope for the first time in months and I, for one, believe in him implicitly."

Nicky recalled his mother leaving Peterhof in tears when she learned of his intention to send his family away. There and then, as the carriage rattled back to Peterhof, Nicholas changed his mind and decided to scrap the Denmark scheme. Secrecy had been compromised from the beginning and if Alix was right about the holy man perhaps there would be no danger in staying. He was influenced by two stubborn women he deeply loved and knew they would both be placated by his change of heart. "Alix, I believe you are correct. Tomorrow we will travel to Tsarskoe Selo instead of Denmark and I will try to make sense of this new manifesto I signed into existence."

Alix leaned over and planted a soft kiss on Nicky's cheek. She nestled closer to him and said, "It will be fine. God wills it so."

Later that evening, at Peterhof, a flurry of preparations had begun so the family could return to Alexander Palace the next day. Since the Tsar was not involved in the activity he retired to the study and took the opportunity to bring his diary up to date. He made a short entry that he had met the man of God and then placed it prominently on the corner of his desk. He then removed his secret diary from its hiding place and proceeded to record his true thoughts and feelings about the monk, Rasputin. He was extremely concerned about Alix's reaction and her gullibility. She was so desperate for miracles and signs that she grasped at anything. His heart was with her and he was one of the few who understood the secret suffering she went through because of Alexei's illness. It was absolutely critical, because of the chaos within the country, that the people did not learn the heir to the throne had a fatal illness. Consequently, Alix suffered in silence, very few aware of the agony she felt, as she watched their two year old son writhe in pain. Although Nicky was not impressed with the "holy man," he knew that Father Grigory had given Alix the gift of hope and for that he was grateful. What harm can come from our meeting again, he thought, as he locked up his diary.

The Imperial family returned to Alexander Palace and as the winter days grew shorter Alix and the children settled back into their routines, blissfully unaware of the bloodshed occurring throughout the country. The October Manifesto did not have the desired result and the nation was still facing widespread revolution. Nicholas, frustrated by the lack of progress, searched for a scapegoat and found one in Sergei Witte. On the eve of the first meeting of the Duma, he requested the Count's resignation, which Witte humbly submitted. That night Nicky explained his reasoning to Alix. "I have never seen such a chameleon. He has changed from a man of peace to a radical conservative and wants to hang or shoot all the opposition. It is not surprising that no one believes in him anymore. I, for one, will never, as long as I live, trust him again with even the smallest of matters." Alix listened sympathetically because she had never liked Witte and was pleased at the news of his dismissal.

The winter season with its heavy snows dragged on but the arrival of an early spring was greeted with enthusiasm by the inhabitants of Alexander Palace. The advent of the summer months found Nicholas busy with affairs of state and time flew by. In the coming months he was forced to dismiss the Duma because of its ineffectual bickering and revolutionary ideas. In July 1906, Nicholas, in what was to be his finest appointment, called Peter Stolypin into service as his Prime Minister. Stolypin was an extremely competent statesman and he handled the crisis in the country with vitality and aggressiveness. He realized reform was impossible as long as lawlessness ruled the land so he ignored the threat of assassination and cracked down on the instigators of violence. Because results were immediately apparent, the Tsar overlooked the fact that the new Prime Minister was acting in some ways much as Witte had recommended. In less than a year over 14,000 revolutionaries were executed and hanging became known as "wearing a Stolypin necktie." The measures were effective and the disturbances in the country finally began to subside. After order had been restored he moderated his stance and promoted land reform and private farming. He was hated by revolutionaries and ultra-conservatives alike, but Nicholas came to admire and respect Stolypin and was grateful to him for returning the country to a semblance of normalcy.

⊰⊱

Nicholas shut his ears to the cries of pain but his heart broke at the sight of Alix's pinched, tired face as she looked at him with pleading eyes. Alexei had been injured again and their precious child was suffering terrible pain from the pressure of internal bleeding. Unable to bear the sight of his suffering any longer, Nicky retreated to his study and pulled out the telegram he had received only yesterday. As he read its contents again his thoughts turned to the mysterious peasant they had met over a year ago and he remembered the hope and joy the "holy man" had brought to Alix. Nicky compared that to the pitiful appearance she presented today and decided he would do anything to relieve her suffering. In the wire Father Grigory had asked for an audience and permission to bring in an icon of Saint Simeon, the miracle worker. The Tsar, overcome by his son's suffering and his wife's desperation, directed his secretary to arrange a meeting that very evening and send a sled to expedite Rasputin's arrival.

When the appointed hour arrived, Alix received the monk in her Mauve Boudoir in the family quarters, because Nicholas wished the visit to be kept as private as possible. Father Grigory presented himself to his rulers and this time his behavior was deferential and correct. He carefully maneuvered his large frame into the delicate chair the Tsar motioned him to. He glanced at them both beneath hooded eyes and quickly took in the situation. Their Imperial Highnesses sat there in the grip of exceptional stress, both with dark, puffy circles under their eyes and Alexandra on the verge of a nervous breakdown. Father Grigory began to speak in a soft but clear voice. "God has seen your pain and sorrow and has sent me to relieve your suffering. Grant me permission to see your son. I know he is gravely ill but God has given me the power to help him." He then removed the icon of Saint Simeon from his jacket, reverently unwrapped it and presented it to the Tsar. "Let me bless him with this holy icon and let its healing power wash over him."

"Come with me," Alix directed him. The three quietly climbed her private staircase to the children's quarters and made their way to Alexei's room. Alix bid him wait in the hall while she dismissed Alexei's nurse. She and Nicky prepared to follow Fr. Grigory into his room but he asked them to wait by the door.

"I beg you, do not interfere with God's work," he told the two. Nicholas was not sure he wished this stranger to touch his beloved child but he held back when he saw the rapt look on Alix's face as she watched the black robed figure walk into the nursery.

Alexei's room lay in semi-darkness with the only light coming from lamps illuminating the numerous icons around his crib. The flickering candles amplified the size of the monk's shadow and made the black form seem twice its actual size. The child lay there, half asleep, fitfully tossing, turning and whimpering as the pain coursed through his tiny body. Alexei looked like a pale cherub with his blond curls lying on his pillow but when he opened his eyes innocence turned to terror as he took in the immense shadowy figure floating over his crib. He let out a blood curdling scream. Unable to see what was happening across the room Nicholas started to intervene but Alix's gentle touch stopped him.

"Please, wait a moment and see what happens," she begged him.

The starets leaned over the crib and carefully placed his hands on either side of the screaming child's head. The cries subsided to a few sobs and Rasputin moved closer to him and stared deeply into his eyes, calmly humming a strange tune while he massaged Alexei's temples. Rasputin loved working his wiles on children, because they were so susceptible to his skills and easily fell under his spell. He whispered a few words to the child then made the sign of the cross and blessed him with the icon. Alexei drifted into sleep and Father Grigory quietly walked over to Nicholas and Alexandra. "God has answered your prayers, the sickness has left him."

Nicholas and Alexandra left the peasant by the door and rushed over to their precious son's crib. Rasputin watched them for a moment and then slipped away. "Oh Nicky, it is a miracle," Alix whispered to him ecstatically as they stood over the crib watching the peacefully sleeping child. His fever had broken, his breathing was normal and even his cheeks glowed with a hint of color not seen in days. "Darling I can never thank you enough for summoning Fr. Grigory. God has worked a miracle through him and healed our son. I feel such joy in my heart." They turned to thank him but the mysterious healer was gone. Nicky placed his arm around Alix, kissed her forehead and together they stood for a time watching their angel sleeping peacefully, his body free from pain for the first time in days.

Chapter 11

January 1907 – London. The winter storm had blown the fog away but it was still a generally miserable day, cold and rainy, and typical of London at that time of year. However, the somber weather did little to discourage the enthusiasm of the large group of men who met that wintry day in a rented hall in the outskirts of the city. The three hundred delegates to this revolutionary conference represented radical elements from all over the continent, as well as Great Britain, and their collective desire was the overthrow of the monarchies of Europe especially the Romanov dynasty of Russia. But on this particular morning the agenda of these anarchists was primarily organizational and they focused on the mundane requirements of putting together the framework of a committee to lead the effort. Among the most dynamic of the revolutionary talent at the meeting was a trio of Russian exiles, Vladimir Lenin, Leon Trotsky, and Joseph Stalin. Trotsky, the fiery orator, so involved in the revolution of 1905, had been able to elude the crackdown instituted by Stolypin and escaped from Russia seething with anger and filled with a desire to return and put an end to Tsarist rule. Together these three managed to dominate the proceedings and before long it was evident they would emerge as the leaders of a new revolutionary party. Also among the delegates attending the affair was a nobleman named Vladislav Zabalia, an intelligent young man, well disguised, and involved in a very dangerous game. He was a spy for Count Benckendorff and was unquestionably loyal to the Tsar. His obvious task was to learn as much as possible about the new movement.

The assembly met for three days and with much fanfare and little surprise, on the last day, elected Lenin as the party chairman. As the conference broke up an event occurred that was to have a great impact on the Tsar and the story of his family. When the revolutionaries departed to return to their homes, a few of the leaders remained behind and by an incredible bit of good fortune, Zabalia overheard them discussing a secret meeting to be held later that day.

It was actually late that night when Lenin and the others were finally able to meet. Taking his life in his hands Zabalia hid himself in a crawl space adjacent to the room selected for the meeting. The dimly lit chamber held only ten people but they were ten whose impact on history would be undeniable. Trotsky and Lenin were among the leaders seated around the circular table and Lenin quickly took charge of the meeting. He was a short, somewhat dumpy man with a round, balding head and his appearance hardly commanded respect. But his keen intellect and ability as a speaker overcame his physical shortcomings and his leadership qualities were never more evident than in the manner in which he manipulated this inner circle. When he began to speak, they listened attentively and he wasted no time in getting to the heart of the matter. "We botched the revolution in 1905 and failed because of the Tsar. He tricked the people and rallied them with his fraudulent manifesto and our efforts to overthrow the monarchy were futile. It will be many years before we have an opportunity like that again especially now that he has instituted his land reforms. The people are relatively happy now and Russia is calm, but if we had assassinated him when the country was in turmoil, we would have succeeded. Tonight, here and now, we must sign a pact, which will remain secret within our group. We must swear to kill the Tsar and his entire family."

"Surely you just mean the Tsar, his wife and son, and not his four daughters. What purpose would it serve to execute them? They are not in the line of succession and it could only hurt our cause to have their innocent blood upon our hands," objected Trotsky rather strongly. He was disturbed by the ruthless suggestion but remembered that Lenin always maintained that "the end justified the means."

"The daughters will die! We do not need their pitiful orphan faces rallying the people to their cause. It would be catastrophic for any of them to live," Lenin argued.

"The imperial family is quite large. What about the rest of that family, all the Grand Dukes and Duchesses that are such a drain on our country," asked Trotsky.

"They are of little importance to us," said Lenin. "They are a group of indolent, rich fools and the people have no love for them."

"What if the Tsar or his children escape to another country?" questioned another of the group.

"Enough," he shouted. "They must all die! Can you not understand there can be no quarter or mercy given? We cannot be weak or shirk our duties no matter how repulsive they seem. We will hunt them to the ends of the earth if necessary, even if it takes years. There must be no survivors. It is far too dangerous for our cause to give hope to the monarchists after we come to power," urged Lenin.

He picked up a sharp knife from the table and melodramatically held his hand over a pale white plate. All eyes were upon him as he cut his hand and dribbled blood onto the small plate. His beady, black eyes glared at the group as if daring them to object. He passed the plate and the knife around the table and one by one the ten added their blood, the bright red a sharp contrast against the white of the plate. Lenin carefully removed a folded document from his jacket. "Tonight we will each sign the Tsar's death warrant and take an oath, swearing to complete this mission even if it means our own deaths." He then stirred the slowly congealing blood with a quill and signed his name in a bright red that quickly dried to a sickly brown color. The others followed in turn, each carefully etching his name with the bloody mixture that served as ink. After each had signed they took an oath to carry out the warrant. With that the meeting broke up.

Vladislav Zabalia heard a creak as the door opened and the sounds of boots tromping across the floor. His heart pounded for fear of discovery but the room emptied quickly and in the dim light no one noticed the access to his hiding place. He waited fifteen more minutes before climbing out, careful to make no noise. The scene he had just witnessed, terrifying as it was, had been worth the risk to his life. He was convinced that divine intervention had put him in position to learn of the meeting and he thanked God for letting him remain undetected. The young man was well aware of the importance of getting the information to Count Benckendorff as quickly as possible but he was unwilling to entrust it to a courier or a coded telegram. The next morning he crossed to France and made arrangements to return immediately to St. Petersburg. He was still shocked by the brutality of these revolutionaries and was sickened at the thought of Russia in their hands.

∞

The Tsar sat in his study at Alexander Palace contemplating the information Count Benckendorff had just relayed to him. The secret pact to murder him and his family was disturbing news to say the least and he was eternally grateful to young Zabalia for risking so much. There had, of course, been other plots to assassinate Nicholas but the sinister nature of this one, which was directed at his whole family, shattered the illusion of security he had created. Under the leadership of his new minister, Peter Stolypin, the country had finally settled into some semblance of normalcy. With this new information in hand he now had to admit that he had been lulled into a false sense of security by the relative calm. The revolution was not over but was, rather, in a period of inactivity and, like the glowing embers of a fire, needed only more fuel to burst into flame. He also understood that Lenin's pact was directed not only at the family but also at the nation and that the next outbreak of revolutionary activity would be better organized and a much greater threat to Russia.

He opened the secret compartment in his desk and reverently removed the box containing the letter from Saint Serafim, given to him by Elena Motovilov, at Sarov, years earlier. Even though the words had been committed to memory long ago, he read it again, and, at long last, pieces of the puzzle began to fall into place. Thanks to Zabalia's efforts the enemy that would hunt his children to the ends of the earth had been identified and he could see now that his simplistic plan to seek safety in Denmark would never have protected the children from Lenin and his thugs. Nicholas was well aware that the letter was only a warning and it was up to him alone to develop a counter-plot to foil the revolutionaries. The task was unambiguous. Save the girls! But how? And why did the letter mention only his daughters and not Alexei? He found this omission confusing and troubling and hoped that the reason for the exclusion of his son from Serafim's letter would become apparent. As the light faded he sat there in the darkened room, lost in thought, wrestling with the vague and shadowy outline of a plan, a plan so complex it would take years to develop.

The Tsar, uncharacteristically, slept late the next morning and awoke refreshed and ready to continue grappling with the troubling aspects of the previous day's developments. He was convinced that within ten years, Russia, as the world knew it, would cease to exist, after being torn asunder by some cataclysmic event. After all, this was what the letter predicted and Nicholas saw no reason to discount Saint Serafim's warning. However, he had to look at the situation pragmatically and unemotionally if he was to be successful in developing a plan to save his children. Unfortunately, for his state of mind, the more he thought about the traitorous anarchists who intended to destroy the Russia he loved, the angrier he became. Nicholas believed in the divine right of kings and considered Russia his birthright. He had no intention of meekly submitting to efforts to deprive him of his patrimony and vowed then and there to fight with whatever means were at his disposal. He knew what the final outcome would be but the Tsar did not allow himself the luxury of becoming fatalistic. He would fight with the tools at hand and, realizing the importance of finance, he decided his first action would be to prevent the revolutionaries from gaining access to Russia's wealth. The revolution might succeed but he would ensure that it was hamstrung by a weak economy. To achieve this result Nicholas intended to transfer vast sums of currency and bullion out of the country and although he was not familiar with the logistics involved he believed the task could be accomplished clandestinely. Valuable resources would not be used to fight a battle, which he knew would ultimately be lost. Eventually, however, the war would be won and when it was, the wealth of the nation would be needed. It was his devout hope that these assets would be safeguarded until such time that a new Russia emerged from the chaos caused by this new breed of reactionaries. The rest of the royal family, and for that matter, the Russian people in general, would never understand the Tsar's actions because they were not privy to the details of Saint Serafim's prophesy.

At present only Alix and Nicholas knew the contents of the letter and the Tsar intended to keep it that way for the time being. Knowing that he would suffer some sort of martyrdom he felt it imperative that a successor be identified as soon as possible. Alexei, of course, was out of the picture because of his disease and the fact that Nicholas intended to shield him from the death threat. He needed an individual, well-respected by all and completely trustworthy and there were very few such men in Russia. His thoughts turned to his uncle Nikolasha and the Tsar knew immediately that he was the one. He trusted him completely and the family respected and feared him. He inspires people, thought Nicky, and he will be the man to rally the people when I am gone. Nicholas' head churned with questions but the answers eluded him. How could he liquidate Russian wealth without arousing suspicions? Who could he trust and who should know about this plan? There was an urgency to resolve these issues, he thought to himself, but first he must talk to Nikolasha and get his agreement.

⊂℘℈∽

That frigid January day in St. Petersburg was hardly the best time to be out and about but Grigory Rasputin was a man with a purpose. He had received word from Grand Duchess Militsa that Empress Alexandra wished him to meet a dear friend and he was eager to comply with the Tsarina's wishes. If he was to continue to have influence he would need to cultivate an insider, someone who was close to the Imperial family and privy to intimate details about their life. Militsa, and her sister Stana, both had a long standing friendship with the Empress but they had their own agenda and were too intelligent, ambitious, and crafty for his purpose. He needed someone he could easily manipulate.

It was a long walk from his lodgings and he arrived somewhat out of breath at Grand Duchess Militsa's palace on the English Quay. Anya Taneyeva, whom Rasputin was to meet, had already arrived and when he entered the imposing mansion he was escorted directly into the drawing room and greeted by Militsa with three kisses. Out the corner of his eye he saw the look of uneasiness that crossed the face of the Empress' confidante. Father Grigory had anticipated some elegant courtier so when Militsa presented him to Anya Taneyeva it was all he could do to contain his surprise. The plump, dark haired young woman seemed a somewhat colorless individual, slightly disheveled and nothing, in appearance, like the meticulously groomed Empress. But Rasputin could be quite charming when the situation called for it and realizing these first moments were of great importance he was careful to treat Anya with deference and courtesy. He gently took her hands in his and stared deeply into her eyes and she responded by blushing furiously. He bade her to sit and they began to converse quietly while Militsa looked on. She was obviously irritated by the attention the black robed "mystic" was paying to Anya and Rasputin quickly sensed that the Grand Duchess looked on Anya as a competitor. In an effort to steer the conversation in another direction Militsa addressed Anya in French, suggesting that she ask the monk to pray for a special intention.

Anya looked up at the starets and timidly asked, "Will you please pray to God that I may spend my whole life in service to their majesties?" Militsa rolled her eyes at this request and unsuccessfully attempted to keep her dislike of Anya from showing. Her influence and friendship with Alexandra seemed to be fading and she was irritated to see this simpleton rise in favor.

Rasputin spoke softly and Anya strained to hear his words, "Your whole life will be spent as you requested, but is there not more you are concerned with my child?"

Anya sensed that this strange man was aware of her innermost concerns and decided to take advantage of his intervention. "I have great doubts about my impending marriage. Her Imperial Highness greatly encourages the match but my husband-to-be is much older and I do not know him very well. He also seems to be suffering some ill effects from wounds received in the war," she replied.

Father Grigory was very careful, in his dealings with Alexandra, to avoid the appearance of opposing her expressed desires, especially in what he considered unimportant matters, as this business with Anya obviously was. His predictions were carefully researched and accurate enough to enhance his influence with the royal family and his apparent ability to alleviate Alexei's suffering kept him in the Tsarina's good graces. When he responded to Anya, therefore, he was deliberately ambiguous.

"You are a woman full grown and thus are free to make your own decisions. This I cannot do for you, but know this, your marriage will not be a happy one." Anya, turned pale, stood up and reached for Father Grigory's hands. "Holy father, this is not what I hoped to hear, but thank you for your kind counsel. At least I know what to expect and for that reason you have set my mind at peace. May I see you again?"

"My child, God has brought you to me and I welcome you into my flock. I shall watch over you always. It is God's will."

After tea and some light conversation Anya departed, but Rasputin remained behind to converse privately with Militsa. When they were alone, he stood up and looked at the Grand Duchess contemptuously. He had no further need of her now that Anya was under his influence and he wasted little time confronting her. "I know that you arranged for me to be investigated, you foolish woman, but it will come to naught and so will your influence with the Tsarina. She is a captive to my will and refuses to believe any accusations against me. As far as she is concerned I am a messenger from God and every word of slander she hears against me is false. I take my leave of you and spit at your feet, you vain and ambitious fool. I will visit no more." With that he left Militsa's palace, never to return.

Rasputin was not too concerned that his tirade against the Grand Duchess would filter back to the Empress. For some time he had been quietly undermining the influence of the Montenegrin princesses through innuendo and outright lies. He knew the Tsarina was concerned that the court be free of immorality and scandal so he voiced disapproval of Stana's relationship with Nikolasha. He did so very carefully, however, because the soldier was highly respected and he was one of the few men Rasputin genuinely feared, especially since Nikolasha had recently turned against him. He was far too sharp and had too much influence over the Tsar. Rasputin intended to weaken this influence by playing Alexandra off against him. His position was solidified by the one factor that dominated all others and that was his apparent ability to treat Alexei's hemophilia. The meeting with Anya had gone well and she would be putty in his hands. He would do everything to encourage Alexandra's continued friendship with her, but he wished she lived at the palace where she could be of more use to him.

 C8&O

Mahogany is a beautiful dark wood with wonderful grain and the architects of Alexander Palace had made generous use of it when the palace was constructed. Unfortunately, on overcast days, the paneled walls and ceiling of the Tsar's reception room made the large chamber seem dismal and uninviting. As Nikolasha paced around the room he imagined that the Tsar's many petitioners were intimidated by the atmosphere, as they awaited their opportunity to see His Imperial Majesty and he could understand why they might feel that way. Nikolasha did not require an appointment to see his cousin but he hesitated before going into the study because, to be honest, he dreaded the encounter. The most respected man in Russia found himself in the unusual and uncomfortable position of a fifty year old supplicant; a petitioner who was, quite frankly, embarrassed by his petition. Cupid's arrow can strike the most unlikely target and he had come to plead with Nicholas to allow him to marry the woman he loved. She was Anastasia, the daughter of the King of Montenegro, and normally would have been considered a suitable match for the Grand Duke. Unfortunately Stana, as everyone called her, brought some unacceptable baggage to the proposed marriage. Not only was she a divorcee but her sister Militsa was married to Nikolasha's brother Peter, and this intermingling of families was frowned upon by the church. Consequently when the Grand Duke came today to appeal to Nicholas he approached the Tsar not only as his Emperor but also as the head of the Russian Orthodox Church. The situation was not promising and the precedents definitely discouraging. His Majesty had dealt harshly with other members of the Imperial family who defied his wishes in regards to their marriages, stripping them of their titles and income and occasionally forcing them into exile. Nikolasha had little hope that the Tsar would grant his wish but he vowed to accept the decision whatever it might be. In spite of his human frailties Nicholas was Tsar and therefore God's representative on earth and he would always defer to that reality. If he was to be denied his love, so be it.

When the secretary came in to announce his uncle's arrival Nicky was sitting in his green leather chair, comfortable in its familiarity, idly straightening items on his desk. He was surprised to learn Nikolasha was here to see him and wondered at the strange coincidence that brought him to the palace just when he was about to summon him to discuss his future plans. Nicky rose to greet Nikolasha when he was escorted into his study and after pleasantries were exchanged asked what brought him to Tsarskoe Selo. A man of few words, and anxious to put an end to the uncertainty he came directly to the point. "Your Imperial Highness, I have come to plead my case. I wish to marry Stana." Nicky was relieved to see that this time he had not unholstered his service revolver to dramatize the situation, as he had on a previous visit. The Tsar turned and looked out the window, contemplating the best way to handle this appeal. The request was not unexpected since everyone at court was aware of the liaison and curious as to how Nicholas would handle the budding scandal. He turned and faced Nikolasha and said, "your request puts me in a very awkward position, as you well know, but I will not stand in your way, uncle. But what you do must be done quietly and without fanfare. I will not embarrass you, but neither will I publicly endorse your marriage." Although he did not approve, and he knew Alix would object, the Tsar intended to ask much of this impressive man and could not jeopardize his acquiescence by humiliating him in this matter of the heart. Nikolasha bowed low and thanked Nicky for his generosity, extremely surprised that he had agreed so readily.

As far as Nicky was concerned, now was the time to bring his uncle into the picture. "I am glad that you called today. I have a subject of the utmost importance and confidentiality which I wish to discuss with you." Nikolasha watched as Nicky carefully unlocked the box on his desk and without any discussion or preparation handed a yellowed letter to him. The Grand Duke took the document and began to read.

My son, give thanks to the Lord God who in his ineffable mercy has revealed to me that a great and calamitous evil shall befall Russia. War and famine will turn the people from God. Russia will be lost, drowning in sorrow in an abyss from which there seems no hope of rescue.

You, Nicholas, must sacrifice yourself and become a martyr. As the Lord said to his disciples, "If ye were of the world, the world would love its own, but because I chose you out of the world, therefore the world hateth you." My son be of good cheer, for from your royal line our Lord will bring forth a great saint. Through her intercession Russia will be saved.

At all costs you must protect your daughters. A great evil will hunt them to the ends of the earth and seek to destroy these instruments of God's grace and mercy. They and their descendants remain hidden until a holy man ariseth. He wears white and travels the earth. The Lord God in his ineffable mercy bequeaths to your family a gift of

fifteen years to prepare for these events. Remember this manifestation
of God's kindness and use these years to plan well.

Serafim

Nikolasha was initially confused when he read through the document but as the meaning began to sink in, he looked at his majesty with concern and said, "Nicky. A martyr? What a burden on your shoulders. I am at a loss for words."

Nicholas was touched by his reaction and surprised that he had not questioned the legitimacy of the letter. "Dear friend, there is more. We met with a holy woman at Sarov some years ago and she confirmed the prophecies in this letter and added a few of her own. She accurately predicted Alexei's birth and Sergei's death."

Nikolasha did not doubt the truth of these revelations and he could tell from the look on the Tsar's face that Nicholas considered it a most serious and urgent matter. "Who knows about this and what is this great evil?" he asked.

"Alix knows. Ella has not seen the letter but she was present when the holy woman spoke to us. You are the third person to read the letter. Alix went through it one time but we never speak of it. She was terribly distraught over the contents. I believe, without any reservation, that the great evil mentioned in the letter is a revolutionary group, which intends to tear our country apart. They have made a horrible pact to hunt down and kill me, and every member of my family. Our intelligence network has verified this."

"Nicholas, this is a heavy load to carry alone. Please allow me to help you bear it."

Nicky thanked his uncle for the generous offer and began immediately to unburden himself of the weight he had carried these four long years. He began with the letter, discussed Elena's prophecies, and talked in great detail about the lost gold and his failed attempt, in 1905, to take the family to Denmark. "I do not intend to make the same mistakes again. I am willing to be a martyr for our homeland, as Saint Serafim has indicated, but I must do everything possible to protect my children. I propose to send them away when the time is right but Alix will remain behind with me to face our destiny together. The arrangements we make this time must be most secret, nothing in writing, discussions that cannot be overheard, and the number involved limited to the smallest and most trustworthy group possible. Just a handful at best."

"Your Majesty, I find the resignation in your voice to be terribly disheartening. Surely the outcome is not written in stone. You have been given a warning and that will give us time to plan. We can rely on the military. The revolution was crushed once before and we can fight and defeat these traitors again," replied Nikolasha with great passion.

The Tsar slowly shook his head. "I am sorry, my General, but you are wrong and I must somehow convince you of that if you are to be of assistance in this matter. Read the letter again, carefully, and then listen for a moment." Nikolasha did as the Tsar directed, leaned back in his chair and gave Nicky his undivided attention. "First you must understand that I am absolutely convinced of the validity of these predictions, written by a Saint, verified by a holy woman, a mystic you might say, and proven substantially accurate by the events of the past few years. I cannot see, nor can I accept any interpretation of the letter except a completely literal one. For that reason I believe Russia will be destroyed and I will be killed, but somehow my children will be saved and you will become the rallying point for the counter-revolution. Therefore, it is useless to squander resources fighting the inevitable. Much better to prepare for the future. Can you accept this?"

Nikolasha was surprised to find Nicky so intense and realized he may have misjudged his nephew. He was not the weakling he was perceived to be and it all made sense to him now. The Tsar had been living under an unbelievable weight for several years and doing it practically alone. Adding to his stress was the unpredictable behavior of his wife and his son's serious illness. It was a wonder he could function at all. Nikolasha knelt on one knee, placed his right hand over his heart, and said, "My Tsar, I have sworn my allegiance to you and I will always be at your service. In the matter of the prophecy I will carry out your instructions to the letter."

"Stand up, my dear friend, the day to fight will come and you will lead an army to liberate Russia from this godless revolution. I am the Tsar, God's representative on earth, and today I anoint you the chosen one."

"Nicholas, I am flattered by your trust but there are others closer to the throne than I. What about your brother or son?" he asked.

"The line of succession will be broken when the revolution comes. My brother is a fine man but he does not have the skills necessary for this mission. Alexei is ill and unlikely to survive to adulthood and even if he does his health will not permit the life of a soldier. Nikolasha, you are the one. The family fears you, Russia respects you, and I trust you with my most precious possession, Mother Russia."

"I am honored and humbled by your confidence and will forever remain your trusted servant but your majesty I will be sixty-two years old when this comes to pass."

"Do not worry, God will give you the strength. Now we have much work to do and many plans to make. Somehow I must send Russia's wealth out of the country. I will not stand by and allow these revolutionaries to have our nation's treasure but I am not sure how to go about it. Perhaps you can suggest a starting point."

Nikolasha walked over to the window and gazed out at the snowy landscape, hoping the view would refresh him. The stunning revelations of the past hour had drained him of ideas but he had the kernels of a solution playing tag in his mind, if only he could pin them down. He turned back and asked the Tsar about the gold. "Do you think you can rely on the methods you used before to move the gold reserve? Now that hostilities have ended, it would seem safe enough to move it by sea in one or two large shipments to a foreign banking concern. The smaller the number of shipments, the less chance of discovery. If you can arrange this, then Peter Stolypin's land reforms may be the answer to the dilemma. These reforms may seem insignificant but they have changed the country and created a whole new class of landed peasant. You own considerable land, Nicholas. Why don't you sell it off and invest the proceeds overseas?"

"The family would fight any effort to reduce the land holdings and you know there is no way to keep something of this magnitude a secret," replied Nicky

"Simply tell them you have decided to sell a large amount of state owned land to the peasants. This action will be popular with the people and you can hide the sale of your own property in the larger transaction."

"You know as well as I they will never agree," Nicky argued.

"Let us concede for a moment that you are right and they resist. You still hold the trump card and can force them to support you.".

"What card might that be," asked Nicky, intrigued by his uncle's unexpectedly devious train of thought.

"Actually it is not complicated at all. You have the power of the throne. Call a family meeting and lay out your plans. If they try to fight you on this you can use your authority as Tsar and threaten to give the land to the peasants outright. If they still object announce that a revenue shortfall has occurred and you will be forced to reduce their annual allowances. They will come around quickly enough and if they ask my advice I will tell them there is nothing I can do. I need to remain in the background as much as possible until we identify who are to be the players in the very dangerous game we are about to begin," Nikolasha replied.

"Why you old fox. I think you may have come up with a practical solution to the first of the many problems we face. I have over ten years to accomplish this and can slowly and methodically implement the sales so that no one suspects. I have been thinking about America lately and the support they gave us during the negotiations leading up to the Portsmouth Treaty. The United States is so isolated from European squabbles that the money should be safe there."

"I think it wise to spread your holdings around, Your Majesty. There is so much uncertainty in the world these days."

'Well, we must talk further about this, but now I must join Alix as she wishes me to meet Anya Taneyeva's future husband. She has been quite anxious that this marriage take place. In the meantime, Nikolasha, go ahead and arrange the meeting."

A few weeks later, a large group of Grand Dukes came together at Alexander Palace to meet with the Tsar. These men were his uncles and cousins and included in the group were the Grand Duke Vladimir and his three sons. Vladimir was next in line to the throne after Alexei and the Tsar's brother, Misha. Nikolasha and his brother Peter were present as well as Nicholas' dear friends, George and Sandro and other members of the extended family. Nicholas dreaded the confrontation that was sure to follow the announcement of his land sale scheme. However, he was determined to brook no opposition because he saw this as the first in a series of steps taken to safeguard his family.

The Imperial family owned about eight per cent of Russian land not including Siberia and the state owned another thirty eight per cent. In addition, the Tsar held title to a large amount of property that his family was not aware of. The history of the Russian monarchy included conspiracy, attempted and sometimes successful coups, and occasionally outright murder at the hands of family members. Consequently many of the Tsars began to accumulate and hide away wealth in different forms such as jewels, currency, negotiable bonds and land.

There was much disagreement among the family members as to who actually held title to revenue producing land. Of course, elements of the family, which consisted of over thirty Grand Dukes and Duchesses and their children, maintained that property which provided income belonged to them and not the Tsar. In fact, Grand Duke Vladimir had held a conference of family members at his palace a few months earlier to which the Tsar had not been invited. At the conference the family arbitrarily decided that the Imperial lands belonged to the Imperial house as a whole and that the Tsar served only as a guardian of these properties. It was determined that he had no right to distribute the income from the property without a family consensus. This meeting had come about because, during and after the war, Nicholas had distributed two million rubles ($1,000,000) to the wounded in the name of the Imperial family and many in the family were quite upset that they were not consulted. The group now gathered at the Tsar's palace was in for a rude awakening. They were about to find out that their earlier meeting had been an exercise in futility and that they did not have the nerve or the authority to force their will upon the Tsar.

After a long, but enjoyable dinner, the group adjourned to the large conference table in the Tsar's reception room. Cigars were passed around and brandy poured and when everyone was generally relaxed Nicholas called the meeting to order. The time had arrived for the Tsar to spring his surprise and he moved directly to the matter at hand. "I have decided to sell to the peasants 1,800,000 acres of imperial land. It is important that we support the land reform and our participation will be popular with the people," he announced.

"Nicholas, what brought about this sudden decision?" asked Sandro.

"Since 'Bloody Sunday' and the loss of the war to Japan, we have been on shaky ground with the people. I think this will be a positive move which will ultimately strengthen the monarchy."

Not surprisingly, Vladimir and his sons vehemently disagreed with his plan. "How can you give concessions to the peasants with our land? I cannot state my opposition strongly enough," said Vladimir. His sons voiced agreement with their father. They were certain the weak willed Tsar would back down in the face of their opposition and the obvious disapproval on the faces of others in the room. Alarm greeted Nicholas' next words and they hardly recognized the man who delivered them.

"I did not invite you here to discuss the matter but rather to inform you of my intentions. If you decide to oppose me I will invoke my royal authority as Tsar and shall present the land to the peasants as a gift. Of course, this will mean a decrease in your revenues whereas if we sell the lands each of you will get a portion of the proceeds," Nicholas argued persuasively.

"The family decides what happens to this land and we have not agreed," Vladimir replied, pompously assuming he spoke for the group.

The Tsar finally lost his temper. "No, my uncle, I am the Tsar and I decide," he thundered.

Vladimir looked around for support but Nikolasha and his brother Peter quickly voiced support for the Tsar's proposal and Sandro and George approved as well. The four glared at Vladimir as if to say "how dare you speak for us." The opposition quickly crumbled and Nicholas dismissed the family members who departed, after the short confrontation, in a state of shock.

Nicky asked George and Sandro to remain behind for a game of billiards. The two brothers followed Nicky into his study and were surprised to find Nikolasha and Count Benckendorff joining their small group. "Nicky, what is going on?" asked Sandro.

"I have not brought you here for billiards. We need to discuss an issue of the utmost importance," said Nicky. "Lives are at stake and you must not talk of these matters to anyone, not your wives, nor my mother, or the Empress. No one. Is that understood?" Sandro and George nodded their agreement. Count Benckendorff then told them of the plot to murder the Imperial family. When he was finished Nicky took over and acquainted them with St. Serafim's letter and Elena's prophecies. He allowed each of them, including the Count, to read the letter and more than an hour went by as Nicky brought them up to date and shared everything with them that he had previously disclosed to Nikolasha. It was with Nikolasha's concurrence that these three had been included.

Count Benckendorff, because of his faithful service to the Tsars, and his cousins because of their long friendship with Nicky. George and Sandro were nearly overwhelmed by this deluge of information and sat in silence not sure how to reply to the astonishing revelations the Tsar had shared with them.

"My friends, do you believe?" Nicky asked.

"I have no reason not to believe," answered George.

"It is mind-boggling but I can see that this is a grave matter and one that you would never take lightly," Sandro said. "I accept your words as true."

"Thank you my dear friends. It is important to me that you have faith. I have the knowledge that my children will survive and I am turning to you, my most trusted friends, to help me."

"Nicholas, I will always be there for you and you can know that your trust is well placed," said George. Sandro also voiced his support and pledged his service.

"What are your plans Nicholas," said Sandro.

"As you have heard we have about ten years to create a strategy to save my children and just as importantly, mother Russia. The meeting we just had with the family was to develop a cover for extensive land sales. I refuse to allow Russia's wealth to fall into the hands of the revolutionaries. We can satisfy our greedy relatives with crumbs while we safeguard Russia's wealth abroad. Knowledge of our plans must be kept to a minimum but the four of you are well known throughout the country so I realize we will have to involve others."

"Tatishchev is an honest and hardworking aide. We can count on him unreservedly," said George. Count Ilia Leonidovitch Tatishchev was an Adjutant General in the Imperial Suite and a Lt. General in the Guards Cavalry. His family had been in service to the Tsars for several generations and George and Nicholas both thought very highly of him.

"Your Imperial Highness, I am an old man and as such I humbly beg your permission to allow my stepson Valia to offer his assistance," said Count Benckendorff. "He is a good and trustworthy young man." Prince Vasily Aleksandrovich Dolgorukov was a Marshall of the Court and a Major General in the Imperial Suite.

At this point Nikolasha intervened. "The gentlemen you have put forth are indeed fine men and we may, at some point, have to call on them. But may I suggest that for the time being we hold off on expanding our group beyond the five in this room. Eventually we will establish cells of responsibility in which the identities of the members are unknown to anyone but the leader. That way, if a cell is penetrated, the entire organization will not be compromised. But we are not there yet. We must also honestly recognize that some cannot keep a secret and Nicky, if you will forgive me, I include your brother, sisters and, unfortunately, your wife, the Empress."

Nicky loved Alexandra completely and without reservation, but he had to admit that Nikolasha was right. Nevertheless no plan could succeed without the involvement of the Tsarina and he realized that when the time was right one cell of the conspiracy would be centered in the Mauve Boudoir.

As the "group of five" discussed the situation Nicky felt as if a heavy load had been lifted from his shoulders. He was among men who were not only friends but individuals of competence and ability and he felt a genuine affection for them all. "Be ready my friends, and when I call for your help know well that the fate of Russia and my family rests on your shoulders. It has been a huge burden, but knowing I now share it with my friends makes it bearable and I do not feel so alone," said the Tsar in a brief moment of weakness and almost overcome by his emotions. The men continued talking late into the night as they sipped brandy and smoked endless cigarettes. They were focused on their mission and none of them would let the Tsar down.

Chapter 12

September 1907 - Gulf of Finland. The Imperial yacht *Standart* was a
magnificent vessel and the envy of European royalty, whose own yachts
seemed small and unworthy in comparison. Built in Copenhagen in 1895,
to the Tsar's specifications, she was, at four hundred feet in length, the
size of a small armored cruiser and was the largest privately owned ship
in the world. Under sail or steam she was sleek and fast, a comfortable
and luxurious floating palace with clean lines and a stately bow. Her
black hull was ornamented with gold leaf and she was an impressive
sight cutting through the surface of the Baltic Sea. Wide, spacious
weather decks made possible a number of outdoor activities even when
the ship was underway. She was much faster and larger than the older
Polar Star, so once launched *Standart* became the primary source of
enjoyment for the royal family. There was no doubt she was Nicky's
pride and joy.

Because of the unrest in the country, and the always present threat of
assassination, the Tsar was asked by his ministers to limit his trips by
land. Travel by train or carriage necessitated elaborate security measures
and since he was loath to vacation too far from the seat of government he
readily acquiesced to their requests. Instead of long stays in the Crimea
or visits to his hunting lodges in Poland he limited the family's trips to
voyages on the yacht. So enjoyable were these excursions that it was not
uncommon for a voyage of a week or two to extend into the next month
if the autumn weather cooperated. Although the yacht generally cruised
only in the Gulf of Finland, the many fjords and islands of those waters
combined to provide wonderful opportunities for exploration and play.

At first light, on this beautiful September day, the captain brought the
ship into a secluded bay and anchored *Standart* a short distance from a
sloping gravel beach. The loud noise created by the chain running out the
hawse pipe momentarily disturbed the peace and tranquility of the
anchorage but soon only the occasional cry of an osprey could be heard
as quiet returned to the rocky shores. Sunlight filtered through the large
pines that grew nearly to the water's edge and sparkled on the mist rising
from the damp ferns and lichens. The family had been here before and
the girls called the cove the "Bay of Standart." They could hardly wait to
be rowed ashore.

The air was festive on the yacht and after Nicholas completed his
morning routine, the band, which accompanied them on every cruise,
struck up a lively tune. This temporarily helped distract the children, who
were impatient to go ashore. Alexei pounded on a toy drum and what he
lacked in talent was more than made up by his enthusiasm. His parents

smiled indulgently at him. Alix found the atmosphere on board totally relaxing and she felt her cares float away the further they retreated from the court. She knew in her heart that these excursions were the key to retaining her sanity and she participated fully in each day's activities. The yacht was one of the few places the family could relax from the tedious formalities that often dominated daily life when ashore. All the sailors and officers on the ship were hand-picked and the children looked upon them as family. For the crew members, service on *Standart* was considered a choice assignment and they helped create an atmosphere that was idyllic, a fairy tale existence where informality reigned. As time passed the military men relaxed their initial reserve and participated with abandon in the games and antics of the children. The officers usually joined the family for dinner and the favor was returned when invitations to tea in the mess were extended. The Tsar enjoyed the company of these unpretentious young men and shared many a game of billiards in the evening. He was more at peace emotionally during these times than at any other primarily because he knew his wife was not usually affected by her migraines and mood swings when they were at sea.

Much to the dismay of the girls, today was a work day for Nicholas, so their first trip ashore was scheduled for the next day. Nicky spent two days a week while under sail responding to the dispatches which arrived on a regular schedule by courier boat or by wireless. He saw that today's boat was moored alongside so he went below deck to his study to read the correspondence and draft his replies. It was tiresome work but he applied himself diligently, eager to complete his task and enjoy the rest of the day. Alix kept encouraging him to engage another secretary but he rejected the idea. Handling the daily workload enabled him to feel in touch with the nation and closer to the people, and gave him the illusion that he knew what was going on in the labyrinth of Russian bureaucracy.

Finally, his day's work done, Nicholas went in search of his daughters. He had promised to teach them how to play dominoes. They were fascinated by the game their father played each evening, with some of the officers on the ship, and were impatient to learn for themselves. He joined his daughters on the fantail under the white canvas awnings stretched over the deck to provide shade from the sun. He was soon seated in a wicker chair and immersed in teaching the girls the fundamentals of the game. Nicholas was a patient and loving father and at times like this he was at his best but unfortunately most of Russia rarely saw this attractive side of his personality. The rest of the day passed quickly as the group dedicated itself to the intricacies of the game of dominoes.

The next morning the sun repeated its performance of the previous day, filtering down through the trees and creating a filigree of glistening light, which spread slowly across the anchorage, and banished, for a time, the darkness of the night. Nicky enjoyed the early morning quiet and generally rose with the sun and then, as he did every morning on board, he checked in with his officers and conducted inspections. The gentle rocking of the vessel at anchor and the salt air usually kept the family and guests asleep past sunrise and the Tsar enjoyed this time alone. Once everyone was up they assembled for breakfast and when they were finished, the day's activities began. Today Nicky was eager to go ashore and inspect the new tennis court he had constructed in a meadow a short distance from the beach. It was a good sport for recreation and he took pleasure in playing the game. The children's anticipation was such that they could barely sit still for the morning meal. Alix had decided to go ashore today as well and Nicky was delighted, as were the girls, that she would join in their adventures.

The launch and gig were lowered away, and brought round to the accommodation ladder where the passengers were ready to board. The strong arms of the crew rowed them to the beach where the enthusiastic group disembarked for a day of fun. A short distance from the beach, Alix happily settled down on a blanket to enjoy a book. Her recently married friend, Anna Taneyeva, now Anya Vyrubova, who had joined the Imperial family for the summer cruise; frolicked in the sand with Alexei and Anastasia. Seaman Derevenko had been assigned to the Tsarevich and was now Alexei's constant companion and he stood a watchful guard over his charge. He had spent so much time with the young boy that he was the one who taught him how to walk but his primary duty was to prevent the heir to the throne from falling or doing any activity that would lead to a bleeding episode. It was an exhausting task since the youngster was so eager to join in all the fun.

Olga and Tatiana ran ahead down a trail to the new tennis court eager for their lessons. They were followed by two officers from the ship, who were drafted to teach them the fundamentals of the game. Maria had a forlorn look upon her face and it was obvious she felt left out. Nicholas reached down for the large net he had brought from the ship. "Come my darling Mashka, let us catch some butterflies." Maria's face lit up with a smile and hand in hand the two set off in search of the beautiful insects, which populated the island at this time of year. As they left the rocky beach with its tall pine trees that seemed to sprout from the granite rocks they followed a trail into the thick dark forest until they reached a grassy clearing. Maria released her father's hand and went running ahead, swinging her net and then, just as suddenly, she stopped. Nicholas caught up to her and was astonished to see fifteen or twenty butterflies fluttering about her and circling her head. He had never seen anything like it. The effect was magical as the bright colors of their wings, various hues of red, yellow, blue and orange blended softly with her white sailor suit and light brown hair. Maria smiled at him, her face radiant with pure enjoyment. She loved butterflies and relished nothing more than a chance to catch them with her father. He sat down beside her and the two enjoyed a quiet, special moment. He knew that it would be memories of moments like these that would sustain him in the trying times to come.

When he and Maria returned to the beach, Nicky was surprised to find Alix with her shoes off and dress rolled up exposing her shapely legs almost to her knees. She was wading in the water and skipping lightly across the rocks along the beach. A few tendrils of hair had escaped her usually tight hairstyle and the breeze blew them charmingly around her pleasantly flushed face. She looked so relaxed and beautiful that when she smiled at him he fell in love with her all over again. Olga and Tatiana, their tennis lesson over, joined the rest of the family by the beach while Anya napped on a blanket in the warm sun. Soon they were all cavorting in the gentle waves that lapped against the rocks of the secluded beach. There was a brief moment of anxiety when Alexei lost his balance and began wobbling but the ever alert Derevenko caught the child seconds before he fell into the rocks. He signaled to Nicholas and Alexandra that all was well and they both breathed a sigh of relief. The slightest bump could bruise the boy and begin the internal bleeding and swelling which could take his life. It was a harrowing existence for the two parents especially since Alexei was an exuberant three year old who had no concept of the danger everyday activities posed for him.

A few days later, in the early afternoon, the Imperial family returned from its outing on the island and the ship's crew began preparations to get underway. Anastasia was now six years old and was becoming quite the imp and even at her young age she was adept at playing tricks on members of the entourage. Most were harmless little childish antics but she had an annoying habit of running and hiding from the nurse, Alexandra Teglyova who was always called Shura. Many a frantic search had taken place while the nursery staff attempted to keep secret the fact they had lost a royal daughter. On this summer afternoon, Shura was preparing the girls' clothes that would be worn for afternoon tea. Their mother insisted they were properly dressed for the daily ritual. Anastasia came bounding in with her sisters all disheveled from the day ashore. Shura began the task of making the Grand Duchesses presentable when Anastasia began to taunt her. "Chase me, chase me, I am going to hide."

"Do not leave Anastasia, you must get ready for tea," pleaded Shura. In the confusion of helping the other girls get dressed she turned her back and did not notice when Anastasia slipped away.

Anastasia closed the door quietly behind her and scampered off to find the perfect hiding place. As she passed the ladder which led below to the crew's quarters and the engine room, she hesitated. She knew those areas of the ship were off limits to her but the thought of hiding where no one would think to look was too much of a temptation for her and she ventured down the steps of the ladder. The young girl did not realize that it was very dangerous to wander off this way, alone and without supervision. At this time of day, with the ship just getting underway, much of the crew was above deck and the engine room personnel were involved in lighting additional boilers, so no one saw her as she explored the passageways of this forbidden part of the ship. She entered a compartment and found what she thought was an ideal hiding place among the equipment lining the walls and stacked around the space. It was a wooden crate on the deck and when she tugged the lid open and she was delighted to find it nearly empty. She climbed in and snuggled down on the packing material inside. *Standart* had gotten underway and after a day of vigorous activity the gentle rocking of the ship lulled her to sleep.

Up on deck the Tsar was enjoying the fine day. The sea was almost perfectly calm and it was so peaceful that he wished the moment would never end. He relished the stark beauty of the Finnish fjords and found contentment in the beautiful vistas they provided. The captain was taking the yacht northward at a moderate speed and there was a gentle breeze across the decks. Nicky found it invigorating and moved away from the rail to stroll slowly aft toward the tea table which had been set up under the taut, white, canvas awnings. Wicker chairs with plump cushions of brightly colored chintz were grouped invitingly around the long table, which was covered with all types of delectable treats. Soon it would be time for tea and he looked forward to the relaxed repast with Alix, his children and their guests. It was so nice to be away from the formality of the palace and its unchanging traditions. The teas ashore consisted of white toast, thinly spread with butter but out here on the open sea court etiquette could be ignored and the traditional tea was much more sumptuous. He sank onto a soft cushion and greeted Alix and his guests as everyone slowly began to gather. The children arrived and Alix immediately noticed Anastasia was not among them. "Where is she?" she asked her daughters.

"Oh Mama, she is hiding again, but Shura and Vasily are looking for her," Olga informed her mother. Anatoly Vasilyev was the sailor assigned to watch out for Anastasia, and the children called him Vasily. "We told her not to go but she ran off anyway."

"Let us not worry about her, I am sure she will turn up when she gets hungry enough," Alix said. She was unconcerned about the missing girl as she knew all about her antics. There was nothing that went on in the nursery that she did not know and the servants often wondered where she obtained her information. She always said, "I am a mother" as if it that was the obvious explanation. At any rate she was quite aware of Anastasia's penchant for pranks and hiding and today she decided enough was enough. She vowed to punish the little imp when she was found and teach her a lesson. Today's tea was exceptionally fine and missing out on the tasty treats should do the trick. How did I ever raise such a disobedient child? she wondered to herself. Alix had faith in Shura's abilities to handle the situation and she began to relax as the string quartet started to play. She joined in the lively conversation around the table and put thoughts of Anastasia from her mind.

Suddenly *Standart* shuddered from bow to stern and lurched to an abrupt stop. The plates and cups of the tea service went crashing to the deck with an enormous racket and the occupants of the wicker chairs were thrown about. The yacht groaned and creaked as if suffering from a mortal blow. Everyone was momentarily frozen in place but jumped to their feet as the ship began to list to one side. Initially there was mass confusion as the collision alarm sounded throughout the ship but soon the disciplined crew began to restore order. Sailors rushed about the deck following the orders of their officers and the lifeboats were lowered into the water. Alexandra, ever resourceful in an emergency, began ordering the women and children into the waiting boats. Disaster seemed imminent since the ship seemed to be taking on water rather rapidly. *Standart* was down by the bow and beginning to list to starboard. The Tsar, not wanting to get in the way of his well trained crew, held onto the rail, calmly pulled out his watch and attempted to calculate the rate the ship was taking on water, at the same time shouting out his estimate of the time remaining.

Anya and Alix rushed below to the staterooms but their progress along the passageway was hampered by the list the damaged yacht had taken on. The deck was slanted, making it difficult to stand, and they kept slipping against the bulkheads. They finally reached the staterooms and removing the bedding from one of the beds they began tossing all of the most precious jewelry and valuables onto the sheets. Realizing their time was limited they quickly tied the corners to form two large bundles, which the two women dragged behind them as they struggled to reach the upper deck.

When they arrived at the area designated to board the lifeboats, they handed off their burdens to the sailors to lower into the boats. The Empress ordered Anya to disembark and as she prepared to follow she heard a cry and turned to see Shura and Vasily running frantically towards her. Out of breath, Shura could barely gasp out the words, "we cannot find Anastasia. We've looked everywhere." She began to weep because she loved the child as if she were her own. Alix looked down at the waiting boats, searching among the upturned faces for her missing daughter, but she was not there. To make matters worse Olga was attempting to leave the boat and climb back up the jacobs ladder to the listing deck. Tears streamed down her face and when she saw her mother she began to scream, "Anastasia, I must go find her. Mama! Mama! She's not here; we have to go find her." Olga had developed into a real leader but this was not the time for her to assert herself and Alix ordered her back into the boat. Meanwhile, Tatiana wrapped her arms around Maria, who was sobbing uncontrollably, and attempted to reassure her. Maria and Anastasia were inseparable and it was unbearable knowing her sister was missing. Looking up at the big yacht as it lurched over ever further she was terrified and buried her face in Tatiana's comforting shoulder.

Alexandra's calm left her and she looked imploringly at Nicholas. "What are we going to do?" she asked.

"We have very little time left. Sunny, you must leave the ship. We will find her," he answered.

She shook her head, "I will go down with the ship before I leave my child here to drown."

Nicholas realized that reasoning with her would be impossible and as they were running out of time, he questioned Shura and Vasily as to where they had searched. He quickly assigned those remaining on deck to look for Anastasia. Vasily spoke up, "Your imperial highness, has no one searched the crew areas and engine room?"

"She would never go into those areas because they are off limits to her. Let us not waste time when we know she is not there," said the Empress.

Vasily left to begin his search anew but some instinct told him the Tsarina was mistaken. He and Shura had thoroughly searched for the missing girl and he knew she must have ventured into the areas forbidden to her. He immediately ran to the ladder leading to the engineering spaces and began the climb down into the depths of the ship.

While everyone was enjoying tea Anastasia had remained asleep in her hiding place until the sudden jerk of the ship woke her. She heard a loud crash as a heavy piece of equipment tumbled down onto the top of her crate, pinning her in. She was very disoriented in the small space and pushed up with her hands to open the box but the lid would not budge from the weight of the object on top. She wedged her little legs upward and pushed with all her strength but the top moved barely an inch. Anastasia became extremely apprehensive as the precariousness of her situation sank in. She screamed loudly for help but could hear no one answer. Her mind began to play tricks and she imagined she could hear voices shouting for her. They will find me soon, she thought. They must know by now that I am missing. Maybe Shura is playing a trick on me. She listened, and hearing nothing, began yelling anew but her voice became hoarse and weak as she continued to shout. As she lay there shaking in the dark box, she felt dampness on her back and legs. At first she thought nothing of it but the water began to slowly rise as it seeped into her hiding place and soon she was soaking wet. It was a terrible ordeal for a young child to endure and she became increasingly hysterical as the water began to cover her. She pressed up as high as she could to keep her head out of the water but It seemed to her that the water was rushing in faster and she began to pray, her little hands folded while her body trembled uncontrollably in the chilly water. Her lips pressed to the top of the crate and as the water kissed at her neck and cheek, she prepared to breathe her last. She was unaware of the frantic search that was taking place to find her.

Vasily continued his search below deck and waded through the knee deep water. It was slow going but he methodically made his way from one compartment to the next. He reached the last room on this deck and used all his weight to shove open the door, which was held closed by the weight of the water pushing against it. He quickly glanced about the room, which held a jumbled mass of equipment in disarray. He turned to leave when a low whimper made him pause. A hoarse voice, barely above a whisper, pleaded for help and he waded into the room with desperation as he realized the voice came from a wooden crate almost covered by water. He quickly assessed the problem and shoved the equipment off the box. When he tore the lid off and lifted the frightened young child up, she put her arms around him, laid her head on his shoulder, and cried and cried. He comforted her as much as possible and then began the struggle to make his way out of the dark, wet compartment. Anastasia's brown curls hung limply around her tear streaked face but finally, in the strong arms of this capable young man, her fear left her. He was responsible for her care and instinctively she knew she was safe and all was well.

Vasily bade her hold onto his neck and sit on his back. The gloomy passageway was illuminated only by a dim amount of light, which made its way from the hatch in the distance. He struggled against the swirling water and the sharp list of the ship and finally reached the ladder, which would lead them out of this ordeal and up to safety. When Vasily arrived on the main deck, he brought the child over to her frantic parents. Alexandra reached out for Anastasia and hugged her wet daughter close, unmindful of the dampness, which soon penetrated her gown. Nicholas ordered the search called off and quickly ensured Alix and Anastasia were safely lowered into a lifeboat. After assessing the situation and being assured by the captain that the passengers were evacuated the Tsar finally left his yacht.

The sailors in the lifeboats began rowing the passengers to the waiting division of cruisers that served as escort to the imperial yacht. The ships had been unable to come in any closer since they drew too much water for the shallow depths. The yacht loomed over the lifeboats as they rowed away but as they cleared the side Nicholas and Alexandra could see the gaping hole in the bow. A few rocks appeared above the surface of the water and it looked as if *Standart* had run aground on one of them. Nicholas was perplexed by the sight. He had reviewed their course earlier in the morning and did not remember seeing this dangerous area on the charts. The ship's crew was extremely experienced and had cruised these waters for years. The Tsar was sure the grounding was just a tragic accident and not the result of human error. He was relieved to see the yacht had not sunk any further into the sea. It attested it to her watertight integrity and the blessing of calm seas. At any rate the beautiful vessel was in for a long period in the dockyards at Copenhagen. The dewatering pumps were beginning to overcome the flooding and the captain had already started the temporary repairs necessary to make her seaworthy enough to be towed to Denmark.

The lifeboats carrying the royal family approached the small vessel *Asia,* and the Imperial family went aboard. *Asia* was a navy vessel and as such was not equipped to handle a large number of visitors. Nevertheless, the Tsar, his wife and the children prepared to stay aboard until another yacht could be readied. With no injuries or loss of life suffered, the Tsar had no intention of canceling the rest of their voyage. He ordered a wire sent to the *Polar Star,* announcing the impending arrival of the Imperial family. In the meantime Alexandra shared a small stateroom with Alexei, while Nicholas slept on a couch in the wardroom. The four Grand Duchesses were crowded into a small stateroom room with four bunks. The rest of the entourage was scattered among the other vessels at the site of the accident. *Asia's* spartan accommodations were a far cry from the luxurious ones the Imperial family was accustomed to but Nicholas, Alexandra and the children were grateful for the hospitality, and not wanting to offend the officers and men of *Asia* they quickly adapted to their austere surroundings. As for the crew they were excited and honored to have the family aboard. Nicky, himself, went in search of basins of water which he brought to Alix to help remove the grime from their ordeal.

As darkness fell, Alexandra went to the small cabin housing her daughters and tucked them in the bunks before turning in for the night. The girls gradually drifted off to a peaceful sleep, except for Anastasia. She tossed and turned before finally falling into a fitful slumber. She started to breathe heavily as the sheets covered her head and then thrashed back and forth. More and more frantically, she kicked her legs up against the blankets covering her. Her little hands grasped and pulled at the covering over her face. She began crying in her sleep, "I can't breathe, I can't breathe, I am drowning." The bloodcurdling scream from below her startled Olga from a sound sleep and she slipped down from the top bunk to see what was wrong.

Olga pulled the sheet from Anastasia's face. The child's face was pale as a ghost and covered in sweat. Olga called, "Anastasia, Anastasia", but she remained in the grips of her nightmare, unknowingly kicking and hitting her sister. Maria and Tatiana in the other bunks were awakened by the loud commotion and immediately came to the aide of their young sister. They surrounded her and Tatiana began to gently caress her hair, attempting to calm her. Anastasia finally woke up and looked around, momentarily confused by her unfamiliar surroundings. Her fear began to dissipate when she saw the loving faces of her sisters. Olga reassured her. "It was just a bad dream, you are safe now."

Maria, unsure how to soothe her sister's fear, began to sing a little song in a soft voice. Anastasia's trembling finally subsided and she said, "I was so scared, I could feel the water over my head."

"No, no little one, it was just the sheet covering your head," said Olga.

"Everything is fine now and we must get back to sleep," added Tatiana.

"No, No," cried Anastasia, "I don't want to drown again."

"We will all sleep with you," said Olga.

The four girls arranged themselves on the bunk and settled down to go to sleep and in the comforting arms of her sisters, Anastasia finally drifted off. The extraordinary relationship between these sisters that was evident on this night, was made even stronger by the events of the day, and was a rare and special bond. Crowded together there on the bunk they were blissfully unaware of what lay in their future. As terrible as the near loss of Anastasia was, the close companionship of the girls would be tested by even more terrifying hardships and ordeals. The sisters would have to draw on the collective strength of their unspoken covenant to confront future trials. It remained to be seen whether it would be strong enough to sustain them.

Chapter 13

March 1908 - Tsarskoe Selo. The grounding of *Standart* and the near loss of Anastasia had been a harrowing experience and not one that was easily forgotten. Quick action by the crew limited the flooding and when all the pumps were brought on line, the captain had taken advantage of the calm seas to get the yacht underway. Escorted closely by Navy vessels she was able to reach the yard in Copenhagen and repairs were begun immediately. A close survey indicated the damage was not as extensive as originally feared. In the interim the family had transferred to *Polar Star* and cruised for several more weeks before returning to Alexander Palace in the Imperial compound at Tsarskoe Selo and settling back into their daily routine.

On this day Alix was nestled back among plump cushions which were piled on a mauve silk armchair to support her pain wracked body. She rested her elbow on the arm of the chair, with her chin in her hand, and stared pensively out of the enormous picture window. The window was made of one large pane of glass and it seemed to bring the outdoors into the room. How she loved this spot and the light it drew into her boudoir. The green of the carpet and the lilac silk wall covering and matching curtains gave the room the look of a spring garden. Through the window Alix could see her children, with their Aunt Olga, setting off for an afternoon adventure and she tried to remember when she had last enjoyed such an outing with her children. She was grateful to Nicky's sister for spending so much time with the children and becoming close to them.

Melancholy seemed to be her lot in life of late and the sunny disposition for which she was once known was now a distant memory buried somewhere in the depths of her depression. Many in the court thought Alexandra suffered from hypochondria but they were unaware of the real situation. The Empress was tormented by a variety of ailments including sciatica, migraines, fatigue and a worrisome heart condition which was probably due to the constant stress and exhaustion brought on by coping with her son's debilitating condition. It was Alexei's illness which made her so vulnerable to quackery and other forms of non-traditional treatment and she would try anything to alleviate the poor child's suffering. As to her own condition, a foolish physician had once suggested to the Tsar that she suffered from a psychosomatic disorder as a result of her nerves. He was dismissed as soon as she heard of his diagnosis. Of course, no one could understand how someone so ill could lay prostrate in agony one minute and then get up the next, with a surge of strength. However, these bursts of energy usually came about when she was needed for some crisis or other and that inner drive of a wife and mother responding to an emergency took over, and consumed her. Afterwards it would take her weeks to recover. Alix was very conscious of the whispers of the servants and relatives, who thought her antics quite eccentric at the very least. All she knew was that she was truly ill. Nicky worried excessively over her, concern always evident on his face as he looked in on her. For Alix, his was the only opinion that mattered.

As her children disappeared from view, she arose and moved over to her desk which was overflowing with neglected correspondence and papers. She began to jot little notes to her daughters and on many days it was her only communication with them especially when she suffered from one of her headaches. The noise and commotion of five children was too much for her delicate nerves on those days and often she would dine with just Nicholas and one of her children, usually Alexei. Alix sometimes felt as if she were losing her influence on the girls and her notes and letters were filled with exhortations to behave and act like ladies. At other times the missives were filled with prayers and good wishes overflowing with love. Today, as she observed her brood scampering off, she was disheartened to see Olga with her dress partially hiked up and her legs showing, as she ran ahead of the other girls. She is thirteen now and old enough to know better, she thought, as her pen began to race across the page.

The brief period of activity tired her so she walked across the room to her mauve sofa and reclined upon it. She was fully dressed because she hated dressing gowns and refused to emphasize her semi-invalid status. So no matter how she felt, she insisted on dressing appropriately every day. Her latest needlework project lay on the table beside her chaise. She picked it up and began to work on the delicate piece. Idle hands were the devil's work and she would never forget her grandmother, Queen Victoria of England exhorting her to not waste time. As they grew older Alix encouraged her daughters to avoid idleness and she began to share her expertise in handiwork with them. When she felt up to their company the family spent many evenings in this room which was filled with mementos and photos of their life together. The maids despaired of ever creating order in the room as the piles of books, papers, and photographs, waiting for their place in an album, continued to grow. In the rigid world of royalty everything had its place but in her mauve boudoir she could indulge the side of her personality that enjoyed clutter and a modicum of disorder.

When Alexandra reclined on her sofa she began to feel a familiar flutter as her heart began to tighten. Her body began to tremble uncontrollably while her heart beat rapidly and as her blood pressure rose she became increasingly dizzy and her head began to throb and ache. Only then could Alix admit to herself that what she desperately wanted and believed that she needed was the presence of Father Grigory and she felt she would die if she could not experience his soothing voice and calming hands. With ever increasing agitation she picked up the telephone and called Anya. She asked her to send a message to Rasputin directing him to come to the palace immediately.

As she placed the phone back in its cradle and reclined against the plump cushions Nicholas walked in and was immediately filled with concern by his wife's condition. She was drenched in perspiration and her face was drained of color. She gave him a pitiful look and cried out, "The pain, I cannot bear it. Why won't it stop? Oh I need him. I must see him!"

"Alix, darling what are you talking about?" he asked her in a soothing voice as he tried to make sense of her words.

"I must see him. I must have Father Grigory."

"Darling, let me call for Dr. Botkin. You must be suffering from one of your attacks."

"No. No," she said with a sob in her voice. "He is no help to me." As Nicky looked at her with concern she grabbed his arm, her fingers digging rather painfully into him. "I need Father Grigory. I want only him. He is the only one who can help me," she pleaded.

"Alix! No! Let me send for the doctor. I am very concerned about your dependency on this Rasputin. It is not healthy for you and I must say your condition seems worse since you met him. He is not helping you and I will not send for him," he gently informed her.

Nicky was upset by her request. As Alix's bouts of illness increased during the past few months she relied more and more on Rasputin's healing presence. For some reason he, and he alone, seemed able to calm her down and ease her pain, especially her excruciating headaches. Nicky could deny nothing to his Sunny and he would give anything to see her cured but Rasputin's influence was beginning to give him cause for concern especially today, when he saw the state Alix was in.

"I must have him and I do not care what you think. He is the only one who can ease my suffering and I have sent for him," she defiantly informed him.

Feelings of jealousy and anger overwhelmed him and he lost his temper. "Fine! Have your Rasputin, but nobody can ever know about this," he shouted at her. "It demeans you, and I, for one, am ashamed of what you are becoming."

Alix looked at him with hurt in her eyes. It was so uncharacteristic of him to speak to her in this manner. "Nicky, I am sorry you are upset but I will not feel guilty for calling a man of God," she replied softly.

The Tsar was so angry with Alexandra he could scarcely think. Even though he felt a twinge of remorse for shouting at her he did not trust himself to continue the argument in a dignified fashion so he turned and stormed from the room. Alix lay back among her pillows taking shallow breaths as she waited in silence for Father Grigory to answer her summons.

Nicholas was totally confused by his reaction to the scene in the boudoir. He was literally seething with rage at the defiance of his wife but he knew the matter went much deeper than a mere disagreement over medical treatment. Although he was considered a mild mannered and somewhat meek individual, the Tsar was capable of great fits of anger and now he clenched his fists and paused to regain his composure before climbing the private staircase to the children's floor. But it was no use and the more he thought about the situation the angrier he became. He faced the dilemma many men have experienced in their married life. Nicholas could accept the situation and maintain peace in the family or he could confront the issue head on, knowing that his opposition to this so-called holy man would lead to constant bickering and disruptive arguments, like the one which had just occurred. And when it was young Alexei who was suffering, Alix had made it quite clear that she was in charge.

He slammed the door behind him and began stomping up the stairs, his anger cooled by the depressing realization that there was no simple answer to the situation. If he did not love Alix so completely it might be easier but he was consumed by his affection for her and the children and ultimately any decision he made would be driven by this deep attachment. He was a captive of his love for them.

As he passed by the school room he noticed his daughters were deep in conversation as they sat around the large table which dominated the room. Their topic of discussion surprised him and he remained standing out of view, listening as they discussed their interest in other religions. "I would be Jewish," said Tatiana in an attempt to shock her sisters. She succeeded.

"Jewish," her sisters replied in unison. "Why Jewish?"

"I like how the men wear those round things on their head and grow their beards so long," she replied. "They get to go to church on Saturday and sleep in on Sunday."

"Those round things are called yarmulkes," said Olga. "What about you Maria, what would you become?"

"I would become a Catholic and then I could live at the Vatican," said Maria. "I have seen pictures and Aunt Ella says it is such a peaceful place."

"You do not live at the Vatican just because you become Catholic, silly. We have Catholics living in our country," Tatiana informed her.

"That's right Tatiana, in fact the Catholics have a church in Tsarskoe Selo," added Olga. She was the oldest child and although only thirteen, her younger sisters looked up to her and respected her opinion. She most often had the last word and if Olga said it was so, then so it was.

"Olga, what would you become?" asked Anastasia.

Olga watched the look of anticipation on her sisters' faces as she carefully thought out her response. She had to top Tatiana's shocking remark. "I would become a Buddhist," she said. Her sisters were suitably impressed. They knew nothing about the strange and distant religion and wondered what Olga would say about it. Olga knew she would have a captive audience with her choice even though she would never really consider becoming a Buddhist.

"That is a strange pick," said Tatiana a little petulantly. She knew Olga's choice topped her own. "Why would you want to become a Buddhist? What do you know of those people?"

"I read a book about Japan. They are all Buddhist and they dress in beautiful clothes called kimonos. They collect these strange but pretty flowers and present them as an offering in a gold house they call a temple."

Although the conversation was light-hearted It was too much for the Tsar. The stress of the day and his dealings with Alix got the best of him and he could take no more of his daughters talk. He burst through the doorway and stormed over to the table. The girls looked up in dismay as the Tsar pounded his first on the table and shouted, "If anyone of you leave the Russian Orthodox faith I will cut off your head." A look of shock and fear came over the Grand Duchesses' faces and Maria and Anastasia started to cry. Olga and Tatiana sat dumbfounded, afraid to speak or move. The girls wondered to themselves what was happening. Their father had been stern with them in the past, but never had he threatened them in this way.

Nicholas quickly came to his senses and as he looked around at his daughters, their eyes filled with tears, he could not help but feel a terrible sense of guilt. What has happened to me that I would threaten my children so? He realized he had taken out all of his frustrations on his daughters and he turned and left the room. Once the door closed behind him he rested his back against it. He could hear his daughters softly crying and talking to each other.

"I do not think he loves us anymore," said Maria.

"He hates us," cried Tatiana.

"You know that is not true," soothed Olga in spite of her own tears.

"What did we do that was so bad?" sobbed Anastasia.

The girls were devastated at what had just occurred and they could not understand what they had done to make their father so furious. The Tsar, listening through the door, could not leave his beloved daughters in such a state. He returned to the room. The girls instantly stopped crying and became afraid, not knowing what would happen next. Nicholas pulled up a chair and sat down at the table.

"I was extremely angry to hear you talking so frivolously about changing your religion," their father began. Olga wanted to explain to him that they were just talking and would never leave their church, but she knew it was best to keep quiet and let her father speak. "My dear children, you must try to understand that the Russian Orthodox Church is the true church. God ordained it so. I am the Tsar, which means I am God's representative on earth." He uses me to guide and watch over his people, the Russian people. You must never speak again about leaving the church even in jest. How would it look to our people if the Tsar's children were heard joking about our holy faith? If you abandon our church, you are abandoning God," he said. "We receive such comfort from our faith and it sustains us. We have many trials to face in the future and we can only persevere through the strength of our faith. As you grow older, you will come to understand all of this. Remember that your mother and I will always love you." The Tsar stood up and made his way around the table, tenderly kissing each one of his daughters on the forehead.

Nicholas walked out of the classroom and went downstairs to his study. He avoided Alix's private staircase as he had no wish to speak to her. The hurt looks and trembling lips of his daughters when he hammered his fist on the table would be indelibly etched in his mind for the rest of his life. He was dismayed at his lack of self-control and began to realize that the very distressing situation with Rasputin was affecting his judgment. His thoughts went back to his earlier confrontation with Alix. He could never remember speaking to her in such a manner and the look of hurt she gave him affected him deeply. He would do anything to repair their relationship, make her better, and bring back his Sunny.

The Emperor's relationship with the holy man was a complex one. On the one hand Nicholas did not trust him past the tip of his finger, and yet he found the talks with him both interesting and intriguing. He admired the peasant's simple outlook on life and the fact that he seemed unimpressed by their exalted position. Rasputin spoke his mind freely in front of them and Nicky respected him for that since such frankness was so rare at court. He had to admit to himself that Father Grigory seemed to have a healing effect not only on Alexei but also on Alix. His words often rang true and he seemed to have the gift of prophecy. Yet despite these positive attributes something about the healer did not sit well with the Tsar. He had to admit the man had unusual gifts but he did not believe for one moment that he was a man of God. Nicholas was beginning to be aware of the rumors surrounding Rasputin's private life, but when the visionary came to the palace he was always cordial and polite and concentrated on the business at hand. Alix would not hear a word said against "her peasant" and until Nicky had something firm to go on, he was not willing to fight that battle with her. He made a quick decision and resigned himself to tolerating Rasputin's presence in their life. And so, reluctantly to be sure, the Tsar cast the dice and Grigory Rasputin's number came up.

It was late in the evening when Rasputin finally arrived at the Alexander Palace and although he did not deliberately delay his visit he was unconcerned at his tardiness. As the Empress grew to rely on him more and more he gained confidence in his power over her. Escorted into her room, he waited until the door closed and then moved in her direction. Alix was relieved that he had finally arrived and as he made his way toward her she was immediately captivated, as she usually was, by his mesmerizing, penetrating hypnotic eyes. She tried, but could not look away from this strange, black robed figure and his dominating appearance. He knelt beside her and grasped her hand.

"Oh, Matushka, what is troubling you so?" he asked.

"Father Grigory, I needed to see you. Please pray with me. I desire your healing powers and no one else truly understands my needs but you."

"Matushka, you must not say such things. It is not my humble presence you need but rather the healing power of God in your soul. I sense that you are in great pain and I am here as God's servant to help you."

He pulled a simple glass vial from his pocket and said, "Drink this! It is made from various Russian herbs and water brought back from the Holy Land and it will soothe your heart and relieve the pain in your head."

As the Empress slowly sipped his concoction and began to relax, he leaned forward and without saying a word motioned her to look into his eyes. Alix gazed into them and her limbs began to feel light and airy. Just when she felt as if she would float away she dropped into a deep hypnotic trance.

Although the Empress suffered from legitimate physical ailments, there was also an underlying emotional condition deeply embedded in her psyche, but one that Rasputin was able to exploit through hypnotic manipulation. After a session with him she would feel better for a number of days before returning to the mental and physical state that led more frequently to his interventions.

It would never do for the Tsar to discover the truth about Alix's illness and knowing their time alone together could be interrupted at any moment, Rasputin quickly whispered his words of suggestion to her. He was still amazed at the control he exerted over her in this hypnotic state and he knew it was her unwavering faith and her belief in anything mystical that made her an easy subject. He had to admit, however, that no amount of hypnotic suggestion could make her stay in bed when she was needed. Whether it was to nurse the Tsarevich through one of his illnesses or care for one or another of her daughters, nothing could keep her down if duty called. The Tsarina's devotion to her family was a recognized and admired trait of her character and was so deeply ingrained that any of her own weaknesses or ill health were set aside when necessary. Nevertheless, when the crisis was over, her melancholy returned.

The Tsar on the other hand was totally immune to his powers of persuasion. Try as he might, Rasputin could never get him under his thumb. Disappointing though this was, as long as he held the Empress captive, he still had immense power and influence. This time he would allow her to recover for a few weeks before she needed him again. He snapped his fingers and Alix slowly opened her eyes to see Father Grigory deep in prayer.

"Amen," he said as he crossed himself.

Alexandra rose to her feet and energy seemed to course through her as the herbs and drugs he had given her began to take effect.

"Father Grigory, our prayers have been answered. Please go and see the children before you leave. They will love to have your company," Alix told him as she escorted him to her private staircase which led up to the children's rooms.

Father Grigory made his way into Alexei's room and was soon surrounded by all five of the children. They sat around him on the floor and all, except Olga and Tatiana, were fascinated by his voice as he regaled them with Russian legends and fairy tales. The two older girls felt a vague sense of unease in his presence and were uncomfortable with the fact they were in their nightclothes. With the natural modesty of early adolescence, they sat a little further back from the others, their discomfort unspoken. The children's nurse-on-duty was Maria Vishnyakova who was known as Mary. She was a passionate supporter of Rasputin and when he came to the palace he used her name to gain admittance. He was then recorded in the police register as her visitor although his visits were really to the Imperial family. With the children gathered around him he dismissed Mary, but when she hesitated to leave, he assured her it was fine with her Imperial Highness. Olga and Tatiana shared a secret look only sisters can give each other and both knew what the other was thinking. They did not like this strange man who had their Mother so enthralled.

"Do the trick, do the trick," Anastasia demanded excitedly.

Rasputin smiled at her enthusiasm but the young girl did not understand that what she considered a prank was no mere sleight-of-hand or magician's trick but something much more devious. Many people, the Empress and her son included, were susceptible to hypnosis and Rasputin took advantage of his rare ability to both heal and entertain. He called Alexei over and peered into his eyes, all the while talking to him in a seductive voice, which the other children could barely hear. Then, on command, the child stood up as if in a trance, dropped down on his knees and began barking like a dog. It amused Rasputin to have the heir of all Russia down on his knees, responding to his hypnotic suggestions. With each change of signal Alexei imitated a different animal. Anastasia and Maria laughed delightedly at their brother's antics while Olga and Tatiana smiled politely. Alexei started to hop around the room like a bunny rabbit but at that moment Aunt Olga poked her head in to say goodnight to the children. Rasputin quickly and discretely snapped his fingers and Alexei ceased his antics.

"See how happy he is to see me," he told the Grand Duchess, as if to explain Alexei's strange behavior. He then grasped Alexei's hand and led him over to the child's bed. He bowed his head and Alexei followed suit and both were soon deep in prayer. Olga was surprised and a little concerned to see Rasputin alone with the children but at this point she had no reason to doubt his sincerity or feel any distrust of him.

"Girls, it is getting late. Off to bed with you," said Aunt Olga. As the girls stood up to go to their rooms Rasputin grasped each in turn by the shoulders and planted a kiss on their foreheads. It seemed to the Tsar's sister that he lingered a little longer with the two older girls, but he did nothing improper that she could put her finger upon. She waited until she was sure he had left the children's quarters before she made her way back to her own rooms.

The older girl's bare feet were cushioned by the plush carpet in their bedroom. In contrast to the luxurious floor covering, the hard camp beds they slept in were downright austere. The girls were victims of a Russian tradition dating back to Catherine the Great. All the royal children slept on these rigid portable beds and everywhere they traveled, the beds went with them. They both lay quietly staring at the ceiling and the ornate vines, flowers and dragonflies stenciled in a border along the wall. Finally Tatiana broke the silence.

"Olga! What do you think about Father Grigory?"

"Why do you ask?" Olga replied.

"Well, he gives me the shivers, but mother says he is a man of God. What do you think, Olga?"

"I just don't know. Anastasia and Maria seem to like him, but I think it is only because Mama likes him. He makes my skin crawl too and no other 'man of God' ever made me feel that way, and heaven knows we have had our share of 'holy men.' The way he tries to stare into your eyes . . ."

"Oh, I know," interrupted Tatiana, "and the way he puts his arms on us and kisses us on the forehead, as if he were our father." She got out of her bed and climbed into her sister's.

"Olga, I am so glad you feel the same way. I am afraid to say anything bad about him to Mama. I think she would be furious if she heard us talking like this."

"I heard that anyone who speaks against him will be immediately dismissed from the palace," Olga added. "I wonder if anyone at court really likes him. If they do not they certainly cannot say so."

"I can't stand the way he controls Alexei, making him bark like a dog or hop around like a rabbit," replied Tatiana. "I tried to talk to Mama once, but she would not hear listen."

"Probably because he makes her jump like a rabbit too," Olga observed.

"Olga, you better watch your tongue," scolded Tatiana.

"I only speak the truth and you well know it. Mama will do whatever he says. It is as if he controls everything," Olga responded with some heat.

"But he does have a way to help poor Alexei when he suffers so badly. His words somehow soothe him but I really think somehow it is that tea he always makes him drink. It smells like sassafras. Still I loathe the way Mama makes us write him nice, sweet notes and be so cordial to him."

"I wrote in my diary once that I thought he smelled funny, and when Mother saw it she make me rip the page right out of my book. She made me so angry that I told her it was true. She said it was blasphemy to say such things about a holy man. That is the real reason she always reads our letters and diaries. It is not to check our spelling as she tells us but to spy. We might as well not even write in them. It is all a pack of lies when you cannot write freely about your thoughts and feelings."

"What are we going to do?" asked Tatiana. "Mama will never get rid of him and after today, I am afraid to talk to Papa."

"Maybe we can find someone to talk to and they can tell Papa how we really feel," said Olga.

"Oh, that is a splendid idea," agreed Tatiana. "I imagine Papa does not know how we feel about Father Grigory. Surely he will do something."

"Papa loves us so much, but he loves Mama more and if she wants him to stay, then what can Papa do?"

"He can make him leave us alone, at least."

"Do not worry Tatiana," said Olga as she gently pulled Tatiana into a sisterly hug. "It will all work out." Tatiana returned to her bed and bid her sister good night. Both girls felt comforted knowing that they were allies, if only in their negative feelings toward this strange man.

The next day was crisp and cool, with a slight hint of spring in the air, although patches of snow could still be seen around the palace grounds. Nicholas, Alexandra, and the children were waiting at the station for the arrival of the train carrying Grand Duke Ernst-Ludwig of Hesse, Alix's dearly loved brother Ernie. Whenever the opportunity presented itself Nicky and Alix loved to personally welcome family members when they visited. Nicky hoped this visit would do Alix some good. She loved her brother and he was one of the few people whose opinion she respected and accepted. The train was on time and when Ernie disembarked he was warmly greeted by the Imperial family. Alix, who was usually very reserved in public, gave her brother a loving embrace and a kiss on his cheek. She was so happy to see him. As soon as the luggage was off-loaded the group departed for Alexander Palace and lunch in Ernie's honor.

Later in the day, Nicholas found Alix and Ernie together in the corner room which Alix used as a formal reception chamber. Furniture was everywhere and the Empress and her brother were debating the proper placement of each piece. Ernie was an amateur decorator and sponsored an artist community in their hometown of Darmstadt. He was an admirer of modern art, particularly art nouveau. Nicholas was not fond of this modern style and he eyed the disarray with distaste especially the open boxes in which he could just make out gaudy vases and knickknacks.

"Oh Nicky, look at the wonderful gifts Ernie has for us," she excitedly told him. Her face was flushed a pleasant pink as she told him of their plans for the room.

"I am sure it will be splendid darling," he said with false enthusiasm. He realized there was not much Alix and Ernie could do to change the classic design of the room. Much to his relief It looked as if they were limiting themselves to rearranging the furniture and keeping the finer pieces. As he glanced around the room, Ernie spoke to him in a jovial, teasing tone.

"So! Can you tell what is missing? I have removed quite a few pieces."

Nicky shook his head and was surprised that he could not tell which pieces of furniture were no longer there.

"Your palaces are like warehouses filled to the brim. Every centimeter of space is covered with furniture. I am not surprised you cannot tell what is missing," Ernie said in amusement.

"So what have you done with my excess furniture, Ernie? You must realize this is some of the most valuable in the palace," he teased with a smile on his face.

"It has been dispatched to the attic, darling," said Alix.

"Well do not let me keep you from your project. As usual duty calls, my dear."

"Do not let your ministers work you too hard, Nicky," Alix admonished.

Nicholas left the room to attend to his affairs but, after several hours of work, he was eager for a break and joined Alix and Ernie for tea in her Mauve Boudoir. The children were present as well and it was a happy occasion. It was enjoyable catching up on all the news of the German relatives and Alix seemed truly pleased to see her brother. Photo albums were brought out and memories of times gone by were relived. Laughter rang out as brother and sister shared a long forgotten joke and Nicky looked on contentedly, glad to see Alix so relaxed.

Before retiring for the night, Nicholas went back to his study to finish his correspondence. As he reflected on the day's activities, he was struck by his visit to the corner room and his failure to notice any furniture missing. If he did not realize furniture was missing from his own house, who else would, he thought. He knew at some point in the future he would send his children away. How wonderful it would be for familiar items to surround them. He thought of the many palaces filled with priceless antiques and paintings by old masters that were out of fashion and stored in attics. Although it was not a practical source of income, these collections were the artistic heritage of his family. He made a mental note to speak to Count Benckendorff about packing and shipping items away. It would be easy enough to use a warehouse in Vladivostok until he knew the final destination and since it was common practice for items to be moved from one palace to another, servants would not be suspicious to see packing crates leave. Servants generally worked at one palace so it was highly unlikely they would speak to their counterparts at another royal residence and inquire about an item.

Nicholas' thoughts turned to his children. Time was passing so quickly and Olga was already thirteen and would soon be a young woman. When St. Serafim's prophecies come to pass she will be twenty-three, a grown woman and old enough to make her own decisions. Nicholas wanted her to have a carefree childhood but as the oldest he knew she would have to be prepared for the future. He removed his secret diary from its hiding place and began to write. It is time to make my plans more firm, he thought and began to jot ideas down on the paper. He paused for a moment, read what he had written then tore up the page and began anew. Although he felt his diary was safe in its hidden location, he did not want to take any chances. He decided that he would code-name his plan the *Masquerade*. The name seemed perfect since a masquerade ball took a lot of planning, people were in disguises and there was much subterfuge and whispering going on. And such parties happened frequently enough that using the name would not necessarily evoke suspicion. He began to write again.

I must protect the sheep from the wolves. I must find a secure pasture with fences to protect my precious sheep. Only my most trusted shepherds will bring the sheep to their new pasture. I must build a strong barn stocked with bales of hay for the long winter. I must gather feed and fill a silo. It must be enough feed to last for the whole winter and to provide for all the animals.

He looked at what he had written and realized that it was very simplistic. But he also knew that the more complicated something was, the more likely that it could suffer breakdowns and be compromised. So he was satisfied with the simple code. The sheep were his children. The wolves, of course, were the revolutionaries and evil ones hunting for his children. The country they would go to would be the pasture. The fences were the foreigners who would protect the children. The shepherds were the Russians involved. The barn would be the children's new home and hay bales were their furniture and household goods. Gold and money sent out of the country would be the feed. The silo was the banks and the animals were the Russian people. He looked long and hard at his list. There was much to be accomplished but he did not feel overwhelmed. The family was moving to Peterhof for the summer and he planned to confer with George during their stay by the coast. He had some new thoughts on the financial aspects of his plan that he wished to discuss with his cousin.

Tired from the long day, he straightened up his desk, putting everything in its place. Nicholas had an incredible memory and at a glance he could tell if anything on his desk had been touched. It was useful knowledge which he kept to himself. He was aware of who came into his study and it enabled him to know if anyone rifled through his papers. His tasks completed, Nicholas retired for the night.

Part Two

The Conspiracy

Chapter 14

April 1908 - Tsarskoe Selo. After tossing and turning for several hours the Tsar finally fell into a troubled sleep that became more peaceful as the night wore on. Tension and stress left his body and his breathing was slow and steady. Caught in the deep webs of sleep he began to dream, but it was not the old, terrifying nightmare that he had finally learned to cope with. No, this was something entirely new. He felt a lightness come over him as if he were being lifted from his bed. A slight breeze chilled him as he stood in his nightshirt and then he began to walk. He was immediately surrounded by a fog so thick that he almost had to push against it to move and he could see nothing at all. After what seemed an eternity, the fog lifted, leaving only a shadowy haze behind. He found himself in front of an archway with elaborate columns, crowned by angels who seemed to be beckoning him to come near. He peered through the arch and saw a room in the distance and through the doorway into the chamber he could make out three dim figures. He was pulled toward the room by some compelling energy, and yet he felt he could resist the force if he desired. Nicholas realized he was being given a choice and he paused for a moment to weigh his options. Evidently he could turn around and retrace his steps or move forward through the arch and face whatever lay beyond. There did not seem to be any urgency and the three figures waited patiently for his decision. He considered his two alternatives and looked again at the archway. Then, his decision made, he strode purposefully through the arch and into the room where the three figures waited.

The trio was standing near a table and chills ran down his spine when he observed that the first figure was a faceless man wielding a small silver ax with curved edges. At the left side of the table stood a figure he recognized as his much beloved Serafim of Sarov, now a canonized saint of the church. The Tsar was instantly comforted by his kindly smile. On the right side of the table stood Pope Pius X and Nicholas was surprised when he offered his blessing as a way of greeting. He drew closer to the man in white and noticed a ring gleaming on his finger. The Pope, aware that Nicholas had noticed the ring, placed his hand out so he could see it more clearly. The ring was make of pure gold and on the front of was the figure of the crucified Christ hanging on an anchor. Behind the anchor was a ship's wheel. The Tsar had never seen anything like it. He wondered at its significance but since no one had yet spoken he did not venture to ask.

After a few moments the silence was broken. Saint Serafim asked the Tsar, "Do you believe in the prophecy I had delivered to you, my child?"

"Yes, most holy and blessed Serafim, I do believe," answered the Tsar.

"Will you accept God's plan for you on this day?"

Without hesitation Nicholas answered, "yes, holy one, and may his will be done in all things for the sake of Holy Russia."

"In the future, long after your life has ended, men will be able to prove your royal lineage through your blood and your skin."

"I do not understand."

"You must sacrifice the first two digits of the smallest finger on your left hand," stated Serafim. "It must be preserved for the future so that all will come to believe that what will be written must be rewritten to reflect the truth. Will you make this sacrifice as proof of your belief and trust in God's will?"

"I will", said Nicholas with some trepidation.

"Then you know what you must do," he said with a consoling look on his face.

Nicholas stood directly in front of the table, which now appeared to be a sacrificial altar, and stretched out his left hand. He made a fist and placed it down on the cold marble and then extended his little finger. He glanced at the faceless man, who had moved in closer to the altar, and everything became clear. This unknown figure was God's instrument and with little warning he stepped forward and with great force severed the Tsar's finger with the gleaming, silver hatchet. The royal blood of the Tsar flowed onto the pure white marble of the table. In shock, Nicholas pulled back his hand and instantly the wound stopped bleeding. When he stepped back, stunned by the violence of the moment, the Pope cradled the severed finger in his hands and raised it up. Nicholas watched in awe as a radiant light began to emanate from between the Pope's hands. As he brought his arms back down, the Pope opened up his palms and in place of the bloodied finger lay a brilliant incandescent pearl. The light shining forth from it was so bright; it concealed the face of the Pope. The Tsar leaned forward to examine the pearl, and, as he did this, the rays of light showered his whole being and he felt an indescribable joy which filled the depths of his soul.

He straightened up and turned to look at Serafim, whose countenance reflected contentment and joy. "God be praised forever," the Saint proclaimed.

"Amen," answered the Tsar.

"My son, in the near future you will be given a tangible sign and then you will know the meaning of this dream. A celestial event of great magnitude will occur in Russia and there will be much devastation. The night sky will be illuminated by an unknown light and for three days there will be no darkness."

Nicholas turned to depart but was stopped by the sound of the Pope's voice. "Come to me, Nicholas, come to me . . ."

"Come to me, come to me," repeated the emperor as he awoke from the dream. When he became aware of his surroundings he reached with the thumb of his left hand to feel his small finger. Filled with relief that it was still there, he turned to Alix who was asking, with concern in her voice,"come to whom, Nicky?"

"Oh, it was nothing more than a silly dream, darling," he replied.

Because of her fragile emotional condition he was reluctant to tell Alix what had occurred. Anyway, how could he explain or share the feeling of contentment that now overcame him as he recalled the details of his startling mystical experience. He was confused by elements of his dream and realized that it would take time to make the pieces of the puzzling vision fit together. For instance, what would he, the head of the Russian Orthodox Church, ever have to do with the Pope. He certainly would have reacted negatively to that part of the experience, if not for the reassuring presence of Serafim, a Russian Saint. And what could the amputation of his finger mean. Normally he would have been dismayed that he had to sacrifice part of his body but the Saint and the Pope seemed so supportive and happy at the event that he could only react in the same fashion. At any rate, for reasons he could not explain, he was filled with a sense of hope, not only about his own future but also about the fate of his beloved Russia. He recognized that he would personally suffer and so would his nation. However, his understanding of the dream was that after the ordeal, whatever form it took, he would be recognized as the good, honest and loving man that he was, and Mother Russia would be released from its tribulation. Nicholas was somewhat concerned about the sign he was to look for and when it might come to pass but he took comfort in the knowledge that whatever it was, it would confirm and possibly explain the revelation.

CRICK

Later that day Alix sat down at her desk and began working on a pile of neglected correspondence. She paused, momentarily, to wonder at Nicky's odd behavior that morning but then put it out of her mind as she just could not spare the time to dwell on it. The next few weeks would be very busy. Her sister Ella had arranged a marriage between her ward the Grand Duchess Marie and Prince William of Sweden. After the wedding Marie's brother Dmitri, also a ward of Ella, was to enroll at the Cavalry School in St. Petersburg and on holidays would live at Alexander Palace where Nicky would assume the role of his guardian. This would allow Ella the freedom to devote more time to her charitable endeavors. The extended family was descending en masse on Tsarskoe Selo to celebrate Marie's nuptials and because the wedding of a Grand Duchess was a state occasion Alix would be required to participate in many of the public events. These official functions always caused her great anxiety because she knew she came across as stiff and aloof. Alexandra felt as if she was being put on display on these occasions, and for all practical purposes, she was. Unfortunately she believed everyone's focus was on her, just waiting for her to make a mistake. As a result she had retired more and more to a secluded life, and for this, she was roundly criticized. It was a problem with no solution. She could appear in public and seem overbearing or remain in seclusion and appear snobbish and uncaring. Alix clearly understood that as Empress she was expected to lead a public life but she was so terribly shy she could hardly function and she was deeply hurt by the suggestion that she was an elitist. In reality, despite her German roots, she had a deep and abiding affection for the Russian people, an affection that she was unfortunately unable to communicate to the nation at large. Only her closest intimates, women like Anya or Ella and, of course, her husband Nicky, knew how she suffered when in the public eye. There was another aspect of the situation that influenced Alexandra's behavior. It seemed to her that all the upper class cared about was frivolity and parties and she was quite concerned about the decadence that had consumed St. Petersburg society in recent years. Her daughter Olga was becoming a young woman and Alix had no wish for her to be a part of such a fast set.

There was a gentle knock on the door followed by the voice of Anya calling out her name. Alix invited her to come around the screen that hid the chaise from view. The Empress was delighted to see her young friend and looked forward to a relaxing break from the tedium of arranging guest lists and answering petitions. Alix felt a sense of responsibility for Anya because the marriage which she had helped arrange for her had been a disaster, and had recently ended in divorce.

She wanted her friend close to her and arranged for her to rent a small cottage only two hundred yards from the palace gates. The quaint little house allowed Alix the opportunity to occasionally slip away from the palace and visit her friend and since Anya's home was beyond the palace walls the comings and goings of visitors to her house were not recorded or listed in the court circular. However, because of security concerns, the Tsarina generally remained at Alexander Palace and Anya visited her there almost every day. Anya had served as a Lady-in-Waiting prior to her marriage and there was some pressure to re-appoint her to an official position but Alix stubbornly refused. She needed to be able to call on Anya as a friend and confidante without the interference and intrigue of court protocol. The children were fond of her and Nicholas seemed to enjoy her company as well, so for the present Alix had what she wanted.

The Empress looked forward to hearing the latest gossip from Anya, who was remarkably well informed about the court. Alix could thus keep her hand on the pulse of court activity without actually participating in it. Unfortunately, the information she received was subject to Anya's interpretations and prejudices so she was rarely presented with an objective view of what went on outside the walls. Anya was very opinionated and, though she never tried to deceive Alix, she was able to exert considerable influence on the way the Tsarina viewed matters. Alix trusted her friend and failed to realize that Anya's lack of sophistication and understanding of human nature made her a poor judge of character. In Anya's mind people fell into two categories. They were either good or evil. Once she characterized someone as evil she did her utmost to ensure the Empress shared her view. As Anya's relationship with Alix strengthened, her ability to influence the Tsarina increased immeasurably.

Many supplicants frequented her small house trying to curry favor with the royal friend. Among these was Grigory Rasputin who, from his first meeting with Anya, had been categorized as a good and loyal friend of the royal family. It was difficult to characterize the type of emotion that women such as Anya, and for that matter the Empress herself, felt for this visionary. There was, of course, a feeling of affection, maybe even love, but not a love with carnal implications. Rasputin was too clever to risk his growing influence on Alix and he acted in a professional manner whenever he was with the family or the Tsarina's close circle of friends. He wanted power and the Empress wanted healing. They both seemed to be getting what they wanted from the relationship so he looked elsewhere to satisfy his appetite for women. The holy man was actually quite cunning and used Anya as a source of information as well as a channel for his ideas and suggestions. Anya idolized him and naively accepted everything he said as truth. What was truth for Anya became truth for Alix.

The most recent gossip involved Rasputin's falling out with Militsa, who had pressured the Russian Orthodox Church to investigate him after he spurned her efforts to be his only contact with the royal family. Alix had once been very close to Militsa and it was at the palace of the Grand Duchess that she first met Father Grigory, but when she heard about the investigation she put an immediate stop to it. She was well aware of the rumors about Rasputin's debauchery but she refused to believe that this saintly, holy man could be involved in any sinful activity. She was convinced Militsa was at fault and Anya, no doubt, supported the notion that the stories and rumors that were circulating about Rasputin were the result of Militsa's efforts to discredit him. When Alix developed a dislike for someone she was never half-hearted in making her distaste well known. Soon Militsa, and her sister Stana, were dropped from her circle of close friends and the two, who were once counted among her most trusted confidantes, were now despised with an intensity that surprised even Nicholas, when he became aware of it.

Alix felt the same way about Nicky's uncle, Nikolasha, and desperately wanted to reduce the influence he exerted on the Tsar. However, of all the Romanovs, the Grand Duke was the most respected and feared and there was little she could do to change the awe in which Nicky held him.

Alix could not alter the situation so she bided her time, determined, at some point, to remove Nikolasha from Nicky's life.

When Alix asked Anya about Brother Grigory she answered honestly, from her point of view.

"You know I just do not understand all the rumors which surround him. I have visited his apartment numerous times and I have never seen anything inappropriate. Your majesty, even you, with your delicate sensibilities, would find nothing to offend." In her naiveté, she failed to realize that Rasputin was always informed of her visits well in advance of her arrival. He was careful to ensure that his scandalous activities remained hidden from her view and that she had nothing but glowing reports to take back to the Empress.

"It is nothing more than jealousy. He is hated because we love him and people will always gossip about that which they do not understand. Now let us talk about something more pleasant," Alix suggested. She and Anya continued their discussion and talked about the plans for the upcoming wedding. After visiting with Anya for nearly an hour the Empress ended the conversation and handed the young woman a sealed packet. "Anya, I have a message I wish you to deliver to our friend. Take it to him personally, as soon as you can," Alix directed her. Anya promised to call on him in the morning.

Such a simple, blameless act. Yet one with great consequences. How could the Tsarina possibly know that this innocent letter to Rasputin, in which she poured out her feelings to him, would come back to haunt her?

cঞ্চ

The trip by train, from Moscow to Tsarskoe Selo, was long and tiring and as impatient as Ella was to reach her destination, absolutely nothing she could do would make the trip seem shorter. Russia was an enormous country and it took only one or two journeys to impress on a traveler the vast extent of the empire. Despite her fatigue, however, Ella always managed to remain upbeat and her disposition was so different from that of her sister, the Empress, that the contrast was startling. The purpose of her trip, of course, was Marie's wedding but she also looked forward to her stay at Alexander Palace and the time she would be able to spend with Alix, Nicky, and the children. In the old days the two sisters would frolic around their home without a care in the world but Alix's declining health had put an end to the carefree days of the past and made succeeding visits more difficult. As for herself, even after three years, she still grieved the loss of her husband Sergei, victim of a terrorist's bomb. Nonetheless, she hoped to spend time alone with Alix reminiscing about the past and those cherished, light hearted days of their youth.

Ella gazed pensively through the coach window at the passing countryside and considered, for a fleeting moment, the upcoming nuptials. She admitted to herself, reluctantly to be sure, that she might have rushed things a little too much. The marriage had been arranged rather quickly and Marie did not seem very happy with the match. Ella understood her ward's concerns but ignored them, for unions at this level were rarely based on love, but on expediency. Marie was a Grand Duchess, the granddaughter of a Tsar and thus required and expected to make a splendid match. Her upcoming marriage to Prince William of Sweden would bring significant political benefits to Russia.

Personally, Ella was glad to see the matter settled since Marie and Dmitri her brother, had been difficult youngsters. Even though she had treated them both as if they were her own children, now that they were of suitable age she was, quite frankly, ready for them to take responsibility for their own lives. Of course, that responsibility did not include picking your own husband or wife, a decision that ultimately, was made by the Tsar.

At any rate, Ella was still a beautiful woman and she had plans for her own future, plans that did not include two immature young royals. She knew that at some point during her visit she would have to approach Nicholas about her future. Since what she intended to propose was somewhat radical, Ella could only pray that the Tsar would hear her with an open mind and react with understanding.

At last the train pulled into the station at Tsarskoe Selo and when the Grand Duchess and her party disembarked, they were met enthusiastically on the platform by the entire Imperial family. Prince William and his family were not due to arrive for a few days so for the present it was to be a family get-together. And, as expected, during the next few days, Ella was able to spend quite a bit of time visiting with her sister. She found Alix to be very distracted and detached but attributed her behavior to the upcoming ceremonies. She knew Alix dreaded these occasions and was sure that was the reason for her state of mind

It was on the third day of her visit she had the opportunity to speak privately to Nicky. He was heading out for his walk, when to his surprise, Ella ran to catch up with him.

"May I join you, Nicky?"

"Certainly, as long as you do not mind some extra company."

Nicholas gave a distinctive whistle and eleven long haired, Scottish sheepdogs came bounding toward them yelping and barking excitedly. Ella laughed at the sound of the whistle, which she had heard many times before. Nicky used it to call Alix and the children as well. It had become a family custom loved by the children and his wife and whenever the whistle resonated they would immediately run toward the source.

Nicholas loved animals, and there was no question that when he went for his walk he would be accompanied by his sheep dogs. The two headed along the path by the lake and the dogs jumped around their feet with excitement. Every once in awhile Nicholas would reach down and pick up a stick and throw it across the park. All the dogs raced after it and ganged up playfully on the winner of the race to retrieve it. Eventually the dogs settled down and it became possible to talk without interruption.

"Ella, perhaps it is because I have not seen much of you lately, but I have noticed a real change in you since we were last together. If I may say so, it is almost as if Sergei's death has released you from worldly concerns and infused you with some deep inner peace. Not that you were not always an exceptional human being before, but then your life was consumed with the court and now all of that seems so unimportant to you. Your spirituality has impressed me and I must say I envy the peace of mind that you seem to have. You now seem more concerned with the poor, suffering soul of a stranger than your own well being."

"You are very intuitive Nicky," Ella replied. "I was more affected by Sergei's death than even my own mother's and dealing with the loss changed me completely. When I gathered up his shattered body I realized how precious every life is and how fragile our mortality. That anyone of us could depart this life at the blink of an eye is not something you normally dwell on. My husband's death made me reflect on how insignificant the so-called finer things in life are and how decadent court life had become. I am certain you do not wish to hear this Nicky, but it is how I feel."

"I understand your search for a simpler way. I too have found my attitude changing about so many things. If it was not my birthright I would gladly give up these royal trappings to live the quiet life of a country gentleman surrounded by my family."

Ella decided it was the right time to bring up an idea which had literally consumed her waking moments for many months. She knew she would need the Tsar's approval and support before she could go any further in her planning.

"Nicky, I have purchased some property in Moscow and I wish to start a convent. The nuns in this convent will have a mission different in purpose from any orthodox orders in the city. They will go out among the people and minister to the poor. The convent will have an orphanage and schools to teach trades," she explained with growing enthusiasm.

"I think that is a wonderful idea, but who have you chosen to run this organization."

"I am sorry Nicky, in my excitement I left out the most crucial detail. I wish to take the veil and become the mother superior. This is not a sudden decision but is one I have pondered and prayed over for some time. My responsibilities to Marie and Dmitri will soon be over and so there is nothing to keep me from going ahead."

"Oh Ella, this is such a drastic step. In time you will recover from Sergei's death and possibly even remarry."

"Nicky, I will never marry again. I feel as if God has looked into my soul and given me this vocation and nothing can dissuade me except your refusal to grant permission."

He was moved by the look of determination in her eyes and could actually feel the goodness that emanated from her. He knew there would be objections from the Church and her family but he could smooth these over. There would be no opposition from him

"My dearest Ella, how could I refuse you anything. You have the permission of your Tsar."

Ella began to weep. She had been so afraid the Tsar might refuse her permission that she was momentarily overcome by emotion when he agreed to her request. When she regained her composure she embraced Nicky and thanked him, joy reflected in the radiance of her face. They continued their walk but Ella, her hopes now completely fulfilled, changed the subject.

"I still feel our individual destinies are somehow intertwined by virtue of the journey to Sarov. It has been years since our visit but it seems like yesterday that we met the old woman. You too have changed and I can not help but think there is more to Elena Motivilov than you have told me."

"Yes, there is much more," sighed Nicholas.

The Tsar was convinced that he could trust Ella completely, but he had great concerns about others of the Romanovs. He would take his time assessing each member of his family as to their loyalty to Russia, but above all to their Tsar. He would decide over the course of several years, whom he could trust and take into his confidence. The planning was in its very early stages and his recent dream, which he accepted as a vision, gave him more details to agonize over. He decided now was the time to bring Ella into the inner circle and reveal to her everything that had transpired.

"Let us go back to the palace," he suggested. "I want you to come to my study. I have something to show you." As the two kindred souls headed back up the path toward the palace the kennel master came forward, gathered up the dogs and returned them to the kennels.

When they reached the palace, Nicky escorted his sister-in-law into his study. After a few preliminaries, the Tsar went to his desk and removed the yellowed letter from its secret compartment and silently handed it to Ella. She carefully unfolded it and began to read. The Tsar carefully watched her expression as she read it. He was not surprised to see her eyes fill with tears as she absorbed the implications of the fragile document.

"Oh, Nicky, what a dreadful burden you have been asked to carry. I do not see how you have continued on with your life as you have."

"The enemies that Blessed Serafim mentions will ultimately have my life, but they will not have my children nor will they destroy my memories of the precious moments spent with them. I refuse to live as if I have one foot in the grave and I decided long ago that I would enjoy life to the fullest. I have not been wasting time and preliminary plans are already in the works to thwart the evil ones. Though I know and accept my own fate there is much I can do in the remaining ten years and this is why I have taken you into my confidence. It is possible that I will have to call on you for help in the coming years and I know I can count on you to be discrete."

Without hesitation Ella pledged her loyalty to the Tsar and for a moment he was nearly overcome by the upwelling of affection he felt for this truly remarkable woman.

"What does Alix think about all of this?" asked Ella.

"She has read St. Serafim's letter and is privy to some information but I try not to speak too much about it. You are well aware of her physical and emotional condition and the pressure Alexei's illness puts on her. Her health has been of great concern to us lately and I do not want to burden her anymore than necessary. Besides, I cannot take the chance that in a period of depression she would inadvertently disclose sensitive information. We have a difficult time as it is keeping Alexei's hemophilia a secret and this is one of the reasons our life is lived in relative seclusion."

"I fully agree with the approach you have adopted. We do not need to cause her any unnecessary worry. Do any of the children know?"

"No, they will be told nothing until it is absolutely essential. I want their lives to be as carefree as possible. They do not need to shoulder such a tremendous burden this soon. It would destroy their childhood. We must maintain everything as normal as possible. If we change any of our usual activities, people may begin to suspect that something else is going on."

"I am truly honored that you felt I was trustworthy enough to confide in. You must know that I will do whatever you need me to do and that I will risk my life if it comes to it," Ella replied.

"It may very well come to that, because the evil that will invade our motherland will use any means to wipe us off the face of the earth," Nicholas warned her.

"But surely with all the knowledge you have about the future you can stop it. You have the power, money and the army," Ella interjected.

"No Ella. You must realize that our country is on a precipice and nothing can be done to prevent it from falling off. Perhaps that is a poor analogy but the coming storm will bring Russia to its knees and I may not intervene even though I am the Tsar of all Russia. I must sit back and watch my country destroyed and even though I know the names of those who will be responsible for the horror that is coming I am restrained from acting. Russia will ultimately be purified and saved but first it must suffer the fires of revolution, war, and all its accompanying destruction. This is the way it must be."

"It reminds me of the Passion of our Lord," Ella observed. "He went to his death without lifting a sword. He was called to surrender his life for us and though he could have refused the cup of suffering, he did not."

"I have reflected on the same passage from scripture, Ella, and I must say it gives me great comfort."

"What brought you to the realization that the country was in such danger and that you could do nothing about it?" Ella asked.

"Well, in addition to the letter which you just read and other information that has been developed, I recently had a vivid dream which I will now share with you. Sit back and prepare yourself, for you will not believe what the future holds for us." Nicholas went on to tell Ella about his dream and to detail some of the plans he had made up to this point. He revealed the revolutionary plot they had uncovered and told Ella of his decision to deny the anarchists any opportunity to seize Russia's wealth. The Tsar did not give her all the details but he valued Ella's opinion and was interested in knowing what she thought about his efforts to date.

The Grand Duchess had listened attentively as he narrated the events that had brought him to this point, and was literally spell bound when he related his dream. When the Tsar finished she asked, "Nicky, how are you going to fund this? It will take millions of rubles. I know you are a wealthy man but even you do not have enough money to prepare for Russia's future."

"Ella, I have wealth far greater than even you know about. Believe me it will be enough. I have already deposited sums of money in Swiss banks but there is still much more to be done. You need not be concerned about the financial aspects as I have someone else working on that." Ella was relieved as she knew so little about financial matters. Sergei had always handled their affairs.

At this point the Tsar decided to divulge the names of the other members of the inner circle. Ella was impressed with his choices and voiced her approval of them.

"Nicholas, you have a long road to travel but remember that you do not walk alone. I believe that our Lord in his great wisdom and our dear Saint Serafim are watching over you. Do not doubt your strengths. God would not have given you this trial without reason and he never gives us a cross so big that we cannot shoulder it. I have the utmost confidence in you and know that you will always have my support and prayers."

He thanked her for her kind words and they continued to talk a little longer until a knock at his study door brought their exchange to an end. "Your Imperial Highness, we have received word that the train carrying the Swedish wedding party will arrive on schedule," the footman announced. It was fortuitous that Ella had joined Nicholas for a walk, for as it turned out, those few precious hours proved to be their only opportunity for a private talk. The festivities and ceremonies for the wedding filled the next few days and Ella left for Moscow immediately following the marriage ceremony.

Chapter 15

June 1908 - Central Siberia. The vast Russian landscape, five hundred miles north of Irkutsk, was virtually uninhabited, and when the meteor punched through the atmosphere and streaked across the morning sky not many, of the very few who lived in this harsh wilderness, were up and about. It was approximately seven a.m. when the glowing ball of molten rock, influenced by the gravitational pull of the earth, and picking up speed as it approached the surface, smashed into the dense Siberian forest with a thunderous roar. The initial collision produced an effect equivalent to a gigantic earthquake which was felt hundreds of miles away. It also created an enormous mushroom shaped cloud which rose nearly three miles above the point of impact. The sky then appeared to split in half while tongues of fire burst through the clouds. From its epicenter in the middle of the Siberian forest, millions of trees fell down in a circle fifteen miles in diameter as if bowing to some mighty force. A searing wave of heat scorched the earth and blackened trees without burning them, but the wildlife of the area was decimated as hundreds of animals and birds succumbed to the tremendous pressure produced by the impact. Residents of a small village miles away ran out of their homes in fright, lay down on the ground and wailed "that the end of the world was here." It was a truly frightful and disturbing example of nature's awesome fury and yet it left very little evidence behind. There were no craters, no iron, no meteorite remnants, and no debris field. The only evidence was the mute, blackened forest, standing in stark testimony to the events of June 17, 1908. In the ensuing years scientists would try, with limited success, to explain the incident. One thing was immediately apparent. *A celestial event of great magnitude,* had occurred.

That night, at Peterhof, the whole imperial family stood on the balcony looking eastward at what should be a dark sky. In that direction the heavens were brightly illuminated and it was so light that it was possible to read a newspaper without difficulty even though the sun had set hours ago and the moon was still too low in the sky to provide any significant light. It was eerie, to say the least, and no one, among the many experts, could explain the phenomenon to the Tsar. Everyone in the area had felt the tremors of what was assumed to be a large earthquake, an event that was not particularly rare in eastern Russia. The northern lights were often a common sight from this vantage point but the light show to the east was an entirely different matter. The children pestered him as to the reasons for the brilliant display but he had no answers for their insistent questions. Nicholas had a vague and uneasy feeling as he looked at the luminous sky and he wondered if this could be the sign St.

Serafim had promised. Despite the mysterious nature of the event the Tsar was not quite ready to commit to this possibility until he had more information. Unfortunately communication with that remote part of the country was not dependable. Word of what had happened would have to make its way by horseback to the nearest telegraph terminus and eventually to St. Petersburg and finally down the coast to the palace at Peterhof. He was troubled, but there was little he could do. Alix was looking at him with concern so he shook off his mood. Time would tell what had happened and in the meantime he, and the family, could only wonder in awe at the heavenly demonstration.

The next morning the Tsar received Count Stolypin who had requested an immediate audience with the Tsar. It was obvious to the Prime Minister that the Emperor was impatient for news of yesterday's events so after exchanging brief pleasantries, Stolypin came straight to the point.

"Your Imperial Highness we have received word of a terrible explosion in Siberia, somewhere north of Irkutsk. The initial reports tell of terrible fires and devastation to trees and wildlife."

"What about the people? Have they been harmed?" the Tsar asked anxiously.

"Strangely enough the report mentions very little loss of life. It seems it happened in an extremely remote area," replied the Count

"God was watching over his people. Are there any indications as to what caused this terrible accident?"

"It was of natural causes but no one knows exactly what took place. There is speculation that it was a meteor but it will be awhile before scientists can examine the area."

"I wish you to mount an expedition," ordered the Tsar. "Staff it with our most qualified scientists and send it to Siberia to investigate. I must know what has happened."

After Stolypin departed, Nicholas gave word that he was not to be disturbed. He sat in his study, quietly lost in thought, and recalled his recent dream. Could the incident Stolypin had described be the sign Serafim had promised him? He remembered that the light would last for three days and knew that realistically he would have to wait to be sure. But then what? If this was his sign, he must take some action. Did this mean he must cut off his finger and if so what was he to do with it? Questions piled up, one on top another, but answers eluded him. He became exasperated at his inability to make sense of all this, so he did what he always did in such situations. He offered a brief prayer and put the whole matter in God's hands.

Nicholas continued to reflect on the dream, especially the confusing ending when, as he awoke, he clearly heard the voice of the Pope calling out, "come to me, Nicholas, come to me." Suddenly he received the inspiration he had asked for and realized that in the cryptic ending of his dream was the answer to at least one of his questions. If this light continues for the three days, as prophesied, then he would go to Rome and see Pope Pius X. He was convinced it was the only way he would have any peace in this matter. "I must know! I must know," he muttered to himself. His hands clenched the edge of his desk, but the stress and tension caused his head to ache and he cradled it in his hands, attempting to find some relief. Yes, in the deepest recesses of his soul he could feel that Rome was the answer. He would see this Pope and hear what he had to say.

But the decision did not give him any great comfort because it generated even more questions, questions that in the present context seemed unanswerable. The Tsar and the Empress both believed in visions, dreams, and mystical experiences but it was almost incomprehensible that a Roman Catholic pope would turn up in the dream of a Russian Orthodox monarch. What could the Vatican possibly have to do with the future of Russia? After all, the split between the church of Rome and the eastern churches had occurred nearly a thousand years earlier and Nicholas was concerned as to how a meeting with the Pontiff might be viewed by his Orthodox subjects. But as he reflected on the matter he remembered that the Vatican was not only a religious entity but one which had significant political influence as well. Historically Catholic churches had always been considered places of sanctuary and the Vatican had served that role in the past. Perhaps there was more to this dream than he realized. At any rate, in a few days he would have his answer.

Despite his impatience there was nothing Nicky could do to make the time pass more quickly. That night the sky was illuminated in the east for the second evening in a row and the next morning he awoke with great anticipation. He tried to work in his study but it was impossible and he ended up pacing back and forth. Finally he went for a long walk in the palace grounds, knowing in his heart that in a few hours his dream would be authenticated. That evening the family gathered, as it had on the previous nights to witness the illuminated sky for the third time. Nicholas had his answer and was now convinced of the validity of the dream. There was much to do but his first thoughts were of Alix. She had been very concerned and knew that something was bothering him. He had not wanted to discuss it with her earlier but felt that now he owed her an explanation of his behavior the past few days. That evening, as they sat side by side on the balcony enjoying the unusual illuminated night, he broached the subject with her.

"My dear Sunny, I must apologize for my actions these past three days. I know you have been concerned about me but many things have been weighing on my mind."

"Dearest Nicky tell me what is troubling you," Alix asked while she gently stroked his hand.

"Two months ago I had a very disturbing dream. In fact the word "dream" hardly seems an apt description of what I experienced. Truly, it seemed more a vision. At any rate, St. Serafim appeared and gave me a message." Nicky than proceeded to give her an edited version of his vision, leaving out any mention of the Pope or the amputation of his finger. He told her about the sign St. Serafim had promised and indicated that as they spoke they were watching the end of it. He led her to believe that the vision was merely a confirmation of the contents of the letter delivered by Elena Motivilov five years earlier. He knew Alix well enough to recognize that she would not understand the rest of his vision, especially as he himself was confused by its meaning and unable to explain it rationally. He wanted to go to Rome before he spoke anymore about it.

For the time being Ella would remain the only person who knew the details of his mystical experience in its entirety and it was not merely the affection that Nicky felt for his sister-in-law that enabled him to confide in her. There was something much deeper, a spiritual bond that tied them together inextricably and allowed him to bare his soul to her in a way he could never do with Alix. His wife had become too fragile and frighteningly dependent on Grigory Rasputin for relief and even though he loved his wife without reservation there were some things he could not share with her. On the other hand, Ella's spirituality was renowned and Nicholas knew she was the only one who could accept what had happened to him without question. Unfortunately she was not visiting again until Christmas so he would not be able to discuss all that had transpired with her for several months.

"It is amazing to think that we are witnessing God's hand at work," said Alix. "He has given us a wonderful gift to know the truth of his words."

Nicky was so relieved Alix had accepted his simplified explanation that he was totally unprepared for what followed.

"We must talk to Father Grigory about this wonderful sign from God," Alix announced. "He will be able to give us spiritual guidance and insight."

"No Alix, we will not discuss this with Father Grigory. If this sign were for him why did he not give it to us?"

"I do not understand your attitude, Nicky. I am convinced he will speak to us about this with great wisdom."

"St. Serafim gave this wondrous sign to me. It is private and sacred. I shared it with you only because you are my beloved spouse but it goes no further. I forbid you to speak of it to anyone," he told her, with obvious agitation.

"Very well, Nicholas," she replied. Although she disagreed with him she nevertheless gave her word to obey him in this matter. But she could not understand her husband's attitude towards Rasputin, especially since he had saved their son. Nicky had lately become sensitive about "their friend" and she did not want to upset him unduly. She had to admit that Father Grigory had said nothing to her to indicate he knew what St. Serafim had foretold. The two continued to sit quietly in the night air and neither broached the subject of Rasputin again.

The remainder of June passed quickly in the idyllic village by the sea and the Imperial family enjoyed the cooling ocean breezes and outdoor activities after the long winter. No more mention was made of the unusual events they had collectively witnessed and eventually the circumstances of those three strange days faded from people's minds. Preparations were underway for their annual voyage on the <u>Standart</u> and the children were counting the days to their departure.

Nicholas was also anxious to get away but he had an urgent piece of business to attend to before departing. He had asked his cousin George to come to Peterhof and Nicholas was eagerly anticipating his arrival. They were to meet privately after lunch and the Tsar had cleared his schedule for the afternoon to ensure they would not be disturbed. He had decided not to tell George about his dream since it did not contain information he needed to know. Visions and dreams just did not seem like a proper topic of conversation between men. Anyway, George was privy to the contents of Serafim's letter and had received enough information to help Nicky with his portion of the *Masquerade*. The Tsar did not feel the need to impart any more than was absolutely necessary. For security reasons each participant would be given only the details needed to accomplish their portion of the plan. Nicky greeted George warmly when he arrived and escorted him to the study where they immediately got down to business.

"I have been giving the financial aspects of our future a great deal of thought," Nicky informed the Grand Duke. "I need to have assurance that our money is secure. My biggest concern is that word of our maneuverings will slip out."

"I totally agree with you, Nicky. I am not sure how much we can trust the European bankers since they seem to have rather flexible loyalties. There is much instability in Europe, especially in the Balkans and I truly believe that if Russia suffers from unrest it will spill over into the west and possibly cause the loss our investments."

"I have come to believe that the United States may be answer to our problem," replied the Tsar. "I do not want to deposit all our gold and currency in one location but I believe the bulk should go to America."

"You are wise to take that point of view and I have information that may provide a solution," George replied. "Through my banking contacts here in Russia and those in Paris, I have heard that the National City Bank of New York City has expressed an interest in opening a branch here. It may just be rumor, but its worth checking out. Our economy has improved so much in the past two years that I can understand the

American's interest. From my research, I have determined they have a solid reputation within the banking community."

Nicky could see where George was going with this and liked the possibilities. "George, we all know bankers are out to make money so if we make it financially rewarding certainly we can ensure their loyalty. I know you will need time to plan but I wish to have a meeting with a senior representative from this bank. Of course, we must select a discreet location for the meeting. An American banker visiting the Tsar would surely warrant unwanted scrutiny."

"Nicky are you planning to go to the Crimea this year?'

"No, not this year but we will definitely make the trip next year. Why do you ask?"

"The Crimea is the perfect location for a meeting. It is far from the centers of intrigue at St. Petersburg and Moscow and no one will be suspicious if I introduce you to my acquaintance from America. We can meet at my place, privately, and develop whatever arrangements are appropriate and since you take pleasure in meeting new people it will not seem unusual if you spend time with my friend." George's estate in the Crimea was within walking distance of the Tsar's Livadia.

"George, I think you have hit upon a great idea. Protocol is so much more relaxed at Livadia and my whereabouts are not so tightly monitored. I will have the freedom to come and go as I please."

"Then with your permission I will make the arrangements. It is important to determine if we can have a secure relationship with National City Bank. I believe it will be in the bank's interest, as much as ours, to keep our dealings confidential. It would not be to the Americans' benefit to have it revealed that they are conducting business with an autocratic nation. I do not mean to offend you Nicky but their people enjoy much more freedom than ours and would not look favorably upon it."

"I take no offense, George. Your words ring true but I think it will all work to our advantage. National City Bank may very well be an ideal partner for the reasons you have indicated. Set the meeting up and we will see where it leads us. Once we have financial ties established they may lead to diplomatic ones as well."

Nicholas was pleased with George's idea. His plan was progressing smoothly in regards to its monetary aspects but the most important element, a safe haven for his girls, would require even more careful investigation and planning. He could almost hear the clock ticking as it counted down his remaining time but he quickly put that concern out of his head. He did not have time for such distractions. The *Masquerade* had begun and he was satisfied with the initial progress. He bid George good-bye and continued with his work.

ᏣᏛᎣ

In mid December the family said good-bye to Peterhof and left behind the frigid winds that were beginning to sweep in across the Baltic. The holiday season was rapidly approaching and at Tsarskoe Selo the palaces were alive with the hustle and bustle of preparation for the festivities. Halls were bedecked with colorful wreathes and many of the rooms contained live evergreen trees covered with ornaments, fruits, ribbons and candles waiting to be lit. The adults had a tree set up in Alexandra's formal reception room where presents from all the relatives were placed. The children had their own Christmas tree set up in the playroom and sometimes at night they would sneak out of their rooms and lie under the tree and sleep there until morning. A special tree was also set up in the hallway for the servants who worked inside the palace and the Empress always insured they received thoughtful gifts, carefully selected for each member of the staff.

In the midst of all the excitement Ella arrived from Moscow and was greeted with enthusiasm by the family. The Grand Duchess brought exquisitely crafted icons for each member of the family and although Alexandra already had many, she cherished each new image as if it were the first she had ever received. Nicholas eagerly looked forward to Ella's visit not only since there was much to discuss but also because he had a special gift for her and could hardly wait to see her reaction when he presented it.

The Tsar waited impatiently for his sister-in-law to get settled into her rooms and it seemed an eternity before the family was finally gathered again at the entrance to the palace. Nicky's continuous fidgeting was setting everyone on edge but at last he strode off to spring the surprise. When he reached his study he picked up the phone and gave instructions to the attendant at the other end of the line. "Please bring the Grand Duchess' gift to the front of the palace. Make sure it is gleaming. I will meet you there in fifteen minutes, so do not be late," directed the Tsar. He then ordered one of the footmen to call for Grand Duchess Ella and escort her to the front of the palace.

"Can we come, Papa," asked Olga, who, as the oldest daughter, had been allowed to tag along to the study with her father.

"Yes, of course. Go get everyone and meet us out front, but hurry, they will bring the gift soon," replied her father. Alexei was not feeling well so he and the Tsarina did not join them. Both Alix and the Tsar were overprotective of the boy and the poor child often missed out on family activities although the presentation that was about to occur did not offer any physical risk. The Tsar hurried to the front entrance to the palace. He wanted to be the first one there in case the gift was brought before Ella arrived but she showed up on time with the four girls in tow. Nicholas greeted them and they all stood there with Ella, in growing anticipation of her reaction to the gift. As for Ella, she was somewhat bemused by all the mystery. She wondered what on earth this present could be.

"You will love this present," said Tatiana.

"Oh, yes Auntie, you surely do not have one," said Olga.

"Now, now girls, we don't want to spoil the surprise," cautioned Nicky. He knew well that when it came to gift giving, the children sometimes got overly excited and gave away the surprise.

"All right, Papa, I won't tell her it goes very fast," Anastasia said.

"Shh, Anastasia, you'll give away the secret," scolded Olga.

"I did not say what it was, I just said it goes very fast," explained Anastasia.

"All right children settle down, it should be here shortly," said Nicholas.

Ella stood quietly, surrounded by the children. She could not imagine what it could possibly be. She hoped it was not a horse, or any other kind of animal for that matter but whatever it was she would receive it graciously. Suddenly a loud horn sounded from around the corner of the palace. The Tsar had planned everything. The children began to jump up and down and shriek with excitement as a brand new Delaney-Belleville touring car pulled up to the entrance. Ella's eyes grew wide as she gazed at the gleaming automobile. It was a truly magnificent machine, the French equivalent of a Rolls Royce. The car was a rich maroon color, trimmed in black and gold, with a plush leather interior. She was momentarily stunned by the extravagance of the gift and though she knew little of automobiles Ella estimated its value at approximately 20,000 rubles.

"Well Ella, it is all yours," said Nicky.

"My goodness! Never in my dreams did I ever imagine I would own a car. I never even considered such a thing," exclaimed Ella

"I know and that is why I am giving it to you," replied Nicky. He then began describing the horsepower of the car and the engine size.

"Nicky," Ella said with a chuckle, "I have no idea what any of that means, I do not even know how to drive."

"I am sorry Ella, it's just that cars are one of my greatest passions and I do ramble on about them," explained the Tsar. "This machine is one of my favorites and is considered one of the finest made. Would you like to take a drive?"

"Yes," shouted the girls in unison and before he could stop them they had jumped into the back of the car.

"We are ready to go, Papa," said Maria.

"No, no children," said Nicholas. "I will drive Ella alone."

"Please Papa, please let us come," pleaded Tatiana.

"Nicky, do let them come, I don't mind a bit," said Ella.

"Very well, girls, you can all join us," said Nicholas, "but you must be quiet so I can speak to your Auntie about the car," explained their father. He opened Ella's door and helped her into the car.

"Nicky, what about the roads, are they safe," inquired Ella.

"Yes, they have been cleared of any snow and salted," explained Nicky. "They won't be a problem."

"Well, let us go then," said Ella. Nicholas drove the car around the grounds and then to the back of the palace. As he guided the car past the window where Alix and Alexei stood watching the Grand Duchesses called out excitedly to their brother and waved and Alix helped Alexei wave back at his sisters. Ella glanced back at the girls, who were giddy with excitement, and it warmed her heart. She had not been blessed with children of her own, but being a part of her nieces' life was the next best thing. She thoroughly enjoyed the time spent with these energetic, mischievous, and lovable young girls. The Tsar drove the car back to the front of the palace where the children's nurse Mary was waiting.

"Girls, this is where you disembark," said Nicholas. They carefully climbed out of the car and went back into the palace eager to share their adventure with Alexei. "Are you ready, Ella?"

"I am not sure, Nicky. Ready for what," inquired Ella.

"To take your new car for a drive," said Nicky.

"You know I do not know how to drive. Sergei would never have permitted it and I am not sure I am ready to try. I will just hire a chauffeur."

"Surely you do not want to rely on someone else to drive you? It is a wonderful freedom. I drive myself as much as possible unless it is an official occasion. Come. You must at least give it a try before you say no," he pleaded with her.

"All right Nicky, I will attempt to drive this machine but you must know I am very uneasy, especially with all this snow. Are you sure it is safe?" Nicky helped her into the driver's seat and looked on in amusement as Ella carefully arranged herself and began looking at the instruments of the car. She stalled for time and adjusted her seat again, and then again, but Nicky would have none of it and urged her to start the engine and get on with the lesson.

"Ella, you saw that the roads were clear when we drove around earlier, so stop worrying, everything will be just fine. Now it is very simple." Nicky proceeded to explain the control mechanisms of the big touring car. He went over everything several times and Ella seemed to grasp the basic instructions quickly. She took a deep breath, put the car in gear, and started moving slowly down the road, the steering wheel grasped tightly in her hands, her brow furrowed in concentration.

"A splendid job," exclaimed Nicky. "It is as if you owned this car for years."

"Oh, if Sergei could see me now, wouldn't he be surprised. He was always so overprotective I imagine he would never have let me drive. What a progressive idea this is, Nicky."

Nicholas and Ella drove around the grounds for nearly an hour. As she began to feel more comfortable with her mastery of the large automobile she moved the accelerator forward and her speed increased. Exhilarated, she threw caution to the wind and began going even faster, her scarf fluttering out behind her, a rosy glow to her cheeks. Just when Nicky began to urge caution, the back of the car started to slide as it hit a patch of ice. The car swerved right and then left as Ella jerked at the steering wheel and then, uncertain as to how to control the vehicle, she made the fatal mistake of engaging the brakes. The Delaunay-Belleville went into a spin, the high performance machine no match for an amateur driver. "We are going to die!" screamed Ella as the automobile spun wildly around in a circle.

"Release the brake," yelled Nicky, but it was too late. The speed of the car caused it to make two complete circles before it slid into a snow embankment and came to an abrupt stop. Ella sat still, visibly shaken, as Nicky got out to look for damage. "Not a scratch Ella," he announced as he walked around to the driver's side of the car. "We can continue with our drive."

"No Nicky, I am through with driving. It is too much for me."

"Don't be silly. I have landed in a ditch more than once. You just need to learn what to do in that situation. Please say you will keep the car," he implored her.

"Very well, Nicky, I will think about it, but you are driving back. How can you be so calm? We were at death's door," she replied in her most melodramatic voice.

"Oh Ella," Nicky laughed. "Minor accidents happen frequently, but people still enjoy driving. I will take over and drive you back to the palace. I am sure you will want to tell Alix all about your adventure."

He helped her into the passenger's seat and then drove slowly back to the palace. During the return drive Nicky glanced over at Ella and saw that she seemed to have calmed down. Though they met infrequently, he had become very fond of her, and now that she was part of the *Masquerade* he felt an even closer tie. This friendship had not gone unnoticed by Alix, who was fiercely possessive, and ultimately the bond between the two sisters would become strained by Nicky's association with Ella. Theirs was a complex relationship. Nicky, on the one hand was the Tsar of Russia and she looked to him for guidance. On the other, she was like a respected older sister and he depended on her for support and advice. He looked forward to a private conversation with her later, but for the present it was time to join Alix for tea and to share their adventure with her. When they reached the palace he turned the automobile over to an attendant and they went in together.

The next few days passed quickly in a blur of holiday activities. Traditionally the family gathered at Anichkov Palace, in St. Petersburg, the city residence of Nicky's mother Minnie, the Dowager Empress. A special Christmas Mass was held in the palace chapel for the Imperial family and everyone participated devoutly in the sacred celebration. The next day, back at Tsarskoe Selo, the Tsar and Tsarina participated in festivities for the soldiers who guarded the palace. The Grand Duchesses were all dressed alike and stood in the receiving line next to their parents. After the tree lighting ceremony they presented gifts to the officers and their men.

The celebrations went on for a number of days, but eventually the holiday season came to a close, and Ella began to prepare for her return to Moscow. She remembered with clarity her discussion with Nicholas a few months earlier and felt that before leaving she should be brought up to date. Nicky was equally anxious to talk with his sister-in-law, and Alix's self-imposed seclusion made it possible for him to slip away. Another driving lesson seemed a perfect cover and Ella suggested that the Tsar take her for a drive in her new car. Nicky had the car brought around, and even though servants, maids, and guards were everywhere, they were confident that they would not be overheard. Ella was fully into the intrigue by now and she knew she must use the utmost discretion to avoid disclosure, but nevertheless she was anxious to get started.

"Nicky, I wanted to talk to you about the secret plans."

"Before you go any further, we must not refer to a "secret plan" anymore. If someone were to overhear one of the discussions about it, they would certainly become suspicious. I have given the whole plan a code name. It will be called the *Masquerade* and we will refer to that name from now on when discussing it. I have informed the others of this."

"Who is involved now?"

"I believe I mentioned some of the participants already. In addition to George, Sandro, Nikolasha and Count Benckendorff there are a few others, including an operative in the enemy camp. This agent does not know of the plan but the information he is gathering is vital to the success of the *Masquerade*. He is reporting on revolutionary activity and it is essential we be kept up to date on the maneuverings of our enemies."

"It sounds quite involved but you seem to be managing things very well."

"It is just like the army. You must have a chain of command to get the mission accomplished. The whole *Masquerade* will be compartmentalized and each participant will only know what is necessary to complete his or her assignment. I am giving you more details than I planned but you will be a major participant. The less people that know, of course, the better."

"I understand," said Ella.

"In time I will need to bring in others to handle different aspects of the *Masquerade*."

"How many people do you think will be involved?"

"It is hard to say. It just depends on how things go. Complications could cause more involvement whereas, if it goes smoothly, we may need less. I think at least fifty people will be involved at different levels."

"Fifty!" exclaimed Ella. "That seems an unmanageable number. Are you sure you want to involve so many? How can you possibly trust fifty people to keep this whole thing quiet."

"Remember, Ella, some will be involved at a low level and know very little. Only a few of the players will know the whole operation. Not even my immediate family will know more than is absolutely necessary. I think we will be able to have some individuals carry out their assignments without ever knowing they are engaged in a much larger scheme," he told her. "There will be much deception in the *Masquerade.*"

"It seems that you have already given this a good bit of thought."

"It is constantly on my mind! How can it not be when my children's lives are at stake? Yet in spite of it all I must continue to be the Tsar, a husband and good father to my children."

"You are a brilliant actor. If you had not told me about this I would not have even guessed that it was going on."

"It is hard, very hard, and sometimes I feel as if I am going to snap but I put my trust in God and he sustains me," said Nicholas.

"Have you decided anything more about the financial aspects, since we last talked?"

"George and I have been working diligently on that subject. After much discussion and research we have decided the bulk of the Russia's fortune will go to the United States."

"How did you come to this decision?'

"Well, we had considered the United States as a possibility from the beginning but it is only recently that we have begun to take action in that direction. Russia is not the only country which suffers from instability and other European nations seem to share many of our troubles. Who knows how far the revolutionaries will spread their ideology if they take over Russia. Their actions could affect Europe and endanger our financial resources. I know I am overly superstitious, but there seems to be a dark cloud hanging over the continent and all I can see in it is death and destruction. The United States, on the other hand, is fairly isolated and tends to back away from European affairs"

"Who will you negotiate with?"

"I do have some financial contacts, as well as funds in a bank in New York City, but nothing of the magnitude we are discussing. George is working on establishing the necessary contacts. He is a very talented financial manager." At this point Nicholas abruptly changed the subject. "Ella I need your assistance. I am going to go to Rome."

"Rome!" she exclaimed. "Oh, your dream. How could I have forgotten? Of course you must go. How can I aid you?"

"You are very perceptive. I received the sign and now I must go. I will never be able to rest until this is resolved in my mind. I just hope the answers to my questions will be found in the Vatican."

"So, you will see the Pope?"

"If he will receive me, and that is how I hope you can be of assistance. I must see him but it cannot be an official state visit. That would be unprecedented and draw much criticism. How would you suggest I go about it?"

"When I traveled to Italy with Sergei, he made all the arrangements, so I am not sure how to go about requesting an audience. However, I am familiar with someone who may be able to arrange it. I do not know if you are aware that I have been working on the project you approved when last we talked. As you may know there is no order of nuns in our Russian Orthodox faith similar to that which I am proposing so I have been doing research on some of the Catholic orders. I am not sure how much you keep up with Alix's friends but her former lady-in-waiting, Maria Bariatinskaya has returned to Rome."

"Yes, I remember her quite well," Nicky replied. "Alix was devastated when she left Russia again but as I recall it was a family illness which forced her to leave our service."

"You are correct. Alix corresponds with her regularly and I have started to, as well. She is assisting me with obtaining the statutes and history of some of the Italian convents. Maybe she could set up your meeting."

"Ella, we cannot bring an outsider into the *Masquerade*. I just do not know enough about her or her family to know if she is trustworthy. There must be someone who can set up a meeting for me."

"Nicky, if you are that concerned, perhaps I can make the arrangements after all."

"You!?"

"Yes. It just dawned on me that I have the perfect reason to go to Italy. I will visit Rome openly, to gather information for the rule of my order. It should cause little attention if I request an audience with the Pope, since I have been to the Vatican before and have been received by his Holiness. I am sure because of my rank I will receive a private audience. At that time I can broach the subject of your visit."

"It is very risky. The Holy Synod would not look favorably on your trip."

"I am not planning on telling any of its members. They already think my ideas are radical enough. No use fanning the flames. If your dream is true and the Pope is expecting you or has a message for you, I am sure he will respond in some way if I bring your regards. And as Tsar you can deflect any criticism that may develop while I am gone."

"Ella, I think this will work. I have a special gift I wish you to bring him, a single perfect pearl of the finest luster. I know that nothing exists on earth like the pearl I saw in my dream but if Pope Pius X has any knowledge of it when he sees the gift it will be a sign for him to trust you. Tell him the person who sent this gift requests a private meeting with him"

"Perfect. I will gauge his reaction to your gift to judge how much I can say. The rest will be easy, Nicholas. You can just wear plain clothes and assume a false name and no one will know who you are."

"You don't mean a masquerade, do you?" he teased.

"Do not be silly," she chided him. The question now is how are we going to get you to Italy?"

"That is actually taken care of," Nicky replied. "I have a visit to Italy scheduled for October."

"Is it an official visit?" Ella asked.

"No. Actually it is a private call on Victor and Elena." The two were the King and Queen of Italy. "Tentatively I plan to go alone. My excuse to leave Alix at home will be her health and that of Alexei."

"What does Alix know about all this?"

"She knows about my dream but I told her nothing about Rome or my poor finger," he said ruefully as he rubbed the digit in question. "I shall miss it," he added.

"Nicky, stop it! Would you like me to talk to Alix? Surely we must tell her about your trip."

"I will tell her in my own time. She would be very displeased that I discussed something with you before I did with her. I imagine I would never hear the end of it and it would not help if she became excessively jealous of our conversations. We have too much work to accomplish. It is not that I wish to keep secrets from her but rather to protect her health."

"Very well," Ella replied. "I will begin to plan my trip as soon as I return to Moscow. It should not be too difficult. Since Sergei was killed I have limited my official duties so I will have all the time I need to make the arrangements."

"I do not have to remind you that secrecy is of paramount importance," Nicholas cautioned her.

"I fully understand, but Nicky something has been bothering me. In all our conversations you have never mentioned what you are going to do with the children when the time comes."

"You are correct, Ella and there is a good reason. At this point I really do not know. Russia will not be safe, so I will send them out of the country. Where, I do not know?

"But people will know they are gone. How will you explain that?"

"Ella, I just don't know yet. I cannot send them away until the last minute. Alix would not be able to tolerate it and I do not want to send them too far from Russia. Once this revolution is over and Nikolasha has freed Russia I want them to return to their birthright. At times though, I must admit that I have doubts and imagine they may never be able to come home. In that case I think they could go to the United States. They are fluent in English and that country is so vast it would be easy to hide them there. At any rate, I do not think I will be able to come to a final decision until I complete this trip to Rome."

"There is time to resolve this very important element of the plan. Do not worry; we will all be with you to help you through this. Never forget, you are not alone."

Nicholas appreciated Ella's support but knew he would not rest until he went to Rome. Once he completed that trip he felt he would have a clearer understanding of what he must do. In his head, he could still hear the refrain, "come to me, come to me".

"I will telephone you when I have made the arrangements for your audience," Ella said.

"No, you must not use the telephone. The lines are unreliable and it is too easy to eavesdrop on our calls. Just send me a telegram and use this code. *'I have sold the pearl.'* I will know all is arranged and you can follow up with the details in a letter, but do not use the regular post. Have it hand carried by your most trusted retainer."

"Yes, I will use the utmost discretion," Ella assured him.

The two had been out for quite awhile and it was very chilly so Nicholas turned back to the palace. They remained silent on the return trip and the Tsar realized his plans were starting to come to fruition. The wheels were turning now and he knew that he could not turn back. Ella was equally pensive but as the car approached the palace she turned to Nicky and asked, "when will I know my real role in the *Masquerade*?"

"All in God's time, my dear, all in God's time," replied the Tsar in a voice full of emotion.

Chapter 16

August 1909 – Livadia. For the first time in several years, the Emperor had decided to spend the late summer and fall in the Crimea, the tropical-like peninsula which jutted out from Russia's coast along the Black Sea. Alix's health had continued to be a cause for concern and Dr. Botkin, the family physician, recommended the mild climate of the Crimea not only for its restorative powers but also for its calming effect on her stress. And so, Alix, the children, and the ever present Anya Vyrubova joined Nicholas for the journey to Livadia, the Imperial palace near Yalta. Dmitri Pavlovich, the Tsar's cousin and ward, was also included in the group.

It was a long and tiring trip and even the luxury of the Imperial train could not offset the dust and summer heat. The journey from Tsarskoe Selo south to Moscow and then on to Sevastopol took days to complete and the sun beating upon the metal roof of the train made the heat in the compartments nearly unbearable. The setting of the sun in the evening hardly lessened the stuffiness of the cars and it was almost impossible to sleep. However, despite the discomfort of the train, there was a festive air during the entire excursion. At each village and town crowds of Russian people lined the route, eager for a first glimpse of the Tsarevich, the five year old Alexei. And when the train made one of its infrequent stops for water or fuel, the enthusiastic throng had to be held back by soldiers posted for the Tsar's protection. The excitement was contagious and spirits were high for the entire trip until finally, after six days, the train pulled into the station at Sevastopol.

Nicky was pleasantly surprised by the warm reception of the local people who had gathered to greet the Imperial family. The excesses of the 1905 revolution seemed to have been forgotten and the festive mood of the town was evident in the waving flags and decorative bunting. The *Standart* had sailed weeks earlier and made its way from the Baltic, into the Mediterranean, and thence through the Straits of Gallipoli to the Black Sea. It was now anchored in the harbor waiting to take the royal party on the last leg of the journey. A red carpet had been laid from the train station down to the pier, where a launch waited to take the royals out to the Imperial yacht. Groups of townspeople were gathered on the hills around the station and lined the path down to the sea. The warm weather, with its light breeze, was perfect for a walk and after the long train ride, the Imperial family was pleased to stroll along the carpet laid in its honor. People began to push in on the police cordon but Alix, who was caught up in the adulation of the crowd, directed the authorities to allow the people closer. The Grand Duchesses and Alexei waved enthusiastically while they made their triumphal way to the wharf. Nicky could hardly believe that Sevastopol had been a hotbed of revolutionary intrigue only a few short years ago.

The family, guests, and retainers boarded the launch and were ferried out to the *Standart* to begin the voyage to Yalta. It was a short sail and they arrived in the afternoon after a delightful cruise around the peninsula. Here, as in Sevastopol, the crowds were enthusiastic and the town festively decorated with flowers. When the yacht was moored to the pier a band struck up *God Save the Tsar* and Nicholas led the family down the gangway. A delegation of officials and local children performed the official greeting and presented the Empress and each of the Grand Duchesses with lovely bouquets of fragrant local blossoms. Then, a troop of traditionally costumed Tatars swept into the square on horseback, each man appearing as one with his mount. The Tatars were an Islamic group indigenous to the Crimea and were renowned for their horsemanship. The escort was led by one of the elders, a noble looking gentleman named Hassan who sat his horse as if born in the saddle. It was an ancient prerogative of the Tatars to escort the Tsar and the duty was considered an honor by these people, who loved and revered the Imperial family. Nicholas was pleased to see that Hassan was still active since it had been a number of years since their last trip. Olga and Tatiana were the only two children who had any real memories of this wondrous place.

The Imperial family and their entourage loaded into carriages and cars for the drive to Livadia. Even though it was late summer, the range of mountains ringing the peninsula and providing a protective cloak from the cold winds of the north, still had a snow cap on its distant peaks. Escorted by the horsemen, the carriages rolled past thick forests and through a lush green valley. The rich, natural vegetation of climbing vines, flowers, and shrubs created an Eden that seemed to have been prepared by God for their very own use. A local flower with a deep mauve color was a favorite of Alix's and it scented the air with a fragrant aroma.

The estate was very large and to ensure additional privacy it was left, as much as possible, in a natural state. When the vehicle carrying Nicholas and Alexandra entered the gates marking the beginning of the Imperial compound they were enveloped by a sense of peace and serenity so intense that it seemed all their cares and worries had suddenly become manageable. It appeared that Dr. Botkin had prescribed the right medicine. The palace was concealed from the main road by a screen of trees and when it finally came into view there was some disappointment expressed by the younger children. The building was a large, rather depressing, wooden structure, surrounded by balconies on all sides. At first it seemed forbidding but on closer examination one had to admit that it exuded a certain warmth and charm. The family had not visited Livadia for five years and the house had been maintained by a skeleton staff during that time. It was slowly falling into a state of disrepair, but nothing could dampen the enthusiasm of the children and soon its gloomy atmosphere was permeated by the sounds of the laughing youngsters. In spite of the servants best efforts to prepare the house for their arrival Alix was not satisfied and soon she had a list a mile long of rooms to be aired, furniture to be polished and flowers to be arranged. After the long train ride she was, to everyone's surprise, bursting with energy and soon the Empress had everyone settled into their quarters and clothes unpacked. When she was finished getting everything organized she settled down with Nicholas in the dining room, the only room in the house that was cheerful and bright.

"My darling sunny, I have a wonderful surprise for you," Nicky eagerly informed Alix.

Her eyes lit up in anticipation, "Oh Nicky, whatever can it be?"

"This old building has served our family well for many years but it is time for something new. I have engaged the local architect Nikolai Krasnov to design a new home for us. You know he is the one who oversaw the construction of George's Harax."

"I have always admired your cousin's estate. It reminds me so much of England."

"It will be so wonderful to have a home we have designed ourselves and I want it filled with all the latest equipment. Krasnov will meet with us and you can give him all your requirements"

"I would love for it to be light and airy, not like these gloomy, old rooms," said Alix.

"I believe we can have the plans completed by the time we leave and then when we return again, it will be to take up residence in our splendid new palace."

The two continued talking late into the night, discussing possible designs, as excited as two young children with a new toy. For the first time in months there was actually something they could work on together and they both looked forward to sharing the project. In the back of Nicky's mind, however, was the nagging awareness that they would not have that many years to enjoy it.

The next day dawned brightly, without a cloud in the sky. Nicholas invited Dmitri to come with him to inspect the guard posts around the palace compound. He had come to love this boy and considered him part of his family. Dmitri had grown into a fine looking young man and would celebrate his eighteenth birthday during this visit to Livadia. It made Nicky envious to look upon the vibrant and healthy Dmitri and realize his own son Alexei, because of his illness, would never enjoy many of the activities the Emperor shared with his ward.

The two made their way to each of the guard posts in turn and the assigned soldiers snapped to attention. The Tsar conversed effortlessly with the men and set them at ease with questions about their families and homes. He dismissed many of the posts because he considered the security excessive. By the time they returned to the main house, Nicky and Dmitri had collected a whole detachment of soldiers and Nicholas was amused by his security chief's reaction when their group marched into the courtyard. The Tsar did not normally interfere with the chain of command but this morning he felt so alive that he had to share his mood with the men he was so attached to. To make matters worse he suggested to the officer-in-charge, in the hearing of all the men, that he give them the rest of the day off. The officer was not pleased, to say the least, but he would never question the Tsar's authority.

Upon completing their rounds Nicholas and Dmitri returned to the house, changed into their bathing costumes and joined the children and their nurses for a swim in the sea. The weather was wonderful, not too hot, nor too cool, just perfect for a day at the beach. All of the children had been taught to swim after an incident when one of the girls had been knocked over by a wave. Nicholas felt it was an important skill for each of them to have, especially since they spent so much time either at sea or in the sea. Each year they grew more proficient. The older girls ventured farther out with Dmitri while the two younger ones built sand castles. Alexei waded in the water while the ever watchful Derevenko looked on. Another sailor named Nagorny, was also assigned to watch him and the two sailors alternated this demanding duty.

The days at Livadia slipped into an easy routine. A daily swim was followed by lazy afternoons relaxing on the balconies and enjoying the cooling ocean breezes. Alix had arrived mentally and physically exhausted from the long trip to the Crimea, but each day away from the stress of the court, she grew stronger and more relaxed. She had started off by just lying on a chaise each day but now she had progressed to driving out into the country side. She had even mentioned to her husband that she was thinking about going shopping, something she would never have considered in St. Petersburg. Here in the Crimea the relaxed atmosphere was conducive to activities never dreamed of in the north and nothing prevented the Imperial family from enjoying the local community. Alix, who always had concern for others, when she was well enough, was aware that many hospitals in the area treated tuberculosis patients. As much as she was able she vowed to help the afflicted victims. In the meantime she, at the least, planned to visit the wards with her children so they could see with their own eyes suffering in the midst of all this beauty. Although they were growing up in great wealth she wished to teach them charity for the less fortunate.

Amidst these lazy days only one thing marred Nicky's sense of peace and that was the lack of any communication from Ella. He began to worry that something might have prevented her from making the necessary arrangements. He realized his concern was misplaced, however, when he received a telegram from her which read, *"I have sold the pearl."* Ten days later a sealed packet from Ella was placed in his hand by a trusted messenger. She had been able to arrange his meeting with Pope Pius X to coincide with his trip to Italy, in October. She wrote that her stay in Rome had gone smoothly and that no one suspected the real reason behind her visit. The Pope had received the Emperor's gift without comment, almost as if he were expecting it and he did not question that the Grand Duchess was the Tsar's legitimate representative. Nicholas was pleased with Ella's efforts. He was to call on the Pope at his villa at Les Combes, which was north of Rome. Nicholas would be staying in Racconigi, near Turin, so he would have to travel south for the meeting. He was relieved that he would be able to avoid being seen at the Vatican. Yes, it was to be an unofficial visit but he knew these things had a way of getting twisted about. He was relatively unknown in Italy so, if he was careful, he anticipated being able to travel without being recognized.

Now that Ella's arrangements had gone so smoothly, he could put aside that concern, for the time being, and enjoy the remainder of his stay at Livadia. He talked Olga and Tatiana into a long walk to Harax, George's estate. He started off with his two daughters at a leisurely and ladylike pace until they were out of the sight of the ever watchful Alix. Then his two girls ran down the trail with abandon. After about an hour hike through the thick forest they reached George's estate. He was happy to greet them and offered everyone refreshments. George had two daughters and soon Olga and Tatiana were happily playing with their cousins. As soon as the girls were occupied, George and Nicky adjourned to the library. Upon entering the room, Nicholas realized they were not alone. A tall man in his early thirties stood up. He had dark hair and warm brown eyes and something about him seemed different.

"Nicholas, I would like you to meet my dear friend from America, Charles Brantingham."

"Ahh, an American," said the Tsar. "You are quite far away from home, my friend."

"Yes, your Imperial Highness, but I go where duty calls and my immediate superior is a very demanding man," said Brantingham. He than excused himself and left the library so the two royals could converse privately.

"I assume this is the representative from that American bank. I am not too pleased, George I specifically requested a senior officer, not this young man who works for someone else."

"Nicky, you are wrong. Charles has all the seniority he needs. He works personally for Frank Vanderlip, the president of National City Bank in New York City. Mr. Vanderlip has given Charles full authority to negotiate on his behalf. Charles is extremely capable and handles 'special situations' for National City Bank."

"He seems so young," said Nicholas, rather doubtfully.

"Do not let his youthful appearance fool you. He is an extremely intelligent and talented young man. I think over the next few weeks we will be able to accomplish much."

"You know I trust your advice in these matters so I will acquiesce and give your Mr. Charles Brantingham a chance. With the amount of money we are talking about I am sure Mr. Vanderlip would not have sent just any banker to accomplish a mission of such importance."

Charles Brantingham was to remain in the Crimea for another six weeks. Nicholas made the walk over to Harax two or three times a week to meet with him. He and George conducted negotiations with Mr. Brantingham in the utmost secrecy. The financial transactions were extremely complex especially since it was necessary for the Tsar's deposits to remain anonymous. A series of secret codes and files were set up that effectively hid the Tsar's involvement. Although the bulk of the money and gold would not be leaving Russia until a later date the procedures to make this happen were put in place. Gold in moderate amounts would be shipped from Vladivostok to Japan from where it would be transferred to another vessel and make its way to Canada. Once safe at a location in Canada it would eventually be shipped into the United States. An alternate route would end in San Francisco. The details of the intricate plan were hammered out over a period of several weeks and both Nicholas and George were satisfied with the results.

On one day, after the negotiations were completed, Nicholas pulled George aside and filled him in on his upcoming trip to Italy. He did not give his cousin the reason behind his journey except to let him know it had to do with their plan.

"I will need Count Tatishchev to accompany me so it is time to bring him into the *Masquerade*," said Nicholas. "He will be my only companion except for my footman and valet, Aleksei Trupp. Make sure he does not bring his uniforms as they will not be appropriate for this particular assignment." He asked George to arrange for Tatishchev to arrive a day or two before he departed for Italy. The Tsar then walked back to Livadia with Olga and Tatiana, who, as usual, had joined him on his walk to Harax.

The last summer days blended into early fall and preparations began for Nicholas' trip to Italy. The selected route was a circuitous one because he wanted to seem a tourist and thus avoid any emphasis on what had become the real purpose of his trip, the clandestine meeting with the Pope. On October 6 he would sail in the *Standart* to Odessa and than complete the rest of the journey by train traveling through Germany and France and then into Italy. A few days before his departure he decided to tell Alix the true reason for his trip. If he were to return with part of his finger missing she would never forgive him for not confiding in her and he braced himself for what he knew would be a difficult discussion. He found Alix relaxing on the balcony, enjoying the view of the sea. They talked comfortably for a few minutes, but Nicky could not postpone the inevitable, and finally, with reluctance, he brought up the subject which he had concealed from her for so many months.

"Alix, I have something I wish to discuss with you," he informed her. "Do you remember the dream I told you about in which Blessed Serafim appeared to me?"

"How could I forget since you were so insistent I not discuss it with our friend, Grigory," she replied.

"That is so, but I withheld some of the details when I related it to you. I just did not feel the time was right."

"What are you talking about Nicky?"

"There was another person in my dream with St. Serafim. It was Pope Pius X."

"The Pope? Surely you are mistaken Nicholas. What could the Pope possibly have to do with St. Serafim?"

Nicholas proceeded to relate the dream to her in detail including the part about cutting off his finger. Alix was incredulous. "I will never believe St. Serafim wishes you to cut off your finger. It makes no sense to me. This dream must be from the devil."

"Alix, I admit that I am confused about some aspects of the vision but I believe it to be true. I received the sign and you saw with your own eyes the brightly lit, night sky. I must make this trip and I will have no peace until I do. When I finally meet the Pope I will know the truth of this dream and maybe more of what lies ahead for us. Surely you understand, my dearest Sunny."

"Are you really going to cut your finger off? It seems so extreme."

"I do not know what is going to happen, but I am prepared for anything."

"Well then, I am going with you."

"No, Alix. You will not be able to go on this trip. I have already made arrangements and they do not include you."

"But Nicky, I do not understand. We are hardly ever separated and I want to be there for you."

"I appreciate your concern Sunny but this is something I must do alone. I will conduct this trip as planned, with my visit to Victor and Elena the apparent reason for it. I am sure Victor will place a motorcar at my disposal and I can slip away for a day or so to meet with the Pope. Even though I will miss you terribly, your presence would bring increased attention, which is something I must avoid at all costs."

"I am not happy about this Nicholas. I cannot believe you did not discuss something this important with me. We should have planned this trip together."

Extremely upset and not wanting to talk any longer, Alix excused herself. She proceeded to sulk for the next few days. Finally the day arrived for Nicholas' departure, and he said good-bye to Alix privately as she refused to leave her room to see him off. He was sorry to see her so out of sorts but as he went down the stairs to get in the waiting car his mind was already focusing on his undertaking.

Alix stood at the window watching Nicholas depart and as his figure disappeared from view she was filled with remorse at her behavior. Who knew what he would have to endure on his trip and she had given him nothing but grief. She had been anything but the loving, supportive wife. Alix drew the curtains to her room, lay down in the darkness, and refused to see anyone, even the children. Later, she would get up and write an affectionate letter to Nicky, but for now she was content to be miserable.

The trip Nicholas had begun was a long and significant one but everything went smoothly and when the train arrived safely in Frankfort, Germany, Alix's sisters, Victoria and Irene, and her brother Ernie, got on the train with Nicky and rode with him for awhile. It was a nice break from the monotonous travel and he enjoyed an early tea with the lively group. They eventually disembarked in Worms while he continued on to France, traveling through the night. Finally at nine o'clock the next morning he arrived at the Italian border. The train then proceeded on to Racconigi where Nicholas was warmly greeted by Victor and Elena. The King and his wife turned out to be gracious hosts and he was relieved that they had not scheduled some activity for his every waking moment. The Italian Court was much more relaxed then its Russian counterpart and it was a real blessing not to have the secret police dogging his every move. As expected, Victor provided Nicholas with a car and the Tsar was free to come go as he pleased. In a few days, when the opportunity presented itself, he planned to slip away and travel to Les Combes for his long awaited meeting with the Pope.

In the meantime the Tsar spent the time enjoying the hospitality of the Italian royal family. In the evenings Nicky spent time with the children. He had brought them an authentic Russian village as a gift and spent many hours with them setting it up. Near the end of his visit, Nicholas set off with Victor in his car for a tour of the local area. They drove around Turin in the morning and visited all the sights and later, in the afternoon, the two monarchs went grouse hunting, an activity Nicholas always enjoyed. The fresh air and camaraderie, as well as the booming of shotguns, distracted him but they could not totally relieve the tension that was trying to build within him. He had made the decision that he would leave early in the morning for Les Combes and it was all he could do to get through the day. So much planning and effort had gone into arranging this secret meeting that the thought something might happen to prevent it was too much to bear. That night Nicky informed the King that he and Count Tatishchev would spend the next two days motoring through the Italian countryside and would find overnight lodgings on the road. Victor offered to provide a guide, a thoughtful gesture which Nicholas, under the circumstances, tactfully declined.

Early the next morning, shortly after dawn, Ilia Tatishchev pulled the car around to the front of the villa where the valet loaded some pieces of luggage. Trupp would remain behind to pack for the return trip to Odessa. Nicholas climbed into the vehicle and Tatishchev sped off, motoring south to get well clear of Racconigi. When they were some distance from the town the Count pulled off the main road and stopped behind a small abandoned house.

He and the Tsar went inside and began to put on their disguises. Tatishchev had made the decision to keep it simple so the costumes were limited to simply cut, dark suits of the design a middle class Italian merchant might wear. They had debated about the Tsar's beard and had seriously considered shaving it off but in the long run they both agreed it would create more problems then it solved. Instead they settled for a trim in the fashion that seemed popular with men here in northern Italy. The finishing touch was a pair of clear spectacles which completely altered his appearance. Nicholas voiced his approval of the disguise. "A fine job, Ilia," he said as he glanced into a mirror the Count held in front of him. "I do not recognize myself."

"Your Highness, the transformation is amazing. You look like an Italian business man. I could pass you on the street and not know you."

"Well, since we do not know the condition of the roads I suggest we drive on and have a quick lunch when we get a little closer. Right now I have butterflies in my stomach and I couldn't possibly eat anything." The Tsar was justifiably nervous because this entire escapade, as involved as it had become, was based solely on a dream, a dream supposedly confirmed by strange lights in the sky. Nicholas was about to meet the man who had called out to him, in his vision, and beckoned him to come. Well, he had come, and in a few hours the long wait would be over.

The Tsar and Tatishchev arrived at the Pope's villa in Les Combes in late afternoon and drove up to the gates of the compound. They were immediately challenged by the Swiss guardsmen on duty, who had no orders concerning the visit of two business men. The Tsar, of all people, understood security measures and was impressed by the efficiency of the Swiss. He asked that a note be carried in to the secretary. It read, *"The man who sent the pearl is here."* The response was immediate and the car was directed around to a side entrance where the two men were met and then escorted into the private office of the Pope. His Holiness immediately stood up to greet the Tsar and his companion.

"For some strange reason I had a premonition that today was the day we would meet," said the Pope. "It is an extraordinary blessing that we have been brought together at this time."

"It is an honor and pleasure to finally meet you, although I feel I have known you for a long time," Nicholas replied.

"I felt the same sensation when you first entered the room and am at a loss to explain just why. Perhaps when we talk things will become clearer," answered the Pope.

"Is it possible that we speak in private?" asked the Emperor.

"Yes, of course." The Pope directed his secretary to entertain the Count with some refreshments and arrange for overnight accommodations in town. In a moment, Nicholas and Pius were alone.

"Please sit down and make your self comfortable," urged the Pope.

"I have been sitting all day and would like to stand for a few moments, if you do not mind. I am here to talk to you about something of grave importance and I am anxious to begin."

"I understand totally, but before you start let me give you a gift I have had prepared for you." The Pope opened a drawer in his desk and removed a small velvet covered box which he handed to the Tsar. When Nicholas opened the box he was rendered momentarily speechless. Nestled in the opened velvet case was a gold ring with an anchor on it and he recognized it instantly as the ring the Pope was wearing in his vision. He took it from the case and clutched it to his heart. He looked up at the Pope and said, "then you do know," as a tear slid down his cheek.

"My son, we are both a link in a great chain. All who work towards the deliverance of Russia are part of this chain. It spans time and it begins with Serafim."

"Then you know of Saint Serafim?".

"Yes, and I know the struggle you went through to have him canonized. Did you even know then it was all part of God's magnificent plan?"

"I only felt in my heart that it was the right thing to do and at that time it was all I had to go on. The Tsarina was the driving force behind it all and if not for her intervention things might have turned out differently. At any rate, during his canonization I was approached by an old woman who had known St. Serafim personally and she gave me a letter written by him years earlier. I want to share that letter with you now."

From his inner coat pocket he removed the yellowed letter and handed it to Pius, who carefully opened it. The Pope was unaware of the existence of the letter and, as he read it, Nicholas could see he was deeply moved. When he was finished he looked up at Nicholas with loving concern.

"My son, you shoulder a great burden but remember you are not alone. Look at this white cassock which I wear. Do you not think that the mysterious man in white referred to by St. Serafim is a future pope of our church? Could he not be another link in the chain?"

Nicholas listened carefully to what the Pope was suggesting. It was possible, he supposed, and would explain plausibly the one element of St. Serafim's letter that he had never understood. However, his anti-Catholic prejudice had prevented him from even considering such an option. This bias against anything Catholic was the main reason his decision to go to Italy had caused him so much anguish. He had to admit, however, that this pope, with his gentle and comforting demeanor, had broken down that intolerant attitude, once and for all. Of course, the ring, in its velvet box, helped quite a bit.

"Perhaps you are right, Holiness, but let me recount to you the details of the vision that bought me here." Then in a voice brimming with emotion he related his dream to Pius, in its entirety.

When he was finished he appealed to the Pope in a voice filled with distress, "why am I here? I am so confused."

"My son, think for a moment what has happened in the short time you have been with me. First, you have been promised the support of my church. I guarantee my successors will know of this pledge and keep it. Next, through the obvious intercession of St. Serafim, working through me, you have had the one element of the letter you did not understand explained to you. And lastly, through the miraculous coincidence of the rings you have had your vision verified once and for all. Although the Grand Duchess was very discreet when she approached me, and disclosed nothing, I could only gather you are making extensive plans and therefore the secrecy. Whatever you are planning will succeed, I pray, most splendidly. Yet I sense something else is troubling you. What is it?"

The Tsar sat quietly, trying to find a way to verbalize what had always been his main concern. Finally he raised his small finger and asked the Pope. "When?"

"You will have to decide when to sacrifice your finger and blood. You will know when the time is right."

"Your Holiness, how will I know these things? What do I do with my flesh? How will I be able to preserve it?"

"Nicholas, the timing of all of this will become clear later, but you must trust in God. The preservation of your finger is not important in the present but will be in the future. I can tell you that you need not worry, for one day the precious vial containing your sacrificial offering will be preserved at the Vatican and protected for the future. In your lifetime you will not understand the reason for this but know that one day it will be the key to proving your children's lineage."

The Pope had referred to Nicholas as "his son" more than once. The Tsar was used to being called "the father" of Russia but he found something comforting in the way the Pope addressed him. He no longer felt that he was carrying the fate of Russia and that of his family on his shoulders alone. He knew he could now share the burden with "each kink in the chain." From the Tsar's point of view that meant each member of the *Masquerade*.

"God in his mercy has given you these signs but he will not make your decisions for you," said the Pope. "But know that we are a resource for you and will assist you, however we can. Now go in peace."

Nicholas had the feeling that Pius knew more than he had revealed and he would have liked to continue the conversation but he recognized that the Pope was tired and the audience was at an end. He stood to leave, bowed over the Pope's hand and kissed his ring as a sign of respect. He could not explain the complete feeling of trust he had in this man in white but he felt that he could count on the Vatican to provide assistance when it became necessary.

The next morning Nicholas and the Count left Les Combes and motored back to Racconigi, changing into their regular clothes on the way. When they reached the villa they were met by Victor and the children who were quick to notice the Tsar's new style of beard. When they pressed him about it he laughed it off and explained that he had to take something of Italy back with him. "You needn't have worried about that Nicholas," Victor exclaimed. "I am sending gifts back for your family. Your man Aleksei has been most helpful and has everything arranged for your final departure. You can leave in the morning if you wish."

"You have been most kind and I hardly know how to thank you for the wonderful hospitality," replied Nicholas.

"Nonsense, Nicky. We have all enjoyed yours and Ilia's company. Your visit has been much too short and I wish I could talk you into staying on."

"As much as I would like to stay, I feel I really must get back to the family. We are rarely separated for this long a period and I do miss them. No, we will leave in the morning as scheduled."

"As you wish, but let us go in. Elena has had a marvelous farewell supper prepared for you and I am sure you will enjoy it."

୧୨୭

The long trip back to Livadia was uneventful and when the train finally pulled into Odessa, Nicholas could see the *Standart* at anchor in the harbor, awaiting his arrival. He sent word to the Captain to bring the yacht into the pier so the luggage and gifts could be loaded and as soon as that was completed the vessel got underway for Yalta and the reunion with his family.

The children and their mother waited anxiously on the pier and watched as the Imperial yacht appeared on the horizon and headed in toward the coast. The children had not seen their father for several weeks and could hardly contain their excitement.

"Here he comes," hollered Anastasia.

"Oh, I have missed Papa so much, I thought I would die," said Maria rather dramatically.

"Mama, how long until his ship gets here," asked Tatiana.

"It looks like it will be at least thirty minutes," answered Alexandra.

"Thirty minutes," wailed Olga. "It might as well be three hours."

"Calm yourselves girls, it will get here in due time.".

"I wonder if he brought us something from Italy," inquired Olga.

"I am sure he has something for everyone," replied her mother.

As The *Standart* drew closer to shore the girls' excitement increased, especially when they could finally see their father on deck waving back at them. Alix was just as excited as the girls, but she had been ill since Nicholas departed and only recently gotten back on her feet. Her face was pinched and drawn and she knew she looked frightful but the tension created by their strained parting had overwhelmed her. Alexandra had wanted desperately to accompany him and she still could not understand why he had not let her go. Nevertheless, she was ashamed of the way she had behaved and anxious to provide a warm homecoming. The Empress was unaware that Nicholas had hardly given their parting a thought, so engrossed was he in the details of the trip. As the ship slowly made its way to the pier she caught Nicholas' eye and knew immediately that all was well with them. He looked very happy to see her and, as she watched, he held up his left hand which, she could see, was clearly intact. When she let out an audible sigh Nicky grinned at her and then turned his attention to the children who were waiting impatiently to board the yacht. Finally, after what seemed an eternity, the gangway was in place and the girls ran to greet their father. In a moment all four girls were nestled in their father's arms.

"Oh, my sweet girls, how much I missed you."

"We missed you too, Papa," answered the girls in unison. They stood there with their father, all trying to talk at the same time, each vying for his undivided attention. Suddenly a loud, screeching noise echoed from one end of the ship. It sounded inhuman, almost as if an animal were in pain.

"What was that, Papa?" inquired Olga with a confused look upon her face.

"It sounded like an animal or maybe a horn," said Tatiana.

"I am going to see," said the bold Maria. The Tsar laughed in delight as he watched his daughter's reaction to the noise. They headed towards the sound of the racket and as they drew near they were amazed to see five sailors struggling to manhandle a braying beast. They were attempting to drag it to the gangway but were having little success.

"Papa, isn't that a donkey," asked Olga.

"Yes, it is a gift to you children from the King and Queen of Italy," said Nicholas. "It also has a marvelous cart that goes with it, but the crew will need to bring it up from the cargo hold," said Nicholas.

"Can I ride in it first," asked Anastasia.

"No," answered the Tsar, "I want Alexei to sit in it first and try it out. Your mother says he has not been able to do much lately and if he feels up to it I want him to try it out, before you girls."

"All right, Papa," said Olga, "but I get to be second."

"No, I called it," cried Anastasia.

"No, you called first, Anastasia," scolded Olga, "and you cannot go first and I called second."

"I call third," quickly interjected Tatiana.

"And I am after Tatiana," called Maria.

"That's not fair," cried Anastasia as she found herself suddenly at the end of the queue. She ran to the nearest deck chair, threw herself down in front of it, buried her head in her hands, and began to cry. Maria looked over at her little sister and could not bear to see her in such a state. The two younger girls were known as the "little pair" and sometimes it seemed as if they were left behind by the "older pair" when it came to receiving attention. Maria had a big heart for a young girl of only eleven. She walked over to Anastasia, bent down, and rubbed her back.

"It is all right Ana, you can take my turn, and I will go last."

"Are you sure Maria?" she asked.

"Yes and maybe, if there is room for two in the cart, you can drive me around," she said.

"Oh yes, that would be so much fun and we can play make believe."

"Yes, we will be the beautiful princesses being chased by the two evil witches. Olga and Tatiana can be the witches," Maria whispered to her sister.

"That sounds like so much fun, Maria. Papa! Can you hurry them along with the cart?"

The Tsar was amused at his youngest. Weeping one minute and radiant the next. Capable of the most outrageous and mercurial mood swings. Sometimes the tyrant, sometimes the victim, but always the prankster. Maria, on the other hand, seemed almost angelic by comparison and the concern she showed for her younger sister was genuine and heartfelt. The girls were all so different and he loved each of them for their good qualities and, like the doting father he was, he tended to ignore their faults. Alexandra was much harder on the girls then he could ever be. At any rate, the scene he had just witnessed reminded him how important his children were to him. All his planning and sacrifice would be worth the cost if his children could live to see the future. The braying of the donkey brought him back to the present.

"Girls we must disembark, so the donkey can be unloaded. We do not want to be in the way. You could get hurt if he starts bucking and kicking." The girls all filed off the yacht with Nicholas following behind. He made his way over to Alexandra, gave her a quick kiss, and rubbed his son on the head. "Oh how I have missed you my precious Sunny," the Tsar whispered to his beloved wife. He wished their reunion had not taken place in such a public location. A tear glistened in her eye as she struggled to maintain her composure. Her Nicky was back safe and sound. She picked up his left hand and scrutinized it carefully. "Oh, thank God Nicky, it is still there."

"Yes Alix, but this is not the time to talk about it. We will discuss it later," he said. Their attention was drawn to the gangway where several sailors were trying to get the donkey off the ship. The animal's lack of enthusiasm for the maneuver was evident as it bucked and lashed out at the handlers. Subdued curses could be heard from the sailors as the donkey landed a few good kicks. The family was so amused by the sight that they could not control their laughter, but their entertainment was cut short when the donkey broke free and ran down the gangway. It avoided capture and charged down the dock toward the road, with the seamen in pursuit.

"Do not worry children, they will catch him," reassured the Tsar. "In the meantime let us examine the cart."

They had just begun to look at the cart, which had been placed on the dock, when a loud shout came from the road. "Watch out! Watch out!" They looked up to see the animal running at a full gallop back toward the ship. When it reached the pier the donkey stopped suddenly next to the cart. He began to sniff the wheels and, evidently, the familiar smells calmed him down. The Tsar signaled for everyone to stay back. He slowly approached the donkey and took up the lead rein that was attached to its halter. He gently stroked the frightened donkey and spoke soothing words to it. "You will be all right, my little friend. You will live here and we will take good care of you." Nicholas directed one of the sailors to take charge of the animal and bring him to the stables. "I think he might need to rest for a few days and get used to his new surroundings before we take him out riding." The Grand Duchesses were disappointed but they knew their father was right and none of them were quite ready for a wild ride.

Once back at Livadia, with supper over and the children down for the night, Nicholas and Alexandra took a few minutes alone so they could discuss the trip to Italy. Since the evening was pleasant they sat quietly in the garden and enjoyed the gurgling of the fountain and, from far below, the sound of the surf crashing on the shore. Finally though, Alix broke the silence.

"I am so sorry darling Nicky. I do not know what came over me but I never want us to part again in anger. I was beside myself and, after you left, I knew I would never forgive myself if something happened to you. I know this trip was important to us and our family and instead of support all I gave you was grief. Please accept my heartfelt apology."

"My dearest Sunny, the past is in the past and we have many things to discuss, so let us not waste time dwelling on what we cannot change. I understood and sympathized with you but it was something I had to do alone. Let us not speak of it again. My trip was very interesting to say the least." Nicky then proceeded to relate the events of the trip including the secret visit with the Pontiff. When he was finished he took out the ring Pope Pius X had given him and showed it to Alix. She would now be brought into the *Masquerade*, but ever so carefully, and in a manner that she could handle emotionally.

"What is the significance of this ring?" she asked. "It certainly is unusual."

"Alix, it is the ring the Pope wore in my dream. During my audience with him he gave it to me as a gift and as a sign of the authenticity of my vision. I was completely amazed and to this day I cannot explain how he could have known. None the less, I am satisfied that I had a mystical experience and the Pope agrees with me. By the way, Alix, I want you to know that this pope is a saintly and holy man, a person that we can trust and depend on. This trip validated my dream, just as the sign from St. Serafim did. We can no longer hope that the predictions in St. Serafim's letter will not come to pass. I am more convinced of its relevance today than when I read it for the first time. I know these things are difficult to believe but we must be prepared to act on them. Until I went to Italy I kept hoping that the letter merely contained the ramblings of a saintly old man and that we would rule Russia for many years. I have procrastinated too long. Now we have confirmation and now we must plan."

"Darling, I am simply overwhelmed by all that has happened. It is so much information for me to digest that I truly do not know what to say. I must admit you seem to have come to terms with all that has occurred. I am glad you have peace."

"Alix, I know this is a hard subject to broach so suddenly but, at some point, we will have to send the children away. It is going to be extremely difficult and the possibility exists that we will never see them again. You are going to have to prepare yourself for that eventuality."

"But what about Alexei, he will never survive without me to properly care for him."

"By the time we send the children away Alexei will be a young man. He will be old enough to care for himself."

"Oh Nicky! It is almost too much to bear," Alix sobbed.

"Alix you must remain strong for the children. I have seen your strength in a crisis and know you have it within you to withstand the evil that will beset us. This will be the biggest challenge you will ever face but do not despair. It is still several years away and we have time to give our children the memories which will sustain them through what lies ahead. They are our legacy and the future of Russia."

"What of these plans you mentioned?"

"Really, there is not much more to tell you at this point other than I am working out the financial details. Now that my visit to the Pope has been completed I can begin to move ahead more quickly. But for the present you should begin to prepare yourself mentally for what we have discussed. I also want you to understand that whatever I tell you must be kept between us. You cannot share it with anyone. I must be your only confidant." Nicholas did not want to leave Alix in the dark but at this stage in the planning he felt it best if she knew as little as possible. He was still troubled by Rasputin's influence on her and was afraid she might let something slip. Anya Vyrubova was another potential source of a leak, not that she would deliberately endanger the family. Anya was really the only close friend Alix had and because she was the conduit between the Empress and Rasputin, she was privy to most of the family activities and thus a potential danger. He rose and led Alix back inside. He felt he had given her enough to keep her occupied. Too much might cause an emotional response and that was something he did not want.

A few days passed and then the Tsar allowed the children to drive around in their new cart under the careful supervision of several seamen. One of these was Anatoly Vasilyev, who had saved Anastasia's life on the *Standart* just two years ago. His loyalty to the Tsar was unquestionable and the children loved him. The Tsar felt a deep sense of gratitude to him and therefore Vasilyev was given many special privileges. Nicholas had promoted him to the rank of junior officer and at the age of sixteen he was the youngest officer in the Russian navy. Due to his youth, the Tsar kept him on the palace staff and assigned him to help with the children, a task which usually went to lower ranking seamen. Vasily did not seem to mind and secretly enjoyed the company of the young girls. One by one he helped the children into the cart and let them have a turn driving around the courtyard.

When Olga's turn came he helped her into the cart and smiled at her blushing face. Olga was engaged in her first flirtation and she thought Vasily was the bravest man in the world. She imagined being married to him and taking his name. Of course, it was all pure fantasy because Olga, the daughter of a tsar, would never be allowed to marry a commoner. The Tsar allowed the innocent flirtations of his daughters with the sailors and officers knowing full well that he would never permit anything serious to come of it.

With the children fully occupied Nicholas decided to go and see George. He was still in residence at Harax so Nicky decided to walk over. He enjoyed this private time and had to admit he was going to miss the warm Crimean air. It seemed like they had just arrived at Livadia and it was hard to believe it was almost the end of October. Soon they would be departing for Tsarskoe Selo.

George greeted him fondly and the two found a quiet alcove in his garden where they could converse. George updated Nicky on the progress of his negotiations and Nicholas was satisfied with the results. Everything seemed to be on schedule and for this he was grateful.

Nicholas told his cousin about his trip to Italy and for the first time revealed to him the real purpose of the lengthy journey. He recounted Ilia Tatishchev's role in the scheme and told him about his audience with the Pope. George was surprised to hear of it but knew that the Tsar would not have left his family unless he considered the reason vital to the development of the plan.

"I was impressed with the Pope and although I conducted some negotiations of my own what I really came back with was the confidence that what we are doing is necessary and right. I feel like a new man and am ready to move forward with our preparations."

"That is good to hear, Nicky. I am glad your trip was so fruitful."

"I would like you to arrange to have a large dowry set aside for each of the Grand Duchesses. I think the Vatican's financial institution would be a perfect place to hide their money. No one would ever think to search for it there."

"I will get started on that as soon as possible. I think we are going about this correctly. The first shipment of gold has started on its way and to the best of my knowledge there has been no suspicion about any of the money leaving the country."

"I am pleased to hear that, but George, one thing that has been weighing most heavily on my mind is the question of where we are going to send the children."

"Have you given any thought to the United States?"

"It is on my list of possibilities but not one I particularly favor. I do not agree with their politics and it is so far away. I want the children to be able to return to Russia as soon as possible, when it is safe again."

"This is going to be a challenge because the first place anyone will look will be where your relatives live," George replied

"Well, that eliminates Germany, England, and Denmark. I have been mulling something over in my head these past few days. What do you think of Japan?" asked Nicholas.

"Japan? Our mortal enemies. Have you lost your mind?"

"Wait, George. Hear me out. Relations have improved between our two countries and in fact last April we hosted a representative from Japan. His name was Prince Kunin and he brought the regards of the Imperial Family. He told me something very intriguing which is what got me started down this path. Do you remember when that maniac tried to kill me all those years ago when I visited Japan?"

"I was not on that trip but I remember hearing about it from your Mother," replied George.

"My point is that the Japanese Imperial family feels dishonored by what happened and even though a war intervened they still want to make amends for what they consider a dishonorable act. I am convinced this is the reason why our captured sailors received such good treatment after Tsushima. At any rate, Prince Kunin expressed their wish to settle this debt of honor. Perhaps we can manipulate the situation to our benefit. I feel certain if we sent the children to Japan, the Emperor would personally ensure their safety."

"I have to admit it has possibilities. No one would ever look to your enemies."

"The cultural differences would pose a problem but it does have the advantage of being close. Unfortunately, the children will not be able to blend in with the locals but I am sure we will be able to come up with a way for them to hide. It is something to think about and I do agree with your point that we cannot look to the usual places. Of course, the most difficult part will be to keep their departure a secret. Five young lives depend upon the success of the plan. One positive aspect of our withdrawal from the social activities of the Court and the secluded life we live at Tsarskoe Selo is that hardly anyone would recognize the girls if they saw them on the street"

"Nicky, so far I find all your reasoning sound. Using code words and keeping the *Masquerade* as compartmentalized as possible will ensure our success. Your idea of having separate cells is crucial. We must keep the participants focused only on their own piece of the puzzle. It is also important they do not know who else is involved as then they cannot discuss their assignment with each other and risk exposure. Although the people who are in the *Masquerade* are all your most loyal subjects and family members we can take no chances. For example, you have already told me more than I should know and now Count Tatishchev knows I am involved. We would give our life for you and we all recognize the dangers but we must be more careful. What have you told Alix?"

"Only as much as necessary," replied the Tsar. "We will be returning to Tsarskoe Selo for the winter. I will use that time to reflect and pray and hopefully come up with some answers. We have much work to do, so put your mind to it, dear friend." The Tsar then left Harax for his solitary walk back to Livadia.

Nicholas used the solitude on the way back to review all the developments of the past few months. He was so engrossed in thought that he was oblivious to the beauty around him. He was anxious to come up with a plan he could commit to but the question of how to save the girls, as St. Serafim had directed in the letter, still eluded him. To resolve all his uncertainty he knew he must work slowly and deliberately, analyzing each step carefully before committing to a course of action. As he continued walking, the fresh air lightened his mood and put a bounce in his step. He looked forward to seeing Alix. He loved her passionately and despite her emotional problems their loving relationship was the one thing that sustained him.

Chapter 17

November 1910 - Tsarskoe Selo. The individuals who made up St. Petersburg society could be likened to a pack of hungry wolves, constantly in search of sustenance. Unlike wolves, however, they found their nourishment in gossip, innuendo, and groundless rumors, all hyped by the newspapers, and eagerly spread by enemies of the royal family. The Empress was the usual target of this vitriolic campaign and it was to be expected, because she had never been welcomed by the Russian courtiers. In fact, they had treated her poorly since the day of her engagement and when the extremely shy Alexandra had reeled back in dismay at this hostility, they disliked her even more. She countered by retreating into the relative seclusion of Tsarskoe Selo and deliberately ignored the howling of the pack. This decision to withdraw from public life was a conscious one, because, as her family grew, she was determined to shield it from what she rightly saw as the immorality of the court scene. When some state function demanded it, she would make an appearance, but she did so with such obvious reluctance that it just added fuel to the fire. She had but a handful of friends to turn too and among them, unfortunately, was Grigory Rasputin

Salacious stories about Rasputin and his involvement with the Imperial family were not uncommon but it seemed to Alix, from the reports she was receiving, that they were becoming more frequent and more vicious. Alexandra decided it might be a good time for Brother Grigory to return to Pokrovskoe to visit his family, in hopes that the talk around St. Petersburg and the Imperial court would quiet down. Rasputin normally traveled with a small retinue of devotees, usually women, so the Empress invited Mary Vishnyakova, the children's nurse, to accompany Rasputin to his home as well. Mary looked forward to the trip as she was an enthusiastic adherent to the "holy man's" teachings and Alix was happy to reward her for her support of "their friend." Alix felt a twinge of envy that she could not join Mary on the journey to the staret's home but she knew it was impossible.

Three weeks later, upon her return from the trip, Mary requested an opportunity to speak to the Empress. When they met Alix was surprised to see that the nurse was emotionally upset, her lips quivering and her pale face streaked with tears.

"Mary, what is wrong, why are you so upset?" she asked with concern in her voice.

"Your Imperial Highness, I have something dreadful to tell you. Father Grigory crept into my room when I was staying at his home. He drugged me and then did terrible, terrible things to me," she sobbed. "He took my virginity."

Alix was speechless. She looked at the sobbing maid and controlled the urge to slap her. This was not merely some rumor from the city but was an accusation by a trusted servant. The Empress felt no sympathy for the maid and looked upon Mary's account of the incident as just another effort to discredit "her friend." Alix was so under the influence of Rasputin that she would not, could not, accept the word of this tearful young woman.

"I have heard enough," she said through clenched teeth. "How dare you slander Father Grigory's good name? I refuse to believe any of your tales. You must have imagined these things." She told Mary to return to her duties with the Grand Duchesses and to speak no more lies about the holy man.

Mary left the Tsarina's presence and climbed the stairs to the children's wing. She was in total shock at what had just occurred and she could not believe that the Empress thought she had made the story up. It made no sense because Mary had always been Rasputin's friend and had no reason to fabricate such a tale unless it was absolutely true. She cringed as she thought of the horrible episode, of those dirty, hairy hands pawing at her and her inability to prevent this person, someone she had trusted so completely, from violating her. When she reached the head of the stairs her whole body was trembling and she paused to compose herself before going into the girls. It would serve no purpose for them to see her like this and, since Mary really had no one to confide in, for the present she would have to hold tight to her emotions in the silence of her heart. Finally under control, she went in to help the girls ready themselves for bed. She ran their baths and set out their nightclothes and dressing gowns and then turned down their beds. Maria and Anastasia shared a room and Tatiana and Olga shared an adjoining room, but they all shared the same bathroom. When the girls were ready for bed they all congregated in Olga and Tatiana's room where they talked about their day. Mary sat on the bed with Anastasia brushing her long hair.

"Why do they say that you must brush your hair one hundred times every night before you go to bed, Mary," asked Anastasia.

"Oh, I think it is just one of those old wives' tales, Anastasia," she answered. "I would imagine if you brushed your hair that many times every day, you would soon have no hair to brush." All the girls laughed when she said this. Mary was like a mother to them and she treated them as if they were her own daughters. She loved them and wanted the best for them and because she was so protective and took her responsibilities so very seriously, the girls felt they could confide in her and tell her things they would not share even with their mother. She spent more time with them each day than any other person at the palace including their parents.

The door opened suddenly to reveal Alexandra and Rasputin standing side by side at the entrance. The Grand Duchesses quickly scrambled for their dressing gowns. Mary rose to her feet in disbelief and it was all she could do to remain calm. She could not understand how the Empress could bring that man up here after what she had revealed to her and she trembled at the thought of being in the same room with her rapist?

Alix could see that Mary was quite upset and dismissed her for the night. As she passed by, Rasputin smiled at her smugly.

"Good evening, Mary, may God watch over you," he said.

Alix had confronted him over Mary's accusations and he denied everything, suggesting instead that the nurse had imagined the whole thing while in a drug induced state and Alix was more than willing to accept his explanation. Mary closed the door behind her and burst into tears as she made her way to her room. It distressed her to leave the Grand Duchesses in the presence of such a libertine, especially when they were in their nightclothes. She could not believe their mother did not notice how uncomfortable they were.

Rasputin blessed each of the children in turn as Alexandra looked on with a smile. She felt honored that this "man of God" was here to bless her daughters. "Matushka, will you leave us," asked Rasputin. "I wish to pray with the Grand duchesses and counsel them."

"Certainly Father Grigory, I know God inspires your every word."

"You are right my dear one, I do not take a breath without his approval," said Rasputin, as Alexandra left the room.

Although all the girls were intimidated by this man in black, they realized there was safety in numbers and they really had little to fear from him if they stayed together. The controlling emotion they felt was one of curiosity as to what this unannounced get together was all about. With the quick awareness of youth they had perceived the unhealthy influence this frightening man had on their mother and each had vowed that he would never manipulate them in the same manner. It was hard for them to understand how a woman as strong as their mother could be exploited by a man like Rasputin. She was so fastidious about everything and even though the monk was fairly well-groomed when he came to the palace there was still the sense of something not quite clean about him. Yet, in spite of themselves, they were intrigued by some of the things he said and did.

Rasputin had given up on his efforts to induce hypnotic trances in the Grand Duchesses and had fallen back on his fortune telling routine in an effort to exert some control over the girls. He was frustrated by his inability to dominate them and he could not understand why he continued to fail when he had success with so many others. He could not recognize what the children knew instinctively. He was no match for a team of strong willed sisters working together. Only Alexei was susceptible to his efforts and that was a different case altogether.

"My darling children, I would like to tell each of you what I foresee in your future," said Rasputin. He sat in a chair in the corner of the room and summoned Anastasia first. She was nervous and looked to her sisters for support.

"Go ahead Anastasia, he will not harm you," said Tatiana. Anastasia walked hesitantly over and sat in the chair next to him.

"Now give me your hand," he said softly. She did as he asked. He held her palm and stared at it long and hard and then looked up at her. "I see you far away in America and you will have many husbands, Anastasia." She pulled her hand back and after determining that this was not the proper future for a princess, she refused to hear anymore.

Maria approached next and sat down. "So Father Grigory, what do you see in my future?" she asked. He looked into her eyes for a long time as if he were lost in them. "Father Grigory, what do you see," she demanded.

"I see you in Poland and you are wearing black but you have a baby growing inside you and it will be a girl," he told her.

"What about my husband? What does he look like? Is he handsome?"

"I see no husband," said Rasputin.

"Then I must be wearing black because I am in mourning and my husband is dead," said Maria with a look of sadness on her face. "My poor child will have no father. Surely you are mistaken Father Grigory. There must be some explanation."

"I cannot say little one, I cannot say."

Maria got up and walked towards her sisters. "Come on Anastasia, let us go to our room, I am tired," she said. Anastasia stood up and followed Maria into the other room.

"I wonder what is wrong with her?" asked Tatiana.

"I guess she did not like what he told her," answered Olga.

Rasputin got up and moved over to where the two remaining girls were sitting. "So what is in store for us, Father Grigory?"

Rasputin looked at the two girls and responded, "One of you will do something very brave in the future, but you will lose your life in doing so."

"And what of the other," asked Olga.

"The other will be vaporized," he said with a very serious look on his face.

"What does that mean," asked Tatiana. Before he could reply, the Empress came in to escort Rasputin out of the girls' room and take him downstairs.

"But Father Grigory, what does it mean," shouted Tatiana. Alix looked at her reprovingly and Rasputin merely smiled as they left the room.

"That was ridiculous," said Olga. "I think he just talks nonsense like that to scare us. He must know how we feel about him. So Tatiana, do you want to die the hero or be vaporized," asked Olga sarcastically.

"I shall be vaporized, whatever that means," she said dramatically and they both laughed.

Lying in her bed in the other room Maria could hear her sisters' laughter but it was a different story for her. She had believed what the staret told her and she could not stop dwelling on the fear that her husband would die before the child was born. How would she manage and what would it be like having a daughter of her own? It was several hours before she fell asleep and even then she tossed and turned the remainder of the night.

The next morning Mary entered Tatiana and Olga's room to help them prepare for the day. "Good morning girls, did you sleep well?" Mary asked. When she was alone with the girls, the atmosphere was very relaxed, with first names used, and titles ignored. Olga and Tatiana helped Mary make the beds and tidy up their room.

"Mary, are you feeling all right?" questioned Olga. She was very observant and had noticed the nurse's pale skin and the dark circles under her eyes.

"I am well. Why do you ask?"

"I noticed that when Father Grigory walked into the room last night you turned pale and I thought for a moment you might faint," said Olga.

"I would rather not talk about it," said Mary, "but I hope that you will both be cautious around Father Grigory. You girls must watch out for each other. Promise me," she pleaded.

"Yes, of course, we will," replied Olga.

"Mary, you must know that Olga and I do not like the man at all," said Tatiana. Mary was surprised to hear this. She had always believed that the whole imperial family supported Rasputin because they always seemed happy to see him when he came to the palace.

"I know what you are thinking Mary," said Olga. "We always seem so excited to see him, but I promise you it is nothing but an act."

"That is true," added Tatiana. "Mama and Papa, adore him, so what can we do but pretend we feel the same."

"If we never saw the man again that would be fine with us," said Olga.

"Well, all I can say is that he treated me very, very badly when I went to his home in Siberia," said Mary. "I would never trust him. What ever you do, never drink or eat anything he gives you. Promise me," she said.

"We would never," said Olga. "But he is always giving things to Alexei and Mama."

"And you should hear his absurd fortune telling," interrupted Tatiana. "He said one of us would be vaporized."

"What does that mean," asked Mary.

"It means nothing, he just made up all these strange tales about our future," said Olga. At that moment Maria and Anastasia walked in from the other room.

"Good morning everyone," said Anastasia. Maria sat down on a chair next to the bed. She had rings under her eyes from her restless night.

"Poor Maria, did you not sleep well?" Mary asked when she noticed the exhausted look on the young girls face.

"No, I did not. Father Grigory said he saw me in Poland with a baby in my stomach and that it was a girl. I was dressed in black. You wear black when you are mourning someone's death and since he said he did not see my husband, I know he must have died," she rambled on. "It was just dreadful. I kept picturing my poor children with no father and me to manage all alone."

"Maria, don't be silly," said Tatiana. "None of that is true; he was just trying to scare us."

"Yes that is right," interrupted Olga. "He said Tatiana would be vaporized."

"What does that mean," asked Maria.

"It means nothing," said Olga. "He just made it up to upset and scare us so we will not speak badly of him."

"Besides Maria, what could you possibly be doing in Poland? There are no princes for you to marry there and I am sure that Papa has already decided whom you will marry and where you will live. Why not ask him," said Tatiana.

"Yes, I think you may be right," said Maria. "Mama wears black all the time and she is not in mourning. I am sure you are right and I will not worry about it anymore, but I am still going to ask Papa whom I will marry. How exciting! Do you think he really knows?"

Mary helped the girls dress for the day and then hurried them off to the classroom for their lessons. She began straightening up their rooms when Baroness Sophia Tyutcheva, the maid of honor came in. "Have the Grand Duchesses left already?" asked Sophia.

"Yes, you just missed them. They are already in the classroom starting on their lessons," said Mary.

"I must meet with them about their schedule."

"Before you go, may I have a word with you?"

"Yes, of course. Something is bothering you, isn't it?" She could see from the look on Mary's face that something was very wrong with her. The two women sat down and Mary's eyes began to fill with tears. The situation was so embarrassing and painful for her that it was difficult to speak of.

"Oh, what is it my dear. It hurts to see you in such a state," said Sophia.

"Something terrible has happened and I have been afraid and so ashamed to tell anyone," sobbed Mary. She went on to recount to Sophia all that had transpired on her trip to Pokrovskoe, with Rasputin. She also explained about her encounter with the Empress and how devastating it had been when she refused to believe her. "She said I should stop telling such lies about Father Grigory and that I should not discuss this matter again. Last night when I was tending to the Grand Duchesses and they were in their nightclothes the Empress walked in with Rasputin. I was so horrified I thought I would faint. She dismissed me but as I left, Rasputin smirked at me. You should have seen the look in his eyes, but of course the Empress was blind to what was happening and thought nothing of it. It was so frightening for me."

"I am so sorry Mary that you had to go through such a horrible experience," comforted Sophia. "Did you say the Grand Duchesses were in their nightclothes?"

"Yes, but they did have their robes on."

"That is completely unacceptable," replied Sophia. "I wonder if the Tsar is conscious of what is going on, and the fact that this man attacked you. I cannot believe that Rasputin would be allowed to roam the palace as he wishes if his Highness was aware of the situation. I will speak to the Tsar about this at once."

"I will certainly lose my position at the palace over this," said Mary.

"You did nothing wrong Mary, and should not have to suffer any consequences. I will see to that. Something has to be done immediately, but try not to worry yourself over this. I will handle it, but please, for the present, do not speak to anyone else of this. We sail on dangerous waters where the Empress is concerned."

Sophia left the room and immediately went to make arrangements to see the Tsar. She left word with Count Benckendorff that it was of the utmost urgency that the Emperor see her as soon as possible. Later in the afternoon, the Baroness was summoned to the Tsar's library where she was announced by the footman and shown into the room. The Tsar put out his cigarette and rose from his chair. "Now what is so urgent that you must speak to me? Are my daughters causing you grief," he asked.

"No, no your Imperial Highness, they are wonderful children." She took a moment to collect her thoughts as she was very nervous about the topic she had to discuss.

"It is about Rasputin. May I speak freely?" The Tsar nodded his assent.

"I spoke with Mary this morning and she said that Father Grigory was in the Grand Duchesses' bedroom last night when they were in their night clothes," she said.

"Was the Empress with him," inquired Nicholas.

"Yes, initially, but at some point she left. Father Grigory stated he wished to be alone with the children."

"What do you think of him," asked the Tsar.

"Again, may I speak freely, your Imperial Highness?" asked Sophia.

"Yes you may, and you need not ask permission again to say what is on your mind," replied the Tsar.

"I think he is a sick individual and no man of God. I believe he is possessed by the devil and I am convinced he will cause great trouble for your family."

"What would you say if I told you that he has done wondrous things for my family," said Nicholas.

"I would say that he has done more harm than good for your daughters," she said.

"What has he done that is so terrible? My daughters love him."

"No, your Imperial Highness, they love their mother, but her friend is not necessarily their friend, and sometimes, as you well know, things are not as they appear. I am very concerned about his penchant for visiting them when they are in their nightclothes. It is just not the appropriate time or place for him to be alone with them. He has a frightful reputation and, if it was my decision, I would not let him near your children."

The Tsar leaned back in his chair. He was playing a slippery game and although he agreed with Sophia completely, he could not, for the sake of his wife's fragile temperament, put voice to his true thoughts. On occasion he had objected to some effort by Alix to include Rasputin in their private affairs. The time at Livadia when she wanted to immediately tell the elder about her husband's dream came to mind. He had been right to put his foot down then but when speaking about Rasputin with others he usually tried to walk a middle path. Still, he was finding it more and more difficult to defend a man who he believed was stealing his wife's mind. Reports such as the one Sophia was now sharing with him just added fuel to the fire burning within but it was a measure of his inner strength that he was able to maintain the gentle demeanor that most people found so appealing. At this point he tended to adopt a *laissez-faire* attitude but he had to be cautious in playing the game. One slip and Alix could find out how he really felt about the man and then who could predict what might follow. Better one "holy man" than a hysterical wife. Of course, he was unaware that his two older daughters were playing the same game and were playing it just as well. It was a shame they did not know each other's true feelings because it prevented Nicholas from drawing on the strength of Olga and Tatiana. What a great treasure to have had someone to whom he could unburden himself.

"Father Grigory is telling the girls all kinds of strange things and he fills their heads with frightening predictions. He even said one of the girls would be vaporized," Sophia continued.

"I do not believe that is even a real word. He must be teasing them. I am sure it is all innocent."

"There is nothing innocent about that man! I have not told you the worst. He is a debaucher of innocent young women. He drugged Mary Vishnyakova and then attacked and raped her." When the Tsar heard this he began to seethe inside, but he would not let it show. He sighed inaudibly then removed a cigarette from an ornate box and lit it. He inhaled deeply and then exhaled a cloud of smoke.

"Certainly you do not believe this story?" asked the Tsar, as he composed himself.

"I do believe every word of it. Have you not heard all the reports about his behavior?"

"Apparently all lies. The Empress questioned Father Grigory and he denied the story. He said she was drunk. If anything did transpire between them she must have seduced him."

"Please your Imperial Highness, think of your children. How could you believe Rasputin would ever admit to such heinous behavior?"

"Why were you not present last night when Father Grigory visited the children?"

"I was informed by the Empress that my services were not needed in the evening. I had the distinct feeling she did not wish me to be present," she told the Tsar.

"Well, now you have new instructions. Every evening I wish you to be in the children's wing until they are tucked away for the night."

"What about the Empress?"

"You have your orders. She will not interfere with you," said the Tsar.

"Thank you," said the Baroness, who was surprised by the Tsar's turn about. When he spoke in support of Rasputin it seemed to Sophia that his words lacked conviction. At least that evil man would not be upstairs anymore, she thought, as she went back to her duties.

The Tsar sat back and puffed away on his cigarette, the smoke billowing upwards, as he considered what had just transpired. Alixs' attitude made it so difficult to have a rational discussion about Rasputin, because she sincerely believed "their friend" was keeping Alexei alive and would accept nothing to the contrary. The troubling aspect, from the Tsar's point of view, was that Father Grigory did really seem to have the ability to alleviate his son's pain and to calm and soothe him during his attacks. Nicholas was unwilling to take any action that might prevent Alexei from gaining some measure of relief from the terrible pain he suffered.

This business of Rasputin's visits to his daughter's bedrooms, however, was a separate matter altogether. He would speak to Alix tonight and explain that he did not wish Father Grigory to go upstairs in the evenings unless Alexei was sick and then only if accompanied by herself or one of the household. He was always to be announced, well in advance, so the girls could be properly attired. After all, it was a question of their reputation. Nicholas knew she would be miffed and demand an explanation but this was one of the times he intended to prevail.

He played his game well. On the occasions when Rasputin came to the palace in the evening Nicholas sat and listened to him with what seemed to be rapt attention. Alix may have had her suspicions, but she never guessed his true feelings.

CR80

While the Tsar was dealing with internal family matters at Alexander palace, on the other side of the world a very different type of activity was talking place. A south bound train had stopped at a small rural station in New Jersey and, in the early morning hours, a number of men began to arrive at the depot in chauffeured limousines. Somewhat furtively they dismissed their drivers and limos, took their luggage and entered the last car of the train. It was a luxurious, private car belonging to Senator Nelson Aldrich, the powerful chairman of the National Monetary Commission and it was carrying the men to a meeting which would later prove to have a significant impact world wide. As the passengers arrived they took individual seats and even though they knew each other, for the most part, they kept to themselves. Once everyone had arrived the private train sounded its last warning whistle, pulled out of the station and picked up speed. Its destination was the small port town of Brunswick, Georgia, and speed was regulated by the engineer to ensure arrival at a time when not too many people were about.

When the locomotive and cars pulled into Brunswick the men detrained and were met by autos, which transported them to the waterfront. From there a launch took the group out to the secluded and exclusive Jekyll Island. Located on the bay side of the island, was the Jekyll Island Club, a bastion of wealth and prestige. Developed by J. P. Morgan, it was a club that catered to the wealthiest in America and its membership was open to only a select few. This loose brotherhood included the Rockefellers, Vanderbilts, Pulitzers, Goulds, Astors, Morgans, and Cranes. It was rumored that one seventh of the wealth of the United States was represented by its membership and it was obviously a very influential group of people.

It was an unseasonably cold November and the group from the train huddled down in their heavy coats to protect themselves from the chilly winds as the launch proceeded towards its destination. Finally, a gleaming white dock appeared in the distance and the craft headed in its direction.

Senator Aldrich was accompanied by Abraham Andrew, the Assistant Secretary of the U. S. Treasury, Frank Vanderlip, President of National City Bank, and Henry P. Davison, Senior partner of the J.P. Morgan Company. Also included were Charles Norton, President of First National Bank, Benjamin Strong, head of Bankers Trust Company, and Paul M. Warburg, a Senior Partner of Kuhn, Loeb & Company, which was part of the Rothschild banking cartel. They were some of the most powerful and influential men in the banking industry and it would have been front page news if word slipped out about their secret meeting.

The bankers looked on with interest as they approached famed Jekyll Island. The dock extended from a shoreline covered with huge live oaks hung with Spanish moss. The screen of trees hid the legendary resort from view. The island had been left in a mostly wild state and was covered with thick vegetation and forests, but through the tops of the trees a few glimpses of civilization could be seen. A tower peeked out, part of the Victorian clubhouse, and from its window a man observed the boat through his binoculars. The arriving group was unaware of his presence in the tower and also unaware that he was the puppet master controlling the strings. J. P. Morgan was pleased to see that everyone he had invited seemed to be present on the boat.

With secrecy the order of the day, only a lone bellman met the launch as it arrived. The gentlemen disembarked from the boat and were directed up the dock to a gravel path which led to the Jekyll Island Club. Not a soul was seen until they entered the lobby of the elaborate Victorian edifice that served as the club house. Senator Aldrich directed the men to settle into their assigned rooms and to meet for lunch in the dining room in one hour. He told them to use first names when addressing each other and to talk to the employees of the club only when absolutely necessary. Most of our staff have been given the week off so we will have ample privacy as we conduct our business," he informed the group. The gentlemen then retired to their rooms while Senator Aldrich went upstairs to get his instructions from J.P. Morgan.

Later that day, after lunch had been served, the men began to address the issue that had called them to Jekyll Island. They were there to write a bill, which Senator Aldrich would present to the United States Congress, establishing what in effect would be a central bank for the United States. These bankers were treading on dangerous ground because the debate over the continued existence of a national bank, one in which the funds of the United States would be deposited, had nearly torn the young nation apart on at least two occasions. The presidential election of 1832 signaled the end of the Bank of the United States because it returned to office the bank's arch-enemy, Andrew Jackson. The president believed that such an institution was unconstitutional because it usurped the power of Congress to regulate money. When supporters of the bank tried to renew its charter four years early he vetoed the legislation, thus slaying what he always called the "monster." His main objection was that the bank loaned more money in the form of bank notes then it had hard currency to redeem. More importantly, while the bank had use of the government's money, it was controlled by a very few wealthy citizens who owned as much as eighty percent of the stock. It was too much power in too few hands.

The group gathered on the secluded island had its work cut out for it because these men were being asked to come up with a plan which effectively resurrected the "monster." The radical blueprint being proposed would effectively weaken the government's constitutional role. Of course, any banking scheme's purpose is to make money for the participants and this was no exception. The goal was to minimize competition in the banking field and thus increase profits, but with the support and backing of the federal government. The Panic of 1907, which led to the failure of a number of private banks, was used as the justification for the new intervention. Rumor had it that J. P. Morgan had engineered the Panic for this very purpose.

Over the next week they hashed out the draft of a bill which would eventually lead to the establishment of a new banking system. The title Bank of the United States was studiously avoided, because of its past history, and the designation Federal Reserve System was substituted instead. It was felt that this would imply Federal involvement in the bank and legitimize it, when in reality the Federal Reserve remained a private entity. To disguise the fact that they were setting up a central bank, twelve regional banks would be established, but the Federal Reserve Bank of New York, from which money would be disbursed to the regional banks, would control the whole system and would have the most power. The chairman would be appointed by the President but the system would remain private.

The men worked long hours as they wrestled with the minutia of financial regulations and as their discussions continued two problems emerged. The first, and most significant, was where the money would come from to set up the Federal Reserve. Second, assuming the Senator could get the legislation passed, how would they get the bill signed into law? For this they must have a man in the White House. The discussion continued with little progress until Frank Vanderlip spoke up.

"As to the problem of funding I can present a partial solution. I have a client who I think would be very interested in this opportunity. He has substantial resources to invest."

"That is very interesting Frank but you do realize the scope and size of what we are proposing. It is bigger than one investor," replied Paul Warburg.

"Let me just say that my man represents varied interests. I am not talking mere millions, but rather billions of dollars."

"All right, now I am interested. Who is this mysterious investor?"

"I think it is best for us all that he remains unnamed. It is for your own and his protection."

"I refuse to get involved in anything illegal," said Paul. "All we need is that trust busting president of ours to get wind of it. I don't know how many anti-trust suits President Taft has sponsored but we have all been affected." The others around the table nodded their heads in agreement.

"His investment will be entirely legitimate but from a political standpoint I believe it is better for him to remain anonymous at this time.

Just know that we will be able to use his gold and other assets for our purposes when the time comes," Vanderlip replied.

After discussing additional options for funding the system, they addressed the thorny issue of getting the legislation passed and signed into law. Senator Aldrich assured the group he had enough clout to get it through committee and felt it would pass by a slim margin on the floor, if they mounted an effective lobbying campaign.

"If you bankers come out as publicly opposed to it, I think it will have a better chance of passing," said the Senator. "

The people are distrustful of bankers and they will think if it is bad for you it must be good for them. Of course, if any one ever found out you had drafted the bill, it would be catastrophic."

"You can get the bill passed Senator, but the area we are going to have a problem with is getting it signed by the President. Taft has said more than once he is opposed to a central bank. He will see right through us and refuse to sign the bill," said Abraham Andrew. He was in a position to know the president's mind on this since he served as Assistant Secretary of the Treasury in Taft's administration.

The rest of the group nodded in agreement. Andrew had a good point. Taft was a popular president and it would be difficult to defeat him when he came up for reelection.

"We need to split the Republican vote," suggested Henry Davison. "If we could convince Teddy Roosevelt to run against Taft I think we would have a chance. We could fund his campaign as well as our man's.

"Just who is our man?" Charles Norton asked.

"We are looking at Woodrow Wilson," said Aldrich. "If we can get him elected to office than we will present this bill to Congress. If it passes, and it should, Wilson can sign it into law and we will be in business.

The financiers were well satisfied with their work and felt they had drafted an iron clad piece of legislation. It would be difficult to pass but the rewards would be immense if they achieved their goal. With their group working behind the scenes they felt reasonably sure of success.

Upon completion of the work on the draft, Senator Aldrich went to report to Morgan, who was extremely interested in who the mysterious investor might be. "Send Vanderlip to see me." Aldrich went to do his bidding.

Vanderlip went into the dark paneled study and was surprised to see J.P. Morgan. He suspected that he had been behind the meeting but due to its secrecy he did not expect to see him in person at Jekyll Island. "Have some bourbon," said Morgan as he poured him a glass from a crystal decanter. After a few moments of small talk he came right to the point and asked Vanderlip who National City Bank's mysterious investor was.

Vanderlip, knowing it would be impossible to dodge the question and aware that Morgan had the resources to find out anyway said simply, "the Tsar of Russia."

Not much surprised Morgan, but he was totally unprepared for Vanderlip's answer. "I now understand your desire to keep his identity a secret, but why do you think he is making these funds available?"

"He is being very secretive but from what I understand he wishes to safeguard his wealth outside of Russia. Perhaps he senses some internal threat, but at any rate he is prepared to deposit a huge fortune here during the next few years. My only concern is that at some point he will want it back and that could be expensive for us."

Morgan and Vanderlip talked for a few more moments and then Frank left to prepare for his journey home. He knew Morgan would be discreet because it was in his interest to do so. As for Morgan, he sat sipping his bourbon and thinking about Vanderlip's explanation. He is right. It could be a huge problem for them if the Tsar suddenly decided to withdraw his money. When the time came the Tsar's commitment would have to be thoroughly examined.

Chapter 18

January 1911 - Tsarskoe Selo. The air in the Tsar's study in the Alexander Palace was so thick with smoke that it seemed that anyone sitting there must surely be asphyxiated. However, love of a good cigar, some fine brandy, and meaningful dialogue with friends diminished the possibility that anyone would expire unexpectedly. As was more and more frequently the case, the topic of conversation was the *Masquerade* and Nicholas had invited his two trusted kinsmen, George and Sandro, to the palace to discuss more of the financial aspects of the plan. Although Sandro was one of the original group of five members he had not, to this point received any specific tasking, so Nicholas had decided to have him assist George with the finances. George had brought his brother up to speed on all the developments and Sandro had begun attending many of the meetings set up to negotiate the transfer of funds. The Grand Duke had been to America before, and the Tsar hoped he could add some fresh insight to their discussion. For the present, however, Nicky was listening with rapt attention as his cousin briefed him on the latest from Mr. Brantingham. George told Nicholas about the possibility of investing in a new central bank in the United States and how plans to do so were being worked out. But he emphasized that the creation of the financial institution was not an economic matter but rather a political one.

"How can that be," Nicholas interrupted, "It seems straight forward enough to me."

"Bear with me for a moment your Highness and I will try to explain," George replied. "You must first realize the American political system is like no other in the world. I have done some research and it appears that the American people in general have a historic aversion to publicly owned banks. It seems they prefer to leave banking completely in the private sector and they ensure that it remains there by voting for candidates that espouse this view. The group that is behind this effort to create what is, in effect, a national bank, is going to great lengths to fashion a financial structure so disguised that it does not alarm the American voter. In fact, they are being so secretive that I doubt it will even be a campaign issue. The public will not become aware of it until the legislation is introduced in their Congress and if the election goes as planned, it will be too late to block it."

"What do you mean by that ?" Nicky asked.

George went on to explain the United States electoral system in some detail and made it quite clear that a well financed group could influence the outcome of a general election.

"The people Sandro and I are working with represent just such a group and they have determined that the man they need to elect is a politician named Woodrow Wilson. If Wilson is successful in his run for the presidency he will sign into law an act establishing the Federal Reserve Bank and when the necessary arrangements are made we will transfer a significant portion of our assets to this bank."

Nicholas had listened carefully to George's presentation and he now gave his complete support to the arrangements.

"I must say, I am very pleased with what you have accomplished in such a short period of time, but let me ask you to consider whether we should contribute handsomely to this Mr. Wilson's campaign. Because our investment in the banking scheme is so important to our overall plan we must ensure that he is elected and that the financial institution on which we are depending comes into existence."

"I am not sure that is wise Nicky," George replied. "Wilson's backers are well financed and have come up with a plan to split the oppositions vote by introducing a third party candidate. You might be interested to know it is our old friend Theodore Roosevelt. At any rate there is little to be gained by chancing disclosure of our involvement.

"You are probably right," Sandro interjected, "but I can see definite advantages to putting Wilson in our debt. Perhaps there is some humanitarian foundation he supports that we could contribute to. That way we could earn his gratitude without becoming involved in his politics. Another option would be to funnel funds through Mr. Brantingham, who is already proving to be such an able intermediary. Either way Nicholas, why don't you let me work this angle and I will see to it that Mr. Wilson learns of our involvement. I might add that I find Wilson an interesting choice for president. I have been following the political news in the United States with great interest. One of Wilson's supporters is a Mr. Charles Crane. His name rang a bell with me and I decided to investigate. He is a wealthy businessman who has traveled quite frequently to Russia and his company, Crane Plumbing, won a contract for the Trans-Siberian railway. Interestingly enough he is very good friends with Count James Rostovstov, the Tsarina's private financial secretary. I think he could be a good contact to cultivate."

"I agree with you," replied the Tsar. "Go ahead and make contact with him and if you feel we can trust him we should use Mr. Crane to funnel money into Wilson's campaign rather than Brantingham."

"American politicians reward their supporters with high public office," George observed. "They call it, strangely enough, 'the spoils system.' It will be interesting to see what position Mr. Crane might receive if Wilson is elected. He could well prove to be very useful to us."

Having exhausted all the new aspects of the financial situation, George raised the issue which weighed most heavily on Nicholas.

"Have you come to any decision on where you wish to send the children," he inquired.

"I am still leaning towards Japan," Nicky answered. It has the benefit of not being too far from Russia, and no one would ever think to look for my children there. Since the Japanese Imperial family feels they owe me a debt of honor I think we should start easing into negotiations with them. We must establish contacts and then decide how we are going to approach the negotiations."

"Sandro speaks Japanese and has visited many times. Is that not correct?" George asked in a lighthearted way.

"Yes, I visited many times but I would hardly consider myself fluent. Besides your experiences are very similar, brother."

The Tsar smiled fondly at the two brothers. "I am quite aware of both your abilities. You have been my friends for too many years."

At that moment there was a knock on the door and a footman announced that Prime Minister Stolypin was here to see the Tsar on a personal matter. "Well, I think we have covered just about everything we had on our agenda so let me see what the Count has for me that is so pressing," said the Tsar. Stolypin was ushered in and after bowing to Nicholas he gave his regards to Sandro and George. He then said, "Your Imperial Highness I have an urgent confidential matter which I need to discuss with you in private."

The Tsar asked George and Sandro to excuse him and they left to continue their assignments. "Peter, what is it that is so personal you could not discuss it in front of the Grand Dukes?" The Prime Minister reached into his briefcase and handed him a thick file. Nicholas looked at it in surprise. "What is this?"

"It is the police file on Rasputin and I must warn you it is graphic and unsettling."

"Who ordered this inquiry and why was I not informed about it?"

"The police wanted to make sure all the information was accurate before presenting it, your Highness. In addition, they thought he might pose a security risk since he has relatively free access to the palace. Considering all the unsavory rumors which surround Rasputin it seemed wise to conduct an investigation and I gave my approval. I take full responsibility for it and I assure you I was acting in the best interests of your family. Unfortunately, it seems all the rumors are true. He has engaged in acts of unseemly debauchery in public places and bathhouses and his home is frequented by women of all classes."

"He ministers to the women who visit his home," the Tsar countered.

"I am sure that is what he calls it," said Stolypin.

"How can you say these things about him when you know him personally? Have you forgotten that he healed your own daughter?"

"I have not forgotten, but this is a very difficult and serious situation. He appears one way to us but in his private life he is completely indiscreet and his behavior has become quite scandalous. Unfortunately that is reflecting negatively on your family, especially the Empress. I will not dignify the rumors by repeating them but it is all there in the report. The papers are starting to print terrible things again and the Duma is up in arms."

"I do not understand why this has become a public matter. It is a private family affair and is no business of yours or the Duma's," replied the Tsar with some heat. But in actuality he was not really angry with Stolypin, who was an honest, loyal, and competent public servant. What disturbed him was the necessity of once again defending a man whom he did not trust, a man whose presence in St. Petersburg was becoming more and more disruptive and whose influence was growing immeasurably. Yet his beloved Sunny was swept up in this cunning monk's web and to attack Rasputin was to attack his wife, and this he could not do. Because he refused to say anything negative about the man, people thought him naive and indecisive. But he truly believed that his public and private life could be kept separate and whenever anyone spoke to him about Rasputin he always maintained it was a private family matter. He was not only the Tsar, but a father and a husband, and as such he felt some things were not open to public discussion. He even refused to discuss it with family members who had begun to voice their concerns. Nicholas was a very private man and regrettably many took his reticence as support for Rasputin when nothing could be further from the truth.

Stolypin did not lack courage and despite the Tsar's obvious annoyance he forged on, aware that the next few minutes would be very difficult. "Your Imperial Highness, your family's good name is being slandered in the newspapers. In addition to all that has gone before they now plan to publish a letter which they claim the Empress wrote to Rasputin. I have obtained the original and I am sure it is a blatant forgery, so we must go after the papers. We can use this letter as justification for our action." He pulled the letter from his pocket and handed it to the Tsar

Nicholas took the letter from the Count and when he looked at it, it was as if a dagger had been driven into his heart. He was looking at the familiar scrolls and swirls of his wife's handwriting. There was no doubt in his mind that it was not a fake. He looked up at Stolypin and said, "Do nothing, it is her hand- writing. Now I do not wish to discuss this further. As I have told you it is a private family matter. It is best that you leave."

"Your Imperial Highness, it would be best for all involved if Father Grigory were to leave St. Petersburg for a while so this scandal can blow over. Please think about it and let me know of your decision."

Stolypin left the study and as he departed he could see that the Tsar was visibly shaken. He could only imagine what Nicholas must have felt when he finally read the short note which seemed to suggest his wife's infidelity.

Nicholas looked at the letter written by his wife and was saddened but not surprised by the words she had penned.

My Dearest Teacher and Savior,

How bleak my life has been since you have left. Beloved, my heart aches for you I miss your touch and wish I could lay my head upon your shoulder and sleep forever in your arms safe in their strong and holy touch. Oh my friend how I need your presence. I ache for your company and your kind words. Oh how you soothe and calm me. I am forever yours.

Matushka

It had been written in the spring of 1908 and the Tsar was surprised that it had surfaced only now, after such a long period of time. It seemed to Nicholas to be innocent enough but he realized that enemies of the Empress would make every effort to attach the most obscene interpretation to her words and do everything they could to discredit her. Nicky knew that she had not conducted an illicit affair with Father Grigory. They shared the same bed and he was rarely apart from Alix. Also, her every move was observed within the palace and he was sure she had no opportunity. In spite of that, the feelings she expressed in her little note indicated a deep emotional attachment to Rasputin. Nicky could not understand that the feelings Alix had for this man were truly spiritual in substance and could not be equated with the enormous love she felt for her husband. Consequently he was deeply hurt and confused as to why his love for her, a love without conditions, did not seem enough for his beloved Sunny.

The Tsar sat at his desk and began to write in his secret diary, a place of refuge for his thoughts that even his wife was unable to read. He was working on a poem that expressed his true feelings, the ones he had kept hidden behind a façade of laughter and cheerfulness. The love he had for his wife was profound, but it had become an unrequited love and although the letters written between them were filled with loving and adoring words, these notes masked the reality of their true relationship. Alix had become a different person and in his desperate efforts to keep her happy he had continued to allow Rasputin into their lives, although it tore at his heart to do so. His wife could never know that he loathed this man and he disguised his feelings so successfully that even his own family believed he had fallen under the spell of a person he inwardly thought of as the mad monk. Nicholas placated the Empress with kind words about "their friend" and he even took advice about affairs of state from his wife and Rasputin.

Nicholas had become resigned to the situation but he was not fatalistic. He realized that it really did not matter what minister was in place or whose advice he accepted, the outcome would be the same. An evil cloud was slowly enveloping Russia, and only he, and members of the *Masquerade*, knew this with complete certainty. So when people said horrible things about him, it hurt, but he had to keep up the charade since he sincerely believed the future of Russia depended on it. Although he had told Alix very little of the plan, and insisted on her silence, he was tormented by the fear that if he allowed Grigory to remain she would unwittingly break her promise and confide in him. On the other hand if he sent Rasputin away and Alix became despondent, how could he be sure that her state of mind would not be just as dangerous to the plan?

The Tsar was convinced that Rasputin had done something to his wife but he could not be certain what it was. It seemed as if she had become addicted in some way to the ministrations of this so-called holy man but the obsession she exhibited appeared to be emotional rather than physical. Addiction was something, that although distasteful, he could understand because his brother George had become dependent on morphine and opium before he passed away from tuberculosis. Because of his brother's experience Nicholas was all too familiar with the signs of addiction. Alix suffered unimaginable pain and emotional distress because of Alexei's hemophilia so he understood her need for relief.

Now though, the appearance of this letter demonstrated that the situation was quite different. After reading Alix's note a second time Nicky concluded that her fixation with him had become much deeper. But love? How could this be true? Rasputin was so repulsive, and yet, Nicky had to admit, women were attracted to him. The tender feelings his wife once had for him were slowly being transferred to Rasputin. Where once he had been her best friend, the one she turned to in times of trouble for advice and aid, she now turned to Father Grigory. She played the part of loving wife well, but in private he could sense the change in her feelings towards him.

His diary was a friend and after recording his thoughts in it he felt a sense of peace. Now he finally felt calm enough to speak to his wife.

Nicholas sent for Alix and had her come to his study. She was very surprised at this and hurried to meet him. When she came in she could see he was visibly upset. Before she could say a word Nicholas said, "sit down Alexandra! We need to speak and please realize that I am speaking to you as the Tsar not as your husband." He knew this was the only way to get her to understand the seriousness of what he was about to say.

"Nicky, what is troubling you. I do not understand," she protested.

"Be quiet, my dear! I need you to explain this." He handed her the incriminating letter, which was undeniably in her handwriting, and placed the police report on the corner of the desk near her.

She looked at it in dismay. "How did you get this? It was a private letter."

"Well, Alix, it is not private anymore. The whole of Russia is probably reading it in the newspapers as we speak."

Alix was mortified. She could not believe that her private thoughts and feelings were now fodder for the gossip and innuendo crowd. She knew Nicky was very angry but she was confused by his anger. Surely he did not attach too much significance to the contents of the note. "Darling you know I write to everyone in that style. What are you so concerned about?"

"Alix do not play the fool with me. Your words are very suggestive and everyone who reads this letter will think you are carrying on an affair with Rasputin. I do not think you understand the seriousness of this. You are the Empress of Russia and this could be construed by some as treason. I have had people jailed for less."

"What are you saying Nicky? Are you going to have me sent to the Peter and Paul Fortress? I cannot believe you are talking to me this way. As if I would have an affair with a man of God. You do not care about "our friend" and never have or you would not believe the lies that this report must contain. I cannot believe you do not trust me," she said in a hurt voice. "Why has your attitude changed? We have always looked upon these sorts of things as private matters and this is just a silly misunderstanding."

Nicholas chose his next words very carefully. He knew Alix was hurt and hoped he had made his point. Now he must soothe her. "Darling Sunny, I can see that you are agitated but we must handle this situation together. What was private is now very public and I cannot bear for anyone to gossip about you. We must do what we can to smooth this situation over."

"I will not kowtow to our enemies. Saintly men are always criticized in their own time. I refuse to believe these negative stories about Father Grigory."

"Alix I want Father Grigory to go home to Siberia until this situation settles down."

"No, I will not allow it. His enemies will not win this time."

"I order it. He must leave St. Petersburg. I cannot guarantee his safety," he told her. "There have been threats." The Emperor really could care less about Rasputin's safety but he knew that his apparent concern would mollify Alix somewhat.

"If he must leave, let us send him on a pilgrimage to the Holy Land. We will have him out of harm's way and our enemies will not see us weakening our resolve."

"I will agree to the pilgrimage but you will have to make a concession."

"What is it?"

"I will not have Rasputin in the palace. Because of the rumors of his indiscretions he can hardly be considered a paragon of virtue. and I do not want our daughter's reputations tarnished. When we wish to see him, have him visit Anya's house. We will be able to see him there without drawing too much attention to ourselves.

"All right Nicky. I will agree to your restrictions but we will see how long they last when your son becomes ill and Grigory is the only one who can save him." Nicky nodded and then gave Alix a warm embrace. "My darling we will get through this situation if we place our trust in God."

A few days later, Alexandra met Rasputin at Anya's house. When she arrived at the cottage she asked for a moment of privacy and Anya left the room. Alexandra wasted no time coming right to the point. "Why did you not destroy my letters? And how did they end up a matter of public record? You must understand how serious this is."

Father Grigory looked at her with his mesmerizing eyes and said, "Matushka, Matushka, these things that upset you are of this world. Turn your eyes to God instead. Remember how our precious Savior suffered for us on the cross. Our sufferings look small and petty in comparison. Do not worry so about cares of this world. We are chosen by God to carry our cross and thus we must suffer the petty jealousies of those not so blessed. Dear Matushka, I saved your letters because I cherished the kind words of an Empress to a lowly peasant. But you are right. In the future I will be more cautious and destroy your letters. I will hold the memory of your words in my heart."

Normally his soothing voice would have calmed her down but now she was simply furious. Every inch the Empress she slowly and carefully addressed him.

"Your mistake has caused me considerable distress. It will not happen again."

Then, having calmed down somewhat, Alix told him that he would not be sent back to his home but instead would be allowed to make a pilgrimage to the Holy Land. Rasputin was inwardly relieved and he thanked the Tsarina profusely for her intervention. A trip to Jerusalem was certainly a better alternative than a return to the squalid village his family lived in.

Grigory was very aware of the rumors surrounding his relationship with the Imperial family but he did nothing to suppress the gossip. He felt the chatter only enhanced his prestige and the innuendo certainly added to his notoriety. However, it was a surprise to him and a source of amusement that anyone could think he was having an intimate relationship with the Empress. When he was in her presence she seemed such a prude that he wondered how she had even had any children. But in this he was totally mistaken. Even though Alix grew up in the Victorian era and overtly seemed always quiet and modest, in truth, she was a very passionate woman.

Anya returned to the drawing room and the three spent a few hours discussing religious matters. Alix had with her a special book in which she recorded all of Father Grigory's sayings and holy words. It was one of her most prized possessions and she treasured it. She would read from it when Father Grigory could not be present and his words always helped calm her soul. Anya and Alix were both excited about his upcoming pilgrimage and were eager for him to record everything he saw and heard in the Holy Land. Neither had been to Jerusalem and they both looked forward to his descriptions and commentary.

CRIO

The following spring, when the young buds were appearing on the trees and the last of the winter snows had melted, Ella came from Moscow for an extended visit. It was so strange to see her dressed in a nun's habit and at first everyone felt a little awkward and uncomfortable around her. But she was the same cheerful, outgoing Ella, and soon Nicky and Alix and the rest of the family warmed up to her and were totally at ease in her company. Nicky and Ella took long walks together and discussed those elements of the *Masquerade* that pertained to her but the conversations were general in nature and no specific arrangements were made during this visit. Ella's involvement, which would be crucial to the success of the plan, was still being worked on by Nicholas and until everything was in order he was not ready to divulge her part in it. He did express his gratitude to her for arranging his visit to the Pope and he gave her a detailed account of the meeting.

One day, as they were starting out on their walk, Alix joined them, much to Nicky's surprise. The Emperor knew his wife's legs gave her much pain and for this reason she rarely wandered far from her boudoir. After exchanging pleasantries Alexandra turned to her sister, and, much to the Tsar's dismay, said to her, "Ella I want to talk to you about Father Grigory. We have all heard the horrible rumors circulating about him in the city but I can assure you that they are all lies. I know that you have reservations with regard to his intentions but if you would only meet with him I am sure you would see that he is indeed a holy man and has only the best interest of the family at heart. Won't you let me arrange a get together at Anya's before you go back to Moscow. I am sure you would then see things the way they really are."

Ella loved her sister deeply and could see that she was crying out for support and understanding, but the Grand Duchess could not play the game Nicholas was so adept at. She could not appear to support her sister publicly while inwardly despising Rasputin and all he stood for. So Ella did the only thing she knew how to do. She told the truth.

"My dearest Alix," she began. "I had planned on discussing this issue with you at some time during my visit and it might as well be now. What I say to you I say with love in my heart and my only concern is your welfare. You are right. I have heard all the rumors about this Father Grigory, but, unlike you, I believe them to be true. I do not ask you to accept my views without some justification so I have brought documents that prove that this man is an evil that must be rooted out. Once you have read them you will see what I mean."

The reaction from Alix was predictable and she flew into a rage. "I do not need to read such filth. It is more of the same, nothing but lies, lies, lies. He keeps my son alive and that is all that matters to me. I do not care what the people say about me," she sobbed. "No one who has not seen my Alexei in pain could possibly understand why I depend on this man."

Ella tried to calm her but it was no use. Alix felt betrayed by her older sister and confused that Nicholas had not intervened in support of her. Ella did not think her sister's reaction was a question of pride or even the stubborn streak that Alexandra was noted for. This went much deeper and she could sense that Alix was suffering tremendous psychological pain.

"Ella, I had hoped that you of all people would see the truth but you have become like all the others. You are ready to accept any calumny about this holy man even though his healing powers are well known. It is useless to talk to you about this anymore." With that she turned on her heel and walked away.

"How long has she been like this, Nicholas," Ella inquired.

"Years, if the truth be known," Nicky replied. "But Ella you must try and patch up this rift. When your role in the *Masquerade* becomes known we will need the Tsarina's support and we cannot have any tension hanging over us."

"I will try, Nicky." However, when Ella said her good-byes before returning to Moscow, the coldness of the farewell was evident to everyone at the station. The two sister's had become estranged and Ella knew the only thing she could do was to pray. Pray for her sister and for Russia.

෮෮

In early September of that year the Imperial family traveled to Kiev for the unveiling of a statue of Alexander II, commemorating the fiftieth anniversary of the emancipation of the serfs. It was a very special occasion and Nicholas was eager to honor his grandfather. They were to stay in Kiev for a week before traveling on to the palace at Livadia in the Crimea. Today the family had participated in a parade through the city of Kiev. Balconies were gaily decorated with bunting and flowers and people were cheerful and obviously enjoying the holiday atmosphere. Crowds lined the route of the cavalcade and cheered the Imperial family as they passed by. The reception by the city's inhabitants was most gratifying and Alexei and the girls could hardly contain their excitement. There was so much crowd noise that the Royal family was completely unaware of an event that took place behind them.

Count Peter Stolypin, the prime minister, traveled in a carriage to the rear of the Imperial family. As he passed by a group of cheering admirers a man, dressed in black, stepped from the crowd near the carriage and began to mumble as he swayed back and forth. Finally he pointed a finger at Count Stolypin, as his carriage passed, and muttered in a loud voice, "beware, death is around us, death is around us." The crowd, frightened by his actions, backed away from the stranger. "Death follows him," he shouted after Stolypin's carriage. Then, his task complete, he forced his way back into the crowd but as he made his way through the throng people began to recognize him.

"It is him. It is Rasputin," cried one man. The crowd surrounding him gasped in surprise and looked at the carriage retreating into the distance. What could he have meant? Did he really think that Stolypin was going to die?

In the mean time Rasputin relished the reaction of the crowd, safe in the knowledge that no one would ever know that one of his friends had made him aware of an assassination plot against Stolypin. He intended to use his prediction, if and when the event occurred, to add to his reputation as a visionary.

The procession had continued until all the dignitaries reached the square where the statue was erected. Impressive marble stairs led up to the large monument, which was hidden from view by white cotton sheeting. The buildings surrounding the square were decorated with colorful bunting, flags, and the Imperial Coat of Arms. Tents and awnings with chairs had been set up for the notables, including a festive arch for the Imperial family. Soldiers were posted throughout the square for security. The ceremony was long and tedious and consisted of prayers and blessings, as well as numerous speeches by various local dignitaries. Finally Nicholas was able to go forward and pull the rope unveiling the monument. It was an impressive work, all bronze, and marble, and the Tsar considered it a fitting tribute to a great man.

With the day's activities concluded all Alix wished to do was rest. She informed Nicholas that this would be the extent of her official appearances. "I am just too weak to participate in anything else," she told him.

"Alix, we are expected tomorrow night at the Kiev opera. We cannot disappoint those who have arranged this special performance," he told her.

"It is too much for me. Olga and Tatiana can go with you in my place. They will more than make up for my absence and they will leap at the opportunity to act the role of young ladies." Nicholas reluctantly agreed. He did not wish to argue with her and it was obvious she was not feeling well. Lately, she had begun spending time in a wheel chair since her legs pained her so much that at times she was unable to walk. The slightest activity seemed to fatigue her and today had been no exception. She was truly exhausted.

The next evening Olga and Tatiana dressed formally for their evening out with their father and they were both very excited. They still wore their hair down and their skirts were those of young girls but it was evident they were both rapidly approaching womanhood. In a few months Olga would turn sixteen and then she would be allowed to wear her hair up and let her skirts down. Both girls looked forward to this adult affair and were pleased their younger sisters would not be tagging along.

It was but a short ride to the theater and soon Nicholas escorted his daughters into the Imperial Box at the Kiev Opera House. Their box overlooked the stage and they were to see the opera *The Sultan Tsar* about which they had heard many wonderful comments. As the girls looked around the theater they recognized many of those in the audience. "Papa is that Prime Minister Stolypin in the front by the orchestra," asked Tatiana.

"Why yes it is," he answered, but before he could say more the orchestra sounded the opening notes of the prelude and the theater darkened. The Grand Duchesses were mesmerized by the music and when the curtain rose they were entranced by the story. They had been provided with copies of the libretto and they followed every word and note with rapt attention. When the curtain came down for the intermission they stepped into the hallway outside their box in an effort to cool off. It was unseasonably warm and the Imperial box had become quite sweltering. Suddenly they heard a loud popping sound and Nicholas turned and went back into the box. He thought someone must have dropped their opera glasses. It was not until he heard a second pop that he realized the sound was that of a handgun being discharged. The girls had followed him back into the box and he put his arms out in an attempt to shield his daughters from the sight, but it was too late. They looked down with horror as Count Stolypin clutched at his chest, his white shirt crimson with blood. The Count looked up at the Imperial Box and seeing Nicholas he made the sign of the cross in the air with his blood covered hand. Then he collapsed.

Pandemonium ensued in the theater as the crowd attacked and began to beat the assassin. Throngs of people poured out the doors, worried about their safety. Nicholas looked at his daughters with concern. Olga, although pale, had maintained her composure and he could see she was absorbing all the activity around her. Tatiana on the other hand, appeared to wilt and looked on the verge of collapse. She had begun to weep and Olga attempted to comfort her. In the midst of this the Tsar's personal security came rushing in and indicated they must leave. They were still unsure if this was an isolated event or part of a bigger plot that could include the Tsar. The frightened girls and their father were ushered downstairs and out a back door into a waiting vehicle and rushed away to their accommodations.

When the girls were finally calmed down and had been put to bed Nicholas told Alix what had happened at the theater and she received the news with little show of regret. Ever since Stolypin had spoken out against Rasputin, she had been lobbying to have him replaced but Nicholas had refused. Peter Stolypin was an experienced and competent minister, one of the best Nicholas had ever worked with. Under his leadership the country was prospering and Nicholas was devastated at the thought of losing him. It was to be a very long night for him as he attempted to make sense of the evenings events.

Over the next few days he kept a prayerful vigil, while continuing his formal duties, hoping against hope that Stolypin would survive. His injury was very serious and when Nicholas attempted to go to him he was informed that the Count's wife would allow no visitors and, though he was Tsar of all the Russias, he respected her wishes. Although his security people urged the Tsar to leave immediately for the Crimea, Nicholas refused to go while Stolypin still lived. Finally on the sixth day, as the Tsar returned from one of his many official functions, he was greeted by Vladimir Kokovtsov, the Finance Minister. The grave look on his face said it all. "Your highness, he is dead."

Nicholas thanked him for bringing the sad news and went upstairs to inform Alix. He spoke softly and shared the tragic news with her. Realizing how upset he was she grasped his hand and squeezed it tightly. "I am sorry, Nicky. I cannot pretend I liked the man, but I know how much you respected and trusted him. It is truly a loss for Russia."

Nicky smiled gratefully at her. He appreciated her attempt to console him. "There is nothing to keep us here now. His memorial service is later today and once that is completed we will leave for the Crimea."

"I will ensure all the arrangements have been made," Alix said, as she left the room. She knew Nicky would need some time alone to come to grips with this terrible tragedy. Secretly, the Empress was content that one of Father Grigory's most outspoken enemies would no longer be able to attack him and spread those terrible lies. She had been advised of the staret's prediction that Stolypin would die and it only strengthened her faith in his mystical abilities.

As for Nicky, he had already made a decision. He would wait until a decent amount of time had passed and then would announce the appointment of Vladimir Kokovtsov as the new Prime Minister. The man was no Stolypin but he was competent and Nicky felt certain he was up to the job.

As Nicholas looked back at the tumultuous events of the past week he had to admit he was surprised and extremely proud of his daughter Olga's conduct. In spite of what had to have been a traumatic and stressful event she behaved with a calm dignity despite her fears. She did not panic, was cool and collected as she consoled her sister, and followed instructions in a disciplined manner, never succumbing to the fright she must have experienced. He wondered if his oldest daughter was the chosen one of Saint Seraphim's letter. Olga certainly seemed to have the characteristics of a leader. Nicholas knew that as a result of this experience some of the innocence of her childhood was gone forever and he was saddened by the thought. On the other hand, she had shown an inner strength that would help her prepare for, and cope with the future, a future that would, unfortunately, make very harsh demands.

Chapter 19

September 1911 – Livadia. It was a somber group that boarded the train at Kiev for the long journey down to Sevastopol on the Crimean peninsula. The events of the past few days had affected all the members of the royal family in some way or another and as they sat in the stuffy coach they each wrestled with their own impressions of the tragic week. Nicholas had lost an able and loyal, public servant and Alexandra lost an enemy. The two oldest girls witnessed a bloody assassination and Alexei, Maria, and Anastasia, too young to really understand what had happened, were totally confused by the funereal atmosphere that surrounded them. But children of that age are irrepressible and as the train headed south and drew closer to the coast their excitement grew. Soon their high spirited behavior became so infectious that it soothed the wounded spirits of the adults, and the remainder of what seemed an interminable journey passed more quickly.

When the Imperial train finally pulled into the port city of Sevastopol the children could see the masts and gleaming black hull of the *Standart*, waiting to take them on the final stage of their journey. The trunks and luggage were quickly loaded and the yacht got underway for Yalta, the port nearest the Imperial estate at Livadia. The arrival at Yalta was always exciting for the children because a troop of uniformed Tatars traditionally met the Tsar and escorted him and the rest of the Imperial family to the royal compound. For this reason, the Tsar always completed the journey in a horse-drawn carriage. Although skilled horsemen, with fine mounts, there was no way the Tatars could keep pace with his Delaunay-Bellville touring car and Nicholas had no desire to embarrass these loyal retainers. Today, though, as far as the girls were concerned the cavalcade seemed to move at a snail's pace and the four Grand Duchesses could barely conceal their impatience. In an hour or so they would see, for the first time, the new Livadia Palace which had been under construction for over a year.

It was a glorious day, bright with sunshine, and a nearly cloudless sky. The procession of riders and vehicles made its way through a forest filled with lush undergrowth and occupied by dozens of singing birds. It seemed once again, as it had two years ago, that they were passing through an enchanted garden. The carriages crested one last hill and below could be seen a breathtaking view of the Black Sea, its rich, blue-green waters reflecting the sun, like so many sparkling diamonds. A short while later the escort turned into the Imperial compound and made its way down the long drive through the thick natural vegetation. As they approached the palace they could see that the woods had been thinned out somewhat, and the road neatly graded. Lush grass bordered each side of the entrance drive and extensive landscaping was already completed. Finally they rounded the last bend in the road and their breath was literally taken away by the sight of the gleaming marble palace. It was absolutely beautiful! The stark white of the marble contrasted sharply with the green of the manicured lawn and was enhanced by vibrant red flowers.

The building was simple in design and constructed in the neoclassical style. It was a perfectly balanced mix of arches, columns, and rectangular spaces. A large square tower rose from the edifice, but the design was so perfect that it did not seem unbalanced. The structure was perched on the cliffs overlooking the Black Sea and situated to ensure the best possible view.

"Oh Papa, it looks like a castle," exclaimed Anastasia. "It is so beautiful."

Alix glanced at Nicky a look of gratitude. "My dearest, it is absolutely breathtaking. Even though we went over the drawings so many times, this is beyond my wildest expectations. Oh darling, it is truly exceptional. It looks like such a cheerful place; so bright and airy."

Nicky was not surprised at her reaction, even when she kissed him in front of everyone. Alexandra had always loved coming to the Crimea but the old wooden palace that served as their home in the past contained bittersweet memories and she was relieved that it had been torn down. Nicky's father had died in that very house those many years ago. She had been betrothed to the Tsarevich at the time and was expected to attend all the ceremonies associated with the burial of a Tsar, but because her command of the language was rudimentary she was treated almost as an outsider. It was an inauspicious start for the young German princess and to make matters worse it seemed as if she went straight from the funeral to her wedding. It was a confusing time in her life but at least, with the old building gone, she would no longer be reminded of those painful memories.

The Tsar had made several trips to the coast to check on the progress of construction and had worked closely with the architect and builders to ensure everything was completed when they arrived. Whereas the other Imperial palaces were treasures of the nation, with changes to them restrained by history and tradition, Livadia was one of the estates he owned privately and he thus had a free hand in the design and construction.

He now took on the role of tour guide and, with obvious pride, beckoned his family to follow him as they entered their new home. They stepped into the front entrance hall through two massive doors and were immediately overwhelmed by the grandeur of their surroundings. The palace was quite large and was built around interior courtyards, which his daughters raced off to investigate. The girls quickly determined that their favorite was the lovely Italian garden, which was filled with roses, and intersected by manicured pathways. Its centerpiece was an ancient well with an archway held up by two marble columns. The columns had been discovered at the archeological excavations taking place at Ai Tudor, the Tsar's sister's estate, and brought to Livadia to grace the garden. The courtyard was surrounded on four sides by marble loggias with arched columns that allowed an unobstructed view of the garden. "I shall spend many an hour here," Alix remarked, as they passed through the garden.

Nicholas and his family continued their tour inside and next explored the main hall, which was the largest room in the building and certainly the grandest. The chamber was completely white except for a gleaming parquet floor that shone like polished glass and it was brightly lit by sunlight streaming in through large, arch-shaped windows. The walls blended into a ceiling that was covered with elaborate, ornamental molding and which added yet another elegant dimension to the room. As the sun momentarily passed behind a fleeting cloud, and the room darkened somewhat, the Tsar flipped a switch on the wall and hidden electric bulbs burst into light.

"It is like magic," Maria exclaimed. "Where are all the lights?" Her father pointed out that they were cleverly concealed in the cornices but still able to emit light.

"Oh Papa, what a good idea. You cannot even see the ugly bulbs or wires."

"Olga, I think we will have your birthday ball in this room," said Alix.

"Oh Mama, it will be so splendid. I can hardly wait for the day," she replied.

Nicholas looked at his oldest daughter and could hardly believe she was turning sixteen. It was as if he had blinked his eyes and she had suddenly grown into a lovely young woman. Her dark blond hair was streaked with highlights from time spent in the sun and she had expressive blue-gray eyes. She was tall for her age and there was an elegance and grace about her that Nicky could see in the other girls as well. Olga was the most outgoing and intelligent of his children and spent many hours with her head buried in a book. The two had become very close in the past year and she loved to go for long walks with her father. She was a fine listener but also a good conversationalist and she often surprised him with her insights.

The initial tour of the house finally ended and the family dispersed to settle into their new living quarters. A little later Nicholas joined Alix on one of the many balconies where she was enjoying the fresh sea breezes and the breathtaking view. From their vantage point they could see a great distance and the azure blue sea seemed to blend in with the sky. The coastline sloped upward from the sea into dramatic hills and cliffs. The manicured grounds of the palace ended at the edge of the forests that surrounded the palace on three sides, and gave them a sense of seclusion which they privately relished. "Oh Nicky, I just love it here. I can already feel my strength returning. The warmth from the sun is such a welcome relief after our long, cold, Russian winter and the sea air must be doing me some good," said Alix.

Nicholas looked at his wife and was pleased to see some color had returned to her face. She had been so pale lately that he had become quite concerned and he hated to see her feeling so badly. Dr. Eugene Botkin had traveled with the family to Livadia and was there to take care of the Empress and his daughters but the girls were so healthy that Dr. Botkin's primary duty consisted of treating the Empress. An additional physician, Dr. Vladimir Derevenko, was also in the party but his sole responsibility was Alexei, whose health required daily attention.

Over the next few days the Imperial household settled into a routine. In the mornings Nicholas would attend to business matters and spend some time with Dmitri. His children spent the mornings attending to their lessons. At lunch time the entire Imperial retinue gathered with the family to share a meal in the palace dining room. Officers from the *Standart* were often in attendance and they made lunch a festive occasion with their youthful exuberance and skylarking. There was an infectious gaiety at these get-togethers that cheered everyone up and made the event the high point of the day, especially for the older girls. They were frequently entertained by members of the *Standart's* military band and when Alix felt up to it she too would join them for the music.

The afternoons were devoted to excursions along the coast but because of the pain in her legs Alix rarely went along. The Grand Duchesses took turns sitting with her so she would not be alone so much and just as Olga was becoming close to Nicholas, a similar relationship was developing between Tatiana and her mother. Tatiana often volunteered to stay behind and let the other girls go off. She was now fourteen and her fabulous good looks were beginning to bring her much attention. With her auburn colored hair and gray eyes she resembled Alexandra as she looked in her youth. Tatiana was much more reserved than Olga and was very conscious of her status as the daughter of an Emperor, and those that saw her, recognized in her the strain of nobility. There was something about the way she carried herself that left no doubt as to her royal lineage. With her mother so ill she had begun to take on many of the Tsarina's responsibilities even though she was very young. She could be very authoritarian and her sisters teased her and called her "the governess" when she attempted to rule the nursery.

Today's excursion, however, was a special event and the children were able to skip their lessons so they could join the fun. Since the journey was a physical impossibility for the Empress she had insisted they go along without her. The entire entourage had been invited by Prince Lev Golitzin to explore the numerous and extensive cave systems found on his estate at Novy Svet and since it could be reached more easily by sea they embarked in the *Standart* for a cruise down the coast. Upon reaching their destination the captain anchored the yacht in a quiet little cove and ferried the group ashore in the ship's launch. They disembarked on a sandy beach and then began the long hike up a mountain trail to meet the Prince. The Tsar, his daughters, and a few officers from the yacht were used to strenuous hikes and did not find the ascent too demanding. But when they reached the top of a hill and looked back down the pathway they could see many of their suite struggling along, as they slowly made the climb. The girl's hearts went out to Seaman Derevenko who had to carry Alexei up the hill when he became overly tired. From their vantage point the girls could look down and see the *Standart* anchored in the cove but their destination above was obscured by the scrubby trees and bushes which clung to the rocky soil on the hillside.

At the halfway point, Prince Golitzin met the Tsar's group and welcomed them to Novy Svet. The prince was from an ancient and noble family and was famous in his own right, but his celebrity was not derived from political involvement or military service.

This unassuming and rather eccentric individual was a vintner and was famous throughout Europe for the quality of his wines. He was considered the father of Russian champagne and had won many awards for his vintages. For this occasion he was dressed in a black suit which contrasted so starkly with his white hair and bushy beard that Maria and Anastasia could hardly contain their mirth. It took a stern look from Tatiana to settle them down but the kindly old man was oblivious to their shenanigans. He had already begun to regale Nicholas with amusing anecdotes and the Tsar and his officers were laughing uproariously. The pause allowed the others to catch up and they were welcomed in turn by the Prince. Finally he turned back up the hill and with liberal use of his gold-headed cane led them, after a short walk, to a huge hall which had been excavated out of the side of the mountain. Here he entertained them with a sumptuous lunch and samplings of his finest wines. Everyone was ravenous after the strenuous climb and enjoyed the meal immensely. During lunch Prince Golitzin explained that underneath the mountain was a huge labyrinth of caves that stretched nearly two miles along the coast. Because the temperature was constant he had fashioned a wine cellar in one of the caves and stored substantial quantities of his vintages there. After lunch he invited everyone to explore the cave system and when most of the group accepted he sent several retainers, with lighted torches, to prevent anyone from getting lost.

Nicholas was very interested in the caves especially after his host told him privately that there were many secret passageways and tunnels leading from his palace and outbuildings to the caverns. It seemed a wonderful place to hide, if that ever became necessary, and he was intrigued by the possibilities the underground chambers offered. But for the present the Tsar merely filed the information away for future consideration. At the end of what proved to be a long but interesting afternoon he thanked the Prince on behalf of the whole company and expressed his appreciation for a wonderful outing.

"Your Imperial Highness, I assure you the honor is all mine," the Prince replied. "I am an old man, but these young people have refreshed me with their energy and enthusiasm and I feel years younger. My door is always open to you." He turned to one of the servants and took a hamper from him. "Please present these few bottles to the Empress and express my regret that she was not able to enjoy the day with us."

"I will certainly do so," the Tsar assured him. "You have been most kind." Then he turned and led the way back down the hill.

The walk downward was less tiring then the ascent so there was much skylarking as they made their way to the beach. At times like this Nicholas was at his best; cheerful and relaxed and full of good humor. The children felt very close to him during these interludes and he indulged them in a way Alix, with her strict Victorian upbringing, could never do. It was easy to forget that these lovely girls and their handsome brother lived secluded lives and were rarely seen by anyone other than a few court officials and an occasional relative. The walls surrounding Peterhof, Alexander Palace, the Polish hunting lodge, and Livadia encompassed their world and isolated them from the Russian people. Consequently, photography was a way in which they could momentarily break through the barriers and bring the outside world a little closer. On this excursion the girls, as usual, were carrying their cameras and stopping frequently to take photographs of the incredible vistas. Eventually, after numerous delays and much clowning for the camera everyone reached the shoreline and waited their turn to be shuttled out to the *Standart*. The weather continued to be clear and the seas calm so the trip home was a smooth and enjoyable one.

The next morning Alix awoke from a sound sleep and felt better than she had for days. Of late Dr. Botkin had restricted her activities and required her to use a wheel chair, but after breakfast the Empress expressed a desire to go for a long walk. This necessitated putting the children's lessons off for the second day in a row; much to their delight. The term "walk," in the vocabulary of Alexandra, had a different meaning then one would associate with such a simple word. At Livadia Alix rode in a pony cart and everyone else walked along with her. This was no rickety farm cart but, as befitted an Empress, a conveyance made of the finest woods and leather, with springs on the axles to absorb the bumps and rough spots. Alix wore a large hat and carried a parasol to protect her delicate skin from the sun and, after being assisted into the cart she, Nicholas, the children, and Anya set off for a hike up into the hills surrounding the estate. Although the cart forced them to stay on the improved roads, the family enjoyed their excursion. A large picnic hamper had been prepared and loaded into the cart with Alix and they intended to enjoy the delicacies in a green meadow further up the road. The Grand Duchesses were so excited to have their mother with them that they chattered continuously and used this rare opportunity to point out all the sights. Nicholas was pleased to see Alix was showing more energy. The fresh air was putting some color back in her cheeks and she was enjoying the company of their children. Although the climate in the Crimea always seemed to have a restorative effect on her, Nicky knew that being away from court, with all its stress and gossip, was a big part of it as well.

Upon their return to the palace, Alix and the children continued their preparations for two special events which were to take place the following week. The children would be participating in the Festival of the White Flower and a few days later Alix would sell items in her booth at a charity bazaar. Both events were held to raise money for the treatment of tuberculosis patients who came in large numbers to the Crimea because of its mild climate. The Imperial family's involvement in this charity was a result of the death of Nicholas' brother from tuberculosis. Seeing the pain and suffering he went through was more than enough to encourage their assistance and whenever they were at Livadia they actively participated in fund raising activities. Alix had used funds from her own personal fortune to have modern hospital facilities built in Yalta and she assigned her friend Anya the duty of inspecting and reporting on the hospital's sanitation and patient care. Anya also had to identify those who were too poor to pay for hospitalization so that the proceeds from the charity events could then be used to support the care of those indigent patients.

The day of the Festival of the White Flower finally arrived and before sending the girls off to join others who were participating Alix insisted that a group photo of all her children be taken. They looked so precious she had to record the moment. Alexei was dressed in a sailor suit with a jaunty white cap, while her girls wore embroidered white summer dresses with navy blue sashes tied around their waists and bows at their neck. To complete the outfits each of the Grand Duchesses wore a large brimmed straw hat adorned with lace, and a badge marking them as participants in the festival. Each child also carried a tall staff covered with ribbons and white daises and topped by a large circle surrounded with flowers. Suspended around their necks by white ribbons were small boxes in which to place the proceeds from the sale of their flowers. All of the girls, except Olga, seemed delighted to be involved in the day's activities. The oldest daughter, however, had earlier staged an unsuccessful mini-rebellion, complaining vigorously that her outfit looked silly and that she did not want to participate. Alix had sighed and, of course, refused to listen to any objections, but now Olga was standing there with a petulant look on her face deliberately spoiling the photograph. Alix looked pleadingly at Nicholas who walked over and whispered something to his oldest. It put a fleeting smile on her face and the snapshot was quickly taken. Although the tension was momentarily broken Alix recognized that Olga was becoming more and more difficult to manage and harking back to her own upbringing she vowed to regain control.

Not wishing to delay any longer she urged the children into the waiting motorcars which would take them into town to sell their flowers. When they arrived, after a short drive, and stepped down from the cars they were immediately surrounded by a crowd and the children quickly sold all their flowers to citizens eager for a memento from the Imperial family. Other children participating in the festival were equally successful in selling their flowers and a great deal of money was raised.

The Bazaar was held a few days later and it was also a huge success. Alix manned her own booth, with the help of Alexei, and completely sold out of everything they brought to the bazaar, with the hand-crafted items she had personally made selling fast and furious. Alix was very pleased with the results of the bazaar and the festival and looked forward to her upcoming visit to the hospitals. She planned to meet with the directors and inspect the facilities and for the first time Grand Duchesses Olga and Tatiana would join their parents in this work of mercy. Alexandra felt it was important for the girls to see and understand the suffering that lay submerged in the beauty of the Crimea. One day, when her daughters came of age, they would inherit great personal fortunes and she wanted them to realize that even though they were forced to endure relative seclusion their lives were, nevertheless, ones of great privilege. She felt that seeing the sufferings of others would help them appreciate their own blessings and good fortune.

A few days later as Nicholas, Alexandra and the older girls prepared to depart for Yalta to visit one of the hospitals, Maria ran up to the motorcar and pleaded with her father, "Please Papa, may I come too,"

"Not this time Maria," said her mother. "I think you are a bit too young for such an outing.

"Mama, I am twelve years old and I will not cause a bit of trouble. I promise! So please, please allow me to go," Maria pleaded. Alix looked over to Nicky and he nodded his assent.

"Very well then, you may join us," said Alix, but you must be on your best behavior

"Oh thank you, Papa, Mama. I will be a perfect angel."

Since this was to be a private visit, protocol was relaxed and Nicholas drove the family himself in one of the many cars he kept at Livadia. They were still followed by a rather large entourage, but because the roads were virtually empty and not many people were about, the cavalcade was able to slip into town without exciting too much attention. When they arrived at the hospital the Tsar helped his wife and daughters from the car and they made their way to the entrance.

"Please wait in the gardens and I will summon you if needed," the Tsar instructed his retinue. "I wish to go in alone with my family. He then led Alix and the girls inside the entrance where they were greeted by the Director of the hospital and several doctors. From the wards they could hear the loud coughs and sounds of distress emanating from the tubercular patients. Nicholas and Alexandra were accustomed to the familiar sounds of the hospital but for Maria it was unfamiliar and very disturbing.

"Welcome Your Imperial Highnesses. It is such an honor to have you join us today," said the Director.

"You know we would never come to the Crimea and not visit the hospitals," said Alexandra.

"I see we have a few new visitors," he said as he looked at the Grand Duchesses.

"Yes these are my daughters," the Tsar replied, introducing each in turn. "Grand Duchess Maria Nicholaievna is a bit shy right now but I assure you she is not normally this subdued."

The Director smiled and turned to Maria and took her hand. "Thank you so much for gracing us with your presence, your Imperial Highness," he said. Maria blushed when her official title was used and she thought it a little silly to be so formal in a hospital where people were probably dying. The Director escorted the family to one of the wards to visit the patients. Even though the disease was very contagious, the Tsar and his wife insisted on speaking to individual patients so everyone was outfitted with gauze masks. "Your visits mean so much to the patients and their families and I think for a brief moment your kindness helps them to forget about their condition. Of course, as you must know, we are extremely grateful to all of you for your fund-raising efforts on our behalf. We are in greater need then ever this year because of a large increase in the number of patients."

"Well, you will be happy to hear we have raised quite a substantial amount of money this year at the Festival and the Bazaar," the Tsar announced. "In fact we almost doubled last year's proceeds. I think it has a lot to do with the increased involvement of the Tsarevich and the Grand Duchesses."

The Tsar and Tsarina conversed with the Director and doctors while Tatiana and Olga distributed holy cards to the bedridden patients. Maria stood in the back of the group, off by herself. Her eyes scanned the corridor walls looking at the icons hanging there, along with pictures of various doctors and past directors of the hospital. She started to daydream, as she often did, but before she could become totally oblivious to her surroundings her attention was attracted by a noise. It sounded like a child singing in the distance and no one noticed as Maria wandered off down the corridor following the faint sound. She entered a small room from which the singing seemed to be coming and was surprised to see a young girl lying alone in a bed. Maria was shocked at the condition of this poor child; she was as pale as a ghost, with dark rings under her eyes and bluish lips. The girl did not notice Maria as she entered the room and she continued to sing, but suddenly her singing was interrupted by the onset of a violent cough. She sat up in the bed and thrashed around trying to contain the terrible spasms. Maria, who was unaware of the contagious nature of the disease and unconcerned about her own well being, walked up to her bed. "Oh, please, can I help you? Do you need some water? What can I do to aid you?" she inquired. The girl was so startled to see someone other than a nurse in her room that she was able to get her cough under control. "Are you better now?" Maria asked.

"Yes," answered the girl, clearing her throat. "Who are you?"

"My name is Maria," she said. "What is your name?"

"My name is Natasha."

"What a pretty name. How old are you?"

"I am twelve. My birthday is June 14th."

"So is mine," said Maria with amazement. She pulled a chair close to the bed, sat down, and pulled off her mask so she could speak more freely.

"It is so nice to have someone to visit with," said Natasha. "No one comes to see me except my father. He is a doctor here at the hospital which is why I am in this private room. I would much rather be with the other children in the ward but my father wanted it this way. Sometimes, though, I get very lonely and I never see anyone my own age."

"What about your Mother, does she come to see you?"

"No, she died when I was eight and now it is just Papa and I."

"Oh, I am so sorry. When you get well, you must come to see me."

"But I will not get well. Do you see that chart hanging at the end of the bed? It has my name on it and I have read it often since I am alone most of the time with nothing to do. It says I only have a little while left," said Natasha.

"Are you afraid to die?"

"I was before, but not now. I had a dream or maybe it was a vision and I saw heaven. It was a wondrous place and words cannot describe its beauty. There was no pain there, no loneliness, no sorrow, only joy." Her face had an expression of complete peace as she recalled what she had seen. "I am ready to go. I will leave my father on this earth but I will join my mother in heaven. She and I will watch over Papa."

Maria's eyes began to dampen with tears. She grasped Natasha's hand and said, "I know it is true. Your Mother will be waiting to welcome you into heaven. What is it like to have tuberculosis? Is it very painful/"

"It feels as if someone has cut a hole in your back right through to your lungs."

"Oh, how dreadful. Do they give you any medicine?"

"Yes, but it only helps a little bit," she explained.

Maria sat quietly for a moment and tried to think of something she might do for this poor suffering girl. If only she had some item she could give her, to brighten her day a little. I could give her my pearls, she thought, but what comfort is that for a dying soul. Then she remembered a special icon that was also hanging around her neck. It was pure gold and had a picture of Saint Nicholas carved on one side and the other had been personalized with her own initials and royal crest. It had been a gift from Aunt Ella who had commissioned one for each of the Tsar's daughters. Maria removed it and gently placed it around Natasha's neck. "I want you to have this icon." May Saint Nicholas give you strength to bear your pain and may he greet you at the gates of heaven."

"You are so kind to me Maria. I imagine that if I were not so sick we would be great friends."

"The best," agreed Maria. Just then the two girls heard foot steps in the hallway.

"You must leave quickly. You will get in trouble for being in here. The nurse said I was not allowed any visitors except my father. I so enjoyed your company that I did not want you to leave."

Maria stood up and leaned over her new friend. She picked up her hand and gently kissed it. "I promise I will come back to see you, Natasha," Maria assured her. She quickly made her way out the door and came face to face with one of the nurses.

"What in heavens name were you doing in there child? Don't you know you can get this disease by just sitting near a patient without a mask on? Now off with you," scolded the nurse, with irritation in her voice.

Maria was unaccustomed to anyone speaking so harshly to her and she was extremely upset. She turned and ran down the hallway, past her parents and out the door. "What on earth is going on with Maria," asked Alexandra in an annoyed voice.

"I will go and see what is wrong," offered Olga.

"No I will go," said Nicholas and he headed down the corridor toward the main entrance.I think she is in the garden adjacent to this building."

Nicholas made his way to the garden and found Maria, sitting on a bench, and praying aloud as tears streamed down her face. "Maria! What is wrong, my precious child?"

"Oh, Papa it just isn't fair. Why does God make children suffer?"

"Maria, we must not blame God for these horrible tragedies in our lives. Remember this was not his plan for us. God once gave us a paradise but that was not good enough for man. Through our sins we created this world and now we must live in it. He allows us to do our own will but we have to live with the consequences of our actions. God does not abandon us and He never hands us a cross so big that we cannot carry it. He is with us always and gives us comfort so that we might survive in this world. Imagine if there were no hospitals or medicines. God gives these things to us as gifts to ease our suffering. It could be so much worse, my little Maria," he said.

"You are right Papa, and I am sure Natasha will be so much happier in heaven with her Mother."

Nicholas was puzzled by Maria's reply and he questioned her about the girl. Maria went on to tell her father all that had transpired between herself and the young patient in the hospital and how she had given Natasha her icon. "I hope you are not angry Papa. She has tuberculosis and is so sick, she will soon die and I just wanted to give her a little joy." Tears filled her eyes again and she cried out, "Oh Papa, my heart hurts so bad I feel as though it is about to burst."

The Tsar put his arms around his daughter and held her tight. Although he loved all his children, he felt a special affection for Maria, whose generous nature and sympathy for others, set her apart from her sisters. As he comforted her, Nicholas realized that they had much in common with each other. In some mysterious way, the two shared burdens that were similar in weight, if different in content and degree. Maria took on the agony of her friend and suffered along with her, just as Nicholas struggled with Russia's troubles, a hemophiliac son, and an eccentric wife. But despite the tremendous pressures placed on him, and with very few to confide in, Nicholas rarely lost his composure and managed to maintain his sense of humor. This was one of the Tsar's most endearing qualities and was a trait he recognized in Maria.

When Maria had settled down the two headed back to the front of the hospital where everyone was gathering to leave. The trip back to the palace was uneventful and all Maria could do was think about Natasha and how she might visit her again. She promised herself that somehow she would come back. After all she had given her word and that meant everything.

Two day later the Tsar had an unexpected visit from one of the doctors at the hospital. Although the doctor was not on his appointment schedule Nicholas agreed to see him, sensing that the visit was of some importance.

"Your Imperial Highness, I appreciate you seeing me. I am Dr. Zorkov from the tuberculosis hospital. I do not know if the Grand Duchess told you but she went in to my daughter's room at the hospital. I assure you if I or the nurse had known we would not have let her in, since my daughter's condition was terminal."

"Yes, Maria spoke highly of your daughter, so do not be concerned. She was deeply touched by her suffering," replied the Tsar. "How is she doing? I know Maria would love to see her again."

"That is why I am here, your Imperial Highness. My daughter died early this morning," said Dr. Zorkov.

"I am so sorry to hear this sad news. May her soul rest in peace. If there is anything we can do for you, please let me know. Maria will be devastated, I am sure."

"There is one thing," said the doctor as he pulled a small package from his pocket. "The Grand Duchess gave this to my daughter and I received the impression it was very special to her, so I wanted to return it personally."

"Thank you. This is very kind," replied the Tsar who was touched by this simple gesture of thoughtfulness from a man who had just lost his child. "Have you made funeral arrangements yet? I am sure Maria would like to pay her respects."

"I will be taking her back to Moscow tomorrow to be buried next to her Mother."

"Then may God go with you on your journey and may He comfort you in your loss," said the Tsar.

The doctor left and Nicholas struggled with the best way to tell Maria about the death of Natasha. Loved ones had died in the past but he knew that in the brief encounter between his daughter and the sickly child a deep bond had been established. It was providential that Maria had walked into that room, on that day and brought a little peace and joy into the life of a poor child who was about to breathe her last. There was no way around it so he called Maria to his study.

"What is it Papa?"

Nicholas took the package from his desk and unwrapped it, revealing the gold icon. Maria saw the necklace and a bewildered look came over her face. "What are you doing with that necklace, father? It is Natasha's. I wanted her to keep it." Nicholas took a moment to compose him self and felt a lump in his throat. He knew how broken hearted his daughter would be and he knew there was little he could do to comfort her.

"She does not need it anymore, sweet one. She left us early this morning. Her father brought it back because he knew it must be important to you."

"No! She cannot be gone. Where would she go? It must be a mistake. She did not tell me she was leaving"

"Maria, she is not on a trip. She has died and is in heaven with God and her mother."

"Please Papa; tell me it is not true. She was just singing and talking with me. It just cannot be true." Maria collapsed in her father's arms and cried and cried. It was all Nicholas could do to maintain his self-control. Minutes went by and Maria finally wiped away her tears and looked up at her father. "Papa, I still want her to have this necklace. I gave it to her to keep. I want to go to her funeral. I promised her I would come back and see her and I want to say good-bye."

"Her father is taking her back to Moscow tomorrow to be buried with her mother, so you will not be able to see her again," Nicholas explained to her.

"But she must have this necklace back. Please can we give it back to her? I want her to have it and she can wear it when they lay her in the ground so she won't be so lonely. Please Papa," implored Maria, fresh tears making their way down her face.

"Very well, sweet one. I will have someone take it to the hospital right away and I will send a personal note directing that the icon be placed around her neck."

"Thank you Papa, thank you," said Maria with a sigh of relief.

It was as if this necklace would somehow connect the two in life and death and the Tsar was relieved that this simple gesture would help his daughter recover from her sorrow. He did as promised, and the necklace with its gold icon was placed around Natasha's neck just before the casket was closed. When the train from Sevastopol arrived in Moscow, Natasha was buried and, as Maria had requested, the icon was round her neck.

೦೫೪೦

The evening of Olga's birthday ball finally arrived and the other girls had gathered in front of the dressing table in her room to help her get ready. The jewels she was to wear were laid out and the four sisters were talking excitedly about the night's events. They had seen the guest list and knew which young men would be there and, as young girls might do, they were discussing who was the most handsome, the most eligible, who was the best dancer and so on.

Suddenly the door burst open and Alexei dashed into the room. He ran over to the dressing table, snatched up the jewels, and began to dance around the room while he taunted his oldest sister. "Look at me. I am the Grand Duchess Olga. I am the most important person at the ball. I am a true lady now that I am sixteen," he sang in a squeaky, childish voice as he pranced around the room.

"Give them back, Alexei," cried Olga. "You are going to break them." The lady's maid began to chase Alexei around the room crying out, "please your Highness, let us have them back."

"No, no, I am the future Tsar of Russia and I can do as I please," boasted Alexei.

"You better give them back or else," threatened Tatiana.

"Or else what," said Alexei. "You cannot touch me. I am very sickly and you know you will be in trouble if you cause me any harm. Mama adores me and she will not believe I did anything wrong." To show his disdain of his sister's warning he began to spin the jewels wildly in the air, but in doing so he did not notice Anastasia sneaking up behind him. She wrapped her arms tightly around her brother and pulled him down, careful to use her body as a cushion when they landed on the floor. He lost his grip on the jewels and Tatiana quickly retrieved them and put them back on the dressing table. At that moment the Tsarina entered the room to check on Olga's progress and found Alexei laying atop Anastasia and unable to escape because of the firm grip she had on him.

"What on earth are you doing, Anastasia," she scolded. "Get up off the floor immediately. Alexei, baby, are you all right?"

"I think so, Mama, but I was very frightened because she was so rough with me. I was afraid I would bruise," he whimpered.

"What were you thinking of, girl? Have you gone mad? You know how delicate your brother is. You will be severely punished. Now go to your room. You will not take part in any of the festivities and you will only have soup for dinner." Anastasia began crying and ran out of the room.

Olga tried to intervene. "Mama, that is not fair," she argued. "He came rushing in here uninvited and snatched my new jewels and was trying to break them."

"Your jewels are still sitting on the dressing table where they were when I left earlier," Alexandra answered.

"That is because Anastasia made Alexei drop them and Tatiana picked the jewels up from the floor."

"Enough," interrupted her Mother. "He is the heir and future sovereign of our nation and you must give him the respect due him."

Olga was at a rebellious age and now she forgot herself completely. "That is so unfair, Mother. Doesn't respect have to be earned? Alexei can run around and do as he pleases and no one does a thing to discipline him. He is not even the Tsar and yet he has complete control of this family. Do you not see how he manipulates every situation and you always accept what he says without question?"

The Tsarina walked up to her daughter, raised her hand, and slapped her across the face. "Do not ever speak to me in that manner again," she said coldly. Then, taking Alexei with her, she turned and strode from the room.

Olga fell back in her chair in complete shock. Alexandra had never slapped any of her daughters in the face before but then again no one had been so bold as to speak to her in such a way. Tatiana and Maria rushed to comfort their sister, but surprisingly Olga was not in tears.

"Poor Olga, and on your special day," said Maria.

"Mama should not have slapped you," Tatiana added. "I am glad you stood up to her about Alexei. It is true that he gets away with too much."

Olga sighed. "I should not have talked to her that way. I deserved what I got." She looked into the mirror and saw the bright red mark on her cheek. "Oh, I must do something about this," she said, as she opened a container of powder and dabbed at her face. In recognizing that her impertinence to her mother was misplaced, Olga had quickly grown up and would rarely see things as a child again This was but one of many arguments she would have with her mother and their relationship with each other would be somewhat strained from this point on.

Tatiana finished styling Olga's hair and then helped her into her dress. It was a light and airy, pink gown that was so pale the color was barely perceptible. Alix had insisted she wear a white dress, which was more appropriate for girls her age, but Olga had resisted. She had made the case that this was only a birthday and not her official debut and since things were more relaxed in Livadia she should be able to pick her gown. Olga was surprised when Alix relented. The dress fit her perfectly and accentuated her graceful figure. Her excitement at being the center of attention at her first ball overcame the lingering effects of the altercation with her mother and she fully intended to have the time of her life.

The White Hall was gaily decorated with arrangements of greenery and hundreds of the fresh roses which the Crimea was known for. Even though the evening was warm and the doors of the hall were thrown open to the fresh breezes, their delicate scent permeated the room. The ballroom was filled with guests eagerly awaiting the arrival of the Imperial party. The men were wearing the dress uniforms of their perspective services and many of the young officers from the *Standart* were guests. The ladies were dressed in brightly colored silk or satin gowns while the younger girls wore the fluffy white dresses considered appropriate for young unmarried women.

On the other side of the entrance doorway Olga stood with her father, waiting for him to escort her into her birthday ball. Her cheeks were flushed and her blue-gray eyes glowed in anticipation of the evening. She looked up at the landing of the staircase and saw her sisters waving at her. They were happy for her but there was a look of envy in Tatiana's face because she wanted so badly to join the party. Alix and Alexei stood inside the hall near the entrance. She was not attending the ball as it was too strenuous for her but she had come down to briefly greet the guests. Nicholas had seen her earlier and was amazed at how attractive she looked. The Crimea was obviously having a positive effect on her. She was dressed in a gown of gold brocade and silk and wore many jewels from her private collection. Her hair was crowned with a diamond and gold tiara which gave her extra height, while around her neck were rows and rows of precious gems. She looked every inch the Empress and the guests, who were used to seeing her in a wheel chair or pony cart, were amazed by the transformation in her appearance.

When Nicholas and Olga walked through the double doors of the White Hall and were formally announced everyone turned to look at the Tsar and his lovely daughter. At a nod from the Tsar the orchestra struck up a lively tune and Nicholas danced the first number with his daughter. When it ended Olga was surrounded by a number of young men and her dance card was quickly filled. She danced with Dmitri, officers from the

Standart and the guard and finally the one she longed to see most. Antoly Vasilyev, known as Vasily, was the young sailor who had rescued Anastasia all those years ago when the *Standart* ran aground. He had been commissioned an officer as a reward for his heroism. He took her in his arms and they floated around the room and she could not have been happier. They exchanged a few words but the dance ended far too quickly for any serious conversation. Soon her next partner was standing by, waiting to whisk her away. She looked wistfully over his shoulders at Vasily, who would dance no more that night. Olga was in the midst of her first teen age infatuation and she and Vasily flirted with one another whenever the opportunity presented itself. Her mother and father did nothing to discourage the flirtations that were beginning to develop among the officers and the Grand Duchesses. They were always properly chaperoned by either Anya or one of Alix's ladies-in-waiting. Alix considered it harmless fun and made sure that each daughter in turn was aware that nothing could come of these relationships. But a "first love" is a strong and passionate emotion for a young girl and Olga was convinced she had found the man of her dreams and would one day marry him. She shared these thoughts with Tatiana, but never with her mother, who she knew would not approve.

The hour grew late and soon it was time for Olga to retire. She wished the night would never end. It had been such a glorious evening. She was young and in love and would remember this ball forever. When the last dance was completed she retired to her room and, once the maid had left, she climbed on Tatiana's bed to share her experience. She described the ladies' ball gowns and the handsome officers. "Vasily was here and asked me to dance," said Olga. "It was the most wondrous thing when he took me in his arms and whisked me around the room. He is so strong and handsome and I adore him."

"Well, do not get too attached. You know you must make a brilliant marriage. I wonder if Mama and Papa will marry you off the way Aunt Ella did when she shipped Marie off to Sweden. She was only sixteen, just like you, said Tatiana."

"Oh they would never do that. I shall marry only for true love and be as happy as they are."

"I have heard the Rumanian Prince Carol is quite a catch. He would be perfect for you," Tatiana teased.

"Oh no, he is horrid and looks like a toad. I could never marry him." Grimacing at the thought of Prince Carol, she threw a pillow at Tatiana and moved to her own bed. "Good-night, Tatiana."

"Good-night Olga, sweet dreams." The two girls drifted off to sleep and Olga dreamt of her sweet sixteenth birthday and the thrill of dancing with Vasili.

Chapter 20

July 1912 - Gulf of Finland. The *Standart* lay at anchor in a well-protected cove, on the south shore of the Gulf, awaiting the arrival of a launch bearing Baroness Sophie Buxhoeveden. Sophie had been asked by the Empress to join the family on their summer cruise and to serve as Lady-in-Waiting and she had readily accepted. This summons to join the group on the yacht was an unexpected honor as usually only members of the immediate family, and friends such as Anya Vyrubova, were invited on the cruise. After a tiring journey from Denmark, first by train and now by boat she was at last approaching the royal yacht and she could hardly wait to get there. The violent pitching of the small craft was making her sea sick and she was anxious to get aboard the larger, more stable vessel.

Years ago, when Sophie had first been called to court to serve as a Lady-in-Waiting, she had made all the mistakes one would expect from an inexperienced teenager. The Tsar still teased her about the time when, during a formal ceremony, she had tumbled down the carriage steps and landed in a heap at the Empress' feet in full view of all the dignitaries lined up to greet the Imperial couple. But as the years passed she became more comfortable in her role and was now a great favorite of the whole family, especially the young Grand Duchesses, who gravitated to her youth and vitality. The Empress wanted Isa, as she was called by the family, to become a permanent member of her retinue but personal obligations had prevented the Baroness from accepting the honor, and so she served only on occasion.

When Sophie climbed the accommodation ladder to the main deck she was greeted with noisy enthusiasm by the girls and with kindness by the Empress. "Come join us for tea, Isa. It will help you recover from what I am sure was an arduous journey," offered the Tsarina. Sophie was touched that the girls had foregone a trip ashore with their father in order to be on board when she arrived. Although she was here in an official capacity she would be given very few formal duties and treated more like a guest. She sat down and joined the light-hearted group and sipped tea while the girls prattled on, catching her up on all the news since she was last with them. When tea was completed, the Grand Duchesses insisted on giving her the grand tour of the yacht.

"My dears, don't you remember that the last time I was aboard you showed me around," Sophie protested.

"Isa, I am sure there is something new you have not seen," insisted Olga. Sophie smiled and went along with them because she knew the Grand Duchesses just wanted to venture into areas they were normally forbidden to go. It was an interesting hour as they explored every nook and cranny, stopping numerous times so Sophie could be introduced to the officers. The girls knew the name of every officer and sailor on board and Sophie noticed quite a few flirtatious glances passing back and forth. She knew it was all very innocent and she had to admit she enjoyed the admiring looks that came her way as well. Still in her early twenties, she was young enough to appreciate the attention but when the girls started below to visit the engine room she called a halt to the tour and went back to her cabin to assist her maid and finish unpacking.

At dawn the next morning, the rising sun tinted the edges of the scattered clouds with orange and yellow hues and held forth promise of a glorious day. A flurry of activity was already taking place aboard the yacht as the non-rated seaman holy-stoned the deck, polished bright work, and put the finishing touches on the morning's house-keeping duties. The Tsar, as was his custom, had awakened early, and gone on deck to conduct a cursory inspection of the Imperial yacht. This, of course, was completely unnecessary because the *Standart* was meticulously maintained, but it gave Nicholas an opportunity to stroll the deck, smoke a first cigarette, and make small talk with the ship's crew. Sophie arose at what she deemed an obscenely early hour and was surprised to find the Grand Duchesses already dressed for the day and gone from their staterooms. They loved to join their father at this peaceful time of the morning and, although the salt air was conducive to sleeping-in, the girls were faithful to the routine. The Tsar and the four sisters greeted Sophie when she finally struggled on deck and teased her about being an old sleepy head. Promptly at nine a.m. the Tsar ushered the group into the dining salon for the day's first meal. There was something about the moist sea breezes that created ravenous appetites and the Grand Duchesses quickly devoured the continental breakfast of sweet rolls and coffee or tea. Forgetting their manners they urged their father to hurry his breakfast and abandon the others so they could go boating. As part of his morning routine, the Tsar liked to row for exercise and occasionally, as a special treat, he allowed his daughters to join him for a turn or two around the yacht. After their ride Sophie and the girls went ashore for a swim. They usually changed into their bathing costumes behind a granite boulder and swam in an area separated from the men who were accustomed to swimming in the nude.

After the morning swim everyone returned to the yacht to enjoy a huge lunch which was much appreciated after the strenuous morning. Once the meal was completed, eyelids became a little heavy, and most of the party enjoyed a short nap in one of the many deck chairs scattered around the fantail. At a little after two, those that were invited went ashore again to join the Tsar for a long walk. Sophie was amused to see how the younger officers competed for invitations from the Grand Duchesses to join them. The older and more portly members of the wardroom, however, tried to stay in the back ground; they had no desire to be included. These hikes were notorious and not for someone in poor physical condition. It was not uncommon for the Tsar to walk as many as twelve miles over difficult terrain, at a fast pace, and it was very fatiguing for some.

Today's walk was to be a lengthy one and Nicholas had made arrangements for the ship's launch to pick them up at a spot about eight miles from the anchorage. The group set out and immediately began to enjoy the crisp air, the aroma of the tall pines and the plentiful wildlife which scattered before their noisy approach. After a few miles of fairly easy going the trail was blocked by a huge rock fall and barriers on either side of the path prevented bypassing it. "I think it can be climbed," said the Tsar and up he went, using toeholds and branches to scale the obstacle. The young officers and Olga, Tatiana and Maria made it easily to the top but Sophie and Anastasia were unable to master the large rock. "Come on Isa, you can do it," shouted Olga, from the top of the boulder. Sophie tried again but slipped and went tumbling down, ripping the sleeve of her dress on the rough granite face. She was mortified when one of the officers climbed down and hoisted her up on his shoulders while a second leaned over from the top and pulled her up. Olga and Tatiana were laughing at her whereas Nicholas used the opportune delay to puff on one of his eternal cigarettes. Anastasia's turn came and soon they were all on their way to the rendezvous with the launch.

Each day was so full of activity that time seemed to race by, leaving in its wake that memorable, idyllic summer of 1912. They played tennis, skated on the wooden deck of the yacht, and went boating, swimming and hiking. The Empress spent most of her days on a chaise lounge on deck with Anya who, as usual, was on the voyage. The two women would laugh and talk the day away while the Tsar, Sophie and the children enjoyed the more strenuous activities ashore. Each evening before sunset a ceremony of sorts took place on deck. The sailors and officers of the crew came to attention while the Tsar and his family stood quietly nearby. A whistle sounded and all bowed their heads and recited the Lord's Prayer. A few minutes later another whistle sounded and the navy personnel saluted while the colors were lowered at the stern. After this everyone went in for dinner.

Although most of the summer cruise was dedicated to relaxation, Nicky put in a number of hours each week on state matters and occasionally hosted an official event. This summer the ordinary routine was briefly interrupted by a state visit from the Swedish King and Queen, Gustaf and Victoria and, since both Alexandra and Victoria were not well, Nicholas decided to receive the couple on the *Standart*. These official receptions were much less taxing while aboard the yacht because of the reduced size of the Emperor's retinue and the smaller number in the King's party. Nevertheless, the relaxed atmosphere on the *Standart* disappeared for a few days. Wild flowers picked on shore and arranged in vases were replaced by large formal arrangements. They were brought to the anchorage from Peterhof by steam launch to add elegance to the state dinner hosted by Nicholas and Alexandra. When the night of the formal dinner arrived, Sophie found herself in a quandary. Dressing for dinner was an ordeal and there was no hair dresser on board. In desperation she attempted to style her hair and attach a diamond tiara but it was a disaster. As she continued to struggle, she heard a knock on the door and Olga walked in. She looked breathtaking in her evening clothes. Olga took one look at Sophie and said, "We must get Tatiana in here to fix your hair, or you will be late. She will not mind helping you. Look at the wonderful job she did on my hair."

"I would greatly appreciate her help. You can see I am a mess."

Tatiana answered the summons and was soon curling and teasing Sophie's hair like a professional hair dresser. After what seemed like hours to the Baroness, Tatiana had created an elaborate coiffure with cascading ringlets.

"Oh, thank you Tatiana; you are a true genius."

"Isa, it is nothing. I enjoy styling hair. Now before you go we must secure this tiara on your head," said Tatiana. I want every young man at the dinner spellbound at your radiance." As it turned out, they were.

Sophie was the Lady-In-Waiting for the Swedish visit and the next few days were taken up with a flurry of activities. She managed to conduct herself appropriately and there were no unfortunate accidents. As for the two royal consorts, they enjoyed each others company and spent as much time together as possible. This was a refreshing change for Alexandra, who was truly comfortable in the company of Queen Victoria. As far as she was concerned the few days of the visit passed too quickly.

A week later another visitor arrived at the anchorage, which by then had been shifted to the "Bay of Standart." From Alexandra's point of view the arrival of the *Polar Star* in the secluded bay was not nearly so welcome since the Dowager Empress was aboard. She was here to celebrate her saint's name day and because it was the same as Maria's she tried to spend it with her granddaughter whenever possible. Her daughter Olga and her son Michael had traveled with her and that afternoon they were rowed over to the *Standart* for tea. It was a surprisingly pleasant afternoon and later, as everyone wandered off from the tea table, Olga took the opportunity to bring up a rather sensitive matter with Alix, her sister-in-law. "Alix, I have something I wish to discuss with you but I am hesitant to broach it," said Olga rather nervously.

"Nonsense, Olga you know you can talk to me about anything," she said warmly.

"It concerns Father Grigory."

"Oh!" Alix stiffened somewhat when she heard what Olga wished to talk about but knowing that Nicky's sister was the most level-headed of all the Romanovs and was certainly not a busybody, she decided to let her continue.

"Alix, surely you must know what is being said about this man. It is all simply dreadful and the worst of it is that gossip mongers are using these horrible rumors to besmirch the reputations of you, Anya and the girls."

"Surely you do not believe I am engaged in any improper behavior."

"Oh of course not, Alix, but I just cannot understand why you allow such a man in your home. His reputation is so terrible."

"Actually, he comes to the palace only on rare occasions, when Alexei is ill. If I need to talk to him we meet at Anya's. At any rate, Olga, I will never believe the things they say about him. I have never seen any evidence of this behavior. I have sent Anya to his apartment in St. Petersburg and also to his home in Siberia and she has never seen anything improper."

"Alix, I do not think you comprehend how serious this is."

"On the contrary Olga, I do not think you understand the situation at all. This is not just about me. My Alexei is very ill and all these years he has remained alive due to Father Grigory's prayers and ability to heal."

"I do not understand. What does he do?"

"Olga, I tell you this in confidence, Alexei has the bleeding disease. It has made him very ill and ruined my health as well. How can I not believe in Father Grigory? The minute he is near Alexei, the child begins to feel better. I have seen the most dreadful of hemorrhages stopped through his intercession. Without him I do not know how we would have survived and even if I believed all of what they say, I would not send him away."

"Alix I had no idea. Why do you not share this? It would help people to understand and they would have much sympathy for you."

"I doubt seriously that the people will ever have sympathy for me, no matter what. At any rate we consider it a state secret. How can we let the Russian people know the heir is ill and could die at any moment? He is their future and it would destroy their hopes."

"Alix, I must apologize for being so quick to judge. How you must have suffered from these vicious attacks. Please forgive me for not being more alert to what is going on."

"God does not give us crosses bigger than we can carry, Olga. Anyway, it does not matter what people say since Father Grigory is not even in St. Petersburg. Nicky sent him to his home in Siberia because we were concerned for his safety. I know you will be tempted to share this news with other members of the family and if you decide you must, please tell them to be discreet. I appreciate your candor today but you must know that I do not wish to have this conversation again."

"Yes, Alix. I understand."

"Please excuse me now. I wish to be alone," Alix said, in dismissing the Grand Duchess.

She needed a few moments to compose herself as it always upset her to think about Alexei's illness. Surprisingly though, Alexandra felt a sense of relief at having been able to unburden herself to someone and was glad it had been Olga, whom she both liked and admired. Usually the Empress reacted negatively to any criticism of Rasputin and this was the first time she had allowed a discussion to continue to a normal conclusion. She did not think Nicky would be upset with her for revealing the nature of Alexei's illness because she knew that he too trusted Olga.

Although she was disturbed by her conversation with Alix, Olga went to join the others knowing she would be missed if she was gone too long. She had long suspected that Alexei had a more serious illness than just the usual childhood sicknesses but she had never considered that hemophilia was the cause of his attacks and now she began to second guess herself.

I have been so blind? How could I have spent so much time with Nicky, Alix and the children and not seen what was right in front of me? Now she understood Alix's obsession with the holy man. Alix had to trust him when she sincerely believed he kept her son alive. Olga wondered how Rasputin did it. She would never believe he performed miracles and despite her acceptance of the fact that he brought relief to Alix and her son, she still considered him a manipulative and evil man. She shuddered when she remembered a time she had been left alone with him for a few moments. He asked her personal questions about her husband and then had the audacity to put his arm around her and attempt to caress her. The Grand Duchess had immediately moved away and he stopped pursuing her when others came back into the room. Olga was sure he was attempting to seduce her and the thought still sickened her, even now. She had told no one about the incident due to her embarrassment, but it contributed enormously to her distrust of the man. It worried her to think of him at the palace, although now she understood the reason.

The next day was Minnie's name day, as well as Maria's, and Nicky's mother had decided to hold a tea dance on the deck of the *Polar Star*. The yacht was festively decorated with satin bows tied to the lifelines and fresh flowers everywhere. The bands from both ships alternated so there was no break in the music. Officers from both yachts were invited and Grand Duke Michael served as host. The few women included the Grand Duchesses and ladies of the suite. Minnie and Alix sat on benches enjoying the high spirits of the young people. The Grand Duchesses reveled in the dancing and the attention they received, and never seemed to tire as partner after partner whirled them around the deck.

Young Olga finally had the opportunity to dance with Vasily and she could scarcely keep in step she was so nervous. As they danced she whispered into his ear, "I will slip away in a few minutes. Meet me at the stern of the ship. I will wait for you there." When the dance was completed she excused herself and made her way to the rear of the ship where she anxiously awaiting Vasily's arrival. She knew that she would never be able to marry this man, but she could not suppress the affection for him that had grown over the years. What had started out as a flirtation was slowly building into a serious infatuation but she could not express her feelings to him because they were never alone together.

Vasily waited until Olga disappeared and then made his way slowly to the stern of the yacht. He was apprehensive about meeting her and was well aware of the risks and yet, he could not deny his feelings for her. He knew that they had no future together and his common sense told him this was a mistake but his heart demanded that he go and take her in his arms no matter what the consequences. He decided that he would have to be the strong one and put an end to this but when he saw Olga standing there in the afternoon sun, in all her beauty, her face flushed from the dancing, his strength deserted him. He approached her and without saying a word took her in his arms.

Olga had never experienced such intense emotions before, but something kept her from telling him how she felt. Vasily on the other hand felt no such hesitation and he refused to bottle up his emotions a moment longer. "Olga, I must share my feelings with you," he said as he looked into her eyes.

"No, you must not. I should not have asked you back here. Just being alone with me could put you in serious trouble."

"I do not care. I have fallen in love with you and I must express this love in the only way I know." They moved closer until their lips met. Olga was nearly overcome with rapture by the innocent kiss. "Oh Vasily," she sighed. "This could never be." And at that moment her world came crashing down around her. She felt a hand upon her shoulder, gently but firmly, pulling her away from Vasily. It was the Tsar. He had walked to the rear of the ship to smoke a cigarette and stumbled upon the young lovers.

"Young lady, make your way back to the dance immediately," ordered the Tsar.

Olga turned and fled, terrified of what her father might do. She was afraid for herself but more so for Vasily and what would happen to him. She hated to leave him there alone with her father because she knew how angry the Tsar could become. Nicholas turned to Vasily, who was standing at attention, and smiled at him. The Tsar was more amused than angry. The scene reminded him of his youth and the times he and Alix had stolen kisses behind the back of Queen Victoria. He put his hand on Vasily's shoulder and looked at him as sternly as he could. "Vasily, you know that I feel very indebted to you, however, I cannot repay you with my daughter. I will say that if you were from a royal family I would welcome you as my son-in-law, but you know that cannot be.

Vasily stood quite still, not daring to interrupt the Tsar, and praying silently that he would not be thrown into prison or sent to Siberia.

"You must never see Olga again. When we get back to port you will be posted to a unit far from my family. In the meantime you will be reassigned to the *Polar Star* so you will not be tempted to obey the yearning of your heart. You will not be confined to your quarters but if you are seen on deck before the yacht sails, you will be thrown in the brig and when I return I will have you put in prison for disobeying me. Now, do not say a word about this to anyone. I do not wish my daughter's reputation to be compromised. You are dismissed."

Vasily saluted smartly, did an about face, and quickly left the Tsar. He breathed a sigh of relief that his punishment had not been more severe. It broke his heart to know that he would never see his precious Olga again, but he realized it was for the best. Being near her every day, but unable to express his feelings for her, would be a torture worse than any prison cell. He was just thankful that it was the Tsar, and not the Empress, who had discovered them together

The Tsar pulled out his gold Faberge cigarette case and removed a smoke but then changed his mind. He walked slowly back to the dance but before he reached it, he was confronted by his Mother. "Nicky, did something happen with Olga. She returned to the dance and seems to be very upset," said Minnie.

"As well she should be, Mama. You know how the girls are attracted to the young officers and have their innocent flirtations with them. Unfortunately, Olga's infatuation was beginning to get more serious, so I had to put an end to it. I am sure she is devastated but I could not let it continue any further."

"Poor dear. It is so hard to be young and in love," said Minnie. "Maybe I should go talk with her."

"No, I think it best to let her be for now. I know she must be very embarrassed and worried since I caught them in a frivolous indiscretion," explained Nicholas.

"Very well, let us go back to the dance. I so enjoy watching my granddaughters twirl around the dance floor." The two walked back to the awning where the dance was taking place. Alexandra motioned to Nicky that she wished to speak to him so he strolled over and sat down on the bench next to her.

"Nicky, I must speak with you. Olga was in such a foul mood that I made her return to the *Standart*. I do not know what has gotten into her lately."

Nicholas nodded in apparent agreement but did not say anything since he had decided to keep this little incident from his wife. He had already handled the situation and felt nothing would be gained by bringing her into it. Nicholas decided that he needed to have a talk with Olga and be straight forward with her concerning the fate of the young officer. "Alix, I am sorry but I need to go back to the yacht and complete some work. I will speak to Olga when I get there."

"But Nicky you have hardly spent anytime with your Mother."

"I know my dear, but she understands. I will try not to be gone too long," he said, and gave her a quick buss on the cheek. When Nicholas arrived back on the *Standart* he went immediately to Olga's stateroom where he found her sobbing bitterly into her pillow.

"Olga I must speak to you. Vasily has been transferred to the *Polar Star* until we get back to port and then he will be reassigned to a unit far away. You will not be allowed to see him again."

"Oh, Papa, he should not be punished just because he cares about me. It is so unfair."

"He is being sent away, but it will not affect his career. No one will ever know about this incident and I trust you not to talk about it."

"But I love him. I wish to marry him."

"You must know that is impossible. You are the daughter of a Tsar and therefore your husband must come from the nobility. I never told you this, Olga, but there was someone else in my life before your Mother. She was a beautiful and enchanting ballet dancer and I loved her dearly, but I knew that duty came first and I could never marry her. It was so hard to give her up and I was sure I would never find another love to match her. In time though, I developed strong feelings for your Mother. My love for her was much greater than it ever was for the dancer. You see, my daughter, you can love again. Our hearts are made to love and you will find another, I promise you. I do understand how you must feel but you are a young lady now and a Grand Duchess as well. Your behavior must always be above reproach. You are suffering enough, I know, so you will not be punished. I have not told your Mother about this, nor will I. This is between you and me, and it will stay that way. If anyone asks about Vasily I will say that he asked to be transferred. That is all I can do Olga. You know I could have exiled him but I have always liked the fellow. I wish things could have been different but I know in time your heart will heal. I would suggest that you return with me to the *Polar Star*. I will make it right with your mother and you can just say you were feeling ill. I think being heartsick qualifies as an illness."

The Tsar left Olga in her stateroom and took a turn around the yacht. He visited briefly with members of the duty section and then called for his gig. Olga was waiting for him at the accommodation ladder, her face freshly powdered, and making an obvious effort to look cheerful. Together they spent the rest of the afternoon with the family and guests taking part in the day's festivities. It was pleasant and relaxing and for a moment the Tsar was able to forget his worries and enjoy himself. He was fond of his Mother and wished he saw her more often but he knew she and Alix would never find common ground. As the celebration drew to a close Nicholas, Alexandra and the children bid good-bye and returned to the *Standart.* Minnie was leaving that evening to return to St. Petersburg so everyone stayed on deck and waved good-bye as her yacht weighed anchor and got underway for the city.

The next day was rather overcast and in the distance a storm threatened to cancel any activities ashore. The Grand Duchesses were quickly bored by the inactivity and pleaded with Sophie to tell them one of her stories. The Baroness was a gifted storyteller and the children loved the somewhat lurid tales she told. Her never ending repertoire of anecdotes had been passed on to her in her childhood by one of her Russian nurses, much to the dismay of her stiff English nanny, and she embellished them at every retelling. "Today I have a very special story to tell you. It is about one of your ancestors, Tsar Alexander I," and with this simple beginning Sophie began to tell her tale.

"It was many years ago and Russia was ruled at the time, by Alexander's father, Paul. Now, Tsar Paul I was a madman, evil to the core, and totally ruthless. Members of the nobility at the court wanted him removed and decided to take matters into their own hands. They went to Alexander and told him what they planned to do and, although he knew what they proposed was wrong, he did nothing to stop them. The noblemen sneaked into Paul's bedroom, fell upon him, and began to stab him brutally with their swords, over and over again. His blood soaked into the white sheets and began spilling onto the floor. Alexander remained hidden in his rooms, covering his ears to block out the bloodcurdling screams coming from his father's quarters. The nobles cleaned their weapons with the curtains and left Paul laying in a pool of blood barely clinging to life. Slowly, as the remaining blood seeped from his mutilated body, he passed into unconsciousness and finally death." Sophie used descriptive gestures to bring the story to life and the children were spellbound by the vivid stabbing motions that went with the gory tale.

"Alexander became the Tsar but he never forgot the terrible night Paul was murdered. He was ashamed that he had done nothing to stop it and, although his father's blood was not directly on his hands, he felt responsible. The guilt he felt about that night haunted his dreams and refused to give him peace and he spent many a sleepless hour struggling with his shame. As the years went by Alexander turned to religion for solace and began to yearn for a simpler life and a way to atone for his sins. His wife, the Empress Elizabeth became ill so he took her to an out of the way fishing village on the Black Sea to rest and recover. A few months later the residents of St. Petersburg received notice that the Tsar had taken ill with typhoid fever and died. The Empress attempted to accompany his body back to St. Petersburg but tragically she suffered heart failure along the way. It was said she died of a broken heart. During the funeral ceremonies the coffin was opened for viewing but the body was in such terrible condition no one could recognize the Emperor. Nevertheless his mother, the Dowager Empress, insisted it was indeed her son and no one had the audacity to suggest otherwise." Sophie glanced around at her audience and became aware that the Tsar was leaning around the corner of the deck house listening to her story. She thought for a moment that he would object to her gory tale but he caught her eye and winked, so she continued on.

"In a small town in Siberia there appeared a man by the name of Fyodor, who was much loved and respected by the townsfolk. Although he lived the simple life of a hermit he did not seem to be the kind of person who normally took up such an austere way of life. He was just too refined and well-educated and seemed quite conversant with the issues raised by the many important people from St. Petersburg who came to visit him. It was said that Fyodor bore a marked resemblance to the late Alexander I. Naturally, rumors abounded and one was especially intriguing. It was said that the body of a criminal, of the same height and build as the former Tsar was buried in his stead. It was also rumored that the Dowager Empress and the new Tsar, Alexander's brother, Nicholas, were part of the conspiracy."

"Oh my word, that is amazing," exclaimed Olga. "You mean he did not die."

"How is it no one knew? I cannot believe this is true, Isa. It is such a preposterous tale," said Tatiana skeptically.

"Oh, but it is true Tatiana," announced the Tsar as he joined the group. "But there is much more to the story."

"Oh, Papa, tell us more," pleaded Anastasia.

"It is so exciting," said Maria.

"Isa, do you mind if I continue your story," asked the Tsar.

"Not at all, your Imperial Highness," Sophie replied.

"Very well. Children, you never knew my late father, and your grandfather Alexander III, who died at Livadia before you were born. One spring, toward the end of his years as Tsar, the Neva River overflowed its banks and there was a terrible flood in St. Petersburg. The flood waters penetrated into the Fortress of Peter and Paul where all our ancestors are buried. It caused much damage to many of the tombs, so when the flood receded, my father ordered those monuments repaired. The law requires that when any Imperial tomb is opened certain officials must be present, including the Marshall of the Court and the military commander of the fortress. Repair work went on during the day in the church where the white marble sarcophaguses lay in state. It was determined that the tomb of Alexander I would need extensive repair and not wanting to open it during the day, in view of the people, the court officials waited until after the final liturgy of the evening. They then entered the cold, dark church whose only lights were the flickering candles in front of the iconostasis. The workers carried lanterns which cast shadows on the walls and as they moved along, the eerie images seemed to leap and jump like angry spirits annoyed at the interruption of their solitude. Everything was quiet and still when suddenly a loud crash was heard," said Nicholas as he clapped his hands dramatically. The noise startled the children and they leaped in their seats.

"What was it Papa?" whispered Maria.

"It was nothing. One of the masons had dropped a tool and the sound filled the church," Nicholas answered.

"Oh, Papa. You frightened me," complained Anastasia.

The Tsar continued. "When they reached Alexander's tomb, they lifted the marble lid and carefully removed it. It took all the workers because it was so heavy. They then maneuvered ropes under the wooden coffin and cautiously raised it up. It appeared that the damage to the coffin was going to have to be repaired from the inside so the lid was pried off and the lid to the inner lead coffin removed. The witnesses made the sign of the cross and the Marshall of the Court directed that lanterns be brought forward. The officials leaned in to examine the body and report its condition and the clerk readied his pen to record their comments. But there was only silence. No one spoke a word or even moved because the coffin was completely empty. No body, no skeleton, no garments, not even a speck of dust could be seen. Finally the Marshall broke the silence and ordered the tomb resealed. He directed the clerk to record that on this date the tomb was opened, repairs were completed and the tomb was resealed. The minister bid no one say a word of what they saw that night on pain of imprisonment. After the work was complete they signed the paper and filed out of the church," said the Tsar, as he completed the tale.

"That is the most extraordinary story I have ever heard," said Olga.

"I cannot believe he left his palace to go live in a hut. Imagine all that dirt," Tatiana protested.

"I am sure he felt the sacrifice was worth it. The poor man. It must have been dreadful for him to feel responsible for his father's death. It was his way of atoning for his misdeeds and was the least he could do," Maria observed.

"Well children, I hope you enjoyed Isa's story but it is time to prepare for tea," said Nicholas.

His daughters kissed his cheek as they left to get ready and Sophie also excused herself. In a paternal way Nicholas was very fond of his wife's Lady-in-Waiting. Although she was young she had a large measure of common sense and nothing seemed to faze her. He would never forget her now famous tumble from the carriage. In spite of her embarrassment she had picked herself up and carried on as if nothing had happened. He admired her spunk and courage.

Nicholas lit a cigarette, walked over to the rail, and looked at the gathering storm. As he inhaled the pungent smoke he thought about the story he and Isa had just recited. It was remarkable that Alexander had been able to fake his death and it was even more astonishing that it took almost a hundred years for anyone to discover the truth. Nicky had a premonition that there was something in this he could use. Just as the coming storm dominated the horizon, so too did the *Masquerade*, in some way, command his every waking moment. Yes, there was some lesson in this but like a life ring, barely out of reach, he just could not grab hold. The Tsar tossed his cigarette over the side and went below to change for tea.

Chapter 21

September 1912 - Spala, Poland. The vast forest was dark and gloomy, its trees growing so closely together sunlight could barely penetrate the canopy of intertwined branches that covered the road. The tunnel-like effect created by the thick foliage often caused mild claustrophobia in travelers hardy enough to brave the deeply rutted track. Into this shadowy world plunged the carriages transporting the Imperial family and its retinue to Spala, the Tsar's hunting lodge deep in the forests of Poland. The condition of the road made the going very slow but eventually the hunting party reached the wrought iron gates that marked the entrance to the estate. In contrast to beautiful Livadia, which was open and airy, everything about this place was bleak and oppressive. The forest pressed in closely to the fence surrounding the compound and although there was a cleared area inside the gates the open space did little to dispel the gloom. The lodge itself was a ramshackle wooden building constructed for men who came to hunt. There was not a single feminine touch in the place, except in the Empress' private rooms, which had been redecorated in her signature chintz. Since they were first married, Alix had insisted on accompanying Nicky to Spala. She knew he loved to hunt but disliked being separated from the family so her presence, in what had previously been a male dominated enclave, solved the dilemma. He loved her company and, now that the family had grown, he enjoyed the youthful exuberance of the children although he knew some in his suite grumbled about the presence of all these women. And so this dreary place, with its tiny windows and dimly lit interior would be their home for the next few weeks. Surrounded as it was, by large trees and foliage, very little natural light penetrated into its darkness and electric lights had to remain on even during the day to banish the gloominess. It was hard to believe that a few, short weeks ago they were having tea on the deck of the *Standart*.

It was a somber group that arrived that day, late in the month of September. Alexei had recently suffered an episode with his hemophilia and was barely well enough to make the trip to Spala. He was still pale and weak from the attack and would have to rest to regain his strength. Nicholas was uneasy about his son's condition but could not put his finger on the reason. He had a sense of impending doom and, though he knew such thoughts were unproductive, this time he could not seem to set them aside.

During the summer cruises the children were excused from their lessons but at other times, whether at Peterhof, Tsarskoe Selo, Livadia and yes, even here at Spala, formal studies were part of the daily routine. Alix arranged for the children's instructors to travel everywhere with the entourage and they had become an integral part of the household. Realizing that during his recovery Alexei would need some diversion, Alix decided to have Pierre Gilliard begin her son's French lessons. The Tsarevich was eight years old now and she felt it important that he learn the language of the court. Monsieur Gilliard had been teaching French to the Grand Duchesses for a number of years and the family had developed a true affection for this gentle man. The Empress had begun to include him at lunches and other activities usually reserved for the members of her suite and, as time went by, they grew to trust him more and more.

The days at Spala passed slowly for the women, but the Tsar enjoyed the outdoor activities, the fresh air, and the hunting for which the area was famous. One day, after returning from a morning hunt, he stepped out onto the balcony of the lodge to smoke a cigarette. Tobacco had become an addiction and it was a rare occasion when Nicholas was seen without a cigarette in his hand. As he leaned on the railing, contentedly puffing away, he was distracted by a child's voice coming from the clearing in front of the lodge. He looked out and was surprised to see Anastasia playing with her dog, Shivbitz, at the edge of the forest. Since It was time for all the girls to be with their tutors he wondered what she was doing out here alone. He knew Anastasia was mischievous and always playing pranks but he did not consider skipping lessons, acceptable behavior. He was also concerned that her tutor seemed unaware that she was missing from the classroom. Nicholas called out to her several times but she did not respond and continued to play with the dog. The Tsar reverted to the special whistle he had for his children and there still was no response.

Nicholas was amazed at the impudence of his youngest daughter and he began to grow very annoyed as she continued to ignore him. "If I have to walk all the way out there my anger will not be contained," he shouted at her. He called her name one more time and then tried his whistle again. There was no reply. Now, thoroughly exasperated, he stubbed out his cigarette, ran down the stairway, and stormed angrily across the green space towards her. He reached her just as she bent over to pick up a stick to throw for the dog, so she was unaware of his presence. "Young lady," he said as he tapped her shoulder. "What is the meaning of this? What are you doing out here? You should be at lessons!"

The girl turned around, obviously startled and confused. She turned pale and her eyes filled with tears and when she realized who this man was. "I do not go to school, your Highness," she said, her lips trembling.

The Tsar stood in stunned silence as he stared at the young girl who appeared to be, but was certainly not, his daughter. Nicholas quickly regained his composure. "Oh! I am sorry I frightened you," he said gently. I thought you were my daughter, Anastasia. It is uncanny how you resemble her, even up close. Who are you and how did you come to be playing with her dog?" he asked.

"They call me Franny Schanzka," she replied, still overwhelmed at meeting the Tsar. "My mother is one of the housekeepers here at the lodge and the Empress gave her permission to bring me along for the day as long as I stayed out of the way and did not interfere with her duties. I met one of the Grand Duchesses and she said I could play with the dog until they finished with their lessons."

"Well. I apologize again for startling you so. I still cannot believe how much you look like my daughter. Continue with your play," he said as he turned and walked back to the lodge.

Later that afternoon, when the rest of the family was already at tea, the door burst open and Anastasia dashed in, laughing boisterously. "Good heavens child have you lost all your manners," complained Alix. "What is all the raucous noise about?"

"Mama, Papa! I have a new friend and she looks just like me. We were pretending that we were Siamese twins, you know the two that were stuck together and could not come apart," excitedly explained Anastasia.

"Calm down child. Whatever are you talking about," asked Alix.

"One of the housekeeper's daughters came with her today. Her name is Franny and I met her before lessons. She looks just like me and we have been having the most fun. We played the best trick on one of the guards. I lent her one of my dresses and hats. She went right up to the guard and asked him a question. He did not know that it wasn't me. He answered the question and called Franny, your Imperial Highness. We laughed so hard afterwards but we did not tell the guard that it was not me," said Anastasia.

"Have you lost your mind child," reprimanded Alix. "Is this the proper way for a daughter of the Tsar of Russia to behave? I am ashamed at your behavior and I will inform the housekeeper that in the future her daughter will not be allowed at the palace."

"But Mama, that is so unfair. We were just playing," cried Anastasia.

"Enough child! Do not argue with me. Now go sit with your sisters and have your tea." Anastasia went to join them, but with a dejected look on her face.

"Sunny, do you remember when you were a child and all the tricks you used to play on your father and sisters?" asked Nicky.

"But I was not a Grand Duchess."

"No, you were a child wanting to have fun, just like your daughter," said Nicholas. "I met this Franny and she is a delightful young girl. Do not forget St. Serafim's letter. We do not know what awaits us, so let the children be children while they have a chance, I implore you."

"Very well, Franny can come back to play with Anastasia, but I forbid them to play tricks such as these."

"It will be as you wish, my dearest," said Nicky.

"Are you patronizing me, Nicky?"

"Of course not, my dear," Nicholas answered, with a twinkle in his eye. He called Anastasia over and told her that she might continue to have her new friend come to play. "But no tricks."

"Yes Papa." Anastasia was excited. She loved her sisters but it was a new experience to have a friend from outside the family.

A few days later as Franny walked to the hunting lodge she was cautioned by her mother again and again. "Now Franny, if anyone asks you why your face looks all bruised, you must tell them you tripped and fell against a rock," said her Mother.

"Yes Mama," was her barely audible reply.

Anastasia spent all her free time playing with Franny. After lessons she found her sitting outside on a bench next to the tennis court. Anastasia immediately noticed the terrible condition of the girl's face. "What happened to you," she asked.

"Uh, I, um. I fell against a rock," she said with some hesitation.

"How did it bruise your face on both sides?" Anastasia was confused and a little suspicious because her friend had a mark on one side of her forehead and another under her chin on the opposite side of her face.

"I don't know, it just happened that way," Franny replied, and Anastasia seemed to accept the explanation.

Technically, Spala was a palace but, since it was used as a hunting lodge and was far from luxurious, court etiquette and rules were not strictly adhered to. The Tsar had given Anastasia permission to invite Franny into her room so the two girls went there to play. Anastasia had many toys, costumes, beautiful clothes and jewels, and she felt a twinge of guilt when she saw the holes in her friend's dress. To balance the inequity Anastasia sometimes gave her an old dress or pair of shoes that to Franny were the height of elegance.

One day as they were playing dress up, Anastasia helped Franny into a costume and, as she turned to button it up, the Grand Duchess was shocked to see the condition of her back. It was completely black and blue with bruises and cuts. Franny had been having so much fun, lost in this world of make believe, that she had forgotten to keep the bruises concealed as she had been told by her mother.

"What in the name of the Lord has happened to you? Who has done this to you?" demanded Anastasia.

Franny spun around, trying to conceal her back. "Oh, it is nothing. I am always falling down and bumping myself. I am very clumsy. It is really nothing. I had better go now."

"No Franny, that is nonsense. You have been beaten. I want to know the truth. You are my friend now, so you must tell me."

"I am too frightened to tell you and if anyone learned that I did I would be in so much trouble. Please do not say anything," Franny implored her.

"Do not be afraid. I am the daughter of the Tsar and you must know I will not let anything else happen to you." She took her hand and led her over to a chair. "Now tell me what happened."

"It was my stepfather. He drinks and then gets very angry and hits me. My Mother says that I deserve it."

"What? Your own Mother! That cannot be. No one deserves to be treated this way, not even the lowest servant or field worker," she said. "I will have your mother dismissed from Imperial service immediately."

"No, you must not. We would starve if my mother lost her job. My stepfather is crippled in one leg so he cannot work. It is only my mother who works to feed us."

"Does your stepfather beat your brothers and sisters," asked Anastasia.

"No. Just me. I am not his real daughter, but the others are, so he does not hurt them. Only me; he hates me," she said and burst into tears, sobbing on the Grand Duchess' shoulder.

"How dreadful for you," she said as she gently patted her on the shoulder. "I will do something. This situation cannot be allowed to continue."

"Please do not tell anyone. I will only be beaten more."

"Very well. I will not say anything," said Anastasia but as soon as the words left her mouth, she knew she would not keep the promise. She could not let the beatings continue. This was her first experience with the harsh realities of life and she was naive enough to believe she could change any unpleasant situation. In her sheltered world such cruelty did not exist. Anastasia intended to approach her father and hope he could solve the dilemma but, before she could talk to him privately, an event occurred that put off, for some time, any opportunity to bring up the matter.

The second day of October turned out bright and sunny and Alix decided a carriage ride would be just the thing to put some color back in Alexei's cheeks. Anya would join them for the outing. The rig was brought around and the three set off, chattering gaily, as the driver maneuvered down the long sandy road. It was rutted and ungraded and the carriage seemed to hit every pothole. A few times Alexei was bounced up only to come down hard on the carriage seat. At first he was happy and smiling, enjoying the rare outing, but soon it became evident that something was quite wrong. The bouncing and jostling had dislodged the clot that remained in his leg from the last bout with his hemophilia and Alexei began to bleed internally. With no outlet for the blood, a painful swelling began, and he began to grow pale. When he leaned back against the seat of the carriage to rest Alix realized something was dreadfully wrong. Alexei's pallor and reaction to the rapidly growing pain confirmed her worse fears. She directed the coachman to turn the carriage around and they headed home at a breakneck speed.

Alexandra pulled Alexei closer and settled him on her lap in an attempt to soften the bumps from the jostling carriage. She pressed her lips to his forehead in the traditional way mothers do when checking for a temperature and was alarmed to find him burning with fever. She felt the old familiar fluttering in her chest and it became difficult to breath but she knew she had to maintain her composure. When her son needed her, the Empress became a tower of strength and refused to succumb to her own weaknesses. Now she looked over at Anya, who was exhorting the driver to go faster, and their eyes met. Alix read the concern in her friend's face and slowly shook her head. Speed was of the essence but each time the carriage hit a bump or rut Alexei would shriek in agony. Time seemed to have stopped and all she was aware of was the excruciating pain her son was enduring. Would they never arrive? She urged the driver on and finally he informed her, "Your Imperial Highness we are at the gates;" but by now, Alexei was losing consciousness.

As the carriage sped up to the lodge it set in motion a flurry of activity. Anya leapt out of the carriage and shouted for Derevenko. He immediately came out to carry Alexei up to his room and Alix followed, refusing to be separated from her precious child. Next Anya sent for Dr. Botkin and the Tsar and then went to see if the Empress needed any assistance, but Alix only waved her away. Fortunately the doctor was not on the morning hunt so he arrived within minutes and began his examination. It took him only a moment to confirm what Alix already suspected. He shook his head at her pleading look and said, "We must send for the specialists. It is a very serious hemorrhage."

At that moment Nicholas came galloping up on horseback. The morning hunt had just ended and Anya's messenger had found him not too far from the lodge. He rushed into the room and looked down at Alexei who was lying on his bed moaning softly at the pain. He grasped his son's hand and gave it a reassuring pat but he was troubled beyond words. He had never seen Alexei look worse and as he caught Alix's eye he knew she shared his concern. It was almost unbearable to watch their son suffer so and yet be unable to help him in any way.

It would take several days for the specialists to arrive from St. Petersburg and time seemed to stand still as Alexei's condition continued to worsen. He suffered not only from the pain in his leg but also from an abdominal hemorrhage, a development that was far more dangerous. As the blood continued to seep into his abdominal cavity it acted like a poison, irritating the nerve endings, and caused indescribable pain. An internal hemorrhage causes high fevers and Alexei's temperature hovered between 102 and 103 degrees. As the swelling increased, blood began to flow into his left hip joint and as it filled the space the pressure caused his leg to be drawn up towards his chest. The poor child was in excruciating agony and nothing could relieve his pain.

Alix refused to leave his side. She sat by his bed hour after hour, barely eating or sleeping and spending days in the same clothes. Each of his cries caused her enormous emotional distress. She could do nothing to make her son better and it was killing her. Finally the specialists arrived from St. Petersburg and they concurred with Dr. Botkin's diagnosis. All they could recommend was cooling compresses and aspirin to reduce his fever and complete quiet and rest. They wanted to give him morphine for the pain but Alix forbade it. Father Grigory had advised her in the past not to let the doctors bother him too much and neither she nor Nicholas had ever forgotten the side effects of the opiate given to his brother George when he was dying of tuberculosis. Although they knew it would relieve Alexei's pain they feared continuous doses of the drug would lead to an addiction. The treatment the doctors recommended was also dangerous because aspirin was an anti-coagulant and could negatively affect a hemophiliac's condition by preventing the blood from clotting properly.

The fact that only a few intimates knew the exact nature of Alexei's illness put additional pressure on his mother. She had to carry on as if nothing was out of the ordinary and at a time when she was most vulnerable, emotionally, she was sometimes called upon to leave Alexei's side and act out her role as Empress. Previously scheduled events had to be held as planned so that no one would suspect the heir's illness was serious and life threatening. And because Spala was small in size compared to the other palaces great care had to be taken to keep the secret from leaking out. When a function required Alix's presence she would make her official appearance and then slip out of the room from time to time. She would run, on her bad legs, down the hallway to Alexei's room to check on him, and then would reluctantly return to what seemed an interminable and unimportant social event.

On one such night she and the Tsar stood in a receiving line as Count Benckendorff introduced and presented the guests. The Empress was very upset but, to her credit, she made a supreme effort to greet each individual with a smile and a kind word. Nicky would occasionally reach over and give her hand a comforting squeeze. Several of the Polish nobility were presented to their Highnesses and introduced by the Count but, although the Tsar was very cordial, the uncertainty of his son's condition, which had worsened alarmingly during the day, seemed to preoccupy him. He was, however, pleased to see Count Alfred Potocki, walk through the door. The Potocki family was one of the major noble houses of Poland and was linked to many of the ruling monarchs of Europe. "It is good to see you Alfred," said the Tsar. "It has been quite a few years."

"Yes, it has been, your Imperial Highness," replied the Count. "Perhaps we will be able to speak later after you have had the opportunity to welcome the rest of your guests."

"I look forward to it," the Tsar responded graciously.

The scions of Polish society were invited tonight and the Tsar met Zamoyskis, Radziwills, and Krasinskis and then finally Baron Carl Gustaf Mannerheim.

Mannerheim, who was Finnish, was known as Gustaf Karlovich by the Russians. He had been educated in St. Petersburg and after joining the Russian army had slowly worked his way through the ranks. He was now Commander of the Uhlan Regiment of the Life Guards and stationed in Warsaw. The Tsar had been suitably impressed with his performance and recently granted him the honorary title of General in the Imperial Entourage. Mannerheim had made a conscious effort to befriend the Poles and many of the attendees at tonight's reception had become his close friends. Nicholas respected his opinion, especially on matters relating to Poland. When he visited Spala, he tried to spend some unofficial time with Mannerheim to catch up on the current situation in Poland. Gustaf was very knowledgeable and he kept Nicholas apprised on Polish factions that were working to create an independent Poland.

"Ah, another familiar face. How are you this evening, Gustaf?" inquired Nicholas.

"I am well your Highness," smiled Mannerheim.

"Poland certainly seems to agree with you. I understand you are quite an experienced hunter. I hope you will join us on one of our hunts, although I'm sure it will seem tame to you after hunting tigers in China."

"I am honored and pleased to accept your invitation. Each type of hunt presents its own challenges, even the smallest of birds and I always find a good chase exhilarating."

The receiving line finally greeted the last of the guests and the Tsar moved to the drawing room to mingle with them while waiters circulated trays of zakuski, the Russian hors d'oeuvres, and glasses of chilled vodka. Alix joined him and briefly chatted with their guests before slipping out to join Alexei. It was obvious to the guests that something was amiss but they were too polite to inquire. After the Empress departed, Count Potocki made his way over to Nicholas.

"I hear the hunting is excellent at your estate this year," said the Tsar.

"Yes," replied Alfred. "We have been very pleased with our success. Archduke Ferdinand and his wife brought in the largest kill this year. The stag was huge and had an enormous rack"

"Well, he does have an unfair advantage. It is said he is the finest marksman in Europe," commented the Tsar.

"That is true and he certainly did not disappoint us last year either. But let me change the subject if I may. How is your dear sister-in-law, the Grand Duchess Elizabeth?" the Count asked. "I met her years ago and found her to be such an extremely spiritual person. She said a change had taken place in her after the assassination of her husband. What a terrible state this world is coming to when a woman must see her own husband murdered before her eyes. It is so tragic."

"Truly; no one is really safe anymore," agreed the Tsar. "But to answer your question, the Grand Duchess has been quite busy. I gave her permission to organize a new order of nuns in Moscow and she built her own convent there a few years ago. As mother superior, she keeps very busy with her daily activities."

"What is the principal mission of the order?" asked Alfred.

"There is no single purpose as such, and although they minister primarily to young women their apostolate is quite extensive. There is a hospital, a home for orphans, a school, and a place for young women to live while they work in the city. She also supplies some of the soup kitchens in Moscow and her nuns make blankets and socks for the poor," answered Nicholas.

"It is interesting to hear of her work because I had a relative who also started a new order of nuns in Warsaw," Count Potocki informed the Tsar. "She died some years ago but the convent she built in the late1880s is very successful. I visited there once and it was very inspiring to see all the good that comes from the place. It sounds as if her convent and the Grand Duchess Elisabeth's are very similar. The religious community in Warsaw takes in girls, mostly from the streets, who need spiritual renewal and moral adjustment. The Mother Superior told me that when a girl comes to the nunnery her past is completely erased and she is given a new name. She in fact becomes a new person and I think that is what is so appealing about the convent. When someone steps through the door, no one asks about her past and a morally questionable girl would be treated the same as a noble woman."

"As it should be in a convent," said the Tsar.

Just then the doors opened, effectively ending their discussion, and the party moved into the next room to enjoy a formal dinner. The Tsar did not realize at the time that his casual conversation with the Count would lead to a breakthrough in the development of the *Masquerade*.

The next morning the heir's condition continued to deteriorate and as the day went on Alexei's screams echoed throughout the halls of Spala. "Lord have mercy on me," he pleaded, over and over. It was so heart wrenching that everyone avoided the hallway to his room, unable to bear the cries of the suffering child. When dawn arrived on the morning of the ninth of October, Alix, faithful to the last, still sat at her son's side, as she had for the past twenty-four hours. Alexei's condition had worsened so dramatically in the past day that as strong as she was when it came to her son, Alix was beginning to lose hope. Mercifully his cries had subsided and he began to speak to his mother in a voice so soft she had to lean forward to hear his words. "Mama, will the pain leave me when I die?

Oh, I want to leave this earth and this agony behind and go to heaven. I just wish I did not have to leave you behind, dear Mama."

Her heart was breaking as she looked down at her dear little boy. His hair was plastered to his head from the sweating of the fever and his skin was pale and waxen, with a gray tinge and he looked so incredibly weak. Alexei's leg was pressed against his chest and he could not stretch it out, and the boy's breathing was labored when he spoke. She gently held his hand and said, "Baby, you are not dying. We will come through this bout like we always do."

"Mama, you must prepare yourself to live without me. When I am gone I wish to be buried outside, but please pick a spot with sunshine to keep me warm."

Nicholas had come to the door of Alexei's room to relieve Alix, who was so exhausted she could hardly keep her eyes open. She remained unaware of Nicholas' presence as she held her son's hand and gently rubbed his brow. She had worn herself out and he was as worried about her as he was about Alexei. He observed their exchange and although he could not hear them, when he saw the expression on his wife's face, it was easy to imagine what had passed between mother and son. She had gone completely pale and Nicholas could not bear it. He ran from the room with tears in his eyes and looked for a place to compose himself. Alexei was dying and, knowing he was powerless to help him, he turned to prayer. He went outside to the tent which served as a chapel and gave explicit orders not to be disturbed.

Nicholas needed this time alone to sort out his feelings and emotions. He walked to the front of the makeshift chapel and lit two candles then dropped to his knees in prayer, pleading with God to spare Alexei. He glanced at the icons hanging on the canvas wall behind the altar and his eyes stopped at the familiar icon of Saint Serafim. "Oh blessed Serafim," he prayed aloud, "in revealing to me, in your letter, God's plans for the future, you have prepared me for so much that is yet to come. But if the loss of the future heir to the throne of Russia is part of the master plan, could you not have warned me? You promised my daughters a future; is my son not included? The holy woman, Elena Motivilov, must have known what was coming, but she said nothing. How was I to know?"

The only answer to his questions was the sound of the canvas walls of the tent as the wind gently rippled them. The Tsar fell to the ground and spread out his arms in the form of a cross. "Lord, God, is not the sacrifice of my own life enough? Must I be like Abraham and offer my only son to you? Lord, I humble myself before you and I implore you to spare the life of my Alexei," he cried out in agony. Just then sunlight broke through the clouds and cast a ray of light through the entrance to the chapel. The Tsar felt the warmth of it across the back of his neck and suddenly he felt a surge of hope which banished the feeling of despair that had engulfed him. "Lord God, have you, in your mercy, heard my prayer?" he cried out. He knew the power of prayer and that anything was possible with God, even the complete recovery of his son. He stood up and gently blew out the candles, his strength renewed and ready to face the challenge of his son's illness.

Meanwhile, Alix was in near despair and beginning to think her son would not live to see the morrow. She rested her head on his bed for a moment and almost began to weep but quickly regained control of herself. She knew if she started sobbing she would never stop and from somewhere she summoned a hidden reserve of strength. "I refuse to sit here and let my son die," she said to herself.

"Anya, come here this instant. I need your help and I must trust in your discretion."

"Oh, Alix, anything! I will do anything for you," she said.

"I need to send a wire and you must take it personally to the telegraph office. I can trust no one with this." Anya handed Alix the necessary writing implements and she quickly wrote out her message. It was very simple.

My dear friend, Baby is dying.

Matushka.

Anya knew the telegram was for Rasputin and was not sure what to do. "The Tsar has forbidden us to have any contact with him," she gently reminded her.

"I do not care. Look at him, Anya," just look at him! Are you willing to let him die?"

"No your Imperial Highness, I will send the telegram."

"Now before you leave we must remember everything Father Grigory does for Alexei. Do you have any of his special tea?"

"Yes, I will brew some. Father Grigory always made sure he was warm. Remember how he would order the bed warmed and cover him with extra blankets."

"I remember now. You are quite correct. Now go, we must get the telegram sent." Before she left Anya brought the tea for Alexei and Alix set it on the night stand. She saw the bottle of aspirin and threw it away in fury. How could she have forgotten and allowed the doctors to give him the medicine. Father Grigory had warned her that the medicines harmed Alexei. She set to work applying his home remedies and trying to make Alexei more comfortable. It made her feel better knowing she was doing something productive.

In another room, the Tsar was conferring with Alexei's physicians and the news was not good. The swelling had reached its peak and now it was a waiting game. The doctors asked him to sit as they gave him their analysis. "Your Imperial Highness there is nothing more we can do. His bleeding has peaked and he will either live or die. We will know by morning but his prognosis does not look good. It is unlikely he will survive the night." Nicholas was devastated by the news but knew he could not succumb to his grief. God's will be done.

"Your Imperial Highness the Empress seems to be suffering some type of breakdown," said Doctor Botkin. "She refuses to allow us to examine Alexei and she has thrown out his medications."

"Do not bother her. It is her way of handling her sadness. You have said that he may not live through the night, so let her have these moments with her son. Anyway, what good have the medicines done except prolong his suffering."

The Tsar then called in Count Benckendorff and together they prepared telegrams to notify the family, and medical bulletins for the newspaper. The country had to be alerted to the possibility that the heir might die and since there had never been a public acknowledgment of his illness the announcement would come as a shock to most of the world. Consequently the bulletins had to be carefully worded. He also ordered that the staff and the rest of the retinue be informed.

Outside in the chapel tent constant services were held throughout the day and night and everyone who had a spare moment went in to pray for Alexei. Even the Polish peasants who worked at the estate, and were predominantly Catholic, were seen slipping into the chapel. They did not know the nature of Alexei's illness, only that it was life-threatening. Father Alexander, the priest at Spala was tireless in his ministrations and prayed continuously for the heir and for Russia. An eerie quiet settled over Spala as everyone waited for news that, one way or the other, Alexei's ordeal was finally over.

One by one the Grand Duchesses were brought in to see their brother. Or course, they knew he was very ill but were not told he was dying. The girls lived such a secluded life that they had little experience with death and Alix was unwilling to burden them with its reality before Alexei actually passed on. Each brought him a little gift and pictures they had drawn for him and Alix allowed them to spend a few minutes with him. Anastasia was the last to come in and she was extremely distraught at his condition. She managed to keep her emotions in check as she talked softly and gave him her gifts. She leaned in and kissed him on the cheek. Then with her lips beginning to quiver, she hastened out of the room and gently closed the door. She leaned against the wall and began to sob bitterly, with an intensity that frightened her sisters, who were waiting for her in the hallway. Maria used her handkerchief to wipe her sister's eyes and Olga spoke soothingly to her. "Let us go to the chapel and pray for him," she said.

Night was falling as the four girls walked across the lawn to the temporary chapel. Dark clouds had rolled in and the sky was forbidding and ominous and they could barely see. The Grand Duchesses entered the dimly lit tent and knelt in front of the altar to pray for their beloved brother but, with the storm threatening to break at any moment, they did not stay very long. Hurriedly finishing their prayers they raced back to the lodge and arrived just as the deluge began.

Meanwhile a hush had come over Alexei's room. Father Alexander brought him Communion and the sacrament seemed to bring him peace. The priest performed the last rites and then waited quietly in one of the chairs set at the opposite end of the room. Nicholas sat with Alix during the liturgy but when Alexei appeared to fall asleep he left the room to make preparations for something he never thought he would have to face; the burial ceremony of his own child. He met with members of his suite in the study and they began to discuss the tradition that would be followed in conducting the state funeral of a Tsarevich.

In the middle of this sad task, the door to his study flew open and Alix rushed in. Nicholas immediately thought the worst but when he saw the look of utter joy on her face he realized something extraordinary had happened.

"He has heard my prayers," she cried out, while clutching a telegram to her breast. "God has heard my prayers and Alexei will not die." She handed Nicholas the telegram which had just arrived from Rasputin.

God has seen your tears

and heeded your prayers.

Your son will live.

Grigory

Nicholas was skeptical but he refused to dampen Alexandra's enthusiasm. Could Father Grigory have healed Alexei from his Siberian exile, he wondered? And what of our own ceaseless prayers? Would they not be heard? Was one prayer more acceptable than another. Did the soul of the supplicant have to be pure?

"Well, Alix. All we can do now is wait and see. We shall know presently, God willing," said the Tsar, as he handed back the telegram. The Empress had expected him to be angry with her but he just stared pensively at the floor. Elated by the wire, and breathless with excitement, Alexandra left to return to her son. The Tsar decided to put further planning on hold and dismissed everyone for the night.

Early the following morning, but well before dawn, the rain turned to snow. It fell gently but steadily and before long the ground was covered with a thick, white blanket. In the sickroom Alix stirred and realized she had fallen asleep by Alexei's bed. She reached over and touched his forehead and immediately came fully awake. It was cool to the touch. His fever had broken and he was sleeping peacefully for the first time in days. In that moment her faith in Grigory Rasputin became complete and unwavering; she truly believed he had saved her son's life. From this point on she would never tolerate a word to be said against him in her presence. Where others saw evil, Alix saw a holy man sent from God and nothing anyone said could possibly change her mind. She would never doubt his healing powers nor allow herself to be influenced by the vicious and spiteful gossip of the court. Alexei was still gravely ill but she had total confidence in his full recovery. Father Grigory had promised.

The Tsar came into Alexei's room shortly after Alix had woken and when he walked over to the bed he understood why she suddenly looked so radiant. "Oh Nicky. Our sunbeam's fever has broken and he is sleeping peacefully," she said as tears rolled down her cheeks. Nicky took his beloved wife in his arms and the two shared the joy of the moment together. For a time all the tension that had built up between them dissipated in the satisfaction of seeing their son sleeping so peacefully. "Sunny, stay with him. I am going to pray for a while," said Nicholas.

The Tsar walked through the snow to the chapel where he had previously poured out his heart. He wished to thank God for the wondrous gift of his son's life. Not for one moment did he believe Rasputin had healed him. His son had been at death's door and a true miracle had saved him, but one which was performed by God Himself, in answer to many prayers, and not by some charlatan peasant. He lit the same two candles and got down on his knees. "Thank you Lord, God, for you and you alone have spared my son's life," he prayed in heartfelt thanksgiving. Nicholas wondered if God had been testing him, in some way, with this tremendous burden. Perhaps this trial was designed to strengthen him for the future. At any rate, he felt at peace.

The gloomy atmosphere of Spala lifted as news of the heir's improvement spread. Although it would be many weeks before his recuperation was complete, things began to get back to normal. Because Alix was completely worn out from her ordeal a chaise was moved into Alexei's room so the two invalids could be together. She relaxed all day while sewing or reading to Alexei. Nicholas began to focus on work and other matters and tried to spend time with his daughters who were beginning to feel neglected by their mother. They understood the seriousness of Alexei's illness and never complained but it was only natural they would miss their mother's company. Nicky also wished to spend more time with her but recognized the recoveries of she and her son were the priority. They normally spent only a few weeks in Poland but now it looked as if they would be here for awhile. The Tsar hoped they would be back at Tsarskoe Selo by Christmas but everything depended on Alexei. He could not risk a reoccurrence of the hemorrhage by traveling too soon. So they all waited.

The line of succession to the Imperial Throne of Russia passed through the male side of the family and if Alexei were to die, his uncle,

Grand Duke Michael, would become the heir. It was a role Michael was familiar with because, prior to Alexei's birth, he had been next in the line of succession. However, he had always feared the responsibility of leadership and had no desire to be Tsar. Now, at a time when everyone was finally recovering from the trauma of Alexei's near-death, Michael created new turmoil in the family. When he learned that his nephew was near death he had eloped in the company of a divorced woman, with whom he was involved, and whose illegitimate son he had fathered. He bluntly informed Nicholas, by telegram, that the possibility he might again become the Tsarevich had forced him into this rash action. Nicholas was angry and upset by the news and disturbed that his brother would act so irresponsibly, especially at a time when the family was undergoing a major crisis. The Tsar responded in the only way he could. He had to protect the integrity of the throne so he refused to allow Michael to return to Russia or to permit his wife, who was a commoner, to assume any title. It was a reaction to the hurt he felt, because he truly loved his brother. Only the shared threat of world war would reconcile the two brothers.

The furor over Grand Duke Michael's elopement finally died down and with Alexei on the mend Anastasia felt the time had arrived to approach her father about her dilemma. Because of the loving relationship Nicholas maintained with his daughters, they did not fear him, and Anastasia knew she could share her concerns with her father and depend on him to resolve a crisis. Still, she was a little nervous as she entered his study. "Papa, may I speak to you?"

"Yes, of course, my little imp. What is it?" asked the Tsar..

"Papa, you must help my friend, Franny Schanzka. Her stepfather beats her and she is covered with bruises. You should see her Papa. It is horrible and wrong."

"Slow down, child. Do not be in such a hurry. Now tell me again what is troubling you."

Anastasia took a deep breath and started over. "I was playing dress-up with Franny and I saw her back. It was covered with bruises and a cut. She kept telling me she fell but I knew that could not be right. I fall all the time and do not have marks like that. She finally admitted that her stepfather beats her. Papa it is simply dreadful what he does to her."

"That poor child. She seems like such a nice little girl," commented the Tsar.

"Her Mother does not care about her at all. Please Papa can we take her with us when we leave? She will not cause any trouble and she can sleep in my room. Maria says she does not mind. I know those people would not even care that she was gone. They are so mean to her and always tell her what a burden she is. And, for them, it would mean one less mouth to feed."

"Anastasia, you cannot just take someone away from their family. Everyone would know they were gone. How would you explain Fanny's absence?"

"I wish I could take her place. I would tell that evil stepfather not to ever hit me. He would be so sorry."

"Well, you do look much alike and although your hair is different you could pass for Franny. But that is beside the point. I could not bear to leave my precious angel behind and allow you to be beaten every day. Now let me think about this for awhile. We are not leaving for a few weeks and I promise you I will come up with a solution," Nicholas told his daughter. Anastasia kissed her father on the cheek and, after thanking him, left the study.

Nicholas leaned back in his chair, lit a cigarette, and considered the conversation he had just had with his youngest daughter. He was particularly intrigued by Anastasia's suggestion that she take her friend's place. Suddenly, as he sat there, his feet propped up on the desk, everything became perfectly clear. It was a moment of rare inspiration and, as the pieces fell into place, Nicholas became very excited. The major obstacle to successful development of the *Masquerade* was the dilemma of how to spirit the girls away to safety. He had suggested to his daughter that if Franny was taken away from her family everyone would know. It would be even more obvious in the case of the royal family if he merely sent the children away. How could he explain their absence? No. They must leave, without appearing to do so, and Anastasia, in her big-hearted innocence, had stumbled on the solution. Ordinarily the idea would never have entered his mind but seeing the uncanny resemblance of the two girls to each other had stimulated his thinking. Still, by itself, the similarity would not have been enough. However, a few months ago he had received an interesting letter from Ella that now came to mind. Her convent had a home for girls and she had written that one of her charges bore a striking resemblance to Tatiana. Surely if this had happened twice it could happen again. What if he could find look-alikes for all his children? Russia was a huge country with millions of children and he was convinced he could find doubles for all his young ones. These look-alikes could be tutored, brought clandestinely into the palace and, at the appropriate time, take the place of the Imperial children. The deception would continue as long as possible and give Nicholas the time he needed to get his loved ones to safety. Once hidden they would never be found.

The Tsar realized it would take major planning and coordination but he did not intend to procrastinate. He felt certain he already had a look-alike for Anastasia and he needed to quickly develop a plausible scenario for bringing her into the *Masquerade*. He had no doubt Franny would be so eager to leave the source of her abuse that she would do anything for the privilege. At any rate he would prepare her properly and ensure that she was willing to cooperate. Initially she would be told she was going to live at a school operated by the sister of the Empress, but under no circumstances would she be forced to participate. For now he must figure out how to get her out of Poland without suspicions being aroused. He poured himself a brandy and sat back to consider various scenarios. He remembered that day on the deck of the *Standart* when Sophie had enthralled them with the story of Alexander I and the rumor that he had faked his own death. In that story Tsar found his answer. Franny's mother and stepfather must believe she was gone forever and the only fool proof option was a faked death. If they thought she was dead that would be the end of it, but he would have to fake her death in such a way that there were no remains. The only way that could be accomplished was with fire and he knew how that could be handled. There was an old cottage on the grounds that the children sometimes played in, and that was where Franny would meet her "death." He would then have word sent to the family informing them that their daughter had been killed in a fire. Of course, he could not tell Anastasia of the plan and, as cruel as it seemed, her grief, when she learned her friend had perished, would lend authenticity to Franny's death. It was just too risky to involve her at this point and she would learn later that her friend had not really died. He intended to be generous with Franny's family and would pension off her mother with a substantial settlement. This would enable her to quit her position at Spala and remove her from the scene of the tragic "accident."

The Tsar called in Count Benckendorff and explained what he had in mind. The Count made a few suggestions and a firm plan emerged from their discussion. Franny would not be informed until the day of the "accident." The Tsar would personally speak to her in some private location and explain what he had in mind for her. If she agreed to accept what the Tsar euphemistically called, her rescue, she would be hidden away and not allowed to speak to anyone. Anastasia would then be informed that Franny was playing in the cottage but by the time the Grand Duchess arrived, the building would be engulfed in flames and unable to be saved. It was a cruel hoax but she too had to believe her friend was dead.

A few weeks later, when Alexei had recovered enough to travel, the Imperial family boarded their private train for the long trip back to Tsarskoe Selo for the winter. The ride to the train station took place on the newly graded and smooth road that now led to Spala. Once aboard, the train got underway and proceeded at a moderate speed to avoid bumping or jostling Alexei. Nicholas looked out the window and watched the Polish countryside slowly pass by his window. Two days ago his plan had gone off without a hitch. Franny was overjoyed to be leaving her oppressive family and cheerfully agreed to the restrictions placed upon her. The cottage burned to the ground as planned and, as expected, Anastasia was devastated by the loss of her friend. When she learned of the pension, Franny's mother, the housekeeper, quit working at the lodge, and seemed none the worse for the loss of her child. She was probably relieved that some peace would come to her wretched household.

As for Franny, she was safely concealed in the baggage car. Boxes and trunks were stacked too high to see over and she lay hidden in what amounted to a secret compartment. Count Benckendorff personally saw to her needs and made sure she was relatively comfortable. Nicholas had made arrangements with his cousin George to meet the train during the night at one of its stops. While everyone was asleep he would take Franny off the train and accompany her to Ella's convent in Moscow where a place had been prepared for her. The Tsar took some comfort in the knowledge that the poor girl would be well cared for there, and would never be beaten again.

Chapter 22

January 1913 – Tsarskoe Selo. The train trip from Spala back into Russia had gone well. As planned, George removed Franny from the baggage car at one of the stops and transported her to Moscow where she disappeared into the anonymity of Ella's convent and school. Alexei seemed to be improving more and more each day and there was a general sense among the travelers that the events of the past weeks could be put behind them once and for all. Even Anastasia, who was still mourning the loss of her friend, looked forward eagerly to their return home, and by Christmas the family was settled into the familiar surroundings of Alexander Palace.

And now, on this second day of the New Year, Nicholas awoke to a typical Russian winter morning. Snow blanketed the grounds of the palace, and icicles, glittering faintly in the early morning light, hung from the eaves of all the buildings. The air was cold but invigorating and the panorama provided by the vast white landscape was one he never tired of looking at. He was filled with a sense of purpose and subdued excitement when he considered the day's two major events. Today was the anniversary of the death of St. Serafim and the occasion would be celebrated with the pomp and ceremony which the royal family felt it deserved. Later this evening the Tsar was meeting with the key participants in the *Masquerade* and it was no coincidence that the conference was scheduled on this particular day. After all, it was the Saint's letter to him that had led to the development of the conspiracy, if it could be called that. The term always seemed to suggest an evil purpose and he studiously avoided using it whenever possible. At any rate he hoped that, on his feast day, St. Serafim would guide their deliberations and inspire them to greater intellectual effort.

Nicholas attended the Mass in honor of St. Serafim with his sister, Olga and his oldest daughters, Olga and Tatiana. Alix was ill with a headache and he did not press her to attend. He knew that under ordinary circumstances nothing would keep her from honoring her favorite saint but she was slow to recover from Alexei's ordeal at Spala. She had remained at her son's bedside for days on end and was literally spent from exhaustion. Her refusal to eat anything of consequence had contributed to her weakness and it would be some time before she recovered enough to participate in any public activity. Nicholas was worried about her and gave her as much support and attention as she would allow. As soon as spring arrived he planned to take her to Livadia where she could convalesce in the peaceful Crimean environment.

At the church the priests and deacons came from behind the iconostasis and began the service. Nicholas tried to concentrate on the ritual of the liturgy but his mind wandered and instead he immersed himself in prayer. He asked for guidance and the clarity of thought necessary to complete his plan. His thoughts then turned to his beloved Alix and their precious son, Alexei and he implored God to grant them improved health. He prayed also for his daughters who would need such enormous strength to face the coming trials. It was difficult to accept the fact that before too long his innocent and sheltered angels would be sent off into the world. They were so loving and caring and so totally oblivious to the fact that evil existed that he could only pray they were up to the challenge. Lastly, he prayed for the beloved Russia with which his destiny was so entwined

When Mass was completed, Nicholas and his daughters returned to Alexander Palace. He went in to visit with Alix and remained with her until the priest brought her Communion. His sister Xenia was joining them for lunch today but Alix felt too ill to participate. Nicky suggested they have lunch in her boudoir but she did not feel up to company. With no other option available Nicky kissed her gently on the forehead and excused himself.

As he walked down to lunch, he thought about Xenia and wondered whether she should be brought into the *Masquerade*. Although she was his sister, he actually had a much closer relationship with her husband Sandro. Xenia was involved in raising her six sons and one daughter and that naturally took up most of her time and energy. No, this was not the right moment to add to her responsibilities and he would include her only if absolutely necessary. On the other hand, he was very close to his sister Olga who was a practical woman and simple in her tastes, much as he was. When they were youngsters they had often talked about running away to live as simple people in the countryside. Olga was not blessed with children of her own so she lavished her affection on her nieces, much to their delight. Olga would definitely be a player, but not quite yet.

When favored guests came to Tsarskoe Selo they generally stayed with the family at Alexander Palace. It was much more intimate, with its mere one hundred rooms, than the vast Catherine Palace across the compound. That enormous edifice was generally used only for formal occasions and rarely visited by the Tsar and his family.

That evening all the children dined early and were sent off to play in their rooms until bedtime. Ella had come up for the Christmas holidays and had remained at Nicholas' request and now she joined Sandro, George and Nikolasha and the rest of the adults for dinner. The social nature of the gathering was a useful charade and allowed the Tsar to gather his trusted advisors together in one place at the same time. Upon completion of dinner, the four men retired to the study for a game of billiards and Count Benckendorff joined them there. Ella visited with the other ladies for a short period of time and then left them with the impression that she was going to her room to pray. She paused in her room, murmured a prayer for guidance, and then slipped away to join the men. Nicholas had also invited Alix because they had reached the point at which she would have to become more involved. He was quite relieved, however, when she decided not to attend. "It is too much for me just now, Nicky," she protested. "I just cannot bear to think about it. Darling you know that I trust you. May God be with you tonight and inspire your deliberations," she had told him. "I will entertain the ladies, lest they wonder at my absence.

The group in the study waited expectantly for the Tsar to begin. Except for Alix and Count Tatishchev anyone who knew of the plan was present in the room and Nicholas looked at each one in turn and then addressed them. "It is no accident that I brought you together on this special day, the feast of our beloved St. Serafim. Let us address a silent prayer to him and beg his blessing on our endeavors this evening." All bowed their heads in prayer. "His words from the past have guided us thus far," Nicholas continued, "and before we get started tonight I think we should refresh our memory as to exactly what it was that he predicted. After all, his letter is what is driving our actions, so let me read it to you." Nicholas opened the yellowed paper and began to read:

My son, give thanks to the Lord God who in his ineffable mercy has revealed to me that a great and calamitous evil shall befall Russia. War and famine will turn the people from God. Russia will be lost, drowning in sorrow in an abyss from which there seems no hope of rescue.

You, Nicholas, must sacrifice yourself and become a martyr. As the Lord said to his disciples, "If ye were of the world, the world would love its own, but because I chose you out of the world, therefore the world hateth you." My son be of good cheer, for from your royal line our Lord will bring forth a great saint. Through her intercession Russia will be saved.

At all costs you must protect your daughters. A great evil will hunt them to the ends of the earth and seek to destroy these instruments of God's grace and mercy. They and their descendants must remain hidden until a holy man ariseth. He wears white and travels the earth. The Lord God in his ineffable mercy bequeaths to your family a gift of fifteen years to prepare for these events. Remember this manifestation of God's kindness and use these years to plan well.

Serafim

The silence in the room was unnerving as the Tsar finished the letter. It was almost as if they could sense St. Serafim's presence and hearing his words read aloud had an impact not felt when reading the letter to oneself. At that moment the members of this small and special group felt they were in the presence of a truly great man and they were honored that he had asked for their assistance. Nicholas looked up as he finished and was encouraged by what he saw in their eyes. Surely, he could trust them with the lives of his children.

"Now let me remind you why we are all here," he continued. "Our agents continue to inform us of revolutionary activity and, despite the calm and prosperity our country is enjoying, there seems to be considerable unrest. As you all may remember, a group of these evil men have signed a blood pact to hunt down and kill myself and my family. As far as I am concerned the Saint's letter lends credence to this information and, as I have told you before, I readily accept my fate.

At this point Nikolasha interjected, "Nicky, how can you blindly accept this. Our army is strong and we have time to plan. Surely we will be able to crush this rebellion."

Nicholas smiled a wan smile, "No, my general, we have been through this before. I do not expect you all to believe as I do. I ask only that you accept that I truly believe it. You may think that I am being fatalistic but I assure you I am not. If I believe the prediction then I have to make plans accordingly. I cannot wait in the vain hope that this is merely a bad dream. I accept God's will unconditionally, and all of you must be willing to accept it as well. But let me give you the opportunity to withdraw if you feel I am asking too much of you. You know I love you all and you have my assurance that if you walk out this door tonight I will still have the highest regard for you. But If you stay then you are fully committed." He looked around the room, not entirely sure what to expect from the group which sat so quietly.

Ella was the first to break the silence. She stood up and walked gracefully over to the Tsar, her gray habit gently swaying as she moved. She knelt in front of Nicholas, grasped his hand, and carefully pressed her lips to it. "My Tsar, I pledge my life, my fortune and all that I hold sacred to you. I am committed with every fiber of my being to ensuring the success of the *Masquerade*."

The Tsar was moved by Ella's eloquence and he began to weep as one by one the others in the room followed suit and moved forward to render their pledges on bended knee. "Well then," Nicholas said when he regained control of his emotions. "I am most grateful. So let us begin. I will not go into the specific financial details at this time other then to tell you George and Sandro are working to remove Russia's wealth from the country. We are in the process of negotiations and have already moved a large portion of our assets to the United States, and smaller amounts to banks in Switzerland, and the Vatican. I refuse to allow the revolutionaries to have access to these resources and we will need the moneys to finance the re-conquest of Russia."

"I have chosen Nikolasha to lead in my absence and I give him the authority to make decisions in my stead. We do not know what the future will bring if the revolutionaries are successful in taking over the country.

And no one can know if Russia's liberation will come as a result of a spiritual or physical conflict. Therefore it is important that you know that Nikolasha has my confidence. Moreover I designate him my regent to rule until one of my children comes of age."

"Nikolasha, I do not mean to question your skill or leadership but we must face the fact that you are getting on in years," interrupted George. "Nicholas, what if the liberation of Russia does not take place in his lifetime," asked George.

"I must say, I truly did not consider that fact. I always assumed this would happen in our generation," said Nicholas.

"George has a good point," said Ella. "St. Serafim stated the intercessor would come from your bloodline. What if it is a grandson or great-grandson?"

"Nicholas, I too have a question. Is not Alexei your designated successor as the law requires?" asked Sandro.

"That is so, but it is important tonight that we be completely honest with one another," said the Tsar seriously. "This evening for the first time I voice aloud something that I have just come to grips with myself. Alexei is unlikely to live to become Tsar. Our experience in Spala last October has made me painfully aware of how fragile he is. We have to face the fact that he may not be here to liberate Russia.

"This is dreadful. With your brother Michael out of the picture due to his marriage to a commoner, Kyril is next in line. There could not be a worse choice," said Nikolasha vehemently.

"You forget, I have five children and St. Serafim was very clear that Russia's savior would come from my lineage. Why would he urge me to protect the girls at all costs if they were not the key to Russia's salvation? Why is it so important unless they are Russia's future?"

"Nicholas, a woman cannot be Tsar. It is against the rules of succession and it is illegal. Russia will not accept this," said George.

"I think you are wrong, cousin. Yes, there would be opposition from the family, but I have given this much thought and I believe I am on firm ground. After all, there are precedents. At one time, as you well know, a woman could rule Russia. Was not Catherine a Romanov and one of our greatest leaders? And before her there were others. Paul I changed the laws of succession out of hatred for his mother but this is not how it was ordained to be. The new law he put into effect, denying women the right of succession, was created to spite her and nothing that is done out of hatred can be from God. I think the reason this issue has never been discussed before is because every Tsar since Paul had a son to succeed him. Now the situation is changed. I am the Tsar, God's anointed ruler, and I intend to order that the laws of succession be changed to reflect what I consider God's will." Nicholas picked up a document from the top of his desk. "This is a change to the laws of succession. Many years ago, before Alexei was born, I contracted typhoid fever and there was a question as to whether I would survive. Since I had no son but only daughters I had Count Witte research the law and draw up this document. Basically it states that if there were no male heir, the thronewould pass to the daughter so designated by the reigning Tsar. You notice it does not mention the eldest because there is always the possibility that she might be incapacitated in some way and not fit to rule. However, as it stands right now. Olga would be next in line after Alexei. There are two significant changes that must be made to this instrument of succession and I need your input and advice on how to word this. First, the requirement that my daughters must marry royalty in order for their children to be considered as heirs will have to be eliminated. The most important thing is that my bloodline flows through them to their children. I do not want restrictions on who they can marry. Secondly, they must not be hindered by their Russian Orthodox faith."

Nicholas looked at the stunned faces that surrounded him and he realized that he must explain himself further. "I can see that you are at a loss for words so let me clarify my reasoning. I believe the revolutionaries will try to destroy the two entities that pose the greatest threat to them, namely the Royal Family and the Church. If they are successful, even in part, then the pool of eligibles, if we retain these restrictions, will be drastically reduced. The world is changing and my daughters' lives will be very different. They will live in hiding for many years and must have the freedom to choose. We will discuss where they are going tonight, but it is likely they may not have the opportunity to practice their faith and even if they did, would this not subject them to exposure? We did not hesitate to ask you Ella, and of course Alix, to convert from your Lutheran faith. The Grand Duchesses may never have the opportunity to meet or marry a royal. Should they be denied love or happiness or the throne? I do not think so. Our laws have served us well, but we must change with the times. Do you not agree?"

Nikolasha said, "I will support you in this Nicholas but what price will we pay? Do you really think Russia will accept the offspring of a Grand Duchess and a stable boy?"

"I just don't know about this Nicky. It seems so radical," Sandro added.

"I think the only ones who will have an issue with this will be the nobility," said Ella. "The Russian people will suffer so much that they will beg for God's mercy and pray their cross be taken away. They would embrace the mingling of their blood with that of the Tsars and accept any offspring of such a union with enthusiasm."

Ella had tremendous influence with these intelligent men and they listened to her with respect. Since becoming a nun she had developed a reputation for wisdom and holiness and, as her spirituality grew, people sought her out for advice and guidance.

"I do understand your concerns, but I have given this so much thought and analyzed the facts so thoroughly that I truly believed that this is the solution. Nikolasha, I would like you to prepare a new version that reflects the two changes I have indicated. I will sign and date it but we will keep it secret until I decide the best way to implement it," said the Tsar.

"Yes, your Highness. May I have Benckendorff assist me?"

"Of course. Now I wish to discuss an idea I have come up with. Ella and George are aware of it, but you will all have to know of it since you will be in and out more and more frequently. It may seem an impossible scenario yet somehow I am convinced it will be a success. As you know from the letter, the years promised for planning will be completed in 1918 and prior to that we will send my children off to new lives. Unfortunately, they would surely be missed and one way or another we would have to explain their absence. I want to avoid that necessity at all costs. I will not get into the details yet but the children will be replaced by doubles. We will continue the deception for as long as possible. That should give us enough time to spirit my children away to their places of concealment.'

"Oh Nicky, can this be done? It seems so very complicated," Sandro interjected.

"It can be done, Sandro. In fact we have already found two potential impostors and they are at Ella's for safekeeping as we speak," Nicholas replied

"It is true," said George. "I brought a little girl from Poland who looks just like Anastasia and except for the fact she was a little rough around the edges I could barely tell them apart."

"This is a very complex plan with many elements, but the ground-work has been laid. Although there are numerous details to work out, I think it is plausible solution," added Nicholas.

"Can you tell us where you will send the children or do you prefer to keep that to yourself at this time?" asked Ella.

"My intention is to send the children to Japan. We have received indications that the Japanese Imperial family feels they owe me a debt of honor dating back to an attempt on my life while I was a guest in their country. We will ask the Japanese to arrange a safe haven for the children at the appropriate time. They will remain in Japan temporarily until they can return to Russia. I want them close, but If things do not work out as planned we will need an alternative hiding place. If Russia's redemption does not occur in your lifetimes, I want the girls to be moved to a location where they can settle down and have a normal life while they prepare for the future. I am afraid that because of the dissimilarity of our cultures Japan would not serve in the long term. The children would never be comfortable there. For this reason I believe the United States is the only option. Sandro I want you to arrange a meeting with Mr. Crane to explore the possibilities. What is your opinion?"

"This is a good idea, Nicky. Since Woodrow Wilson was elected President it seems Mr. Crane has considerable influence, which is not surprising since he was the largest single contributor to Wilson's campaign. It is rumored that he is responsible for getting Wilson elected," said Sandro as he passed Nicky a knowing look. A substantial portion of Crane's campaign contributions had been funneled to him from the Tsar's personal fortune.

"Well, it seems as if our hard work is beginning to bear fruit. Sandro, it is important that your negotiations take place behind the scene. I do not want any type of official overture and I am sure I do not need to remind you of the need for secrecy. I would like you to travel to the United States and verify our arrangements with the American banks. With Wilson elected President it should not be too long before the Federal Reserve Act is passed and signed into law. We need to ensure all our arrangements have been completed prior to that occurring. Since you have been to the United States before I do not think it will cause much comment if you visit again but to be on the safe side I think you should be as circumspect as possible."

Ella, Nikolasha, and Count Benckendorff were mystified by this exchange so Nicky explained that George and Sandro had been working on the financial aspect of the *Masquerade* for some time.

"Now George, I need you to continue to explore the idea of the children going to Japan. Although Japan has been our enemy in the past, I have total trust in the integrity of the Japanese Imperial family. If they think they have a debt to repay me then let us allow them to settle their debt. Sandro! Work closely with George on this. I know it is a long train ride but leave for America from Vladivostok and on your way stop off in Japan. You can go unofficially and determine if they are sincere about their intentions. Keep in close contact with George so that he can exploit anything that you may find out."

"I will leave as soon as I can make the necessary arrangements," Sandro replied.

"I appreciate that, Sandro. I think we are about ready to finish up so let me summarize. Count Benckendorff will continue to operate his spy ring, which has generated such important intelligence for us and will assist Nikolasha on the succession issue. Ella will work on finding more doubles and then begin the process of turning them all into Romanovs. Sandro will begin negotiations with Japan and the United States and George will continue to handle the finances. I would like to remind everyone that Nikolasha is my right hand man and I expect each one of you to give him the support he needs, especially after I am gone. I trust him to make the difficult decisions and I am counting on everyone to make this work. If anything new develops, I will be in contact."

Nicholas dismissed his friends and family members and sat quietly in his study, analyzing the momentous meeting and all that had taken place at it. He felt the *Masquerade* had finally solidified into a concrete plan. There were many details to work out, especially the manner in which the impostors could be utilized most effectively, but it gave him something to focus on and now instead of worrying about the future, he was preparing for it. Everything was beginning to feel more manageable and he was especially pleased that to this point only eight individuals were involved.

As George and Sandro made their way back to their rooms it was apparent they were engaged in serious conversation. The two brothers were very close and often shared their feelings on various subjects. "George, I must tell you that although I am totally committed to do whatever the Tsar asks of me, I am somewhat skeptical about this plan," said Sandro. "The Tsar seems to be basing everything on dreams and mystical experiences. I admit that I am not as devout or accepting of these spiritual events as he is, and frankly I have reservations about aspects of his plan. The fact that money has been deposited at the Vatican bank seems a strange course of action and gives me some pause."

"Exactly what anyone would think," George replied. "Who would suspect the Vatican was aiding the Tsar and Russia, especially in light of our persecution of Catholics. It is really quite brilliant and remember, we are not talking about large sums. For some reason, which he has not disclosed to me, the Tsar believes the Vatican is completely trustworthy in this matter. It is no different than his dependence on the Japanese, who were at war with us not so long ago."

"Yes, but the Japanese still feel that they owe the Tsar," said Sandro. "What does the Vatican hope to gain?"

"To put it simply, the Vatican just wants peace," answered George. "I think that the Tsar and the Pope are kindred spirits and much alike in their hopes and dreams for the future, not only of Russia, but of the whole world. Let us not forget that it was the Tsar's diplomacy that led to the Hague Peace Conferences. They both want a new world, a better world and maybe that is what this is about. And do not forget the Vatican has connections all over the world. People underestimate its influence."

"Yes, but the Russian people would never accept a word that came from the Vatican and can you imagine the attitude of the Russian Orthodox Church. What if the Vatican betrayed us? Do you think the Tsar has even considered these things?"

"I do not know Sandro," said George. "I assume he is carefully developing the plan and looking at every possible consequence but it is impossible to anticipate every eventuality especially when whatever approach he takes may very well change the course of history."

"I understand that he is still putting it all together and things may change but I am concerned that he is not considering all the repercussions of the decisions he is making."

"That is part of the reason he has brought us in. He welcomes our input," said George.

"I understand that, George, but what I do not understand is why he feels it necessary to remove such a large portion of Russia's fortune at this time. Surely the Russian people will suffer tremendously."

"Sandro you forget that it is the Tsar's wealth. When he ascended the throne all of Russia's riches became his. He is the caretaker of these assets and for now we must trust that he knows best. Yes, as Ella reminded us, the Russian people are destined to suffer, but you cannot believe for one moment that these madmen who will foment insurrection care a bit about the Russian people. They would hoard this money and the people would still suffer. Then by what means would we be able to bring about a new Russia? All would be lost," said George, with some passion.

"Yes, I see your point, but I will not pretend to understand all of this and I just hope my skepticism is not too obvious. As I have said before, I am available and willing to do whatever the Tsar asks of me. He is family, one of my closest friends and above all the Tsar. I trust in him and his decisions even though I may disagree," said Sandro.

"There are many things I do not understand either but like you I trust in the Tsar and will put myself at his disposal."

"Do you think this whole mess will come to pass in our lifetime, George?"

"I just do not know, but evidently the Tsar is preparing Nikolasha for events he thinks will occur in the near future. It is my impression that Nicholas thinks that Russia's torment will not be drawn-out but I have a strange premonition our country will be in distress long after we are gone. I just do not know what will happen when that time comes. Who will take our places? What will happen to our families? There are just so many questions, but we must put them out of our minds and focus on our assignments. I can only assume that the children will know what to do when the time comes.

"Only time will tell," said Sandro. "By the way, I meant to ask you. Has Mr. Brantingham approached you about depositing your personal assets in the United States?"

"Of course, but I explained to him that I already have money invested outside of Russia. I assume he spoke to you."

"Yes, but I thought it was inappropriate of him to approach me about a matter that is none of his business, and I have to say I was offended. I told him my money will stay in Russia just as my loyalty will. He seemed surprised at my answer and I assume that was because it came at a time when the Tsar is sending out billions in gold to America. I may change my mind later once I see if things are really going bad. We have plenty of time."

"Sandro, do not be a fool and wait too long. If you procrastinate you may lose everything. Think of your family. I find it troubling that at a time when I will be encouraging other family members to set up funds outside of Russia I cannot convince you."

"What do you mean encourage the family to invest?"

"Sandro you know, as well as I do, that the Romanovs will be targeted by the revolutionaries and once they are in control it will be nearly impossible to get money out of the country. Of course, the Tsar cannot tell the family to set up accounts outside Russia so he has entrusted me with the task. Basically, I am giving simple financial advice and suggesting to anyone who listens that keeping all ones eggs in the same basket might be unwise."

"I think everyone will react the way I have. They will feel as if they are somehow betraying Russia and I can assure you right now that my mother-in-law, the Dowager Empress, will not take kindly to your suggestion," said Sandro.

"Well, if everything happens as the Tsar has predicted, we will either be dead or living destitute in some foreign country," George countered. "It is not as if there will be jobs for former Grand Dukes. We have a chance now, knowing what we do, to make arrangements for our futures and if we do not act on this warning then we have only ourselves to blame for the outcome. The Tsar is focusing on his children and the fate of Russia and not on us, which is as it should be. We will have to be responsible for ourselves and because we are privy to information from the *Masquerade* we have ample time to plan. Anyway whom do you think would come to our aid if we have not made other arrangements?"

"I really haven't a clue," answered Sandro. "If the Japanese come through for the Tsar, and I have no doubt they will, we couldn't possibly risk asking them to accept additional Russian exiles. It would be far too dangerous for the Grand Duchesses. As it is, I do not know how the Tsar will keep all of this a secret," said Sandro.

"It will be difficult but not impossible," George replied. "Discretion is the watchword. Now let us go to bed."

When Sandro entered the guest suite he found his wife, Xenia, still awake. "That must have been some game of billiards to have lasted this long," she observed.

"It was. We made a pact that we would not leave until someone beat Nikolasha. I think we just wore him down in the end. At any rate I'm for bed. Good night my dear."

A day had passed since the conference and Ella wanted to meet with the Tsar to formulate a more precise plan for selecting the impostors and to obtain answers to several questions she had formulated. Ella understood that this was by far the most critical aspect of the

Masquerade and she was honored the Tsar had chosen her for such an important task. She knew that God worked in mysterious ways and she believed with her whole being that he had brought her to this point in her life for this special purpose.

When Ella entered Nicholas' study she found him at work on a draft of the new succession document. "Is this a bad time to discuss my role in the plan?" she asked."

"Not at all. In fact the sooner the better. Please take a seat and let us get started. I know you must have many questions and concerns but I must confess I have only recently considered the use of doubles," said Nicholas. "It was your letter, in which you mentioned a girl who looked like Tatiana, and my meeting with Franny at Spala that turned me in this direction. I took action to send Franny to you without much thought and only the shadowy outline of a plan, so the how and when of it have not been worked out. I would like to get your input now that you have had a day to think about this. Have you come up with any ideas?" He knew that Ella did not waste time and that in a day she could have come up with a number of possible scenarios.

"Well, certainly some of the impostors could come from the convent or school," said Ella. "Among the peasant classes you are thought of with great reverence and many of these girls would lay down their lives for you. As I wrote you, there is one young lady at the convent who is the mirror image of Tatiana and now that I have seen Franny I am convinced we have the beginnings of a workable plan. I have heard it said that there is a double in the world for every person alive."

"I have heard that as well, but let us hope my children's doubles are here in Russia."

"I have made up a list of questions that will need to be answered," said Ella.

"You must be sure to commit the list to memory for there can be no documents that would allow someone of intelligence to discover our plan. When it is all over and done with the *Masquerade* must never seem to have existed, lest the children be endangered," said the Tsar.

"I understand Nicky. First I must know how much time I have to locate and enlist the other look-alikes."

"I would like to have them all ready to start training by the end of the year," answered Nicholas.

"That does not give me much time. But at least we have two of the five."

"Actually I want to have more than five. Of course, the first consideration is that the impostors look like my children but we also have to judge their ability to learn, their trustworthiness, and especially their loyalty to their Tsar. Find as many as you can in the allotted amount of time. Initially you will probably just look for a marked resemblance to the children, then later you can determine which ones will work out. We must have backups in case one of the children becomes ill or does not fit in. Children grow at different rates and their looks change as they age. A child that resembles one of my children now may not do so in five years. We do have one significant advantage and that is the fact that they are rarely seen in public and then only in passing."

"I understand," Ella said as she jotted down some notes. She used her own personal code and it was unintelligible to anyone other than herself. "This makes time the critical element but perhaps we can find some of the doubles on the streets. My convent takes in the homeless and we have an orphanage as well. We are constantly finding abandoned children in the slums around the city and there are literally hundreds to choose from in Moscow alone. If possible, however, I think it would be better to obtain the children from outlying locations. I assume they must be orphans, abandoned by all."

"Absolutely. That is critical. We cannot risk anyone recognizing them. And they must willingly participate."

"Yes, I agree. Now, I thought that as I locate these girls I would keep them in with everyone else for the time being, so that no one notices any special treatment."

"The only problem I see is that the girls might strike up lasting friendships with others who will not be involved."

"Nicky, I really do not see that as a problem," said Ella. "But if necessary, as soon as they come into the orphanage, I can separate the girls who may become doubles and keep them in the cloistered part of the convent."

"We really need to think this through. There are so many details to be concerned with." Nicholas sat for some time without saying a word. Ella could tell that he was formulating the outline of a plan and she remained silent until he was ready to share it. Finally he spoke, "I think I have an idea. Bring all of the girls you find into the orphanage. When you have a sufficient number of candidates, you will announce that some of the girls have been chosen to be trained for domestic duties in one of the Grand Duke's palaces in the Crimea. Before they are separated from the other girls, you can question them and see how you think they will work out. It will give you the opportunity to weed out anyone whom you think is unsuitable. Take many photographs of them so we can track their features for dramatic changes and then determine which ones look most like the Grand Duchesses. Remember you must be circumspect and low key about the business and act as if it was something you did every day."

"Yes, I understand I must be discreet," Ella replied. "No one will suspect new children at the orphanage. Unfortunately it is a weekly occurrence. May I ask if anyone else is involved in searching for doubles?"

"Not at this time," said the Tsar. We need to keep the number of people involved to a minimum and you are least likely to raise questions if you are seen in the presence of unknown children. Your work with orphans is well known. However, if you run into any difficulties other people can become involved if necessary. Do you feel you can handle this on your own for now? Of course, you are not really alone; you can turn to me or anyone who attended the meeting the other night."

"Yes I can manage this but I do have a request. I wish to have my companion, Sister Barbara, assist me. I have known her for years and in fact she was my maid while I was married to Sergei. She is a dedicated friend and has given her life to the Lord. I have no doubt as to her faithfulness to me and loyalty to Russia. She followed me into the convent in spite of being offered a generous pension and now she is my constant companion when I travel.

"Yes, I will agree to that Ella, but please tell her only what she needs to know. It is for her safety as well as ours."

Ella looked down at her notes and gathered her thoughts. "Let me go over what we have discussed once more. I want to be sure that I have a clear understanding of what I need to do. First, the impostors will be found in locations outside of Moscow and St. Petersburg, the further away the better. Secondly, they will be grouped with the other children, and I will, to the best of my ability, insure that they are truly orphans with no family. Once they are at the orphanage I will assess their capabilities and determine their suitability. Our goal is to have a group ready by the end of the year. Next, the girls will be separated from the others, ostensibly to be trained for service at a Grand Duke's palace. We can teach them everything from table manners to the history of the family."

"Languages will be a problem since these girls will likely speak only Russian. But much can be achieved in four years and we will do the best we can. Lastly, I assume that after the training is well along you and Alix will select the final group. Let me suggest that at this point they be slipped into Alexander Palace to meet their alter egos and continue with the most important phase of their education; learning to act as a Grand Duchess. You will, of course, have brought your children to the *Masquerade* by then."

"You seem to have everything covered, Ella, but as you know even the best laid plans often fall apart. We will just have to make decisions as issues arise. Now one last but very important element that we have not discussed is an impostor for Alexei."

"Finding a double for Alexei may prove difficult but we do have an outreach with boys and, of course the orphanage includes both boys and girls. I am sure we will be able to work something out."

"Very well then, we are well on our way to putting this whole thing together."

"I plan to get started as soon as I return to Moscow. With your permission I will leave in a day or so. May I have your blessing?"

"You have it; and may God smile on your efforts," replied the Tsar.

After Ella left the room the Tsar sat back and thought about the day he received that fateful letter and how confused he had been. He hadn't a clue as to what needed to be done or how to proceed. Now here it was, nine years later, and the plan was finally being put together. For the first time in years he had hope for the future. This is going to work, he thought, especially with Saint Serafim guiding the way.

Chapter 23

February 1913 – St. Petersburg. In the city that was Peter the Great's gift to the Russian people, there was an atmosphere of excitement and anticipation, for this was the year of the tercentenary of Romanov rule. Three centuries earlier, a frightened, unwilling young boy named Michael, had been induced to accept the throne of Russia and that reluctant act had resulted in an unbroken chain of Romanov rulers which had continued for three hundred years. Although the city's winter social season was in full swing, the jubilee itself would be commemorated with a series of balls, receptions, theater productions and religious ceremonies and, in order to be closer to the festivities, the Imperial family moved from Tsarskoe Selo to quarters in the Winter Palace. It was the first time in many years that Tsar Nicholas chose to reside at the palace because, if the truth be known, he was a country boy at heart and hated living in the city. He recognized, however, that the size and luxury of the palace was more suitable for entertaining the large number of diplomats and foreign dignitaries who would be attending the various celebrations.

Anyone viewing the expressions of loyalty and affection pouring in from all over the country in the form of letters, gifts and flowers would have found it difficult to believe this was a nation on the verge of revolution. On a drive through the city of St. Petersburg almost every building seemed to be adorned with a giant Romanov crest, on which were displayed the dates 1613 – 1913, and the number 300. Some were simply decorated with bunting and flowers while others were more elaborate, with electric lights and simulated jewels. The people of St. Petersburg obviously intended to impress visitors as much as possible and have their city suitably reflect its role as capital of Imperial Russia.

The February day was clear and unseasonably warm and the pleasant weather brought out crowds of people who lined the Nevsky Prospect in hopes of getting a glimpse of the Imperial family. The carriages bearing the Royal family passed quickly along the street, which followed the course of the frozen Neva River, and made their way to the Cathedral of Our Lady of Kazan. This church was an architectural masterpiece, modeled after St. Peter's Basilica in Rome, and in it was enshrined the miraculous icon of Our Lady of Kazan. This icon was venerated by the Russian people and over the years, in times of celebration or sorrow, many voices had been raised in prayer in this magnificent church. It was a fitting location in which to open the official celebration of the tercentenary and the cathedral was packed with a crowd of worshipers that included dignitaries and the nobility of Russia. Shortly after the Imperial family arrived and were escorted to their places the solemn

Mass began. As the sound of the Te Deum filled the church, Nicholas felt a tug on his sleeve and he glanced down at his son Alexei who was pointing urgently at the dome of the cathedral. Two white doves had entered the church and seemed to be circling over the heads of the Tsar and his son. The pair made several passes over them and then gracefully disappeared from view. Nicholas wondered if this could be a sign of God's blessing on the house of Romanov or just one of those lovely happenings that could be enjoyed without need of explanation. He patted Alexei on the shoulder and smiled down at him. It was a very special moment and Nicholas was grateful to God that Alexei was able to share it with him. He was still shaken when he reflected on how close they had been to losing him. The liturgy was quite lengthy and the Tsar directed that chairs be brought for both Alix and Alexei. Everyone else stood through the ceremony which was rich in pageantry and uplifting in its solemnity. The polyphony sung by the choir was so absolutely gorgeous that it caused chills to run up and down the backs of those in attendance. Eventually though, the Mass, with its prayers and blessings for the continuance of the dynasty, came to an end and the congregation dispersed.

Nicholas and Alexandra rode in an open carriage on the way back to the Winter Palace and they were cheered by the vast crowds lining the route. "Look how much the people love you, Nicky. It is difficult to believe that one day they will turn against you. They seem so devoted," commented Alix.

"Russians, like people everywhere, are fickle by nature and they blow in the wind. Have you forgotten how it was in 1905 when everyone was ready to throw us to the wolves," Nicholas replied.

"I know you put great store in St. Serafim's prophecies and you are certainly right to do so but when you see this outpouring of affection, which seems so genuine, I sometimes wonder if we are not misinterpreting his words. And you know Father Grigory says we shall rule for many, many years."

"I hope you have not shared St. Serafim's letter with him."

"No! You asked me not too and I have not. You must trust me, Nicholas"

Nicholas breathed an inward sigh of relief and then tried to change the subject. He mentioned the doves he had seen in the cathedral and how excited Alexei had been.

"I did not see them, but it must be some kind of sign. I will ask Father Grigory," the Tsarina replied.

"Alix, that will not be required. It is not necessary to make Grigory privy to everything that happens between members of our family. I took this as nothing more than a sign that God has blessed us on this special day. Let us leave it at that. Anyway, I still cannot believe there have been Romanov rulers for three hundred years."

"And you will be the last," Alix said sadly.

"I have to admit my thoughts drifted in that direction during Mass but I put it out of my mind, as you must do as well, my dear. We must continue to plan to the best of our ability and entrust God with the rest."

"We only have five years left," said Alix with a touch of melancholy in her voice.

"I know, but we shall try and make those five years splendid ones, full of memories for our children to cherish for the rest of their lives. Alix, you, and I have had a wonderful life. Not many are blessed with a strong love such as we have shared and I for one could die tomorrow with no regrets," said Nicholas as he gently kissed his wife's hand.

"I, too have no regrets. Never has there been a finer husband."

During the next few days a series of receptions was held at the Winter Palace to receive delegations from all over the world, as well as the length and breadth of Russia. Each day the reception rooms of the palace were packed with people who had been invited to meet the Tsar and other members of the royal family. In the evening there were state dinners and trips to the theater or opera where special performances were presented in honor of the Imperial family. It was a taxing schedule and was especially difficult for Alix and Alexei who collapsed at the end of each day in total exhaustion from the fatiguing work of receiving hundreds of people.

The girls did not participate in many of the evening events. Maria and Anastasia were too young and neither Olga nor Tatiana had been officially presented to society. However, on the night that the noble families of St. Petersburg gave a ball in honor of the Tsar and his family, Alix surrendered to the gentle prodding of Nicholas and the pleading of the girls, and allowed the two oldest to attend. Olga had been to a few balls but other than some tea dances this was a first for Tatiana, and the importance of the occasion was not lost on her. On the night of the ball the Grand Duchesses could barely contain their excitement as they dressed for what promised to be a splendid event. Alexandra was not extravagant but for this occasion she allowed the girls to have dresses made and now they were debating over which hairstyle was most flattering and which jewels best complimented their new gowns. Maria and Anastasia eagerly offered their unsolicited opinions but were more a hindrance then a help. Looking on in amusement was their favorite Lady-in-Waiting, Sophie Buxhoeveden, who had been asked by Alix to oversee the preparation.

"Isa, the pearls you have on really will not do," said Olga. "Please wear these instead."

Sophie looked in amazement at the exquisite emeralds Olga was holding out to her.

"I could not, Olga. They are much too valuable."

"I do not understand," said Olga. "We sisters always share our clothes and jewels and you are like a sister to us."

Touched by her generosity Sophie agreed to wear the emeralds which matched her gown perfectly. She then assisted the two girls in adjusting the red sashes which displayed the diamond stars of the Order of St. Catherine. The sash draped across one shoulder and attached at the opposite hip. With the trio now perfectly coifed and gowned they left their quarters to join the Tsar and Tsarina and their entourage for the carriage ride to the Assembly Hall of the Nobility where the ball was to take place.

Olga and Tatiana were impatient with excitement and eager to arrive at the ball. They both hoped the official ceremonies would be over quickly so they could enjoy the dancing. Upon entering the Hall, Nicholas and Alexandra were presented with the customary bread and salt by selected members of the Russian nobility and they accepted graciously. When the ceremony of the salt concluded Nicholas led his wife onto the dance floor, and without further ado opened the ball with a lively polka. With that first dance at an end the official duties of the night were completed and Nicky escorted Alix to the royal box which was set up on one side of the hall. Alix was grateful that the box allowed her to sit away from the hundreds of guests attending the ball. She was not a social creature and was very uncomfortable in such settings, but she did enjoy watching her daughters dance.

As she looked out at the couples, Olga waltzed by in Grand Duke Dmitri's arms, her cheeks glowing with enjoyment while Tatiana shared the dance with her father. Alix smiled indulgently at her daughters and was relieved to see they had suitable dance partners. She found dancing on her weak legs so taxing that she rarely participated except for the required opening number. She tried not to look impatient as she sat and waited for enough time to pass so that she could leave without causing offense. Occasionally someone would speak to her but on the whole she was left alone. Around the box she could hear conversation and merriment as the various Grand Dukes and Duchesses of the extended Romanov family laughed and gossiped.

Finally Alix felt enough time had passed, although she had been at the ball little more than an hour, and she made a sign to Nicholas that she wished to leave. Olga and Tatiana were devastated when she told them they must return to the Winter Palace but the Tsar, seeing their disappointment, arranged for Alix to be escorted home and stayed behind with his daughters. Olga and Tatiana were thoroughly enjoying themselves and Alix, remembering her husband's admonition to let them relish what little time they had, made no objection. With their father as escort, they knew they would be able to dance the night away.

Olga danced again with Dmitri, knowing full well the gossip it would cause. She was aware that their names had been linked together as a possible match but she looked upon him as a brother and never considered him a romantic interest. Dmitri was the Tsar's ward and was treated like a close member of the family with which he had lived for a number of years; except for the periods when he was away at school. If the truth be known she had not forgotten Vasily, her first love, and their enforced separation only increased her feelings for him. Unlike her sister Tatiana, who had a certain regal bearing and attitude, Olga was attracted to simpler things in life and as a result she always had a much easier and natural relationship with the numerous maids, nurses, tutors and ladies-in-waiting. Tatiana was generous and good-natured but tended to be a little more aloof, more like her mother.

However, the young Grand Duchess did not lack dance partners, although none really struck her fancy. Tatiana was growing up into a beautiful young woman, tall and very elegant, the epitome of what a Tsar's daughter should be, but none of the officers vying for her attention could break down her natural reserve. Of course, she was not used to being at the center of things and was somewhat in awe at the continuous adulation of so many young men. Consequently she was a little shy at the start but, after the first few dances, she relaxed and began to enjoy herself, so much so that for once she put her mother out of her mind. It was thought that Alix preferred Tatiana over her other daughters and there was some truth in this. Tatiana was very solicitous of her mother during Alexandra's many illnesses and the two had become fairly close. But as the wonderful night continued Tatiana began to realize how secluded their lives had become and for a moment she felt a bit of resentment towards her mother who kept them from attending any of the social events held in St. Petersburg. She was painfully aware of her mother's dislike of these activities but could not understand why she and Olga were not allowed to attend. There were plenty of suitable chaperones to escort them, but she knew it was useless to argue with her mother about this aspect of their lives. It was fortunate that the tercentenary provided opportunities that otherwise would not have existed. At any rate none of the girls were old enough to understand the enmity that existed between the Empress and St. Petersburg society and Tatiana was content to let her sister Olga argue their point of view, as she did more and more frequently.

As the night ended and early morning arrived the Tsar finally refused to hear any more entreaties from his daughters to stay on and, taking leave of the hosts, he escorted them back to the Winter Palace. "Young ladies," he commented, as they climbed into the carriage, "you have probably gotten me into big trouble with your mother. I am sure she will not consider three in the morning an appropriate time for two young girls to be returning home, even in the company of their father."

"Oh, Papa do not be cross with us," exclaimed Olga, "it was all so wonderful."

Nicholas smiled as the two girls excitedly exchanged anecdotes on the evening's entertainment and argued over who had the most memorable dance partner. They talked incessantly all the way back to the palace and he was happy to hear them go on because, more than anything, he had wanted them to have a glorious evening. He was inordinately proud of their grace and beauty and loved to show them off but he was somewhat concerned that excessive exposure might undermine his plan. He also knew Alix did not want them associating with the extended family because she felt they were a bad influence on innocent young girls. Still, he did not see the harm in a properly chaperoned event.

After Olga and Tatiana retired for the night, they sat up in their camp beds and talked about the evening. Tatiana teased Olga about Dmitri but it did not seem to embarrass her. "Oh please, Tatiana, he is like a brother to me and, although I have to admit he is handsome, my heart belongs to another."

"Olga, surely you don't still have feelings for Vasily. It has been at least a year since you have seen him."

"It is true but my feelings seem only to have grown stronger with his absence. It is a cruel torture not knowing where he is."

"You must put him out of your mind. You know father will never allow you to marry him."

"What you say is true and my head agrees, but my heart refuses to accept the reality. I cannot put him out of my mind and I keep hoping that somehow things might change and I would be permitted to marry him. Maybe father could give him a title."

"Silly girl. Now you are really dreaming. In a hundred years it will never happen."

"I love him enough that I am prepared to wait that long."

"Well, you shall be an old maid."

"Better to be an old maid than imprisoned in a loveless marriage."

"Mama and Papa will never force us to marry against our will. I for one will marry according to our station. There are plenty of eligible members of royal families to choose from."

"We are two very different people, Tatiana. Love is the most important consideration for me."

"You are very naïve if you think that way," Tatiana replied. "We are Grand Duchesses of Imperial Russia and appropriate marriages are expected of us. How can you even consider turning your back on your heritage?"

"Tatiana, I cannot control the feelings I have in the silence of my heart and I did not choose to fall in love with Vasily. If I am pressed on the matter I will respond as Papa always does. It must be God's will."

"Well, this is all very enlightening but we should get some sleep. Tomorrow will be another busy day.

CR80

It was early afternoon and the weather was just dreadful. Alix was laying on the chaise in her Mauve Boudoir in the Alexander Palace trying to regain her strength after the last few weeks in St. Petersburg. The endless round of festivities had exhausted her and she was grateful to be home. Anya Vyrubova had joined her a few hours earlier and her endless prattle was giving Alix a headache. She wished Anya would return home and leave her in peace but she did not want to hurt her feelings by sending her away. In the initial years of their friendship Alix had appreciated her simple outlook on life and welcomed the novelty of a friend who was not part of the court clique. Anya's companionship was a balm which soothed the hurt caused by all the gossip and lies of the Empress' enemies. She had become part of the family and Alix usually saw her everyday. Of late though, their relationship had become slightly strained but Anya, in her naiveté, failed to notice the cooling in Alix's attitude towards her.

The source of this disaffection was Grigory Rasputin and Alix was ashamed to admit to herself the feelings of petty jealousy that were consuming her. She acknowledged that he was a holy man of God and a treasure of all the people but she still felt that he belonged to her more than to others. However, due to the gossip and innuendo surrounding Rasputin and the Empress, Alix could not see him freely or even contact him, unless it was an emergency, without going through Anya. Of late, Nicky had relaxed his restrictions somewhat, primarily because of the strange events at Spala but he still did not like her to receive Father Grigory at the palace except on rare occasions. For the Tsarina it was galling to have to relay notes and messages as if she were a mere schoolgirl. She envied Anya's freedom and access to the holy man and thus resentment had begun to build within her.

She sat working on a piece of needlepoint as Anya chattered on. Talk turned to the tercentenary celebrations. "My Olga and Tatiana certainly are growing up. They were the belles of the ball last week," Anya observed.

"Yes, they have definitely blossomed into attractive young women. Soon we shall have to start thinking about husbands for them," Alix replied.

Anya remembered her own disastrous marriage, which the Empress had personally arranged, and wondered if Alix intended to force unwanted matches on her daughters. "Are they going to have arranged marriages?" she asked as innocently as she could, while hoping the hidden meaning in the question would escape Alix.

"My children will never be forced to marry someone they do not love, however, I will encourage them in the proper direction. I have already found a suitable match for Olga which I will propose to her shortly."

"Who is it?"

"I would rather not say at this time. There is still some negotiating going on between the two families. You will be the first to know, when everything is settled."

"Oh, I understand," said Anya but, of course, she really did not. When had she ever broken a confidence? Her feelings were hurt and for a moment she was at a loss for words. To cover her embarrassment she changed the subject. "By the way I visited Father Grigory yesterday and he sends his regards. We had such a wonderful talk. He is so perceptive and he shares things with me that he tells no one else."

Alix stabbed at her needlework and fumed silently as Anya went on and on about her latest visit to Rasputin's apartment. As far as Alexandra was concerned it was extremely presumptuous of Anya to think that somehow she had replaced the Empress as Father Grigory's special confidante and for a moment she felt pity for her poor disillusioned friend. Alix pressed her hand to her breast and felt the familiar icon that Grigory had made with his own hand and given her as a sign of their special friendship. She wore it under her outer garment and its comforting presence enabled her to put aside her annoyance at Anya's impertinence. She smiled to herself, confident in the knowledge that she alone had an elevated spiritual relationship with the holy man. After all, he had even requested that she transcribe his teachings.

Poor Alix. Her illusion of pre-eminence was shattered when Anya pulled on a cord around her neck and lifted out a hand carved icon. The Empress was speechless.

"Your Highness, look what Father Grigory gave me. He told me not to show anyone but I thought it would certainly be all right if you saw it. He made it himself out of wood from his village and it is very special. He said it was a unique token of our friendship and a reminder to think of him in times of trouble.

Alix had heard enough. "Anya you must leave now."

"Alix, is something wrong?"

"I feel one of my headaches coming on, so I must ask you to excuse me. You may show yourself out."

After the door closed behind Anya, Alix stood up. She was extremely agitated and in a fit of anger she tore the icon from around her neck and threw it to the floor. She looked with disdain at the image which only moments before had been one of her most treasured possessions. She was very upset with Father Grigory and could not imagine what kind of game he was playing. Alix knew he had told Anya not to show anyone her gift because he did not want the Empress to see it. When Rasputin gave Alexandra her icon he told her that he had carved it himself and implied that it had mystical powers to protect her. It was a token that only she was to have and was a mark of the esteem in which he held her.

Alix was beside herself and could not believe "her friend" could lie so blatantly. She was used to the intrigue and treachery of the court but to experience deceit from this unexpected quarter was almost more than she could bear. She made up her mind to confront him and she intended to do it on her own ground, not at Anya's cottage. Throwing caution to the wind she summoned Rasputin to Alexander Palace at half past ten the next morning.

When he finally arrived and was escorted into her mauve room, she was still so angry and hurt that she could barely think straight. Alix glared at him and Father Grigory could see from her visible anger that he was on dangerous ground and he knew instinctively he must exercise caution. He did not know why she was upset, and so he gently prodded her. "Matushka, you seem distressed."

"I am hurt and angry that you have lied to me," she replied as she pulled her icon from the bureau drawer and threw it at him.

"Dear Matushka, I do not understand," he said, as he removed the carved icon from the floor. "I made this for you. It was my gift to you."

"I and who else?"

Rasputin immediately recognized that this was about jealousy and that if he was careful he could manipulate the situation to his benefit. He had no intention of telling the Tsaritsa that he made many of the little wooden icons for his female followers. They were such gullible creatures and each liked to think she was the most pre-eminent in his circle of admirers. He played upon this blind devotion and used it to his advantage, but now it seemed he was caught like a rabbit in a trap. Thinking quickly, he addressed the Empress.

"Matushka, I see you are learning the lesson well. I am deeply sorry your feelings were hurt but I did this for your spiritual growth. This jealousy you are exhibiting is beneath you. You are the Empress of Russia and more is expected of you than ordinary people."

Alix was speechless and truly there was nothing she could say. She had acted like a jealous shrew and all she could do now was swallow her pride, humble herself, and beg his forgiveness.

"My dear Matushka, you are forgiven, but remember what I have taught you. It is only through sin that we can truly be redeemed. You have sinned, but now you are forgiven, so enjoy this redemption and know that you are favored by God. He has sent me to guide you through these difficult times in your life. Did I not choose you, Matushka, to record my words? Surely you know this is a special honor given only to you?"

Alexandra was perplexed and confused. Only a few moments ago she had been consumed by what she considered righteous anger but now she was empty of any emotion except guilt. Rasputin was very clever. He espoused and preached a decadent and dangerous philosophy which held that without sin there was no forgiveness and without forgiveness, no salvation. She had heard it all before but she was unaware that he used this flawed logic to justify his sexual escapades. In his mind these excesses were justified because they provided his women disciples the opportunity to sin and thus be redeemed. Of course, redemption was granted through God's holy man, namely Grigory Rasputin. It was all nonsense, but he was such a smooth liar he was able to make it all work.

Rasputin could see that the anger had left the Empress and inwardly he relaxed. He knew he had won this round, but in the future he would have to be more careful. The staret knew that without the Tsarina's silent support his prestige would evaporate and he could not let a careless mistake cost him everything. Knowing that his presence at the palace placed him in a precarious situation he asked and received permission to return to the city.

Alix was appeased by his visit. Once again he had smoothed her ruffled feelings and once again he was in her good graces. However, it was somewhat ironic that Alix, who would allow no one to speak ill of him, had been so quick to accuse him of lies and deceit. After he departed, Alexandra considered her relationship with Anya and recognized that she could not let jealousy ruin their friendship. Alix needed Anya, not only as a friend, but also as a conduit to Father Grigory so she resolved then and there to put aside the kind of behavior that could destroy their fondness for each other.

CBEO

The snow covered streets of Moscow were normally silent in the early hours of the morning and Ella used this quiet part of the day to catch up on her enormous workload. She had already been awake for hours but this was nothing unusual for her. After Morning Prayer and breakfast she could usually be found hard at work in the office she maintained in the convent of Saints Mary and Martha. The blue and white curtains in the windows filtered out the pale morning sun and left the room in shadows and, although her large wooden desk was covered with paperwork, this morning she left the lights off and sat there in the semi-darkness. After the loss of Sergei the monastic life had been her salvation and she fully embraced it and all the hardships it entailed. Ella rarely slept more than a few hours a night and worked diligently to meet all her responsibilities. As she sat enjoying the quiet of the early morning hour, she considered everything she must do to carry out her part of the *Masquerade*. The Tsar had left it to her to make momentous decisions and she knew he had complete confidence and trust in her. Ella recognized that if she was to succeed it was important that she continue with her normal activities. Nothing could be allowed to cause her efforts to receive unwanted scrutiny and she feared any change in her normal routine might do just that. She had established the convent in 1910 and had continued to expand over the past few years not only at Saints Mary and Martha but also through sponsorship of hospitals, schools, and orphanages all over Russia. Although the majority of her time was spent in Moscow she also traveled extensively during the year, visiting her various interests and occasionally making a pilgrimage to some holy site. Despite her busy schedule Ella felt certain she was up to the challenge of the Tsar's mission. It was as if the fate of Russia had been placed in her hands and she took the responsibility very seriously.

She got up from her desk and began to pace round the room, the gray robes of her habit rustling gently as she moved about. The large ceramic stove in the corner kept the chill out of the office and she was able to concentrate on the most important aspect of her part in the deception. Ella was not really concerned about finding one set of doubles, but the requirement to find more than one for each child could be difficult, if not impossible. She already had two in residence at the convent, one for Anastasia and another for Tatiana, but the search was just beginning. Well, she would do the best she could over the next few months and at the end of that time they would have to begin training with what they had. She also was aware that working with teenagers, from whatever background, would not be easy. Young girls could be unpredictable, and boys even more, so the doubles had to be fully committed to the charade. Loyalty and reliability were the watchwords. Ella had a fleeting moment of doubt that she could pull this off but it was soon replaced by her eternal optimism. She had several visitations planned in the coming months and she hoped in her travels throughout Russia she would find what she was looking for. At any rate the trips would be a perfect cover for her quest.

She rang the bell on her desk and a few minutes later Sister Barbara arrived at the office. The day she returned from Tsarskoe Selo, Ella had called her dear friend in and explained to her the task they would soon embark upon. Although she trusted Sister Barbara without reservation she kept her promise to Nicholas and told her only of the responsibility to find and train orphans to serve as doubles for the Tsar's children.

"Sister, I have been sitting here trying to develop a course of action for our assignment from the Tsar. My biggest concern right now is the education of the children. They have to pass as a member of the royal family."

"You have to find them first," joked Sister Barbara.

"I think that will easy, compared with the task of converting them from street urchins," replied Ella with a smile. Let me share with you the Tsar's suggestions for accomplishing this goal. She then outlined for her friend the plan, as she and Nicholas had discussed it.

"I think you have the beginnings of a good solid plan for achieving your ends but other than traveling with you, where do I fit in?" queried Sister Barbara.

"I have decided to begin their training immediately, and we will start with the two we have. We cannot afford to wait until they are all identified; too much time would be lost. With the experiences you have had working for me, I know you are the perfect person to begin with the children. You know how a large household is managed and can share what you know with them and as they learn from you, they will help pass it on to the newcomers. I am counting on you to personally supervise this schooling. No one else can be involved."

"I think it is important to separate them from the other children as soon as possible, as you just indicated. Their education will go way beyond what we are providing the others and we do not need to contend with any petty jealousies. I am also concerned about what the other nuns will think when we single these children out. You will probably have to address them and call for their silence under their vow of obedience," Sister Barbara suggested.

"I had not even considered that. Oh, I am so thankful you will be here to help me. The children's education will be extensive and we do not want to forget anything. We must assume that they know nothing. I happened to view our Anastasia and Tatiana eating their meals yesterday and I must say I was appalled by their lack of table manners and the coarseness of their conversation. We definitely have our work cut out for us."

"I think we should start with their appearance. If they look and feel the part I believe the rest will come," said Sister Barbara.

"You have a point, but we may not be able to solve that dilemma in the early going. We certainly cannot have eight Grand Duchesses wandering the halls of our convent dressed in gowns and jewels. That would immediately tip our hand. But there is no reason to delay teaching them correct bearing and posture and for the time being a simple uniform will be sufficient."

"The more I think about this the more I realize how very difficult it is going to be," Sister Barbara observed, somewhat despondently.

"Dear friend let me put you at ease. I neglected to tell you the story about Franny that His Highness shared with me when I visited at Christmas. It is quite amusing and yet very significant. It seems that imp, Anastasia, dressed Franny up in one of her outfits and they managed to trick the guards into rendering honors to the little impostor. The only change was the dress and to me that indicates that in most cases the mere illusion will be enough. Later on, as they get closer to moving into the palace we will do more. I just cannot gamble at the beginning that someone might recognize their resemblance to the Imperial children."

"Then Mother let me ask you this. Do you think it is wise to keep them here at the convent? There is so much activity in Moscow and we have so many visitors interested in our service to the poor that they could be seen. Have you considered moving them out of the city as soon as they are selected? Why not take them to Ilinskoe?"

"Why, I never even thought of that," Ella replied. Ilinskoe was her beautiful country estate outside Moscow. Situated as it was on the river, and well outside the city, its most attractive feature was its isolation. It was an hour by carriage to the nearest railroad station and although other estates were in the area they were miles away. "Since establishing our order I have rarely visited there but now that you mention it, the estate would be an ideal location for our school." Sergei had loved Ilinskoe and for that reason she could not bear to part with it, instead reserving it for the use of Marie and Dmitri. However, she could not remember the last time they had been there. It was too far from the glitter of St. Petersburg.

"If I remember correctly there are quite a few buildings on the grounds. Didn't you have a hospital set up there during the war with Japan?" asked Sister Barbara.

"We did, and it is not in use at the present time. It could be used as a school and there is enough room upstairs for a dormitory. The only drawback is that I cannot be there to oversee the program."

"No, you have too many other duties, but if we had additional teachers, I could do it. I do not have the knowledge or experience to instruct them in everything but with the proper help, it could be done."

"You are right and I know exactly who can help you. Sister Irene and Sister Catherine were both born to the nobility and are well educated young women, devoted to God and the Tsar. They also speak several languages. I could have you out there at first until we get everything organized and then move them out to assist you. I am sure I could manage to visit at least every two weeks to check on your progress. It makes sense to remove the children from Moscow and it is certainly quiet at Ilinskoe. The fresh air and outdoor activity will be good for them and, since the Tsar and his daughters are very active, it will immediately give them something in common."

"There are so many things to teach them, but most importantly, they will have to learn French and English if they are to have any chance of passing as a Grand Duchess," Sister Barbara added.

"I wonder how long it takes to master a language. When I first married I spoke no Russian and it took me quite awhile to speak comfortably, but even now I still have a slight German accent."

"We must immerse them in the languages at once and we must only allow them to speak French or English, perhaps on alternate days. I have heard it said that children can learn a second language much easier than an adult and since we have several years I am confident it can be done."

The two continued to discuss the training of the Imperial doubles for the remainder of the morning and it was decided to focus on the basics. Appearance, bearing, and table manners would be emphasized in the first lessons, with language training overlying the whole effort. Eventually they would have to learn the protocol of the court, study art, and music, read the books the Imperial family read. The list went on and on. At one point Sister Barbara thought she had identified an insurmountable obstacle. "How will they recognize the people they are supposed to know," she asked in a worried voice.

"Actually that should not be a problem. All the children are avid photographers so we will have a number of photos to aid us in the recognition of the family members and their key retainers," Ella assured her.

"These poor children; they will be in school for hours."

"I know from experience that they have short attention spans so we will first have to insure that they want be a part of this. It is imperative that the children be treated with dignity and made to feel they belong. Besides the schoolroom we will have to be creative with games, play, and other activities to help them learn," said Ella.

The two nuns continued expanding the list they had started as the ideas began to flow. They were excited at the possibilities and, after breaking for a light lunch, they were hard at it through the afternoon, stopping only for Vespers. And so the process of transforming rough stones into beautiful, glittering jewels, had begun. The most intricate and dangerous element of the *Masquerade* was now in the capable hands of the Tsar's sister-in-law and her associates.

Early the next morning Ella awoke in an austere room, similar to those of all the nuns in the convent. She stretched to relieve her aching body, but there was no escape from the hard wood of the bed, which dug into her skin, its firmness unrelieved by the thin layer of blankets she slept on. She arose and, after washing her face with cold water from the pitcher in the corner of the cell, she donned her habit. Then, a quick look at the sickest patients in the hospital, and on to the chapel, where she could pray privately until her sisters joined her for Morning Prayer at half past seven. She knelt on the stone floor before the altar, oblivious to the discomfort, and prayed silently for the success of the *Masquerade*. Her fervent hope was that she would quickly find doubles for her nieces and for Alexei and she had lain awake most of the night contemplating this task. She knew it was critical and she wanted to make sure that her part would be successful. Here it was weeks after the meeting with the Tsar and she had yet to find anyone who she really believed would be able to pass as a member of the Imperial family. She had a few girls in mind who might be used as alternates but their resemblance to the Grand Duchesses was slight at best.

She looked up at the iconostasis and began to pray in earnest. "Saint Serafim, you warned the Tsar of the coming tribulations. I pray that you will not abandon us at this critical time. I entreat you to guide me through the streets of Moscow and beyond, and lead us to the children that will be crucial to this complicated plan." Ella remained in prayer until her sisters began arriving for the liturgy of the hours. After Morning Prayer was completed she greeted each nun in turn and bestowed her blessing, as was her custom. As soon as they went off to their various duties Ella bade Sister Barbara join her on a trip to one of the soup kitchens they sponsored in Moscow.

At that time of day, Moscow was a busy city, teeming with people going about their business. The crisp winter air could not dispel the combination of a dozen odors which blended and then were wafted away on the morning breeze. The pealing bells of the many churches called the faithful to worship but, when they fell silent, they were replaced by the cries of hundreds of crows which had taken refuge in the city. Street vendors plied their wares, while beggars weaved in and out of the crowd pleading for coins or a bit of bread. Shopkeepers swept the sidewalks and fidgeted with their displays hoping to encourage people to come and buy their goods. This was Ella's new home. The city she had known as the wife of the Governor, with its grand palaces, balls and banquets, did not exist for her any more. Since she had dedicated her life to helping the poor and suffering, she quickly learned about the other side of Moscow. It was a place where people suffered, where orphaned children ran in the streets, dressed in rags filled with vermin, their pinched faces hidden by dirt. Ella knew that somewhere behind the filth were the sweet features that would answer her prayers.

Despite the attention it attracted Ella drove the car which the Tsar had given her as a gift. It was a luxury she allowed herself because it enabled her to get around the city quickly and accomplish her tasks in less time and by now most citizens were used to seeing it. Upon arrival at the soup kitchen, the two nuns set about the business of inspecting the facility. Ella looked into every nook and cranny and as she identified a shortage her companion made note of the needed item and quantity required. When they completed the inspection Ella took a few minutes to visit with the staff and complimented them on their hard work. She exhorted them to serve the poor cheerfully, with dignity and compassion. "Remember dear friends that the only sustenance many receive today will be what you provide them from your facility. God be with you."

The car was parked in a street beside the soup kitchen and while the nuns were conducting their inspection, two young boys had entered the alley. Screened from view by the large touring car they knelt and began to gamble with an old pair of dice. They seemed to be about twelve years old and each was covered in grime, their faces smudged with dirt and soot. One appeared to have blond hair but it was so dirty it was hard to be certain. The larger of the two boys was dark -haired and it was obvious both of them were tough youngsters, hardened by life on the streets and alleys of Moscow.

The dice game was not a friendly one. The blond lad lost continuous-ly and finally resorted to cheating; yet he still continued to lose. He became desperate as his few pennies rapidly disappeared and he made the mistake of trying to steal the pile of coins and run away. His opponent tripped him, knocked the money from his hand, gathered it up, and, for a moment, considered beating him. Thinking better of it he turned and began to walk away, but realizing he had forgotten his dice he went back. The smaller blond youth was on him in a flash and delivered a number of stinging jabs. Caught off guard the bigger youth reeled back and then was tagged with a skillfully administered left-right combination that left him bleeding form the nose and mouth.

At this point Ella and Sister Barbara rounded the corner and entered the alleyway. Thinking quickly, the aggressive youngster grabbed the bigger boy by the front of his ragged coat and pulled him down on top of him. After making sure that the free-flowing blood had liberally doused his face and shirtfront he began to cry out "help me, somebody please help me." The dark-haired boy, still dazed from his beating, pushed himself off and stood up. As he prepared to give his tormentor a well deserved kick he became aware of the approaching nuns and, panicking, he ran past them, almost knocking Ella to the ground.

"Perhaps we should call for the police," said Sister Barbara.

"It will not do any good, but we might be able to help this one," Ella replied. They approached the urchin and knelt beside him. He sat up and began to cry and Ella who had no children of her own, but possessed a strong mothering instinct, was immediately sympathetic. It never entered her mind that this child was anything other then what he seemed, the innocent victim of a street bully. She calmed him down with soothing words and removing a handkerchief from her habit she began to wipe away the blood and dirt from his face. With each stroke more of his face was revealed and when Ella finished cleaning him she had to stand and seize control of her emotions. Sitting in the alley in front of her was a handsome young boy who could pass, without any trouble, for her nephew, the Tsarevich Alexei Romanov. The Lord had answered her prayers and delivered into her hands the perfect double!

She and Sister Barbara assisted the boy to his feet and Ella asked him if he would like to sit in her car for a moment. The boy was surprised that the nuns had been so easily deceived and he played it up as only a street wise child could, even adding a newly acquired limp. Once he was seated in the car, Ella began to question him, doing the best she could to restrain her excitement. Where did he live? Did he have a family? Where was he from? All of his answers were what she hoped to hear. He was a homeless orphan from a small town outside of Moscow and had been living on the streets for a number of years. Ella felt this young boy was the one she had been searching for so she began to explain to him the purpose of her convents and schools. When she had finished she offered him the opportunity to come and live at her orphanage.

The boy sat back and thought for a moment about his life on the street. He was miserable and starving most of the time, no longer welcomed at the soup kitchen because he stole from them every chance he could. He almost froze when the temperature dropped suddenly and he would huddle for warmth with some of the other children in the alleys. He had no other clothes but the ones on his back. It was a miserable life and he was ready to give it up and so he had lied to Ella and Sister Barbara. He had known better days because he was not an orphan, as he had told them, but rather a runaway from a middle class family in St. Petersburg. He had been an only child but was a constant burden on his parents because of his stealing, lying, and sudden outbursts of violence against his mother. He had no desire to go back to his home, nor would he be welcomed there, but neither did he want to continue to live on the streets. "Yes, thank you sister, I would love to have a real home," he said in a dramatically pitiful voice. "I will come with you."

At that moment a policeman walked by. He noticed the urchin in the car with Ella and Sister Barbara. "Is this child bothering you?" he asked the two nuns.

"Not at all," replied Ella.

"May I speak with you in private for a moment," he asked.

"Yes, of course," she said as she exited the car and walked a few steps away with the policeman. The boy in the car strained to hear what the two were talking about but they were too far away.

"I know you wish to help the less fortunate, sister, but you must be distrusting of these street children, they are liars, cheats and thieves and nothing but trouble," said the policeman.

"What you say may be true, officer, until you treat these children with kindness. Then their true personalities emerge. These are good children trapped in bad situations, forced to do ugly things just to survive. This boy is different, he was beaten by another boy, and if I had not come up when I did he surely would have died. He is now my concern."

"Do you even know his name?"

Ella walked back to the car, "Child, what is your name?"

"It is Dalek Rakyovich," he said.

"I doubt that is his real name," said the policeman. "I do not know this one though so I will leave it to your judgment but please remember what I told you, and be careful."

Ella thanked the officer for his concern but her mind was already made up. She had found Alexei's double and was not about to let him slip away. Sister Barbara allowed Dalek to sit in the front seat on their way to the orphanage and the young boy was suitably excited by his first automobile ride. When the group arrived Sister Barbara turned Dalek over to the orphanage staff who soon had him bathed, into clean clothes and fed.

At the convent Ella went to her office and prepared a telegram to Nicholas, which she sent out immediately. The wire read:

"One male sheep wandered into the convent yard today.
We caught him and sent him to a farm."

Her task completed Ella began to make arrangements to move Dalek from the orphanage. Since they found him in Moscow she did not want to risk having him remain in the city. He was sure to know somebody and until she assessed his suitability for their purpose she did not want to put in jeopardy everything they were working towards. He would leave in the next few days for Ilinskoe along with the other impostors and Sister Barbara.

Chapter 24

June 1913 – Japan. The merchant ship rolled gently as the long swells of the north Pacific began to influence the motion of the vessel. The port pilot had been dropped off an hour ago and, as the steamer headed out into the open sea, Sandro leaned over the railing and watched the twinkling lights of the city of Nagasaki fade from view. He had booked passage on this vessel because it carried a limited number of passengers and would afford him a welcome anonymity as he began the second leg of his long journey. Now, as he gazed at the receding shoreline, the brisk salt air cleared his head and he felt totally invigorated. His brief stop in Japan was very successful. He was met in Nagasaki by His Imperial Highness Prince Kanin Kotohito, a cousin of Emperor Yoshihoto, the Mikado. Kotohito was an esteemed member of the Japanese Imperial family and he held the trust and confidence of the Emperor. It was Prince Kanin who worked behind the scenes and handled the Emperor's private and personal activities. The meeting of the Grand Duke and the Prince had been arranged through diplomatic channels in as circumspect a manner as possible. Sealed messages had passed back and forth in the diplomatic pouches of the two embassies in the preceding weeks and the rendezvous was finally organized. Sandro's visit was treated as an unofficial one and he was able to meet with the Prince, in the relative privacy of a secluded estate, to discuss the Tsar's request.

More than twenty years earlier Sandro had performed military service in the Russian Navy in His Imperial Majesty's corvette *Rynda*, which at that time was a unit of the Pacific squadron. During this period of naval development the Japanese were very interested in the ships and training level of their competitors so the government encouraged port calls and the *Rynda* made frequent and lengthy visits to the city of Nagasaki. As a result the young sub-lieutenant became very familiar with the culture of Japan, so much so, that he followed the practice among Russian sailors of taking a Japanese "wife." The small town of Inassa, a short distance outside of Nagasaki, was the traditional home of these "wives" and Sandro was able to choose his "bride" from among a number of women eager to improve their economic situation even if only for a short time. Sandro's two year "marriage" was an enjoyable one and he learned not only the customs of this strange land but became quite fluent in the language.

Toward the end of his tour, he was called upon by Tsar Alexander III to make an official call on the Japanese Emperor. Initially the visit went smoothly and would have been considered a success but for an incident which occurred at the formal dinner on the last night of his stay. While seated next to the Empress, Sandro decided to impress her with his mastery of the Japanese language. Now the Japanese were extremely polite and never wished to cause embarrassment but in this case the Empress could not control herself. As he spoke, the Empress began to smile and then she suddenly lost her composure and laughed outright, as did the courtiers surrounding them. The official interpreter explained to Sandro that he was speaking Japanese slang, which was unique to the Inassa village, and used by women of ill repute. Everyone laughed about the incident but it was an unacceptable social gaff and one of the reasons that Nicholas decided to use Sandro only as the point man. Since he could not speak the language of diplomacy, negotiations with Japan would be conducted by another. The Tsar could not run the risk that his envoy would be the butt of jokes and not taken seriously. This mission was too important.

The meeting with Prince Kanin had gone extremely well. The two had sipped sake and exchanged pleasantries before getting down to the business at hand. Sandro then explained that the only purpose of his visit was to request that an envoy be received by the Emperor of Japan to discuss a matter of grave importance to the Tsar. The emissary would be his brother, Grand Duke George Mikhailovich. Prince Kanin was privy to the "debt of honor" that the Emperor felt he owed Nicholas and knew that this debt transcended the fact the two nations had fought a war against each other only eight years ago. Therefore he was quite receptive when Sandro broached the possibility of a private audience and went so far as to guarantee that he could arrange a meeting between George and the Emperor. To avoid involving anyone else Prince Kanin, who spoke several languages, would serve as interpreter. If all went according to plan, George would travel to Japan in a few weeks and negotiate a safe haven for the Tsar's children. He would also tour the country and, with the help of Prince Kanin, settle on properties suitable for the children and a small group of carefully selected retainers. The Grand Duke would also arrange for the transfer of funds to subsidize the endeavor although, according to the Prince, it was more likely that the Emperor would insist on financing the project himself. At any rate George and Sandro would arrive back in Russia about the same time and were scheduled to meet with Nicholas upon their return.

Sandro had wired Nicholas, informing him of his success, and was now continuing his journey to America, traveling first to San Francisco and then on to the Isthmus of Panama. He could have taken the shorter route across the United States by train but he was intrigued by the American effort to complete a canal across the isthmus and felt that he should use the opportunity to learn as much as he could about it. It was a feat of engineering he could not help but be impressed with and it increased his respect of America's drive and ingenuity. He was anxious to discuss the effect the canal would have, not only on the United States, but on the rest of the world as well.

After crossing to the Atlantic side by motorcar Sandro boarded a ship to New York City where he was to stay with Cornelius and Grace Vanderbilt. Cornelius, known as Neily by his friends, and Grace were famous in New York society for their parties. In fact Grand Duke Boris Vladimirovich, the Tsar's cousin, still talked about an event he had attended in their Newport home. Grace kept in contact with many of the foreign ambassadors in Washington and when she became aware of Sandro's visit she extended an invitation to stay in their home in the city. Her contacts were one of the keys to her social success and in the past she had elevated her standing in society by providing the only private home to be visited by the Kaiser's son and heir when he came to the United States.

Sandro had been introduced to Neily on his last visit to America but had not met Grace. Nevertheless, he gratefully accepted their invitation as he wished his visit to be as private as possible. Staying in a hotel would have provoked unnecessary publicity but certainly not much more than was generated when it was learned he was staying with the Vanderbilts. The Russian Ambassador, of course, knew of his trip and notified the State Department but emphasized that this was strictly an unofficial visit. He tried to keep it low key and did not issue any press releases. Sandro's plan was to stay in New York City for a few days with the Vanderbilts, while discreetly conducting his business. He would then link up with Charles Crane, who was arranging a meeting with President Woodrow Wilson. After his business was completed he planned to meet the Vanderbilts in Newport, Rhode Island for a taste of the summer social season for which it was so noted.

Unfortunately when Sandro disembarked in New York, he was greeted by a throng of photographers and society reporters jostling for position and shouting out questions. The flood of publicity was exactly what he had hoped to avoid but he was naive to think that Mrs. Vanderbilt would have kept silent about this social coup. He was disappointed by this development and knew it would make his mission more difficult. Conducting office calls with bank presidents was now out of the question so he decided to keep up the pretense that his visit was strictly a social one and hope the situation would sort itself out. After getting settled in with the Vanderbilts he spent some time alone in his rooms wondering how he could attend what were sure to be a number of social events and still take care of the financial matters which were the purpose of his visit. It was most important that he meet with Frank Vanderlip. Mr. Brantingham had informed his superior that the Grand Duke would be in the United States for a short period of time and somehow a quiet meeting had to be arranged. Sandro decided to take an afternoon nap and struggle with the dilemma later, when he was more rested.

Later that evening while at dinner, the problem solved itself. The conversation had turned to a discussion of Sandro's itinerary during his stay in the United States. Neily suggested they start the next day with a round of golf at the country club he belonged to. Sandro was not an accomplished golfer but he could play well enough to avoid embarrassment and when he learned that the Sleepy Hollow Country Club included Frank Vanderlip among its members he immediately agreed to the outing. The club had been founded by Vanderlip and William Rockefeller, who had purchased the estate, known as Woodlea, from Neily's aunt. They then had the course and clubhouse designed and laid out by the finest architects. Situated in Scarborough, New York, it became a very exclusive club with a fully subscribed membership when it opened for play in 1911.

The next morning, Neily and Sandro motored out of the city to the town of Scarborough. Fortune smiled on Sandro, for when Vanderbilt arranged a tee time for early afternoon, Vanderlip and Rockefeller preempted the other members and insisted on being included in the foursome. As founding members, they were not going to miss the opportunity to spend time with Russian nobility. The match went well and the four men enjoyed the comfortable camaraderie that enormous wealth allows. However, Sandro struggled with an annoying slice that kept him from being competitive and he was frustrated with his game. On the twelfth tee Vanderlip, hitting third, sliced his ball into the right rough and Sandro, teeing off last, followed suit, his ball landing only a few feet from Vanderlip's. As the two men walked together down the fairway Sandro saw an opportunity to open a dialogue and took advantage of it..

"Mr. Vanderlip, I am sure you know why I am here in the United States. Unfortunately the situation, as it exists, does not allow for any intimacy, but somehow we must arrange a private meeting. Do you have any suggestions as to how we might get together?"

"Please call me Frank, your Highness. I feel as if I have known you for some time."

"Well then, you must reciprocate. My friends call me Sandro."

"Then that is settled. How would you like to join me for lunch and a tour of my estate tomorrow, Sandro? The others have been there many times and won't be insulted if I do not include them. It will give us the opportunity for total privacy. I will send a car in the morning to pick you up. Will that satisfy you?"

"By all means," Sandro replied. "You have been most understanding."

With the match completed Neily and Sandro returned to the city to dress for a function that evening at the Astor's home. Since his arrival,

Sandro had received a number of invitations and he had been grateful for Grace's help in sorting them out. Soon the wealthy would depart for their Newport summer homes and Sandro had decided to wait and do most of his socializing in that quaint Rhode Island town. For the present he wanted to limit his engagements until after he met with Charles Crane. However, Grace had encouraged him to accept the Astor's invitation and since he had met the family on his last visit he felt obligated to attend. It turned out to be a very pleasant evening and he enjoyed it immensely.

The next morning he made the trip back to Scarborough in the car sent by Frank Vanderlip. Upon arriving he was introduced to the family and then they all had lunch together. As soon as they could Sandro and Frank adjourned to the library so they could converse in private. Their main point of discussion was the Federal Reserve Act which Vanderlip expected to be passed by the end of the year.

"Before the Tsar commits any money he wants more specifics. He wants to know who will be in charge and how the banks will to be set up and supervised. Most importantly he wants assurance that his accounts will remain anonymous," Sandro began.

"I understand his concerns. Once the Federal Reserve Act is passed I anticipate the Federal Reserve Banks will be up and operating by the summer of 1914. As soon as the act is passed in Congress and the covenants under which the banks will be established and operated are finalized I will send Brantingham to Russia to meet with you and sign the documents. National City Bank will continue to hold the Tsar's funds until the time comes when the transfer to the Federal Reserve can take place. Is this acceptable?" asked Vanderlip .

"Actually the funds you have on deposit at National City Bank will remain there as an anonymous account, for the Tsar's personal use. We will be shipping gold and other currencies to the Federal Reserve Bank once our negotiations are finalized." Sandro then passed a slip of paper to Vanderlip upon which was written the amount the Tsar intended to deposit in the future.

Vanderlip was used to working with large amounts and normally retained a poker face when talking about money, but he blanched when he saw the number on the slip of paper. "Why this is the reserve of an entire nation. You could fund the whole Federal Reserve with this amount of money. Why is he moving this much money out of Russia? Is it his?"

"Frank, you are serving as the Tsar's banker and that is all you need to know. If it will relieve your mind, however, you must know that Nicholas is the wealthiest man in the world. His holdings are vast and the amount you see on that paper is only a portion of his net worth. These transactions, though unusual, are totally legitimate, but if you have any reservations about them you must let me know now so I can make alternative arrangements."

Vanderlip grew weak in the knees at the thought of the large fees he would lose if Sandro looked elsewhere for investment opportunities. "No, that will not be necessary. National City Bank can handle the amounts you have indicated and we are pleased to serve your financial needs."

"It is good we understand each other. I am pleased with Brantingham and the Tsar likes him as well. Please see that he remains our point of contact."

With their discussions complete they adjourned for coffee, and then, after a quick tour of the estate Sandro was driven back to the city.

The next few days passed quickly, filled as they were with shopping, sightseeing and social events and Sandro thoroughly enjoyed his time with the Vanderbilts. Grace was a vivacious woman and was skilled in the art of good conversation, which added to the enjoyment of his stay. Finally, his visit at an end, the Vanderbilts escorted him to Grand Central Station to catch the train to Cape Cod. They said their good-byes but agreed to meet in Newport in about a week.

Sandro arrived in Cape Cod and was personally met at the station by Charles Crane who then drove him to his estate. The mansion was built on Juniper Point and was blessed with breathtaking views of the Atlantic. Sandro found the natural landscape and expansive vistas a welcome change after the hustle and bustle of the crowded city. On the drive out Charles explained to Sandro the arrangements he had made for his meeting with the President. In two days they would travel by train to Cornish, New Hampshire, where Woodrow Wilson had established his summer White House. Cornish was a quaint New England town, primarily noted for its artist's colony, and a visit to this somewhat avant-garde community would provide the rationale for Sandro's presence. The Grand Duke was very pleased with the arrangements, and looked forward with enthusiasm to his long awaited meeting with the President.

On a beautiful summer morning Charles and Sandro drove to the station and boarded the train for Cornish. Mr. Crane's cook had put together an elaborate picnic lunch and rather then use the dining car they remained in their compartment and consumed it with much appreciation, as the Massachusetts's countryside rolled by. They arrived at their destination well after dark and were met by a close friend of Crane, with whom they would be staying.

The following day, after an early breakfast, the two men walked to the family estate of Augustus Saint-Gaudens in which the artist's colony was located. Sandro and Charles strolled through the exquisitely landscaped grounds, under expansive, old growth trees that provided shade from the summer sun and added to the beauty of the estate. Many of the artists were women and they looked very bohemian in their softly flowing robes and loosely bound hair. Sandro, who had an eye for attractive women, would occasionally stop to admire a work and discuss its merits with the artist. He was obviously enjoying himself, although Charles, who had been there frequently, seemed somewhat impatient and kept glancing at his watch. Finally, about half past twelve, they were approached by a young man, as if by chance, and quietly invited to a late lunch with the President and his wife. It was a very convenient arrangement since Hacklenden Hall, the summer White House, was also located on the grounds of Saint Gaudens and was only a short distance away.

The aide accompanied the two guests and together they walked, at a leisurely pace, to Hacklenden Hall, a stately white mansion situated on a slight rise overlooking the grounds. They were escorted into the drawing room and Charles introduced Grand Duke Alexandro Mikhailovitch to President Woodrow Wilson and his wife Edith. No one else had been invited for lunch, due to the nature of the meeting, so they all moved into the dining room where an elaborate buffet awaited them. Edith inquired after Sandro's family and kept the conversation moving along but once the dishes were cleared away the three men quickly adjourned to the study. Edith was an intelligent and able woman and was often included in her husband's deliberations, but this time she recognized she was not invited and graciously withdrew.

Wilson was a plain spoken man and not one for idle chitchat so he wasted little time in opening the discussion. "Charles has informed me how generous your Tsar was in contributing to my campaign. It was a key to my election as President, although I could never publicly acknowledge the fact. Both you and the Tsar understand, I am sure."

Sandro was surprised by Wilson's direct approach as he was more accustomed to the devious nature of the Russian Court where very few spoke their true thoughts. He decided that he too would be candid and open during this conference, secure in the knowledge that such an approach would avoid misunderstandings. "Yes, Mr. President we do understand. Now, as I am sure you are aware his Highness has expressed interest in investing in your national bank and wants to assist in any way possible to ensure this bill passes through your legislature."

"I appreciate his offer but you can assure him we are well on track and will have the Federal Reserve Act passed by the end of the year."

"The Tsar will be pleased to hear this. He wished me to express to you personally that he understands the troublesome nature of the recession you are experiencing and is willing to deposit an amount that will make the Federal Reserve instantly solvent. As Mr. Crane knows I have been in touch with Mr. Vanderlip and he assures me that he can make all the necessary arrangements. This is the sum we are discussing, " said Sandro as he passed a folded piece of paper to the President.

For once the president was caught off guard and his eyes widened as he noted the large amount written on the paper. "This is a very large sum of money."

"Most of it will be in gold," Sandro added.

"What, then, is the quid pro quo?" asked President Wilson.

Once again Sandro was surprised, yet refreshed, by this American's candor.

"There is no quid pro quo," he replied.

At this point Crane interrupted. "What the President is trying to say is, what does the Tsar wish in return?"

"I fully understand, but I am not sure that you do. There are those of us who believe that Europe, or at the very least Russia, will soon be in embroiled in turmoil and these financial dealings are for the purpose of safeguarding our nation's assets. Since we intend to leave our funds on deposit for a minimum of five years, and possibly much longer, from our point of view the United States seems a wise choice. When this turmoil is resolved the Tsar will want to return the money to Russia."

"Please pardon me if I seem rude, but I find it hard to believe that you came all the way to Cornish just to discuss bank transactions," the president replied.

"You are very perceptive Mr. President. There is another reason, but it is more in the nature of a request. You need not feel an obligation to comply but if you could accede, our family would be most grateful."

"What is it you want from me?"

"The Tsar is considering the idea of sending his children out of Russia if the conditions deteriorate to a point that he feels it is unsafe for his family. As you know, Russians have a long history of solving political differences by use of terror and assassination. The Tsar watched his own grandfather die as the result of an assassin's bomb and, although not a relative, the Prime Minister, Peter Stolypin, was killed not too long ago," Sandro replied.

"Every President is very aware of the dangers of assassination. In the last ten years both President Garfield and President McKinley were felled by the bullets of an assassin," interjected Charles Crane.

"Well then, you understand the Tsar's concern for his family. If it becomes necessary for him to send his children away for a long period of time, he wants them to come to America. They will have to establish new identities but the Tsar believes they could live here anonymously without too much trouble if you authorized it."

"Your Highness, you must forgive me but I find this a little confusing. Your Tsar's line is unbroken for three hundred years and there has not been an assassination in your family since Alexander was murdered two generations ago."

"Sir, that is not so. Less than ten years ago the Tsar's uncle Sergei, the Governor of Moscow was killed by an assassin's bomb."

"If it was so dangerous why did he not send his family away at that time?" asked the president.

Sandro sighed. "It is a long story, but to make it short, the Tsar did try to make arrangements at that time. However, the war with Japan and other circumstances disrupted his efforts and his plan did not prove feasible. He realized at the time that if he was ever in the same situation again he would need outside help."

"If I am to help, then we must be totally candid and at this point I am not comfortable with your request," replied the president. "You must understand that Americans have a deep rooted suspicion of kings, emperors and royal families. If it was learned that the Tsar contributed to my campaign or that Russia was investing heavily in our financial system I would be in trouble politically and unable to help you. It is almost impossible to keep a secret in this country so unless you can assure me there is real danger to the children I would be hard pressed to play a role in this intrigue. I do not want to appear unfeeling, but you must give me more information. I hope you understand my predicament."

"Let me apologize, President Wilson. I do understand your concern about this state of affairs. Please let me explain the situation. The Tsar has an extensive network of spies which works directly for him and is not controlled by a governmental bureaucracy. A plot to overthrow our government and murder the Tsar and his family, including the children, has been uncovered. It is an extensive plan that is international in scope. There is much more to it than that and even I do not know all the facts, but for security reasons I cannot say more."

"If he has uncovered the plan then why doesn't he take action right now?" asked the president.

"It is much bigger than that, and many of the conspirators are out of reach."

"That is ridiculous. If he knows of the plot surely he can stop it."

"President Wilson," replied Sandro in a grim and serious voice, "you must believe me when I say that the Tsar is in great danger and so is his family. He is an honest and kind man and would never invent something so insidious as this conspiracy. What would be the purpose? Nicholas sent me personally, a member of his own family, to visit with you, to look you in the eye and assure you of his sincerity. He wanted us to meet face to face to emphasize the seriousness of this situation. He has great respect for the United States, which is why I am here today."

"Is the Tsar planning on abdicating or abandoning his country?" asked Mr. Crane

"Absolutely not," replied Sandro, with some heat. He paused for a moment, embarrassed at losing control. "I am sorry for my outburst but you must understand Russians are a very spiritual people. We believe the Tsar to be anointed by God to rule us. Nicholas believes this to be so and accepts his role humbly, but is very aware of the enormous responsibility entrusted to him. His actions reflect what he thinks is best for his family and for Mother Russia and he would never abandon her even if it meant the loss of his own life."

Sandro had spoken passionately to the president and he hoped his words made sense but in his heart he felt he was losing control and that his mission might end in failure. He could never explain to Wilson and Crane that everything he was doing was predicated on the prophecy contained in a hundred year old letter, the contents of which were known to only seven individuals. If he had not seen the letter with his own eyes he doubted he would believe it himself. He looked at President Wilson to gauge his reaction and was relieved to see that he seemed to soften.

"Your highness, you have pleaded your case well and have convinced me of the gravity of the situation. I know that there is more to it than you are telling me but I understand the need for secrecy. It is clear to me now that you have a dangerous situation and I am willing to help. What can I do?"

Sandro felt as if an immense burden had been lifted from his shoulders and his sincere gratitude was evident when he spoke. "Mr. President, the financial arrangements are nearly complete, as I am sure Charles has informed you, and funds have been deposited in National City Bank for the maintenance of the children. All we need is your approval to make deposits in the Federal Reserve and your assistance in finding a safe haven for the Tsar's children. Of course, as time passes more will be revealed to you but I suggest we provide you with as much deniability as possible and work exclusively with Charles in the matter of the children. As you might expect the Tsar will want to thank you for your assistance in some substantial manner."

"That will not be necessary. I have been a secret admirer of your Tsar ever since he organized the International Conference held at The Hague back in '98. His call for peace through disarmament and non-aggressive settlement of disputes was brilliant. I fully endorsed his ideas at the time and have long believed, as your Tsar appears to, that the world needs an international body to settle disputes without the necessity of war. Although I do not know Nicholas personally I do believe he would welcome the establishment of an organization that prefers peace to war. If such a body had existed perhaps that unpleasantness with Japan could have been avoided. No, I do not need any further inducement to support the Tsar. You have my word. I will help you." The two men stood up and shook hands. As Charles Crane sat there he realized he was witnessing a very significant event, but one that would never appear in the history books.

When they left the house Sandro was mentally drained and Charles decided to delay their departure until the following day. Arriving back at their lodging Sandro excused himself, went to his room and stretched out, fully clothed, on the covers of his bed. He lay there thinking about the just completed meeting and concluded that he had been successful in pleading the Tsar's cause, although at one point he thought he might fail. Sandro was impressed with President Wilson and felt he was dealing with an honest man. He had been surprised when the President brought up The Hague Peace Conference. In Russia, it had been looked upon as a project of a new and inexperienced Tsar and was not taken seriously. He was delighted, therefore, to see how foreigners viewed the conference. It was interesting to note the regard in Wilson's voice when he spoke of the Tsar's ideas, and when Sandro contrasted that with the chilly reception his views had received in Russia he realized he was developing a much deeper respect for Nicholas.

Chapter 25

September 1913 – Livadia. The Tsar stood in his study at Livadia smoking a cigarette and looking out the window at the breathtaking view of the sea and the horizon beyond. Although he appeared outwardly calm he was a little worried that he had not received more word from Sandro or George. Of course, they had to be very careful, so their telegrams were cryptic at best, and he was forced to read between the lines. From what he could surmise, however, everything was going well and he took comfort in the knowledge that he had sent two of his most trusted advisors to conduct the tricky negotiations in Japan and America.

Nicholas had instructed George to make arrangements for all of the children to go to Japan, if necessary, but it was the Tsar's intention to actually send only two of the girls. The Grand Duke was to have so informed Prince Kanin and the Emperor of this fact. Nicholas was uncomfortable with the idea of separating the girls but Count Benckendorff had convinced him that it was necessary to improve the odds that at least two would escape. If a long term exile seemed to be called for then Sandro's contacts with Charles Crane would come into play. The dilemma now, was where to send the other two girls and of course, the Tsarevich.

The two brothers were due in the Crimea next week and he knew they brought with them answers to many of the questions which troubled him. Consequently he awaited their arrival with great anticipation. Nicholas turned away from the window, with its glorious view, and walked over to the wall where a globe of the world sat upon a credenza. As he idly spun the globe he wondered how long his children would have to remain in their temporary homes. He still held out hope that Russia's upheaval would be short-lived and his children would be able to come back to their homeland in short order.

He stared at the sphere as it spun round and round and was mesmerized by its slow rotation, so much so, that he was momentarily startled when it stopped spinning. By chance it had come to rest in its cradle with Eastern Europe and portions of the Russian Empire clearly in view. Where, he wondered, among all these nations could he find a haven for the other children, one where they could realistically be safe-guarded. He had eliminated nearly all the European nations because they either had dangerous revolutionary movements of their own or because they were too obvious. Nicholas lit another cigarette, walked over to the bookcase, and took down an atlas which displayed the entire Empire. With his finger he traced the outlines of the nation, from the frozen Arctic to the Crimea, then eastward to the vast, sparsely inhabited expanse of Siberia.

Finally he was drawn to the western border and the dark line which delineated the province of Poland. Even though one of his titles was King of Poland, Nicholas had always thought of Poland as merely the location of the lodge at Spala with its wonderful memories of the hunts, and the easy camaraderie of men born to privilege. Although the Tsar was fond of the Polish people he had never seriously considered hiding the children in Poland because he reasoned that without political protection it would be too easy for the "evil ones" to hunt them down. But now as he pored over the atlas he began to have second thoughts. Frankly, he found the idea of using Poland as a safe haven, an intriguing one; a concept worthy of further discussion with his fellow *Masqueraders*.

In the past, the situation in Poland had been a frequent topic of conversation because the Tsar openly toyed with the idea of granting independence or some sort of autonomy to the Poles. His ministers, however, were adamantly opposed to any loss of Russian territory and warned that the people would never accept such a radical course of action. At times like this, when Nicholas was acting on an emotional plane, he generally ignored the lack of support he received and made his decisions unilaterally. Even though they had suffered greatly at the hands of some of the Tsar's predecessors, the Polish people were always gracious and kind to the Imperial family. Nicholas knew that the Poles wanted what most of the peoples of Eastern Europe desired, namely the right to select their own leaders, to practice their religion freely, to speak their own language and to enjoy their own culture. The Tsar realized that if he encouraged this nationalism in Poland he would be placing himself on a collision course with most of the monarchs of Europe, as well as his own people. And who could he deal with? There had been a number of uprisings over the past decades and there were active revolutionaries in Poland at this very time, but Nicholas looked upon them as nationalists rather than anarchists. Perhaps someone would appear from among these groups with the stature to negotiate a change, someone he could place in his debt, someone who could help him with the children when the time came, someone he could trust implicitly. He decided to get in touch with Count Carl Gustav Mannerheim, who commanded the Uhlan Regiment in Warsaw, and have him make some discreet preliminary inquiries as to who might be an acceptable negotiator.

The beautiful and restful environment at Livadia was conducive to thoughtful contemplation and the Tsar continued to dwell on the Polish situation and how he might manipulate it to his advantage. At this time last year the family was gathered at Spala and Alexei was near death, his frail body wracked with pain and the doctors unable to provide any relief. As much as he enjoyed his visits to the lodge he knew he would never see Spala again and it was painful to accept the reality. But during that last visit something significant had occurred and he was struggling to dredge it up from the recesses of his memory. He went back over everything that had happened during their stay and finally it came to him. Nicholas remembered a conversation he had with Count Alfred Potocki during a reception the Empress had given at Spala. The Count had spoken of a convent in Warsaw, a place of complete anonymity, a place where identities could be hidden. Perhaps this was the answer. The key, of course, was to get the doubles in place, for once they were acting out their roles it would be fairly easy to spirit the girls away and hide them. Nicholas reasoned that once the switch had been made there would be no motive for anyone to search for them unless, God forbid, they were betrayed. Discovery of the *Masquerade* was always a possibility, and none of the players, especially the Tsar, were so naive as to underestimate the dangers they faced. But the convent in Warsaw seemed to offer at least a temporary solution and, if it was all Potocki said it was, he was willing to take a closer look at it. He rubbed his temples, trying to relieve some of the pressure that was building inside his head and then reached for his cigarette, but it had burned to ash. Nicholas moved over to his desk, sat down, and reached for his silver cigarette case. He took out another cigarette, lit it with a platinum lighter, embossed with the Imperial Emblem, and inhaled deeply. He decided, then and there, to put Nikolasha in overall charge of what, in the future, would be referred to as the "Polish situation." The Tsar would leave everything to his uncle and let him determine to what extent Mannerheim and Potocki should be involved. Nicholas recognized that there would be friction over the question of Polish independence but he thought he could adequately make his case. At any rate, Nikolasha had a knack for assessing character and the Tsar was confident that his uncle would be able to identify the individual they needed to talk to. When you came right down to it, personal preferences had to be suppressed. The goal, after all, was to save the girls and whatever served that end is what they would do. One of the factors that disturbed Nicholas the most and weighed heavily on his mind was the question of how much he should involve Alix. The Empress already knew some elements of his plan including the effort to find safe haven for the children. She had also been told about the use of substitutes and although she had not been too enthusiastic about the idea he knew she would come around. Alix had been surprisingly cooperative up to this point and Nicholas wanted her to be as informed as was possible. He needn't have worried, however, because Alix often eavesdropped on his meetings and was more familiar with the deliberations then he realized. His greatest fear was that somehow Rasputin would get wind of their actions. Since the events at Spala Alix had surrendered completely to the belief that the "holy man" had healed their son and nothing would convince her otherwise. She was now firmly convinced that he was necessary to the continued well-being of their son and after her ordeal and the suffering she had endured there was no way Nicholas could cut her off completely from his influence. Alix had assured him that she would not divulge anything to Father Grigory and up to this point she seemed to have kept that promise. Nicholas would continue to monitor the situation and take action if necessary, but at this point he would just have to take Alix at her word.

The next few days passed slowly as Nicholas waited impatiently for word that George and Sandro had arrived in the area. Ella was staying with the family at Livadia while Nikolasha waited at Chaeer, his Crimean estate. The plan was for everyone to meet at Harax the day after the two brothers returned from their separate journeys abroad. Finally a message from Harax announced the arrival of George but also informed Nicky that Sandro had been delayed by bad weather on his Atlantic crossing and was running a few days behind. By the time Sandro did arrive Nicholas had everybody on edge and so it was with some relief that on a beautiful sunny morning, in late September, Nicholas set off for Harax accompanied by Ella, Count Benckendorff and his two oldest daughters. Everyone was to have lunch together and then Olga and Tatiana would spend the afternoon with George's wife and daughters while the others held their meeting. The lovely weather made the long walk an enjoyable one and the girls chattered continuously as the group made their way through the forest. The Tsar stopped frequently to allow the Count to catch his breath so it was nearly two hours before they arrived at Harax. Nikolasha, George, and Sandro were waiting for them when they finally walked onto the verandah and the host, realizing their appetites had been sharpened by the long hike, ushered them immediately into the dinning room where a sumptuous lunch was waiting. Despite the air of anticipation which everyone felt, they deliberately kept the conversation light-hearted, well aware that soon enough they would be engaged in a momentous discussion.

With lunch completed the *Masqueraders* adjourned to George's library where he had a large conference table. The Tsar took his seat at the head of the table and the others filled in around him. Nicky looked at each of them in turn and was nearly overwhelmed by the affection he had for these five individuals, who were risking so much for his family. Finally, his emotions under control, he began. "Before I receive your reports I want to share with you some actions I have been considering while you were all going about your affairs. As you know, George has been attempting to place two of the girls and he will brief us this afternoon on the success of that effort."

"Why only two, Nicky?" asked his uncle.

"Because, Nikolasha, I have been convinced by Benckendorff that we should make it as difficult as possible for anyone to trace the children and two of the girls together will certainly be less noticeable than four. What has given me pause was where to send the others and I have made a determination that will probably surprise you."

Everyone looked at Nicholas in anticipation for they were all aware of how much distress the dilemma had been causing him.

"I will send them to Poland," he announced. Nicky looked around the table and was met by looks of absolute shock, so he prepared to rebut the objections that were sure to come. He did not have long to wait and as expected Nikolasha, the "terrible uncle," was the first to voice his objections. "To send them to Poland is no different than to keep them in Russia. Poland is Russia. Surely you are not serious?"

"Please hear me out, Uncle. Believe me, you cannot imagine the hours I have spent considering this option and I did not come to the decision lightly. You must all know that there is no way I can send the children to a country that has family ties to the Russian Imperial family; and that rules out most of Europe. The first place assassins would look for the children would be among my relatives. The best solution is to send them to a country that no one would even consider and that is why George has been in Japan. But to accommodate Count Benckendorff suggestion that we split the children up we need a second destination."

"But what about its proximity to Russia," persisted Nikolasha? "How safe would the children be?

"We must constantly remind ourselves that if the *Masquerade* is successful no one will be looking for the children. You know I have talked frequently about granting Poland its independence and now could be a good time to make a gesture in that direction. Dear Uncle, I know you will have the strongest objections to what I am about to suggest and for that very reason I intend to use you in this matter. You will see all the obstacles to my course of action and bring your extensive talents to bear in overcoming them. I want you to get in touch with Gustav Mannerheim and have him assist you in identifying someone from among the Polish leadership with whom we could open private discussions. There is always someone who stands out among the rest as a potential leader and who has the trust of the people."

"Nicky, you are their leader," said Sandro.

"I know, but if Poland was made independent I would no longer be its King. My place would probably be taken by some nationalist who has the trust of the people."

"What! You would negotiate with a man who is revolting against the crown of Russia," Nikolasha practically shouted.

"You do not see it the way I do, Uncle. If not for Serafim's letter I doubt we would be having this discussion and I freely admit that I have changed. Since I am fighting to save the children I see things differently and these Poles are not the anarchists we battle in Russia, but rather a group wanting the independence of their country. I have not heard of any violence in their quest for freedom."

At this point George could contain himself no longer and spoke up. "I was going to wait to discuss my negotiations with the Japanese until later but what I have to say may be relevant to the current topic. May I speak?"

"Certainly, "Nicholas replied.

"You know I have been working with the Japanese and, of course, they were curious as to why we were only sending two daughters to Japan. I had to be very careful not to give offense because they felt they were fully capable of safeguarding all the children. However, when I explained your reasoning to them they understood immediately. Then the most amazing thing happened. When they asked me where the other children were going I replied that the decision had not been made. At that point, and here is the strange part, Prince Kanin suggested we consider Poland. I was caught off guard and was literally speechless.

"Surely you are jesting," said the Tsar in disbelief. "How could they have possibly come up with that idea? This is the first time I have mentioned it to anyone."

"Evidently the Japanese have had contacts with Polish nationalists since their war with us, in 1905," explained George. "It seems a man named Joseph Pilsudski, who apparently represented a number of Polish revolutionary factions, visited Japan during the war and offered to assist in their fight against us by opening up a western front. He asked the Japanese for money and weapons and they agreed to some of his proposals. In return for his help he wanted a free and independent Poland but, before anything could come of it, the United States negotiated a settlement."

"That must have been a very delicate conversation. What was the Japanese attitude during this discussion?" asked the Tsar.

"They were obviously embarrassed to bring up the Pilsudski matter, especially since the relationship between our two countries has improved so much, but they honestly want to help us. In spite of their discomfort, they suggested Poland because of their contacts there and the possibility that they could help in negotiations," George replied.

"This Pilsudski certainly does not sound like a friend of Russia," the Tsar observed. I wonder if he is still one of their leaders for I must admit I have never heard of him."

"As I understand it he is still the leader of an organization called the Rifleman's Association, and is actively agitating for Poland's independence," George replied.

"Well, we need to find out for certain," said the Tsar. "Nikolasha, you see what you are up against? Find out everything you can. Mannerheim will know if this Pilsudski is the man we are looking for, but we do not want to show our hand too quickly in case he is not. This is a separate issue, for the time being, so discuss the idea of Poland's independence only with Mannerheim and whatever you do, protect the *Masquerade*. However, we are running out of time and if we are to grant Polish independence we must do it before everything falls apart in Russia.

Otherwise the "evil ones" will have access to the sanctuary we have worked so hard to create.

"Have you thought about where the children will live in Poland," asked Nikolasha.

"Yes, I have given it a great deal of thought. Count Alfred Potocki, who calls on us every year when we visit Spala, told me of a convent founded by one of his relatives. It intrigued me because once a woman enters the convent her past is erased. This enables an individual to make a fresh start in life, whether she was a prostitute, or escaping from a bad marriage or any number of other reasons. The women can choose to become nuns or they can leave the convent after a period of time, with some education and, most importantly, a new identity. My daughters could be slipped in and no one would be the wiser. They would probably dress like nuns and live among the Sisters there. Nikolasha when you are meeting with Mannerheim you should be able to get more specific information on the convent but be discreet in your inquiries. Find out the details and determine if what I propose is feasible.

"May I make a suggestion," interrupted Sandro. The Tsar nodded his assent. "I assume the American leadership will be kept in the dark as to the whereabouts of the children unless, of course, we determine they must go to the United States. But why not encourage President Wilson to back the independence of Poland? If the United States supports the idea, other countries may fall in line as well. President Wilson seems to be more concerned with foreign affairs than most of his predecessors were, and is known for his anti-imperialist sentiments. When I met with him I was surprised to find out he was an admirer of your efforts at the Hague Peace conferences, Nicky. He may talk like an isolationist but I have feeling he is a supporter of national self-determination, especially in the Balkans and Eastern Europe. After speaking with him I am sure that a free Poland is something he would gladly support."

"It is certainly worth a try, but we should not be seen by our European neighbors as the driving force behind any independence movement," said Nicholas. "Maybe he could make a public statement of some sort that we could use as a basis for negotiations with the Poles.

"You helped put the man in office. It is the least he could do for you," said Sandro.

"I think he will be inclined to cooperate. Yes, Sandro you broach the subject and see what you can accomplish. Now tell us about your trip to America and where we stand there," said the Tsar.

Sandro stood up and began to speak about his trip. He related in some detail the particulars of his meetings with Vanderlip and Charles Crane. He did not dwell on the banking arrangements other than to indicate that funds would be transferred as soon as the Federal Reserve banks were ready to receive their deposits. He also mentioned that working capital was located in accounts with National City Bank.

"It is amazing that you were able to accomplish so much and still not arouse suspicion since you managed to be in all the papers," teased Nikolasha.

"Well, you can imagine my dismay when I disembarked in New York City and was greeted by a contingent of press and photographers. So much for my discreet visit. But the Americans were very skillful at moving me from place to place and I was able to accomplish my mission while, at the same time, maintaining my persona as a Grand Duke on holiday. Had I been on my own it would have been almost impossible. At any rate, it all went well so let me move on to my meeting with President Wilson. Although he acceded to all our requests, it took some convincing, and at one point I actually thought I had failed. But in the end he agreed to everything we asked for," announced Sandro, with satisfaction in his voice. He then went on to describe the meeting in detail and share his impressions of the President with the others. When he had finished he made a final observation. "This Charles Crane is a man who commands respect. It is hard to put into words, but when he spoke I found his commentary and arguments quite compelling. He is a very intelligent man and I can see why he has the President's ear. Charles will be visiting Russia later in the fall and will have documents prepared for your signature. You can meet him at that time, if you wish, or I can hand-carry the documents back and forth between you."

"An excellent report, Sandro. I am very pleased with your effort in America."

"Thank-you Nicky, but I do have some concerns. We are putting so much faith in foreigners. What if they betray us?" Have you considered some sort of backup plan if this all goes awry?"

"We can only do so much, Sandro," said Nicholas softly. "We cannot plan for every eventuality nor can we allow ourselves to be forced into situations where we can only react. For this to work we must remain on the offensive and in control of our own destinies. As for me, I must trust in God and the people that have been chosen to participate in the *Masquerade*. That is all I can do."

"When should I start encouraging the rest of the family to prepare for a future outside of Russia," asked Sandro.

"Well, I admit I have not given that much thought but my instinct tells me they will be on their own, for the most part. The country is doing well right now and the family may not be open to financial advice, but keep at them. Maybe you could bring up the unrest that occurred in 1905 and suggest they make some foreign investments or move funds to banks in Switzerland. But whatever you decide, do not allow Brantingham or Crane to have contact with anyone other than yourself or George. The *Masquerade* must be separate from any family plans. Does everyone understand that," asked the Tsar, as he looked around at the group. They all concurred.

"Remember," Nicholas cautioned, "we must not leave any clues that will allow people to discover what we have done. If the details of the *Masquerade* were never revealed I would be pleased, but at the very least we must make it work for as many years as possible.

The Tsar looked around the richly paneled room and noticed that George had displayed the Imperial flag in his library. Nicholas stood up, walked over to the flag, lifted it from its stand, and brought it back to the conference table. "George, I hope you don't mind." He laid the flag across the table and everyone assisted in smoothing it out, not exactly sure what the Tsar was doing. But his purpose became clear when he asked them all to place their right hand on the flag. "I know that all of you have pledged your fealty to me, as Tsar of Russia, but I feel that we must all swear to be loyal to the dangerous undertaking we have embarked on. If I am dead and gone, your oath to me is no longer binding, but the *Masquerade* will go on and will need your unwavering support far into the future, as will my children. Will you do this for me?"

Ella had been quietly listening to the discussion and had waited patiently for her turn to give an update on her work but now she spoke up, for at times like this, the others tended to follow her lead. The Tsar's unexpected request touched her and although her loyalty was unquestionable she could see that such an oath would add additional emphasis to the need for secrecy. Without any discussion or request for clarification she said simply, "I will swear." Nikolasha, George, Sandro, and Benckendorff immediately followed suit.

No one in the room realized that the swearing of the oath was an unplanned and spontaneous act on the Tsar's part and that he had no idea what he was going to say. Everyone watched him intently and wondered what this promise would entail. For his part the Tsar hoped that he would be able to come up with words that would inspire this small group of beloved friends to even greater effort. He paused momentarily to jot down a few sentences on a piece of stationery and then said, "I want you each to take this oath separately so that everyone here will be a witness to your commitment," said the Tsar. "I will be the first." The Tsar placed his left hand on the flag and raising his right hand he began. "I, Nicholas Alexandrovich Romanov, give my word before God and all present that I will strive with all that is in me to protect the *Masquerade* and all its secrets and I will do my utmost to ensure its success. I pledge my allegiance to this plan for I believe that the salvation of Mother Russia depends on it. So help me God." The Tsar turned to Ella who was standing to his right and passed her the paper. She took the oath and when she finished the others followed in turn.

There was dead silence in the room when the last one made the pledge and all stood still, looking down at the Russian flag on which they had just sworn. The symbolism was not lost upon them. They recognized the fate of the country was truly in their hands and all realized the significance of the oath. Nicholas finally broke the spell and asked everyone to sit down. He carefully picked up the staff and placed the flag back in its base, where it stood as a visible reminder of what was really at stake. The Tsar turned to George, "Now back to business. Please give us your update on Japan."

"The Japanese are committed to helping you and are very willing to accommodate your request. Prince Kanin and I drafted documents which the Emperor signed stipulating that he will give refuge to your children. I have the paperwork for you to review and countersign and then we can send their copy back via the Japanese ambassador. Emperor Yoshihoto is pleased that Japan will finally repay the debt to you that has been owed for so long. He said he is willing to do whatever is necessary to protect the children. I might add that I did not spend too much time with the Emperor. Once he gave his approval he left the details to Prince Kanin, and I worked closely with the Prince on all the arrangements. I discussed with him the possibility that the children might eventually go to the United States if the situation in Russia became untenable. He will rely on the Japanese ambassador to keep him up to date on the conditions in Russia. If for some reason the ambassador is expelled from our country by the anarchists the Prince will have to come up with alternate sources of information. He suggested we establish some type of intelligence network in Siberia, perhaps in the vicinity of Omsk, under the cover of a trading mission. He thinks it is important to have some people close at hand because we would obviously move the girls through Siberia to Vladivostok and on to Japan. I will need to send word to him as to your decision," said George.

"Yes, I think the idea of a Japanese trade mission in Siberia has possibilities, especially if it is established right away. George, since the financial arrangements are on track, I am assigning you the additional responsibility of working with the Japanese to get this network established. If something were to go wrong when it came time to evacuate the children it makes good sense to have an additional way to get them out."

"I will send word right away," George replied. "And by the way, the Emperor has categorically refused payment of any kind. He said this will repay the debt which his country has long owed since the vicious attack on you. But consider this. Although I am sure Japan will provide support for the children, I think we need to make some alternate financial arrangements for them. We have not really discussed the matter yet but we need to decide how the girls are going to handle their own finances. Your children have led sheltered lives and although Olga is maturing rapidly, I doubt she understands the nature of finance or the value of money. Do you have any plans to prepare the children and when are you going to tell them what the future holds?

"In regards to the financial arrangements, I have been contemplating the idea of giving the children jewels instead of large sums of money or gold. Jewels will always have value and a large bag of diamonds and rare pearls, liquidated a few at a time, would be more than enough to cover their needs. And, of course, they will have access to the maintenance accounts we have established in various locations. But you are right George. Go ahead and find a reputable Japanese bank and deposit funds in their names. But use gold. If Russia goes down, the ruble will certainly devalue. You all need to think in those terms. If we use Poland we will also have to make some arrangements there. Now in regards to your other concerns, I have made no decision, but it is something that Alix and I will discuss. We will decide together when the children will be told. Do you have anything else, George," asked Nicky.

"No, that is everything. The Japanese understand that we are in the initial planning stages and that specific arrangements will be finalized at a later date. I did forget to mention that Prince Kanin will visit Russia, when it is convenient, to meet the children and discuss life in Japan. The Emperor has chosen him to be their guardian while they are there. He is an honorable man and I was most impressed with him. I would trust my own children with him."

"Well, it sounds as if things are starting to fall into place," said the Tsar. He turned his attention to Ella. "How is the search for substitutes coming along?"

"At this point we have identified a total of seven doubles. I have not yet found one for Maria but I have two for each of the other girls. I also located a young boy who is the image of Alexei. Because the Tsarevich is more easily identified I think it is imperative that his double look like him as much as possible. It is not as critical for the Grand Duchesses as their features are usually hidden under hats and their pictures have not been distributed as widely as those of the Tsarevich. Their training has already begun at Ilinskoe and is progressing much better than I had hoped. The boy we found is smart, a quick learner and carries himself as if he was born to nobility."

"That is good news, but I am concerned that we have no one for Maria yet. Do you have any leads?" Nicky asked.

"I will be taking an extended trip to visit my outlying convents and am also planning a pilgrimage to Solovetz," Ella replied. "I hope since I will be in areas we have not visited recently that we will find her. I leave in a few days. My plan is to travel from the Crimea and complete my search before returning to Moscow."

"I pray God will favor your efforts and provide a suitable impostor. Of course, she will have to be as strong as an ox, otherwise no one will believe it is Maria," joked the Tsar.

Ella smiled at the comment because she was well aware of the stamina of her niece. Maria was unusually strong and had been known to lift one of her tutors in the air. "God willing we will find her," said Ella.

"Ella when this year is up we will have to go forward with what you have. They must start training to play the parts of the Grand Duchesses and the heir. You will have much work to do."

"Well, as I mentioned we have already begun their education and the children are making great progress, especially in the area of languages. Two of the nuns from our convent, Sisters Irene and Katherine, are highly educated noblewomen and they have undertaken the academic education of the substitutes. Sister Barbara, who you already know about, is taking care of other matters such as protocol, etiquette and manners and I conduct classes on the genealogy of the family when I visit Ilinskoe. I have decided it is too early to begin altering their appearance. They are isolated, of course, but we are taking great care to ensure they do not look like your children. Someone who knows the Imperial family might see them and wonder what is going on. I know it is unlikely, and perhaps I am being overly cautious, but I see no reason to take risks at this point.

"Ella, how much have you told these nuns? You have not brought them into the plan have you?"

"Nicky, I have been very discreet and have told them only what they need to know to accomplish this part of the training. You must remember that I am the Mother Superior of an order of nuns and one of our vows is that of obedience. Although they must wonder what the purpose of this school is, they would never ask and their involvement will not be an issue."

"Well, I am satisfied that you have things under control, Ella," Nicholas replied, "and I think we have covered enough for today. It is getting late and I want to get back to Livadia before dark. I do not think we need to meet together again as a group for a while, as we will all be busy. If anything comes up, however, or there are any questions or problems, do not hesitate to contact me. I will keep Benckendorff fully informed and if for some reason I am not available, consult with him."

After the meeting broke up, the Count started back to Livadia while Nicholas and Ella went to retrieve the girls. When Olga and Tatiana joined them the Tsar had to admit that George was right. At eighteen and sixteen his daughters were no longer children but fashionable young women of marriageable age. But what did his precious daughters know of the real world? They were innocent and full of trust, yet he knew that somehow he would have to destroy those endearing qualities and prepare them for the transition from fantasy to reality. It was something he dreaded because it meant creating cynicism where none existed and making the concept of trust a liability rather than an asset. And what of the younger children? Would he have to subdue their high spirits and force them to abandon their childhood? He could already envision the scene when he informed them they would be separated, not only from their parents, but from each other. He knew how they would react and how painful it would be for everyone. But the alternative was worse, and he knew when the time came he would find the strength to do what was necessary. He could only hope that Alix would be able to shoulder her share of the burden and be strong for all of them. At any rate he realized it was not only the impostors who needed special training but his children as well.

They started their walk back to Livadia and the Tsar let his daughters and Ella set the pace but Nicholas fell behind as he continued to dwell on the questions of when and how to bring the children into it. Up to this point he had always considered the *Masquerade* as his plan but at this moment he suddenly realized that though he was arranging everything, the fate of Russia would ultimately be in the hands of his children, and not his. Through the intervention of one of the girls Russia would be saved; but which one? He knew now that it was time to bring Alix into it. She had left everything to him, up to this point, but he knew she would never forgive him if he made a decision about the children without consulting her. Frankly, he felt intimidated by the prospect but he could not shrink from his duty no matter how much he dreaded it. He decided to discuss the situation with his wife at the earliest possible moment.

It was not too early to start planning for the substitution even though it would be months before the doubles were ready. Who in the palace would need to know? Once the impostors assumed his children's identities, who would they come in contact with? Hundreds of people worked at the palace and there were numerous security personnel on hand as well. However, most of the workers saw only brief glimpses of the family and very few actually interacted with his children on a regular basis. He would have to seriously consider this and start narrowing down the list of those who would be allowed contact with the family. Access to their rooms would be severely restricted after the family returned from Livadia.

He realized he was falling way behind so he sped up to catch Ella and the girls. His sister-in-law gave him a look of understanding when he approached for she knew he had needed a moment alone. Ahead they could see the distant form of Benckendorff and set the pace to accommodate his tired old legs.

CR80

A few days later, when Nicholas came back from his morning walk and inspection of the guards to join Alix for breakfast he was surprised to find she had ordered the meal to be served out on the terrace. He walked out to find her sitting at a table set for two and sipping tea. She greeted him with a radiant smile and beckoned him to join her. She looked so healthy and happy for a change. "What is the occasion?" he inquired.

"You have been working too hard my darling. I am feeling wonderful and would like to share the day with my husband," said Alix. "I would love to walk in the garden today."

He had to admit she looked lovely this morning. Her hair was loosely piled atop her head with a few tendrils escaping to frame her face. She was simply dressed in a crisp, long white skirt with a fitted jacket to match

"Why not go after we finish breakfast. The weather is delightful today and I do not have anything on my calendar until after lunch. Will you need your wheelchair or can you do without?" Nicky hoped she would walk because she got so little exercise and he was pleased when she indicated the chair could be left behind. They enjoyed a leisurely breakfast and when they were finished Alix retrieved a hat and her cane from their room and together they strolled through the garden and down to the paved path which overlooked the beach area and allowed unobstructed views of the sea. After walking for a while Nicky led Alix over to one of the many benches placed along the pathway. Before they departed the palace Nicholas had directed that they were not to be disturbed and the two were quietly enjoying the luxury of being alone together without their usual entourage. He sat down beside her, grasped her hand, and pressed it to his lips.

"Darling, I hate to interrupt this idyllic moment but I need to talk with you about our future and I wonder, since you are feeling better, if this might not be a good time to do it. I know what we have to discuss might distress you, so if you are not up to it I will wait for another time, but I cannot put it off much longer," said Nicholas.

"My dearest husband, what better time than this? I know that this has been a difficult period for you but I will try and be strong and you must believe I will stand by your side through this all."

"Dear Alix, thank you so much for your support. Now please hear me out. I and a small group of advisors have come up with a plan which addresses the predictions in St. Serafim's letter. We have called this plan the *Masquerade* and it has many elements, most of which do not involve you. You made it quite clear some years ago that under no circumstances could I induce you to leave the country without me. Is that still your feeling, Alix?"

"Nicky, how can you ask this? You know I would never leave you."

"Very well, then. Beginning right now, you and I must embark on the most difficult and dangerous part of the plan; the replacement of our children with doubles. When the substitutes are installed in the palace, Alexei and the girls will be spirited out of Russia to places of safety. I mentioned this to you earlier but we have progressed so far that it is time for you to become actively involved."

"Do you have any of the impostors identified yet," Alix asked.

"I have put Ella in charge of the search and, I must say, it is moving along quite well. We have seven doubles so far and they are in training at Ilinskoe," Nicky replied. Your sister has done a marvelous job finding the children and they are making great progress. For the present they have been told they are being trained to work at one of the family palaces. When the time comes you and I will select the final candidates and the others will indeed go to the summer palaces here in the Crimea."

"You said you had located seven. I am afraid I do not understand," Alix said, with obvious confusion in her voice.

"We have located one for Alexei and two for each of the girls except Maria. Ella left yesterday to complete her task and it is our hope she will find one girl, and possibly two, who fit our needs. At any rate, two of her nuns were from noble families, and well educated, so they have become the primary teachers and along with Sister Barbara are turning these street urchins into grand duchesses and the heir apparent. You will be amazed. Ella is very impressed at how quickly they are mastering second and third languages. This was the area of their education she had expressed the most concern about because if they cannot speak the court languages it might pose a problem. Of course, they needn't be fluent but at least as conversant as our children. Do not forget, it is only recently that you insisted Alexei take up French."

"Oh, now I understand. It sounds as if everything is coming together although I am certain I will have difficulty pretending these impostors are my own children."

"You will have time to adjust to the idea, Alix, but this is not what has been bothering me. Walking home from George's the other day it struck me that we have done very little to prepare our children for life outside the palace walls. I have arrogantly assumed that I hold the fate of Russia in my hands but in reality it is in the hands of the girls and I fear we have done little to prepare them for the coming trial."

Alix could understand why he was so troubled. Their children were so young and innocent, and such unlikely candidates to carry the burden that would soon be placed on them. She was determined to help her husband as much as possible. "Oh Nicky, do not worry so. We will just have to prepare them," she said with German practicality.

"I want them to be ready for the future but at the same time I want them to have as normal a childhood as possible," Nicky replied. "I toyed with the idea of at least telling the older girls but then decided it is too soon.

"I could not agree more. I do not want the children to suffer for five years with the knowledge that at the end of that time, we might well be dead. It is too much for a young mind to cope with. Perhaps with a few changes in their education curriculum we can help them out. Your daughters have very simple tastes; they make their own beds and assist with cleaning their rooms, so they are not totally helpless. But I must ask you, how do you see their future? How will they live?"

"That is a difficult question to answer. All of this is still in the planning stages. The two who go to Japan will undoubtedly live in comfort, whereas the two who go to Warsaw will live anonymously, in a convent.

"A convent! Oh Nicky, what kind of life is that for a young girl, if she has no vocation?"

"It will be a temporary stay. Remember, we can only speculate as to the duration of the catastrophe that will befall the nation. If things do not change for the better in Russia the children will be moved secretly to the United States. False identities will be established for them and they can live a quiet private life. I am still working out the details but that is the general idea."

"How do the impostors fit in?"

"They will replace our children until we get them safely out of the country. And then the substitutes will stay with you and I for as long as we can maintain the *Masquerade*."

"If these doubles are going to pass as my children I must have some interaction with them. Is there some way we could hide them in the palace?" asked Alix.

"When the training with Ella and her nuns is completed and we select the final five we will bring them to the palace and into our lives. Although it is important for you to be involved I think it is even more important for our children to interact with their look-a-likes. They will be able to tell them things that we do not know and share little confidences we are unaware of."

"When do you think this will happen?"

"I am looking at the latter part of 1916. They will need enough time to become totally acclimated before we make the exchange, which I anticipate would take place early the following year."

"So soon Nicky? We have until 1918."

"Yes we do Alix. But when? January or December? What if this revolution erupts in the beginning of the year? We would not have time to move the children."

"Would they have to leave Russia so soon? Could we not keep them somewhere close so we could see them from time to time before the final parting?" At this she lost her composure, buried her head in Nicky's shoulder, and began to weep.

"There, there Alix," he said as he gently rubbed her back. "We must stay strong and, as hard as this is, we cannot dwell on our sadness. It is best that when we send the children off, it be to a place of safety and we cannot jeopardize the arrangements we have made by waiting too long. But I will promise you this. I will wait until the last possible moment."

Alix pulled herself together. "Nicky, when do you think we should tell the children?"

"I would like to wait as long as possible before we tell them, perhaps a week or two before we bring in their doubles. I want them to have a little bit of time to adjust to the idea."

"My poor Nicky, you have so much to prepare for." She wished there was some way to convince her husband to confide in Father Grigory but she knew this was not the time to bring it up. Nicholas was adamant that "their friend" not be informed about Serafim's letter. The Tsar worried that if Rasputin found out what was going on it would only be a matter of time before all Russia knew. Nicky maintained that if Rasputin was supposed to know about the *Masquerade*, his mystical powers would have already made him aware of it, and Alix could not fault his logic. Despite her blind faith in the man and her fervent hope that he would somehow become involved, she had given Nicky her word that she would say nothing and she meant to keep her promise, even though it was very difficult. She kept hoping that somehow Father Grigory would learn of the plan on his own, and once aware of it, be able to advise her on how to act.

Alix looked down and began gently stroking her husband's hand. "What about your finger?" she asked

"My finger? To be honest I just haven't thought about it at all. I don't know. I cannot cut it off too soon as I am sure someone will notice it is missing. Maybe I will wait to the last moment and just have Dr. Botkin whack it off."

"Oh, Nicky how can you jest about it?"

"I am sorry darling and, of course, you are right. It is not a laughing matter. I think I have had enough for today. You now know your role in this, but tell no one, lest you endanger us all. Now let us talk about something else for awhile. Have I told you how beautiful you look today?" Alix blushed a little and smiled at her husband. The two resumed walking through the garden, enjoying their rare moment alone, reluctant to return to the palace.

♋♋

Ella had departed Livadia for her convent visitation and pilgrimage but the trip was only a cover for the real purpose of her long journey, which was to locate a substitute for Maria. She planned to visit the Solovetz Monastery which was located on an island in the White Sea, but before doing so she stopped in St. Petersburg to pick up Felix Yusupov, heir to one of the largest fortunes in Russia. He would soon be a member of the Imperial family as he was to marry Sandro's daughter Irina. Felix was a complex young man who had suffered from many emotional problems in the past. He had grown up an extremely spoiled youth but, in spite of all his troubles, he was a delightful scamp. He had sought Ella

328

out a few years ago for spiritual guidance and she was instrumental in setting him back on the right path so he was anxious to make this pilgrimage with the woman who had such a profound and positive influence on his life.

Getting to the monastery meant traveling to the port of Archangel on the White Sea, in the extreme northern part of Russia. At the port city they boarded a ship which took them out to the island where the entire community of monks had gathered at the quay to greet them. The Grand Duchess was dressed in her habit, as was Sister Barbara and they were touched and humbled by the monk's kind reception. A carriage brought them through the thick stands of fir trees and around numerous lakes en route to the monastery. The country side was breathtakingly beautiful, the lush evergreens contrasting with the crystal blue waters of the northern lakes. The first snows of the season were still a few weeks away but the air was crisp and chilly. The monastery itself had been constructed in the fifteenth century of gray and red granite and was an imposing sight. The monks escorted the nuns and Felix to the spartan cells which were to be their accommodations for the next few days. Ella was used to the simplicity of monastic life but she wondered how Felix would fare.

The week at the monastery passed quickly for Ella, who immediately succumbed to the tranquility and the aura of spirituality which enveloped her. She attended all the services and joined the monks for the chanting of the office but most of her time was spent in private prayer in which she entreated God to grant success to her endeavors. Felix on the other hand had a short attention span. For the first day or so he attempted to follow Ella's routine but quickly tired of it. "I just feel I am becoming too holy," he joked to Ella.

"Felix, I live a contemplative life and I enjoy this but please do not feel you must do as I do. Explore the island. You do not have to stay by my side."

For the remaining days, Felix met Ella in the morning for a simple breakfast and then departed for a day of exploration, while she continued her meditations. Although he did not spend too much time in prayer himself, the silence of the monastery, combined with the natural beauty of the area, was conducive to contemplation. Away from the decadence of St. Petersburg it was possible for Felix to see there was more to life than dissipation. Something called to him spiritually and he began to wonder if he should abandon thoughts of marriage and consider a monastic life. Finally after much soul-searching, he broached the subject with Ella. She quickly brushed his doubts aside . "Felix, you must marry the woman you love. That is God's plan for you. Some are called to the religious life and some to the married state but both are paths to holiness. Use your gifts to glorify God by helping people to lead better lives. Follow Christ and you will find true happiness in this world and the next." Felix appreciated her advice and her honesty and was thankful that his life had been so enriched by his friendship with this saintly woman. He knew no matter what the situation he could always count on her for guidance.

When their day of departure arrived all the monks escorted the pilgrims to the dock where they caught a ship back to Archangel. When they pulled into the port Ella told Felix she would meet him later at the train station. He set out to explore the city and she set out to find a double for Maria. A nun from the local convent agreed to serve as her guide. Ella explained that she had established a school in Moscow to give young girls the chance to learn a trade and she wanted to see if there were any in the area who would like to avail themselves of the opportunity. She was particularly interested in orphans who had no other options.

The sister from the convent was most helpful and brought her to the area of the city where most of the poor lived. The slums were depressing and dirty but it was no different from what she experienced everyday in Moscow. Ella, Sister Barbara, and their guide visited several hovels and they gave what spiritual comfort they could and distributed some coins as well. The poverty often depressed Ella, especially when she considered the meals she used to serve at her palace. These people could have eaten for a week from the leftovers. She intently eyed the faces of a number of girls but no one seemed to fit the bill. Nevertheless she gathered a few young girls to take back with her. She knew they were one step away from prostitution unless someone provided some type of assistance. She sent them back to the train station with Sister Barbara and decided to take one last look around. Just as she was about to give up and go back she saw a child sitting on the side of one of the streets. Ella could not explain what drew her to the girl or how she knew this was the one she was looking for. From across the street it was impossible to see in this pathetic child any resemblance to her niece, and yet something about her reminded her so much of Maria. The girl was filthy from head to toe and sat dejectedly with her feet in the gutter. As the two nuns approached she brushed a stringy tendril of hair out of her face and looked up and Ella could sense her utter despair. There was a stronger resemblance to Maria but she would not know for sure until she was cleaned up. "What is your name child?"

"Sophia", she whispered.

"When was the last time you had anything to eat?"

"It has been two days, Sister."

"Where is your family?"

"They are all dead, even my little brother who died last week. Taking care of him was my only reason to live. He was so sick and I had no money for medicine," she cried.

"You poor girl. Would you like to travel to Moscow with me? I have a school for young ladies such as yourself and you will be able learn a skill and support yourself."

"You would help me?" she asked, with trembling lips.

"Yes we will. Now let me help you up. We have a train to catch." Sophia began to stand but was so weak she fainted into Ella's arms. They were able to revive her but Ella knew that she needed to eat so she carried her to a nearby stand where they were able to purchase a cup of nourishing soup. Sophia sipped it and gradually began to feel better.

"I think I can walk now, Sister."

"Good. The station is not far." Ella and Sophia bid good-bye to the nun who had been so kind and helpful and made their way to Ella's private car. Ella helped Sophia aboard, showed her where she could clean up and gave her one of her habits to wear, as she had no other clothes. Once Sophia was cleaned up, Ella introduced her to the other girls who would also be traveling to Moscow. They were missing only one passenger. Felix was late, as usual. Ella began to worry that something might have happened to him but just as the engineer started to couple her car to the St. Petersburg train he showed up. "I apologize for being late, Ella," he explained, "but I was considering purchasing a huge white bear that was on display near the market. The bidding went so high, however, that I decided against it. So you see, there is hope for me after all."

The train started off on time and the girls were all very excited. None of them had ever been in a railcar before and they stayed glued to the windows until the sun went down and night fell. Then, exhausted by the day's events, one by one they fell asleep in their seats. As for Ella, she was elated. She had found the double she was looking for and had enjoyed some much needed time for contemplation. She felt the trip had been good for Felix as well. Ella knew that many young men felt doubts before an impending marriage and she thought the pilgrimage had given him a chance to really analyze his feelings for Irina. He had asked her for counsel and she had given it in her usual no-nonsense manner. She truly wished him well and was glad he was settling down. He and Dmitri were known to carouse excessively and perhaps Felix would no longer be a bad influence on her nephew once he was married.

Ella said good-bye to Felix at the station in St. Petersburg. She then had her car coupled to the Moscow train. The Grand Duchess knew the private car was an extravagance but it did allow her to move people around circumspectly and she needed the anonymity it provided. With the exception of Sophia all the girls would go to the convent school. Sophia would be moved immediately to Ilinskoe to begin her training as Maria's look-alike.

Before leaving the capital she sent a telegram to the Tsar at Livadia. It read:

"I found a pure white lamb on my trip and I brought her home."

Chapter 26

January 1914 – Tsarskoe Selo. The winter season of 1914 was to be one of the happiest in memory for the Grand Duchesses. The two younger girls' days were still filled with lessons but were interspersed with visits to the city to shop. For the two older girls, formal schoolwork was beginning to taper off, although fluency in languages was still given much emphasis. As was customary in most of Europe, members of the royal families were given positions in their country's army and navy and the Tsar's oldest daughters were no exception. Olga had been appointed colonel of the 3rd Hussars and Tatiana proudly wore the uniform of the 8th Ulans. Although these were honorary assignments the girls took their postings very seriously and were active in the parades, reviews and social activity of their units. As they grew older they also began to fill in for their mother, when she was too ill to attend to her duties, and various local committees and societies vied to have the girls serve on their boards. All this activity posed a great dilemma for their father. On the one hand, Nicholas wanted his girls to enjoy their teen years and receive the attention he felt they deserved, but on the other he worried that the increased exposure would make the substitution of doubles much more difficult and consequently endanger the plan. In the end he decided that keeping the children in seclusion at a time when they were expected to be active would be more likely to raise suspicion. He could only hope that Ella's efforts were bearing fruit and that when the time came, the substitution could be made without too much difficulty. One item they had overlooked was the necessity for the look-a-likes to be comfortable on horseback, but that could be easily remedied.

Each Sunday included a trip into St. Petersburg for lunch with their grandmother, at the Anichkov Palace, followed by an afternoon visit to Aunt Olga's. The Grand Duchesses endured the formality and stiffness of a formal meal at Minnie's with great fortitude. They politely answered her questions while counting the minutes until the ordeal was over. While they loved their grandmother, they adored their Aunt Olga and eagerly anticipated their afternoons with her. Olga often held tea dances at her home which allowed the girls to enjoy the company of people their own age. If the weather was nice she would take them on excursions around St. Petersburg to places they would not normally see. Aunt Olga spent more time with the children then any other member of the Imperial family and she knew the children's personalities very well. The girls loved her like a second mother and trusted her with all their little secrets. They really felt they could talk to her about anything and knew that she would never be judgmental.

The highlight of the winter for Olga and Tatiana was a ball held at the Anichkov Palace, given in their honor by their grandmother. Minnie felt it was past the time that the girls should be officially "introduced" and when she learned that Alexandra had no plan to present her daughters to society, she took charge of the whole matter. Minnie knew that neither Nicky nor Alix would challenge her on this so she threw herself wholeheartedly into the preparations for what turned out to be the grandest social event of the season. It was a smashing success, as were all the functions hosted by the still energetic Dowager Empress.

As bad as she felt, it was pure torture for Alix to attend, but this was one time she had no option. Nicholas and Alexandra escorted their two daughters to the event and that was the last they saw of them for several hours as the girls dance cards were quickly filled and they were immediately whisked off to dance the night away. Alix left at midnight to return home but Nicky remained until four-thirty in the morning with Olga and Tatiana. They returned to Tsarskoe Selo by train and Nicholas enjoyed the excited chatter of his daughters as they reviewed the entire ball in great detail. Although he had a full schedule that day, and would be exhausted, he was glad his daughters had such a wonderful time and he would remember the contentment on their faces, this early morning, until the day he died.

CR&O

While the Imperial children were enjoying the winter season in St. Petersburg, several hundred miles away, at Ilinskoe, four young women, three girls and one young boy were going through a very different experience. Ella had decided to look no further for substitutes and, since time was of the essence, training of the seven young people was proceeding at a rapid pace. Their two teachers, Sister Irene and Sister Katherine, were competent and demanding instructors yet, despite the steady and unrelenting pressure they put on the youngsters, the atmosphere at the little school was one of kindness and good nature. Ella knew that she had to offer these young people a better life than she had taken them from and to do that would require love and patience as well as firmness and discipline. Ella had impressed upon the two nuns the importance of this approach to educating the children because it differed so much from the usual manner, in which physical punishment was considered a teaching tool. As for the sisters, they had to quickly gain the trust and respect of the substitutes if they were to be successful. They were told to make ladies and gentlemen out of their charges and no matter what it took, that was what they intended to do. The task was made a little easier by the fact that all of the doubles were relatively uneducated and were starting at the same level, so the need for duplication was, for the most part, eliminated. Regardless of age they all received the same instruction and, though some were not as quick to learn, the others helped to bring them along. The program thus became a team effort, an effort filled with laughter, enthusiasm, and high spirits. As for time, Ella would only say that the nuns had at least two years to complete the transformation.

Sisters Katherine and Irene were initially optimistic about their chances for success; that is, until they met their pupils. Then the two nuns quickly realized they had their work cut out for them. For the most part they were faced with unrefined, uneducated Russian peasants from poor backgrounds. Only the young boy, Dalek Rakyovich, came from a more middle class environment, but he was careful not to show it.

The two oldest girls, Ekaterina and Elizabeth doubled for Olga, and Tatiana's alter egos were named Helena and Anna. Sophia, the newest arrival, would stand in for Maria. The two look-a-likes for Anastasia were the irrepressible Franny and a girl called Louise. The teachers quickly realized that a schedule of lessons that utilized only part of the day would not be sufficient to teach the children everything they needed to know. Lessons therefore would take place every hour of the day except the full eight hours allotted for sleep. Sister Irene was convinced that a well-rested child was more receptive to instruction and the response of all the students proved her right. Classroom time was devoted to subjects best handled in a structured environment. French and English were used on alternating days and the nuns spoke the languages exclusively except when they were instructing in the classroom.

Time away from the classroom was used to teach deportment, manners, and all the other intangibles which identify a person of the nobility. Sister Barbara, who was herself a peasant and could identify with the girls, took on this aspect of their training. Sister Katherine introduced the children to classical music and the classics of literature which, at this stage of their education, had to be read aloud to them. Meals were devoted to learning table manners and the art of conversation. This had initially been very difficult, since the children would wolf their food down as if they did not know where their next meal was coming from. The nuns knew from their own work with the poor exactly what was happening but gradually, as the children began to trust them and become accustomed to their surroundings, they began to relax. Meals slowed down and the pupils began to eat with proper utensils and began to open up to their teachers.

The day began at 6:00 am with a short prayer service followed by a simple but hardy breakfast of bread, milk, cheese, and fruit. All the nuns shared meals with the children and made a conscious effort to establish a family environment at the table. They attempted to make the atmosphere as pleasant as possible while encouraging conversation in the language of the day. With the exception of Sophia, they had been working with the children for six months and were very pleased with the progress they were making, especially in French and English. By immersing the children in the language they were forced to pick it up quickly and, although they needed work refining their accents, they had made remarkable headway.

After breakfast, lessons began. History and literature were taught, as well as the intricacies of court life. They learned why the train on the Empress's gown was longer than any other woman at court, how nobility was ranked, and what the responsibilities of a lady-in-waiting were. Ella took a hand in many of these sessions because, as a Grand Duchess, she knew all the details and could pass them on without seeming too imperious. The girls were hard working and even if one or two of them struggled with the demanding schedule the others helped them along. Dalek on the other hand was a challenge. He was lazy and a smart-aleck, but he was also extremely intelligent and managed to keep up with the other children with a minimum of effort. The two nuns sensed that this youngster had a special purpose, for why else was he the only boy in this gaggle of girls? Whatever the significance of his presence at the estate the sisters were determined to see that he succeeded in his studies and privately gave him extra encouragement.

When morning lessons were completed they adjourned for lunch which was followed by a period of exercise. Long walks provided an opportunity to learn about flowers and their importance in decorating a manor home. The time was also used to learn croquet and tennis and other games the nobility might play. Then it was back to the classroom for more lessons until dinner time. In the evening they viewed motion pictures and newsreels. None of the children had ever seen a movie and this became their favorite part of the day. They also used stereoscopes to familiarize themselves with points of interest in Russia and in Europe as well. Ella frequently sent Sisters Barbara boxes of photographs with captions penciled on the back of each picture. Their students studied them intently and learned to recognize the person or place in the photos. The nuns often divided the children into two groups and had competitions to see who could correctly identify the most. It was fun for the children but, of course, they did not realize it was one of the many important facets of their instruction.

One afternoon a messenger arrived from Moscow bearing a short note from Ella to Sister Barbara. It seemed that the Tsar had identified a number of other areas that the group might need to exhibit some expertise in. Since Ilinskoe had a well-stocked stable, horsemanship and the handling of hunting weapons were added to the curriculum and Dalek excelled in these two areas. These activities were generally scheduled in the afternoon of a day when classroom instruction had been particularly rigorous and provided an outlet for pent-up energy. He was less enthusiastic, however, when in the evening the students were introduced to dancing, but he was never forced to learn the girl's steps, and it turned out he was a natural at this too.

Sister Barbara prepared weekly reports on the children's progress which she forwarded to Ella in Moscow. The Mother Superior tried to come out of the city once a week but sometimes her other duties prevented a visit to Ilinskoe. It was just as well, because Ella did not want anyone to notice how much time she was suddenly spending at the estate. When she was able to come she inspected the school and interviewed each child privately so she could personally assess their progress. In the initial weeks, although she tried to be positive, she doubted they would be successful, but as time passed the students got better and she was pleased with their advancement. If they kept improving at this rate they might complete their training at Tsarskoe Selo within the allotted time.

As the winter neared an end and the last remnants of the snows began to melt away Ella traveled out to Ilinskoe for what was to be the first of an especially important succession of visits. She came armed with the finest camera money could buy and was there to conduct a series of photo sessions of her eight charges. The Tsar had decided it was time to make the first of many comparisons and had requested the photos so he could see for himself how well things were going. Outfits similar to what the real Tsarevich and Grand Duchesses might wear had been prepared ahead of time and the children were directed to change for the photography session. When they were all ready Ella took a few individual shots but concentrated primarily on group photos. She skillfully maneuvered the children around, from one pose to another, so that even the smarter children did not notice that Dalek and Sophia were always included in the group shots especially when there were only five of the impostors involved. Ella took many pictures and allowed some skylarking and silliness to be captured on film in order to hold their interest and eventually she had all the combinations she needed. She would sort the prints later and get them off to the Tsar by special messenger.

After she completed her photography she gathered the children around her and began to talk to them about a subject they had discussed in the classroom during history lessons. She explained to them the role of the Tsar in the scheme of things and told them that Russians believed he was anointed by God to rule and to lead them in times of trouble. Ella was aware that these youngsters had only the most basic understanding of a concept she liked to call, "love of country." She was certain, however that for the *Masquerade* to succeed the children who were chosen would have to demonstrate, in some way, their belief in the Tsar's divine right to rule and their total loyalty to him and the Mother Land. Ella decided this might be a good time to feel them out although she realized that in a group setting they might be less likely to open up. "I want to ask you something and I want you to answer honestly without any fear that I would be cross or upset with you. Here is my question. How much do you love your country?"

"Sister, I love my country with all my heart," said the innocent Sophia, the one child who had suffered the most by far.

"Yes, mother, I would do anything for my country," added Ekaterina.

"Dalek, what about you?" asked Ella.

"I would die for my country," he answered, with no hesitation.

"What about the Tsar? What if he needed you?"

Franny chimed in before all the others. "I would give my life for him. He saved me when I was in danger and I owe him my life. I would do whatever he asked of me."

"I am not sure what I would do but the Tsar has never done anything for me," said Elizabeth. "You and the other sisters are the only ones who have shown us true love and kindness.

"I have to agree. I cannot imagine the Tsar would give his life for me," Anna added.

"I think you might be surprised what the Tsar would do for you and for Mother Russia," Ella said. Many times I have seen his generosity to the poor. He loves the Russian people and would give his life for all of you if called upon to do so. He is a warm and loving person unless he perceives a threat to his beloved country and then his vengeance can be terrible. You have seen the family photographs and know that his wife, the Empress, is my sister. I have known him for many years and I know the truth of which I speak."

"Well, I just don't know," said Louise. "I was starving before you rescued me, Mother, and no one helped me before. Where was the Tsar then?"

"I understand your confusion dear child," Ella replied, "but who do you think made it possible for me to help you. I could not do what I do without the Tsar's assistance, and my convent and hospital are just two of many he supports. So you see; he was indirectly responsible for your rescue.

As the children answered her questions, Ella was surprised to learn that over half the group expressed at least a philosophical willingness to give their life for Russia or the Tsar. For the present, she knew it was just talk and she was not sure how they would react in a real situation. It was quite evident to her that she would have to carefully observe those who were negative in their responses. The qualities Ella considered the most important in the doubles were loyalty and physical courage and she could now understand why the Tsar wanted more than one stand-in. There would obviously be some weeding out to do.

CBⒺꝹ

Some days later the Tsar could be found in his study at Alexander Palace hard at work on the myriad of paperwork he dealt with on an almost daily basis. Alix kept begging him to retain a personal secretary to assist him but he refused to do so. The fact was that Nicholas honestly enjoyed the work because it made him feel alive and in touch with his empire. He often received requests in the form of letters or petitions from common people, peasants, soldiers, housewives, and the like. He would generally assign one of his aides to look into the various matters but occasionally, when a request was extremely heart wrenching, he would handle the matter personally. The Tsar took great pleasure in being able to make a difference in someone's life.

This particular morning, however, he was full of anticipation and rushed through the day's correspondence, delegating nearly all of it to his staff. When he finally completed his required work, and was alone, he got up and closed the door to his study. Returning to his desk he opened a drawer and took out a sealed packet. It was from Ella and had arrived yesterday and he knew it contained the photographs he had requested. His schedule had been so full that this was the first time he had a moment of privacy in which he could look at them. He carefully removed the photographs from the packet, spread the pictures across his desk, and began to examine each one thoroughly. Ella had included individual photos of each child, full face and in profile, as well as group shots of five children together, carefully posed in a manner reminiscent of photos of his own family. The Tsar paused for a moment to take down one of the albums which contained the most recent pictures of Olga and her siblings. As he paged through the book Nicholas was amazed at the strong resemblance of the figures in the photographs on his desk, to those of his five children in the album. It was uncanny to say the least. With a change in hairstyle and an expanded wardrobe he felt certain the look-a-likes could pass for his children. He and Alix would rely heavily on Ella's recommendation when the time came to make the final choice. She had done a marvelous job and any doubts he might have had about this phase of the plan were diffused by the faces smiling at him from his desktop. This was going to work.

Nicholas looked down at his pocket watch and checked the time. Nikolasha would be arriving any moment. He had phoned Nicholas the previous evening to make an appointment to discuss the Polish issue. The Grand Duke did not elaborate but it seemed there were some difficulties with the plan. When Nikolasha was announced, Nicky stood up expectantly. He and his uncle quickly exchanged the normal pleasantries and then Nicholas proceeded directly to the matter at hand. "Nikolasha, I have been waiting on word from you for some time. What have you found out about this man in Poland?"

"I am not sure where to begin because the news is so bleak. I received a report from Count Benckendorff in which he discussed the attitude of the Poles towards Russia and it is not what we hoped for, Nicky," said Nikolasha. "His spies have infiltrated a group in Poland and found out that plans are being made for the establishment of an independent Polish state. Since your plan addresses an autonomous state, rather than an independent one, we are looking at the possibility of full scale insurrection. As soon as I read the report I realized I must talk to you because we may have to find an alternative to sending the girls to Warsaw. It would be very dangerous to set them down in the middle of a rebellion. If they were discovered by the revolutionaries the *Masquerade* would be exposed and the girls could be used as bargaining chips in negotiations with our government."

"But don't you see uncle?" replied Nicky. "We must go forward, confident that the *Masquerade* will work. Then none of these factors of which you speak will matter at all."

"Well, we can address that situation once you have heard my entire summary. The information I am about to brief you on was gathered by one of Benckendorff's spies and was included by the Count in the report I just mentioned," Nikolasha continued. "Sometime last year, the political parties in Poland met and created a governing body called the Provisional Commission of the Confederated Independence Parties. The acronym for this commission is TKSSN. Now you understand, I am sure, that at the present time these parties have no real power but I must warn you that they are gaining in strength and support with the local populace. The partition of Poland into three entities took place long before our time, Nicky, and we cannot change what your great, great-grandfather achieved. I do not need to give you a history lesson but perhaps a little refresher might help. When Napoleon defeated Prussia back in 1807 he created the Grand Duchy of Warsaw from territory seized from the Prussians during the war. Although the Duchy was later dismantled at the Congress of Vienna in 1814 its short existence had the important historical effect of encouraging Poles in their quest for independence. Russia was awarded the major part of Poland and in the ensuing hundred years there have been at least four insurrections. From my point of view the problem is not going to go away."

"Where are these modern day independence parties most active?" Nicholas asked.

"They are strongest in Galicia where the Austrians turn a blind eye to their activities. The Germans run a tight ship in Saxony and there does not appear to be any underground activity there, but in Russian Poland there has been evidence of cells here and there."

"Is there any evidence to support your concern that an insurrection might be brewing?" the Tsar asked his uncle.

"Well, of course, there is always the historic quest but according to Benckendorff's man, the TKSSN seems to be much better organized than previous groups. This commission has the duty of putting together a detailed plan for Poland's independence and to prepare a military response in the event of war between Austria and Russia. They are very aware of the tensions between our two countries and would hope to exploit any outbreak of hostilities to further their interests. They have some funding from sources outside the country and they have established a military command and made Joseph Pilsudski, commander of the underground forces. It is estimated that he can put a division of 10,000 men in the field on short notice although they have little equipment. Another item of great interest is their ongoing discussion of who they would side with if Russia and Austria were to go to war.

"I am quite amazed by this. What if Germany was to ally itself with Austria?" asked Nicholas.

"In my opinion the Poles would put aside their animosity towards the Germans and back the alliance," said Nikolasha.

"Does anyone support me in that country?" asked Nicholas.

"Well, you do have the loyalty of the Polish nobility. Have you considered having them suppress the independence movement?"

"No," the Tsar replied. "It would never work. The upper classes derive their power from their wealth. In the event of war or revolution their riches would be lost and with them what little influence they possess."

Nicky was surprised to hear Nikolasha suggest that the ordinary Poles would side with the dreaded Germans. Had their hatred of Russia grown that deep, he wondered? "What about Pilsudski? What is his agenda?" Nicky asked

"As far as we can tell, he will go along with the TKSSN. He is said to be very loyal and committed to the Polish cause but we have not yet approached him to discuss his views on total independence. If he sides with the Austrians and Germans he is in effect abandoning Gallicia and Saxony to their continued domination. There would be no united Poland and that may give him pause. At any rate, there is another man that may suit our needs. His name is Roman Dmowski and he is a bitter rival of Pilsudski's. Interestingly enough, he was in Japan at the same time as Pilsudski but his goal was to prevent him from entering into an agreement with the Japanese to fight against Russia. Dmowski's dream is to unite Poland under the scepter of the Tsar," said Nikolasha.

"We cannot use a man who publicly espouses such a position. If what you say is true he would never have sufficient influence to make a difference and if I am seen to be supporting him, his followers, however many there are, would abandon him. Besides, if as you say, Pilsudski controls an army then he has the real power. No, the Japanese seem to think he is the man we should turn to. If we have their backing perhaps that will be enough to influence him and bring him to our way of thinking," the Tsar replied.

"I see danger in this approach. We cannot take a chance that our secret alliance with Japan be made public prematurely, so we certainly cannot use it as a negotiating tool," said Nikolasha.

"I wonder what effect it would have if he knew that in the event of a war the Japanese would be a Russian ally. That might make a difference in his willingness to deal with us," suggested Nicky.

"Regardless of his relationship with the Japanese, he seems to hate Russia more than anything and I believe he would give up his association with them quickly if he knew they were our allies. I just do not think it would have any effect on him," Nikolasha observed.

. "Well if he is looking for Polish unity and freedom from the Germans or Austrians, he will be utterly disappointed," Nicky replied. I may be wrong, but my instinct tells me he is still our man. The Japanese spoke highly of him and they are not easily impressed. Now we have the daunting task of bringing him around to our way of thinking. Money and power are normally what every man wants but if he is a true patriot I doubt he would be swayed by an offer of riches; in fact he would probably be insulted. Nikolasha, do not be discouraged. Go ahead and have Mannerheim make contact with Pilsudski and see if he is at least receptive to listening. Although I would prefer to have you handle this, you are easily the most recognizable man in Russia, so perhaps it would better for Mannerheim to manage the talks. I know this is a long shot because if I was Pilsudski and someone from the royal family approached me to discuss Polish independence I would be highly suspicious."

"Well, it is worth a try and at the very least we will be able to verify what Benckendorff's spy has told us. When it comes time to make the substitutions the atmosphere in which we will be operating will be clear to us and that will be very helpful," said Nikolasha. "And remember, Nicky, you have been ordained by God and certainly he would not lead you astray at such a critical point," he said. "Look at how far he has brought us. You must trust your instincts."

"My confidence has been shaken so many times, by so many people, that it is sometimes hard to know the right thing to do," confessed Nicky in a rare moment of weakness. "As far as Poland is concerned we do not know how it will turn out, but this phase is not critical to the overall plan so I am not overly concerned. Now to change the subject. What have you found out about the convent?"

"Well, there is good news on that front and I think you will be very pleased to hear what I have learned. The nuns who operate it are called the Sisters of Charity and they run a hospital, orphanage, and home for women. The complex is quite large and it seems to function much the same as Ella's convent, in Moscow, except for the fact, of course, that it is Roman Catholic."

"I would not care if it was a Buddhist monastery! My daughters would be safe there because no one would suspect the Tsar of making use of such a refuge. I know my children will not be able to practice their Russian Orthodox faith when they initially go into exile as it will be far too dangerous but I have hope that in time they will eventually have that freedom. All Alix and I can do is pray we have built a solid spiritual foundation that will carry them through the hard times. You know the Russian Orthodox Church is well established in America, especially in the western part of the country. If ultimately they go to the United States the children will be free to practice their religion. We have not always been kind to the Catholics so tell me about these Sisters of Charity. What sort of reception can my daughters expect?" Nicholas asked.

"This order, I believe, is quite unique. They have connections all over Poland and throughout Europe. They use these contacts to wipe away the past of the young women who come to them."

"Yes, I know. Potocki told me the same thing, but how on earth do they accomplish it. I must say you have me completely baffled, Uncle. How is it possible to wipe away a person's past?"

"Be patient, Nicky, I am coming to that. Young women come to the abbey from the streets but once they enter the convent they are submerged in its culture. If a petitioner wants a new identity they forfeit any documents they might have and later are provided with new ones. The transformation almost always includes relocation and through their connections in Poland and throughout Europe, they place the women in a new life with a new name and documents to support the change. The woman who enters the convent leaves it a completely different person. Sometimes it is a matter of months and for others it could mean several years. The convent accepts women from all walks of life, not just girls from the lower classes but members from the middle class and nobility as well. Once they enter, however, they are all treated alike. And not all the women are looking for a new life in the outside world; many are called to embrace the religious life and take vows. In many ways It is similar to what Ella is doing with the substitutes except for the fact that these women do not have to look like someone else."

"That is remarkable," said the Tsar with great enthusiasm. "It is as if my prayers had been answered."

"Yes, it is a perfect place for the Grand Duchesses to stay until it is safe to have them relocated. Will you inform the mother superior of their identity?"

"I want to say no. If someone showed up at the convent looking for the children she could honestly say she was not aware that the Grand Duchesses were there. At a later time she might need to be brought in, but not initially. The less anyone knows the less there is to deny. We would of course inform the Vatican and if the need arises the children could be assisted through their diplomatic mission."

"Have you considered who you would assign to take them to Warsaw?" asked Nikolasha.

"I have given it some thought and the most loyal, trustworthy men I have known in my life are our Cossack guards, Peter and Boris Pavlovich. Their fathers, grandfathers, and great-grandfathers have been loyal protectors of the Imperial family since the time of Nicholas I. Several of them lost their lives in service to the Tsar and you cannot find men more dedicated to my family. These are the type of retainers who would stay with my children and watch over them their whole lives. That is what they have sworn to do. You know that I trust the *Masqueraders* implicitly, but we are all too well known to serve as escorts to my children. I may assign a Cossack to each of my daughters for their protection although that might prove difficult when the impostors are introduced. At any rate I have not made a decision yet. We will just have to see how things work out."

"It sounds as if the plan is shaping up nicely," Nikolasha observed. The United States, the Vatican, and Japan all appear to be very supportive."

"I just wish we could get a definitive answer on Poland. It may not be the right time for negotiations but I do at least want to move forward with some preliminary details."

"What are you referring to?" asked the Grand Duke.

"I want you to make arrangements to buy a house in Zakopane, Poland."

"Yes, I am familiar with the area, but for what purpose?"

"Soon I intend to start shipping some furniture and other items to Japan, for the girls. It will make their exile a little easier if they have familiar items around them. We have already moved some things to a warehouse in Vladivostok in preparation for transportation to Japan. All of our palaces are overflowing with furniture, artwork, and knickknacks. I could set up several complete households from what is unused and no one would have an inkling anything was missing. The attic area in Alexander Palace is completely full. There are some old servants' quarters there that have been unused and locked up for some time. I want to clear it out and make some alterations so the doubles can live there. Now to answer your question. Even though we do not have the Polish situation resolved, I want to make similar arrangements there, just in case the girls who go to Warsaw can leave the convent. That will be one less thing I will have to worry about later."

"What exactly are you looking for?"

"Certainly nothing ostentatious, just something they will be comfortable in. We will use it for storage in the meantime so once you have made arrangements for the purchase inform Count Benckendorff and he will organize transportation of the items.

"Very well," Nikolasha replied. "I assume George will open a line of credit for me. When I find the right place, I want to be able to move quickly on it."

"I can tell from the look on your face that you are wondering why I am getting involved in these mundane details, so let me explain. I would like to have everything arranged now so that when we move the doubles into Alexander Palace there will be no unresolved issues. That is why I intend to convert the attic area immediately, even though we will not use it yet. In a few years no one will remember that anything was done upstairs and if we have to move more expeditiously than expected the rooms will be ready. When we finally bring the look-a-likes into the palace, it will be done quickly and in great secrecy and only a trusted few will know of it. The area I intend to renovate is right above the private family rooms. All of the suite and staff except for our personal servants are housed in the other wing of the palace. I believe it will work out."

"When do you plan to bring the impostors to Tsarskoe Selo?"

"Probably sometime in 1916."

"You are planning to keep them in your attic for two years?" asked Nikolasha incredulously.

"Think about it, uncle. You are assuming we have all of 1918, but Serafim's letter does not promise that. The catastrophe could be the first day of the year, for all we know, so if we bring them in during the latter part of 1916 we are looking at just about a year at most. And something could happen to move that day forward although I pray that will not be the case. Nikolasha, it is not as if they are going to be imprisoned. As soon as they arrive here they will begin acclimating to their new surroundings and have get togethers with my children. I have not yet worked out all the details but we will begin with simple exposures such as walks and picnics; activities in which they will only be seen at a distance. They will dress like my children everyday and when the substitutes are filling in for some event the Grand Duchesses will go to the attic for study and play. Sometimes we may use only one or two at a time so that they have the support of my daughters. Someone who knows the ropes, so to speak and if, heaven forbid, there was a slip up, one of my children might be able to smooth it over. We can also make use of the secret passages to move them around. There are many ways to get in and out of rooms, and the palace itself, without anyone being aware. I know it will be hard for the impostors at first because they have had a certain independence at Ilinskoe but there will be so much going on they will not have time to become bored. Can you imagine the first time Tatiana's look-a-like takes the salute of her regiment while on parade? You or I will have to be riding at her side and I know the poor child will be terrified. At the same time their lives have improved immeasurably. Most of the children arrived at Ella's from the streets and several were half starved. They will never be hungry again and will wear only the finest clothes, and they are receiving an excellent education, as well. When the *Masquerade* finally ends, if it ever does, they will be amply rewarded from accounts which George established for them at the Vatican Bank." Nicholas placed his elbow on his desk and rested his forehead in the palm of his hand. "Uncle, there is so much to consider. What if I forget some detail or the plan goes awry? What if someone betrays us?" the Tsar asked rhetorically.

Nikolasha, not realizing that the Tsar was thinking out loud, took it as a question. "Earlier Nicholas, you were entreating me not to be discouraged now let me reciprocate. I know you have been chosen by God and he will not abandon you." The Tsar looked up at his uncle with weary eyes and the Grand Duke could see the worry that was reflected in them. Nikolasha cupped his hands as if he were holding onto something. "Look here, Nicky. You hold Russia in your hands and yet as we all know she is on the verge of falling from them. Hold tight," said Nikolasha as he clasped his hands forcefully together. "Do not let her go; hold on to her with all your might Nicholas; save her!"

The Tsar's eyes moistened and he felt a tightening in his chest as his uncle's words washed over him like the gentle surf at a beach. In the past there had been disagreements between the two and at times their relationship had been quite strained but Nicholas knew these words came straight from the heart. "Thank-you," he said as he composed himself.

As their conversation drew to a close and Nikolasha prepared to leave he asked the Tsar, "do you wish me to see Alix before I leave?"

"No, that will not be necessary. I am not sure if she even knows you are here today. Although she knows the basic elements of the *Masquerade* she is not privy to all the details and I will be honest with you; her health and mental state are such that I cannot burden her with anything else right now. It is all she can do to manage her health and take care of Alexei."

"I understand. It is no secret to me that her feelings toward me have changed."

"Dear uncle, please do not put me on the spot."

"Nicky, I do not take her feelings personally and I understand the reason for this dislike of me and I do not hold her accountable."

"What do you mean?"

"Nicholas, you well know her intense dislike for me began when my opinion of Father Grigory changed and I publicly disavowed him. But how can I be angry with her? It will always be to my shame that it was through my house the evil man was introduced to your family. He has mesmerized Alix like he did me, but my eyes are now open to his true nature. Unfortunately the same cannot be said of Alix. She is still blind to his numerous faults."

"Do not be too hard on yourself, dear uncle. I, too, allowed him into my home and now that Alix is convinced he can heal Alexei it is almost impossible for me to prevent all contact. The best I can do is deny him the palace but allow the meetings at Anya's house to continue. In fact I join them when I am available in order to monitor the situation and keep an eye on him. When I am around his advice seems harmless enough and there has been times when his words have given me comfort. It is easy to see how one can fall under his spell and there have been occasions when I felt as if he were trying to read my mind. As for Alix, he has given her peace and comfort in her suffering and for that I am grateful."

"You do not have to justify yourself to me Nicky and, as I said, I bear no ill will towards Alix."

"My biggest fear is that she will slip up and disclose our plan to him. I have her promise that she will not tell him and I have never known her to break her word but the staret is very cunning and if he gets wind of anything he will draw it out."

"Yes, that is why he is so dangerous. He has this ability to mesmerize people; more so the women, I think. I am grateful I came to my senses and I must say I can understand your concern as regards the *Masquerade*. However, what we are about to do is so compartmentalized that even if he learned something and attempted to disclose it I truly believe no one would believe him. He is considered a drunken peasant by the public and is not taken seriously except by his intimate friends. Nevertheless, we must never relax our guard, and always assume the worst. Once the switch is actually made perhaps we will be able to relax a little"

"I have never spoken of this to anyone but I feel I can unburden myself to you. I wish the evil, vile man were dead and we no longer had to worry about him. However, I cannot allow my true feelings to be known as it would hurt Alix deeply and make her look ridiculous, since it is well known she has faith in this man. No, I must maintain a public silence on the matter. It is a difficult price to pay but ever since Alexei's illness at Spala the Empress is convinced that it was Rasputin's prayers and his alone that were responsible for my son's recovery. What can I do? There is no convincing her otherwise."

"We must keep going on as we have. I do not think we need to worry about Rasputin just now but if the situation takes a turn for the worst, I will see to it that our Father Grigory is properly cared for."

Nicholas shook his head at this. "No, Nikolasha, this is a private family matter, as you well know, and I hope you understand that if it becomes necessary it will be my responsibility to act, and mine alone."

"I do understand and will accept your wishes in this matter, but know that I am available if you need any assistance or advice. As I said before, I hold myself responsible for this situation."

"I do agree we must soldier on and confront each obstacle as it presents itself," said Nicky. "Now I think this is enough for today."

Nikolasha bade his farewell and departed the Tsar's study with a purposeful stride. Nicky straightened his desk, put away the photos, and then joined his family for tea. He was grateful that he and his uncle had been able to discuss Alix in a calm yet candid manner. It was always a relief to speak of things that concerned him and it never ceased to amaze him how voicing his anxieties aloud made them less troubling.

Chapter 27

February 1914 – Paris. Despite the blustery weather of that cold winter afternoon, the rented hall was packed with a throng of supporters, secret police, spies, and curious French citizens. The crowd had gathered to hear the articulate and fiery Josef Pilsudski verbalize the hopes and aspirations of Polish nationalists and urge support for an independent Poland, completely free of Prussian, Austrian, and Russian influence. The generally enthusiastic audience was not disappointed and frequently interrupted the speaker with applause as he traced the history of his divided nation for the past hundred years and eloquently laid out his justifications for independence. Seated in the midst of Pilsudski's most ardent sympathizers, but unknown to them, was a gentleman wearing a dark tweed suit and spectacles. At first glance he seemed to fit in and, intent on the lecture, those sitting around failed to notice the fine quality of his clothing and his natural yet aristocratic bearing. Although he appeared to be attentive, and applauded along with the others, the gentleman was not there to listen to the history of Poland, about which the orator spoke so passionately. He had already made the decision to carry out his plan, so when the speech drew to a close he reached into his jacket and withdrew a note he had written earlier. It was carefully folded and the name Pilsudski was written on the front.

The crowd rose and some of the audience made their way to the front of the hall to offer their congratulations to Pilsudski on his fine speech. The Pole had come down from the stage to mingle with his supporters and answer a few questions and the man in the tweed suit took this opportunity to wedge his way forward. Finally after several minutes of being jostled about, he found himself face to face with Pilsudski. He looked directly into his eyes and said in a low voice, "a wonderful presentation, Josef. Congratulations." With a firm handshake he passed the folded note to Pilsudski, slipped away into the crowd, and was soon lost from sight.

Pilsudski immediately opened the note and read its contents;

Urgent to meet with you tonight.

11 pm at the De Belfort Hotel, room 20.

The fate of Poland is in your hands.

He looked at this strange communication with some confusion and wondered who could be behind it. His attention was brought back to the room by the voices of his many admirers so he slipped the note into his pocket and continued to shake hands and greet the attendees. Later, when he finally returned to his hotel room, he removed the paper from his pocket and read it again. Whoever sent the note obviously knew quite a bit about him and he wondered if this was from an enemy who was attempting to sabotage his efforts or a friend who had important information. The note was cryptic but whoever wrote it must know he was working towards Polish independence and was Commander-in-Chief of the Polish Legions. With Europe on the brink of war and Poland divided between three countries he knew there would be attempts to enlist his support. Perhaps this was the beginning of such an effort. There was something vaguely familiar about the man who slipped him the note but he did not seem to pose a threat and Pilsudski wondered if he might have met him before. He decided then and there, that for the sake of Poland, he would take a chance and attend the meeting even though there was some element of danger.

He looked at his watch; it was 6 o'clock in the evening. He had five hours until the meeting and he utilized the time to make some necessary preparations. He first went down to the lobby and talked to the concierge to determine the location of the De Belfort Hotel. Having learned it was only a few blocks away he decided to walk to the meeting place and survey the best route to use when proceeding there later in the evening. Although it was but a short distance Pilsudski decided it would be safer to take a taxi at that late hour. He returned to his own hotel, telephoned one of his traveling companions, and told him that he had a business meeting later that evening. It was not unusual to have such meetings, but he always kept those concerned with his security fully informed. Someone from the movement would accompany him to and from the meeting and maintain a discreet watch on the door to room 20, while Pilsudski conducted his business there. Unfortunately the note provided few details so he was unable to give his friends much information as to the purpose of this clandestine rendezvous.

Remembering that the man with the note was well attired Pilsudski decided he should dress in the same fashion and, after resting for a while, prepared for his meeting by donning a smart, well cut suit, which adequately hid the holster strapped to his waist. He removed the revolver and carefully chambered a round so that it was ready to fire. He could take no chances if this turned out to be a trap.

Finally the time drew near and, accompanied by his bodyguard, the Pole made his way to the front of the hotel and waved up a taxi. The Russian secret police had always tracked his movements but it was difficult to keep a twenty-four hour watch on someone, especially on unfamiliar ground, so Pilsudski was fairly certain his departure went unnoticed. At this hour the streets were practically deserted so it was easy to see if he had unwelcome company. As far as he could tell they were not followed.

When he arrived at the De Belfort he strode through the lobby to the elevator as if he were a guest, and with his confident walk and aristocratic air none of the staff presumed to question his presence. He exited on the second floor and slowly walked down the corridor until he found himself in front of room 20. He glanced at his watch, which read 10:58 pm. He motioned his security man to take up position in a nearby alcove and took a moment to catch his breath and check one last time for the comforting feeling of his revolver. He then gently knocked on the door, careful not to disturb the other guests in the nearby rooms and draw unwanted attention. The door opened immediately and Pilsudski saw the man who had given him the invitation earlier that day. "Please come in," he said as he gestured him into the room and to a table by the window. "May I offer you some refreshment?"

"No," Pilsudski answered bluntly. "I want you to tell me who you are and what this is all about. You obviously know me and although there is something familiar about you I feel I am at a distinct disadvantage. You have approached me in a very unusual manner and if I am not mistaken you are here as a representative of someone else."

"You are right, of course, and I apologize for seeming so rude. Please allow me to introduce myself. I am Gustaf Mannerheim and I recently took command of the cavalry brigade in Warsaw," he said.

"Yes, I recognize your name. Have we met before?"

"I believe we were introduced some years ago at a party in Warsaw. You are well known in the circles I frequent. I believe you are acquainted with the Potockis, Counts Maurice and Adam Zamoyksi and Prince Zdzislaw Lubomirski and his wife Marie."

"Yes, now I remember, but who sent you and what is this about?"

"I am here as the direct representative of Tsar Nicholas II of Russia," said Mannerheim. "The Tsar believes that you, of all the men in Poland, have the ability and charisma to lead your people in the troubling times that are coming. He wants to help you unify Poland and eventually put you at the head of the country."

"And where did the Emperor get the idea that I was the man to achieve this?"

"Please sir, do not fence with me. Time is short. You are a well-known nationalist, and as such you must know that your activities are monitored as closely as possible. The Russian government has an extensive file on your activities which includes, I might add, an account of your trip to Japan during the Russo-Japanese War and an analysis of your motives. We know you are building an army and that you strive for an independent Poland. The Tsar fears that if war breaks out in Europe, Poland will become a battle ground and he wants to know what position you will adopt in such an event. In other words, who will you side with?"

"Ah," said Pilsudski. "Now we get to the meat of the matter. The Tsar is looking for support if Russia declares war."

"The Tsar will never unilaterally declare war, but he is well aware of your inclination to support Austria and Prussia against us. Pilsudski, I consider myself a friend of the Poles and I must caution you that this would be a terrible mistake. If, God forbid, the Germans were to occupy the part of Poland controlled by Russia do you honestly believe they would give it to you, even if you supported them? Wilhelm would merely add you to his empire and you would be worse off than before. Poland will never be free under the Germans."

"And has Russia done better? The Tsar promised independence but nothing ever came of it. Now with danger looming on the horizon you are making overtures to me, as if I were a head of state. If war breaks out the Tsar has concluded that he may lose Poland and so he has decided the time is right to make a gesture of goodwill. It seems a bit late, as far as I am concerned."

"Hear me out," said Mannerheim. "Russia does not control all of Poland but the Tsar is giving his word that in the event of a Russian victory in any future conflict he will give your country its independence and then work to unify it with Saxony and Galicia under the scepter of the Tsar."

"That sounds like an autonomous Polish state, subject to Russian hegemony, and not the independent nation, free of Russian influence, that I and my fellow Poles envision," replied Pilsudski.

"Poland has been ruled by Russia for nearly a hundred years and this is the first Tsar to even hint at Polish independence. He cannot give you what you desire all at once; there is just too much opposition to such a course of action. What he is asking you to do is to give him more time."

'And then what? Will he just hand everything over to me?" asked Pilsudski sarcastically. "I think not."

"The Tsar is asking for your oath of loyalty and your support in the event of a conflict. In return he wipes clean the slate listing your revolutionary activities and promises a united Poland under your leadership. How can you refuse such an offer?" asked Mannerheim.

"In the past Poland has given the Tsar many an opportunity to achieve just such a result and he has not responded. Now you are asking me to believe that he has changed. No, Count. Although I do not doubt your sincerity I think the future of my country depends on support of the Germans. You must understand that I do not speak for all Poles but the sentiments I have expressed to you are representative of those held by most of the people."

Mannerheim knew Pilsudski was an honorable man and he could see that he was getting nowhere with his arguments. Nevertheless he tried one more time to convince the Pole that Nicholas was making an honest effort on behalf of Poland. But alas, he just could not crack the shell of

Pilsudski's skepticism, a shell that had been hardened by repeated disappointments.

"At this point, what would it take to induce you to give your allegiance to the Tsar," asked Mannerheim.

"Nothing on earth could compel me to take such an oath," replied Pilsudski.

He had made his decision and would stand by it. He would back Austria and Germany in the event of war.

"Is there nothing I can offer to persuade you to change your position?"

Pilsudski shook his head. "Only immediate and unconditional independence and a promise to support re-unification would satisfy the Polish people."

"Then my trip here was doomed to failure," said Mannerheim as he shook his head in disappointment. Pilsudski got up to leave but the Count stopped him. "Wait, I want to give you a contact in case you should change your mind or want to negotiate with the Tsar. Mannerheim handed him a card bearing the name and address of a trusted intermediary who could make any necessary arrangements. Pilsudski took the card, shoved it into his pocket, and walked out the door.

Mannerheim watched him depart and wondered if they would ever meet again.

◌৪৪◌

Nicholas and Alexandra sat in the garden at Livadia enjoying a cup of tea as they discussed a letter the Tsar had received from King Carol of Romania. The Imperial family had moved to the Crimea at the beginning of April and Nicholas was planning to stay through the spring. "It seems Carol would like us to come for a visit this summer so he can return the hospitality we provided his son and grandson when they visited St. Petersburg last winter," said Nicky. Crown Prince Ferdinand, his wife Marie, and their son Prince Carol had been guests of the Tsar and his family for several days during the height of the social season.

"You and I both know that is not the real reason for his invitation. He wants to marry his grandson Carol to our Olga," exclaimed Alix.

"You know we must honor his invitation to visit. It is only proper, and we can work it into our return to Tsarskoe Selo."

"Oh, I know you are right but I just cannot stomach the idea of Prince Carol as a partner for Olga. He is not suitable."

"I totally agree with you, Alix. He is not the man for our Olga. Anyway, I do not see any of the girls marrying in the near future as it would introduce too many complications and render it almost impossible to hold the *Masquerade*.

"How are we going to discourage this alliance?"

"I do not think we need to worry about it. Olga will never agree to marry Carol and it is a well known fact that we will never force our children to wed someone they do not love. I propose we act as if we are unaware of the king's plans and then leave it up to Olga and Carol. We will visit Romania in June and I believe when we leave, after a short stay, no more will be said on the subject."

"Oh, I do hope you are right, Nicky. I would so dislike having this turn into a diplomatic incident."

"Do not worry. There have been no official negotiations as of yet so I think our visit will nip it in the bud."

"I must speak with Olga."

"No dear, just let it be. I want her to feel and act naturally, not as if she knows she is being inspected by the Romanian royal family."

"You have a point. I remember how shy and nervous I was when my grandmother, Queen Victoria began to present potential husbands to me. I felt so much more comfortable when I met you because no one seemed to be rushing us to the altar. It was a very natural way to fall in love."

"Yes, my dearest Sunny, I knew you were the one for me and I would have no other. How does that old saying go? Love conquers all. It seemed to have worked in our case. So many were opposed to our marriage and look how wrong they were."

"I like to think Grandmama is looking down from heaven and is smiling at our joy. I just hope when everything settles down, our children will find the happiness that we have known," said Alix.

"I am sure they will."

The relaxing days at Livadia passed quickly in a blur of activity and Nicholas enjoyed the leisure time with his family. He was relieved to see the tension and stress seem to flow away from Alix after a few days on the coast. These were the days he treasured, time away from the pressures of court, in the loving presence of his family. Although he still had his usual work to attend to, he had fewer visitors and was able to enjoy more outside activities with his children. The days were filled with swimming, tennis, hikes in the hills surrounding the estate, and excursions to sites of interest in the area. Before they knew it summer was upon them.

It was a pleasant day in early June and the balmy breeze that wafted in off the water provided a cooling breath of fresh air. Pierre Gilliard was enjoying a rare moment of peace and quiet. Of all the elaborate palaces of the Romanovs, he enjoyed Livadia the most. An atmosphere of relaxation seemed to dominate all of the activities, even though he still worked very hard tutoring the Imperial children. They would often take the first few days off when they arrived, intent on squeezing the last drop of enjoyment from the brief interlude, before eventually returning to the books. As the years passed Pierre became more and more a part of the family. He had initially been retained to teach the French language to

Alexei but his duties expanded when the Tsar and Empress saw the positive influence he had on their extremely spoiled son. Gilliard became Alexei's primary teacher and was placed in charge of organizing his education. He now lived with the Imperial family and was assigned a room next to the Tsarevich, in whatever home they were residing. He was aware of the heir's illness and often conferred with Alexei's doctors prior to making decisions on his education. As Nicholas and Alexandra's trust in him grew they began to share with him some of the concerns and worries they had about their son. It was very unusual for a teacher to become a trusted confidant of the Russian royal family but young Pierre Gilliard was an exceptional individual. His relationship with the heir was a complex one but after his initial difficulties establishing a regime of discipline with Alexei he grew to care deeply for the child. He suffered intensely when the Tsarevich was felled by a bout of hemophilia. At those times lessons were canceled but he made an effort to spend some time each day reading to him and trying to keep his mind off the pain.

A few seagulls flew over and he watched as they swooped low over the palace before flying back towards the sea. He became lost in thought and oblivious to his surroundings. It was a truly idyllic moment, the kind that one treasures when reminiscing about past good times. At that moment, when he was deeply engrossed in thought, a faint hint of a delicate perfume shook him from his reverie and he became aware that Olga had come up beside him. She was fetchingly dressed in a white summer dress and wore a large hat, adorned with fresh flowers. She had a unique sense of style and he recognized that all of the Grand Duchesses had that talent. In spite of the fact they were often dressed alike, according to their mother's wish, they each managed to add a little something to their ensemble to express their individuality. Olga smiled up at him, "Monsieur Gilliard you seem so far away today."

"No, not at all, I was just enjoying the view. It is so clear today that you can see forever."

"Tell me, do you know why we are going to Romania in two weeks?"

Pierre was taken aback by her frank question but he should have expected it. He had taught her for many years and watched her grow from a child into a stunning young woman. Of all the Grand Duchesses, he was closest to Olga. She was the most intelligent and industrious of his pupils and he had encouraged her to speak freely during their lessons. Theirs was the innocent relationship of a trusted teacher and respectful student but Olga looked upon him as more than a tutor. He was a friend, a big brother, someone she could confide in. Pierre, of course, had heard the rumors of a betrothal between Olga and Prince Carol. It had been the subject of gossip for many weeks now. Even though he was well aware of the gossip, in answering he chose a more diplomatic approach.

"I believe it is because your father has decided to finally accept King Carol's invitation. It was, after all, made some time ago."

Olga smiled at him impishly. "Monsieur, surely you are not that naïve. I believe they mean to try and marry me off, but I shall not agree. I am a Russian through and through and that I shall remain. Beside my heart belongs to another, as you very well know." Although Nicholas and Alexandra had not wished Olga to know about the potential match it was inevitable that she would find out. Nicholas had spoken to her once he became aware that she knew. His only request was that she keep an open mind and he promised once again that he would never force her to marry against her will. So when Olga interrogated Pierre she already knew the answer and was just having fun.

Her friend responded in kind. "Well, you are getting up in age. If you do not marry soon you shall be an old maid," he teased her.

"Better to be an old maid than married to a toad."

"Now really your highness. Is that any way for a Grand Duchess to speak?"

"Oh Monsieur, you know I am only teasing. I shall behave perfectly, as is expected of a Grand Duchess," she said before wandering off.

Pierre looked after her and could not help but wonder what her life would be like. Would she remain in Russia as she wished, or be married to a member of one of the European royal families? He often felt a sense of sadness when he considered the Imperial children. They were so sheltered from the world and rarely interacted with people outside their own small circle. It would be interesting to see how the Romanian trip turned out.

Two weeks later, on a fine June day, the *Standart*, with the Imperial family on board, got underway from Yalta, on the Crimean peninsula, and put to sea. No one in the family, least of all the children, realized, as the coastline faded in the distance, that this was the last time they would visit their beloved Livadia. The series of events that would change their lives forever, and prevent them from returning, were only a few short weeks away but no one had any premonition of what was to come. On this occasion the yacht's destination was Constanta, Romania's major port on the Black Sea and, since this was to be an official state visit, the family was accompanied by the Imperial household with its contingent of ladies-in-waiting and aides-de-camp.

The next morning, the royal yacht sailed into Constanta, and despite the early hour, was received with honors by the many ships anchored in the harbor. Nicholas, Alexandra, and all the children stood on deck awaiting the official welcome. As the ship moored to the pier, a band struck up the Russian anthem, "God Save the Tsar" while members of the Romanian army snapped to attention and an artillery battery fired a salute. The Russian Imperial family made their way down the gangway and were greeted affectionately by the Romanian royal family, who were all present to greet them. The Russians were to be in town for only one day, so King Carol had gone to a great deal of trouble to showcase the town of Constanta. Once the official welcome was completed the two families attended a service at the Cathedral and then were escorted to a palace on the coast where a lavish lunch had been prepared in an open air pavilion overlooking the sea. The girls loved these lunches because they were allowed to taste dishes they rarely saw at home.

Later, after an extended rest period, the two families gathered on the *Standart* to begin the day's serious activities. Alix was hosting a formal tea and to her dismay more guests showed up than were expected. She found herself in the unusual position of worrying if there would be enough refreshments for her company. However, the ship's stewards were up to the task and the tea was a success.

Olga had become the center of attention and after tea was served and an appropriate amount of time passed, she excused herself. She felt she had to have a few moments of privacy away from the intense scrutiny of the Romanians, who were sizing her up as a potential Crown Princess. It was a trying time for Olga and her stomach was in knots. It was not only the fact that she was in love with a Russian naval officer but, truth be known, she found young Carol a distasteful fellow, a conclusion she had come to last winter, when he had visited Alexander Palace. Olga had done her best to avoid shrinking away from the unwanted advances and attention she was receiving and hoped her true feelings were not transparently obvious. She dreaded the banquet which was to be held that night for she expected she would be seated next to Prince Carol, but she knew she only had to get through this one evening and it would all be over. Olga was afraid that time had been set aside for Carol to be alone with her and she shuddered at the thought. But for the time being the Grand Duchess was grateful for the opportunity to slip away, if only for a moment.

It was well after sunset when the Russians departed the yacht for the gala banquet. King Carol had rolled out the red carpet for his royal guests and built a new room onto his palace especially for the occasion. The evening activities began with champagne toasts presented by the two monarchs to their illustrious company and then tray after tray of delicacies were served by servants in spotless livery. Olga was seated next to Prince Carol and she chatted pleasantly with him, a smile frozen on her face while inside her stomach churned with nervous energy. Her sisters, who were seated across from her, gave Olga suggestive looks whenever they thought they could get away with it. Tatiana nearly burst out laughing when her sister looked at her and rolled her eyes before assuming her role again. Finally the banquet ended and Crown Prince Ferdinand and his son Carol escorted their guests back to the *Standart* which was scheduled to get underway at first light.

The next morning as they cruised towards Odessa, Olga, and Tatiana sat in the wicker chairs on the deck of the *Standart* watching the activity of the sailors as they tended to their duties. They sat undisturbed, enjoying the cooling breeze wafting across the calm sea. Olga glanced at her sister. "This trip was such a waste of time. Papa knows I do not love Prince Carol."

Tatiana laughed, "Yes that was very obvious. It was written all over your face that you found him distasteful."

"Oh no, I hope I did not offend any one."

"I am just teasing you sister, dear. You were the perfect lady and only someone who knew you very well could tell your true feelings."

"Well, they must know I would never marry him. Every time I was around him all I could think of was my feelings for Vasily."

"I know how much you care for him Olga. It makes me sad to think that Papa had to send him away."

"I just wish he could understand that this is not some schoolgirl crush. We have known Vasily forever. I fell in love with him gradually over the years. We spent time together almost everyday when we were on the *Standart* or at Livadia. Someday I will find a way to see him again. I often wonder how he is and what his life is like. My heart yearns for him and yet I feel him slipping away from me, and there are times when I forget what he looks like," she said sadly.

"We lead such a privileged life, and I appreciate that, but sometimes it feels like we are imprisoned in a gilded cage," said Tatiana. "Mama and Papa would never force us into a loveless marriage but we do not have the freedom to fall in love as we wish. If we are to marry it must be to a man of suitable rank and that really limits our choices. It is almost as if they do not wish us to marry. I sometimes wish that we could just disappear and become someone else, other than royalty. I would just love to eat whatever I want, when I want to," she said.

"Or wear what I want," interjected Olga.

"Yes," agreed Tatiana, "and walk down a street and have no one recognize me."

"Or marry a sailor if I so desired," teased Olga. Tatiana laughed at her response.

"Of course, I would want to keep my jewels in a box and take them with me wherever I go."

"I do not know how you would walk down the street draped in diamonds, sapphires, and pearls and not be noticed," Olga argued.

"Well, silly, I would not wear them down the street. I said I would put them in a box and take them with me."

"What if you had to choose between your jewels and freedom? Which would you choose?" Olga asked.

"I think I could live without my jewels, except for my pearl necklace. I would have to keep that."

"Well, in this imaginary world we have created I imagine it would be allowed. I will keep mine as well." The two giggled at the foolishness of their conversation. As if they could ever be anything but Grand Duchesses.

Part Three

The Masquerade

Chapter 28

July 1914 – Peterhof. The winds of war that swept across Europe, that dismal summer of 1914, were not unexpected, because the cauldron of friction, antipathy, fear, and dissent had been simmering for a number of years. It needed only to have the heat turned up a notch to send the evil brew boiling over the sides of the pot to engulf most of the world in an unimaginable cataclysm of horror and destruction. The event which precipitated the conflict was the assassination of the Austrian heir, Archduke Francis Ferdinand, and his wife Sophie, while on a state visit to Sarajevo, the Bosnian capital. The plot that led to their deaths was hatched by a group of ultra-national Serbs called the Black Hand, who ostensibly had the goal of uniting all Serbians in a single state, a course of action which the Austrian government vehemently opposed. Although unable to prove the Serbian government's involvement in the murder, Austria-Hungary determined to punish the Serbs and presented their government with a list of demands which no sovereign state could accept. When Serbia vacillated, the Austrians mobilized their army and, on July 28, declared war. In the tense context of European affairs the assassination of the Archduke and his wife became an after thought as the entire continent slid toward war. To avoid being isolated, most European nations, during the past decade, had entered into an entangling web of secret alliances which divided Europe into two camps and tied them to one side or the other. Oh, there were many other reasons to explain the coming apocalypse. There was the arms race, which included the British and German naval buildup. The inept statesmen, whose diplomacy should have led to a peaceful solution. The unwillingness of the United States to emerge from its isolation. There was rampant nationalism in the diverse empires of the continent. The list seemed endless, but after all was said and done, when Austria mobilized its army there was no turning back. The process of bringing an army to readiness was so cumbersome and time consuming that full mobilization was tantamount to a declaration of war. When Russia mobilized against Austria it was acting as a protector of its Slavic brother, Serbia, and the die was cast. The dance card showed Russia, France, Serbia, Japan and, soon thereafter, Great Britain and Italy on one side and on the other Germany, Austria-Hungry, Bulgaria and the Ottoman Turks. Others would follow, primarily the United States, which entered the war in 1917.

Nicholas was against the war from the start but had received much pressure from his hawkish Foreign Minister, Sergei Sazonov, and an influential military clique to mobilize not only against Austria but

Germany as well. The move made sense because everyone knew Germany would fight alongside the Austrians. The Tsar initially supported the order to mobilize but then changed his mind for he alone realized, it seemed, that Russia had the least to gain and the most to lose in the coming war. Finally, having been convinced that his indecision was wreaking havoc with the mobilization, he reluctantly agreed to allow it to proceed. The anticipated German declaration of war on Russia was delivered by the German ambassador to Sazonov on August 1.

⋘⋙

The thud of a sharp ax slicing into an oak log reverberated from the wood yard behind the palace as Nicky used his favorite exercise to work off tension. He had been splitting logs for about forty-five minutes in an attempt to clear his head and relieve a little of the stress that threatened to overwhelm him. Nicholas took a short break and wiped the perspiration from his forehead. He needed this time alone to gather his thoughts because tomorrow he would travel to St. Petersburg where, from the formal rooms of the Winter Palace, he would officially announce Russia was at war. He was devastated that circumstances had brought the country to this juncture and his heart was heavy at the thought of what his people would suffer. Up until the moment his government had received Germany's formal declaration of war he had hoped to avoid the conflict. Most Russians were unaware that secret negotiations had gone on for days and many telegrams had passed between the Tsar and his cousin, the German Kaiser. Nicholas had counted on family affiliation to prevent the war but he could not stop the ponderous mobilization and these efforts bore no fruit. Now there was no turning back.

It was hard to accept that in the space of four short weeks the intransigent attitude of Austria and Russia had brought Europe to the brink of war, a war which the victors would ultimately blame on Germany. And when the necessary millions had died and the guns of that August finally fell silent, the short-sighted conquerors would impose a series of peace treaties on the defeated nations which contained in their harsh provisions the seeds of an even greater conflict. The suffering about to occur would be for naught.

As was usually the case, when some unexpected event occurred, Nicholas tried to place it in the context of Serafim's prophecy. He was stubbornly convinced that 1918 was the year of decision yet he was troubled by the scope of the events taking place in Europe and the speed at which they were occurring. Could something as dynamic as this terrible war upset his time table? And how long would the war last? Nicholas, like nearly everyone else, suffered under the illusion that hostilities would be short, and was unwilling, or unable to grasp the fact that tactics had not kept up with technology. The costly, massed infantry assaults early in the war would be replaced by the stalemate of trench warfare and the conflict would drag on. He could not know this, of course, so he was understandably disturbed, especially since some of the key elements of the *Masquerade* were not yet completely in place. The line between faith and fatalism was very narrow but Nicholas could not afford the luxury of giving in to doubts about the proper course of action. He was determined to proceed as planned and treat this war as an obstacle to be overcome, like all the others. After all it was not too long ago that the big concern was finding impostors and they had worked through that problem. The Tsar was determined to remain optimistic and not succumb to negative thoughts even though he knew it was going be difficult to hold the *Masquerade* in the middle of a war. One of his main concerns, when the fighting commenced, was that the tide of battle would flow on to Russian soil. Nicholas, therefore, favored an early offensive to drive the enemy back, on a long front. But for the present he would not be making such decisions.

As if the stress he was feeling, as he prepared the country for war, was not enough he had to deal with problems on the home front as well. Two events had occurred over the summer which turned the family upside down and threatened Alix's equilibrium as never before. The first was an attempt on the life of Grigory Rasputin in his home town of Pokrovskoe. He had been assaulted by a young woman, one Khionia Guseva, who waited for him near his house and, when he approached, pulled a knife from under her blouse and stabbed him in the stomach. Rasputin turned and fled down the street with Guseva in pursuit, hoping to strike a fatal blow. Finally he stopped, picked up a stick, and knocked her down, whereupon she was set on by a crowd. Rasputin collapsed and was near death for several days but eventually recovered, much to the relief of Alix. The Tsar's reaction to his recovery could only be described as one of disappointment. There were, of course, rumors of plots and conspiracies and so on, but nothing was ever proven. Guseva was locked up in a mental institution where she remained until the revolution. Alix was convinced that had Rasputin been in the capital, instead of languishing in the hospital, she would have been able to use him to convince Nicholas to ignore the war party and opt for peace.

The second incident involved Alexei. The heir had a minor accident which contributed to a serious bout of hemophilia and although it was not as severe as his experience in Spala it left him temporarily unable to walk. It was a terrible setback for Nicholas and Alexandra who had hoped Alexei would be able to present a healthy appearance at the formal ceremonies declaring Russia at war.

Alix was vehemently opposed to the war and for the past few weeks had argued steadfastly against it. There was a major confrontation when her husband began the mobilization because she knew as well as anyone it would be seen as an act of war and not merely a show of strength. Nicholas would never forget the expression on her face when he informed her Russia was at war. She was very hurt that he had ignored her advice and made the final decision without her input, yet, in a way, Nicholas had considered her point of view. It just came in the form of a telegram from Rasputin who exhorted the Tsar not to get involved in the war and prophesied endless horror and bloodshed. Was this not Alexandra's perspective on the issue?

As Nicholas thought about this telegram he resumed chopping wood. He remembered how angry he had become at Rasputin's unprecedented interference in governmental affairs. Even now he found himself becoming annoyed and imagined for a moment that it was Rasputin's head on the block. He began to apply the ax with greater vigor and slowly his frustration dissipated as the number of logs to be split dwindled away. Finally, totally relaxed, he made his way back to the palace to bathe and continue the work on his Polish manifesto, a document he hoped would have a significant impact on the war effort.

The next day, one of the hottest in memory, the Tsar, Tsaritsa and the four Grand Duchesses traveled by boat, from Peterhof to St. Petersburg and up the Neva River to the palace. Alexei, much to his distress, was left behind because of his illness. He was much too weak to make the trip and no amount of pleading would change Alix's mind. Despite the heat, the short journey did much to raise the spirits of the disheartened Nicholas because from the time the launch turned into the Neva, the crowds of citizens lining the banks of the river showed their support for his decision by waving flags and cheering wildly. Nearly every building was festooned with the national colors and, as the launch passed under each of the many bridges, enthusiastic crowds waved and chanted his name. Upon reaching the quay the Imperial family disembarked and walked up the steps on the red carpet leading to the Winter Palace. Millionnaya Street which ran in front of the palace was blocked to traffic and filled with a crowd jostling to catch a glimpse of the Tsar and his family. Police officers and soldiers struggled to control the throng and prevent it from spilling over on to the pathway prepared for the Tsar. More than five thousand dignitaries had gathered inside the gates of the famed palace. There were diplomats from the embassies, nobles in court dress, government officials, and officers in field dress. The common people were represented by a company of conscripts fitted out with new equipment and uniforms for this momentous event.

Nicholas, Alexandra, and their party made their way through the crowd and entered the gleaming white marble room known as Nicholas Hall. A special altar had been set up for the simple ceremony and on it was displayed the precious icon of the Virgin of Kazan. As required by custom, Nicholas presented the manifesto declaring war to the witnesses in the hall. Before reading it he glanced around at the assembly and was touched by the devotion in the eyes of those attending the event. His listeners seemed to be filled with confidence and, after the inner turmoil he had experienced during the past week, this expression of trust gave a tremendous boost to his self-confidence.

He then read the manifesto and when he had finished Nicholas took a solemn oath in front of the many witnesses. "To the officers of my guard and to my whole army, I greet you and bless you. I solemnly swear that I will never make peace so long as one of the enemy is on Russian soil."

Upon completion of the ceremony, he and Alix moved to a balcony overlooking the palace square and the Tsar repeated the manifesto which took the nation to war. It was received calmly, but with enthusiasm, by the multitude gathered there and when Nicholas raised his hand to bless the people most fell to their knees and crossed themselves. He was relieved to see that the crowd was orderly because he could not bear another tragedy such as occurred years ago at his coronation, or more recently in 1905, on Bloody Sunday. As he looked over the crowd his thoughts drifted back to that dreadful day when so many innocents were killed in this same square. He would have been devastated if even one person had been injured on this day. The Imperial family remained for some time on the balcony, waving to the people and basking in the adulation which reflected from the square below. Privately Nicholas wondered how long the passion would remain if the army suffered defeats.

With the ceremonies complete the Imperial family returned to the quay and boarded their yacht for the return trip to Peterhof. It had been an eventful day and despite Alexandra's opposition to the war both she and Nicky were pleased at the way the day had gone. They stood on deck and, with the Grand Duchesses, waved to the crowds until the Neva flowed into the sea the people gathered along the water front faded from sight. The enthusiasm of the people lifted Alix's spirits and fueled her belief that the people adored their Tsar. The fervor of the crowds made it easy to forget that today, in fact, was a solemn occasion. The declaration of war would send millions of Russians to their death, but in the burst of patriotism that flooded the country very few considered the reality of war.

Nicholas devoted himself to the new responsibilities that a wartime monarch is faced with and the remainder of August flew by in a flurry of activity and work. He did take a break for a short period of time on the 12th of August when he paused to celebrate Alexei's tenth birthday. Nicholas and Alexandra were nearly overcome with emotion during the somewhat subdued festivities as they realized their precious son had survived the dreadful ravages of his disease for another year. But the guns were thundering along the front as the Russians began their offensive into eastern Germany and so the next day Nicholas was back in his study, hard at work on a document he hoped would help the war effort. The paper was a heartfelt message to the Polish people and although the Tsar was pessimistic about its potential impact he felt it was worth a try. Ever since Nicholas received word from Mannerheim that Pilsudski had refused his offer, he had been wrestling with the problem in the hope he could come up with some way to turn the situation around. Although he never would have chosen war as a medium in which to transmit his appeal he felt he had to make some overture to the people of Poland. Following the declaration of war he had worked with Foreign Minister Sazanov to prepare a manifesto. Originally he planned to deliver the message personally but Sazanov had talked him out of it.

"Your Imperial Highness, you must think this through carefully. Large sections of Poland are presently under German and Austrian control and we cannot anticipate that we will be successful in recovering those provinces. If we fail to do so this document is meaningless and you would seem foolish for having proclaimed something you cannot deliver. I recommend that you have Grand Duke Nikolasha present the manifesto. As Commander-in-Chief of the army it is certainly within his area of responsibility, and if he succeeds in liberating the Slavic peoples in the coming campaign it will be to your credit," Sazanov had advised him.

Although Nicholas had personally wanted to command the troops, his ministers urged him to remain in the capital where many urgent matters awaited his attention. The Tsar acquiesced and in his stead he appointed his universally respected uncle, Nikolasha, as head of the army. He really wanted to deliver the statement himself but he agreed that Sazanov's recommendation was a wise one. He read over the words one last time to see if any changes were necessary but concluded the document should be published as written.

Poles!

The hour has struck when the dream of your fathers and forefathers may be realized. A century and a half ago the living body of Poland was rent asunder, but her soul has not perished. She has lived in the hope that the time will come for the resurrection of the Polish nation and its fraternal conciliation with great Russia.

The Russian army brings you glad tidings of this union. May the frontiers which have divided the Polish people be broken down! May the Polish nation be united under the scepter of the Russian Emperor! Under this scepter Poland will be born anew, free in faith, in language and in self-government.

One thing Russia expects of you: an equal consideration for the rights of those nations with which history has linked you. With open heart, with hand fraternally outstretched, great Russia comes to you. She believes that the sword has not rusted which overthrew the foe at Grunwald. From the shores of the Pacific Ocean to the Polar Sea, the Russian war-hosts are in motion. The morning star of a new life is rising for you. May there shine, resplendent in the dawn, the sign of the Cross, the symbol of the Passion and Resurrection of nations.

As he read over the completed draft of the manifesto he knew in his heart it was the best thing he had ever written, both in its content and spirituality. Deep within his soul he felt a yearning for this union of the Polish nation. He could not explain his sentiments but somehow he knew it was the right thing to do. And he had to concede that a united Poland would be a safer place for the two daughters who would be sheltered there. Tomorrow he would review the document with Nikolasha, who was leaving for the front. The Grand Duke would then submit the manifesto to the troops and later it would be published in newspapers in Russia as well as the area of Poland under Russian control.

The next day when Nikolasha arrived he brought a gift with him, a German machine gun which had been captured in one of the initial skirmishes of the war. He had it set up in the garden and the Tsar and Alexei spent some time examining it with great interest. Later the two men retired to the study to review documents and discuss strategy for the future. First they went over the manifesto which Nikolasha would present on Sunday. The Grand Duke was pleased with the wording and assured the Tsar it would be received favorably. They then spent some time reviewing the war plans and discussing long term strategy. Then the Tsar broached a topic which was causing him some discomfort.

"Nikolasha, I want to talk with you about your position as Commander-in-Chief. You must understand that I have assigned this position to you only temporarily. However, you are the only person who knows this."

"I must admit I was rather surprised you honored me with the appointment. I felt sure you would take command yourself as did tsars from our illustrious past," his uncle replied.

"Yes, well let me explain my reasoning. I need you in command while I take care of the work the various ministries are loading me down with. More importantly I have to finalize key elements of the *Masquerade*. You have the trust of the army and are the logical person to put in command. The problem, as I see it, is that when I am gone you will have to see to the success of the plan and you will not be able to do that if you command the army. I think you should stay on at least until sometime next year and then we will look at moving you to a different position where you will have more freedom to move around. I will have to arrange things to ensure it does not appear as if you were relieved of your command. I am not sure yet how to do that."

"I appreciate your concern, but it is not necessary," the Grand Duke replied. "When the time comes do not worry about the perceptions of other people. My only desire is that I be able to carry out God's will and I intend to follow the course that best ensures the success of the *Masquerade*."

Nicholas was touched by Nikolasha's words and knew he had chosen well when he brought him into the secret plan. "I wish you Godspeed on your journey to the front." The Tsar then blessed his uncle. "May your battles be successful and God keep you safe." The two men exchanged handshakes and then a hug as Nikolasha departed, on his way first to St. Petersburg and then onto the Austrian front.

A few days later, on the morning of August 17th, the Imperial train pulled into the station in Moscow. A row of carriages awaited the family to transport them to the Kremlin where members of the extended royal family were gathering for the traditional ceremonies held to ask for God's blessings on the Tsar and his people. The route took them past thousands of inhabitants who lined the road and filled windows and balconies, hoping for a glimpse of the Tsar. It was a repeat of the excitement and enthusiasm the family had experienced some days ago when they journeyed to St. Petersburg for the reading of the war manifesto. There was wild cheering and applause and many joined in the spontaneous singing of the national anthem. The carriages eventually made there way through the Iberian Gate, the traditional entrance the Tsar used when he visited the Kremlin. Both Nicholas and Alexandra were overcome by the reaction of the crowd and filled with a sense of awe at the adulation that was heaped on them. Unfortunately the short ride reinforced Alix's rose colored view of events and she sincerely believed that her husband, with the proper advice, could do no wrong. She would learn, to her sorrow, how fickle the people could be.

The next day a religious ceremony was held at the Cathedral of the Assumption. There was some frantic discussion as to whether Alexei would be able to attend, because his recent bout of hemophilia had left him unable to walk and when he awoke that morning he was still unable to stand. Nicholas believed the ceremony was too important to the country and the family for the heir to be absent and Alix agreed. Seaman Derevenko would carry Alexei to the service and he would be allowed to remain seated while the others stood through the long liturgy. When all the members of the family, invited dignitaries and selected soldiers had gathered in the cathedral the Mass began. It was celebrated by the highest members of the church's hierarchy and was a moving and fitting tribute to those about to go off to war. The Mass ended with the presentation of holy relics, and when Nicholas and his family had venerated them they left to make a private visit to the Monastery of Miracles and pray at the tomb of Saint Alexei. It was an emotional moment for Nicholas and he could see that his children were also affected by the solemnity of the occasion.

Nicholas planned to stay a few more days in Moscow before return-ing to Tsarskoe Selo. Because of the war there would be no cruise on the *Standart* this fall nor would there be a visit to Livadia in the spring. The day after the celebration, as he sat in the room in the Kremlin which served as his study when in Moscow, the Tsar received two messages of importance. The first was word from Sazanov that the Polish Manifesto was being positively received. The press was unanimous in its satisfaction and many editorialists spoke in glowing terms of the possibility of reconciling the Russian and Polish nations under the umbrella of Slavic brotherhood. In addition, a telegram from Mannerheim arrived announcing that in Warsaw, at least, the manifesto was being received with enthusiasm by the Poles he was in contact with. Unfortunately, much to Nicky's disappointment, Josef Pilsudski was not included among those supporting the manifesto.

As critical as this news was, the other message he received was personally devastating and most troubling. The Italian ambassador had informed him that Pope Pius X had passed away early that morning. It was quite a blow and he was not quite sure how to react. As he sat there reflecting on the implications of the Pope's unexpected passing, the arrival of his sister-in-law, Ella, was announced. He had forgotten they would be meeting this morning to catch up on the details of the plan, particularly the progress of the impostors. He rose to greet her when she came in and gave her a kiss on the cheek. He still found it strange to see her dressed in the gray habit of her order. "How are you, Ella? I almost forgot we were meeting today."

"I am fine, but oh Nicholas, have you heard the news? The Pope is dead," said Ella.

"Yes, I received word earlier," said Nicholas. "You can imagine my dismay Ella. First the war and now this. It is so disheartening to see these obstacles being placed in our path just when everything seemed to be on track. I met the Pope only that one time and did not know him very well, but there was something about him that inspired confidence and trust. I am at a loss to know how this will affect our efforts," said the Tsar.

"Certainly the Pope would have made some arrangements for his successor to be informed as to what was discussed by you and Pius."

"Well, there really is no need for me to be concerned because he promised me the support of his church and assured me his pledge would be honored by future popes. Ella, there was something so remarkable about that man that the idea of working with anyone else will take some getting use to. I assume the next pope will send a representative to meet with me at some point and we will see what develops. But now that I have had a chance to verbalize what was on my mind I realize the death of Pius X will have no impact on the *Masquerade*. In my anxiety over his passing I thought I was losing confidence in myself but I recognize now that what I actually felt was a deep sense of loss. Dearest Ella, I will certainly miss his calming influence. I may have told you that in my dream the Pope was accompanied by St. Serafim, so I was always convinced of the legitimacy of his involvement. The only part of my dream that was unexplained when I left the meeting was when, how and why I would sacrifice my finger. Pius assured me I would know when the time was right, and evidently it has not yet arrived. It is so strange! I had made up my mind that when it happened I would send my finger to the Vatican for safekeeping, but now I think not."

"I do not understand Nicky," said Ella. "What has happened to make you change your mind?"

"Ella, I am not a scientist and I cannot pretend to understand the significance of safeguarding my finger and blood. Frankly, the idea is grisly and distasteful but I imagine in the future there will be some way to connect me with my descendants, by using this finger."

"Did the Pope tell you about such a test?"

"Oh no, I merely reasoned that with all the advances made in science it must be something of that nature. It is the only answer that makes any sense."

"Well, what has changed in regards to the Vatican."

"The death of Pius was completely unexpected. I thought he would be the one involved with us and I was completely comfortable with the idea but now that he is gone, I am not so sure. If a piece of my finger is to have some significance in the salvation of Russia perhaps this relic would be better placed with our Russian Orthodox Church. Pius never suggested it be sent to the Vatican, only that when the time came I would know what to do. So I am going to make alternate arrangements to have the finger safeguarded by our Church and I vow from this point on, to quit worrying about it. When the time comes I will know and that is that. If the future of my country and the recognition of my descendants somehow depends upon this finger business then let it be a Russian matter and a Russian concern."

"Won't there be documents to verify the actions you have taken?" asked Ella.

"Of course, but they will be held outside Russia. My flesh and blood will lend credence to these papers and let the Russian people know that I did not waste my life in frivolous activity but ended it working for their future."

"Nicky, if everything takes place as prophesied I cannot believe that there will be a Church left in Russia," said Ella.

"Yes, I thought about that but the Russian Orthodox Church has congregations in the United States and Europe as well as Japan. I have even financed the construction of a few churches. I think it will be a Church in exile for a period of time but, whatever the case, my finger will have to go to a Church outside of Russia. Perhaps, after all, we should send tissue and blood samples to the Vatican and possibly the United States. Sometime in the future everything will come together and I am convinced that tests on my blood and flesh, as well as the documents we will have prepared, will prove to be of great importance."

"What additional samples are you planning to use?"

"It must be blood and skin. I know I must sacrifice my finger," the Tsar answered. "The dream made that quite clear but there are other options. Maybe a piece of my toe could be used."

"Oh, Nicholas, it sounds so dreadful, mutilating yourself just to send samples all over the world. The dream only asked for part of one finger. Why not use something else? Maybe something that was already removed like nail clippings or a lock of hair."

"No, it must be flesh and blood."

"What about a tooth?

"That may be a possibility but only if it contained blood. When I make my decision I will have George and Sandro carry out my wishes. I am not sure what is going to happen now that Pope Pius X is dead but we must continue on.

"My poor Nicky, it all seems so complicated," said Ella.

"It may be time to bring Maria Bariatinskaya into the plan. She is a dear friend of Alix and serves as one of her ladies-in-waiting. I believe she is extremely loyal and trustworthy and more importantly she is Catholic and has ties to Rome. We could send her to Italy and she could act as our conduit to the Vatican and the new Pope once he is elected. At some point she should be able to ascertain whether or not the future Pope will honor Pius X's agreement with me."

"I have met Maria many times and have been impressed by her quiet spirituality. I concur with your opinion of her character and am certain that she is completely reliable," said Ella. "I think she is the perfect person to have as your private representative in Rome. Her family background is impeccable and they have many connections within Italy as well as the Vatican. Of course Alix will not want to give her up. How much of the *Masquerade* are you going to reveal to her?"

"As much as I trust her, it will be as little as possible. After she evaluates where we stand with the new Pope, I want her to enlist his support for our plan to send some of the children to Poland. A letter from the Pope to the Mother Superior of a certain convent in Warsaw should go a long way in establishing the needed cooperation."

"Exactly. It would be the same as if you were asking something of me. There would be no question and it would be taken care of immediately."

"That was my thought. If we have the support of the Pope there will be no opposition from the Mother Superior. The question is, will we have the endorsement of this as of yet, unnamed Pope?"

"Only time will tell Nicholas, and we must pray continuously for the success of our mission."

"I agree, now tell me, how are the children doing? I want to hear all about them."

Ella spent some time updating Nicholas on her charges and he was pleased at their progress. That aspect of the plan at least, was coming along very well. Nicholas asked many detailed questions to which Ella responded in depth. She felt the doubles would be ready by the end of 1915, possibly sooner. My training with them will be complete by then but they will still need some additional time with your family in the palace before they will be ready to pass for your children."

"I understand. I am working on where they will be staying when they come to Tsarskoe Selo. I have not yet decided when the move will take place but I will keep you informed. Thank-you Ella for all of your hard work, I am very pleased with your progress."

"It is nothing Nicky. We are all in this together and it is what families do. We take care of one another, especially in times of hardship or trouble. Now I must ask to be excused. I have much work waiting for me at my convent."

The two said their good-byes and Nicholas returned to his work. Talking out the situation had been most helpful and he felt refreshed by the two hours spent with Ella. He had a very busy schedule for the next few days and had much to attend to before he and the rest of the family could return to Tsarskoe Selo.

⊂Жᗡ

It was the first week of September and Nicholas had been back at Alexander Palace for a few days. As usual, at this time in the evening, he sat at his desk working his way through the stack of paperwork he had to attend to on a daily basis. The news from the front was grim and he paused for a moment to reflect on the telegram he had received from Nikolasha reporting the decisive defeat, in late August, of a Russian army in the four day battle at Tannenberg, in Prussia. Nicky stretched his legs for a moment aware that in stressful times, when the news was bad, it was comforting to be in a familiar place, surrounded by the people and things he loved. As he finally reached the bottom of the pile he picked up a letter which he had set aside earlier and wished to reflect on. It was a request from a peasant woman named Maria Bochkareva, from Tomsk. Maria's petition was unusual to say the least. She begged the Tsar to allow her to go to war and help save her country. She asked permission to join the Russian Army and be sent to the front to aid in the war effort. It seemed she had attempted to enlist previously but had been refused. Her last hope was to appeal directly to the Tsar.

He read the telegram again and though he was moved that a woman wanted to join the troops going into battle, he was not really surprised. There were a number of historical precedents, of course, but in Russia the only authorized positions for women were as Red Cross nurses or in other auxiliary roles which did not involve combat. What could possibly motivate a woman to want to carry a rifle and associate exclusively with men? Could women actually be of use as soldiers? Would not a woman's femininity be much too disruptive and impact negatively on the morale of a unit? Nicholas remembered back to his days on active service and wondered how a woman would have fared in his regiment. It certainly would have changed things in the barracks. Of course, if she dressed and looked like a man it would be less unsettling for the troops. He wondered how strong this Maria was but suspected that with her peasant background she probably possessed strength greater than anyone might expect. The Tsar thought of his own daughter, Maria, who was very strong. She often carried Alexei on her back and he had seen her lift one of her tutors completely off the ground. She was certainly as strong as any boy her age.

Nicholas quickly made up his mind and pulled out a sheet of paper. It was the official imperial stationary of the Tsar with his crest centered at the top. He briskly wrote a reply to Maria Bochkareva and granted her permission to enlist in the army. But first he laid out conditions that she would have to agree to. She must cut off her hair and wear the same uniform as the male soldiers and secondly she must successfully undergo the training program for new recruits. If she met these requirements, than she would be allowed to go to the front with her fellow soldiers. The Tsar was satisfied with his decision and he drafted a few follow-up notes to his commanders to ensure his orders were carried out. He also requested regular reports on Maria's progress. Nicholas would not stand in the way of anyone who was willing to give their all for Mother Russia.

He leaned back in his chair and wondered if his daughters should have some special military training. It would not be a bad idea for the girls to know how to defend themselves. He made a mental note to discuss this with Nikolasha the next time he saw him, and, if past experience was any indicator, that would happen as soon as the Grand Duke received the directive allowing the peasant woman a combat assignment.

Chapter 29

September 1914 - Tsarskoe Selo. While Nicholas immersed himself in the affairs of state and followed, with concern, reports of the battles raging along the entire front, Alix shook off the real and perceived ailments that plagued her and plunged headlong into the war effort. She focused her energy on the area for which she was most suited and began to help organize the medical evacuation effort. This included the preparation of special trains to move the wounded to the rear and the establishment of hospitals to receive them when they arrived. Realizing that the enormous Catherine Palace stood empty most of the time she had it converted into a multi-ward hospital which, because of the terrible losses in Prussia, was soon filled to overflowing. Alexandra did not limit her efforts to administration, however, and she, along with her close friend Anya Vyrubova, and daughters Olga and Tatiana enrolled in a nurse's course and were studying for their Red Cross Certification. Maria and Anastasia were considered too young for exposure to the sights of the operating rooms but they were expected to visit the wounded each day and assist in rolling bandages and making handicrafts for the troops. Alix was like a dynamo, and one would never guess that the Empress, with her boundless energy was practically an invalid only weeks earlier. Her wheelchair was now parked in a corner and barely used as she went back and forth to the hospital and her various meetings. Only a few of her closest associates really understood what this complex and intriguing woman was going through as the war began. When she agreed to convert to Russian Orthodoxy and give up her German heritage to marry Nicholas she did not do so half-heartedly but threw herself into her new role with all the energy she could muster. In reality she became more Russian than the Russians and was the strongest and most vigorous supporter of the Romanov dynasty. Sadly, the personal sacrifices she made were never understood or appreciated by the people and yet she labored on without complaint to make life easier for the wounded. She quietly earned the gratitude of the many who were recipients of her ministrations.

Her two eldest daughters served on various boards and committees but they were each eager to participate more directly. Alix had considered them too immature to take the nurse's course, but they had insisted and when Nicky sided with the girls, Alix finally relented. At nineteen and seventeen, respectively, Olga and Tatiana were growing up and, anticipating what was ahead for his girls, the Tsar encouraged them to learn as much as they could of the real world in the short time that remained. He did not relish the thought of the suffering they would see as nurses but he knew it would toughen them both up, and that could only be good for their future. The two girls often traveled into the capital to attend the meetings of their committees and to visit the many hospitals in the area. The Tsar had changed the name of Russia's most important city, by official decree, to the more Russian form. It would be called Petrograd, until after the revolution.

While his wife and daughters were involved in their duties, Nicholas focused on one of the most crucial areas of the *Masquerade*; the preparation of quarters for the impostors when they came to Tsarskoe Selo. Nicholas had previously directed Count Benckendorff to begin, as unobtrusively as possible, to remove some of the furniture from the attic in the south wing of Alexander Palace and store it in a warehouse until it could be sent to Poland. The Count also had a substantial number of household items pre-positioned in Vladivostok awaiting transport to Japan. Today the last shipment of furniture was leaving the palace and the task would be completed. That is not to say the attic was empty, however, as there was still a substantial amount of furniture and other pieces still remaining. As usual, packing the items into nondescript wooden crates with no labels indicating what they contained was a major production, but by now Count Benckendorff was an old hand at this. He had developed a special coding system to identify the destination and contents of the crates and everything went smoothly.

Some time ago Nicholas had asked the Count to inspect the south attic and see if the old servants' quarters were still there and after he verified that they were Nicholas concluded the space would be a perfect spot to conceal the impostors. That was one of the reasons why the Count had not stripped the storage area bare but had left enough behind to furnish the children's rooms when they finally arrived. The attic was located directly over the family quarters and would afford quick access when the substitutes had to be hidden away in a hurry. By comparison to the magnificent Catherine Palace across the grounds, Alexander Palace seemed quite small, but it was, by any standard, a large building and the space over the family's wing, once it was renovated, would provide a comfortable and roomy hideaway.

Count Benckendorff had worked diligently to fulfill the Tsar's wishes. Nicholas had given him a general idea of what was needed but left it up to his discretion as to what items would be removed and what would remain. The attic held numerous pieces of priceless furniture, art work and household items that had been stored there ever since Nicholas and Alexandra had moved into the palace and completed extensive renovations between 1897 and 1903. This large storage area had been locked up at that time and seldom if ever did anyone go up, except to add to the growing collection. Over the years the once cavernous space filled to over flowing. Some of the furniture was wrapped in blankets or canvas coverings but many had been stored with no protection and were covered with dust.

Great care was utilized in moving the pieces, some of which dated back to the time of Catherine the Great. The crates containing the furniture were taken out of the attic and down a flight of stairs to the second floor. From there the workmen carried the boxes down the main staircase to the center of the palace near the Parade rooms and then out the doors to the waiting trucks. Although this was near the public entrance of the palace the size of some of the pieces necessitated utilizing the larger entrance. Benckendorff had hired some local day laborers to move the furniture to avoid discussions among the palace servants. The men had been hard at work since the early hours of the morning and Benckendorff hoped to be completed before the daily visitors to the Tsar and Tsarina began arriving.

Unfortunately, an early arriving minister, hurrying to deliver a report, happened on the loading operation just as the men were finishing up. Curious as to what was going on he approached two of the workers. "What are you doing?" he inquired of the laborers.

"We were told to report here this morning to load crates onto trucks," said one of the workers. "That is all we know."

Just then Count Benckendorff came out of the palace to inspect the progress and saw the minister. He realized immediately that this was a touchy situation and he offered a quick prayer for guidance. "Good-day to you," he said to the official.

"Oh! Good morning, my dear Count. What is being taken from the palace? Is the Tsar moving to another location?" asked the Minister. There had been rumors that the Imperial family was considering relocating to Moscow for the duration of the war.

"No! Of course not. The Emperor and Empress have decided to sell off surplus from the palace to support the war effort and these crates will be shipped out later today. Sometimes I am overwhelmed by their generosity and I am sure you will agree that parting with these prized possessions is an act to be admired."

"Yes," said the minister. "The Imperial family has done much for the war effort with their private donations and active support of the hospitals." He then excused himself and hurried to his meeting.

Benckendorff had deliberately down-played the incident and unintentionally provided a perfect cover story for the movement of the material. No one could keep a secret for long and he was sure that the Tsar's secret generosity would be soon be an item of gossip in the city.

The laborers continued their work and finally the last load was in place. Count Benckendorff walked around the trucks and conducted a quick inspection before sending them on their way to the station at Tsarskoe Selo where the crates were to be loaded onto a train. Once the workers were gone Benckendorff went back into the palace and climbed up the stairs into the attic. Each of the palace's two wings had attic space but the areas were separated from each other by the two-story Parade rooms which occupied the central portion of the palace. At the top of the stairs was an oversized door that opened into the large room which had been used for storage. It occupied approximately half the space over the Imperial family's wing of the palace. The attic was dimly lit by a few electric light bulbs which hung by wires from the eaves and he had to carefully pick his way through the remaining pieces to the end of the room where he found the door he was looking for. He had been here before to verify the layout, as the Tsar had requested, but it had been very difficult because of all the items that were haphazardly stored there. Now, with the larger pieces removed, he was able to get the door open without too much trouble. It gave access into a long corridor with doors on either side. He walked up to one and attempted to open it but the wood of the door had swollen and it resisted his efforts. The Count was no longer a young man and by the time he finally forced it opened he was breathing heavily. There was a large cobweb blocking the entrance and he impatiently pushed it away. He was looking into a room that many years ago had housed one of the lesser servants of the Imperial household. It was filthy with years of accumulated dust and dirt and only a bit of light filtered in from the grimy windows which were high up on the wall, just below the ceiling. He went through the other rooms and they were in much the same condition. He turned around, went back into the large room, and then picked his way in the dim light back to the staircase. As he walked down the stairs he realized that use of this exit would expose the plan to some risk. The impostors would certainly be coming out of the attic from time to time but if they came this way they would exit on the first floor right near the Parade rooms and the public entrance. The Count knew this was a major problem and he determined to make it one of the first item of business when he met with the Tsar in the morning to discuss the renovations.

The next day Benckendorff made his verbal report to the Tsar. He explained the status of all the furniture and other items which were awaiting shipment. "We have enough to fill five households," the Count explained. "The goods in Vladivostok are ready for shipment whenever you give the word. I hope you will not think me impertinent but I must ask you, have you decided where you will send the Tsarevich?"

"No, I have not. As you are aware, two of the Grand Duchesses will initially be sent to a convent in Poland and the other two will go to some secluded location in Japan. On my cousin George's advice I am leaving the exact details to Prince Kanin but it would seem that Japan offers the safest option for Alexei. I cannot imagine that the presence of a young boy at a girl's school in Warsaw would go unnoticed, however careful we are. So that leaves Japan. At any rate whatever decision I make will be influenced by the state of his health and that is always an uncertainty. So for the present I am at a loss to know what to do."

"It is possible he could out grow his illness," said Benckendorff, in an attempt to encourage the Tsar.

"Yes, perhaps he will, but this is talk for a later time. Now tell me. What did you find in the attic? Is it feasible?"

"It is quite filthy and much work must be done to make it habitable but as far as space and suitability are concerned it is perfect. However, there is a major problem."

"What is it?" the Tsar asked.

"Access to the attic is from the stairway at the front of the parade rooms. I do not know how we could bring the children in and out without someone seeing them."

"Certainly there must have been some other stairway to access the servants quarters," said Nicholas.

"Yes, I thought about that," said the Count. "I have been in your family's service for many years and if I remember correctly, there was once another set of stairs. But that was many, many years ago and I do not know if it still exists. There have been so many changes and renovations to the palace over the years and when the old servants quarters were turned into storage rooms they may have been taken out."

"Do you remember if it was in this wing or the other," questioned Nicholas hoping to jog the memory of the Count.

"I only went up the stairway one time but as I recall it was in this south wing towards the front."

"Let me see if I still have the second floor plans. We can look them over and see if you can recall where the stairs were located." Nicholas walked over to a bookshelf near the fireplace and removed a sheaf of yellowed papers containing what appeared to be architectural drawings, and brought it to the table.

"Please join me," directed the Tsar as he paged through the plans. Eventually Nicholas found a second floor layout and the two men bent over it, looking for the lost staircase. They searched the plans carefully but were disappointed when they could find no trace of it. They looked at some older plans and still, nothing. Benckendorff tried to recall where he had seen it, but after so many years his memory was not up to the task and he apologized to the Tsar. Nicholas felt sure that there must be something that could revive the count's memory. "Do not be concerned, old friend. We will find it. Do you remember what the staircase looked like?"

"It was very narrow and steep. I remember walking through a doorway," the Count replied, and then mimicked opening a door. "Once through the door I turned left to go up the stairs. Oh, I remember something. The staircase was unusually narrow because it was constructed between two walls."

"Are you sure?"

"Yes. Please let me see the second floor plan of the children's wing again." The Count studied the plans intently. "The hidden stairs were near the front of the palace, if my memory serves me."

The Tsar looked at the drawings with him. "Then the staircase must have been behind this wall, here, in the children's dining room."

"Yes, I believe so, or possibly this wall," the Count said as he pointed to the next room.

"We will just have to examine the dining room and find out if an opening still exists. We can wait until everyone has retired for the night. The children's dining room is far enough away from their rooms that we can complete our search without disturbing them or their nurses."

Would you like me to make the arrangements? I can ensure that we will not be disturbed."

"Very well. In the meantime I will inform the Empress of our plans. We will use her private staircase leading to the children's floor. As you know it has access to the dining room and will allow us to go up without using the main corridor."

"Would you have any objections if I bring my stepson Valia along. He is a much younger man and will be able to assist us and if I swear him to secrecy you can depend on his loyalty."

Nicholas looked at the Count, who was beginning to get up in years, and quickly agreed. "He will be quite a help. Now, I am not sure what we will need, but have Valia bring whatever tools he thinks are appropriate and some type of lighting."

And so, to find a staircase, the *Masquerade* grew by another player, albeit a necessary one. Nicholas had been careful to keep the plan compartmentalized but he knew it was time to start bringing in trusted members of the palace staff. When the impostors were smuggled into the palace more people would certainly have to know at least some of what was going on. But for the time being, even after several years of preparation there were still only twelve.

Count Benckendorff spent the rest of the day preparing for the evening's quest to find the hidden stairway. He made sure that the servants would be finished with their work and in bed for the night so that he, his stepson, and the Tsar could look for the staircase undisturbed. Late in the evening he and Valia went to the Imperial couple's private rooms to join them for tea. It was customary for Nicholas and Alexandra to end their day with tea at eleven each night and it was usually a private time when they could catch up on the day's activities and unwind. Occasionally members of the personal staff or family were invited so Benckendorff and Valia's appearance did not raise any suspicions. The two sat down in Alix's Mauve Boudoir and were soon sipping tea and nibbling on small cakes. The conversation immediately turned to the secret stairway.

"I am so surprised. I never heard anything about it," said Alexandra.

"Well, I had completely forgotten its existence until the Tsar jostled my memory," said Count Benckendorff.

"I do hope it is still there. With all the redecorating and refurbishing of this palace over the years, it may very well have been torn down. Now where exactly do you think it might be?" Alix asked the Count.

"After looking at the plans I am pretty certain that it is behind one the walls of the Grand Duchess's dining room," said Benckendorff.

"Is it near the stairs we had built from my rooms up to the children's rooms?"

"I am not sure, your Highness. It literally ran up between two walls. It was very steep and little more than two feet in width. Some of the servants were housed up in the attic and there were rooms for them up there."

"It is very intriguing and exciting. A secret staircase in our own home and I never knew," said Alix,

"One of the dangers of intriguing and exciting things is the nearly irrepressible desire to share knowledge of them with others," Nicholas pointedly observed. "We must be very careful with this."

"Oh, I understand all that. Just let us pray it is still there," said Alix. "It really would be ideal to bring the doubles in and out through the dining area as very few people are ever in there and it is certainly not a public part of the palace."

"That is correct," said Nicholas. "No guards and no courtiers."

"What about the children's servants," asked Valia.

"When the time comes we will "retire" the newer ones or transfer them to other houses and keep only the most trusted. For instance the Empress's maids who came with her to Russia and a few others."

"What about the ladies-in-waiting? Will they be informed," asked Benckendorff.

"I have not addressed that issue yet so we will have to wait and see," Nicholas answered.

"My ladies-in-waiting are called to the palace for six months at a time and when their tour is completed they do not expect to return any time soon. I would be able to choose two and we could keep them on duty as long as necessary," said the Empress.

"We can decide this later but now it is time to get to work," said the Tsar. He stood up and excused himself. He was joined by Benckendorff and Valia who bowed to the Empress before following the Tsar through the Imperial Bedroom and Alix's dressing room to her private staircase. They went up the stairs and entered the children's dining room. Although the palace had electric lights the Tsar did not turn them on in the dining room. Instead he reached into his pocket and pulled out a small silver flashlight. It was three inches long and very ornately decorated with his initials. It had been a gift from one of his cousins and was specially made for him by Tiffanys. The Tsar loved gadgets and had used a flashlight since they were first introduced in 1903. Valia and the Count were also equipped with hand-held lights and when they all switched on there was sufficient illumination. The three proceeded towards the first wall of the room.

The Tsar turned to Benckendorff and asked, "Where do you think we should start?"

"I do not recall exactly where the entrance was but I believe it was near a window. I think this wall would be a good place to begin."

"Then let us commence at the far right corner here and make a small hole and see what we find," recommended the Tsar. "We will need to move this small table first." Valia stepped forward, picked up the table, and moved it off to the side.

"I will remain outside the door while you conduct the search," suggested Benckendorff. "That way I can head off anyone who might come up, although at this hour I doubt there will be any activity."

The Tsar nodded his assent and began the search. "Valia, look in the bag and see if there is some sort of pick or awl and maybe a hammer we can use to make an opening." Valia looked through the bag, removed the tools the Tsar had asked for and passed them to him. Nicholas took the hammer and awl and began tapping at the wall while Valia held the flashlight. He gently picked away at the plaster until he finally poked a hole through the wall. He worked to enlarge the opening, careful to ensure that the table they had removed would hide the hole when they replaced it. He took his flashlight from Valia, put his arm into the hole, and looked through the opening. He could see very little but it was enough to determine that there was a wall directly opposite the hole he had made. There were no stairs, although there appeared to be a space of at least two feet between the two walls. However, when he looked to the left he could see another wall which appeared to have no function and which seemed out of place.

"There is enough space between the walls for the stairs but there is a wall on the left. That does not leave enough room for a staircase. I do not see any stairs and I can not get a good enough angle so that I can see above the hole. I do not want to make the opening any bigger as it would be too obvious and I want to have that table cover up the hole until we can get it repaired. Valia please have your father come in to take a look." The young man went to get the Count from the hallway.

"Did you see anything your Majesty," asked the Count.

"Well, there is space between the walls, but I do not see any stairs and there is a wall to the left."

Benckendorff took a look and suggested they make another hole in the wall past where the Tsar saw the partition that blocked his view. "I think our attempt was too far over. Why don't we try several feet to the left."

Valia moved to the spot the Count indicated with his light. "But there is a large hutch here."

"Yes it was here when we moved into the palace," said Nicholas. "It is built in so you cannot move it. You know, it might very well have been put there to hide the entrance door to the stairs."

Valia offered to crawl into the hutch. It was a huge piece of furniture and the bottom section was as high as Valia's chest. It had two doors that opened to reveal a large space with shelves. He removed the linens stored in the cabinet and then the shelves. Using the Tsar's flashlight he saw that the back of the hutch was actually the wall so it would be easy to make an opening. Valia was able to sit up in the cabinet and the Tsar passed him the tools so he could begin to chip away at the plaster. When he had made a hole big enough to get a good view, Valia climbed out of the hutch so that the Tsar could have the first look.

Nicholas climbed into the cabinet and shined his light into the aperture. He could see a space much like the one they had worked on earlier but this time when he looked to the left he could make out what appeared to be a staircase heading up to the attic. Excitement overcame him and he climbed out of the cabinet. "It is there," he whispered. Valia went back in and enlarged the opening so that a man could fit through. The Tsar motioned to him to go ahead so Valia carefully moved into the opening. The staircase was thick with cobwebs and dust but they did not deter him and he climbed up the stairs checking the stability of the structure as he went. When he reached the top, the stairs ended below what appeared to be a trap door. He shined his light on it and looked for a lock or latch, but could see nothing. Valia pushed and shoved at the door but could not budge it. It was obviously blocked from the other side so he backed down the stairs, crawled out the hole, and told the Tsar and Benckendorff what he had found.

"It is as you remembered it Count," said Nicholas. "They must have removed the door, plastered over the opening and then set the hutch in place. I wonder why they went to such trouble? Now we will have to go up into the attic and see if we can find the entrance."

"I will go with you," said Benckendorff. "Valia, give us about ten minutes and then head back up the stairs. When you hear us, start knocking so it will help us locate the door."

The Tsar and Benckendorff walked down the long hall and out of the children's wing to the entrance to the attic. They quickly made their way up into the garret and worked their way through all the furniture until they reached the servants' quarters. The two went to the last room on the right and entered. Valia could hear their footsteps above him and began knocking on the hatch. Following the knocking sounds, Nicholas and the Count rapidly located the source. A large trunk blocked the opening and when they shoved it out of the way the trap door was revealed. Nicholas pulled on the handle of the door but to no avail. He leaned down and yelled to Valia "On the count of three push as hard as you can and I will pull on this end." The Tsar counted and then the two pushed and pulled with all their strength. The force caused the hatch to fly open and the Tsar tumbled backward to the floor.

"Are you all right your Majesty?" asked Benckendorff.

"Yes, I am fine. Well, this is it. We have our secret passage. Eventually we must work on cleaning up this filth and making the place habitable for our guests. But not quite yet. I have an idea that I will share with you after we get some rest." The three men climbed down the stairs and, when they had removed the traces of their nocturnal activities, parted for the remainder of the night. Nicholas went immediately to tell Alix the good news.

When he entered the boudoir the Empress was still awake. "We have found the stairway," said Nicky.

"Really, that is wonderful news. Where is it located?"

"It is too late to take you there tonight. Do you have those recent photographs of you and the girls in their dining room?"

"Yes, I have not put them in my album yet."

Nicholas retrieved the photographs. "Here, look at this picture," said the Tsar. "We put a hole in the wall here and found nothing but we decided to try a little further over." He then recounted the discovery they had made.

"That is amazing. All the years we have lived here, not to even know it existed."

"It is remarkable. When the stairs were no longer in use they must have walled off the entrance and built this cupboard in front of it. It is perfect. We will go ahead and open up the original door and strengthen the framing. I will have large strap hinges mounted on one side of the hutch so that it can swing away from the wall. It will need a special concealed latch to allow the cabinet to be opened from either side but that should not be a problem. Finally we will have to cover the back of the hutch with thin paneling so that when a servant gets out some linens they will not be able to see the doorway. When the work is to be done we will have to get everyone out of this wing so I want you to come up with some plausible reason to move the staff to the other side. Perhaps we can reward their service and devotion with a party or dance and announce that it will be an annual affair. I leave it up to you. In the meantime I will have Benckendorff arrange for some trustworthy workman."

"It is as if God is guiding us through all of this and giving us the means to achieve our goals."

"Alix, you are right, of course. We are all God's tools and he uses us as he sees fit. Now you must understand that I have been very careful to involve as few people as possible in the *Masquerade*. But before too long it will be time to bring in your maids because they will play a key role in making this work."

The Empress had two personal maids, Madeleine Zanotti and Marie Tudelberg. They were both women of strong character and were fanatically loyal to the Tsarina. Zanotti and Tuddles, as they were called, refused to wear the caps and aprons of the Russian servants and instead dressed in simple black gowns. The two did not socialize with the other servants and Nicholas intended to capitalize on this situation to prepare the upper rooms.

"For the present we will do nothing but when the time comes they will be the ones to clean and furnish the rooms for the doubles," said the Tsar.

"They will not be happy about that," Alix replied. "They are ladies maids, not scullery staff. They are not used to cobwebs and dirt and Zanotti does not clean at all. She feels it is beneath her. Tuddles, on the other hand, will do anything that I ask her to, but she is very slow and methodical."

"This is a dilemma you will have to work out. At first you can tell them enough to insure their cooperation but do not reveal everything. Later, as the plan evolves, they will be brought more fully into it, but they must comply; they have no choice. Alix, these are the first that I will allow you to tell about the *Masquerade* so you must reiterate the need for secrecy, especially in their relations with the other servants. And as for your friend Anya Vyrubova, not even she is to know at this time. She is not secluded like the family and I just cannot risk an involuntary disclosure. The same is true of "our friend," Grigory. His circle of admirers contains too many gossips and gossip can lead to ruin. I am sure you understand."

"Of course. You have reminded me often enough," Alix replied in a hurt voice. "How long do I have to get the rooms ready?"

"I had thought to have you start immediately but I realized that all the activity would be obvious to the children and staff and it is just too soon to explain all this to them. I will have Valia change the locks on the doors leading into the attic so no one has keys. We will alter the hutch as I explained to you and then do nothing else until the time is right. The dining room will look as it always has. When we begin the actual work you will have to use the hidden staircase to go up and down. Once the rooms are ready we will have to maintain them continuously because the substitutes may arrive on short notice. Are you sure you will be up to the challenge, my darling?"

"I have helped to amputate the leg of a man in the hospital and have sledded down the hill and I certainly can manage a narrow set of stairs. Besides, I do not intend to give my maids a free hand in deciding how to enhance the rooms."

Over the next months, and well into the following year, the Tsarina continued to dedicate herself to her work with the wounded. But in the back of her mind she was making preliminary plans to prepare the attic for her "new children," as she began to think of them. There was much work to be done to accomplish the task. The place would have to be thoroughly cleaned and painted, then furnished. Alix would not spend too much time in the attic, as it was too risky, but she planned to occasionally slip up the secret stairs to check on the progress. She had a number of ideas to make the place a comfortable home and she embraced the challenge of the decorating project. To avoid suspicion Alix would use as many items from the attic as possible but she knew she would have to order a few things to add a more personal touch to the rooms. There were six in all, and she had discussed with Nicholas the feasibility of leaving the one that housed the trap door in disarray so that if someone discovered the staircase it would discourage them from exploring any further. But since the stairway was so narrow it was decided to clean the room and install a sturdy railing around the upper door so the children could safely come down without risking a fall The other rooms would comprise a dining room, a drawing room, a bedroom for Alexei's double, and two rooms for the Grand Duchesses' doubles. The older girls would share a room as would the two younger ones, just as the Imperial children did. Alix intended to decorate their rooms as much as possible like her own children's, although on a smaller scale due to the size of the rooms. The large attic room would be cleaned and used as a classroom and common area for the two groups of children to interact.

The biggest challenge was the fact there was no indoor plumbing in the attic and installing it was absolutely out of question. It was decided the doubles would use chamber pots as well as pitchers and bowls for personal hygiene. Once a week they could come down and use the maids' bathroom which was on the same end of the children's wing as the dining room. Alix would institute new rules that allowed only her senior maids to use this bathroom. The others would be required to use the bathroom at the opposite end of the wing. Nicholas and Alix had talked it over and decided this made the most sense as the children's dining room was rarely used because as of late, the Imperial family dined together. Late in the evening no one was ever at this end of the wing so the chance of discovery was slim. Alexandra was determined to see that everything went smoothly and she began to prepare checklists which outlined the priorities and sequenced the work. She kept them locked in her desk and would destroy them when the work was completed. She also anticipated the need for duplicate wardrobes and began to order a few outfits at a time for her "new children." Zanotti was an excellent seamstress so when the time came she would be able to alter the clothes if necessary.

Alix made several trips up the secret passage to analyze the layout. She estimated it would take no more than two or three weeks to complete the preparations. Once she had prepared her work lists there was no more to do except wait for the Tsar's order to proceed.

In the meantime there were the wounded.

Chapter 30

September 1914 –Tsarskoe Selo. On September 5, the Cardinals assembled in Rome for the conclave had finally elected a new pope, who took the name Benedict XV. When news of the election reached Nicholas he was immediately assailed with doubts about his clandestine relationship with the Vatican. Would this new man be anything like his gentle predecessor? Would Pope Benedict be cognizant of the Tsar's secret meeting with Pius X and would he be fully aware of the nature of their discussions. Nicholas was in a quandary. He knew that because of the war there would be no opportunity for a personal assessment of the new pope and he would be forced to rely on the opinion of others as to whether the strange pact between Pope and Tsar would remain unchanged.

And now, several weeks later, word reached Count Benckendorff that an emissary had indeed been dispatched by the Vatican and was making his way through war-torn Europe for a meeting with the Tsar. The situation was so fluid at the front that he could arrive at the palace at any moment. Nicholas had resolved some days earlier to quit worrying and to rely on Pius X's promise that his successors would continue their support. So it was with hopeful anticipation rather than any sense of dread that he waited for the appearance of this unknown messenger. Nicholas would greet him with courtesy, but say little, and would allow the Pope's man to dictate the direction the discussion would take.

As he paced back and forth in his study he reflected on the conversation he had about a week ago with Maria Bariatinskaya. She was more than willing to be of service to the Tsar and pledged her loyalty to him. She took a vow of secrecy, as well. She was leaving at the end of the week for Rome where she would begin her mission for the Tsar. It would have been fortuitous had she been able to meet the emissary face to face but at any rate Nicholas was convinced, because of her extensive connections, she would have no trouble obtaining an audience with the Pope. After he received her report, then he would decide the role the Vatican would play. There was an outside chance that the messenger would arrive before she departed for Italy in which case he would arrange a meeting.

A few days later, as if on cue, Benckendorff came into the study and announced the arrival of Father Edmund Walsh. The priest, who was dressed in ordinary street clothes, greeted the Tsar with a firm handshake and exchanged pleasantries. Nicholas directed the Count to remain at this first meeting because he wanted his analysis when they finished. They sat down in the comfortable leather chairs which dotted the study.

"Your Imperial Highness I bring greetings to you from Pope Benedict," began Father Walsh in fluent Russian. "He expresses his thanks for the spirit of religious freedom you have fostered in your country, which allows your Catholic subjects to practice their faith." He was speaking, of course, of western Russia and Poland.

The envoy had an aura of confidence about him and when he began in Russian, Nicholas knew immediately that the Pope had sent a man of special ability, not just some low level diplomat. Although it was not yet apparent, Walsh was an authority on Russian affairs and Nicholas felt instinctively that this was a man with whom he could work. He wondered what this priest's actual position was in the Vatican but then realized that just as Sandro, George, and Benckendorff had their agents, so too must the Pope have his own group of trusted men to assist him. Nevertheless, despite his initial positive impression, he wanted to hear what this Father Walsh had to say. And what he had to say was, surprisingly, very little.

"Your Highness, I was not made privy to the reason for this interview but my instructions were quite simple. I am to deliver a note to you." At that point he stood up and handed the Tsar a sealed letter. "Pope Benedict prepared this personally for you and asked that you read it privately. I am to remain at your disposal in case you have questions you wish me to relay to him either verbally or by sealed letter. Or if you wish to make other arrangements I am here to assist in any way I can.

"Father, thank-you for your time and may I ask you to wait a few minutes as I believe I will need to speak with you again."

Father Walsh nodded his agreement and the Count escorted the priest to the Tsar's reception room. Nicholas broke open the seal as soon as the door closed behind them and quickly read the words written by the pope:

My Dear Son,

On the night I was elected I received a sealed packet from the private secretary of my predecessor explaining everything. Cease your worries. Your secrets are safe and will remain so. Preparations continue as were discussed and we remain at your service. Father Edmund Walsh is my most trusted emissary. He is at your disposal and you may trust him with your most precious possessions. My blessings and prayers are with you.

Benedict XV

The Tsar could not explain it, but the minute he read the message from the Pope he found the peace he had been seeking. He decided to put his trust in Father Walsh and utilize him not only to facilitate Maria's meeting with the Pope and but also to assist her in making arrangements at the convent in Warsaw. As a direct representative of the Pope, he had immense influence and could exert pressure if necessary. His decision made, the Tsar stood up, opened the door, and asked Father Walsh to join him. He spoke to him privately for a few moments about the mission to

Poland and what part he hoped Father Walsh would play in this *Masquerade*. Again, as he did with most of the characters in this complex drama, Nicholas told him only what he needed to know to carry out his part. The priest was most receptive, asked a few questions, and then pledged to assist him in any way he could as long as what was required of him would not compromise the Pope or the Church. Nicholas assured him that he had nothing to fear in that regard. He then asked his aide-de-camp to send for Maria Bariatinskaya, who arrived after a short delay. The Tsar was pleased to see that she was immediately comfortable with Father Walsh and at the Tsar's urging the two emissaries agreed to meet in Rome in a few weeks, at which time Father Walsh would arrange for Maria to meet the Pope privately. With all the details settled he dismissed the two and then turned his attention to the most immediate and pressing concern; the conduct of the war.

A few days later the Tsar left in his private train to visit the front. At this stage in the conflict the General Headquarters of the Imperial Army, the Stavka as it was called in Russian, was located in Baranovitchi, a small Polish town between Minsk and Brest-Litvosk. The Stavka was approximately behind the center of the Russian lines and consisted of a group of rail cars pulled off onto a siding. Nicholas looked forward to the company of his men and once he settled in at the Stavka he took side trips everyday to visit his troops at the front, returning to headquarters each night. Usually there were letters from his wife and children waiting for him in his study on the train. This was the first time they had ever been separated for more than a week or two and they missed each other immensely. Initially the time passed slowly but after the first bout of homesickness faded Nicholas began to enjoy his time among the men. In truth it was somewhat of a relief to get away from the perfumed bastion of femininity the Alexander Palace had become as his daughters grew into attractive young women.

One brisk, fall night at headquarters the Tsar had the stove in his private car working overtime in an effort to warm the room. He sat at his desk and attempted to work through the huge stack of paperwork that was piled in front of him but he was exhausted from a day spent in meetings with various military personnel, ministers and foreign ambassadors. As he sat in his chair he felt his eyelids becoming heavier and heavier and when he could fight his weariness no longer he leaned back and fell into a deep slumber.

He dreamed he was on a train, late at night, but it was not moving and sat motionless as if it were switched onto a siding. It was a passenger train and he was seated on an ordinary bench quite unlike the luxurious furnishings of his own car. He glanced over to see a tall man, dressed in a suit and holding a heavy overcoat, sitting next to him. He did not recognize his face and yet as he looked carefully at the gentleman there was something about him that made Nicky feel at ease, almost as if somehow this stranger with the kindly, reassuring face knew him.

The man reached into his pocket and pulled out a small case. It was made of brown leather and was in the shape of a boat. It had an opening at the top of one end and was fashioned with two light leather straps which tied around the opening to hold it closed. The stranger passed the boat to Nicholas and said, "Have each of your daughters choose one." The Tsar untied the straps and opened the top but he could not see the contents of the bag. Just then his daughters appeared from nowhere and walked up to him. He held the boat-shaped case out in front of him and one by one each daughter reached into the bag and took out what appeared to be a ring. He could not see the details of the ring and it frustrated him. When Anastasia stepped up to reach into the bag he asked to see her ring but just as she began to open her hand she disappeared.

He turned to the man in a state of confusion. "I saw that they were taking rings out of the boat but I could not see the details of them."

"What the rings look like is not important," said the stranger. "Know that one ring is slightly different than the others. It contains a hidden code and the one who receives this ring is the chosen one of whom Serafim spoke in his letter. In the future she will learn how to unlock the secret of the ring." The Tsar looked down at the empty leather boat and then turned to give it back to its owner, but the man had vanished.

Nicholas was awakened by a tapping at his door that grew increasingly louder when he did not respond. He finally cleared his head and said "come in." He was expecting Count Benckendorff and indeed his aide opened the door to announce and usher in the Count. Nicholas wondered what was so urgent that his trusted advisor felt it necessary to come all the way from Petrograd at this late hour. The telegram which indicated he would be arriving gave no information as to why the Count wanted a private meeting and since the Count was involved in so many aspects of the *Masquerade*, it could be anything.

"Please have a seat," said the Tsar. "You must be tired from your long journey. Perhaps we should wait until morning to address the purpose of your visit."

"Thank-you for your concern but there have are some troubling developments that you need to be aware of and which, for security reasons, I did not want to entrust to the mail. Since I did not know when you might return to the capital I decided to come down to brief you."

Nicholas could see that the Count was quite visibly upset. In all the years he had known him Nicky had never seen him lose his composure and usually, even in the most dire emergencies, he could depend on him to react with stoic reserve. He urged him to have a seat and then poured him a generous serving of vodka. "It is all right my friend, take your time."

Count Benckendorff took a breath, gathered his thoughts together, and began to speak. "As you know there are a number of revolutionary groups working for the destruction of the monarchy and we have managed to infiltrate all of them. Some are more active than others and the developments I alluded to concern the most fanatical group. Apparently these men have much more in store for Russia than I ever imagined. They are rabid atheists and they are determined to destroy religion in Russia by shutting down all the churches including our own Russian Orthodox Church. God plays no part in their world and once they come into power they plan on spreading their message throughout the continent. They intend to export this insidious movement from Russia and ultimately destroy all religion, eventually returning us to a world wide pagan society. It is just an evil, evil plan," said Benckendorff shaking his head sadly.

"It does not seem possible?" said the Tsar, now sitting upright in his chair. Benckendorff had his full attention.

"I still cannot believe it myself, but it is true. These men intend to organize the peasants and workers by talking about rights for the people, and promising them the moon, but it is only a cover for their real plan. Their goal is to use the Russian people to erase every trace of God from the world."

"My God, have they gone mad?" questioned the Tsar.

"Indeed. It is so," the Count replied.

"When you first brought me the intelligence on this group I believed that only Russia would be affected," said the Tsar. "I had no idea these madmen had their sights on world supremacy. This is obviously a plan on a much larger scale than we assumed. I cannot imagine a world without God. If they deprive the people of their faith than they will also deprive them of hope and without hope there is no life."

"Someone else must be aware of their plan of action. Certainly the burden of this would not rest on your shoulders alone."

"It may fall on my children's shoulders. This is a very grave development. There may be no safe place for the children after all." Nicholas sat quietly and became lost in thought.

Finally, after some time the Count broke his reverie. "Is there anything else that is pressing, your Imperial Highness?" Benckendorff asked.

"Oh excuse me, I was thinking about something else. You know, old friend, this may work to our advantage after all. These revolutionaries are very ambitious and they may be overestimating their abilities. Although the Vatican has no army it will be a formidable adversary to any atheistic crusade, in whatever form, and I cannot imagine the United States will remain uninvolved. Or the other western nations for that matter. No, the ambition of these anarchists may lead to their ultimate destruction. Is there any other word from your spy?"

"Well, as you know, young Zabalia has infiltrated this group at the highest levels and his primary source is a man who seems to be quite free with his tongue. I can tell you that his position is such that he is privy to all sorts of information. Nothing gets past him, so be assured we are well informed. Now on a lighter note, your daughters asked me to deliver this to you personally," he said as he handed the Tsar a letter.

"One letter from all four," questioned Nicholas?

"Apparently so."

"I do not know if I tell you this often enough, but I am extremely pleased with your work and grateful to you. You have been a good and trusted friend to my family for many years."

"It has been my honor to serve you and your family," replied the Count.

Nicholas smiled and dismissed Benckendorff. The Count would spend the next several days at the Stavka continuing to update the Tsar in greater detail about the *Masquerade* and the goings-on at Tsarskoe Selo and Petrograd.

After Benckendorff departed for his quarters, Nicky moved over to his couch and sank down into its cushions, taking out his ever present cigarette case. He lit one and puffed a few times before setting it down. He picked up the letter from home the Count had delivered and examined it with curiosity. The writing appeared to be Olga's and he immediately recognized the stationery as Maria's. Interesting he thought. He had received letters from his daughters before, but this was the first that they had written together. He opened the correspondence with anticipation and began to read. Again, he noticed Olga's handwriting at the beginning of the letter. It read:

Dear Papa,

We four miss you terribly and cannot wait for you to come home again for a visit. We decided that we would write you one letter because we all have the same request. You are probably wondering what it is. Well, we will tell you. Please Papa, may we use your big bath. Alexei is allowed to use it and he has such fun. Mama would not give us permission since it is your private tub. She said we would have to take it up with you. Please Papa may we. We have already made plans. Tatiana and I would bathe first then Maria would share with Anastasia. We really would love to use your big tub. Why do you call it a tub when it is really more like a small swimming pool? Please! You can telegram Mama with your answer when you decide. Now we would each like to tell you what we have been up to lately. I am the oldest, so I am going to tell my tale first.

I have been working very hard with my nursing duties at the hospital. You would be so proud of me, Papa. I am also in charge of several committees. I usually drive out with one of Mother's ladies-in-waiting to my meetings in Petrograd. I have become quite busy and I am so glad that our security is not as restrictive as it was. We can go to the hospital as much as we please and we do not have several guards following us. It is quite nice as you know how much I dislike being watched like a child. I am grown now and really should be able to come and go as I wish and besides, Aunt Olga has purchased me the most beautiful gun you could ever imagine. It is called a Derringer and it is perfectly lovely. It has a mother of pearl handle. Of course I could shoot it right away without trouble. It is much easier than the guns I use when we are in Spala. I only told you because Aunt Olga said she had your permission to buy it for me. Tatiana had something new too, but I will let her tell you about it. I love you Papa.

Hello Father. It is I, Tatiana. I am glad Olga did not give you all the details of my new gift. Anya has given me the cutest little dog. It is a French bulldog and I have named it Ortipo. Mother must love him because he always wants to be with her. When she is at her writing desk, he sits on her feet. She says he keeps them warm. I too have been busy with committees and work at the hospital. It is so hard sometimes to see our soldiers come in with such wounds. I treat them very well Papa, so they might be able to come back to you and fight for Russia. Aunt Olga also wanted to buy me a gun but I refused her offer because I did not want one. They scare me terribly and I just do not think I need one but if you think I should have one than I will ask her to purchase one for me as well, but only if you say so.

I Love you Papa.

Hi Papa. Maria here. I have to say that Mother does not love Ortipo. She found a surprise on her new Persian rug that he left for her. She was not happy at all. I have been very busy myself lately. I keep busy at my hospital even though I am too young to be a nurse. I visit my patients often and they seem quite content to see me. I have been horse riding more and now I am even able to jump a little hurdle that Anastasia and I set up. Do not worry Papa it is not too high. We go often to Anya's house now because Mother is not feeling so well lately. Poor thing, her heart bothers her so. I hope you will give permission about your tub. I will love you so much more if you will.

Bye Papa.

"I am always last. Even in letter writing. I guess you know who this is since everyone else went before me. They do say the best is last or something of that sort. Papa, will you have a talk with Mama. She always makes us go to Anya's house to visit with Father Grigory since he is not allowed to visit the palace unless Alexei is sick. Sometimes it is fun, but other times he is frightening and scares us. We want to have fun and not talk about the things he does all the time. Can I get a gun too? Papa, it is not fair that Olga should have one and not I. Just because Tatiana does not want one does not mean I do not. Please think about it Papa, all

right. Olga is trying to take the pen from me because she wants to sign the letter from all of us.

I should sign the letter, right Papa, because I am the oldest. We love and miss you. Our very own, dear, sweet, much loved, Papa.

Love OTMA

Up to this point the letter had amused the Tsar and he enjoyed it immensely, but when he saw the signature he was puzzled. He knew, of course, that the initials OTMA stood for Olga, Tatiana, Marie and Anastasia but he also had the feeling that he had seen these letters before, in another context, and it frustrated him no end that he could not immediately recall the circumstances. He kept searching his memory and finally it came to him. He remembered that four of the red seals on St. Serafim's prophetic letter, written so many years ago, were imprinted with his daughters' initials. Nicholas did not believe in coincidence and he took this as further affirmation that the letter was authentic and, indeed, written in Serafim's own hand. The letter was back at the palace but Nicholas had read it so many times he knew it by heart. The information the Count had brought concerning the expanded plot substantiated the Saint's description of the great evil that would befall Russia, but other elements of the letter remained unexplained and he realized he might never know what everything meant. For instance why was the fifth seal blank? Who was the man in white? The fact that these questions remained unanswered did not trouble the Tsar. If the *Masquerade* was successful, every eventuality would be met with the appropriate response. He could see, however, that it was evolving into a plan with greater purpose and that ultimately, despite its complexity, it would simply be a battle between good and evil.

And in that sense the man in white was probably the key. Logically he would be the one to come forward and say what was to be done. He would have to give instructions to the children, tell them when to come out of hiding, how to claim their birthright and most importantly, identify the chosen one.

The Tsar's thoughts turned to the dream he had earlier. Bencken-dorff's arrival had broken the spell but then OTMA had forced him into this mental exercise and he was quite content to continue with it. How amusing, and fitting, if it was St. Serafim masquerading as the man on the train. The Tsar decided at that moment to have signet rings made up for his daughters. The seals in all four of the rings would be identical and would be used by the Grand Duchesses to access the individual accounts that had been established for them. But in addition, one ring would have to contain the code to which the stranger in the dream had referred. This ring would be used by the bearer to gain access to the funds secretly deposited for Russia in the Federal Reserve Bank. At some time in the future, when he gave the rings to the girls he would impress upon them the need for secrecy and would insist that they wear them on chains around their necks, but inside their garments. He would have Carl Faberge work out the details and produce the rings. Nicholas already had an idea of what he would like him to fabricate and he knew Faberge had the capability of converting a simple suggestion into a magnificent piece. The jeweler was also adept at fashioning hidden compartments and this talent would be severely tested by the Tsar's commission for the rings. Over the years Nicholas had entrusted many projects to the master artisan and he knew him to be a man of discretion, a man who could be trusted to keep a secret.

Nicholas was aware that Father Walsh would be coming to see him again so he promised himself that on his next trip home to Tsarskoe Selo he would have tissue samples prepared. He would send them along with documentation to Rome with Father Wash, when he returned.

Before retiring for the night the Tsar prepared a short telegram to his daughters.

OTMA! You may use the bathtub.

Love Papa.

ᏏᏄ

Maria Bariatinskaya and Father Walsh traveled separately from Rome to Switzerland in the early weeks of November. Arrangements had been made for the two to board a train that was sponsored by the International Committee of the Red Cross (ICRC) and bound for Warsaw. The ICRC was founded in the mid-1800s as a relief society to aid victims of war. Most countries respected the Red Cross and although war was raging across Europe, the trains displaying the committee's placard were able to run with little interference. The train arrived in the wee hours of the morning and Maria and Father Walsh disembarked wearing the uniforms of Red Cross personnel. As they climbed down from the car they were horrified to see hundreds of men lying on the platform, all injured and many dying from their wounds. Although the fighting was intense, Warsaw was still in the hands of the Russian Army and these men, for the most part, were Russian soldiers awaiting transportation back to Russia where they could receive further medical treatment. There were very few doctors and nurses at this location and the conditions were appalling. Father Walsh looked around in sadness at the carnage and although the sight of such suffering moved him, there was little he could do. His mission took precedence and he could not stop to minister to the wounded. All he could do was offer his blessing as he passed through them and made his way out of the station. Maria's eyes filled with tears and she covered her mouth with a handkerchief to stifle her sobbing. Father Walsh urged her to get control of herself as he did not want to draw attention to their arrival. A member of the Red Cross would not normally behave in such a manner. Maria Bariatinskaya was a strong woman but in her whole life she had never been exposed to such horrifying sights, sounds and smells and it took a few moments to gain control of her emotions.

Father Walsh arranged for their transportation to the Convent of Our Lady of Czestochowa and the two climbed into the car. He patted Maria's hand and she smiled wanly at him. "I apologize for my moment of weakness, Father. It was just so shocking and I did not expect it. I promise to stay in character in the future. I know how important this trip is."

"My child, do not be too hard on yourself. I too, found the situation very distressing but we must remain focused on our purpose in being here." Maria nodded her agreement and they rode the rest of the way in silence. Word had been sent ahead to the Mother Superior to expect their arrival and when they reached the convent, which was located in the heart of the city, they stepped down and rang the bell at the main entrance. They waited a few minutes but no one came to the gate so Maria tried again. It was quite early, but these large convents usually had a nun assigned as a porter so it was distressing to be left standing in the dark. The priest was becoming impatient so she tried again but still no one came. Finally, just as Father Walsh reached out to try the portal a small window in the door slid open and a nun peered through the opening. It was obvious she was quite agitated. "Yes, what is it," she said rather sharply.

"We are here to see the Mother Superior," Father Walsh answered.

"Do you have an appointment at this hour?" she asked in disbelief.

"No, but I believe . . . "

"Then, I am sorry. Mother is much too busy and unless you have an appointment you will be unable to see her. As you can see there is a war going on and she has many responsibilities."

Maria was about to speak but Father Walsh motioned her to remain silent.

"Mother is expecting us," the priest said sternly to the nun. "Please inform her that we are here."

"I am not aware that she is expecting anyone."

It seemed that even in a convent there was an established bureaucracy and this nun took her role as "keeper of the gate" quite seriously. Maria was amused as she watched Father Walsh try to break down the defenses of this aged nun and wondered if he would prevail. Finally, in exasperation, he raised his voice and said, "Sister it does not concern you. Please give Mother this card."

The little window slammed shut and Father Walsh and Maria waited. "I am concerned Father. I thought they were expecting us and that our welcome would be a little warmer."

"It will be fine Maria. The Mother Superior received word to expect us but due to the nature of our visit I am sure she did not inform the rest of the convent."

A few minutes later the nun returned and her attitude had changed completely. "I apologize for my obstinacy, Father. It is a confusing time and people act so differently when faced with adversity. It is a dangerous time and we must be so careful."

"Do not fret about it Sister. We quite understand," said Father Walsh.

The porter unlocked the gate and escorted the two travelers across the courtyard to the convent. She led them through a large wooden door into a foyer, down a hall and into the reception room, where she asked the two to have a seat at the table that stood in the middle of the room. A fire burned in the fireplace in one wall and a crucifix hung on the wall opposite, next to an icon of Our Lady of Czestochowa. In spite of its austerity the room was quite comfortable. The nun who had escorted them withdrew and quietly closed the door behind her. Father Walsh and Maria conversed in low voices discussing what they would say to the Mother Superior.

A few minutes later the door opened and the two stood up to greet Mother Superior. Sister Mary Joseph had been at the head of the community for many years and was admired by the locals and loved by her sisters. "Good morning," she said. I must apologize for the confusion at the gate. With the war going on we have had a few incidents which have necessitated having our gates locked at all times. I was not sure when you would arrive so our sister at the door did not know who you were. Again my apologies."

"Yes, I understand, Sister. Let me introduce myself. I am Father Edmund Walsh and as you know, from the message you received, I am a special emissary from Pope Benedict XV and am here at his bequest. This lady is Maria Bariatinskaya. She is a personal representative of the Tsar of Russia, Nicholas II." Mother acknowledged the introductions and suggested that perhaps they would like to rest for awhile and have breakfast before getting to the purpose of their visit. But the priest replied that they could rest later and nodded at Maria to explain the purpose of their long journey.

"Greetings Mother. We are here to ask for your help," said Maria. She reached into her bag and pulled out a formal portrait of the Grand Duchesses and passed it to the nun, who studied the photograph intently. "These are the Tsar's children and they are in grave danger. The Tsar has been advised that your convent is a haven of sorts and he understands that you have the ability to erase a woman's past and give her a new identity. This is what he seeks for two of his daughters."

"I am sorry you have come such a long way but I am not sure this is the right place for the Tsar's daughters to be hidden. All of our nuns are treated equally and have daily chores and work very hard. We have had women of noble birth but they have renounced their former lives," said Mother Joseph. "Since the war began our focus has changed somewhat and the women we help now are very active working with victims and refugees of the fighting. I am really sorry but I do not think that it is a good time nor is this the right place to be sending the Tsar's daughters. Besides the city may soon fall to the enemy and the danger to them would increase."

"Mother, I cannot reveal too much other then to alert you to the fact that it is not the Germans or Austrians who pose a threat to the children. No, the danger comes from another source and the anonymity you provide would shield them. And please consider this," argued Maria. "The Tsar's daughters are not pampered young women of leisure. His older girls are school trained nurses who have handled some of the most difficult cases."

Mother Joseph was not convinced. "Assuming I agreed to attempt this, when would the girls arrive?" she asked.

We are planning this move for sometime in the future. The Tsar would wait until the last possible moment, of course, but early in 1917 has been suggested."

"And what if the war is still ongoing?"

"All the more reason to obtain your cooperation now and plan for every eventuality"

The Mother Superior remained skeptical. "I do not understand your role in this, Father."

"The Pope is very involved in this plan," said Father Walsh. He reached into his jacket and pulled out a document with the Papal seal and handed it to Mother Joseph. She opened it and was surprised at what it contained. The Pope had explained the situation with the Grand Duchesses and requested, in the letter, that she take in the daughters of the Tsar and safeguard them. He assured her that he was fully involved but that few knew of the plan and he trusted her discretion in this matter. It was of the utmost importance that she use prudence and it would be left to her as to whom she would involve in this most important undertaking. The last sentence directed her "to do whatever is necessary to protect the Grand Duchesses." The letter was signed by Pope Benedict XV.

"Why didn't you show me this document immediately?" she asked. "I owe no spiritual allegiance to the Tsar but you know I could not refuse the Pope."

"Please do not be angry, Mother. It was my hope that by having you look at our request objectively that you might come up with an argument that we had overlooked, one that would force us to consider other options. But it seems, so far, we have provided plausible solutions to any potential problems."

"I will need to consider this carefully but I will do whatever I can to ensure the plan's success and I am at your disposal from this minute forward," said Mother Joseph.

"The first thing you must do is burn that letter," said Father Walsh. "There can be no trail left that might jeopardize these girls."

"Yes, I understand," said Mother Joseph. She rose from her seat and went over to the fireplace and threw the letter in. The fire flamed up and quickly burned the letter to ashes. "Now what do I need to do?"

"The Tsar is presently working on arrangements to remove his daughters from the country," said Maria. "He has not formulated an exact plan yet but you will be informed when the time draws near."

"I cannot personally offer help now in the transportation of the Tsar's children but I have a small group of men who were formerly members of the Polish Legion. They grew disillusioned with its policies and withdrew from the organization. These men have been loyal supporters for a number of years and have performed invaluable services for me. They have helped us get documents for some of the women who have come to us for aid so they can travel to other countries and I trust them completely. Would you like to meet the senior member of this group? He is here today assisting us in getting supplies. Of course, I will not give him any information without your approval."

"The Pope, as well as the Tsar, are placing their complete trust in you to carry out this mission," said Father Walsh. "If you feel he is trustworthy than so be it but I would not mention the Tsar's children at this point."

"Of course, but it is sometimes helpful to be able to attach a face to a name so I will let you meet him and we will go on from there," replied Mother. She left the room and returned a short while later with a man in his mid-thirties. Mother Joseph introduced Stanislaus Wojtyla, whom she had known since he was a child growing up in the same village.

Stanislaus reached out his hand to greet the two strangers. "It is a pleasure to meet you," he said. Maria and Father Walsh each acknowledged his greeting.

"Stanislaus, I wanted you to meet my guests. They are here on an assignment very dear to our Holy Father. In the future they will need our help, especially when our convent returns to the mission of helping young women."

"Certainly, Mother, you know I am available for whatever you need. Now if you will please excuse me I must return to my work. We have many supplies to unload today."

"Yes, of course, and thank you Stanislaus," said Mother Joseph. He departed the room and the three returned to their discussion. "Has the Tsar decided which of his children will be coming to Poland," she asked as she picked up their photograph and looked at it intently.

Maria walked over beside Mother and began pointing out the children by name. "It has not been decided which of the four will come to Poland but one of the older girls will be paired up with one of the younger ones. This is Olga, the eldest and she is nineteen." She went on to point out each child with her age.

"They certainly are beautiful children. How tragic they must be sent from their home. Now what about the young boy, the Tsarevich? You have not mentioned his name."

"Alexei is in ill health so his disposition has not been decided. There is a possibility that the Emperor would send him to Poland, as well, but for the time being, we, and now you, will concentrate on two of the girls. He has purchased a house in Zakopane which will be used as storage for furniture and household items for his children. It will be made available to you when it is safe for the children to leave the convent and assume their new identities," said Maria.

"I think the Tsar's daughters will have to remain in the convent for quite some time, especially if someone is searching for them. Certainly people will know they are missing."

"Mother, the Tsar has made arrangements so that will not happen. It is not something that concerns your part in this. More will be revealed when the time is right," explained Maria.

"When you return to your Tsar and the Pope please inform them that I am completely at their disposal. I will do whatever is necessary to protect these girls. They should be safe here. Even though we are at war, our convent has thus far remained unharmed and the enemy usually respects churches and the monasteries and convents."

"Mother, there is one more detail we need to discuss," Maria interjected. "I am a Catholic and that is why I was chosen to be an intermediary. I understand the differences between Catholicism and Orthodoxy and God willing I can, in some small way, bridge the chasm between the two faiths. You must understand that the Tsar is a deeply spiritual individual and devoted to his faith and he has passed this devotion on to his children. The Tsar is concerned, and understandably so, that once separated from the practice of their faith they might lose it. He is hopeful that in some way the girls will be able to remain faithful to their religious heritage and free to say their familiar prayers."

"Well, to change their identity might entail using Catholic means to conceal them, such as dressing like a nun or appearing to be overtly Catholic," said Mother Joseph. "But certainly no pressure will be placed on them to renounce their faith and in their private moments they could carry on as they wished. However, it could jeopardize their anonymity if they openly professed their Russian Orthodox faith."

"I can well understand the Tsar's concerns. No one will try to convert his children," said Father Walsh. "But the Tsar must realize that we will deny our faith to no one who is open to it and asks for instruction."

"I believe the Tsar will find that an acceptable risk," added Maria.

"Then to summarize what we have discussed, two of the Tsar's daughters will come to our convent and I am to erase their identities. If the situation changes or becomes more dangerous we may need to send them to another convent or one of our rest houses. I am to ensure their care until I hear word from the Vatican or am approached by an emissary from the Tsar," said Mother Joseph.

"That's it then, and as soon as we know the details of their arrival you will be informed. I will be your contact and you may reach me in Rome," said Maria as she handed Mother a card with all her information on it. I will be your go between with the Tsar. You are not to try and contact him personally. It is very important that you understand that."

"Yes, of course."

The two travelers had done what they could to prepare a safe haven for two of the Tsar's daughters. They bid the Mother Superior farewell and made their way out of the convent. Maria was heading back to Rome where she would await word from the Tsar or Tsarina as to what her next assignment was. Father Walsh would be busy for the next few weeks on a private mission for the Pope. He sent word to Count Benckendorff that he would meet with the Tsar at the Stavka after the first of the year. At that time he would discuss the arrangements made at the convent and examine possible ploys that might be used to move the two girls to Warsaw. He would then return to Rome to report to the Pope and wait until he was needed again.

೮₰

Doctor Botkin had not yet come to grips with the tragic news he had recently received. His beloved son had been killed in action and now, as he sat at his desk, head in hands, he wept quietly and unashamedly at his loss. His assistant hesitated to interrupt his superior in his grief but after a few minutes he brought in the Doctor's mail, hoping that it would provide a diversion. Botkin was thankful for the interruption and grateful to the young man for being so thoughtful. He needed some activity to take his mind off the death of his son. He sifted through the pile and his eye was caught by an official looking envelop with the Tsar's seal on it. He opened it and read a note of condolence from the Tsar on the loss of his son. He paused for a moment to consider the kind words of his monarch and then continued looking through his mail. The last envelop was plain and nondescript and he was surprised when recognized the Tsar's handwriting. There was no seal or any indication of where it came from. His curiosity aroused, he slit open the envelope and pulled out a note. It was short and to the point.

Stavka, 17 December 1914
Eugene,

I will be returning from the front to Tsarskoe Selo in a few days. I must speak with you on a very personal and confidential matter. Request your presence at the Alexander Palace in my personal quarters on the 22nd. When you visit please bring your surgical kit and several vials. I will explain all when I see you.
Nicholas

After reading the letter the doctor sat in his chair for a time, somewhat confused by the unusual directive and wondering at the implications of the Tsar's request. One thing was certain. This was to remain confidential, as was the case in so many of his dealings with the royal family. He put aside his personal grief and began to gather the instruments he would need for his bag.

Five days later the Doctor made the short trip to Tsarskoe Selo and the palace. He was still unsure as to why the Tsar had asked him to bring his medical kit so he had equipped himself with everything he thought he might need to meet his request. When he arrived at the palace he was escorted to the Tsar's study. Nicholas was anxiously awaiting his arrival and greeted him at the door. "Do come in Eugene," said the Tsar. "I know you must be curious as to why I requested your presence today."

"Your Highness, you are certainly correct in that observation. If I may ask, do you have a wound?"

"Please sit down so I can explain something to you. I will get right to the point as I have so little time before I must return to the Stavka and I must have time to heal. Eugene, I need you to remove the ends of two of my toes," said Nicholas. "Just the fleshy part, not the bone."

"I do not understand. You wish me to cut off pieces of your toes?"

"I can only tell you this for now. In the future, my children will be in grave danger. In order for them to have a future, I must do this," said the Tsar.

"Certainly that cannot be so."

"It is the truth. I must preserve a part of me, so that in the future my lineage can be proven."

"How can that be possible?"

Nicholas quickly explained. "I believe that in the future scientists will somehow be able to use blood and tissue to identify my descendants. I am not asking that you accept this notion but you are a man of science and you must know such things are possible. It does not matter if you believe me to be correct, it only matters that I believe. At any rate you must take these samples now. That is why I asked you to bring the vials and your kit. I will tell you more about all of this later when we have more time but for now we must carry on with this."

"Do you want me to do this here, in this room?'

"No, I thought we could set up in my bathroom. It is large enough and we will have water available."

"Are you absolutely certain about this?"

"It must be done," said the Tsar.

"I am very troubled by all of this, Nicholas, but my family has served yours for two generations. I will do what you ask of me."

"Then let us go and get this over with."

The two men walked down to the Tsar's bathroom. Nicholas had made arrangements so they would not be disturbed. He had explained to Alix what would take place today and she had been distraught and insisted on being present so she could comfort him. Nicky knew it was better if she was not there so he placated her by offering to let her change his bandages. He knew she could be overly dramatic about things and he just wanted to get this over with, quickly, and without any fanfare. She had reluctantly agreed to his request and he was relieved she would not be present.

Doctor Botkin set up an area in the bathroom to perform this unlikely procedure on the Tsar. The bathroom was a large room which not only had a huge tub the size of a small swimming pool but also held chairs and a small end table. Nicholas sat down in a chair and propped his leg up on the table which Doctor Botkin had covered with layers of surgical linen. Botkin opened his bag and removed several instruments. This would be a relatively simple procedure but although he had performed many surgeries he was surprised to find himself nervous. Not wanting to alarm his patient and make him feel uncomfortable, the doctor took a deep breath to calm himself. Nicholas was completely oblivious to him. He had pushed the chair far enough back from the table that he was able to stretch out and rest his head on the back of the chair. Before she departed Alix had given her husband an icon of Saint Nicholas and he held it in his hand and methodically rubbed it with his thumb.

"Nicholas, I am ready to begin but first I want to be certain that I am doing exactly what you want."

The Tsar raised his head up and looked at the doctor while lifting up his foot. He pointed at his toes and said, "I want you to remove a piece of my toe, the pad of skin underneath the tip. Use the toe next to my big toe and the one after that. Then I need you to collect six small vials of blood."

"Yes, that should be relatively easy to accomplish. I want to put your mind at ease. You will feel some pain during the procedure and you will probably limp for a few days but it will not affect your stride after it heals."

"That is good news. I had not thought about a limp. I will explain it as a bunion, if any one inquires."

"Very well then. I will begin now." Nicholas laid his head back and attempted to put himself in a relaxed state. Doctor Botkin knew that the Tsar was not interested in a step-by-step explanation of the procedure, so he planned to get through it as quickly as possible. He took a small needle and drew out a substance from a vial. He washed the toes with an antiseptic solution and then held the foot tightly with one hand. He inserted the needle into his toe and injected it with a numbing substance. The Tsar clenched the icon tightly in his hand as he felt the pain from the needle. He wanted to cry out, but he knew he could not. Doctor Botkin said nothing and continued in a professional manner to numb the second toe. For a moment Nicholas felt as if his foot was on fire but within a few minutes the pain faded and the Tsar breathed a sigh of relief.

"That is the worst of it," said the Doctor. "You should only feel a little pressure on your toe but no pain." He then proceeded to cut the tip of the toe with a scalpel. The blood trickled out and he collected a small amount in four of the six open vials sitting on the table. The vials contained a chemical that would preserve the blood indefinitely. He then continued with the removal of the tissue. He sutured up the wound and did the same procedure with the next toe. The tissue samples were placed in the remaining two vials. Less than an hour had passed and the whole ordeal was over. Botkin bandaged the foot, carefully put his boot back on, lacing it very loosely, and then helped the Tsar up. "When the anesthesia wears off I have some pills for you to take for the pain. Have the Empress change the bandages daily and then you must tend to it when you get back to headquarters," he continued. "You should be healed in about two weeks, but try to stay off your feet for a bit."

"That was not as painful as I thought it would be," said Nicholas. Botkin, still totally confused by what had just occurred, saw himself out and Nicholas slowly walked across the hallway to his bedroom. The Tsar walked into the room with a slight limp and Alix, who was waiting anxiously for him cried out, "oh Nicky, how are you, my darling? Here let me help you to bed."

"Sunny, I am fine and have no pain at all. And as you well know there are soldiers lying in our hospitals that have had far worse done to them. Really it is nothing. You must not fuss over me so. I will take a little rest then I have a meeting with Benckendorff," said the Tsar.

"You cannot meet with anyone today," said Alix. "You must rest and take it easy for several days."

"No, I am only here for a few more weeks and then I must return to the Stavka," explained Nicholas. "We cannot let anyone know about this and if I change my routine it will raise questions. We must carry on with our usual schedule."

"You are right, of course, my love, but I cannot help but worry about you."

"Doctor Botkin instructed me to have you change my bandages once a day and he gave me medicine for pain. You should probably replace the dressings at night after the children have gone to sleep"

"Very well. I understand."

Later that day Nicholas met with Count Benckendorff and his cousin George. He was feeling some discomfort but he ignored the pain killers so he could keep a clear head. The Count informed him that he had arranged for Carl Faberge to come to the palace the next day for a meeting with the Tsar. Nicholas was pleased because he had completed the design for the seals which would be incorporated into the rings Faberge was to create. Not many people realized Nicholas was an accomplished artist and had designed many pieces of jewelry for himself, Alix, and his mother. He even kept a detailed inventory of all his jewelry, which contained sketches of each piece.

The Tsar then gave the Grand Duke and the Count instructions for completing the documents which were to be sent to the Vatican and to America. Both sets of papers would include the imprint from the signet rings which he was having made and a specially designed case containing one of the tissue samples and two vials of blood. The documents going to the United States would contain, in addition, a sealed envelope with a facsimile of the code etched in one of the rings. All the information necessary to legitimize the Imperial children's accounts and generate their identification numbers would be included. Nicholas was confident that everything could be completed quickly so that when Father Walsh paid his visit to the Stavka, Nicholas could give him the complete package. Also George was making a final trip to Japan in March and had arranged a rendezvous with Charles Crane. He would pass on the package destined for the United States during his mission to Japan. Nicholas spent more than two hours with the two men going over, in minute detail, every piece of paper and examining them for any mistakes. Nicholas was pleased with what they had been able to accomplish and with the work complete he bid his two friends good day and returned to his room for a pain killer, as his foot was beginning to throb.

Because time was of the essence he knew he would have to pressure Faberge to drop everything and focus on completing at least one of the rings. That was all the Tsar needed for the present. He planned to show him his preliminary sketches at tomorrow's meeting. Nicholas envisioned a large flat ruby or sapphire, surrounded by diamonds, and placed in a platinum setting. Somehow the seal would be revealed but he wanted there to be some sort of ingenious method of opening it that would be obvious only to the owner. He liked the idea of pressing one or two of the diamonds in sequence to open the rings. Nicholas was sure that once he presented his ideas to the jeweler he would be able to resolve the technical issues. After all, his Easter eggs were artistic and technological works of art and Nicholas hoped he would be able to resolve any problems with the design.

Chapter 31

January 1915 - Tsarskoe Selo. The beginning of the New Year was a difficult time for Alix, both mentally and physically. She had thrown herself head long into hospital work and, in addition, took frequent trips all over the country to tour facilities and visit wounded soldiers. These activities had taken a toll on her and she was exhausted and needed rest. Unfortunately, she would have no time to recuperate because on the second day of the new year, her friend Anya Vyrubova, en route to visit her parents in Petrograd, was involved in a horrible train accident and was gravely injured. The locomotive pulling the train had derailed and as the cars jumped the track they piled up like an accordion. When the rail cars collapsed, one after another, the injured were trapped in the mangled wreckage. Anya sustained a severe blow to the head, two broken legs, and a spinal injury, as well. She and the other victims of the accident were taken by special train back to the station at Tsarskoe Selo. Nicholas, who had not yet returned to the front, along with Alix and the four Grand Duchesses, met the relief train at the platform and greeted Anya when she was taken off in a stretcher. The initial diagnosis indicated her condition was very serious and the prognosis for her survival was not good at all. She kept drifting in and out of consciousness.

When Anya was transported to the hospital and made as comfortable as possible the Empress sent for Rasputin and he arrived on the next train from Petrograd. He was taken directly to the room where the young woman laid, in a state of semi-consciousness, her medical condition such that nothing more could be done for her. All visitors were ordered from the room except for the Imperial family. Grigory lifted her hand and Anya opened her eyes. The monk peered down at her and then turned and left the room. Alix followed him into the hallway. "Father Grigory, what will happen to her?"

"Dear Matushka, if she is not from God, and is not good for you, she will not live. But if she lives, know that God has sent her to you as an ally and friend. Respect her words and treat her as one of your family and as one sent to you from Our Lord," answered Rasputin.

The monk was worried about the situation because he could not control the outcome. He desperately wanted this confidante of the Tsarina to survive her injuries, not because of any affection he might have for her but because she was his conduit to the goings-on at Alexander Place and his primary source of information. It was through her that he could determine what the Empress wanted and it was through her that he was able to tailor his advice to reflect Alexandra's wishes. Without Anya his role as Alix's secret advisor would begin to suffer.

Alix was surprised that Rasputin had made no effort to pray over her or to attempt to cure her injuries. For a moment she wondered if there was any truth to the stories she had heard, that when confronted with real physical injuries Grigory had no power to heal. But she had only to think of her son Alexei to wipe away any doubts she might have entertained. The Empress said good-bye to Rasputin and went in to sit with her friend. Nicholas took his distraught children back to the palace where they entered the chapel and prayed for Anya's recovery.

As Alix sat at the bedside she considered what Grigory had said about treating Anya like a family member and as one sent from the Lord. Of late her friendship with Anya had entered a worrisome phase and was on shaky ground. Alix was understandably irritated that her friend flirted with Nicky, the more so because he seemed to enjoy it and encouraged Alix to include this vivacious young woman in their private time. The Empress was also jealous of the access Anya had to the strange individual whom she considered her private holy man and she chafed at the restrictions the Tsar had placed on his visits to the palace. It was a frustrating situation and but for Rasputin's insistence that Anya was to be treated as one of the family Alix was sure their friendship would be strained to the breaking point. The Tsarina was tired and distraught and certainly did not need the added stress that this unusual friendship was causing her. But as she looked down at the broken body of her friend and imagined the pain she was suffering Alix began to weep. How could she be so selfish? She would banish these destructive thoughts and concentrate on the daunting task of making her friend well. Whether Anya would live or die only time would tell. Alix vowed to stay by her side in the hospital until her fate was decided. Outwardly, she would exhibit all the signs of a good friend and, if possible, nurse her back to health but she knew it would be much harder to resolve her inner feelings and accept Father Grigory's guidance to her.

For the next three days, Alix stayed by Anya's side, supervising her care. She rarely left her but every time she departed, even if only for a few moments Anya, upon her return, pouted at being left alone. The Empress was annoyed but held her tongue and at the end of the third day, when the doctors informed her that Anya would definitely recover, she finally ceased her vigil. After that she visited once a day and devoted the rest of her time at the hospital to the wounded soldiers. Anya, of course, complained that Alix had abandoned her but the Empress refused to change her schedule. Alix felt sympathy for her friend but she conveniently ignored the fact that in the past Anya had always been at her side when she, herself, was ill. It was not a situation she was very comfortable with.

The weeks slipped by and gradually Anya recovered, but she would remain crippled by her injuries. She was finally able to move back to her little house and life began to return to normal, if anything could be called normal in that chaotic time. The Grand Duchesses continued to be busy with their committees and hospital work. Alix worked as much as she could but she often had bad days and she had to take to her bed. But even when she was ill she still sewed or knitted for the soldiers.

❦

The trip across Siberia was a long and tiring one and it was late March before George arrived in Vladivostok to prepare for his visit to Japan. A few weeks earlier the Grand Duke had sent Count Tatishchev on ahead with instructions to arrange for the trans-shipment of the crates of furniture and household items that were stored in a warehouse near the docks. Prince Kanin had suggested Nagasaki as the port of entry since much of Japan's international commerce passed through that bustling seaport and a Russian vessel unloading there would not be out of the ordinary.

When George arrived in Russia's far eastern port he was met at the station by Tatishchev, who greeted him warmly and filled him in on everything he had been able to accomplish. The Count then escorted the Grand Duke to the ship in which he had chartered space for the shipment, as well as passage for himself and George. The winter had been relatively mild and George was relieved to see that the ice had already broken up and the waterfront was a beehive of activity.

"When do you think we will be ready to sail?" George inquired.

"Sir, I talked to the Captain earlier and he informed me that the loading is just about complete. We can sail on the morning tide if you so desire."

"Excellent, Ilia. You have done your usual splendid work. Now I must get a telegram off to Prince Kanin informing him we are on the way."

The next morning, just after dawn, the Captain took in its mooring lines and headed the ship down the channel to the open sea. George had been awakened by all the activity of getting a vessel underway but rather than get up and go on deck he lay in his bunk, enjoying the gentle roll of the ship as it began to react to the ocean swells. It had been a restless night and it was very late before he finally fell asleep. George had been entrusted with an extremely important mission by the Tsar and he had spent much of the night considering, then reconsidering what he was about. His task was to finalize all the arrangements made for the Tsar's daughters and actually see for himself what had been prepared. Then he was to meet with Charles Crane, who had already sailed for Japan, and turn over to him the documents and vials that he, Benckendorff and the Tsar had prepared for safekeeping in the United States. The Grand Duke sometimes found his part in the *Masquerade* to be a little intimidating, but he could not shirk the responsibility, even when it seemed so overwhelming.

When the ship arrived in Nagasaki, after a short voyage, George was met by Prince Kanin who whisked him away for a tour of the secluded estate he had selected for the children. Tatishchev remained behind to arrange for the unloading and transportation of the furniture to the estate. The home Prince Kanin had selected was outside of the city and a little bit of a drive so the two men used the time to discuss the details of George's visit. After a quarter of an hour they arrived before a large walled compound. Due to the height of the wall all that could be seen was the tip of a roof peeking out. A retainer opened the barred gate and the Prince led George into a paved courtyard that was partially surrounded by substantial stone buildings in the typical Japanese style. George was very impressed. The high wall afforded complete privacy once inside the gate and he was pleased to see a beautifully landscaped garden with a stream flowing through it.

"Your Highness, this exceeds my most optimistic expectations. The Emperor has been most generous. This will be a perfect home for the Tsar's children once it is safe for them to come out of hiding."

"It was what the Emperor desired," replied the Prince. "The other part of your request, however, is more difficult to satisfy. When we initially began to plan for the extended stay of the children I envisioned moving them immediately into this estate, as soon as they arrived. I did not realize that the Tsar would want to hide them in a convent for a period of time."

"Have you had any success locating one that meets our needs?" George asked.

"As I am sure you are aware there is not a large Christian presence in Japan but I believe I have found what you are looking for in Yokohama. There is a small orphanage and an order of western nuns who care for the children. The Mother Superior will accept the girls, although I did not make their identity known. I will leave that up to you," said Prince Kanin.

"It sounds like what we are looking for."

"Very well then, I will arrange for a visit before you depart Japan. It is quite some distance from here but it is quiet and would be a good place to hide the children. But George there is something else I need to discuss with you. I feel very strongly that I should meet the Tsar's children, the ones who are going to live here in Japan."

"That would be Grand Duchess Tatiana and Grand Duchess Anastasia. The Tsar has still not decided where he will be sending Alexei."

"I think it is important that they recognize me and are comfortable around me since I will be overseeing their affairs. With their parents gone and no contact with their other relatives they will feel totally abandoned. I think it is essential that we meet and have a chance to spend some time together."

"I certainly agree with you that a familiar face would be very helpful when the time arrives to spirit the girls away and I am sure the Tsar will have no objections to your spending some time with them. However, because of the course of the war it will be next to impossible for the girls to come to Japan for a visit. Even though you are our ally in this conflict It would be too difficult to arrange their travel and would surely raise questions, questions that we are not prepared to answer. As I see it, the only time Tatiana and Marie will leave the palace for an extended time is when they, in fact, are being escorted to their hide-away in Yokohoma. We will use the escape route only once and then dissolve it to eliminate any traces. So we will have to arrange for you to visit Tsarskoe Selo under some pretext or other."

"You are right, of course," replied the Prince. "Do you know when the Tsar plans to send the children out of the country?"

"I believe it will be in April 1917 or thereabouts. He does not plan to tell the girls until sometime in 1916."

"Very well then. We have plenty of time to make the necessary arrangements. But I will wait until I hear from you that the children have been informed before making the trip. In the meantime I will make tentative plans to travel to Petrograd in September of next year on some type of official business. I can meet the children at that time."

"Excellent," said George. "I will inform the Tsar so we can prepare for your arrival. I must say, it is a good idea. My heart goes out to his children, as they will have so much heartache to endure in their lifetimes. I am glad, that for now, they are having a reasonably pleasant childhood, but unfortunately that will soon change. As you say, a familiar face in a foreign land will be very welcome to the Grand Duchesses."

George and Prince Kanin continued touring the estate and the Grand Duke was pleased with everything he saw. Tatishchev arrived and they discussed the disposition of all the items from the ship. It was determined that the furniture should remain in the shipping crates until the Grand Duchesses needed it, so as to protect it from any damage. Once the inspection of the estate was completed Prince Kanin arranged to meet George later in the week at which time he was to bring the Grand Duke to the convent in Yokohama. The Prince took his leave and George and Tatishchev departed for their lodgings.

The next day, around noon, George left for his meeting with Charles Crane, while Tatishchev continued supervising the transfer of the crates of furniture to the estate they had toured yesterday. The Grand Duke walked briskly through the throngs of people to the restaurant where the meeting was to take place. He had reserved a private room, so the two men, who were now on a first name basis, could converse freely. Since Crane's first meeting in America, years earlier, with George's brother Sandro, Charles had been to Russia on a number of occasions, but this trip to Japan was for a special purpose and today's meeting was to be the last one for a while. When George arrived at the restaurant, Charles was waiting for him in the private room. The two greeted one another and quickly got down to business.

The documents that George carried in his briefcase reflected the results of endless hours of discussion and planning. They established procedures for the children to gain access to the funds which were held for them in the United States. In order to do this, they would have to verify their identity utilizing special identification numbers assigned to them by the bankers, know their passwords and account numbers and produce their seals. In addition there was a special set of instructions describing the method that would allow one child or her descendent to gain access to the vast deposit in the Federal Reserve, a deposit which represented the bulk of Russia's wealth. These documents would be given to Crane who in turn would hand carry them to Frank Vanderlip at National City Bank where they were to be stored in the bank vault. In addition to the documents, George carried a special box no larger than his hand which contained three vials, two of which held a sample of the Tsar's blood and the other a tissue sample. This box, with a note from the Tsar, would be given to President Wilson to be held in a special vault in the White House that only the President had access to. This vault contained top secret communications that a president's successor would need in event the incumbent was incapacitated or died in office unexpectedly.

Once their work was finished, and in spite of the early hour, they shared a bottle of sake and toasted their two leaders. They also drank to the successful completion of their mission. It had been many years in the making but now they could call the financial aspects of the plan complete.

A few days later, George again met Prince Kanin and they boarded a ship bound for Yokohama. It was a short voyage but the sea air was refreshing and George was grateful for the chance to catch his breath, as it were. Everything had fallen so effortlessly into place that he wondered if some important detail could have been missed, but he had such total confidence in Prince Kanin that it was easy to brush any doubts aside. He was extremely grateful to Kanin for his expertise in arranging every detail. It was easy to see why the Emperor placed such trust in the Prince. George had anticipated being in Japan for many weeks working on all the arrangements but with Kanin's intervention everything was quickly completed and he would soon be able to return home to Russia. He knew the Tsar would be pleased with the results of his trip.

When they arrived in Yokohama they immediately went to the convent, where they were welcomed by Mother Superior. George and Prince Kanin quietly discussed their requirements with her. Having already been briefed by Prince Kanin, she quickly agreed to their requests. There was really no chance she would refuse since the continued existence of this tenuous bastion of Catholicism depended on the good will of the Emperor. What she was being asked to do was unusual but not unreasonable and so she assured the two gentlemen that the convent would be prepared to receive the children sometime early in 1917. George expressed concern about the language barrier but Mother Superior assured him it would not be an issue. Many of her nuns were from other countries and had not spoken Japanese when they first arrived, but learned in time. There would be sisters in the convent who could converse with them while the Grand Duchesses learned the language.

After the meeting with the Mother Superior was completed, George spent a few more days in Japan with Prince Kanin finalizing the details of the plan to move two Russian Orthodox Grand Duchesses across the breadth of Russia, into an obscure convent of Catholic nuns in the middle of a Buddhist country. It was mentally exhausting yet extremely interesting work and when he was finally en route to Russia he was able to relax knowing that the planning was thorough and complete. When George eventually arrived in Petrograd, after a long and tiring trip, he was disappointed to learn that the Tsar was at the Stavka. He knew, however, that Nicholas would be anxious to hear his report so he continued on to headquarters, arriving in time for lunch. After the meal, in the solitude of his private car, Nicholas received his cousin's report and, as expected, was very pleased.

CR&O

It was the beginning of April and at the Stavka the weather was finally beginning to warm up a bit. The Tsar hoped the changing seasons would relieve the discomfort of his troops who had suffered through another harsh winter. He felt somewhat guilty that he was able to sit in the relative warmth of his private car while his men suffered malnutrition, frostbite and all the other maladies associated with a poorly equipped and meagerly supplied army. He put those thoughts away, however, and stared pensively at three letters that lay open on his desk. They were a mixed lot but each was important in its own way. The first was a report from the front providing him an update on Maria Bochkareva, the woman who had requested his permission to join the army when the war first began. It appeared that In the course of a fierce battle in the trenches at Polotsk she had acted with incredible bravery. Under her own initiative, and without orders, Maria crawled through the wire in front of the enemy positions and began to systematically evacuate the Russian wounded from that deadly space between the lines. She was very strong and managed to carry or drag a number of men to safety before being herself wounded in the leg. She was presently recuperating in a hospital in Kiev. Of the two hundred fifty soldiers in her unit only forty eight survived the engagement unscathed. Maria had become a heroine and a respected comrade to the men of her unit and it seemed that Nicholas had made the right decision in allowing her to serve.

The second letter was from Alix, and Nicholas now reread it with suppressed amusement. In it she rambled on and on about a legion of women who had supposedly set up a training camp outside of Kiev. *"What are these women about?"* she wrote. *"Why are they organizing and who gave them permission to do so? I have heard terrible rumors about these women. They are not training to be nurses and it has even been mentioned they want to go to war and, even more horrifying, they are wearing trousers."* Her letter went on and on in this vein. *"I just do not think they should serve as anything other than nurses. I know other countries have tried to introduce these liberal ideas but our Russian women are less educated and have no discipline. I cannot imagine how they will manage and I wonder who allowed them to form themselves into a military unit."* Alix was very insistent that women should serve the country only in traditional roles.

Nicholas did not have the heart to tell his wife that he had known of the existence of the female unit in training at Kiev for some time and had been intrigued by the possibilities this experiment offered. His sister Olga, who was working in a hospital in Kiev, had given him a thorough report on their progress. This information, coupled with the report on Maria Bochkareva, offered him a way out of the dilemma posed in the third letter.

This communication was a coded message from Ella who sent word describing complications with the double for Maria. It seemed the girl wished to take vows and enter Ella's convent. The problem was that she was the only double for Maria and if they allowed her to become a nun they would have no one to take Maria's place. It was a very complex situation but Ella felt they should not stand in the girl's way if she truly had a vocation. So the Grand Duchess was referring the whole matter to Nicholas for a final decision, well aware that time was running out.

It was quite a blow to their plan because they were so far into the *Masquerade* that it would be very difficult to train a replacement. Yet the options were clear. The Tsar could insist the girl continue, or he could find another Maria. He rummaged through the papers on his desk until he found Olga's letter describing the women's brigade. He read it again and then looked at the account of Maria's heroism. He immediately made his decision. He would send George and Sandro to inspect the unit and see if they could find anyone who resembled Maria. It was a long shot but worth the effort. This girl, if she existed, would be behind in her education but he felt her other skills would make up for her deficiencies. A trained soldier, someone with the strength of his own daughter, would certainly be an asset to the group and in the event that no one could be found he would have Maria's current double put off taking vows until later.

Nicholas prepared a telegram to Ella in which he explained his course of action and assured her that the minute he knew something he would be in touch. He then summoned George and Sandro to the Stavka to inform them of their latest assignment and discuss the manner in which they were to carry it out. To ensure the security of the *Masquerade* Nicholas preferred to explain additions or changes to the plan face to face with the principals. However, with the war going on it was sometimes difficult to schedule meetings and arrange for the persons involved to come in from another town or even from the front. But George and Sandro were both military men and their arrival a few days later, in uniform, aroused no suspicion. After pleasantries had been exchanged the Tsar immediately got to the purpose of the meeting. "I have a mission for you both. Sandro, I know you are aware, as is your brother, that a number of impostors have been located and will take my daughters' places in the palace at the appropriate time. We have two for each child except Maria and Alexei and even as we speak they are being educated and prepared for their mission. Unfortunately a complication has developed with Maria's look-alike and we have to come up with a replacement. That is why I have called you here. You two, my dear cousins, have accomplished everything I have asked of you and I am most grateful. I hesitate to lay another burden on you but if you agree I want you to become the search team for the new girl, one who looks like Maria, if possible, and is about the same age."

"Nicholas you know you can call on us, but how are we going to find this girl?" asked George.

"Be patient, my kinsmen, and all will become clear. When the war started I received a petition from a woman wanting to join the Russian Imperial Army. She had attempted to enlist several times, but was refused," said Nicholas.

"Surely you are joking," interrupted Sandro. "A woman in the army, how utterly preposterous."

The Tsar smiled at Sandro's outburst. "That was my initial reaction as well, but after considering her request I responded to her petition and allowed her to join the Army, with certain conditions, of course."

"What," said George. "Are you serious? What possible benefit could a woman provide the army?"

"Actually the reports are very good and she has done surprisingly well. She has been wounded in action and has performed an act of heroism for which she will surely be decorated. The others who were later accepted into the army have also done well," said Nicholas. "But I did not call you here to debate the merits of women in the military. I have been informed that a group of women have set up a training camp outside of Kiev. It seems they have aspirations to become soldiers and have been preparing as a unit for some time now. They are organized as a battalion and have officers. From what I gather, the commander has retained a veteran drill master to direct their training and he is very demanding. He does not tolerate displays of weakness and refuses to let the recruits take advantage of their supposed frailty. Their training is nearly complete and I anticipate they will petition to go on active duty as a unit. I will have to work that out with Nikolasha when the time comes. He is sure to offer objections."

"But how does this relate to Ella and the look-alikes?" inquired George.

"Cousin, open your eyes. Here we have a whole battalion of women gathered in one place. That should make your task easier and avoid the necessity of a lengthy search. Certainly there should be at least one candidate among so many recruits. The reports I have seen indicate some of these women are as strong as men, if not more so. If we could find one that looks enough like Maria she could be brought in as an impostor. Her formal education at Ella's would begin immediately and her military training would allow her to act in the role of a bodyguard if the need arose."

"I must say, that is a brilliant idea," said Sandro. "It offers so many possibilities."

"I am glad you approve," said Nicky with a touch of sarcasm in his voice. "I want you and George to go to Kiev, inspect this camp and see if one of the women could pass as my daughter. I will prepare orders so that if you find someone, you can direct the commandant to release her to you for a special mission. Your visit will be an official one and to give it plausibility there should be a formation and the presentation of some awards. You can handle those details but there should be enough ceremony to encourage the women in their training and cover the real reason for your tour of the camp."

"Yes, we could conduct an inspection of the entire battalion and present training medals or something appropriate. It will give us a perfect opportunity to examine the women closely without causing undo attention. We can then close with a formal parade." said Sandro.

"Excellent. I will alert those concerned that you are coming as my personal representatives to examine the progress of this training battalion. If God smiles on us and you do find a suitable candidate she will surely volunteer but before you take her on to Moscow and Ella's school she will have to be told the same story that the other children were and she must come of her own free will. For this to be a success we must constantly think through every action we take lest the *Masquerade* be jeopardized," said the Tsar. "I trust you both and will leave this to you but do plan on arriving at least a day before the formal activities so you can put your ears to the ground as it were. Now let us coordinate our calendars so we do not interfere with your other military duties. Remember though that time is of the essence and we must start the girl's education as soon as possible. We have a little over a year to turn her into a Grand Duchess."

After George and Sandro compared their schedules, George spoke up. "We should be able to make the trip down to Kiev in a week, two at the latest."

"I need an exact date to schedule the formation. This cannot be a surprise visit."

The two brothers looked at the calendar and agreed on the 20th of April.

"I want to be informed as soon as you have completed this task. God willing, this will work," said the Tsar

About a week later George and Sandro met in Petrograd to begin the trip to Kiev. Sandro made all the travel arrangements for the two of them. Their private car was coupled to a supply train heading towards Kiev and they had hopes it would not be diverted since military traffic had priority on the rails. Both had been very busy working on their divided responsibilities and they would now use the time on the train to coordinate their efforts. The plan was to present each recruit with the Medal for Zeal, fourth class. It was an honor given to those who served Russia in times of war or peace and there were no restrictions on presenting the medal to women. George was in charge of the awards and had verified arrangements with the commandant of the camp for their visit and inspection of the battalion. As they settled in for the long journey they discussed what they hoped to find. "Personally I think this trip is a waste of our time," said Sandro. "It took Ella almost a year to find all the doubles and even then she was only able to find one for Marie. I believe the odds are truly stacked against us."

"Sandro, Sandro, you are so negative," admonished George.

"Not negative George, just practical."

"I, for one, think it is worth a shot. We may be lucky and find the perfect woman. It is better to at least try than to do nothing. At this point we have run out of options and the Tsar's plan has merit."

"That is why I am here. It is not like I had something better to offer."

After a long journey they finally arrived in Kiev where they were met by a driver from one of the Imperial Palaces. After settling in, the two brothers discussed their plan for the next day when they would travel twenty miles south of Kiev to inspect the Women Legion's training camp. "Our visit should go smoothly," George observed. "The commandant of the camp, Oksana Chekovna will have her troops prepared for inspection and will be in formation when we arrive. I think we should conduct the inspection as soon as we reach the parade ground. When we are finished we can announce that we are pleased with their progress, so much so that the Tsar himself has authorized us to present medals to each and everyone. This will allow us a second walk-through to look at their faces one more time. Passing through the ranks twice will take a while but if anyone meets our requirement we can have them pulled out of formation to interview separately. I already wired the commandant that we were interested in talking to a few of the women so we could accurately report back to the Tsar, and she evidently did not seem to think that this was an unusual request. If we find our Maria in the ranks, she can serve as our guide around the camp and that will give us more opportunity to speak with her."

"You know there are protocols we must follow. The camp commandant and her entourage will be glued to us," said Sandro.

"That is true but I still believe we will be able to get a sense of her bearing and whether she will suit us or not. Now let us study the pictures of the Grand Duchess again to sharpen our ability to pick someone out. I have not seen Maria for a while and I had quite forgotten how pretty she is. This will make it even more difficult."

"Quite right, brother," said Sandro. "You know I am really looking forward to this. I cannot imagine what we will see. I will have to try and control my amusement. Women soldiers. What next?"

"This is no laughing matter," said George.

"George you are becoming so stodgy in your old age. I am as aware as you that this is serious business and we must be careful how we conduct ourselves. We do not want to appear to be looking for someone so this must be a real inspection and not just a walk by. I suggest we move down the ranks side by side inspecting each woman in front of us. If we see someone we can use they can be pulled from the ranks later, during the medal presentation. Our military bearing and appearance must be superior to those in the ranks. I just hope my back will remain ramrod stiff for several hours."

"Have we covered everything?"

"Everything except the most important item. How will we get this look-alike out of the camp?"

"I really do not see that as a problem. I think we must visit the camp and see if we can find our girl. If we are successful we will use the Tsar's order to overcome any obstacles. Anyway these are dedicated Russian women and I would wager my best mare that every last one would volunteer for a special mission. We need only pick the one we want, collect her duffel, and have her depart the camp with us. Let us not make this overly difficult."

Early the next morning they drove out to the camp. As their car drew up to the large stockade fence which surrounded the compound, they became aware of a sentry on duty dressed in an army uniform with no insignia of any kind. "I wonder how they coerced a man into standing guard duty for a group of women training to be soldiers," said Sandro. He had to admit to himself that he did not approve of women as soldiers. His own experience in a military unit had shown him how harsh the life could be and he wondered how a pretty little woman with her hair all done up could ever be a real Russian soldier.

The soldier on guard duty snapped to attention, rendered a sharp salute, and then opened the two gates to allow the car to pull forward into the camp. Upon stepping down Sandro and George paused and glanced out at the small parade field. Their jaws nearly dropped as they looked at the soldiers standing at attention awaiting their inspection. They stood proudly in their freshly starched and ironed uniforms with highly polished boots and not one looked anything like a woman. The Grand Dukes could not believe what they were seeing.

"Lord," muttered George. "I never expected them to look like men. Their heads are as bald as a billiard ball and they are wearing pants. Aside from their small frames, I cannot tell they are women. I did not anticipate this."

"I agree with you George, I never expected this either. I thought we would see women in skirts with their hair pulled up, playing at being soldiers. How strange they look. Just like men," said Sandro.

After a moment they recovered from their surprise and walked over to greet the Commandant as she marched towards them with her aide. She was wearing a man's army uniform with insignia indicating the rank of colonel. She introduced herself as Colonel Oksana Chekovna and seeing the look on the faces of the two Grand Dukes was quick to explain. "I wear this rank to instill discipline and respect in my soldiers for the chain-of-command. When the war began I disguised myself as a man and fought in many battles but presently I was wounded and lost sight in my right eye. It was at that time, during my hospital stay, that my superiors discovered my secret. Although I am not able to return to combat I am more than capable of training these women. I might add that I have received medals for valor."

"Thank-you for your loyal service to our country," said George as he shook her hand.

Sandro shook her hand and said, "Madam."

"Your Imperial Highness, my title is Colonel and I ask that you address me by that rank. These women are patriots and have gone through much to achieve what you are here to see. It would not be helpful to slight me in front of them, so I ask this small favor of you. Now, shall we begin the inspection." The Colonel turned and marched off to call her battalion to attention.

Sandro, who was not in favor of this scheme to begin with, was taken aback by her abrupt, no nonsense attitude and stood rooted to the ground. As he was about to respond to her George grabbed his sleeve and whispered "do not even think about it, Sandro. This mission is too important to let her manner get to you. Please pull it together." George knew his brother well and was afraid his famous temper would ruin everything. Thankfully Sandro got control of himself, smiled, and said to his brother, "I had better do what the Colonel says. She looks as if she could handle me with very little effort and I would hate to be humiliated in front of all these women.

George and Sandro moved over to the front of the formation of women and after exchanging salutes with Colonel Chekovna, proceeded with their inspection. They gave each recruit a thorough going over, from a military perspective, but used the opportunity to discreetly examine the face of each woman. They tried to imagine her with flowing hair and dressed like a Grand Duchess but in reality they were immersed in a sea of bald heads. At the end of the inspection, George and Sandro moved to the side and briefly conferred.

"Did you see anyone who fits the profile," asked George.

"I have never seen so many ugly women in my life and not one that looks even remotely like our Maria."

"Well then, let us present the medals and take another look. But I admit it is very difficult to visualize Maria when they do not have any hair. I never realized what a difference it makes in a woman's appearance. Very discouraging indeed."

George and Sandro informed the commandant that they were so pleased with the results of the inspection that they wished to present medals to each person in the unit. Sandro motioned to their driver who brought over a tray with the medals laid out on it. They moved through the ranks of women presenting each with a medal and saying, "the Tsar thanks you for your loyalty and service to Russia." When they had finished George and Sandro looked at each other in dismay. The one they were searching for was not among the ranks.

At the completion of the inspection and award ceremony Colonel Chekovna escorted the Grand Dukes on a tour of the camp and its facilities. When the tour was over they thanked her on behalf of the Tsar and turned toward their vehicle but were stopped by a sudden loud crash from behind one of the barracks. "What was that!" said George. "It sounded like a training grenade." The three went running to the other side of the building and to their surprise found several more women soldiers, in uniform, unloading a large truck of supplies. Two of the women had not been strong enough to remove a large crate from the truck and it had dropped to the ground and shattered. They scurried to clean up the mess but to the amazement of the Grand Dukes another soldier walked up to the truck grasped a crate of the same size, lifted it and carried it into the building.

"Are you thinking what I am," Sandro asked of his brother.

George nodded and turned to the Colonel. "Who are these soldiers?"

"They are some of the women, who like me, disguised themselves and joined the army. Some never made it to the front and a few were injured in combat. The girl with the remarkable strength did more damage to a Russian soldier who tried to get fresh with her than any ten

Germans could have." George and Sandro laughed at the thought. "I did not include them in the formation because they have already proven themselves"

"Well then. Form them up. We wish to present them with a medal as well. They certainly are the most deserving"

"Yes sir," replied the Colonel and called the women to attention. George and Sandro walked slowly over to them and stood in front of each one in turn, hoping that one of them could pass for a grand duchess. The disappointment continued but turned to suppressed excitement when they came to the last woman. She had a very pretty face, with fine features, and although she was a little plump she bore a striking resemblance to Grand Duchess Maria. This was the woman with the exceptional strength and when George pinned the medal on he asked her where it came from.

"I was an only child Your Highness," said the girl. "My father desperately wanted a son and he just got me. I did man's work and became the son he never had."

"What is your name and how old are you?" asked Sandro.

"My name is Dalida Lukin and I am seventeen," she replied.

Sandro looked at George and nodded imperceptibly. Dalida was the one.

George took the Colonel by the arm and walked her out of earshot of the others. "Colonel, although this inspection was very important, there was another reason for our trip to Kiev. Yes, the Tsar has had some favorable reports concerning women such as yourself and he wanted a first hand report on the training that is going on here. And I can tell you we will be advising him that there is a cadre of trained women soldiers available for service. I cannot make any promises but I think the Tsar will be pleased with what you have accomplished. As to the other matter, much depends on your counsel." Seeing the confused look on her face George reached into his tunic and removed an official army document." I have here an order from the Tsar authorizing me to solicit, from your battalion, a volunteer for a special assignment. I was going to discuss this with you at a later time but it occurs to me, after meeting this last group, that there is no better time than right now. Do you think that among these women we might find a willing soul?"

"I have no doubt of it, Your Highness," the Colonel replied.

"Then let us lay it before them."

George and the Colonel walked back to the group of twenty or so women still standing rigidly at attention. He addressed them formally. "Women of Russia, your Tsar requests a volunteer for a special assignment. I cannot give details of this mission to anyone except to say that it could be dangerous. At any rate, you will not be returning to this unit and that means forsaking the friendships you have made. If you wish to volunteer take two paces forward."

Each of the twenty-three women stepped forward. George was not surprised nor was their colonel. Sandra joined them and they discussed the possibilities. "Colonel I was impressed by the Lukin woman. Her strength would certainly be an asset. What do you think?" Sandro asked.

"If I was to select anyone in this group it would be Lukin. She is an excellent marksman, well disciplined and completely reliable. You could not make a better choice."

"That's it then," said George. "Colonel, will you do me the honor of informing the unit of our selection."

"Certainly, sir." Chekovna did a sharp about face and in a rather quiet voice announced "Attention to orders. Dalida Lukin has been chosen by the Grand Dukes to carry out the Tsar's directive. Lukin, stand fast. The rest of you, fall out."

Seeing the disappointment on the faces of those who were not selected Sandro intervened momentarily. "Ladies, your willingness to serve has been noted and if your Colonel will supply me with a list of your names I will make them known to the Tsar. I am sure he will wish to thank you in some appropriate manner." The Colonel nodded in the affirmative and the women were dismissed.

"Come here girl and try to relax," directed George. "We are not going to bite you. We will tell you what is required of you later and it is possible that you will change your mind, in which case we will have to come back and go through this drill again.

"I can assure Your Highness that I will not change my mind. The Tsar has honored me with this assignment and no matter what it entails I will not fail him," the girl replied.

"Very well then. Gather what you need but be aware that you cannot remain in uniform. Colonel, can you outfit her in civilian clothes? Something simple will do. And oh yes, a large scarf to cover her head. Dalida this mission requires a woman, so you must allow your hair to grow out and keep your head covered until we reach our destination. I would like to leave today, on the evening train if possible, so Colonel, if you could expedite this little charade, we would be most grateful."

"I will see to it immediately," Cheknova replied.

Two hours later, after partaking of the refreshments the Colonel had prepared, George and Sandro drove out of the compound accompanied by a peasant girl in a long skirt whose head was covered by a large, light blue scarf. Well aware that they seemed an odd group George ordered the driver to proceed directly to the station. Their private car was on a siding and would later be coupled to the evening train bound for Moscow, so they were able to slip aboard unnoticed.

The young girl was somewhat apprehensive about traveling alone with these two imposing men. Some of the Grand Dukes had reputations as womanizers but the two she was with treated her with courtesy and deference. Later that afternoon George informed her that she was being taken to a special school run by the Tsarina's sister where she would join other young people training for the same mission. "Now Dalida, the others are sure to ask you what happened to your hair. You are to answer that you have just gotten over a bout with the measles. The Grand Duchess will give you any other instructions you might need when you reach the school. This is all I can tell you at this time. Are you comfortable with this? "

"My only desire is to serve the Tsar and Mother Russia," Dalida replied.

Shortly before the train was to depart Kiev for Moscow, Sandro slipped out and made his way to the telegraph office. There he sent two identical wires, one to Nicholas, the other to Ella. They read:

We have found a lamb and are taking it to the farm.

When the train arrived in Moscow, Ella was there to meet it.

Chapter 32

August 1915 - The Stavka. During the spring of this terrible year the German onslaught had wrested most of Poland from the Russian army. In response to these setbacks, the Commanding General's headquarters, the Stavka, had been relocated to a less vulnerable position at Mogilev on the Dnieper River in Belorussia. Nicholas was spending more and more time with his generals, not that he had any winning military strategy to suggest, but because he felt it his duty as Tsar to be with his men. He never pretended to be a tactician, in fact just the opposite, and he refused the opportunity to interfere with the decisions being made by the staff. The reality was that the Russian army was terribly overmatched and the enormous, heart wrenching casualties, numbering in the hundreds of thousands, made it impossible to go on the offensive.

Nicholas wondered how many more would give their lives before this evil war came to an end. He would stop it tomorrow, if he could, but he knew that the allies on the other fronts depended on Russia to tie up a number of German and Austrian divisions and prevent them from being diverted elsewhere. As a result of the series of defeats Nicholas had decided the time had come to assume the role of Commander-in-Chief and send Nikolasha to lead the troops in the Caucasus. It was something they had discussed several times in the past and Nikolasha was always aware that the Tsar would assume command at some point. Alexandra had been urging her husband to take this action for some time and would surely think she had influenced him, but nothing could be further from the truth. The decision was driven by the *Masquerade* and Nicky's fervent desire to protect the reputation of the nation's most respected individual. It was important that when the Tsar was gone at least one Romanov would emerge with character untarnished; respected, and capable of leading a counter-revolution. From a personal standpoint Nicholas wanted to assume the role that traditionally belonged to the Tsar, that of leading his people in war.

This was the truth behind Nicky's decision but he knew it would be said by the gossips that Alix's influence had forced him to relieve the Grand Duke. She had despised his uncle ever since he had spoken out against Rasputin and lately she had become obsessed with the idea that Nikolasha was plotting to steal the throne and send her to a nunnery. The Tsar knew these fantasies were the product of her increasingly unstable mental condition but he had no doubt she was supported in these notions by Rasputin and Anya. Alix's letters to him over the last month spoke of little else than the fact he must get rid of the "evil uncle". It was something he had been unwilling to do before now, but circumstances had changed and it was time for Nikolasha to move on. Nicholas was content to let her think he had acquiesced to her demands and hoped her letters of advice would taper off. But it was a vain hope and the endless notes continued, with requests to replace this minister or that one, along with detailed instructions on how he should behave, and pointed suggestions that he become more autocratic.

And so today was Nikolasha's last at headquarters. All the official paperwork had been completed and signed during the preceding week. After the morning report, the Tsar and his uncle went for a long walk so they could converse privately. The Grand Duke had accepted the Tsar's assumption of command as a necessary measure and there was absolutely no acrimony between the two men. Nicholas had written a decree announcing the change of command and it was so full of praise that any one who read it, or heard it read, had no doubt that the Tsar's decision was based solely on historical precedent and his desire to shoulder responsibility for all that had happened. The two men walked quietly for a few minutes lost in their thoughts. Nikolasha was the first to break the silence. "Nicky, I do not want to offend you by offering advice on how to command. You will have to feel your way into the role of leadership. I have assembled the best staff I could to support you and I believe you can trust your officers to do their utmost to defend the motherland."

Nicholas accepted the advice in the spirit it had been offered. "Uncle, I wish you could remain."

"No, Your Highness, if I stayed on, my presence would only cause confusion among the generals," said Nikolasha. "It is important that I leave now so I do not hinder your effectiveness. Because of the distances involved, my assignment to the Caucasus will make it difficult for any one to monitor my activities and I should be able to implement any part of the *Masquerade* that you wish me to, without arousing suspicion."

"Yes, I know. This has always been our plan since the beginning of the war but I feel so bereft at the thought of you leaving. I shall miss you, Uncle and I wish you God speed."

"I may not be physically present but know that my thoughts and prayers will be with you," said Nikolasha, his voice choked with emotion. The two men shook hands and Nikolasha walked back to headquarters to board his train while Nicholas remained behind to have a few moments alone. From this point on he would reside at the Stavka on a permanent basis with only short trips back to the palace to break-up the overwhelming loneliness he felt at the separation from his family.

In mid-November, with the concurrence of Nicholas and the help of Benckendorff, Valia, and the maids, Alexandra began the cleaning, painting and renovation of the secret attic. The time was drawing near when the substitutes would be moved from Moscow to Alexander Palace and Alix felt she should not delay any longer in making the changes. Unfortunately, the only access that could be used was the concealed doorway behind the hutch in the children's dining room. There was, of course, absolutely no way to suppress the children's curiosity when they first became aware of the activity, and Alix had to tell them something. That first night, therefore, when they had gotten ready for bed, Alix called them all together in Olga and Tatiana's room. They arranged themselves on the two camp beds and looked expectantly at their mother.

"Children, although your desire to know what is happening cannot be ignored, you must understand that what is going on is a great secret, the most important one you will ever be asked to keep. For this reason you must pledge on this relic of St. Serafim not to discuss what you see and hear with anyone. You cannot even talk about it among yourselves, or with the trusted few who know, lest you be overheard and everything be ruined. Will you do this for me?"

"Oh yes, Mama," they cried out in unison and then each in turn pledged their silence.

"Very well, my dears. I will not tell you everything just yet but do not be disappointed because when your father returns from the front in a few weeks he will give you more details. For the present all you need know is that sometime after the New Year, a small group of young people, whose identities must remain unknown, will arrive here and be lodged in the rooms that we began to prepare this morning. You will be interacting with them from time to time, but when and for what purpose your father will have to explain."

"What of Father Grigory and Anya?" asked Olga. "Will they know?"

"Although I would wish they be informed, your father has absolutely forbidden it and of course we will obey him. You must be on your guard around everyone or you will let something slip. Now let us pray for the assistance to carry this out. Your father will tell you the rest."

Over the next few weeks preparations in the attic continued. There were setbacks, of course, and the lack of plumbing meant that the amenities consisted of portable commodes and chamber pots, an inconvenience that was unavoidable. Alix cautioned the children that if they ever found the hutch unlatched they were to close it immediately to protect the secrecy of the upper rooms. By the end of the month everything was prepared and it took only some light housekeeping to keep all in readiness.

Nicholas left headquarters at Mogilev in mid-December and began the long journey to Tsarskoe Selo, where he would spend most of the holidays. He freely admitted to himself that he felt guilty at leaving the army behind but this trip to the palace was much more than a Christmas vacation. It was time to introduce his children to parts of the *Masquerade* and prepare them for the arrival of the impostors. Their role in this was very important because they would have to spend time with their doubles and assist in training them. He was not sure how much he should tell them but Alix had communicated to her husband that the children were on pins and needles and he would not be able to delay for very long bringing them together to discuss the strange goings on. Ella would be arriving a week after Nicholas and he would have preferred to have met with her first, before talking to the family, but he realized he had to play the cards he was dealt, and that meant disclosing elements of the plan as soon as he reached the palace. The Tsar's train was delayed and he did not reach the station at Tsarskoe Selo until late afternoon but when he stepped down from his car he was mobbed by Alexei and four exuberant young women. Alix normally frowned on such public displays of affection but she was caught up in the excitement of the reunion and looked on with a rare but happy smile. When the horse drawn sleds reached the palace and everyone stepped down Anastasia could not resist the urge and pelted her father with a snowball. The Tsar was up to the challenge and a melee quickly broke out with sides forming up based on age. Nicky and the two oldest girls began to get the best of the youngsters and would eventually have triumphed if an errant toss had not struck the Empress, who then demanded they put an end to the "silliness." It was a special moment and they all hated to let it go, but Nicholas brought them back to reality. "Children, I have some things to talk to your mother about," he announced, as he took Alix by the arm. "We will all meet later in your mother's boudoir for I have something of importance to discuss with you. Now why don't you go in for some hot chocolate and I will see you later."

When Nicholas and Alexandra were finally alone the Tsar kissed her tenderly and they embraced for the first time in many weeks. "Oh Nicky, I am so glad you are home. The children have been angels but their curiosity is about to get the better of them and the sooner they know what is going on the sooner things can return to normal."

"I am sorry I have to say it, Sunny, but from this point on, I doubt anything will ever be normal again. Now you must explain to me exactly what you have told the children. Perhaps then I can get some insight as to the best way to handle tonight's little get together."

At the appointed hour Nicholas walked into the Mauve Boudoir. The whole family was assembled, the older girls on chairs and the younger ones and Alexei sitting on the floor around their mother. The Tsar looked at them and hesitated, not really sure how to begin. Alix knew at least part of what was coming but until this point the planning of the *Masquerade* did not directly involve her or her children so she too, was curious. She sat erect on the chaise lounge waiting impatiently until the silence became unnerving, wondering how the Tsar would introduce his children to this elaborate production. Finally Olga spoke up, "What is it, Papa?"

The Tsar sighed and then began. "My darling children, I need to speak to you about an unusual matter," said Nicholas. "I have decided to bring into the palace some young adults and children who will, on occasion, act as your doubles. They have been in training for sometime now, so that in the event a situation arises they will be prepared to take your places. That is why we are preparing quarters above your rooms."

"What kind of situation are you talking about, Papa?" asked the ever alert Olga.

"Well, let us pretend for a moment that I wanted to send you some where, the Crimea for example, but I did not want anyone to know. I would disguise you and send you on your way and in the meantime I would ensure that your doubles were seen around the palace grounds or even at official functions. The possibilities are endless and we can make this into a great game. Remember the time at Spala when Anastasia tricked the guard into saluting her friend. Your mother was furious but it worked." Nicholas looked at Anastasia and saw a tear trickling down his youngest daughter's cheek. "Oh dear. How thoughtless of me to bring up such a painful memory. But who knows, maybe you will become great friends with your double."

"But won't they feel like prisoner's penned up in that attic all the time," Tatiana interjected.

"Absolutely not. Say that you wanted to go for a sleigh ride. You could take Olga's double, or if Marie wanted to visit the hospital she could go with your look-alike. As I said before, there are endless combinations. I think this will be great fun. You know, this has been done before, but usually with only one person. That is why your mother stressed the need for secrecy and asked for your pledge."

"Does everyone have a double?" asked Maria.

"Yes, you all have doubles. I believe it was your Aunt Ella who once informed me that everyone living on earth has someone else living on earth who looks just like them."

"Like a twin?" asked Anastasia.

"Yes, like an identical twin," answered the Tsar. "We have found your twins and have invited them to come live in the palace."

They all seemed satisfied with this answer except for Olga who looked at her father skeptically. He was not surprised, as she was very perceptive.

"If any of you breathe a word of this," said Olga, while looking at her siblings as only a big sister can, "you will have to answer to me." She could not explain how she knew but Olga realized there was more to this then her father was telling them.

The other children had numerous questions about their doubles and their father answered as many of them as he could without divulging too much. Nicholas had made up his mind that the real reasons for this charade would be revealed at a better time. He knew the children would recoil from the suggestion that they were to be separated from their parents and until they had established some rapport with their doubles he did not intend to let them know how much danger they were in. After they had exhausted their curiosity he sent them off to bed but as they scampered up the stairs to their rooms Nicholas pulled Olga aside. "My wise little owl, I know you have seen through me but for all our sakes do not discuss your doubts with anyone. Play the game for now and eventually all will be explained to your satisfaction. Can you do this?"

"Yes, Papa, of course I can."

"Then off with you, my dear. I know I can depend on you."

When Olga reached the room she shared with her sister, Tatiana wanted to know what she was talking to their father about. "He wanted to make sure that you and I kept an eye on the little ones during all this. You know Anastasia cannot keep a secret and he wants us to be extra alert so the presence of the doubles is not exposed." The two older girls got ready for bed but before turning off the lamp Tatiana turned to Olga and asked if she remembered the time they had talked about leaving the palace and living like normal people. Olga laughed. "If I remember correctly you wanted to bring your jewels along. How normal is that?"

"Oh fiddle faddle, silly, you must see what I am getting at. If we have doubles we can try and do some normal things. Papa will be at the Stavka and Mama will not be able to keep track of everything. What an opportunity."

"You know Tatiana, you really are a very wicked, naughty girl. Now let me go to sleep."

The next morning the Tsar called in Baroness Sophie Buxhoeveden and proceeded to explain to her the role she would play in all this. Once the impostors arrived at the palace she would take over from Ella the responsibility for their continued education and training. The Countess would oversee the interaction of the young people and polish the rough edges. She would, of course, have to spend a substantial amount of time with Dalida who had only recently come into the *Masquerade* but, according to Ella, the girl was a fast learner. Sophie was at first somewhat intimidated by the awesome responsibility the Tsar was asking her to shoulder but then, as she thought about it, she realized that she was fascinated by the intrigue and excited by her part in it. She assured the Tsar that he could depend on her and the short meeting came to an end.

⋘⋙

As Ella's train neared the station at Tsarskoe Selo the Grand Duchess looked one last time at the photographs spread out on the table before her. The pictures were the most recent ones taken of the impostors and she had made her final decision as to which of the group they would use. Dalek and Dalida, of course, were automatic choices as they were the only doubles for Alexei and Maria. As for the others she could only go with her instincts and the subtle differences in them that she had come to recognize. A most important factor was their perceived loyalty to the Tsar and since she sensed this quality more strongly in three of the girls, she chose them. Ekaterina, Helena, and Franny would join Dalek and Dalida for the next phase of their education at Alexander Palace. Ella had already sent her recommendations on to the Tsar for his final approval but she knew it was only a formality. He had given her carte blanche in the selections since she had been working so closely with the doubles. Once she talked to Nicholas and received his official approval she would break up the group and find positions for the other girls in towns far from the capital. Maria's first double, Sophie, had already entered the convent. The remaining girls would be sent to a separate location and Ella knew it would be hard on them since they had formed lasting friendships. But the plan had to be protected and anyway the lives they would now lead would be far superior to life on the streets of some big city. But, of course, the main purpose of Ella's Christmas visit was to finalize arrangements for bringing the impostors into the palace.

When Ella arrived at the station at Tsarskoe Selo she was met by Count Benckendorff and his driver and escorted to Alexander Palace. She was amazed at the amount of activity in the Imperial compound and asked the Count about it. "Well, Your Highness, since Catherine Palace has been converted into a hospital, there are constant comings and goings of ambulances and medical supply trucks. All the wards are full and there are nurses and doctors and aides of every description. It all seems quite disorganized but I can assure you the Empress has everything running smoothly. And as I am sure the she will mention in your meeting with her, we intend to use the activity to cover the arrival of the doubles."

As the car approached the entrance to the Imperial family's home Ella began to feel that old familiar pit in the bottom of her stomach. The build-up of tension was caused by the strained relationship that had developed between her and her sister and could be traced directly to the presence in Petrograd, of Grigory Rasputin. It was no secret that Ella distrusted the man and worried that the advice he was giving Alix would some day lead to disaster. Ella and Nikolasha were the leaders of a group of royals who wanted to bring him down but, of course, Alix considered any criticism of the staret to be a direct and personal attack on her. With the Tsar spending almost all his time at the Stavka, she had turned more and more to Father Grigory. It was clear that he had cast some sort of spell over her and now it appeared that Alix was unable to make a decision or take action without first consulting him. Ella was just glad that the Tsar was here for the holidays and that she could concentrate on her real reason for coming.

The next day, after Ella was settled in, Alix made arrangements for Mademoiselle Zanotti to show her the secret stairs and give her a tour of the upper living quarters. When the tour was complete, Ella met Alix in her Mauve Boudoir. "You have done an absolutely fabulous job in preparing all this, Alix, and it is better than my most hopeful expectations," said Ella. "I know Dalek and the girls will be so pleased with the living arrangements. I was concerned that the attic would not be a fitting place for anyone to spend so much time, but now that I have seen it, I must admit it is just perfect. Anyone would be quite comfortable living up there. "

"The rooms are a little smaller but I am still going to have the girls share, since mine do," said Alix with little enthusiasm. Ella was surprised at her attitude for when they were younger this was exactly the sort of intrigue Alix would have enjoyed. Unfortunately Ella did not understand the divided loyalties that were tearing at her sister. Alexandra knew she must be involved with the *Masquerade*, because her husband had directed her to, but quite frankly she did not believe this plan was necessary. Rasputin, whom she often referred to as "our friend," had frequently stated that everything would be well with Russia, but this directly contradicted the prediction of St. Serafim for whom she also had great reverence. So she kept her own counsel and put her trust in Father Grigory, who was here in the flesh, and not the Saint who was a nebulous figure from the past. In her mind, all these preparations were needless and she was content to wait out the future believing that as long as Rasputin watched over her and her son, Russia was safe. She was firmly convinced that someday she would see her son on Russia's throne. To the Tsarina's credit she never broke her pledge to her husband and did nothing to hinder the plan. In fact she did much to insure its success, going so far as to suggest that the doubles never be allowed to visit Father Grigory. She knew the minute he was alone with them he would immediately recognize them for what they were. But protecting the plan was made more difficult for Alix because she could barely tolerate the other players in the elaborate scheme. The Tsar had carefully chosen individuals who were not aligned with Father Grigory and though this infuriated Alix she managed to keep her true feelings hidden. Ella did not know all this but she was aware, as the conversation continued, that she must be very careful

"It is amazing how the staircase was hidden for all these years. Don't you think this plan will work?"

"Yes, I believe it will," said Alix. "But you should know that "our friend" has stated many times that everything will be well with Russia if we hold true to our faith. He told me before that Alexei must never leave the country or he will die." There was an appeal for understanding in her voice but her sister missed it completely.

"Alix," said Ella, with a look of shock on her face. "Please tell me you did not inform him of the Tsar's secret plan."

"How dare you even suggest that," said Alix with anger in her voice. "He is a holy man and knows of things on his own," she said. "I would never betray the Tsar's trust." An uncomfortable silence followed and Ella was aware that she had missed an opportunity to draw a little closer to her sister. She could kick herself for not being more alert for the mood swing that came when anyone was critical of Grigory.

"Now, I must ask you to excuse me Ella. I am not feeling well."

"Very well, I shall leave you to your needlepoint. Shall we meet later for tea?"

"No, I am afraid it will be too much for me."

"Nicky told me when I arrived that you would give me the preliminary details of the plan to bring in the doubles, and the Count made some mention of it when we drove over from the station. What time shall we meet tomorrow? Do you have a preference?" asked Ella.

"Yes," said Alix wearily. "Come to see me at half past eleven"

Ella left the room with an ache in her heart and the knowledge that she was slowly losing the sister she once knew and loved. She blamed all the tension in their relationship on that vile insect, Grigory Rasputin. She was sure that the only thing that would bring her sister back to her was to somehow remove him from their lives. As she walked down the corridor she knew she must speak to Nicholas about her conversation with Alix, as it had left her feeling very uneasy. Despite Alixs' vehement protest Ella wondered if she had revealed their secret to Rasputin.

At 11:30 the next morning, Ella arrived at the boudoir to find Alix in an almost cheerful mood. It was a welcome contrast to yesterday's unpleasantness and the Grand Duchess was determined that she would say nothing to ruin the atmosphere. The plan to bring the doubles in had to be finalized during this Christmas visit so she would step lightly around Alix and make every effort to keep her younger sister calm and focused on the matter at hand.

"Well good morning sister," said Alix. "We have much to discuss today."

"Yes, we certainly do," Ella replied.

"Nicky and I have considered the issue of moving the doubles and have come up with a plan that we believe will enable them to enter the palace undetected," said the Empress. "As I see it, the move will take place in several stages. First you will divide them into two groups, the boy, and Olga's double in one party, and the remaining three girls in the other. On the appointed day take the first group to the station in Moscow where they will be met by their escort, Count Tatishchev. Dress the boy as a hospital orderly and the girl as a nurse's aide. The Count will bring his two wards all the way to Catherine Palace and with all the medical personnel about they should blend right in. He will then conduct them through the tunnel connecting the two palaces and up and into their quarters here in Alexander Palace. Two days later you will repeat the scenario with the remaining girls, all disguised as aides, only this time they will be met at the station by Count Benckendorff's stepson, Valia. I will arrange for you to meet him before you leave but, just in case, you will both be provided with a sign and counter-sign. Nicky thinks it would be unwise to tell the doubles the purpose of the move until they have safely arrived and are settled in. Since the Tsar will probably be at the Stavka when the move is made it will be up to me, Sophie and Benckendorff to insure a smooth transition. I wish you could be here for the first days at least. Do you think you could delay your return? A familiar face would be so helpful."

"I hadn't thought about it but you are absolutely correct. If we could send a trusted courier to Sister Barbara to inform her of the plan she could take charge in Moscow and I could remain here until the children arrive."

"And who is Sister Barbara?" asked Alix.

"She is a woman who was in my service before I became a nun. She followed me into the convent and has been invaluable in preparing the doubles. I certainly could not have accomplished this alone. She has been a close companion and I would trust her with my life."

"Of course, my dear. It is just that I worry that more people are becoming involved," said Alix.

"Well, as you are aware, only a few individuals know the entire plan and Sister Barbara's involvement has been limited to training the children," explained Ella. "This additional assignment is well within her capabilities but I know she will be saddened to see the children leave."

"Then what do you think of the plan I have described?" Alix asked her sister.

"I think it is a brilliant idea," said Ella. "If you can arrange for a courier I will get word off to Sister Barbara immediately. Then all we need do is send a telegram with the dates Tatishchev and Valia will make contact. I pray for hours everyday that God will be with us and that we are doing everything as he wishes."

"I pray daily as well," said Alix, "and you should know that Father Grigory also prays for the Tsar and his family."

Ella knew Alix was testing her so she looked up and smiled..

"Yes," she said, "we all need many prayers."

For the first time in quite a while the two sisters sat and chatted as if there was no tension between them. Alix talked about her hospital work and Ella in turn gave her sister a complete update on the effort to create believable doubles for her nephew and nieces. It was a pleasant interlude but one that was too good to last.

"Ella, I must ask you to excuse me now. I feel a headache coming on and I must rest before it aches too badly. I do want you to know how glad I am that you will be in the palace when the children arrive. I was worried as to how I would react to them, but with you here to make the introductions things will go much easier"

Ella left Alix reclining on the chaise in her Mauve Boudoir. She was extremely worried about her sister's state of mind and was anxious to talk to Nicholas about it. Something was not right and although she could not identify exactly what the problem was she was sure it had something to do with Rasputin.

The next afternoon, while Alix was resting, Ella joined Nicholas in his study. "I have so much to discuss with you Nicky that I scarcely know where to begin."

"I have several things to talk over with you as well," replied Nicholas, "but why don't we start with you."

"I hesitate to bring this subject up as I really do not like to even talk about the man but I feel I must. Nicholas, I am extremely concerned about Alix's relationship with Father Grigory and her dependency on him. Something is not right with my sister. It is as if she is slipping away and becoming another person. If I dare say a critical word about that despicable fraud she ends the conversation immediately. Her favorite technique is to complain that a headache is coming on. As if. I do not know what has happened to her but it is my firm belief that Rasputin is practicing some form of mind control over her. She is just acting so strangely. I have noticed it gradually happening over the years but now it is quite apparent."

"I am well aware of what you speak, Ella, and although I have managed to keep him out of the palace I must at least appear to be sympathetic to my wife's concerns. He can come in when Alexei has an attack but only under strict supervision and his contact with the girls must be kept to a minimum. After the impostors begin to fulfill their roles there will be no reason for him to come into the palace and access will be denied. Ella, you will not be able to influence the situation, but do not worry. When the time comes he will be dealt with appropriately. But for now, if anything unpleasant was to befall him, Alix would be beside herself with grief and I think the possibility exists that she could have a breakdown and disrupt the plan. My biggest concern is that when I am away at the front she will be unduly influenced and there is no one who could intervene for me. We have to put our faith in God that all will work out"

"It is indeed a troubling situation. If there is anything I can do Nicky, I will. She just does not seem to want to talk about it. You know there are rumors that people want to kill him. Maybe something will happen to him."

"Yes, I am aware of the rumors but I pray that for now nothing is done to the man. He keeps Alix calm and we desperately need that. I do not know how he does it but he does help with Alexei"

"Well, brother, I felt I had to share my observations with you. But now to the *Masquerade*. I must say that when Alix explained the plan for bringing in the impostors she was clear, concise, and right on the mark. We did make one change which I am sure Alix will discuss with you. I will remain here to meet the children when they arrive. It will help smooth the transition. Sister Barbara will handle the Moscow details. My only question was about the guards. How will they slip past them?"

"They will be distracted at the appropriate time. Count Benckendorff is arranging that. I will be at the Stavka but I have complete confidence in the Count, who has assured me all will go as we intend. Everything has been planned out and Alix and Baroness Sophie Buxhoeveden will begin working with them immediately. You know Sophie don't you?"

"Most certainly. She is very capable."

"They will tutor them and continue with the lessons you prepared. I think it is important that Alix become comfortable with the impostors as quickly as possible since she will have to pretend that they are her own children. Much of the instruction will take place late in the evening when it is quiet in the palace. Alix's personal maids will be involved in the care of the doubles. They know nothing else of the plan but they had to be brought in since they are literally right in the middle of everything. Because they are foreigners they do not often interact with the rest of the staff and they rarely leave the palace so we are not concerned about security. Anyway they are extremely loyal, just as the nuns you chose from your convent to help you. I will return from Headquarters at the end of January to meet my second family. I just wish I could be here to see the look on Anastasia's face when she meets her double. Alix, of course, will tell the impostors basically what she told our children and we will slowly begin to work them into our daily activity, introducing one, or another while hiding the real child in the attic. By the way Olga is on to me already."

"She would be the one," Ella replied. "Nicholas, I hesitate to ask you this question but we have not discussed the topic before. What will happen to the doubles after your children are spirited away? Surely if your life is at risk will not their lives be in danger as well."

"Certainly they will, and this has been weighing on my mind since the beginning. Benckendorff's man reported that the revolutionaries took an oath to kill the whole family but I just find it hard to believe that they mean the children. They are not guilty of any crime, perceived or otherwise, and when I look at their innocent faces I cannot imagine anyone wanting to harm them. Nevertheless, I have agonized over the possibility that they might somehow be harmed. Everyone would certainly look upon me as a monster if that happened so I have come up with a tentative plan. Once Alexei and the Grand Duchesses are safely out of the country, sometime in April of 1917, I will send Alix and the impostors to Livadia. Once they are there we can consider several options. You know when I staged the death of one of the impostors at Spala, it went off brilliantly. I thought we might try the same ploy again although it would certainly be more difficult with a large group. Another more intriguing idea is to put everyone on a neutral flag ship and send them off to Alixs' cousins in England. It would be easy to slip them away from the coast of the Crimea and that would certainly confuse the search and buy even more time for my children. I know either course would be risky but if it succeeded they could all go on to live happy, safe lives in another country. I would provide them with enough money to live comfortably for the rest of their lives."

"Although the plans both have merit," Ella replied when the Tsar had finished, "I think they are too complicated to be successful."

"I know," Nicky sighed, "but I must try, and if I do not succeed, then so be it. One thing I will not lose sight of is the fact that it is one of my daughters who will prove to be Russia's savior and not one of the impostors. Thus, as brutal as it may sound, these look-alikes are expendable. They are like the soldiers I send off to battle, not knowing whether they will live or die. Time is of the essence and the doubles must buy us time. While they are playing out their roles no one will be looking for my children. Ella, I will do everything in my power to save them but if necessary they will be sacrificed for the cause. The difference is that they will not be alone. I will be there with them, to share their fate."

"This is all so tragic but if God ordained this who are we to question his will," Ella replied. "If something should happen to any of the impostors they would be martyrs for their faith."

"I do not know if I would go so far as to say that but they are definitely brave soldiers."

"If you bring them into the palace in a few weeks they will be hidden in the attic for over a year. I wonder if such a thing has ever been done before."

"Who knows, Ella, but maybe we are establishing a precedent. At least they will be able to get outside for fresh air now and again and as soon as they are comfortable in their alter-egos we will bring them out more and more."

"When will you have the impostors take the places of your children for good?" Ella asked.

"Well we have decided on April of 1917 as the month the children will leave the country but I have changed my mind as to when I want to make the switch. I have spent much time trying to work this all out. Nikolasha is at his wits end. He thinks I must make a plan and follow it to the letter."

"That is typical of a man who has devoted his life to the Army," said Ella.

"He does not always understand the twists and turns this plan is taking."

"I think you have developed a very workable plan up to this point and I see no reason why it will not be successful."

"Thank you for all your support, Ella. I am not a coward but I am afraid. Russia is losing the war and when it is finally over our ravaged motherland will have to face an insidious enemy from within. I sometimes weep when I realize what this country has yet to face."

"Nicky, I cannot lessen your worries about the war but let us focus on what we can control and that is the *Masquerade*."

"You are right, of course. Now where were we?"

"We were speaking about the doubles taking over full time."

"I have decided to make the switch as late as we possibly can."

"How late?" asked Ella.

"If I have the doubles assume the role of the Imperial children too soon it would leave many months during which someone could uncover the plan and realize the doubles are not my children. Everything would be lost. My solution to this problem is to do the turnover in January or February of 1917. We would just reverse the procedure we are using now to smuggle in the doubles. My children would be hidden in your convent until the final arrangements were made to send them out of the country.

"I believe you make a good point," Ella observed. "It makes sense to wait as long as possible and leaves less opportunity for discovery."

"I will need you to arrange to transport two of the girls and Alexei to Vladivostok in April."

"That will be no problem. Our order is all over the country now so it will not seem out of the ordinary for several nuns and orphans to be traveling eastward.

"The representative from Japan will probably be Prince Kanin. He will meet the group in Vladivostok and escort the children back to Japan. The Mother Superior at the convent in Warsaw has some trusted supporters that can be used to escort the other two daughters to Poland. I have yet to work out those details."

"I will be a nervous wreck until the children arrive and are safely in the palace. Nicky, please let me know what you think of the job we have done with these youngsters. You will like them I think, and I pray they will be up to the task.

"You need not worry. But for you, none of this would be possible. Let me also thank you for agreeing to stay on for a few weeks. I was worried about Alix but with you here everything should be all right. Now let us enjoy the few days we have left before the *Masquerade* begins in earnest."

Chapter 33

January 1916 - Tsarskoe Selo. The calm, cool and usually collected Ella, was a bundle of nerves, for in this third week of the new year, word was received that Count Tatishchev had arrived in Moscow, made contact with Sister Barbara, and was on his way back with Dalek and Ekaterina, Olga's double. Ella could not be in two places at once and she had agreed that things would go more smoothly if she were at the palace when they arrived. All seemed to be going according to plan and Ella offered a quick prayer of thanksgiving that she had someone as capable as Sister Barbara to oversee the send off. It had been decided that Tatishchev and his two fellow conspirators would not change trains in Petrograd since the Count was well known there and might be recognized. Instead they disembarked at the stop before the capital where Alix had an ambulance waiting. The Count posed as a doctor, carried a medical bag, and was accompanied by his orderly and a nurse's aide. The ambulance took them directly to Tsarskoe Selo and then on to the Catherine Palace. It was a well orchestrated plan and as in most such plans timing was a critical element. They were to have arrived later in the day but the train was ahead of schedule and the ambulance made good time despite the snow. Tatishchev decided to forge ahead and hoped his early arrival would not upset things. He would have to telephone Count Benckendorff at the first opportunity, but unfortunately such a chance did not present itself.

There had been a major battle two days earlier and the casualties were starting to come in so everything was much more confused then usual and the organized chaos worked in favor of the Count and his two wide-eyed companions. Ambulances unloaded wounded at every entrance, so no one at the hospital took notice of the arrival of additional medical personnel when their vehicle pulled up and they stepped down. Dalek and Ekaterina had been instructed to speak to no one and to follow the Count closely as they made their way into the hospital, but the scene that awaited them, when they walked in, literally took their breath away. The assembly area was filled with wounded and dying soldiers, limbs missing, blood soaking through hastily applied bandages and, most disconcerting, the groaning and cries of men in terrible pain. Although the impostors had seen their share of suffering they had never experienced it on such a monstrous scale and their isolation of the past few years had left them unprepared for such misery. They reeled back in horror, and though Dalek was able to cope with the sight, Ekaterina was terribly affected.

The Empress and Grand Duchesses Olga and Tatiana were all at the hospital that day to create diversions if necessary and to intervene if anyone stopped the impostors. Dressed as they were in their Red Cross habits they looked just like nuns and there was little danger that anyone would see a resemblance between Olga and her counterpart. Count Tatishchev was somewhat at a loss as how to proceed and was standing there motionless, with the two frightened children, when the Empress noticed him and sent Olga over to help. "Good day to you," said Olga. "I am Tsar's oldest daughter, and Sister Ella, whom you know so well, is my aunt. She is waiting for you, so if you and the good doctor would follow me, I will get you on your way." As they began walking into another wing of the palace, Olga quietly explained to them that the Empress and several others were watching over them so they need not be afraid. "I reacted the way you did my first day here and though I am resigned to the misery I never get used to it."

They were almost out of the ward when one of the patients reached out from his bed and grasped the arm of Ekaterina as she walked by. "Please Sister, I am dying. Help me! Pray with me sister, please," cried out the delirious soldier in a voice filled with pain. The small group stopped and Olga looked back nervously while the Empress and Tatiana watched from across the room. They had been so close to getting clear of the ward and really had not planned for any unexpected delays. But Ekaterina was up to the situation and immediately demonstrated the effectiveness of Ella's training. The young woman took a cloth from her pocket, handed it to Dalek, and motioned to him to wipe away the perspiration from the wounded man's forehead. Then she sat on the side of the bed, took the soldier's hand between her own, and calmly stroked it while quietly reciting a familiar prayer. Her gentle voice calmed the patient and he released her hand. Ekaterina stood up and blessed him on the forehead and then followed Olga and the others from the room. The whole affair had happened so quickly that hardly anyone else in the ward noticed and the little group passed on into the next room where the Tsarina and Grand Duchess Tatiana joined them and were introduced by Olga. Needless to say, the two impostors were spellbound at being in the presence of the Empress of Russia but at this point there was no time for explanations.

Alexandra slipped through another door of the ward and out into a hallway which contained access to the basement. A guard was standing his post there but the Empress bade him follow her and Tatiana to assist in retrieving a heavy box of supplies from a nearby medical storeroom. Once the guard entered the storeroom, Olga, who had been watching unobserved from the other entrance to the hallway, led her group midway down the hall, then through a door and down a staircase to the basement. Once everyone was accounted for she led them through the basement to a wrought iron gate marking the entrance to the tunnel. Olga pulled an old fashioned key from her pocket, unlocked the gate, and motioned everyone through. "I will say good-bye for now but do not worry because the Count knows the way and someone will meet you at the other end." She handed them each a small flashlight and demonstrated how to switch them on. "Now God be with you. I must go, said Olga." As Ekaterina and Dalek started through the tunnel Tatishchev turned back to Olga and said, "please telephone Benckendorff and tell him we are on the way." The Grand Duchess nodded and locked the gate behind them. She then returned to the main floor to rejoin her mother and sister, quite pleased with the way things were going.

The three companions, on what was turning out to be an exciting journey, walked slowly down the tunnel. In spite of their lights, it was dark and gloomy but they were all so full of anticipation that they hardly noticed. The Count, of course, was relieved that the heavy burden of responsibility was about to be lifted from his shoulders. However, the impostors, who had been told only that they were going to serve in the Tsar's household were feeling much different emotions. Excitement, of course. Some trepidation assuredly. But mostly wonder. Wonder at the sudden change in their lives. Wonder at the secrecy. Why all this if they were merely to be servants in a big house? Dalek, immature as he was, could barely contain his impatience but Ekaterina knew that all would be explained in time and from what she understood the others would be joining them soon and she took comfort in that thought. When they reached the end of the tunnel, Count Benckendorff was waiting for them. He unlocked the gate and escorted them to the other end of the basement which was lined with storerooms. He led them into one that was empty of stores. Prior to their arrival he had set an empty crate up as a table with a meal of milk, bread, cheese and fruit laid out. "You made better time then we expected, Tatishchev, so these two will have to remain here until later tonight when we will be able move them upstairs unnoticed." He then addressed Dalek and Ekaterina. "I have set up some food for you and there is a chamber pot behind that makeshift curtain. I ask that you keep as quiet as possible and I apologize for the long wait but it is imperative that no one become aware of your presence. The reason will become apparent later."

The two nodded their agreement. "We understand," said Ekaterina. "I can assure you that we will remain quiet." Both were more than a little intimidated by the imposing figure of Count Benckendorff. Assuring them that they had nothing to fear, he left the room, locking the door behind him.

During most of the day and well into the evening the honor guards stood their post just inside the entrance to the Tsar and Tsarina's private quarters. But each night they moved outside the doors and closed them, effectively sealing off the family wing. Later, the guards were relieved by night watchmen, who roamed the halls of the rest of the palace but never entered the family's private quarters. Count Benckendorff would wait until the guard was relieved and then move the impostors into their newly renovated rooms.

Late that night, when the palace was totally quiet, the Count made his way down the stairs which led to the basement. He carried a flashlight to illuminate his way through the darkness and walked over to the storeroom. He unlocked the door to let out his two charges, who were groggy from lack of sleep. They had been too nervous to drift off while they waited. The youngsters followed the Count up the stairs and then into the Empress' quarters. Mademoiselle Zanotti, Alix's maid, met them there and quickly escorted them into the Empress' dressing room, Count Benckendorff remaining behind. Everyone remained silent as they climbed the stairs to the children's wing. The impostors were in awe at the incredible furnishings they glimpsed as they were whisked up the stairs. When they completed the climb, Zanotti asked them to wait while she insured the way was clear. She opened the door into the children's dining room, saw that it was empty, and quickly ushered in the two doubles. The maid locked both doors and then unlatched the cupboard, which swung out to reveal the staircase leading to the attic.

"Quickly children," she whispered, "go up the stairs." Dalek led the way and M. Zanotti brought up the rear closing the hutch behind her. The impostors were dismayed when they climbed through the trapdoor into the attic. They were in a bare, depressing room, the boredom of it relieved only by the sturdy railing built around the trap door entrance. "Certainly this will not be our new home will it, Miss?" asked Dalek.

Zanotti looked at their crestfallen faces and knew what they were thinking. "This is not where you will be staying." She opened the door to the room and motioned them to follow her down the hall to the next room on the left. It was named the Crimson Room after the children's room directly below it. She turned on the electric light which illuminated the room and the two doubles followed her in. Never before had they seen such an exquisite room. The walls were covered in a rich red fabric similar to the room below. Gilded frames hung on the wall with pictures of the Imperial Family. Furniture of the finest quality filled the room while shelves laden with books lined one of the walls. On the wall opposite the door hung thick velvet draperies which totally obscured the windows behind them. Zanotti pointed at them and said, "Only open the curtains during daylight hours to allow sunlight into the room. Once it is dark and you turn on the electric lights you must ensure they are kept tightly closed. They are special blackout curtains which will keep the lights from being seen from the outside. It is important that you follow these instructions. I will be going below now to meet with the Empress. She will address you all in a few days once everyone is here. Sister Ella will see you in the morning. Miss Tudelberg will be up shortly with your tea and to help you get settled into your own rooms which are just down the hall. I think you will both be very pleased. Now wait here quietly until she arrives. By the way, Ekaterina, you will be sharing a room with Helena. Dalek you have a room to your self."

The minute she left Ekaterina and Dalek walked around the large room looking at every detail and caressing the beautiful furniture. "I cannot believe that we shall be living here," Ekatrina remarked. "And to think the Tsar is only two flights of stairs away from us. Can you imagine it, Dalek?"

"I don't like this place," said Dalek. "It has too many flowers and smells like a garden." He had a point because Alix had ensured that fresh flowers filled the room. "I can tell you, I am not going to be happy here."

"Dalek, you should not be so ungrateful. You don't even know what our service is going to consist of."

Dalek walked to the other side of the room and began playing with the curtains, pretending to let light out of the room. "Dalek," Ekatrina exclaimed, "you better not ruin this for all of us."

Just then they heard noise in the corridor and Dalek was immediately on his best behavior, any hint of his true personality quickly concealed. Miss Tudelberg entered the room carrying a large wicker basket which contained a meal for the two. She quickly introduced herself and had her new charges move next door to the dining room where she laid out the food. "I am Miss Tudelberg but you can call me Toodles if you like. It is what the Tsar's children nicknamed me." She puttered around the room while the two sat at the table. Ekaterina used all the proper table manners she had learned in their training and had become quite the lady. Dalek on the other hand ate like an animal, shoving food in his mouth every time that Toodles was not looking at him. He was not liked by the girls at all. Most of the time he was rude and nasty but the minute someone outside the group joined them he had the truly amazing ability to become quite charming. Only the other impostors knew the truth and they were afraid to tell for he was a rough neck and frightened them with his threats.

After the meal, Toodles showed Dalek and Ekaterina to their rooms. She was gratified by their reaction as she had worked extremely hard to make them comfortable. Alix's maids had gone up and down the staircase so many times preparing the rooms that it was no longer difficult for them to traverse the two foot wide stairwell. Fortunately, Benckendorff had left enough of the heavy pieces, wardrobes, dressing tables, armoires and the like, to furnish all the rooms, and after a little dusting and polishing they looked like new. It was impossible to move large items up the narrow staircase but smaller things such as fabrics, linens, and such could easily be brought up.

The impostors were very impressed with the Crimson Room and even more so when they saw their bedrooms. Each of the Grand Duchesses had donated some of their personal belongings such as mirrors, combs, and their favorite perfume to their secret guests. They wanted their doubles to get to know them and what they liked as well as make them feel welcome. Alix had ordered duplicates made of all her children's clothes so matching wardrobes hung in the armoires of their rooms. Each day the doubles would wear what the Imperial children wore. Toodles got them settled for the night in their new nightclothes while explaining the rules and sanitary arrangements. During the day they would be required to use chamber pots as there was no plumbing in the attic. Every other day they would be allowed to have a bath in Toodles and Zanotti's private bathroom. None of the other maids were allowed to use it and it was easily accessible from the children's dining room.

Two days later the same procedure was repeated. Helena, Dalida, and Franny, arrived in an ambulance and, accompanied by Valia, entered the Catherine Hospital. Alix, Olga, and Tatiana were on duty again but this time the process went off without a hitch. The doubles were unobserved as Olga escorted them down the stairs leading to the basement. Once they were all ready she unlocked the gate and ushered them into the tunnel. Valia led the way and the three girls followed him through the passageway to the palace basement where they were met, this time, by Sister Ella. There was a brief tearful reunion which emphasized the relief the girls felt at seeing a familiar face and later that night they were slipped into the palace to join their comrades. As were the others, the three newcomers were very impressed with the living arrangements. Now the *Masquerade* could truly begin.

At the end of the month, Nicholas returned from the Stavka, arriving at Tsarskoe Selo early in the morning, and anxious to learn how everything was going. But as filled as he was with anticipation he knew he would have to wait until that night to finally meet his "second family." The day dragged on, but as usual, when he returned from the Stavka, he had an abundance of work awaiting him. His calendar of appointments would take up most of the day and when he finished his meetings there was a mountain of official documents awaiting his signature. He worked diligently through the day, stopping only briefly for light meals, which were served in his study, and finally he cleared his desk. It was time to go up but before doing so he went to the boudoir where Alix was waiting for him. "Well, Sunny, what do you think? Will they pass muster? Give me a feel for the situation before I meet them."

"Nicky, I had my doubts about all this, but Ella has done a truly amazing job. The girls are perfect ladies, and even Dalida, the new girl who is Maria's double, shows remarkable poise. And you should have seen the way Ekaterina handled a touchy situation at the hospital when she arrived. I am not so sure about the boy. I cannot put my finger on it but he does not seem as gentle as Alexei. Of course, that could be because he does not suffer from a horrible disease. As to their resemblance to our children all I can say is that it is truly remarkable. But you can judge for yourself in a few moments. We have spent the past weeks getting them acclimated but except for Olga and Tatiana none of our children have met them yet. I think Olga recognized Franny but if she did she is keeping it a secret. I must admit to you that I have found myself drawn to this scheme and I want it to work. But I pray we never need to use it."

"Have you told them anything about the plan?" asked Nicky.

"Nothing. I left that for you. But they are intelligent and when they were dressed that first morning they immediately realized they were not here to be servants," Alix replied.

Meanwhile, the five impostors sat in their common room anxiously awaiting the arrival of the Tsar. Franny was the only one who had ever met him or even seen him in person and she had been awestruck in his Imperial presence. Even after so much time had passed the nervousness she felt at their first meeting was starting to return. The realization that they were about to meet Nicholas II, Tsar of all the Russias was almost overwhelming and the emotions of the children ranged from apprehension to near panic. Ekaterina, Olga's double, was pale and nervous and Helena kept straightening her dress and smoothing down her hair. The girls, in particular, wanted to look their very best. Isa had helped them to prepare and they wore beautifully embroidered blue dresses. They had only been at the palace for a few weeks but already they were accustomed to the finer things that were provided by the Empress and her daughters.

Dalek sat leaning back in his chair. "Why are you so concerned about meeting the Tsar? You act as though God Almighty is getting ready to walk through that door," he said irreverently.

"How dare you speak of the Tsar in that manner," shouted Dalida as she jumped to her feet. "The Tsar is God's representative on earth and in his presence you will stand, be respectful and greet the him in the manner you were taught. I have my eye on you, Dalek and if you betray the confidence placed in you I will personally ring your scrawny little neck." Occasionally, when Dalek provoked her, she forgot her training and reacted like the soldier she was. Frankly, the addition of this young woman had been a Godsend for the other girls because Dalida was absolutely fearless and would brook no nonsense from Dalek nor allow him to harass the others.

"Dalek, what is the matter with you? You have been taken away from a terrible life and now you live in total comfort. Why would you want to throw it all away?" asked Helena.

"I am tired of being inside," he said. "I do not like it here. I feel like a caged rabbit."

"You are too impatient Dalek. The time will pass quickly and when our service is completed the education we have received will enable us to start new lives."

"Well, maybe," said Dalek.

"You will not ruin this for the rest of us. We have worked too hard for it all to be thrown away because of you. Now straighten up and behave yourself," Dalida ordered.

Dalek started to object, but seeing the looks on the faces of the others, he thought better of it.

The Tsar had made his way with Alix up to the attic. Count Benckendorff and the others involved in the plan ensured that they were not detected or missed. They were being a bit overly cautious since this was the part of the night that belonged to the Tsar and his family and no one had the temerity to intrude on their private interlude. As they reached the top of the stairs and entered the attic, they could hear raised voices. "Listen Sunny," said Nicholas with a laugh. "They argue just as ours do."

"Yes I can hear them. I wonder what it is all about."

"They are confined to this space all day with only each other. I am sure they feel a bit irritable." As they walked down the hall to the large room at the end the noise stopped as the occupants of the room realized the Tsar was approaching.

"Be gentle with them darling. They are very nervous, so please try to help them relax. They must get comfortable with us if people are to believe we are their parents. I for one must admit it is forcing me to be more patient."

Helena heard the approaching footsteps and became very flustered. "He is here, am I presentable?"

"Yes, you look beautiful," said Ekaterina. They all quickly stood and waited to be presented to the Tsar. The door opened and Nicholas and the Tsarina walked into the room.

"Greetings, your Imperial Highness," they all said in unison, as they bowed and curtsied.

"And greetings to you all," answered Nicholas with a broad smile. The smile concealed the absolute amazement he felt as he looked at each of the doubles. Ella had shown him pictures and described them but the transformation they had made in just a few weeks was remarkable. Dressed as they were in his children's clothes, with the same hairstyles, their resemblance to the Imperial children was remarkable. "I am astounded," he said to Alix. "I truly believe that at a distance even someone who knew our children quite well could not tell these are substitutes." He then turned back to the children and said. "You have been selected to perform a service for Russia which requires that you look as much as possible like my own children. I will give you more details later but for now let me say how very, very pleased I am with the way you look and what you have accomplished so far. When you finally meet your counterparts you will understand my enthusiasm. Now Your Highness," he said, with a twinkle in his eye, "will you introduce me to our children."

They all smiled at this and Alexandra began the introductions. "This is Ekaterina, and obviously she will double for Olga," said the Empress.

Nicholas extended his hand expecting her to shake it but instead she bowed to kiss it. "It is such an honor, Your Highness to meet you and to be of service to you. I have thanked God over and over that you chose me and that I now have the opportunity to thank you in person," said Ekaterina as tears streamed down her face. The Tsar took a handkerchief out of his pocket and wiped away her tears. "Thank you for saying yes my dear. You are doing a great service for your country."

He moved to Tatiana's double and Alix introduced her. As the Tsar reached for her hand Helena fainted but with his quick reflexes he caught her before she fell to the floor. He placed her in a nearby chair while Alix waved smelling salts under her nose.

"Poor girl, I hope she will be able to manage better in the future."

"She will be fine Nicky. It is the combination of the excitement and the fact that her stays are too tight." As they spoke, Helena sat up, mortified that she had fainted in front of the Tsar, and full of apologies.

"I understand my dear. This must seem overwhelming but just rest there for a minute and you will be fine. I even get that way at times myself," the Tsar whispered to her.

Alix intervened and said, "Nicholas, come and meet the rest of the group." The three youngest had remained standing, not sure what to do when Helena fainted.

Nicholas moved to Dalida and Alix introduced her. "So you are my little soldier?" queried the Tsar. She snapped to attention as if she was still on parade and rendered a sharp salute.

"No need for that here," said Nicholas. "You will be impersonating my daughter and although I hear you are strong like Maria you must leave your soldier ways behind and act like a Grand Duchess."

"Yes, your Highness," she replied.

Nicholas then looked over at Anastasia's imposter and smiled at her. Franny's nervousness vanished and she remembered how kind he had been to her. She had heard people refer to the Tsar as "Bloody Nicholas" but in her mind he was the hero who had rescued her from a life of misery. "How is my little Franny," he asked. "Not so little anymore, I see." Franny blushed with pleasure that the Tsar had remembered her. "I know Anastasia will be overjoyed to see you."

"Yes, but we may have little time to see each other," she said.

"That is true, but it is for a good reason. We have a task to carry out and we must all remain focused on our mission. It is critical for our safety that no one know of your presence here," he reminded everyone.

The Tsar came to the last impostor. Dalek stood with his head bowed as if the Tsar might recognize him for the scoundrel he was. He had fooled everyone but he was not sure if he could fool the Tsar of Russia.

He knew that he would have to be on his toes and not slip up. "You must be the Tsarevich?" said Nicholas.

"Yes, Your Highness. Evidently I am to be your son's double," he replied.

"It is good to meet you," said Nicholas, turning to the others. "It is good to meet all of you." He motioned them to take a seat and they all settled in around the table with the Tsar at one end and the Empress at the other. "I have much to discuss with you tonight but first we must examine the serious issue of why you are here. Each of you is a soldier in a small but important army. During the coming months you will continue your education but more importantly you will learn my children's likes and dislikes, their mannerisms, their family relationships, everything you can that will enable you to successfully imitate them. If and when the necessity arises your task will be to fill in for my children in what could very well be a dangerous situation. There is even the possibility your lives could be in danger. It is important to understand that this is not a lark but a very real state of affairs. I know it is exciting to come and live in a palace but you are here, first and foremost, to train for an assignment, a most important one. Just as Dalida trained to be a soldier and knew her occupation would be dangerous and that she could die, so is it true for you. Remember first and foremost that what you will be asked to do is for Russia, and your love for your country will help carry you through. And I myself, or the Empress, or both of us, will be with you at all times. You will never face danger alone. Can I count on you?"

The group at the table nodded their assent and Nicholas continued. "I hope you have all grown in your faith since you first joined Sister Ella and began your preparation. Our Russian Orthodox faith is extremely important to us and it has sustained us through many trials and tribulations. It will strengthen you as well and give you the fortitude to be successful on your mission. If you only practice the faith, hope for the future, and love one another, all will go well."

Nicholas could see that they all had a hundred questions but he was not up to spending the night answering them. "My children I know what I have told you may seem somewhat vague but be patient and much will be revealed in the coming days. I will tell you that I do not know at this point how long you will be with us, but when I no longer have need of your services you will be released to make new lives for yourselves and will be generously provided for. One other concern you probably have is whether you will be able to leave the palace. For the present your world will consist of these upstairs rooms and the occasions when you go to the second floor. By the way, you may never come down without one of the trusted staff as an escort. This is not a prison but we must protect our secret. We will do everything in our power to keep you occupied. If we can find a way to get you outside from time to time be assured the Empress will arrange it."

The impostors were not surprised at this because Miss Zanotti had already spoken to them about the need for secrecy but it was different hearing the words from the Tsar himself. It gave added weight to the need for concealment. There was no need to belabor the point so Nicholas ended the conference with some simple instructions.

"You must act naturally around me, and this may be difficult for you, since I will be at the front most of the time and you will not see much of me. So we will keep it simple for the time being. My children call me Papa and give me a kiss on the cheek every night and so must you. Now I think that is enough for tonight, but before the Empress and I go down I would like each of you to have a small gift from me. It is an icon of St. Serafim of Sarov, a great saint who is much revered by this family." Nicholas handed each of the doubles an icon which he had commissioned for each of them. They were all touched by his gift, even Dalek, who now had something he could call his own. When the Tsar had finished he stood up to leave and all the doubles immediately stood up as well. "We will have none of that," said the Tsar. "Come and give your Papa a kiss good-night." Each of his new children nervously approached him and kissed his cheek. "Good. Now let that be a lesson to you. The simplest of things could give you away." Nicholas and Alexandra made their way to the hidden staircase, followed it down, and then returned to their quarters.

It had been an extremely long day for Nicky and Alix and it was after midnight when they finally retired for the night. With the lights turned off the room was dim except for the flickering of a few candles which illuminated the icons on the wall. Alix sighed with pleasure as she lay back among the many down filled pillows which covered her side of the bed. "Nicky, I was wondering about something," said Alix.

"What is it my dear?" asked Nicky. It was a struggle to stay awake but he did not want to be rude to his darling Sunny, who seemed to be rejuvenated by this intriguing escapade.

"When our daughters finally come out of hiding, how will the family know if they are our royal children or the doubles? I have to admit that I am still stunned by their likeness to our children."

"Well, certainly my mother will know her own grandchildren and besides, the doubles will assume different identities once they complete their mission." Alix's question had caught Nicky off guard. It was something he had not considered and he was instantly alert in despite his fatigue.

"We can not rely on that Nicky. Several times you have failed to recognize our relatives when a long period of time has past since we have seen them."

"That is hardly fair. Sometimes it has been years since I have seen them and people change. Besides, they will have their rings"

"Exactly my point. It had been years and they had changed considerably. We do not know how long the children will be in hiding and they will certainly look different when they reappear. They will not be able to pull out an identity card that tells your mother who they are, if she is even still alive. And as for the rings, they can be lost or stolen. As far as the doubles are concerned, what if they decide they like the royal life? They could try to assume one of our children's identities and step forward to claim their fortune. There has to be something we can do, Nicky, to prevent anything like that from happening."

"Well, you need not worry about anyone obtaining access to the money. Only someone who knows the code and the special provisions I have established will be able to withdraw any funds. It is not possible to simply walk into a bank and walk out with funds I have placed there. However, you do have a point. Money corrupts and although we may forge a tight bond with the doubles there is always the possibility that one could have her head turned by the thought of great wealth and come forward to claim she is a Grand Duchess. But I think you are wrong about my mother, she would know her grandchildren any where. Our daughters would be able to answer any questions she could ask.

"Well, perhaps your mother is a bad example but the likely course is that she will not be around. The impostors will have lived in the palace long enough to know all kinds of personal family information and they might not fool an Empress but certainly they could deceive more distant family members or other nobility."

"Poor Sunny, you worry too much and it is not good for your heart. I believe we have everything under control. The doubles will be very well taken care of in the future and I cannot imagine anyone would have the audacity to approach my mother posing as a Grand Duchess unless she really was. It is preposterous," said Nicky.

"You of all people should know that we must consider everything and try to imagine scenarios which could endanger the plan. I think you need to take what I am saying seriously."

"I am sorry Sunny. I do value your suggestions but it has been a long day and frankly I am exhausted. There is so much to consider and many loose ends to tie up but I will give your concerns some thought and see if a solution comes to mind. When I head back to the front this time everything must be in place. Now darling, go to sleep and let me take this burden from you."

"Thank-you dearest, but it is no burden. My love for our family is all consuming and I only desire the safety of our children."

"I love you, Sunny," Nicky said as he rolled over to kiss her good night. A few minutes earlier he had been struggling to keep his eyes open but now, as he lay there on his back, he was wide awake. Their conversation had put his brain in motion and he found he was unable to sleep. Nicholas appreciated his wife's advice because it indicated to him that she was committed to the *Masquerade*. She was an intelligent and well-educated woman and in spite of her many infirmities she remained a valued confidante. He wondered if the concern she had voiced about identifying the children was really a problem and after considering the issue he had to concede that it might be. But as the minutes turned into hours he could think of no simple solution. He knew that unless he came up with some answer he would not be able to have a restful night, one that he so desperately needed.

He glanced over at Alix and in the dim light he could see the rhythmic rising and falling of her breast and hear the gentle sounds that indicated she was fast asleep. He carefully slipped out of bed, donned a dressing gown, and quietly left the room. Nicholas walked across the hall to his bathroom, an elaborate room large enough to accommodate his exercise equipment. He had installed a chinning bar which he used on a regular basis and on sleepless nights such as this one he found the rhythm of chin-ups relaxed him and helped clear his mind. He removed his dressing gown, placed it on a chair, and moved into position under the bar. He jumped up, grasped the bar, and began a set of pull-ups. As he continued the exercise he noticed the rippling muscles in his upper arms. Nicholas was a small man in stature and because of this he devoted much time to working out, even going so far as to installing an exercise bar in his private car on the Imperial train. He was now in his late 40's and no longer considered a young man but his exercise kept him in fairly decent physical shape.

As he pulled himself up he noticed the mark that had been tattooed on his arm by a Japanese artist when he had visited Japan in his youth. He dropped from the bar and looked at the tattoo in the dim light. This is the answer, he thought. His children's identifying mark, known only to selected members of the *Masquerade*, would be a tattoo, located in an inconspicuous spot on their bodies. Where would be a good location? The arms and legs were occasionally exposed so that was not acceptable. He discounted the torso for fear that the mark might be discovered during a medical exam or by one of the maids who assisted the children with their baths. Finally it came to him. The ideal spot was under the left buttock, an area that posed little risk of discovery. He hesitated for a moment at the thought of his daughters having to expose their bottoms and he knew that Alix would have a hard time accepting the idea. But a tattoo did provide a response to her concerns and since he could come up with no other idea she would have to solve the dilemma herself, or live with his solution.

His answer to the problem created many more questions. Who could he possibly get to do the tattoos? What would they look like? And when would he have it done? He felt relief that he at least had an idea. He would have discuss this with some of the others and get their viewpoints. But for now he wanted only one thing. His bed.

When morning dawned and light began to filter into their room, Alix was the first to awake. As she stretched her limbs she saw that her husband was still in a deep sleep. He was usually an early riser so she assumed he was probably awake half the night wrestling with a solution to her problem. Alix really did not want to wake him but he was here for such a short time and there was so much to do that felt she must. She smiled as she gently prodded him awake. "Nicky, wake up. Did you arrive at a solution to the problem we discussed last night?"

"Could you not have allowed me another moment or two of sleep, darling," he responded sleepily.

"I am sorry my dear but you have a very busy schedule today and must wake up. Besides you have to tell me what your solution to our dilemma is. I know you thought about it during the night and it is very important to me."

"Well yes, I have an idea, but I fear you will be opposed to it."

"Let me hear it at least."

"We will have each of the girls tattooed with a small but distinguishing symbol."

Alix laughed aloud. "Oh Nicky, be serious and tell me what you have come up with."

"I will have you know that I am dead serious. How could I joke about such a thing, woman?"

"Do I hear you correctly? You spent hours on this and all you could come up with is a plan to brand our children like cattle. The poor girls, they will be horrified. I cannot even imagine how painful it will be. Certainly there are other alternatives."

"It is as I thought," the Tsar replied angrily. "You do not approve." Nicky had just been awakened from a deep sleep and was tired and irritated and the combination made him lash out at Alix.

"How easy it is for you to lie there and criticize me. Can you offer anything substantive or do you plan on spending your time carping away while I break my back trying to save Russia, and our children."

Alix was quick to realize she had touched a nerve in her usually patient and unflappable spouse. "I am sorry Nicky. It is just that I had not expected such a drastic solution. Please tell me more."

"The catalyst for this idea was my own tattoo, which by the way was not painful. It itched terribly when it was healing but other than that, it was not a problem. I have decided that this will be done and the only discussion will be answering the questions when? how? and by whom? I am sorry if you find it disagreeable but my mind is made up. The tattoo will be very small, not much larger than a kopeck and will be in an inconspicuous place."

"And where might this inconspicuous place be," inquired Alix, in a rather subdued voice.

"On the back of the upper left leg, right under the buttocks."

"I am not sure I understand the location."

"Under the derriere, right here," said the Tsar as he rolled over and pointed out the location to Alix.

"Let me make sure I understand this. You are going to have a total stranger, a man I assume, tattoo your daughters on their backsides like common whores. Now please explain to me why this is a good idea. It just sounds preposterous to me." She paused and her face became flushed and her breathing labored. She felt the beginnings of a heart palpitation and clutched at her chest.

Nicholas observed her with concern. He felt sure that if he could not calm her down she would be incapacitated for the rest of the day. He picked up her hand and kissed it. "Sunny," he said gently. "You must not worry yourself over this. Now I want you to rest during the day. You have been over exerting yourself with all of your nursing and war work."

"Nicky please think about what you are planning to do. Do not ask your daughters to disrobe before a stranger and have their bodies marked forever with some horrible tattoo."

"Alix, this is the perfect solution for the concerns you expressed to me only last night. You have never indicated any distaste for my tattoo."

"But you are a man."

"Please, help me, Alix. We can design a beautiful symbol, something that will be special not only for us but for our children. I have not had time to consider a design but I thought the Russian Imperial double eagle should be incorporated into it," said Nicky.

Alix began to calm down, and as she put aside her initial doubts she had to admit Nicky's idea of a mark that could never be removed had merit. It was the procedure itself that caused her distress and she wondered if there was some way it could be done without compromising the girl's modesty. "Nicky, we cannot just have our daughters expose their bare bottoms to a total stranger. If you can assure me that proper decorum will be observed then I will not object to your plan. I would like to add something to the design, my special symbol, the swastika. It is the ancient sign of movement, the four rivers flowing away in different directions."

"Yes, I remember, the sign for Atlantis. How fitting, four daughters and four rivers."

"What about Alexei," inquired the Empress? "We cannot have him tattooed. Not with his condition; it would be far too dangerous."

"I agree that with his health it is not feasible. I have made arrangements for his double but I am unsure about his future as he was never mentioned in St. Serafim's letter. Remember, it is one of our four daughters that is the bridge to the future of Russia. It is through her that Russia will be reborn. Maybe she will be a future leader or the mother of a future Tsar. It is so hard to know what their prospects are; only time will tell."

"Nicholas, you are frightening me. Do you think Alexei is going to die?"

"No my darling, but his health is frail and I cannot foretell what the future will bring."

"Father Grigory assures me his future is secure. Do you sometimes wonder if we are placing too much trust in the words of a dead man when we have a living, breathing man of God among us?"

"Alix, do you forget that it was your personal intervention that led to St. Serafim's canonization. It is too late for you to have doubts now. I firmly believe in Serafim's words. I have staked my life and that of my children on them. I need to know that you share with me that same confidence."

"Oh Nicholas, I do. It is just every now and then that I allow my fears to overwhelm me. Forgive me darling."

Nicholas sat up and reached over to the night stand for the pencil and writing tablet he kept by the side of his bed. "Let me sketch the two symbols and see what they look like together." He drew various versions using the two symbols but was unhappy with his efforts.

"Why not take this and put it above the other," Alix suggested.

Nicholas was a very talented artist and was meticulous in his illustrations. One of his portfolios contained drawings of each piece of jewelry he received from family members. Some of the renderings were so lifelike that it looked as if the jewel could be lifted off the page. Nicholas carefully drew another version according to Alix's directions.

Her face lit up as she gazed at it. "That is it Nicky," she said with enthusiasm. "It is perfect." Alexandra took the drawing from the Tsar and gazed at it with a far off look in her eyes. The double eagles were above and appeared to be holding the swastika in their talons. "Always to be recognized by my sign," she murmured. "I like the design but I dread telling our daughters about this."

"Do you want me to be the one to tell them?"

"No, this will be rather embarrassing for young girls. It will be easier and less frightful for them if I explain it. When do you think we should have this done?"

"It will have to be done after we tell the children what is in store for them and, as we have discussed before, we will put that off as long as possible.."

"I agree with you. There is nothing to be gained by telling them now and having them worry about it for months. Who will do the tattoos?"

"Obviously I have not had time to come up with the answer to that," Nicky replied. "We do have tattoo artists in Russia, but maybe the Japanese could send someone. This must be done with the utmost secrecy. I will speak with Sandro about it."

"Why Sandro?" asked Alix.

"He has spent so much time in Japan learning about their culture that he may have a suggestion. Maybe he could formulate some sort of plan." He leaned over to kiss Alix. "Well Sunny, let me get dressed and started on my day." For Nicholas another hurdle had been crossed. Each of the Grand Duchesses would receive a tattoo and only select members of the *Masquerade* and possibly his mother and sisters would be made aware of the secret mark. The impostors would never know.

Later that morning Isa gathered the Imperial children in their dining room to prepare them for their first visit to the attic. Ella had returned to Moscow shortly after the doubles arrived, staying just long enough to see them settled in, and now the Baroness was responsible for the ten youngsters. But this morning the Empress had indicated to Isa that she wanted to be there for the initial introductions so Alexei and the girls were waiting impatiently for the arrival of their mother. They knew, of course, of the existence of the secret stairs but had been forbidden to go up until the renovations were completed and the doubles settled in. At last the day had arrived and there was a palpable aura of anticipation at both ends of the staircase, for neither group had any sense of what it meant to have or be a double. Isa had them all dressed alike and she was as excited as everyone else to finally see them standing side by side. When Alix arrived in the dining room the children jumped to their feet and ran to the hutch which concealed the entrance to the upper rooms.

"Settle down for a moment, my dears, while Toodles locks the doors, and remember to keep the noise down. Some sounds carry a long distance and we do not want to ruin things the first day."

When all was ready Isa unlatched the cupboard, swung it out from the wall and motioned the young people to follow her up the narrow stairs. Alix brought up the rear and, when she had gone through the opening, Toodles sealed the entrance behind her.

At the top Alix took the lead and ushered them down the hallway to the large common room where the impostors were gathered, eagerly awaiting the arrival of the Imperial children. When the door opened they jumped to their feet and in unison said "good morning Mama." Alexandra's children were shocked at this familiarity and when the Empress saw the look on their faces she hastened to explain that this was what their father wanted. Reassured, they each approached their double and introduced themselves.

"Hello, I am Olga," the Grand Duchess said, by way of introduction. "We met briefly at the hospital when you came in."

"Yes, I remember. I am also Olga." The two young women smiled at each other and then burst out laughing for indeed, they did look like each other. Their exchange broke the ice and soon they were all talking to their counterparts. The most poignant moment occurred when Anastasia recognized that her double was her old friend from Poland. "Oh Franny,"

Anastasia exclaimed. "Can it really be you? I thought you had perished in that terrible fire. I cried for days."

"Yes it is really me. The fire was necessary to hide the fact that I was leaving but I knew eventually we would be re-united. Everyone has been so kind to me."

The Empress looked at the animated group and smiled. Dalida was explaining to Marie why her hair was so short, and Tatiana and Helena seemed to have found some common ground. Even Alexei, who had a tendency to lord it over his few friends, seemed to have hit it off with Dalek. After the introductions the Empress had intended to gather everyone around the table to explain the routine and go over some of the dos and don'ts but they were all so involved with each other that she hated to break the mood. She arranged with Toodles to serve lunch up here and then slipped out of the room. They could continue their interaction until the newness of the situation had worn off, then Isa could take over. Alix was pleased at the way things had turned out and was anxious to share her observations with the Tsar. Ella had done a marvelous job. They really did look alike.

Chapter 34

February 1916 – Tsarskoe Selo. Several weeks later, as Olga made her rounds in the hospital, an event occurred which would have a profound effect on her life. Some additional casualties had been brought in and one of the doctors asked for her assistance in determining the extent of their injuries. She moved from soldier to soldier examining them carefully and then marked the forehead of each of the wounded with a letter indicating his status. When she neared the end of one row of cots she leaned down to assess a patient and then stepped back with a gasp as she recognized the dirty face of the unconscious soldier. Despite the battlefield grime that covered his face Olga had made out the features of her first love, Anatoly Vasilyev. She stood there in a state of shock, staring at Vasily and unable to move, so pale that one of the other nurses asked her if she was all right.

"What?" Olga replied.

"Is there something wrong Your Highness? You look as if you had seen a ghost."

"No. Everything is fine. I thought I recognized this officer, but perhaps not." She smiled at the other nurse and leaned back over the wounded man. It just cannot be, she thought. What are the chances? She wiped his face with a damp cloth and yes, assuredly, it was her Vasily.

She quickly assessed his condition and made the appropriate mark so he could receive the proper care. Olga wanted to linger and be with him when he regained consciousness but she did not want to draw undo attention to him and she had other patients to evaluate. She carried on her duties as best she could but found it very difficult to concentrate. She had been a young girl when she had fallen in love with Vasily but he was deemed by her father to be unsuitable and was sent away. Now she was a young woman of twenty-one and despite the intervening years her love for him was as strong as it had ever been. When she had a chance for a short break, she rushed off to find Tatiana and tell her what had happened. Tatiana slipped away from her station for a moment to look at the new patient. "Olga, you are right. I am sure it is him," she said. "In spite of all the dirt, he is more handsome than I remembered."

"Oh, I cannot wait until he regains consciousness," said Olga. "I have so much too say to him"

"Olga, you must not let your emotions run away with you. It would be very dangerous for you, and for him, if your feelings became known. You know how Mama and Papa feel. You must be very circumspect and treat him like any other patient."

"Times have changed, Tatiana. I know he will eventually recover and have to return to the front but I have this premonition that something is going to bring us together again, maybe not right away, but in due time. I pray it is so. It is this hope that keeps me from becoming depressed at the idea of losing him again."

Vasily was suffering from a severe concussion, dysentery, and a number of shrapnel wounds which had weakened him considerably. On the third day after his arrival at Catherine Palace he regained consciousness and during the next few weeks started down the road to recovery. Olga attempted to see him everyday, for a few minutes at a time, and although she tried to hide her feelings it soon became obvious to those that worked in the hospital that the Grand Duchess had a new flirtation. She had a glow about her and she had increased her hours at the hospital but, to her fellow workers, it all seemed harmless enough. When Vasily recovered enough, and was able to speak, he talked to Olga about everything that had happened to him in the years they were separated. She responded with words of endearment and soon learned that in his case, at least, absence had made the heart grow fonder. Yet, despite their love for one another, they had matured enough to realize, that as things now stood, there was no future for the two of them. So they took what comfort they could in the few quiet moments they shared with each other, and relished the beginning of each new day, secure in the knowledge that it would bring them together again if only for a few fleeting minutes. Olga's mother was well aware that something was going on but she knew nothing would come of it and the Empress had no intention of intervening in her daughter's innocent relationship with the young officer. The girls would face so many challenges in the coming year that the idea of depriving them of any enjoyment was beyond her.

Vasily was a strong young man but his wounds healed slowly and it was a while before he could get up and move around. But for Olga the weeks had seemed to pass by so very, very quickly and she knew from experience that before much longer the doctors would discharge him from the hospital. The Grand Duchess had become a young woman of strong determination and though she dreaded the day his name would appear on the return-to-duty roster, she vowed to be strong and not succumb to her emotions. On this particular day she had just finished her shift at the hospital and had made her way to the officer's ward to read to Vasily. These special moments spent at his bedside were precious ones, and were the only times that she could, in whispered words of affection, express her love for him. As she reached his bedside she was surprised to see him sitting on the side of the bed fully dressed in his uniform. "What is going on?" inquired Olga, although she knew without a doubt.

"The doctor came by this afternoon and pronounced me fit and ready for duty. I am to return to my unit," said Vasily. "I knew this day was coming but it caught me totally by surprise. I thought we would have more time together before I had to leave."

"I am stunned. I heard nothing from the doctor. I must speak with him."

"No Olga, my dearest love," he whispered. It is my duty and I have to admit I have not rushed my recovery. But they need every available bed for new casualties and it is not right for me to take up a space when others need it so desperately. I am no longer a casualty and even you must admit that I am fit for duty."

Olga leaned forward and in a low voice said, "I must see you alone before you leave."

"I too was hoping for that. The last time we had a moment alone together was when you were sixteen and your father caught us trying to kiss."

"Yes, I remember. I felt so sorry for you and, of course, I was mortified."

"You should know that they are sending me off first thing in the morning," said Vasily.

"Then we must meet tonight. It will be our only opportunity."

"Are you willing to take the risk again, as we did so many years ago? I would not relish being interrupted by your father again. He can be very intimidating."

"Vasily, do not be such a sissy. All fathers are like that. It is my decision to see you alone one last time. Will you meet me?"

"If you will risk everything, my dear, so will I. Do you have a plan?"

"Not yet," said Olga. "Let me think about it and I will come back and let you know. I am sure we can meet undetected somewhere on the grounds. Besides, officers do not have a bed check so you should be able to slip away at any time. I will be back later with the arrangements."

Olga left and immediately went to search out Tatiana. She wanted to talk this secret meeting over with her sister and try to come up with a plan. She found her alone in one of the surgical rooms cutting bandages. "Tatiana, I need your help," said Olga.

"Of course, dear sister, what is going on?" she asked as she continued to cut and fold the bandages.

"I just spoke with Vasily and they are shipping him back to the front, first thing in the morning. I was caught totally off guard because the nurses usually get advance notice. I want to speak with him alone and share my true feelings with him."

Tatiana knew all about Olga's feelings since her older sister kept her up many a night talking about Vasily. She could see her sister was deeply and truly in love and she could see what attracted her. Vasily was tall and handsome in his uniform, which was now covered with ribbons and medals for bravery. "Why not meet him outside tonight? Tell him to take a smoke break or go for a walk and meet you in the park near the hospital. No one will recognize you in your nursing outfit. Of course, it will be easier for him than for you. You realize that you will be expected at the palace for dinner."

"Couldn't you tell everyone that I am staying late at the hospital. Mama knows we are expecting more casualties in the morning and we will need many more bandages and supplies. Tell Papa or Mama that I have arranged for an escort to walk me home."

"I think that will work. You have stayed late before and no one commented on it."

"Well then, let me go tell Vasily our arrangements."

"No Olga, let me talk to him. That way no one will see you together before he goes outside. And wear a wrap. It is still quite cold."

"Very well," said Olga. "Set the meeting for nine o'clock. That will give me time to go back to the palace after dark and get a gift I made for Vasily." She had embroidered a handkerchief for him and she wanted to present it to him as a remembrance of her love. She could not let him leave without it.

"Olga, what are you thinking? You will certainly be seen by one of the staff and then my explanation for your absence will seem ridiculous," objected Tatiana.

"I have a solution for that," Olga replied. "The hard part is getting into the palace unseen." She reached into her pocket and took out the key to the tunnel gates. "Count Benckendorff forgot to get this back when the impostors were brought in. I will sneak back into the palace through the tunnel and retrieve the gift from our room. Then I can leave by one of the side doors and make my way across the grounds to meet Vasily near the hospital. It should work."

"Well, all right then, but don't be caught. If you are, it will appear to Papa and Mama that I have lied to them and I never have."

The trip through the tunnel was uneventful and Olga was able to slip into her room and get the handkerchief. Tatiana had set up the rendezvous with Vasily and explained Olga's absence to her parents. The Grand Duchess was anxious to meet her sweetheart and at half past eight she left the palace. She had thirty minutes to elude the sentries, who for the most part were on the outer perimeter, and make her way to her tryst. Olga had considered going back through the tunnel but she did not want to be seen by any of the hospital staff. They all thought she was at Alexander palace and everyone at the palace, except Tatiana, of course, thought she was at the hospital. It was a perfect situation but she knew if she was detected that she would be immediately brought back to the palace and turned over to her parents. So Olga was very cautious when she moved away from the shadows and into the bright moonlight. If she had delayed a minute longer, she would not have seen a figure sneak out from the corner at the other end of the palace. Olga was confused. Could it be Vasily? But why was he coming from that direction? They were to meet on the other side of the park nearer to the hospital. Whoever it was, and it appeared to be a young boy, was being very secretive as he flitted from tree to tree. Olga moved back into the shadows as he approached and finally recognized who it was. Dalek, of all people. He was forbidden to leave the attic so whatever he was doing out here could only be mischief and she knew, without a doubt, that he was up to no good. Ever since the day she had overheard him complaining about his present situation she had ceased to trust him. Now she wished she had brought it to someone's attention.

She knew that she could not call on the palace guards or the secret police. They knew nothing of the secret plan and it would be catastrophic if word got out. She knew she had to keep her wits about her. Dalek ran for another tree and Olga dashed after him. The Grand Duchess had long legs and despite her nurse's gown, which she clutched in her hands, she was able to quickly catch up to him. Olga grabbed his arm and ordered him to stop. "What on earth are you doing out here this late?" Olga asked the boy. "You know that you are not allowed out of your quarters."

"I am leaving. I am finished with this place," he answered defiantly.

"That is impossible. You cannot go like this. You gave your word to my father that once you came into the palace you would stay until he made arrangements for you to leave."

"So I lied. What of it. You think I am some orphan like the others but you are mistaken. My name is Dalek Rakyovich and I am the son of a very important man, a revolutionary. I had run away from home but Mother Elizabeth found me on the street. How naive they were. They believed I was a homeless, orphaned beggar so I played them along. I am small for my age so they thought I was a young boy but I am now eighteen years old. I had hoped to get a little money, food, or something out of the deal. Little did I know that I would end up living in the palace."

"That is correct. You were given this incredible opportunity so why are you trying to leave? You will have it no better on the streets and if you stay you will be handsomely rewarded for your service to the Tsar," said Olga, as she tried to reason with him. If she could just get him back to the palace they could deal with him there.

"I have better plans for myself now. I will be a true hero of the people. The information I have to bring back to my father will be of great use to his movement and then he will respect me. The walls have ears and on many a night I slipped out of my room to listen to conversations on all sorts of topics. I heard plans about money and accounts abroad and secret codes. Oh, the things I have heard." Olga's face turned pale as he continued his hateful tirade. "Do you not know that many Russians are planning and scheming to bring down the Tsar. He will have to pay for the suffering he has caused the workers, soldiers and peasants."

"How dare you speak of the Tsar that way? He loves Russia more than he loves himself and he has suffered along with his people."

"We will not be his people for long, but that is another matter. I am leaving, I have much to report," he said as he turned toward the wrought iron fence.

"I have heard enough," Olga replied. "You are an evil, hateful person and you are not leaving the palace grounds."

"Oh, and will you stop me. I doubt it.

Olga knew that if she allowed Dalek to climb over the fence her family would be endangered. She had to do something. She reached into her pocket, pulled out her gun, and aimed it at him. The little derringer fit snugly in her trembling hand. "I said, you are not leaving."

Dalek laughed as he turned back around. "And how are you going to . . . . "he became silent when he saw the gun. Olga stood there like a statue, holding the gun with both hands, trying to keep it steady. Although she was an accomplished marksman she had never pointed a gun at anyone, especially when the stakes were so high. She hoped that Dalek would do as she said and that somehow she could get him back to the palace without alerting the guards. Then her father, who was briefly home from the Stavka, could deal with the situation. Luckily they were in an isolated part of the park surrounded by woods. "You aren't going to shoot me are you?" Dalek asked.

"I will do whatever is necessary to keep you from going over that fence. Now walk slowly back toward the palace," she said and motioned to him with the gun.

"Just don't shoot me with that thing," Dalek whined.

"Then do as you are told. But make no mistake if you try to run I will shoot." Dalek began to walk and Olga followed closely behind with the gun to his back. She was frightened but she knew that this might be the most important thing she would do in her entire life. Vasily was probably wondering what had happened to her but there was no way she could avoid this responsibility. She had to see it through. Suddenly Dalek slipped on the icy path and appeared to fall forward, opening the distance between them. Olga was caught off guard and almost dropped the gun but it was all a ploy. Dalek caught himself, spun around, and lunged at Olga. He grabbed for the gun and a struggle ensued. As they flailed back and forth trying to gain possession of the derringer it was pressed between them. Suddenly there was a report as the gun went off but their thick cloaks muffled the sound. The struggle ended as Dalek and Olga both fell to the ground.

Several moments passed before Olga's eyes opened. She had fainted at the sound of the gunshot, but otherwise was unhurt. She pushed Dalek off of her and sat up, dazed and somewhat confused. The boy lay there motionless, covered with blood, his glassy eyes staring up at her accusingly. Although the derringer fired a small caliber bullet it was quite lethal at such short range and the round had passed between the ribs and directly into Dalek's chest. Olga's medical training took over and she knelt at his side. As she leaned down across his face to listen for the sound of breathing she felt a hot breath on her cheek and with the last of his strength Dalek mumbled, "I will tell all." She felt for his pulse, but there was none, and she realized that he was dead. Olga was horrified that she had shot and killed a man but she also felt a sense of relief. She looked at the body and whispered,"well, Dalek, who can you talk to now?" Then she leaned against a tree and began to weep. Later she prayed, "God you have spared my life and taken this wretched soul away. Please have mercy on it and when the time comes, I beg you, do not judge me too harshly. But your will be done Lord; your will be done." She realized that if God had not brought her there at that exact time, Dalek would have escaped and exposed the existence of the doubles. She could breathe easy now, knowing that with his death all he knew about the impostors was safe. Olga regained her composure but she was unsure what to do next. She remembered her meeting with Vasily and wondered if he was still waiting for her. Olga had to find out so she pulled Dalek's body further into the trees, covered it with brush and then went to meet Vasily. To her utter relief he was still there. "Oh Vasily," she cried as she fell into his arms. "The most horrible thing has just happened."

"What is it Olga? Are you all right," he asked as he looked at her disheveled appearance and bloodstained clothing.

"I am fine but there is no time for long explanations. A man attacked me near the palace when I was coming to meet you and I shot and killed him with a pistol my Aunt Olga gave me," she said as she stood trembling from her ordeal. "He grabbed at the gun and we struggled and it went off. He is laying under a bush in the woods at the far side of the park. I know who the vile creature is but I can only tell you that if anyone finds his body it will put my family in great danger. I do not know what to do."

"Calm down, everything will be all right." Vasily knew there was more to the story than she was telling him but there was no time for that now. He fired a series of questions at her. "Did anyone see you leave the palace? Do you think anyone heard the gunshot? What about the guards?" he asked.

"As far as I can tell no one saw or heard anything. Everyone at the palace thinks I am still at the hospital."

"Then you have to go home. You know what explanations you will have to make to your father. But first I will get a pick and shovel from gardeners tool shed and then you can take me to the body. The snow is not too deep in the trees and I will bury it there and no one will be the wiser." Vasily found the necessary tools in the shed and Olga led him to Dalek's corpse. He shoveled the snow aside and began to break up the ground with the pick.

"Oh, Vasily," Olga cried. The ground is so hard you will never finish."

"You forget that I have all night. The transport does not leave until after breakfast. I will smooth the ground, put the snow back and when the thaw begins in earnest no one will notice. Now you must go, and when you see your father assure him I have taken care of the matter and will say nothing."

"I had so much to say to you but all this has robbed me of my chance." She reached into her pocket, took out the packet with the handkerchief, and when he laid down the pick, handed it to him. "A little something to remember me by."

"But I have nothing for you," he protested.

"Yes you do," Olga replied "and I have waited many years to receive it from you. May I have it now?"

Vasily took her in his arms and kissed her tenderly and when she began to weep he tried to kiss away her tears but there were too many. "Olga I love you and always will."

"And I, you," she answered. Then, without looking back she made her way to the palace. In the morning she would have to explain to her father why there was now a missing impostor. Once in her room she removed her blood stained clothes and washed up. When the girls had been at the hospital most of the day their clothing was often spattered with blood from working in surgery so a few stains were not unusual. She quietly crept over to her camp bed and slipped under the covers but her hope for a few moments of peace was quickly dashed. "Well, big sister, do not think you are going to go to sleep until I hear every little detail," whispered Tatiana. "What did he say when you told him how you felt? How romantic with the full moon; did he kiss you?"

The stress of the night, and the realization of what she had missed overwhelmed her and she burst into tears. Olga knew she would have to tell her sister the truth because they shared everything and right now she needed to confide in someone. She sat up in bed and turned on a small lamp. Tatiana knew immediately by looking at Olga's face that something dreadful had happened. "Olga, what is wrong? He did not hurt you did he," asked Tatiana with deep concern.

"No, no, this has nothing to do with the way Vasily acted. I hardly got to see him. It is much, much worse. Alexei's impostor is dead."

"Dalek dead? How can that be?"

"Shhh, you will wake the little ones," whispered Olga. "I will tell you everything." Tatiana sat completely dumbfounded as Olga described in detail everything that had transpired earlier. "Vasily was so strong and brave, he handled everything."

"What if he tells someone about the body?"

"He would never. He knows how much I risked sneaking out of the palace at night to meet him. And we did kiss, Tatiana, and it was so delicious."

"Oh, Olga you will have to tell Papa. And what are we going to do about Alexei? There is not enough time find a replacement for Dalek. To think of the years wasted on that creature. Mama will be devastated."

"I know, I know. I will tell Papa first thing in the morning. I want to talk to him alone and then he can tell Mamma. I just cannot face her."

"You were truly a hero tonight, Olga. I would have collapsed in fear. Do you realize what you have done? Had you not been there that boy would have told everything to those people? It gives me cold chills to even think about. But you must try and rest. Tomorrow will be a momentous day. Good night, dearest sister."

Olga could not sleep a wink that night. She tossed and turned as she relived the events of the evening. Her greatest regret was not Dalek's shooting but rather the loss of those precious moments with her beloved Vasily. She was at peace with what had happened but wondered if she had been the one who pulled the trigger; not that it mattered.

Tatiana awoke the next morning to find Olga's bed empty. She knew that her sister had gone to break the news to their father and she wished she could have joined her sister for moral support. She bent her head and said a prayer for her sister asking God to grant her strength to weather the coming storm.

It was early in the morning when Olga entered her father's study, well before his first appointment of the day. She was relieved to see he was sitting alone at his desk. "Good morning dear, what has you up so early this morning," asked Nicholas.

Olga fell to her knees at his feet and laid her head on his lap. "Papa the most terrible thing has happened. You must be told everything but I do not know where to begin," cried Olga, tears streaming down her cheeks.

The Tsar lifted her chin and wiped away her tears. "Olga, is that anyway for a Grand Duchess to act? Now get up off the floor and sit here in the chair and tell me what is troubling you so."

Olga got up and sat in the chair next to her father. "Papa, I am sure mother has told you that Vasily was a patient in the hospital and that I have been spending some brief moments with him. In my nursing capacity, of course."

"Yes, I was aware of the care you have been giving him, in your nursing capacity, of course," her father replied, with a twinkle in his eye.

"Well, since he was being returned to duty this morning, I wanted to see him one last time. So last night I left the palace to meet him."

"Tatiana told me you were at the hospital."

"I was, but I came back through the tunnel to get a handkerchief that I had embroidered for Vasily, then I returned to the hospital across the grounds."

"Olga, how could you do that? I have always insisted you have an escort at night. Why would you disobey me?".

"Please Papa, do not be angry. Allow me to tell you everything before I lose my courage."

"Very well then, continue."

Olga then related to her father the events of the past night, starting with her discovery of Dalek trying to escape, and ending with Vasily disposing of the body. It was when Olga told him of the information Dalek had gathered in the short time he had been here, and what he intended to with it, that the Tsar's face took on a look of dismay.

"Papa, he cannot hurt our family now that he is dead," said Olga..

"I know that Olga. I am consumed by anger, relief, and pride, all at once, and I scarcely know how to react, or what to say. I am angry that you disobeyed me, relieved that you did and proud of your resourcefulness in handling what must have been a truly frightening experience. I will need time to sort out everything that has happened and we will have some major decisions to make. Now tell me Olga, is Vasily trustworthy? Will he tell anyone where the body is buried?"

"Oh no Papa. He asked me to assure you that he would take care of everything and say nothing. We love each other Papa and he would never do or say anything to endanger me. And remember, we would not have Anastasia, if not for him."

"How could I forget. You are right, of course. You may go now but speak to no one about this until I decide what will be done," said Nicholas.

"Yes, Papa, but I have already told Tatiana."

"Then find her immediately and tell her to say nothing."

Just as Olga reached the door it burst open and the Empress stormed into the room. She was in complete hysterics and out of breath. "Nicky, Dalek Rakyovich is gone. He missed breakfast and is not in his room and the girls do not know where he is. What if he left the palace? What are we to do?" she gasped. "This will ruin all our efforts."

"Calm yourself Sunny He did not escape and the boy has been dealt with. Olga you may be excused, I need to speak privately with your mother." Olga left the room with a heavy heart, troubled by the anxiety her mother was feeling, and aware that she was indirectly responsible.

"Nicky, what is going on," Alix asked

Nicholas decided that due to her state of mind he would give her an abbreviated version of the previous evenings startling events. "Last night, about nine o'clock, Olga slipped out of the palace to meet her Vasily, near the hospital. It was providential that she did so because on her way she came upon Dalek trying to leave the grounds. She tried to force him to return, using her little gun, but he attacked her and in the ensuing tussle Dalek was shot and killed. His body has been secretly buried so he is no longer a threat to the *Masquerade*."

"Nicky, can this be true? What was she doing sneaking out in the middle of the night?"

"I am not going to worry about that Alix. There are too many other concerns which need our immediate attention. Our Olga, in spite of her disobedience, saved everything last night. She has been through a horrible experience and I think that is punishment enough. Now, since you are here, let us work through this situation together. We never had an alternate for Dalek so now there is no double for Alexei. We must decide what to do about that. As for the girls, we will simply tell them that Dalek had an accident and is no longer with us. They do not need to know the details. From what I gather they will probably be relieved they no longer have to deal with him."

"Oh Nicky, I know you say we cannot include Father Grigory in this plan but I really think his advice would . . ." Nicholas cut her off before she could go any farther.

"Absolutely not," he stated emphatically. "Do not dare to even consider his involvement in this." It was bad enough that he had to tolerate Rasputin's meddling in affairs of state but he was determined that the *Masquerade* would never include "our friend." But Alix would not leave it alone and was constantly after him to give in. He took small comfort in the realization that if Alix had already revealed the plan she probably would not be asking his permission to do so. The whole situation caused him tremendous stress and was one of the reasons he spent so much time at headquarters.

She tried again. "I just do not understand Nicholas. We have always turned to Father Grigory for everything and now when confronted with the most important event in our lives you refuse to seek his guidance. Look at what has happened. Our friend could have prevented this."

"Enough woman," the Tsar replied in a determined voice. He had enough to worry about now that Alexei's impostor was dead. He did not need his wife nagging him about bringing Rasputin into the picture, a man he loathed and distrusted. Yes, he had involved him before but the matters were inconsequential when measured against his plan to save Russia. He could not allow a flamboyant, talkative, reprobate to ruin what so many had worked so hard to achieve. Yet with the critical months just ahead he could not banish Rasputin from their lives for fear of creating an intolerable climate at the palace. Alix believed Father Grigory kept their son alive and he knew that if the "holy man" was exiled and Alexei died, Alix would blame him forever. It was not a burden he was prepared to accept. Not quite yet.

"Now, Sunny try and concentrate. What do you think of this idea?" The Tsar proceeded to lay out a scenario that he thought might meet the needs of the *Masquerade* and at the same time satisfy Alexandra's concerns. "Even though Serafim only mentioned safeguarding the girls, and said nothing of a son, we have always included Alexei in our planning. It is natural that we would do so. But what if we read into the letter something that is not there. Perhaps Alexei was never meant to leave us. If that is the case then Dalek's death will have no impact. Our son will continue to function as the heir and when the time comes to send the girls into hiding Ekaterina and the others will step in and take on the roles of Alexei's sisters. Alix, the truth of the matter is that his disease is so debilitating he might not survive it and I would hate to know that he was suffering alone, in some foreign land, without you there to care for him. It is not very complicated is it? When our precious daughters leave Tsarskoe Selo, Alexei will remain with us. What do you say, Alix?"

"Oh Nicky, I say yes, yes and yes again. I know you do not want to talk about Father Grigory but he said something to me which now seems very prophetic."

"Yes," said Nicky, trying not to look irritated. The last thing he wanted at the moment was another tiff over Rasputin. "What did he say?"

"Father Grigory has maintained that as long as Alexei remains in Russia he will live, but if he leaves the country he will certainly perish. Your solution to the problem is an answer to my prayers."

"Then Sunny, I will allow him to remain with us no matter where the future takes us."

"Then he will live," cried Alix as she kissed Nicky in happiness. "Our son will live."

Nicholas viewed his wife's irrational joy with skepticism, knowing that it had no basis in fact. He had been told time and again by his physicians that Alexei was unlikely to survive to adulthood and it had mattered little if he left or stayed. But Dalek's death had settled the issue. Alexei would share his parent's fate, whatever that might be.

After Alix left the study she went to the attic where the children and the maids had gathered. They were all, with the exception of Olga and Tatiana, confused and somewhat agitated at the furor Dalek's absence had precipitated. Toodles and

M. Zanotti were especially apprehensive that they might be blamed for Dalek's disappearance. The Empress called them all to the table and, avoiding her usual melodramatic style, laid it out quite simply. "Dalek has been grievously injured in an accident and will no longer be with us. Do not make a big to do about this because we will continue without him; nothing will change. When I go back down that will be the end of it. You will not discuss the matter with each other and you are never to mention his name again. Is that understood?" They all nodded. "Then let us get on with your work. Enough time has been wasted this morning."

Nicholas sat in his study staring out the window. He had remained fairly calm throughout that turbulent morning, getting through his appointments without succumbing to the inner turmoil that tried to overwhelm him. Poor Olga. What a terrible burden for her to bear. And yet Nicholas felt tremendous pride in the way she had confronted Dalek and mastered the situation. He always knew his first born had an inner strength that made her a natural leader and it had been evident in the way she handled herself the previous night. The Tsar stood up and began to pace the floor, vexed by his inability to pull up from the recesses of his mind an idea that he knew was somehow connected with Olga. Finally it came to him. He walked over to his desk, unlocked it, and took out the final draft of the Writ of Succession. Nikolasha and Benckendorff had prepared it for him nearly three years earlier but despite its significance the press of other matters had driven it from his mind. Olga had the strength of character to lead the nation and the other girls were beginning to exhibit similar traits. Now, as he reread the proclamation, he realized the time had arrived to do something with it. There was no question of making it public, especially in the middle of a war, but there was another option. He would have three exact copies made and they would go the route of all the other items. One copy to Prince Kanin when he visited in the fall. One to Father Walsh for safeguarding at the Vatican. A third to the White House and the President's safe. The last to Nikolasha, the only copy to remain in the country. They might never be used, but then again, maybe they would.

Chapter 35

April 1916 – Moscow. The slim young man, conservatively dressed in a dark suit and sitting at the bar of the Hotel Savoy, in downtown Moscow, was hard at work. To the casual observer, however, he seemed innocent enough, as he sipped his tea and inhaled the smoke of a thin cigar with obvious enjoyment. This ability to blend in was but one of his numerous talents and of the many agents employed by Count Benckendorff, Vladislav Zabalia, the man in question, was without doubt the most able and competent. At the direction of the Count he had moved his operation to Moscow, which had become the hub for much of the revolutionary activity in the country, and through persistent espionage he had been successful in penetrating one of the revolutionary factions at the highest level.

Zabalia had been at the Savoy for the past three nights in the expectation that he could generate a "chance" encounter with a mid-level reactionary from this group of dissidents. He had been cultivating this source for some time and had learned from the barman, who was in his pay, that the man he hoped to meet loved his vodka and was a fairly regular customer at the Savoy. Now, after three nights, Vladislav was beginning to think that his contact had found some other place to drink, but he was a patient man and decided to give it more time.

He had the barman take away the tea and replace it with a vodka glass half full of water. It must appear that he was a drinking man for he intended to use the large bundle of rubles in his pocket to get his acquaintance very inebriated. It was his experience that his man was a braggart and tended to give him everything he needed after a few drinks. The information he received was usually general in nature but occasionally there was a useful tidbit that, when added to other intelligence he had gathered, painted a more complete picture. But tonight he was just fishing and would be satisfied with anything he could get.

Zabalia was just about to give it up when, to his delight, the reflection of Ivan Rakyovich appeared in the mirror behind the bar. He turned to greet him but thought better of it. Since he wanted the meeting to appear spontaneous he would wait until the revolutionary noticed him and initiated contact. Rakyovich walked up to the bar, sat two seats down from him, and ordered a large vodka. Zabalia tossed down his water and had the barkeeper fill his glass again. The agent then gave Rakyovich time to get well into his second drink before remarking to the barman in a loud voice, "this vodka tastes like water. Give me a sealed bottle and a fresh glass." Ivan immediately turned to the familiar voice. "Ah, comrade, what a state you must be in to order a bottle for yourself. What troubles you?" he asked.

"Comrade Rakyovich, what a pleasure, my friend. Nothing troubles me. I am on a mission to get drunk. Do come join me upstairs and we will make friends with this bottle," he replied. The Savoy had an upper loft with seating which was perfect for the interrogation he had in mind.

"Oh, he has been my friend for a long time, comrade," said Ivan. "I will gladly join you." The two men made their way up the stairs and sat in one of the corner booths. They were alone because it was still too early for most patrons of the bar.

Zabalia poured a glass for each of them and they toasted the revolutionary movement, but each in their own fashion. Ivan tossed his drink down while the Count's man merely sipped at his. "There is nothing like good vodka," he said. The two men made small talk and continued to drink and before long it was obvious that Ivan was getting quite drunk. Vladislav never divulged any real truths about his own life to anyone and any piece of personal information that he shared was a fabrication to protect his true identity. Ivan, on the other hand, his tongue loosened by the liquor, was eager to share his own experiences and told Vladislav that he had been a teacher at one time but lost his job because of his radical beliefs. Now he had to work at odd jobs to make ends meet. Zabalia needed to know more than details of Ivan's personal life and he decided that his comrade was now a plum, ripe for the picking, and ready to divulge what the revolutionaries were up to. The agent had a meeting scheduled with Benckendorff in three days and thus far there was nothing new to report.

"Drink up comrade, drink up," encouraged Zabalia.

"You know, comrade, I am getting ready to embark on a great adventure," said Ivan. "I am going to Petrograd and then to Tsarskoe Selo and the Alexander Palace."

"That is the vodka talking, my friend. What possible reason could you have for going to the palace?"

"No, no, it is true. We have heard of some strange things going on at the palace in Tsarskoe Selo. I know I told you that I had a son who ran away some time ago and he is connected to these rumors"

Zabalia could hardly contain his excitement. He felt as if Ivan was on the brink of revealing something important, if he could only keep him focused. "What does all this have to do with you going to the palace?"

"Well, there was a girl named Natasha whom my brother was in love with. She had a position at the palace as a scullery maid but she was accused by a housekeeper of stealing some silver and when they found it in her room she was dismissed and thrown into prison. Somehow my brother found out she was there and went to see her. During the short time he was allowed to speak to her she told him she was sure she had seen my son at the palace. I personally find it hard to believe but my comrades feel that it needs to be looked into. Apparently there have been rumors about things going on in the palace."

"Things? What kind of things? Ghosts?"

"Ha! Vague, nebulous comings and goings. I do not know for sure, but they want to send in a . . .," he leaned drunkenly towards Zabalia and whispered, as if worried someone might hear . . . a spy. They want to check up on our great Imperial family and I have insisted that they select me to go because my son might be involved. They said they will have to wait and see how things develop. There are so many factors to consider."

"Now how do they suppose you would get into the palace. Oh, I know. You would just stroll up to the palace door, knock on it and say I am Ivan Rakyovich and the Tsar would invite you in," ridiculed Zabalia.

"Oh, but you underestimate our comrades. They have their ways."

Zabalia was worried and wondered how he was going to get him to reveal the plan to infiltrate the palace. "That is interesting, my friend but you will never get into the palace. The security is very tight."

"Not tight enough. From time to time the palace publishes a list of vacant positions and we have access to that list. It may be several months but when something opens up I hope to be the one to fill it. At any rate we will be sure that no one else applies for the vacancy, if you know what I mean," said Ivan. Zabalia knew exactly what he meant. These men would go to any lengths to end the Romanov reign. They were vicious, dangerous men; all of them.

"But what are you qualified to do," Zabalia asked.

"As I said earlier, I was once a teacher and I specialized in foreign studies. Perhaps a teaching position will open up."

"Perhaps," replied Vladislav. Before he could illicit anything else, Ivan Rakyovich passed out on the table. With the assistance of the hotel porter the agent put him into a taxi and sent him to his lodgings. He had hardly touched his stack of rubles.

Three days later the agent detrained at Tsarskoe Selo and was met by Count Benckendorff. Zabalia gave him a detailed verbal report of his meeting with Rakyovich and was somewhat surprised at the Count's reaction to the news.

"Vladislav, my dear young man, you have brought wonderful information. I see a great opportunity here. How does that proverb go? 'The devil you know, is better than the devil you don't know.' Consider this. If we do nothing they will eventually get someone into the palace and we will not know who it is. And if we expose their intrigue now, they will still keep trying and may succeed. But what if we facilitate their plan? What if we advertise for a tutor to give a two or three week seminar to the Grand Duchesses on Egypt and India, for example. Do you think a certain Ivan Rakyovich might apply for the position? We would have a spy in the palace, but one whose movements we could manipulate. I guarantee we would have him so confused by the end of the period that he could only report to his superiors that everything seemed absolutely normal at Alexander Palace."

"A dangerous, but intriguing idea," Zabalia observed.

"I will take it up with the Tsar immediately. In the meantime, I want you to return to Moscow and have some men keep an eye on our tutor. As soon as I have approval I will let you know and we can put the plan into action."

Count Benckendorff wasted no time in bringing to the Tsar's attention the newly discovered scheme to introduce a spy into the palace. At first Nicholas was reluctant to approve the Count's suggested counter-plot but the more he thought about it the more intrigued he became. "You know Benckendorff, we could take this a step further."

"I am not sure what you are getting at, Your Highness. Does my plan not suit our needs?"

"Most certainly, my friend," the Tsar replied. "But we have been preparing the doubles for a long time and I have always known that at some point we would have to test the effort we have made. What better time than this when, as you say, we can control the situation. We will advertise a teaching position, to start next month, making sure that Zabalia notifies our revolutionary, so he can apply. I am sure Vladislav can do it in such a way that suspicions are not aroused. When you have hired him and arranged for his accommodations he will come each day to tutor the four Grand Duchesses. They just will not be the real ones. The impostors will be on stage."

"Ah, yes," said the Count. "I see. And Alexei will be with you at the Stavka, a fact which can be easily verified."

"That is correct. I will be returning on the 24th so you, Sophie and the Empress, of course, will have to pull this off. I must admit, old comrade that ever since the Empress agreed to allow Alexei to accompany me to headquarters I have felt a peace and contentment that I have not enjoyed for a long time. To be able to spend time with my son and do things with him has been a great gift. So as much as I would like to see our four girls perform in their initial test I will return to the front as scheduled and leave it in your capable hands. Now I would like you to brief the Empress and everyone else involved as to our intentions. As for the doubles, I will personally inform them at a meeting here in the study tomorrow morning. Please arrange it."

⋘⋙

Ekatrina and the other girls were somewhat surprised to be summoned to the Tsar's study since all of their other meetings had been held in the attic common room. They were naturally excited and impatient to go down but there was a delay as Baroness Sophie inspected the security arrangements. Anyone not involved with the plan was excluded from the private family quarters and Sophie, after insuring that the way was clear, went up to the attic and escorted the doubles down the secret stairway and into the children's dining room. From there they used the Empress' private staircase to access the bottom floor. Most of the rooms on Alexandra's side of the first floor corridor were interconnected so Sophie was able to lead them from the stairwell, through the Imperial bedroom and into the Mauve Boudoir. Next came the Pallisander room and finally the Maple room which was located directly across the hallway from the Tsar's study. It was just an extra precaution but by utilizing this route it was unnecessary to enter the long corridor, and the risk of discovery was thereby reduced. Unfortunately everyone was becoming a little paranoid but in reality if the impostors had been seen by someone unauthorized it could only be assumed the real Grand Duchesses were on the way to visit their father. Sophie checked the corridor and then led the four young women out of the Maple room, across the hall and into The Tsar's study.

The Tsar had decided that the rich paneling and decor of his study was a more appropriate venue in which to announce to the doubles that their training was about to be tested. Alexandra had decided to attend this important "family" get-together and was there with Nicholas to greet the group when Sophie ushered them in.

"Good morning Papa. Good morning Mama," they dutifully chorused.

"Good morning children," replied the Tsar. "Sophie please close the door and remain in the corridor. Keep an eye on things if you would."

"Of course, Your Imperial Highness."

"Girls please be seated. I have something of importance to discuss with you."

Nicholas looked at each of the girls and still could not believe how much they resembled his daughters especially now that they were dressed in similar clothes and their hair was styled to look exactly like the Grand Duchesses. Nicky was sure that at a distance he would not be able to tell the difference, so striking was the similarity. At close range, however, there were subtle distinctions such as the slight slump of a shoulder or an altered facial expression. But he was sure these were things that only he or Alix would recognize. "By now you all know that Dalek suffered a terrible and tragic accident from which he did not recover," began the Tsar. "I am fairly certain that you are not unhappy he is no longer with us but his loss, if you wish to call it such, has created some problems. But I wanted to assure you that your situation has not changed in the least. You will remain with us as we have always planned."

The girls breathed a sigh of relief for they had feared Dalek's death would alter their relationship with the Tsar and his family. Dalek had been nothing but trouble. He had tormented them constantly and offended them in the worst possible ways. But of all the annoyances they had despised him for the most egregious were the terrible things he had said about the Imperial family. They were always worried that he would ruin this opportunity for them to be in direct service to the Tsar. They loved being treated as members of the family and had grown to love the Imperial family as if it were their own. Now they did not have to worry, Dalek was gone and they could continue in their roles.

"I know now that Dalek was a very troubled young boy and that had he lived, we would all now be in grave danger," continued Nicholas. "We have learned that his father is a member of a revolutionary group that hates us and is plotting the overthrow of the monarchy and the destruction of this family. As we speak they are making an effort to place one of their group in the palace to ferret out whatever information is available. Now, we have no reason to believe they are aware of your existence but there have been rumors that Dalek was seen here. So I have come to a decision that will have a dramatic impact on you. You do not need to know all the details, in fact, the less you know the better, but here is the bare outline. We will advertise for a tutor to conduct a two week seminar for the Grand Duchesses and allow our adversaries to fill the position with their spy. We have some assurance that Dalek's father will be the one who applies and Count Benckendorff will engage him to conduct the course of studies. What is your part in this? Your role will be extremely important for you will act in the guise of the Grand Duchesses when Ivan Rakyovich is in the palace."

There was a gasp, and a look of consternation came over the faces of the girls when they realized they would be asked to stand in for their counterparts. Up until this point they had always thought their interaction with people would be limited and their primary responsibility would be to portray the Grand Duchesses at a distance. They had never envisioned being in such close proximity to an outsider especially one who loathed the Tsar and could very well uncover their secret. "Imperial Highness," interrupted Helena.

"No, you must always call me Papa. Remember that," said the Tsar. "From this point on we will no longer use your given names unless for some reason all eight of you are together for a meeting. But we will limit such gatherings because, if you think about it, the only time you could be exposed is if you were all seen together. You must become so familiar with your new names that it is second nature to respond when you hear it. Now what is your concern, Tatiana?" asked Nicholas.

Helena blushed at being called Tatiana by the Tsar. Never had she dreamed that one day she would become a Grand Duchess, even if only temporarily. "I do not know if we are ready for this yet. We are still making mistakes and it terrifies me to think that one of us might slip up and this man would know something was wrong," she explained.

"Do not be overly concerned, replied the Tsar. We have several more weeks to train before he comes in. You must remember that you are now members of the Imperial family. Your relationships with those around you in the palace will be very different from that of an outsider.

Rakyovich knows nothing of court life so he will be instructed on the proper etiquette to be observed in your presence. For instance, he will be forbidden to converse with you about personal matters. He will only ask or answer questions relating to his lessons. And I want you to ask questions. It is important that he see you interacting as sisters would in a classroom environment. When he returns to his friends we want him to be able to report that he is now an expert on the abilities and characteristics of the Grand Duchesses. If you treat him with courtesy, as well-bred young women would, you will be successful. And since he is new to the palace Mama or Sophie will be sitting in the back of the classroom to monitor the situation. This man will only be tutoring you for a short period of time, two to three weeks at the most. That will be just long enough for him to determine that Dalek was never here and that everything else seems to be normal. So you must not worry since the situation will be under control and the tutor will be watched very carefully."

Franny, who had taken on the role of Anastasia said, "You know we would do anything for you, Papa." The Tsar smiled at the earnest look on her face.

Dalida echoed her sister's sentiments. "I would offer my life in a moment to save you Papa, and I believe all of us here feel the same way. You have been so kind to us. It is an honor to serve you and we will do whatever you ask of us." The three other girls solemnly nodded their heads in agreement.

"Thank you Maria, and all you wonderful girls. I truly believe that I have been anointed by God to serve as Tsar of Russia and when you support me He showers His blessings upon you. And when you say yes to me, you are saying yes to Him. Now tomorrow you will begin your preparations with the Empress. I mean your Mother, of course," he corrected himself. "Sophie will also be there to aide in any way." Nicholas rose from the table and looked at his watch. Everything in the *Masquerade* ran on a tight schedule, especially when the impostors were out of the attic. "Let me make sure Sophie is ready to take you back to your rooms," he said as he cracked open the door. He saw her standing a short ways down the corridor and when she saw him she walked briskly to his study.

"I have cleared the way," she said. "Are the ladies prepared to return to their rooms?"

"Yes, we are finished here. Tomorrow the Empress and you will begin preparing the girls for the arrival of the new tutor." He then moved a little closer and spoke softly so the doubles could not hear him. "They seem a bit anxious about the whole business but they have indicated they are willing to do whatever I ask of them," said Nicholas.

"That is good to know. I will do whatever I can to make them more comfortable in their roles." She and the impostors quickly slipped across the hall to the Maple room and then retraced their steps to the stairway. In a few minutes they were safely returned to their attic home. Once the Baroness had departed the girls chattered excitedly about this newest challenge and Ekaterina reiterated what the Tsar had said. "From now on we use our counterparts names. Ekaterina, Helena, Dalida and Franny are no more. We must do our part to avoid any silly slip-ups. Do you all agree?"

"Of course, Olga," they replied with laughter in their voices.

The next morning, an announcement was made that the Empress was indisposed and was not to be disturbed under any circumstances. When all was in order Alix, Sophie and the Count then slipped upstairs to the attic quarters and popped in just as the impostors were finishing their breakfast. "Good morning, my children."

"Good morning Mama," responded the four girls.

"I know the Tsar spoke to you yesterday about your new tutor," said Alix. "Today we are going to go over the manner in which you are to conduct yourselves when in the presence of a man we know is here to cause mischief. Before Monsieur Rakyovich teaches you for the first time he will meet with Count Benckendorff who will instruct him in the proper protocol. You will be introduced to him initially by your full title but after he is presented to you he will be allowed to address you by your first name, as all the other tutors do. Usually when my children have a new instructor I sit in for the first few lessons, then one of my ladies-in-waiting takes over. In this particular situation Sophie will be present whenever I am unable to be with you. A grand duchess must always be properly chaperoned. I will always appear aloof and imperious because that is the reputation I have and it is what an outsider would expect. I will, however force myself to treat him courteously and you must do the same. But always remember that this man is not a loyal subject of the Tsar. You must constantly be on your guard when he is around and make sure you do not slip up. Much depends on you, my dears. Now, Count Benckendorff please explain to my daughters what you will tell the tutor. I want them to hear what you have to say so that when Monsieur Ivan Rakyovich comes to the palace they will know what to expect from him."

"Of course, your highness. Now girls, I will first interview candidates for the position and, of course, I will retain Monsieur Rakyovich. I will require him to begin on Monday of the second week of May, so you will have nearly four weeks to prepare. He will not stay in the palace but will receive a generous stipend so he can arrange for lodgings in town. A car will be sent each morning to bring him to the palace and it will return him to his lodging when his instruction is completed. Sophie let us pretend you are Monsieur Rakyovich and are receiving my instructions."

The Baroness nodded her assent.

"Very well, Monsieur. There are strict rules to be observed once you enter the palace grounds. A car will pick you up early enough so that you can be cleared by the guards at the gate and still arrive in the palace in time for your lesson to start. You must be exactly on time, neither early nor late. Once you have passed the guards the driver will take you to the entrance of the palace where you will be turned over to a member of the Tsar's household. You will then be brought to the Grand Duchesses' classroom. On your first day the Empress will wish to review your lesson plans. When she has finished, and is satisfied, your pupils will be sent for. After your formal introduction to the Grand Duchesses you may address them by their first names while in the classroom. Court protocol prohibits you from speaking to the Grand Duchesses about personal matters. The lesson will begin at nine o'clock and last for two hours at which time you will be escorted out of the palace and a car will return you to your lodging. You must be accompanied by a member of the household any time you are in the family wing of the palace. If you are discovered violating this prohibition your teaching position will be immediately terminated. Do you understand Monsieur?"

Sophie nodded her head. "Yes, Count Benckendorff. I understand."

"See my dears," Alix added. "You have nothing to worry about. If for any reason one of you has a difficulty we will be there to smooth over the situation."

"If I may ask," inquired Olga. "What will he be teaching us?"

"It is my understanding that when he was a teacher, he taught a class in foreign studies," answered the Empress. "Monsieur Gilliard has suggested we allow him to lecture on Egypt, the Middle East and possibly India. I think we would all find that interesting. By the way, although Pierre normally accompanies the Tsarevich when he is at the Stavka with his father, this time he will remain at the palace when Papa and Alexei return to headquarters. He will help keep an eye on things and will serve as Monsieur Rakyovich's primary escort. So you see, everything is under control."

In the course of the next few weeks, while Benckendorff conducted interviews with the applicants for the coveted position, the girls rehearsed their roles. The doubles became more comfortable now that they understood the situation and how the classes were to be conducted but they still worried that one of them might slip up. Alix was especially concerned that Helena, Tatiana's stand-in, might become so nervous and agitated that she would give the whole thing away. Of the four girls she seemed the most fragile and Alix had considered having her miss the lessons altogether due to a feigned illness but after discussing the problem with Nicky they both agreed it was better to forge ahead. This would be the impostor's first test and if they failed then the *Masquerade* would likely fail. Better to know it now than later.

Count Benckendorff had advertised only in the Moscow papers in order to limit the number of applicants, and the revolutionaries did their best to frighten away the faint of heart. So it was no surprise that in beginning of the second week of May, the new tutor Ivan Rakyovich, a revolutionary spy, sat in the Imperial children's classroom with Pierre Gilliard, awaiting the arrival of the Empress. As directed he had come early this day so his curriculum for the short session could be reviewed by the Empress and Gilliard. Rakyovich was obviously nervous but Pierre made no effort to put him at ease other than to make small talk. Finally the door opened and Alexandra swept in followed closely by Sophie. The two men stood and Pierre made the introductions.

"Your Imperial Highness may I present Monsieur Ivan Rakyovich, the gentleman who has been retained to conduct this seminar."

"Monsieur, may I introduce you to Her Imperial Highness Alexandra Feodorovna, Tsarina of Russia."

Ivan Rakyovich bowed low and in a firm voice said, "I am honored to make your acquaintance, Imperial Highness." The spy had made up his mind that if he was to be effective he could not allow himself to be intimidated by his surroundings.

Gilliard continued. "The lady accompanying Her Highness is Baroness Sophie Buxhoeveden who will be in attendance whenever the Empress is not present. You will probably hear the Grand Duchesses refer to her as Isa, so do not be confused." The tutor bowed again.

"Well then," Alix directed, "let us see what you have prepared for us."

Ivan had been provided with all the maps and other study materials he had requested and he now proceeded to outline for the Empress the abbreviated course of studies that he would present over the next two weeks. Quite frankly, Alix was impressed, and readily approved the lessons. She paused momentarily and then nodded to Sophie to bring in the four impostors.

Her hesitation, which Rakyovich failed to notice, was due to the fact that the room set aside for classes was located right next to the children's dining room, wherein access to the attic was concealed. Alix and Sophie had been concerned that too much movement, so close to the classroom, would jeopardize the whole exercise and they had considered having the eight girls exchange bedrooms for the two week period. But after some discussion they decided against the move. It was just too involved. Instead, the real Grand Duchesses would go to the attic immediately after breakfast and remain there until Monsieur Rakyovich had departed for the day. The four impostors would await his arrival in the dining room. So when Sophie departed to get the girls, the real Grand Duchesses were already safely ensconced in the common room of the attic where they were quietly working on various projects. The Baroness went into the dining room to fetch the girls, who were waiting there with barely concealed apprehension. "Well, my darlings the time has arrived, "she announced. "Your Mama has approved the lessons and the tutor is waiting to begin. Be calm, remember what we taught you, and everything will go as planned. Now when we enter the room I will make the introductions, so wait for my cue."

Rakyovich had received a thorough indoctrination on how to conduct himself and was feeling much more at ease. When the door opened the Empress remained seated but once again the two men stood for the introductions. Sophie turned to Monsieur Rakyovich and announced, "Monsieur, may I introduce you to their Imperial Highnesses, the Grand Duchesses Olga, Tatiana, Maria and Anastasia Nikolaievna." The girls nodded politely to him and then Isa and Pierre excused themselves and the first lesson began

Everything went fairly well, although Tatiana was pale and upset at being in such close proximity to Dalek's father. The other girls were perfect, however, and Rakyovich was never able to focus on Tatiana; he just assumed she was somewhat shy and unassuming. When the session ended Alix and the four young women left the room and proceeded to the Mauve Boudoir. When they arrived Alix hugged each girl in turn and then thanked them for their performance, careful not to comment on the way Tatiana had reacted to the tutor. But tomorrow was another day so she cautioned them to be constantly on their guard. It was ironic that she did so because Alix had herself already made a serious error. She had forgotten to summon an escort for Rakyovich at the end of class and the spy was loose and unattended in the family quarters.

Ivan, in the meantime, was acknowledging to himself that he was out of his depth. With the strict protocol how would he have the opportunity to uncover any information or learn whether or not his son had ever been at the palace? He was an intelligent man but he knew nothing about the workings of the court. How could he possibly know if anything seemed unusual? He put away his study materials and realizing he was alone, he began to snoop around. He opened up every cabinet and drawer in the room searching for what, he did not know, but hoping that something would give him an indication that his son had been there. He tried the other door only to find it locked. Strange he thought. I wonder why they lock that door. He was only alone for the few minutes it took for the Empress to realize her mistake and inform Count Benckendorff who rushed off to find him. In that short amount of time he had managed to rummage through the whole room and had just tried to open the door into the dining room when the Count walked into the room. "What sir, are you doing?"

"I was looking for the water closet," he answered.

"You must not wander about. I thought we were very clear about that. This must not happen again. Now let me take you to the facilities." Benckendorff was not fooled by the tutor's explanation and his sharp eye caught the fact that a drawer was left ajar. Once Rakyovich was finished the Count escorted him downstairs and out of the palace.

The tutor came to the palace everyday for the next two weeks. After her initial hesitation, Tatiana had calmed down and fallen into her role very well. She liked to playact and once she got over her nervousness she was fine. Besides, the tutor was very entertaining and his lectures were quite interesting. It was Ivan Rakyovich who was beside himself with frustration for by the last day of instruction he had been unable to learn anything about his son. He had talked to one maid who thought she might have seen a boy matching his description but she could not be sure. At last Ivan admitted defeat and after he finished with the last lesson and said his good-byes he was escorted out of the palace for the final time. Count Benckendorff had kindly provided a car to take him to the station and, as he waited on the steps for it to be brought around, he saw a young boy in the distance who bore a remarkable resemblance to his son. He called out to him but the boy did not respond although he continued walking towards the palace. Ivan was sure it was his son and he called out again, "Dalek, Dalek." The boy looked in his direction but did not respond. When he finally reached the steps, Ivan realized it was not his son. "Who are you?" he asked.

"I am Dr. Derevenko's son," answered the boy, concerned he might be in trouble for wandering around without his father. "He is the family physician."

"What are you doing here?"

"I usually come with my father to the palace to play with Alexei. I mean his Imperial Highness, the Grand Duke Alexei," he said. "But he is at the Stavka with the Tsar. My father said I could accompany him today."

Ivan looked at the boy and realized that although the coloring was the same, it was the distance, and wishful thinking, which made this boy look like his son. He realized the scullery maid Natasha, who had claimed to have seen his son at the palace must have made the same mistake, as did the serving girl he had talked too. It was absurd to think that his son had ever been there. His car arrived and he left the palace, never to return.

When Ivan Rakyovich returned to Moscow he submitted a written report to his superiors. However, they were dissatisfied with it and he was called in for interrogation. But Comrade Raykovich stood by his report. He had been in close proximity to the Empress and Grand Duchesses for two weeks, as well as other members of the Imperial household. He had not seen the Tsar or Tsarevich because they were away at the front. The boy thought to be his son Dalek was in reality the son of the family physician and although there was a resemblance it was purely coincidental. He was surprised to learn that despite all the opulence and wealth, the Imperial family lived a fairly simple life. As far as he could ascertain there was nothing out of the ordinary going on at

Alexander Palace. The revolutionary council then accepted the verbal report since it was delivered with such certainty.

Ivan Rakyovich would see the Imperial family again, but under much different circumstances, and his testimony would unwittingly help preserve the *Masquerade*.

Chapter 36

August 1916 – Mogilev. The time had finally arrived, the moment he had dreaded most, and Nicholas Romanov, the most powerful man in Russia was afraid. He was not consumed by a physical fear, not the kind that sometimes made cowards out of brave men, but rather an emotionally draining apprehension at what was about to occur. It was time to break his own heart and the hearts of those he loved most in this world. It was time to reveal to his children the details of the *Masquerade*, knowing as he did, that it would hurt them beyond belief. He could only hope that the strength of character which his off-spring had demonstrated in the past would carry them through this distressing time, because he had no intention of sugar coating the bitter pill. His son would be the first to learn the details, not only because he was the heir and it was his right, but also because the death of Dalek had emphatically changed Alexei's part in the plan.

The day was hot and muggy, with no hint of a breeze, and Nicholas found the room he used as an office at the Stavka unbearably hot. Sitting there in the oppressive atmosphere, contemplating the task that faced him, was more than he could bear and abandoning any attempt to work he stood up and left the room. He found Alexei playing outside and motioned for him to join him in a walk. The Tsar had discussed all of this with Alix weeks ago and they had agreed that Alexei's introduction to the *Masquerade* should occur in a "man to man" talk. Nicky had been putting it off, but he realized he could no longer procrastinate because Alexandra would be arriving tomorrow with his daughters, and it was only right that Alexei be informed before they reached the Stavka. And so, on that stifling summer day, father and son walked slowly down the partially shaded path in search of a cool spot to discuss their destiny, a destiny that had been dramatically changed by the intervention of Olga on that fateful night in March.

As Nicholas strolled through the grove of trees with Alexei, he wondered how his son would react to the revelation he was about to make. The time they had been able to spend together at headquarters had been good for Alexei. The Tsar hoped the interaction his son had with the men would prevent him from being afflicted by the same overwhelming shyness his father had experienced as a young man. It seemed to be working but the Tsarevich still suffered from his physical ailments and was just a little boy, babied by his mother and pampered by his sisters. It remained to be seen how he would respond.

Nicholas stopped under a large shady tree, sat down, and rested his back against the sturdy trunk. He patted the ground next to him and Alexei joined his father.

"You know Alexei," he began. "You are the last of an unbroken line of Romanovs that stretches back over three hundred years. It is hard to admit, but not all of our countrymen love the Tsar. We have made mistakes over the centuries and as a result have created enemies who have tried to harm us. But that is all in the past. It is the present that concerns me and I freely admit to you, my son, that I too have made errors of judgment. As a result of these errors my throne, and thus yours, is in serious danger from several groups of revolutionaries who are dedicated to my destruction. It is for this reason that the doubles were introduced. The original plan called for you and your sisters to be replaced by the impostors and then removed to a place of safety, outside of Russia. The death of Dalek changed all that and it is too late to find a replacement. "

"Father, you need not be concerned about finding someone else. I realize I am very young and do not understand everything that is going on, but one thing I do know is that my place is in Russia, at your side. I could never leave you."

"But Alexei it will be very dangerous. I am marked for death, and who knows what will be the fate of your mother. And as for you, the revolutionaries would never allow you to succeed me. If you were imprisoned how would you survive one of your attacks? There would be no one to care for you."

"Please father, I know that I have not always been brave in the face of pain but, I implore you, do not deny me this opportunity to show you my courage. Let me stand at your side and face the enemy with you. Carry out your plan with my sisters but allow me to remain in Russia. Persuade Mama that this is the only honorable course of action."

Nicholas was deeply moved by his son's declaration. Deep inside he had known this was the way it would be and tears came to his eyes. They were tears of sadness but also of pride. Pride in this son, who had always been so frail and sickly but who today was a true Romanov in every sense. "Dear Alexei. I am so proud of you. It shall be as you have asked. And do not worry about your mother's reaction. Father Grigory has convinced her that as long as you remain in Russia you will be safe. She will be absolutely ecstatic when I inform her of our decision. But say nothing of this to anyone, especially your sisters. I must tell them what is coming in my own way and it is something I do not look forward to. Now let us go back." The two rose from their seats under the old tree and the Tsar gave his son a careful hug. They walked quietly back to the Stavka, each immersed in their own thoughts. Nicholas was somewhat surprised that his son seemed so unaffected by their talk and he smiled down at him. Perhaps because Alexei suffered so much from his disease he did not consider some future martyrdom a thing to be feared. Or maybe he was just to young to really understand.

That same morning, back at Alexander Palace, Alix and her daughters were making final preparations to depart for the station at Tsarskoe Selo. There they would board the Imperial train for the long anticipated journey to Mogilev and a visit with the Tsar and Alexei. The Grand Duchesses were very excited to be making the trip because women were not normally invited to visit the Stavka. It was felt that the presence of females, especially attractive ones, caused unwanted distractions and disrupted the routine of the staff. But occasionally Alix flaunted the normal conventions and persuaded Nicholas to allow a visit and when such an outing was permitted it always proved to be a welcome break from the tedium of day to day life at the palace. And despite the unspoken prohibition against such activity, in the middle of a war as it was, inevitably there would be social activities and many opportunities for innocent flirtations with the many handsome young staff officers. The girl's enthusiasm, however, was tempered by the mood of their mother. Alix had agreed with Nicky that the time had arrived to tell the girls about their future and to begin preparing them for their new lives. Soon they would be departing Russia, maybe never to return, and it tortured her to even think about it. Try as she might she could not keep the look of utter sadness from her face, especially when she considered that once gone she might never see them again.

At last the group went aboard and after a long and tiring journey the Imperial train finally pulled into the station at Mogilev. The cars were uncoupled and moved to a special siding reserved for the Tsar, where it would remain for the length of the visit. The coaches served as temporary lodgings for the Empress, her daughters and the accompanying retinue.

Nicholas and Alexei stood on the platform eagerly awaiting the arrival of the family and as soon as the train stopped they leapt aboard and were enveloped in hugs as the family was reunited. Alexei could not contain his excitement and insisted on showing his "treasures" to his sisters then and there. The Tsarevich had collected odds and ends since he was a small child and the family always referred to his collection as "Alexei's treasures." Now that he was older, he was more sophisticated and the box of treasures included medals and insignia of rank from the various foreign visitors to the Stavka, as well as other interesting bits and pieces. His sisters all made the appropriate expressions of wonder as Alexei showed them the latest items. Nicholas looked at the happy, smiling faces and wondered if he had the strength to tell the girls what was about to occur. He knew it would destroy their happiness forever and he decided he would wait until the day before Alix and the girls departed before telling them his devastating news. At least they would have a few days to enjoy themselves.

Later that night he broached the subject with Alix and she agreed with him on the need to wait until just before they departed to inform them. "They have so looked forward to this visit and that I hate to spoil their fun too soon," said Alix. "But I dread the train ride back without your strong shoulder to lean on. Nicky, could you not come back with us for a few days, so I do not have to face them alone?"

"I am afraid that is out of the question at this time, Sunny. You are the woman who sat patiently for days at Alexei's bedside when he nearly passed on at Spala. I am confident you will weather this storm. Now I must share something of importance with you."

"What is it Nicky? You sound so serious."

"I am very serious. Alix, it was most difficult but I finally worked up the courage to talk with Alexei about the purpose of the doubles and the impact Dalek's death has had on the overall plan."

"Oh, my poor baby. He must have been terrified. How did he react?"

"Sunny, I have never been so proud." Nicholas went on to describe in detail the conversation with his son and by the time he was finished they were both in tears. Nicholas embraced his wife, gently kissed her and then held her in his arms while they both struggled to gain control of their emotions. "It seems," Alix observed through her tears, "that we have cooperated in producing a lion, after all."

"It is settled then. Alexei will remain in Russia with us, as you have always wanted and the girls will be sent away. But how I will cope with their absence only God can possibly know."

Everyone at the Stavka went out of their way to ensure that the family's short visit would be enjoyable and the next few days were filled with activities. The Tsar would attend to his work in the morning while Alix and the girls visited peasant families in the nearby village. The Empress looked on wistfully as her daughters interacted with the little children and wondered if they would ever marry and have children of their own. Grandchildren whom she was sure she would never see. Later they would all gather together for lunch on the train or in the mess before embarking for an afternoon of hiking or motoring around the area. In the August heat a drive in an open car was always the preferred method if Alix was along. As for the girls, they enjoyed being themselves, flirting at every opportunity but most of all, enjoying being together as a family.

The week flew by and before they knew it the visit was almost at an end. Early in the morning, on the day before his family would depart and return to Tsarskoe Selo, Nicholas awoke from a restless sleep. He sat on the side of his bed, rubbing his eyes, and remembered that today he would have that long delayed conversation with his daughters. No wonder he had tossed and turned throughout the night, unable to fall into the deep slumber he was usually blessed with. Nicholas peered out the window of the sleeping compartment and noticed that although it was beginning to lighten in the east the sun was still below the horizon. It would be some time before the others awoke so he carefully slipped out of the bed without awaking Alix, donned a dressing gown and quietly made his way to the study.

From a drawer in his desk the Tsar withdrew a lovely little box, hand-crafted by Faberge, and containing a brown leather case shaped like a boat. He removed the leather boat and marveled at how much it resembled the one in his dream. Carl was a true artist, for Nicholas had only described what he needed one time and yet the man had produced exactly what he wanted. He held the case for a moment then opened it and emptied the four signet rings into his hand. The Tsar examined them carefully and once again shook his head in absolute awe at what Faberge had created. But despite their beauty, the rings produced a terrible sadness inside him, for he knew that when this jewelry was given to his daughters it would mean they were about to leave him forever. He wrapped his hand around the four rings, grasped them tightly and held them over his heart. It was as if he was embracing his four precious daughters all at once and he savored that feeling for a brief moment. "Oh Lord God, please inspire me," he prayed. "Help me to be strong and do not allow me to weaken in the face of the tears and supplications that will surely result when I tell my children what is planned for them." Nicholas composed himself and returned the rings to their special pouch. He would explain their purpose when he gave them to the Grand Duchesses at the appropriate time and place.

He began to hear stirrings in the train so he hurried back to his compartment to dress for the day. He had arranged with Alix to meet with their daughters after breakfast but had decided not to have Alexei in attendance. His son's role, in all of this, had been greatly simplified and the less the young boy knew of the overall plan the better for all concerned. So when the dishes had been cleared away an aide arrived to take the Tsarevich on an outing. The girls also rose to leave but Alix motioned them to remain seated around the table. Nicholas sat there at the head of the table and covered his face with his hands. No one spoke and the silence became deafening. The girls looked at their mother in confusion but she motioned to them to be patient. They sat there wondering whether they had done something wrong or if some exceptionally bad news had been received.

Finally Olga could stand the silence no longer. "Papa, Mama, what is it?" she implored. "You are frightening us."

Nicholas took his hands away from his face and his daughters could see the tears on his cheeks. Alix touched his arm and said gently, "go ahead my dearest and tell them what you must. Then they will understand your tears. And girls, hear your father out. You will know when a question is appropriate but try not to interrupt unnecessarily. Now please begin, my beloved husband."

"Very well." the Tsar replied. "My darlings, some years ago Count Benckendorff's agents learned of a revolutionary plot to overthrow the government. Now, we have dealt with such activities before but this particular group is especially virulent because in addition to a change in the government they wish to destroy any vestige of Romanov ascendancy. To put it simply they mean to murder our entire family."

"What have we ever done that would make someone want to kill us?" cried Tatiana.

"It is because you are my flesh and blood. These evil men do not want my lineage to survive and they have vowed to hunt us to the ends of the earth if necessary. So we intend to make it as hard as we can for them to achieve their wretched purpose. But please, not too many questions just yet."

The girls were obviously troubled but had the sense to remain quiet when their father continued.

"Many years ago; thirteen to be exact; we visited the town of Sarov for the glorification of St. Serafim. You girls probably remember what a festive occasion it was and what an enjoyable excursion. While we were there an old woman named Elena Motivilov gave me a letter from St. Serafim and the time has come to share its contents with you. It is in the form of a prophecy and after I have read it to you I will explain its meaning as myself, and others close to us, understand it to be." Nicholas carefully removed the aged letter from the inside pocket of his tunic, unfolded it and read it to his daughters. St. Serafim's words resonated across time and touched the hearts of his children and although they were utterly confused by the contents of the letter they nevertheless sensed its magnitude and importance. They looked at their father expectantly as they waited for him to explain this curious document, which he held so reverently in his hands. Nicholas looked at their trusting faces, bowed his head for a moment to gather his thoughts, and then explained the letter.

"This letter is really easy to understand if you keep in mind what I told you earlier. The great evil is, of course, the revolution and the men who will perpetrate it. I will suffer martyrdom for Russia at their hands and though I know you will weep about this later, be assured your mother and I came to grips with this aspect of the letter long ago. One of you will be the salvation of Russia, either directly or through your children and since I know not which of you it is, I must protect all of you. I cannot explain the man in white and I can only assume his role will become clear in time. So my primary responsibility, as I see it, is to ensure that you are safe. To that end a select group of loyal friends have been working for years on a plan to thwart these evil men, a plan which is called the *Masquerade*. The period of time given me to make plans and take action is drawing to a close and it is for this reason that I am telling you about it now.

"Father, in explaining all this you have not once mentioned Alexei. What will become of him?" asked Maria.

"In good time my dear, but not quite yet. I am sure you have wondered about the impostors and I must confess I have not been completely candid with you. Olga has long suspected that there is more to their role than I have previously told you. They have been in training for a number of years and are at the palace to take your place. When the time comes, in just a few months, they will assume your identities and you will leave the country to a place prepared for you."

"But father," protested Olga. "Will not the danger we are in then be transferred to Ekaterina and the others?"

This was one question he had anticipated and prepared for. "You are very perceptive Olga. Yes, they will be in jeopardy, but this possibility was made clear to them and they volunteered anyway. They are true daughters of Russia. Anyway, it is my intent to carry on the charade as long as I can and then if they are threatened in any way I will do my best to protect them."

Olga kept her composure but the faces of the other three girls registered disbelief as they began to realize the implications of what they had just been told. Alix could see that the tears were about to come and she quickly intervened. "I know this is a great shock to you but I am counting on you to be brave. You certainly were not prepared for this but I know that you comprehend the gravity of the situation. Many people have worked very hard, for many years, to ensure your safety and well being. You must never discuss what you been told lest you be overheard and always be careful because spies are everywhere. Now let your Papa continue."

""I will not go into all the details of the plan now, but later on you will be given all the information you require. I will say that two of you, Tatiana and Anastasia, will be living in Japan, for at least a while. Next month, Prince Kanin, the Japanese representative will be coming for a visit. In addition to making final preparations for your move, he is also coming to meet you personally. He is a fine and honorable man and I think you will like him very much. He will spend time with you and answer the many questions you must have about his country. Olga, you and Maria will be hidden in a convent in Poland until it is safe to move you to another location. I did not want to split you up but I felt, and everyone agreed, that keeping all four of you together was too dangerous. More of the plan will be revealed in time and I assure you all of your questions will be answered."

Olga ventured to ask the Tsar that which was weighing on all their minds, "What is to become of Mama, Alexei and you? You said you would tell us. Surely we could all leave together."

"Olga, what a wonderful target we would make, all grouped together. No. I must remain in Russia because it is what I have been called to do.

Your mother feels her place is at my side and since Alexei no longer has a double he has asked to stay and we have given him our permission."

"Then if we have a choice, I choose to stay as well," Olga stated emphatically.

"Me too," echoed her three sisters.

"My dears," Nicholas replied, "it is apparent that you do not realize the significance of this letter. I realize it is difficult for you to accept what it contains when you have just heard it for the first time but your mother and I have had years to consider its meaning and for us it has become a matter of faith. No, my darlings, you do not have a choice in the matter and neither do I. I will be required to sacrifice my life for Russia and for you, so please do not ask me to forgo this burden. You must help me to be like Christ. You certainly must know that I want this cup to pass from me, but His will must be done. I am not alone in this. You too must make a sacrifice and that will be to leave your family and country behind. We must do as St. Serafim has asked of us."

"We will be abandoning our Motherland. How can that bring about anything good for Russia?" asked Olga.

"If I knew the answer to that I would not hesitate to share it with you. Only time will reveal how this can be, but at the moment my responsibility is to see that you are protected, and that is what I intend to do. Tears and recriminations are a luxury we do not have time for. I have had to carry this burden for many years and it has caused me much pain, more than you could ever imagine. Be grateful for what we have had together, the love we have shared, and all the wonderful times. You have had a sheltered existence, but that is about to change. You will now live your lives with new identities and when the time comes for the great event that will transform Russia, the man who travels the earth dressed in white will know what must be done. He will have your answers."

"How will we know who he is and how will he contact us?" asked Tatiana.

"I have analyzed this letter for over a decade but I do not have the answer to your question. The answer lies somewhere in the future and I cannot see that far ahead, but I do know that God will protect and aid you, as He has me."

"Faith is the willingness to accept something that you do not understand," Alix interjected. "You must pray for this gift and have complete trust in God. If you place all your worries and doubts before Him, He will guide you."

"Your mother is correct," said Nicholas. "Now let us bow our heads and pray as a family that God will give us the grace and strength to get through this trial. Lord, from the depths of our souls we cry out to you. Shower your mercy upon us as we offer ourselves as your instruments to be used as you see fit. I also ask Mary, our ever present mother, to protect and watch over my daughters and help them to understand your son's will for them and for Russia. Amen."

"Amen," replied Alix and the Grand Duchesses and then, finally, the tears began to flow and there was no holding them back. After a period that seemed like hours but was only a matter of minutes, the Tsar intervened.

"I must return to headquarters and finish some work before lunch. I do not want this discussed here at Mogilev or anywhere else unless your mother or I say it is safe to do so. The slightest slip up could jeopardize the plan and with it, your lives. Do I make myself clear?"

"Yes Papa, we understand," said his daughters.

"Good. Well now, I have a special treat planned for your last day. We are to have an excursion down the Dnieper River and a picnic," said Nicholas, who then bid them good-bye.

After the Tsar departed the girls turned their sad eyes to their mother who gathered them together for a hug. She knew what they must be feeling and it broke her heart to know how utterly devastated they must be. Nicky had handled the difficult task as well as could be expected but nevertheless the girl's world had come tumbling down around them. Alix was proud of them, however, for they could have reacted hysterically. Instead Olga had been a rock, and her reaction had influenced the other girls. All in all it had gone better than expected, but there was no way to put a happy face on what had just occurred. "Pray that our Lord's will be done," she said as she kissed each on the forehead. The girls went to prepare for the afternoon outing and left Alix sitting alone with her thoughts.

It was to be later that night before Nicholas and Alix had a moment alone. The afternoon activities turned out to be a disaster with everyone pretending an enjoyment they did not feel. The young officers who were in the party knew something was amiss because the Grand Duchesses were usually exuberant and full of life at such times, but they knew better than to make inquiries. More than once Nicholas caught an unguarded look of melancholy on his children's faces and he was filled with sadness knowing that he was the cause. Many photographs were taken that day and the Tsar was sure that when they looked at the pictures later it would be quite obvious his children were not their usual selves.

Alix sensed his mood and put her arms around him. "Nicky, it had to be done."

"Yes, but I never imagined it would be so difficult. I just wish I could have spared them this, but I could think of no other way."

"Darling, they are not little girls anymore. They are young women and I think you will be surprised at how strong they are. If you could see their work at the hospitals you would have more confidence. Also they have at least one person to share their problems and concerns with and that will be a great comfort to them."

"I just wish that I could be there to protect and guide them."

"Nicky, it is not quite the same, but I am sure you would feel this way if they were leaving to get married," Alix suggested in an attempt to lighten the mood. She felt a little strange acting as the comforter, but this role reversal was necessary because she could see how dejected her husband was. "You have faith that Our Lord, through His chosen one, St. Serafim, has guided you to this point in time. There is absolutely every reason to believe that He will do the same for our daughters. So please, my dearest, try and put your mind at ease. We have done everything we can to prepare and now we can only pray and hope for the best."

"You are correct, my Sunny. If our Lord has guided me thus far certainly He will continue to do so." The two then turned in for the night knowing it was to be many weeks before they saw each other again. The next day Alix and the four girls, all of them sad and disconsolate, departed for Tsarskoe Selo.

A few days later Nicholas left by train for Kiev to call on his mother, the Dowager Empress. It was not a visit he looked forward to because its purpose was to bring her into the *Masquerade* and he honestly did not know how she would react to all that he was about to reveal. Minnie was still very vibrant and healthy and likely to live many more years so it was quite probable that at some point she would come in contact with the impostors and, if she refused to receive them as her granddaughters, the whole plan would unravel. He had vacillated all these years because his mother could be very intimidating and he had been unwilling to risk her potential opposition. But with the plan about to be put in motion he could delay no longer; too much depended on her support.

When the Tsar arrived in Kiev, he and Alexei were met at the station by Sandro, who was assigned to a unit near the city. Nicholas had brought his son because he realized, at the last minute, that this might well be the last time the Tsarevich would see his Grandmama. They greeted each other fondly and Sandro joked with Nicholas about his upcoming visit to the "Dragon Lady" as he referred to his mother-in-law, Minnie. "Have you decided what you are going to tell her yet?"

"Well, after my experience with the girls I am convinced the best way to approach her is to lay it all out and then answer directly any objections she might have. You know how stubborn she can be so I am counting on your presence for moral support," said the Tsar.

"Your wish is my command, your highness," said Sandro teasingly. But what of young Alexei here? Is he to attend the meeting?"

The Tsar put his hand on his son's shoulder and smiled down at the boy. "Alexei has become my strong right arm and we have come to an agreement about his role in this. He understands the need to compartmentalize the plan so he will rest while I try to beard the lion, as it were." Sandro felt only sympathy for Nicholas because Minnie was notoriously opinionated and had no qualms about voicing those opinions.

Sandro's driver delivered them to Minnie's palace in Kiev and they were escorted to the drawing room where she had tea waiting for them. Minnie stood up to greet Nicholas and Alexei with a kiss but merely nodded politely to her son-in-law, Sandro. They spent some time expressing the usual pleasantries and catching up on family news.

When there was a lull in the conversation Nicholas informed his mother he wished to speak to her on a matter of the utmost importance. Realizing that her son was deeply troubled by something, she nodded her assent, dismissed all the servants from the room and sat quietly waiting for her son to speak. Alexei was led off to take a nap and Sandro sat down in a comfortable chair.

"Mother, I asked Sandro to be here because he is privy to most of what I am about to tell you and he can fill in the gaps if I forget something. I do have one favor to ask. Please allow me to speak without interruption. When I am finished I will answer all your questions."

Minnie was somewhat surprised by the Tsar's attitude because although she loved him dearly, she had always considered him to be somewhat weak. However, as the story of St. Serafim's letter, and her son's subsequent actions began to unfold, she realized that Nicky had an inner strength of character that she had been totally unaware of. The tale of intrigue continued and though the Empress itched to interrupt she kept silent while the Tsar explained everything. He spoke for almost two hours and when he had finished he was exhausted and his mother was stunned. "Now, Mama, it is time for your questions."

"My dearest son, for once in my life I am nearly speechless. What is it that you want from me?"

"Mother, I want your support and cooperation."

"Then, Nicholas, answer these three questions. Do you really believe in this prophecy?"

"Yes, mother, I believe in it without reservation," the Tsar replied.

"And this revolution. Is it not in our power to prevent it?

"Mother, the shortages of food and other necessities created by the war have produced a climate of unrest that is bigger than our ability to deal with. You are isolated from this but our trusted agents have verified the conditions "

"Then my last question is this. Why did you wait so long to tell me?"

It was the question he most feared, but he intended to answer it honestly. "To be truthful Mama, I was afraid you would not agree with my plan and would refuse to identify the impostors as your granddaughters if it became necessary to do so."

"Oh stuff and nonsense," Minnie exclaimed. How could you think such a thing? I know your father was hard on you but today you have shown me a side of you I have never seen before, and I can say I am very proud of you. I am not completely comfortable with your dealings with the Vatican but I will do all in my power to ensure the success of this *Masquerade.*"

"Mother, there is one other matter that relates to this situation. Because of Alexei's condition, some years ago I changed the laws of succession." Nicholas went on to explain the alterations he had made and the disposition of the four original copies. His sister, Olga, had recently divorced her husband and married a commoner and Nicholas had acquiesced to the marriage because he could not deny to his sister what the new, yet to be promulgated laws would allow his daughters to do. "I have placed my complete trust in Nikolasha to issue the proclamation at the appropriate time."

Mother and son sat and spoke softly for a while and then Nicky broached the subject of her future. He explained what he had in mind and it was this which brought out a strong response from her. "I am a Russian now and I will never leave my country," she informed her son.

"Mother I have arranged for Sandro to take care of you, Olga and Xenia. The financial aspects are all in hand and he will ensure your safety. Think of your grandchildren and think of Russia. You are greatly loved in this country and your survival will be a symbol of hope," said Nicholas. His impassioned plea silenced her, and after Sandro explained his role in trying to encourage the extended family to make foreign investments, she agreed to wait and see how things played out.

Over the next few days, Nicholas spent much of his time with his mother, answering her many questions and attempting to prepare her for the future. She did surprise him with one of her suggestions. "If the Japanese are to be responsible for the safety of two of my granddaughters I think I would like to meet this Prince Kanin when he comes to Russia next month. Send him to Kiev for a day or two so I can look him over and form an opinion of him. See if it can be arranged," she directed.

"Mother, I assure you, the man is totally trustworthy. It is not necessary for him to come all the way down here."

"Do not argue with me Nicholas," she replied. "Just make the arrangements and keep me informed."

Nicky smiled and replied, "of course, Mama." This woman, with her imperious manner, was the mother he was more acquainted with, but he was no longer intimidated by her. In fact, these past few days with her had been some of the best in memory.

Chapter 37

September 1916 – Mogilev. As the crow flies, the distance between the Russian port of Vladivostok and the ancient city of Moscow, was a mere four thousand miles. However, the tracks of the Trans-Siberian Railway did not run straight between the two cities and under most conditions, what would have been considered a long journey was, in reality, an interminable one. The only other option a traveler had was to go by ship around Asia and Africa, a voyage that took months to complete. Prince Kanin decided to travel by rail so Nicholas had sent Count Ilia Tatischev on ahead, with a special train, to meet the Prince when his ship arrived at Vladivostok. The members of the Prince's retinue were assigned compartments, the luggage loaded and, with a minimum of delay, the long journey began. At Moscow the train would be switched onto the spur line leading down to Mogilev. But in the meantime the delegation from Japan would be exposed to the stark beauty of the steppe, the vast Siberian landscape, the many lakes and deep rivers and finally the imposing mass of the Urals as the plateau rose to join the craggy peaks. Once through the mountain passes there were still miles to go but eventually the train passed through Moscow and proceeded down to the Stavka at Mogilev where the Prince was to be met by the Tsar and his cousin George. Nicholas had recalled the Grand Duke from his unit to assist during this important visit because George had developed a close friendship with the Prince during his trips to Japan. He was the logical choice to act as escort during the remainder of the Prince's visit. The Tsar had yet to meet the Prince and therefore relied heavily on George's evaluation of him. But when Nicholas greeted him on the platform at Mogilev he sensed immediately that this was a man of honor, a man who could be trusted, a man of discretion.

The presence of a Japanese delegation at headquarters did not evoke any surprise because the two nations were nominal allies in the war against the Germans. Of course, everyone knew the Japanese had entered the fray to snap up German possessions in the Pacific and had been quite successful in doing so. But that was a political matter and had little to do with the Prince's visit, which was strictly personal. Nevertheless the presence of military attaches in Kanin's retinue provided a convenient cover for what the Tsar considered a pivotal meeting.

George made the introductions and the Prince commented that it was indeed an honor to be met personally by the Emperor. "It is a small thing considering what you are doing for my family," Nicky replied. "I have looked forward to your arrival with great anticipation." Prince Kanin could see the gratitude in the Tsar's eyes and though he did not let on, he was touched by it.

"And may I present my son, Grand Duke Alexei. Alexei is serving here at the headquarters with me, learning to be a soldier."

The Prince bowed to the Tsarevitch. "I am deeply honored, your Highness," he replied.

As they walked to the waiting cars Nicholas touched George on the arm and whispered, "you must speak with the Prince alone as soon as you can arrange it."

"Quit worrying, Nicky. I have arranged to take him on a drive in the countryside later today and I will handle everything as we have discussed. Trust me, I know this man."

"Very well then, I will leave it in your hands."

The entire entourage motored back to the Stavka where a meal had been prepared for the visitors. A high pressure front had passed through two days earlier, bringing with it some cooler air, so tables had been set up outside to take advantage of the weather. The informal setting helped break down the natural reserve of the Japanese and before long a number of animated conversations were in progress. After lunch the staff briefed the visitors on the military situation which, if truth be told, was an unmitigated disaster. In the meantime the train was shunted onto a siding to serve as accommodations during the visit and after the exhausting journey and heavy meal most of the visitors were happy to nap for a while. Late in the afternoon George invited Prince Kanin to join him for a ride in the country and the Prince readily accepted. The Japanese security team was not happy with the arrangement but he waved them off.

When the car cleared the compound George drove at a leisurely speed down one of the country lanes and then pulled over at a convenient spot. They made small talk for awhile but finally turned to the reason for the Prince's visit. "Your recent letter was very interesting," said Kanin. "So the Tsar wishes to have another Japanese tattoo. You may inform him I have brought one of the finest tattoo artists in Japan with me. He has on occasion done work for the Japanese Imperial family. Has the Tsar mentioned what type of design he would like to have rendered?"

"I apologize that I had to mislead you in my letter but the tattoo is not for the Tsar," said George. "He has decided his daughters need to be tattooed. I know that may seem shocking to you but there is a valid reason."

"No, on the contrary, Japanese women are often tattooed. But what about the Tsarevitch; will he be included as well?"

"No, he has a medical condition that would make it very unsafe for him. It could even cause his death."

"I am sorry to hear that. If I may ask, why has the Emperor decided to do this?"

"He is concerned that in the future the features of the Grand Duchesses may change so much that no one would recognize them. This would indeed be a problem if they attempted to claim their patrimony and he wants to ensure that there is a way to identify them. He came to this decision because he remembered once attending a family gathering and failing to recognize some of his relatives whom he had not seen for many years. We can take care of this when we travel to Tsarskoe Selo to meet the Grand Duchesses. In the meantime he has suggested, with your approval, of course, that your man be allowed to tattoo some of the officers who have expressed an interest. This would justify the artist's presence among your retainers."

"I understand completely. The Tsar has put his plan together with great imagination and he seems to think of everything."

"We Russians believe that the Tsar is God's representative on earth and because of this we believe that God directs and guides him."

"It is an interesting concept. The Japanese have a similar belief although I would have to say it goes beyond what you have described."

"I am sure that some higher being has a hand in the monarchies of all countries," said George. "Now If I may, I would like to discuss your itinerary."

"Yes, what are the plans?"

"The Tsar's mother, the Dowager Empress wishes to meet you. She has been told that the Grand Duchesses will be sent out of the country for their protection. She wants to meet the man who will be responsible for the safety of at least two of her granddaughters, so we will be going down to Kiev for a short visit. However, I must warn you ahead of time that she can be quite difficult."

"I will gladly meet with her and hopefully put her mind at ease," said Kanin. "Everything is ready in Nagasaki and I know the young ladies, if not happy with their circumstance, will at least be comfortable. I will personally meet them in Vladivostok and take them back to my country. The Empress will have nothing to worry about for even if there is a suspicion they have taken refuge in Japan, it would be almost impossible to breach the security we will have in place."

"Very well then. After we meet with the Dowager Empress we will travel to Tsarskoe Selo to meet the Empress and her four daughters. At some point during your visit we will have your tattoo artist complete the tattoos. The Empress is making the necessary preparations as we speak but she will not tell the Grand Duchesses until the last moment because she obviously does not want them to feel the stress of such an ordeal too far in advance."

"It can be a painful process but there is an ointment that can be rubbed in ahead of time which deadens the area and eases the pain."

"That is comforting to hear. I dread the thought of those poor girls having to go through this procedure but the Tsar has ordered it and it must be done."

"The Tsar is very wise to utilize this Japanese artist for he must know that complete discretion will be maintained. I can assure you that once I have given him his instructions and he has completed his task nothing more will be said."

"That is good to know," George replied, "but we will be taking some added precautions. For instance, the ladies will be under a covering with an opening that reveals only the area of the tattoo. The artist will, of course, realize his subject is a young woman, but a special screen will prevent him from seeing her upper body and he will not know who he is working on. Only the Empress and Baroness Sophie Buxhoeveden will be in the room, one on either side of the screen and there will be no conversation. The Empress will explain any other details when we meet her next week and there will probably be changes so I do not want to be premature in laying out the way things will occur."

George started the car and drove back to the headquarters building. "When do you anticipate we will leave for Kiev," Prince Kanin asked, as the car glided to a stop.

"The Tsar has cleared his calendar for tomorrow and wishes to spend the day talking with you. So I thought we could go down the day after tomorrow if you are rested enough."

"That will be just fine," replied the Prince.

෬෮

With the Tsar spending more and more time at headquarters many of the intimate details of the *Masquerade* were being left to Alix to arrange, and she found herself depending on Isa to assist her with these new responsibilities. It was not that she had abandoned her old friend Anya but she knew that anything she told her would find its way back to Father Grigory and though she desperately wanted to include him in all this she would not break her pledge to Nicholas. Anyway, Alexei was at the Stavka with his father so there was no reason for Rasputin to visit the palace and thus the presence of the impostors remained a well-kept secret.

This morning Alix paced nervously in her Mauve Boudoir as she waited for her daughters to arrive for a meeting. In a few days time Prince Kanin and his entourage would arrive from Kiev and she had to break the news to her daughters that they would soon be getting a tattoo. The thought of it made her slightly dizzy and she sat down to keep from falling. She was sitting there, resting her head in her hands, when Isa and the girls came trooping in. They were not their usual boisterous selves for they had not been able to come to grips with the idea that they were soon to be separated. In fact, they were now apprehensive anytime they were called together and this morning was no different. "I will wait outside," said Isa.

"No," said Alix. "Please stay and hear what I have to say. You are very much a part of this now and I will need you to help me."

"Yes, your Highness." The girls gathered round their mother's chaise lounge, Olga sitting on the end, Tatiana taking a chair and the two youngest on the floor.

"When your father talked to you at the Stavka a few weeks ago he said that as time went by you would learn more about the *Masquerade*. Do you remember?" Alix asked.

Olga answered for them all. "Oh Mama, how could we forget something as heart rending as that terrible morning. We have been waiting patiently to learn more but the suspense is almost more than we can bear, especially since you told us not to talk about it."

"Yes, my dears, you have been very patient and today you will learn more. Now, in addition to the letter from St. Serafim, which your father read to you, he has received additional inspiration in the form of dreams. So everything he disclosed to you at Mogilev, and the entire plan he has developed, is not based merely on the letter but on other experiences as well." The Grand Duchesses hung on her every word and though they had many questions, by unspoken agreement, there were no interruptions.

"Your father has allowed me to tell you," Alix continued, "that he has drawn up a document of great significance, an instrument which changes the laws of succession to the Imperial throne. Although males will have precedence there will no longer be an absolute requirement that the successor be a man. Thus Olga, if something were to happen to Alexei, God forbid, then you would be next in line, and your sisters after you. More importantly, from your point of view, are the marriage requirements. In the past, marriage to a commoner was prohibited because the offspring of such a union was considered to have broken the blood line. If you married while in hiding, it would most likely be to a commoner, and your child would not have any rights or titles. No longer is that the case. This document changes that fundamentally, by stating that as long as your royal blood flows through your child, he or she will be a Romanov with all the rights of succession."

"Are you telling us that we have our parents' blessing to marry a commoner," asked Olga, as she thought back to her recent encounter with Vasily.

"Naturally our first choice for you would be someone of equivalent rank but that would probably be too dangerous, with all the attendant publicity. So the answer to your question is that it will be your decision to make. Lastly, you will not be required to maintain your Orthodox faith if doing so would jeopardize a suitable marriage."

"But Mama, I could never give up my faith," Maria cried out.

"It is not so much a matter of giving it up as it is changing the manner in which you practice it. You may have to keep it in the silence of your heart, but Our Lord will surely guide you. Now there is one other matter I wish to discuss and it is really the reason I asked you here this morning. In a few days, Prince Kanin, the Japanese Emperor's personal representative will be visiting the palace to meet you and tell you about his country and the arrangements he has made for you. He is also here to assist us in a more sensitive matter."

"What is it Mama?" asked Marie.

"We are convinced that your father will be martyred in some way, probably by a revolutionary assassin, as was your great-grandfather, and that the monarchy will be destroyed. As for your brother and I, we can only speculate as to what our fate might be. We may even survive the cataclysm that is rapidly approaching. Father Grigory has predicted such an outcome, although your father thinks it unlikely. These are heavy burdens for all of us to bear but we must do so with heads held high and pride in who we are. Now, it is possible that in your life time there could be a restoration of the monarchy but as history has shown, in such situations, there are often illegitimate claimants. As people grow older their features, as well as their mannerisms, change with time. Your looks could change dramatically and you must have a way to prove your identity.

"Certainly Mama, we will know our own sisters," said Olga.

"Yes, my dear, of course you would, but there are other family members besides yourselves and some of them would be very happy to claim the throne and deny you your birthright. And there is another factor. We all love your doubles very much but if they survive the revolution, they will have places in the world and someone could try and manipulate them for their own ends. They have been trained to replace you and could easily fool someone who did not know you well. It is an unlikely scenario but we must be prepared for everything. Your father and I felt it critical that you each have something to distinguish you from the doubles."

"What might that be, Mama?" asked Tatiana.

"We have decided that each of you shall receive a tattoo."

"You cannot be serious," said Olga.

Alix just gave her a look that only a mother can and Olga said no more.

"Mama, what is a tattoo?" asked Anastasia.

"Anastasia, you know very well what a tattoo is. You have seen your father's many times."

"I meant how do you make one," explained her youngest daughter.

"It is a very detailed process during which colored ink is applied to the skin with special needles."

"Ugh, it sounds absolutely dreadful and very painful," said Tatiana. "Is this really necessary, Mama?"

"Yes it is. Your father has ordered it to be done and that is the end of it. Now let me show you the design. It is something very special." Alix got up, walked to her desk and withdrew from it a carefully executed drawing of the proposed tattoo. "You know that I consider the swastika to be a special sign. It is an ancient sun symbol and represents four rivers moving away in different directions, which is what you four will eventually be doing. The Romanov double eagle at the top symbolizes your heritage."

"Mama just where is this tattoo going to be placed?" asked Marie.

"It will be placed very high on your leg just under your derriere." The girls' eyes widened when the location was revealed and they giggled at the thought. Alix explained to them that Prince Kanin was bringing a special artist all the way from Japan to tattoo them. "The tattoos will be rendered as soon as he arrives and arrangements to protect your identity and your modesty are well in hand." The Grand Duchesses then peppered their mother with numerous questions which, considering her condition, she answered with great patience. Finally, with the subject exhausted, they departed to continue with their schedules for the day.

A few days later Prince Kanin, accompanied by Grand Duke George and a greatly reduced retinue, arrived from Kiev. The Japanese military contingent remained at the Stavka and would rejoin the Prince later, in Moscow, for the long journey home. The diplomatic mission continued on to Petrograd and were to be housed at the Embassy.

To everyone's relief the audience with the Dowager Empress had gone very well and Minnie had been impressed with the Prince and the manner in which he conducted himself. The Empress was not always a good judge of character but in this case she sensed in the Prince a strength of purpose, a willingness to do whatever was necessary to satisfy his own Emperor's long standing debt of honor. Minnie had questioned him at great length concerning the arrangements he had made and was convinced by his answers that nearly every eventuality had been anticipated. Yes, his visit with Minnie had been a success.

When George and the Prince arrived in Tsarskoe Selo they were met by cars which whisked them away to the palace. Alix was aware of both the importance of the visit and the need for secrecy so she had decided to honor the Prince by inviting him to stay with the family at Alexander Palace. This greatly facilitated his access to the Grand Duchesses and allowed him to get to know them in an informal setting. The fact that Kanin's retinue consisted only of a secretary and two man servants, one of whom was the tattooist, also made it easier to maintain a relaxed atmosphere. Alix knew that the official receptions and entertainment that she had arranged in the evenings were hardly the venue in which to establish intimate relationships so she was quite pleased with the way things developed.

As for the girls, there were mixed reactions. They all were introduced to the Prince and spent time with him because there was always the remote possibility that all the Grand Duchesses would have to go to Japan. But Tatiana and Anastasia immediately formed a strong attachment for the Prince, which he reciprocated in kind, whereas Olga and Marie felt somewhat left out. The Prince brought gifts for everyone and the girls were particularly pleased with the elaborate silk kimonos, which he presented to them. Alix countered with a family picture enclosed in a Faberge frame. During their time together he showed them many photographs of his country and explained, as much as he could, the rich culture of Japan. Despite the cloud hanging over them Tatiana and Anastasia were very excited about their new home while Olga and Marie were slightly despondent that they would not be going to such an exotic land. They knew Poland well from all their trips to Spala and were familiar with the culture, which in many ways was so similar to that of Russia. They were slightly envious of their sisters who were going to Japan, a fascinating place that only their father had visited.

It took a full day for Matsui Kobiyama, working from the drawing the Empress had provided, to prepare the rice-paper patterns he would need to execute the tattoos. The artist had been told very little about his assignment, only that he was to create the same image on four different individuals and that he was to begin as soon as he was ready. The Japanese, with the exception of Prince Kanin, had been led to believe that the immense Catherine Palace was the Tsar's home and that Alexander Palace, where they were staying, was the residence of a minor prince. It was an unnecessary deceit because none of the retainers spoke Russian and they had all been trained from birth to maintain silence while in the Prince's service. Matsui was honored that Prince Kanin had selected him for this trip because he was in his mid-seventies and would not be working much longer. But even at this age he had a steady hand and was renowned for his artistry. Nevertheless, Alix and Isa had taken every precaution they could think of to keep the family wing empty of anyone but *Masqueraders* and, of course the two Japanese.

The routine for creating the tattoos was much as George had earlier explained to the Prince. The actual tattooing would be done in the Mauve Boudoir and Alix had decided to start with Olga, the oldest, and work her way down. When all was ready Isa would bring her down the Tsarina's private staircase, through the Imperial Bedroom and into the Boudoir where she would be prepared for the tattoo. At the same time, but from the opposite direction, Prince Kanin and Kobiyama would be escorted by Count Beckendorff into Alexandra's formal reception room, through the Maple Room and finally into the Pallisander Room where Alix would meet them. Prince Kanin would sit by the partially open door to the

Boudoir to act as interpreter if necessary and Alix would escort Kobiyama into the room and remain with him until he had completed his work. No one was sure how long it would take but Alix and Prince Kanin had agreed to allow two mornings and afternoons, although Matsui thought he could finish sooner.

On the appointed day Alix entered her Mauve Boudoir and was pleased to see that Isa had all the necessary furniture rearranged. She had moved Alix's chaise out into the room and fashioned a makeshift screen out of sheets. Next to the chaise was an end table for the artist's tools and equipment and a low footstool for him to sit on.

The Grand Duchesses were waiting anxiously in their dining room for the ordeal to begin. Alix had been deliberately vague about the process so they were quite nervous and wondered if it would be painful. When the Baroness walked in they looked up in anticipation and she smiled at them. "You can stay here if you want to but it is unlikely that he will finish everyone today, so you may want to wait in your rooms. And remember, say nothing about this to anyone. Now Olga, let us get this over with."

Once in the boudoir, Isa instructed her to remove her skirt and pantaloons and lay face down on the chaise, which was just long enough to hold her reclining body. Isa quickly covered Olga with a sheet, which had a circle cut in it to expose a small portion of her upper leg. She arranged the vertical screen, swabbed the exposed area with alcohol and covered it with a towel. Isa then went to the door and said, "everything is ready your Imperial Highness." Alix stood up and nodded to the Prince, who directed Kobiyama to follow the Empress into the next room.

Alexandra led the artist to the chaise and noticed that his face remained impassive when he saw that the screen shielded him from his subject. He quickly set up his equipment and got down to work. After carefully examining the picture Alix had given him and comparing the exposed area to the patterns he had prepared, Matsui began. As his first needle punctured her delicate skin, Olga let out a startled squeal. The pain was not unlike getting an injection over and over and she bit down on a pillow to keep from crying out again. Isa held her hand and gently rubbed her neck until the procedure was over. Once Kobiyama was finished, Alix led him out of the room. The whole business had taken about an hour and a half and the old man needed a rest, so it was decided to do Tatiana after lunch. There was an exchange of guttural Japanese between the two men and the Prince turned to Alix. "My man said to tell you that the tattoo would look fine for a few hours but that it would begin to scab over and itch terribly as it heals. Have them wear loose clothing and try not to pick at the scab; it will fall away of its own accord in about two weeks."

When Olga returned to the dining room, she was immediately surrounded by her sisters, who wanted to know everything that had happened. She explained that it was somewhat painful, but not unbearable and certainly no worse then going to the dentist. The trick was to get past the first needle without crying out and she advised them to bite down on a pillow when the tattooist began. Of course, they wanted to see her tattoo so she lifted her skirt and carefully pulled down her undergarment so they could see it.

"It is beautiful," said Marie as she looked at the small yet intricate tattoo adorning her sister's leg. At that moment Alix entered the room to tell Tatiana about the delay and she too examined the tattoo. "It is exactly what I had hoped for," the Tsarina exclaimed, "truly a work of art." She went on to explain what would happen during the healing process and after Olga adjusted her clothes they washed up and sat down for lunch. Alix told the younger girls that because the tattooist was an elderly man he would be unable to complete all the work in one day. "Oh Mama, that means we will have to think about this for another whole day," Anastasia cried out.

"Yes you will, but I assure you there will be far greater adversity to face in the coming months than some childish apprehension over receiving a tattoo," she replied rather sharply. Alix had access to the medical supplies at the hospital and had considered giving the two youngest a small amount of morphine to ease the pain. But in the end she had been unwilling to deprive a wounded soldier of the scarce drug merely to alleviate a child's minor discomfort. A little pain might do them good.

After lunch Tatiana received her tattoo and the following day Marie and Anastasia went through the ordeal. There were some tears but no hysterics and it actually went much more quickly the second day. Once the last procedure was completed Prince Kanin and the artist returned to their private quarters in the guest wing of the palace. Before departing the Empress had presented Kobiyama with a small token of her appreciation and the old man's normally impassive face was visibly moved by the kindness. Over the next few days Prince Kanin visited with the Grand Duchesses as often as could be arranged. He continued his talks on Japan and the girls were all fascinated by the folk tales and descriptions of his country. But all too soon his visit came to an end and the Prince departed on his return trip to Japan. Before leaving he was allowed a private moment with Tatiana and Anastasia and during this final meeting he assured them that though it would be months before they would see him again, when the time came he would be waiting on the pier.

෴

The next two months proved to be very busy ones for the Imperial family. The Grand Duchesses, in addition to their normal duties, were busy preparing for their future. They also spent time, face to face, with their doubles reviewing the scrapbooks and photograph albums each girl kept. They worked together to intersperse photos of the impostors among those of the real daughters and went over the lives of the Imperial children again and again. Sophie was convinced that the girls, all eight of them, were ready for the great *Masquerade.*

But despite the success they were all having, a troubling situation had developed. During the past year, with Nicholas at headquarters so much of the time, Alix had become increasingly involved in the running of the government, going so far as to conduct meetings with the Tsar's ministers on a weekly basis. This interference in governmental affairs was met with intensifying enmity from the Russian people who, after all these years still questioned her loyalty, and referred to her as "that German woman." As she became increasingly isolated Alix began to play a very dangerous parallel game and as might be expected she turned to her spiritual advisor, Grigory Rasputin, to help her. If Nicholas and Alexandra were poorly prepared for the demands of governance, Rasputin was totally clueless, and a worse choice could not have been found to give political advice. The Empress did not have the power to replace ministers but she hounded Nicky at every opportunity and, burdened as he was with the war, he inevitably gave in to her incessant demands. Thus the Empress, Rasputin, and Anya, the go-between, became a shadow government, one which through inept statesmanship ultimately contributed to the overthrow of the Romanov dynasty. To add fuel to the fire there were the personal attacks on her moral character that appeared in the newspapers, vicious allegations of debauchery that were totally untrue. And there were rumors of plots against Rasputin, which worried her no end but over which she had little control. All of these factors, as well as the demands of the *Masquerade,* were reflected in her increasingly erratic behavior and everyone around her felt that she would shortly suffer some type of breakdown, one which could have disastrous consequences. Something had to be done, but only Nicholas, who was miles away, had the power to intervene.

Part Four

Sanctuary

Chapter 38

November 1916 – Mogilev. The Tsar sat at his desk at the Stavka reading the latest in a long series of notes and letters from his wife. He was very angry, not only at Alexandra, but also at himself, for it had just dawned on him that his own selfishness was partially responsible for the rapidly deteriorating situation in Petrograd. In isolating himself at headquarters he had fulfilled his desire to command the troops but he had also made it possible for Rasputin to increase his influence with the Tsarina, and the staret had taken advantage of his absence to do so. Nearly every letter from Alix contained detailed advice on how various matters should be managed and she always closed with the suggestion that "our friend" approved. Nicholas had been slow to respond to the threat posed by Father Grigory's interference but today's letter pushed him over the edge and drove him to a course of action, which he had fervently hoped to avoid. Alix had included with the note, a comb used by Rasputin, and suggested that if he combed his own hair with it he would receive some kind of mystical protection. Nicholas realized that his wife had become totally irrational where Rasputin was concerned and he made up his mind to remove this cancer infecting his government, once and for all. He knew from the police reports that the so-called "holy man" was a notorious womanizer but he never believed for a moment the vicious rumors that Alix and Rasputin were somehow romantically involved. The Tsar had hoped he could handle the matter quietly and salvage something from the situation but he feared Alix had created such a mess that there was now only one way out.

Nicky's thoughts were interrupted by the arrival of his ward, Grand Duke Dmitri Pavlovich, who invited him outside to enjoy a smoke. It was as if providence had intervened, for the plan Nicholas had decided on required a person who was absolutely loyal, and he suddenly realized, when he saw Dmitri, that he was the man for this most delicate assignment. Yes, his young friend would be the key to success if he chose to participate.

It was a quiet night in Mogilev and the two men stepped outside to smoke and drink some iced vodka. The fall air had turned chilly but it was still very comfortable, compared to the smoke-filled headquarters. Dmitri was like a son to the Tsar and the Grand Duke was one of the few members of the extended family whom Nicholas trusted implicitly. Nevertheless, the Tsar hesitated, for what he was about to ask of Dmitri would change the young man's life forever. Nicholas was irritated with himself for waiting so long, but he had only himself to blame and he accepted responsibility for his serious lapse in judgment. Count

Benckendorff had repeatedly warned him that from a security standpoint the most difficult, but important task, was to keep the overall plan secret from Anya Vyrubova and Rasputin. Unfortunately the Count's agents had reported that at one of the drunken soirees, which he hosted, Father Grigory held forth on a variety of subjects, and made a number of comments about the Imperial family. Since he tended to ramble when he was drunk what he said made no sense to the guests, but Benckendorff felt Rasputin might be close to sniffing out the *Masquerade* and that would lead to disaster. Thus there was now an urgency, whereas before the Tsar had been content to let things just move along at a leisurely pace. There was also the danger that Alix, in her irrational state of mind, might renege on her promise to Nicky without realizing she was doing so. It was time to act.

"Dmitri, I want to ask you a question and I want you to be completely frank in your answer. Will you do that for me?"

"Of course, your Highness."

"Then tell me. What is your opinion of Father Grigory? Answer me as you would a friend, not as if you were speaking to the Tsar," said Nicholas.

Dmitri was caught completely off guard by the unexpected question. He knew very well how he personally felt about Rasputin and he had no difficulty expressing those feelings to his friends, but this was the Tsar. Dmitri knew that for the most part Nicholas had always defended the "holy man" and he felt uneasy discussing the subject with his guardian. "I think I should keep my opinion of that man to myself. I would not want to offend you."

"No, that will not do. I must know where you stand and I will tell you why when you have answered me. I know most, if not all of the family, despise him and if you feel the same, I will understand. But you must verbalize your opinion of him."

Dmitri took a deep breath and began to explain to the Tsar his feelings about the man. "I have spent time with Grigory Efimovich in settings much different than the one you and the Empress have at Tsarskoe Selo. He has shown me the kind of person he really is and I loathe the man, not just because of what I have heard others say about him, but also because of what I have seen and heard with my own eyes and ears. I have heard him say things about you and the Empress that made my blood boil. You have been like parents to me and you know my loyalty lies with you and the Empress. To hear him tell lies about what he does when he comes to the palace is unforgivable. I think the man should be shot. There are many who would like to see him dead but no one has the courage to lift a finger against him."

"Thank-you for your honesty, Dmitri," said Nicholas. "I have another question which you may find more difficult to answer than the first. What do you believe is my opinion of Father Grigory?"

"I would never presume to guess what you think. May I ask what this is all about? I really do not understand where this is leading."

"I will tell you, once you have answered my question."

"Very well. He seems to have a great deal of influence over you and the Tsarina. I think that you honestly believe him to be a man of God who was sent to help you rule Russia. I also think you believe the reports of his debauchery and obscene public behavior to be lies. You seem unwilling to discredit him and as a result there have been vicious attacks on the family. In short he seems to have cast a spell on you both." Dmitri was almost certain the Tsar was going to be angry with him but when he glanced over at Nicholas it was impossible to guess what he was thinking. The Tsar's reaction was not long in coming.

"You are correct in your observations Dmitri, as far as the Empress is concerned, and you have accurately stated the case. Now what I am about to tell you must never be discussed with anyone else. I must have your promise on this."

"I will not repeat this conversation. You have my word."

"The truth is that I despise Grigory Efimovich. He is not a man of God and I think he may even be the spawn of Satan. I know all that is said about him is true."

Dmitri was shocked. If the Tsar really felt that way, how could he have welcomed that man into his home? It was incomprehensible to him. "But why have you allowed this? The family thinks Russia is being ruined because you let that man influence you. The Russian people think he is running the country."

"Dmitri, you must calm down. On a number of occasions, as you well know, he has provided relief for my son during one of his attacks. So for my wife and son's sake I have played along with Rasputin for many, many years. It may seem to you that I have been naive and I admit that at times I have been, but be assured, that is about to be put behind us."

"What do you mean by that?"

"There are plans in motion that it would be too dangerous for you to know, especially considering what I am about to ask of you. But I am not standing idly by while the government comes down about my ears. Now this Rasputin situation has reached a crisis. It is possible that he has learned of some secret information and, if he has, it is likely that he will share the details with others. It is extremely sensitive and cannot be revealed. The time has come for Rasputin to be removed."

"Are you exiling him?"

"No. We need a permanent end to his interference. He must be executed."

"Executed?"

"Yes. He will be punished for crimes against the state and the Imperial family."

"Will you throw him into the Peter and Paul Fortress? Will there be a trial?"

"No, this is a private matter, not for public record. This situation is very complex and no one must know that I am the one who called for his execution."

"I do not understand. What are you saying?"

"Dmitri, I am asking you to be the official executioner of this evil man."

The Grand Duke did not hesitate even for a moment but cried out, "I willingly accept this mission for you and for Russia."

"No, Dmitri. You must take some time to think about this. It is a terrible thing to take a man's life, even if it is justified. It is something you will remember until the day you die. And there will be some repercussions. If you are caught I will have to punish you in some manner. At a minimum you will be banished from court but it could even mean exile or worse. The Empress, of course, will never forgive you, so you must reflect very carefully before you decide," said the Tsar.

"Will I have to act alone or can others be involved?" asked Dmitri.

"You may involve others but it must appear as if this is your own idea, and none of the participants must ever know I ordered it. That a Romanov did this will not be surprising in view of the hatred the family has for this man, but it cannot be traced back to me."

"I believe I know someone who would willingly assist me."

"Do not mention any names to me. I do not want to know any details. Now I want you to think this over carefully and let me have your answer in the morning, after you have slept on it. Agreed?"

"As you wish, your Highness."

"Good. Then let us go in. I feel a chill." The two finished their cigarettes and returned to the Tsar's office for a brandy. There was no more talk of Rasputin that night but before Dmitri left the room he had made up his mind to accept the Tsar's commission. He was honored that Nicholas trusted him for such an important assignment. He said goodnight to the Tsar and made his way back to his quarters.

The Grand Duke awoke the next morning refreshed, and with a clear head, and immediately began to consider the great responsibility the Tsar had placed on his shoulders. The first person to come to mind as a potential accomplice was Prince Felix Yusupov, who was a very close friend. Felix was married to the Tsar's niece and was encouraged in his dislike of Rasputin by his mother and father who were both vocal in their condemnation of the staret. But the more Dmitri analyzed the situation, and its repercussions, the more he came to believe that the assassination should be carried out without the assistance of anyone else and that if at all possible he should act alone. It was too heavy a burden to place on anyone else's soul, even if the execution was totally justified.

The Tsar hoped the young man would think the situation through, but he knew in his heart that Dmitri would accept the commitment without much thought. He had already been awarded the St. George Cross, one of Russia's highest honors for bravery in combat, so he obviously had the physical courage that would be required. Nicholas found it strange that the solution to the problem of who to use had come to him just the night before. He had given it much thought and he realized that his unwillingness to use any members of the *Masquerade* had caused him to put off making a selection. His most loyal friends and family members were involved in the master plan, and he had to eliminate these co-conspirators from consideration. As someone outside that group Dmitri became an obvious choice.

After breakfast the young Grand Duke waited for a break in the Tsar's morning routine and when an opening occurred he knocked on the door to the room Nicholas used as an office, the room where the night before he had been presented with this great opportunity to serve his nation. When he entered Alexei was sitting on the floor playing with his tin soldiers. Nicholas asked Alexei to go outside as he needed to speak with Dmitri privately and the Tsarevich gathered up his toys and cheerfully left the room. As soon as the door closed behind Alexei, Dmitri said, "I accept the assignment because I know this action is crucial to the welfare of Mother Russia. I just pray that we have not waited too long."

"You are sure you want to do this?" questioned the Tsar.

"Yes and I have decided to act on my own, although I have someone in mind to assist me if I cannot come up with a feasible plan. Now when must this take place?"

"As soon as possible I should think, but by the end of the year at the very latest." The timing was critical because the Tsar wanted Rasputin out of the picture before he switched his daughters with the impostors. "You must be certain that the execution takes place while I am at the Stavka. It would be too easy to connect me if I am at Tsarskoe Selo. As I emphasized last night, there can be no hint that I am involved in anyway. Once he is dead, I will, of course, receive official notification. It would be best if you can simply make him disappear but that might prove difficult. At any rate, when the deed is done I will return home to comfort Alix. I hope I will be able to strike the right note of sympathy, but who knows what condition she will be in."

"Does anyone else know about this?"

" Ella is the only one who knows of my decision. As I have said, I do not want any of our family members to know."

"Ella condones this?"

"I would not say she condones it, but she agrees with me that there is no other way. You may speak with her if you have any feelings of guilt or remorse. She has a good understanding of why this must happen."

"I can assure you I will have no such feelings. The whole matter is best kept secret but if my involvement becomes known the family will consider me a hero."

"Yes, I believe they would, but I forbid you to speak of it at all, not even to your sister. I am not sure what will happen after the man is dead. The Empress will be devastated but the rest of the Imperial family will be elated and hopefully Rasputin's demise will help resolve some of the internal strife our government is suffering. I do not want you to let this drag on. I want this over and done with as soon as you can arrange it."

"I will leave for Petrograd first thing in the morning. I am due a furlough and that will explain my presence in the capital," Dmitri replied. "And thank you for entrusting this to me."

The Tsar nodded at him. "Dmitri I may not have the opportunity to speak to you in private once this is all over, but know that whatever I say to you in front of others or whatever is written by me concerning you is done because it must be. You will always know I love you like a son and am proud of what you are about to attempt. Hopefully your involvement will not come to light but if it does I will be required to speak out against what you have done. If I do not, I will give the impression that I was somehow involved or that I show favoritism towards members of the family. Some day you will have the gratitude of your countrymen for your patriotism and hopefully I will be able to repay you for your devotion."

"Please do not speak of repayment. I understand what must happen and God willing I will succeed," said Dmitri. The next day the young war hero departed the Stavka for what his comrades believed to be a long and well deserved rest in the city of Peter the Great.

For Nicholas the clock on the wall of his office seemed to suddenly stand still. He knew it would take Dmitri time to come up with a plan but nevertheless he was unable to control his impatience. Each morning he awoke with the expectation that today would bring the official report detailing the death of Rasputin. But there was no word and his subordinates quickly became aware that something was troubling the Tsar. He normally displayed an equanimity that put his staff at ease, but now he was short tempered and irritable and they were not sure how to respond to this uncharacteristic mood swing.

Finally a courier arrived from Petrograd bearing a sealed note from Dmitri. Nicholas was surprised because there was to have been no direct communication between the two men, but he put aside his frustration at this breakdown and eagerly tore open the note, hoping beyond hope that it would contain some good news. It was, therefore, with extreme disappointment that he read the few lines written in Dmitri's fine hand.

My first attempt has been a failure. I have not forgotten

my promise to you, but for the sake of my soul I must speak

to Aunt Ella. When you receive this I will be on my way

to Moscow. I will explain all, later. Dmitri.

The Tsar was disappointed at the news and confused by his ward's reference to the state of his soul. He had expected much more and could only sigh in absolute frustration at the let down he was feeling. And so the wait would continue and Nicholas, who was not very good at waiting, did not look forward to the coming weeks with any enthusiasm.

To make matters more confusing he received another letter from Alix in which she paraphrased a message she had received from Father Grigory. It was not addressed to the Tsar in particular but with everything that was going on he had to believe it was directed at him. Supposedly "our friend" had predicted that if he, Grigory Rasputin, were to be killed by the "people" of Russia, the Tsar need have no fear; he would continue to rule. But if "our friend" was to die at the hands of the ruling Romanovs, Russia's blood would flow and the throne would be lost within the year. Nicholas was already prepared for that eventuality, and it was for this reason the *Masquerade* was about to begin, so he paid little attention to the staret's prediction. He was curious to know, however, if Rasputin had concrete evidence of a plot or if he was just speaking in general terms. But it made no difference; the Tsar had no intention of calling off the execution. In fact, this cryptic prophecy lent an even greater urgency to the matter. Nicholas could only wait to learn if Dmitri was up to the task.

CRBO

Grand Duke Dmitri Pavlovich was chilled to the bone and had inched his chair as close as possible to the warmth emanating from the coal-fed iron stove. He was seated in the austere office of the Mother Superior, in the Saint's Martha and Mary convent, in Moscow. Across from him sat his dear Aunt Ella in her simple gray habit, seemingly impervious to the numbing cold in the room. Dmitri had come to Moscow to seek guidance from the one person he felt he could unburden himself to. The fact that he had botched the attempt on Rasputin's life was causing him to have second thoughts and he needed to talk to someone about his doubts. It was not a coincidence that Sister Ella was the one person the Tsar had entrusted with knowledge of the plot for she had long been an enemy of Rasputin. And it was to be expected that Dmitri, her former ward, would seek Ella out for advice and spiritual guidance on a matter that was eating at him. "Dear Aunt, thank you for receiving me on such short notice but I have a troubling matter to discuss with you and since time is of the essence I came unannounced."

"My son, I can see that your heart is heavy. Speak freely and give peace to your soul."

"Aunt Ella, I tried to kill Rasputin," he blurted out. "I was successful in introducing poison into his drink at a party but other than causing him to complain of a headache it seemed to have no effect. I used enough to kill an elephant but I accomplished nothing and failed miserably. I am beginning to think that he is a man of God, after all, and is protected by some mysterious force. When I took on this assignment I was full of purpose but now I am starting to have doubts. How could I have agreed to assassinate someone protected by the Almighty?"

"Dmitri," Ella cried out, "never for a minute think that Rasputin is a 'Man of God'. If he is protected, then it is by Lucifer himself. This man is indeed the devil's disciple, the spawn of Satan and therefore he must be destroyed. Scripture tells us not to judge, but this is a prohibition against judging unjustly. I sincerely believe that in this case we judge justly and it can never be a sin to destroy evil. As there are just wars so also are there just deaths, so pick up your sword and complete God's mission. Do not fear what our Almighty Father has in store for you."

Dmitri was astonished at Ella's reaction. He had expected a mild reprimand from her, not this passionate cry for justice. The manner in which she addressed him, and her promise of support gave him the strength of will he needed to carry on, confident in the righteousness of his act. "You have helped me immensely, dear Aunt. I have peace in my soul now and will find a way to complete my mission."

"It is important that we carry out the Tsar's mission as soon as possible but I think I will send him a wire and ask for a little more time. I would like to give Alexandra one more chance to give him up of her own volition. If she publicly distances herself from him it will do more than anything to smooth over the scandal which has erupted around her. The Empress is my sister and I feel we owe her the opportunity." But even as Ella spoke these words, she knew it was a hopeless cause. Nevertheless, she felt it was her duty to make the effort, as much for her own peace of mind as anything else.

Dmitri returned to Petrograd to await the outcome of Ella's effort to intervene. In the meantime the Grand Duchess arranged to meet the Tsar at a small town a short distance from Mogilev and despite the snow Nicholas was able to pick her up in his car. He drove Ella to a secluded spot a short distance from the train station where they could converse privately. Once Nicky turned the engine off, Ella spoke to him about her conversation with Dmitri. "Nicky, he was so upset and worried that he was doing the wrong thing. I assured him that it was God's will but I said I would ask you for more time so that I could try and persuade my sister to give up Grigory Efimovich on her own. It would go a long way with the people if she would publicly banish him. I know I have little chance of success but I believe we owe her the opportunity."

"I agree, but when will you come to see her," asked Nicholas.

"I will visit next week. Dmitri will remain in Petrograd and when I leave Tsarskoe Selo I will direct him on how to proceed. I have little hope that I will achieve anything with Alix so he is already working on a plan which I am sure will be successful.

"I hope so. I believe we are running out of time. I do not think Alix has told Rasputin about the *Masquerade* but I cannot help but think that he knows something." Nicholas then revealed the contents of the note containing Rasputin's prediction about his own death. "I think he suspects the plot against him, which is why we must take care of this matter as soon as possible."

"I agree with you and I know that Dmitri is convinced of the urgency and necessity of his mission."

"Good, and now since we have a little time before your train leaves I want to speak to you about the *Masquerade*. I will be sending the girls to Moscow two at a time. They will be dressed as nuns, so when Sister Barbara meets them it will appear as if they are returning to the convent after a pilgrimage or some such thing." He then unfolded a map of Russia and showed her the tentative route they would be taking. "We will slip them on the Imperial train just before we leave Tsarskoe Selo and they will stay with me until we reach Likoslavl. At that point the train will be shunted onto the line going down to Mogilev. The girls will slip out and proceed to the station where they will purchase tickets for Moscow." Nicholas pointed to the map where he had circled the location of the small town of Tver, north of the city. "I would like to have Sister Barbara board the train here and escort my daughters on to Moscow and thence to the convent. Does that seem feasible?" Nicky asked. Ella nodded her assent but wondered aloud about the timing. The Tsar had anticipated her question and explained his solution. "When you receive a telegram which says it is time to pick-up the medical supplies, that will be your signal to meet the Grand Duchesses at Tver. I believe this will take place sometime in March but I am still working out all the details. I hope your trust in Sister Barbara is well-placed because she plays a pivotal role. The girls would be totally lost in a large city without a guide. By the way I have decided that once we have the girls out of the palace, Alix will travel to the Crimea with the impostors, but I am worried about the week or so before they depart. I just do not want anyone to realize the doubles are not my real children."

"Nicky, there is no need to be so worried about it. We have trained the impostors very well and I know they will pass for your children. But if it really concerns you there is something you can do."

"What is that?"

"Why don't you have them come down with a contagious disease such as the measles? It would certainly keep people away from them and Alix is known for nursing her family on her own, without outside help. It could be easily accomplished and would keep the doubles out of sight. It would also provide a realistic excuse to move everyone to Livadia in the middle of the war. The last thing we need is the suggestion that you are sending your family on a holiday and are therefore somehow unpatriotic"

"That is a brilliant idea, Ella, and it also solves another of my dilemmas. Once Alix and the doubles arrived in the Crimea and we were sure my daughters were safely out of the country, I was going to have to come up with an elaborate plan to fake the impostor's deaths. Nothing plausible came to mind and I have been agonizing over it for weeks; but your idea works perfectly. Once at Livadia they will remain very ill and become more so as time passes. Finally, they can succumb to their illnesses and be buried at their beloved Livadia, in closed coffins, of course, due to the contagious nature of the disease. I will, of course, be devastated by the loss of my children and everyone will understand when I leave the Stavka to be at my wife's side for the funerals. A change of clothes, different hair styles, and the impostors can assume the role of new household domestics, which is what they originally trained for. Alix can find them places in the Grand Ducal palaces along the coast. Once the war is over Nikolasha can make arrangements for them to travel to new homes outside the country and, God willing, no one will be the wiser. Thank-you, dear Ella," he said and kissed her on the cheek. "It will take some planning but I think you have solved my problem."

"I am glad to have rendered you assistance," she replied. "Now I must get back to Moscow. By the way, will you be there for my confrontation with Alix?"

"Yes, I will, and depending on the outcome, I then will decide how long to stay. I do not want to be at Tsarskoe Selo when Rasputin is executed. It is important that Alix never suspect I am involved in any way. She would never understand." Nicholas started the car up and drove Ella back to the station. "May God go with you, dear sister."

"And with you as well," said Ella, as she bid Nicholas adieu.

A week later, with arrangements in hand, Ella departed Moscow for Alexander Palace, and her confrontation with Alix. When she arrived she was greeted by the entire family, including the Tsar, who had arrived only that morning from Mogilev. Alix had arranged for them to have tea together and then dinner, later on. It seemed to Ella that Alix was avoiding any opportunity to be alone with her, which indicated she was well aware of the reason for her sister's visit. Ella wanted to get the dreadful ordeal over and Alix wanted to avoid it altogether so finally Ella asked Alix if she could have a moment alone with her in the morning. The Empress reluctantly agreed to meet with her older sister at half past ten in the formal reception room.

The fact that they were not meeting in the informal confines of the Mauve Boudoir alerted Ella to the fact that she was in for a difficult time. Alix had long ago stopped seeking advice from her sister and made it quite clear that if they were not yet estranged it was only a matter of time. Alexandra had no wish to speak to her sister privately because as far as Alix was concerned Ella was numbered among the enemy. Anyone who opposed Father Grigory could not be her friend, even the sister she had once so loved.

The next morning the two met in the reception room, which the Empress had deliberately chosen to impress upon her sister just who was in charge. It was a wasted gesture for there was little that could intimidate Ella. Anyway, as it turned out, the conversation was short and one-sided.

"Alix I wish to speak to you about Father Grigory," said Ella quietly.

"I do not want to discuss him with you. I have told you that repeatedly."

"You must! The country is falling apart around you, and your good name, and that of your family, is being slandered because of your involvement with him."

Alix stood up. She had heard these accusations before and had no intention of listening to them again, especially from someone she expected to support and comfort her. In her anger at the injustice of it all, she crossed the line and lashed out at Ella. "Get out," she shouted at her sister. "I will not be talked to as if I was a child, I am the Empress of Russia and I will not allow it. Your visit here is at an end. I wish you to leave immediately. You are no longer welcome here." She glared at her sister in a manner which left no room for argument.

The short, rapid fire nature of the attack had actually frightened Ella and for once she was shaken and at a loss for words. But because it was so important, she tried one more time. "Alix, surely you do not wish to part in this manner."

"We are finished," Alix replied, in a more subdued voice. "My only association with you from now on will be that which the *Masquerade* requires." She crossed her arms, walked over to the window, and turned her back on her sister. "Now leave me," she ordered.

Ella left the reception room and started down the corridor and as she did so Nicholas came out of his study and joined her. "It was no use. I am sorry I wasted your time in this manner," she told the Tsar as she struggled to maintain her composure. Alix's attack had hurt her deeply especially since she had spoken only out of love and concern. Nicholas looked at Ella's grief stricken face, reached out, and squeezed her hand in a gesture of comfort. Aware that they only had a few minutes before Alix came out he said, "Ella, I heard it all. There is no reasoning with her when it comes to that man. You gave it your best and our consciences can be at peace because we have tried everything to avoid what comes next. You must inform Dmitri to complete his mission immediately." He gave Ella a quick hug and then went back to his study and closed the door. He did not want to get in the middle of this dispute. Ella gathered her things and prepared to depart for the station. She was surprised when Alix came out with Olga and Tatiana.

"We will see you to the station," she said coldly, before entering the car. Olga and Tatiana did not understand. Ella had just arrived and was leaving already, obviously because of an argument with their mother. They could not imagine what it was but they knew they would soon learn from the palace grapevine. The ride was completed in silence and once on the platform, Alix said good-bye to her sister. It was the last time they would ever see each other.

Ella boarded the train to Petrograd and once she arrived she went to visit her friends, the Yusupovs, at their palace in the city. Their son Felix was present as well as Dmitri. The family was part of what Alix termed the evil Moscow clique, which she suspected was out to do Father Grigory harm. Ella did not wish to get into the private details of the meeting with the Empress and merely informed the group that she had failed to obtain Alix's agreement to give up her staret. Still emotionally affected by her conversation with Alix she was happy to accept an invitation to stay for tea. Later, when she had relaxed somewhat, Dmitri offered to drive her to the station so she could catch the evening train to Moscow. There was no conversation as he walked her to his car but as he closed her door she leaned forward and passed on the Tsar's message. "Dmitri, complete your mission and fulfill God's plan."

He nodded and kissed her cheek, "His will be done."

Ella watched him as he drove off aware that to some he would be seen as a hero and to others, a vile assassin. She immediately left for Moscow and the convent where she would await word from Dmitri about the outcome of his mission. The Tsar departed Tsarskoe Selo the next day so as to quickly distance himself from what was to come. The next few days would pass very slowly for the two conspirators as they anxiously awaited the results of Dmitri's plan.

CRBD

By mid-December 1916 the Neva River, which flowed through Petrograd, was iced over, but not so thickly that it could not be breached. The frigid weather, which produced these conditions, kept most citizens indoors so it was unusual to see activity near the river when the cold morning air penetrated even the warmest clothing. Yet at one of the more remote bridges on the outskirts of town there was some suspicious goings-on. A black automobile had pulled up near the embankment and one of the three men inside jumped out and made his way, slipping and sliding, down to the edge of the ice. The car continued to circle the block while the man on the river bank attempted to break a hole in the ice with a fire ax. In the thin, cold air it was exhausting work but he was driven by some sense of urgency and kept hammering away at the ice until finally he broke through. He signaled the car to stop and then continued to enlarge the hole until it was big enough to accept the bloodied body that the other men were dragging down the bank towards him. Together the three forced the body into the water and as far back under the ice as they could reach. It was back breaking work but eventually they were satisfied. All three symbolically rinsed their hands in the icy water, crossed them selves, and climbed back up the embankment. They glanced back at the river, then got back into the auto and drove off. Grigory Efimovich Rasputin was no more, but for Russia it was to prove too little, and too late.

A short time later, at the Alexander Palace, Alix woke in her bed, dripping with perspiration and screaming that she was drowning. Madeleine Zanotti, who was sleeping in the next room, ran in and attempted to calm her but to no avail. The maid then called on the house phone to Isa who was the Lady-in-waiting on duty. Isa rushed over from the other side of the palace but by the time she arrived Alix had passed out. Isa immediately called for Dr. Botkin but it was a while before he arrived at her bedside. He examined Alix thoroughly but could find nothing wrong and yet he was unable to revive her from her coma-like state. Dr. Botkin and Isa maintained a worried vigil, unsure as to what exactly was happening to the Empress. After a few hours, her labored breathing calmed and Alix woke to find two very worried faces peering down at her. "What is wrong," she inquired and Dr. Botkin explained what had happened.

"Well, all I know is that I feel wonderful. It is as if I had awakened from a great night's sleep."

Dr. Botkin examined her again and he had to admit her eyes were remarkably clear. They no longer had that red dazed look that had so unnerved everyone. "I cannot explain this episode other to say that you must have had a very bad dream." He did not mention that he had once attended an exorcism and that there were parallels in what he had seen occur and the symptoms the Empress had just exhibited.

"I wish all dreams made me feel so rested," she replied as she smiled at the doctor.

Later that day, the city of Petrograd reeled from the news that Rasputin could not be found, and was presumed to have been murdered. He was initially reported missing but two days later his body turned up in the Neva River the victim of what appeared to be a vicious assault. The assailants did nothing to hide their involvement and before long it was common knowledge that a plot to kill Rasputin had been uncovered and that the key conspirators were Grand Duke Dmitri Pavlovich and Prince Felix Yusupov. Alix had them put under house arrest until the Tsar could return from the Stavka. An investigation was conducted by the police and was completed by the time Nicholas returned from Mogilev. He examined the facts and after some consideration the Tsar exiled Felix to his country estate. Dmitri, however, received a harsher punishment. He was ordered to the Persian front for the duration of the war. No amount of pleading from family members could dissuade the Tsar from awarding this punishment. As it turned out, the sentence was a generous one for when the revolution occurred Dmitri was out of reach of the Bolsheviks and was able to make his way to safety.

Chapter 39

January 1917 - Tsarskoe Selo. The death of Rasputin did not turn out to be the dreadful blow to the Empress that her enemies expected and, in fact, quite the contrary was true. Alix, of course, had been saddened by the loss of her friend, but surprisingly she did not dwell on it, reasoning that it was the inevitable outcome of the intrigue which had surrounded him. Each day she seemed more like her old self, as if she had been released from some sort of spell, and though no one close to her would comment on the changes in her personality, everyone welcomed the improved atmosphere. In the trying months that were coming it would be Alexandra's strength and fortitude that helped hold the *Masquerade* together.

As for the Tsar, he was relieved that up to this point his role in the removal of Father Grigory had remained undetected. He knew that Alix would have looked upon his involvement as a betrayal and he hoped to avoid causing her any pain. Nicholas harbored no guilt about Rasputin's demise but he did feel a sense of remorse over the manner in which he had treated Dmitri and he planned on mitigating the young man's punishment once a reasonable amount of time had passed.

The Tsar realized, that although the last few weeks had been pivotal ones, the dawning of the New Year would bring the first of the major tests of his plan to save his daughters. And so, as he sat in his study in the early hours of the morning, wondering what the future would hold, he was inundated by a flood of wide-ranging emotions. He felt hope; hope that he had done everything he possibly could to prepare for what must come. And there was fear and concern for his wife and son. He knew what his fate would be, but what would become of them? There was deep sorrow that before too long he would be saying goodbye to his beloved daughters, for the last time. He felt anger at the evil men who were making it all necessary. And lastly he felt a deep sense of gratitude for the wonderful friends and family members who helped put the *Masquerade* together. It was finally completed, except for a few minor details, and was just waiting to be implemented. Of course, there was always the unexpected obstacle but the plan had flexibility and the Tsar was sure the key players had the ability to adjust to changing situations.

Nicholas planned to remain at the palace for an extended period; several months, if necessary. He wanted to spend as much time with his daughters as possible, not only because he would never see them again, but also because he wanted to go over what was expected of them, again and again, until they were totally comfortable with the roles they would play. He put his study off limits and kept it locked at all times. The walls were soon adorned with war maps, but that was just a ploy since Nicholas had weeks ago conceded that if things continued as they were, the war was lost. So he pretended to be involved in the conduct of the various campaigns, but in reality he was working with the girls on the *Masquerade*. He tried to spend some time with them each day, one-on-one, reviewing details of the plan and testing them on their knowledge of it. It was extremely important that they commit everything to memory, especially the financial details. It appeared to some in the household that the Tsar was spending more time with Olga than the others but she was the oldest, and with the changes made to the Laws of Succession, Olga needed more preparation. Nicholas never mentioned it to anyone but he often wondered if she was the chosen one of Serafim's letter.

While Nicholas was focusing on the future, Alix could not help but be drawn to the past. Although she was improving each day there was a residual concern that stemmed from Father Grigory's prophecy that if he died at the hands of a Romanov, her son Alexei, would die within six months. Today, she sat in her mauve room and carefully unwrapped a package of the staret's writings, which his family had sent to her. It had been found among his personal effects in his Petrograd apartment and Rasputin's daughter thought that Alix would like to have them. The Empress removed a tattered journal and loose scraps of paper with nearly undecipherable writing on them. The cover of the notebook was filthy and Alix slipped on a pair of gloves to avoid soiling her hands. As she glanced at the contents she recognized many of the spiritual treatises that he had shared with her and which she had faithfully recorded in a book of her own. Father Grigory was considered by many to be illiterate but his thinking was clear and concise, although his handwriting was almost illegible. It was only through years of practice that Alix was able to read the documents.

As she flipped through the pages, a folded piece of paper slipped out and dropped to the floor. Alix bent over to retrieve it and when she straightened up the heading at the top of the paper immediately caught her attention. It was labeled 'Alexei's tonic' and appeared to be a list of ingredients to be used in preparing some sort of potion. She turned it over, looking for some clue as to its meaning, but the reverse side was blank. She turned it back over and looked at the list again. Some of the items, such as sassafras, were familiar to her, but others were not. At the bottom of the list was some faint writing and she had to strain her eyes to see what was written there but eventually she made out the words, *a pinch of opium*. She quickly looked through the rest of his papers but could find nothing else about Alexei. Alexandra had always had a strong belief in Father Grigory's healing power so she was confused by what she had discovered. Alix remembered the packets of tea and herbs he had given her for Alexei and wondered if they explained the "holy man's" seeming ability to heal the child. Now that she was thinking more clearly, she recalled the time in Spala when she had been convinced Father Grigory healed her son with a telegram from Siberia. As she thought about it more carefully she remembered that Anya had brought a supply of Grigory's "tea" with her and near the end of the episode had administered a draught to Alexei. Alix had been too exhausted to object, but the fact remained, the child recovered soon thereafter. Could this recipe be the elixir that Rasputin used to heal and which now, more than ever, she needed to keep her son alive?

Alix immediately went to find Nicky and tell him about her discovery. She found him in his study poring over some documents. "Nicky, you are not going to believe what I found among Father Grigory's papers. I still cannot believe it myself."

Nicholas looked up from his desk at Alix and wondered what she could have found. He thought they were rid of Rasputin, but looking up at Alix's animated face it seemed as if the staret had risen from the dead, and was once again the topic of an unwelcome conversation. He suppressed a sigh of annoyance and asked, "what is it Sunny, what did you find?"

Alix laid the folded piece of paper on his desk and said, "I believe this is how he healed our son."

He looked at the list and recognized Alexei's name across the top. "Do you know what this is?" he asked.

"It is obvious to me that this is some sort of tonic to help treat his bouts with hemophilia. I just do not know how often he should be given it or in what dosage. I think we should find these ingredients and have them on hand for Alexei's next spell. I must say though that I am worried about the reference to opium. You know we have always discouraged its use."

"That is true, but if Grigory mixed opium in this concoction it certainly did not make Alexei's illnesses any worse; quite the contrary. But it must have been introduced in small amounts or we would have seen symptoms of its use," said Nicky as he perused the list of ingredients. "Most of these seem harmless enough, although there are a few I do not recognize. As for the opium we will just have to wait and see. I will have Dr. Botkin research this and render an opinion and if he is satisfied it is safe we will surely do what you suggest. I am sure Petrograd has an herb shop of some sort."

The next day the Tsar discussed the tonic with Dr. Botkin. The doctor looked at the list of ingredients and recognized the combination as an old folk remedy. "I believe I can find all the necessary items," he informed the Tsar, "but I must tell you quite frankly that I believe it was the opium in the tea that ultimately provided relief. I think it relaxed the child's body enough so that natural healing could take place. As for the tea itself, it will do no harm. I will obtain whatever is necessary and work out the dosages, but I must know if you wish me to include opium."

"If the situation warrants its use I am sure the Empress will agree. Anyway what other option is there?" replied the Tsar.

The timing of all this was fortuitous because several days later Alexei suffered an accident while playing outside. His sled flipped over and though he fell into the soft snow he struck his elbow sharply on one of the runners. He was brought quickly to his room and Dr. Botkin was summoned immediately so the injury could be assessed. By the time the doctor arrived the discoloration and swelling were already apparent and Alexei was beginning to feel pain. Knowing there was nothing else he could do, the doctor mixed up a batch of "Rasputin's potion" as he called it and administered it to the boy. Alexei drank it and shortly after, drifted off to sleep, seemingly relaxed by the warm drink. Later that day, when he awoke, the pain in his arm was almost gone and the swelling was noticeably reduced. Anticipating the worst, however, Alix insisted he stay in bed for several days and since Alexei liked the taste of sassafras, the doctor continued giving him the elixir each day. These follow on treatments were completely innocuous and did not include "*a pinch of opium.*" After a number of days passed it was quite obvious that Alexei was healed. His arm had never swollen into the huge mass it usually did with this sort of injury and in less than a week Alexei was back up, feeling like his old self. The Tsar, his wife, Dr. Botkin, and Gilliard his tutor were amazed at his quick recovery.

Later when Nicholas and Alexandra were alone they discussed what had occurred. "Nicky, I just do not understand why Father Grigory kept this from us," said Alix with sorrow in her voice. "He acted as if God was working through him to cure our son when in reality it was not his power but rather this special tonic. To think of all the suffering our poor Alexei went through and all it took to alleviate his pain was a few sips of the drink. You know that I have been agonizing over Father Grigory's prophecy that Alexei would die in six months? I am beginning to wonder if withholding this recipe from us was his way of ensuring his prediction would come true. Just listen to me. Did you ever think I would talk about him this way? I cannot believe that he did not share this with us. It is unconscionable."

"Do not be hard on yourself, dearest Sunny, and do not dwell too much on the past. It has been very difficult for you. Although there were many attempts to warn you about this man, for the most part it was impossible to penetrate your concern for our son. And he manipulated the situation to his benefit. But now he is gone and I need you at my side, strong and courageous to face what is coming." Nicholas loathed Rasputin even in death and it angered him to think that he was still influencing their lives. "Sunny, God was looking out for us and sent an angel down to deliver that paper into our hands, so we would have it to help our son. I know with the passing of Father Grigory you thought Alexei was doomed, but now we have hope again," he said

Alix gave Nicholas a tender kiss and said, "I must go and get a long letter off to Ella. I can imagine what she must think of me, but before I go, do promise me that we shall always have this medicine for Alexei." Nicholas nodded his agreement and explained that Dr. Botkin had already laid in a good supply.

Several days later, after Alexei's full recovery, Nicholas summoned Count Beckendorff to his study. "As you know, dear friend," he began, "I have been working individually with Alix and the girls to prepare them for the future, but I think it is time to meet together as a family to go over some of the arrangements. Much thought and effort have gone into this, almost a decade of work, and the test of all our efforts will soon be upon us. I have prepared for this meeting over the past few days and I think now is a good time. My calendar is clear for the next two hours so would you please ask the Empress to bring in the Grand Duchesses and Countess Buxhoeveden as well? It is not necessary for Alexei to be here. The less he knows of the other elements of the plan the better. I will want you to attend, of course, but before you join us make sure you brief the guards that no one but regular staff members are to be allowed in this wing of the palace"

"Yes, your Imperial Highness, I will see to it immediately."

When Alix received the summons she called her daughters down from the attic, where they had been working with their doubles, and within a short period of time everyone was gathered together around the Tsar's large conference table. Nicholas greeted everyone and, noting the expectant looks on all their faces, got right to the point. "I feel the time has come to begin meeting as a group to review our plan and see how the various aspects of it are coming together. I have finished assessing all of our efforts and I believe we have addressed everything. Today we will review step by step some of the actions we will each be taking as part of the overall plan." Nicholas picked up his notes, shuffled them together, and glanced at each one of the participants in turn. The faces that looked back at him were set with determination, but he recognized that underlying their grim resolve was a deep feeling of sorrow.

In the five months since the Grand Duchesses had been informed of the plan they had all changed. It was inevitable, of course, and even Anastasia, usually so full of exuberance and excitement, now seemed older than her years. They all understood the significance of what they were about to do and because of the great importance their parents attached to this plan, they now viewed their lives differently. Gone were the days of a structured existence replete with constant guidance from their parents and those who surrounded them. Now they were expected to make the leap from reliance on others to virtual independence. The concept was exhilarating and frightening at the same time.

Although it was envisioned that only two of the girls would go to Japan, all four had spent their free time studying about their neighbor to the east. Prince Kanin had given the girls an extensive library about the country and had also brought language books. They had been to Poland many times, throughout the years, and were familiar with the culture so they spent a minimal amount of time revisiting their "western refuge." They did, however examine how people in the United States lived, on the off-chance they might end up there. In addition to their country studies they poured over materials on mundane topics such as how to set up a household, shop for their necessities and conduct banking. Without exception they had all applied themselves to this change in the focus of their education and the results were gratifying. Nicholas was pleased with their progress.

The Tsar lifted a sheet of paper from the stack in front of him. "I have prepared an agenda and we will go down the list item by item to ensure we do not overlook any details. There is much to consider so I want you all to listen very carefully. Olga and Tatiana, as the eldest you will help guide your younger sisters over the next few years, until they attain their majority. Maria and Anastasia, I expect you both to listen and obey your sisters, as if it were your Mother and I who were giving you guidance." The Tsar expected some smug looks to pass from eldest to youngest but instead their newfound maturity asserted itself and the two younger girls solemnly nodded their assent.

"From now until the time you leave the palace, you will all be preparing for the journey itself. Whatever comes later you will have to address on your own. My immediate task is to get you to safety and to provide sufficient funds for your upkeep, so the first thing we need to discuss is how you will support yourselves. I have analyzed the expenditures involved in your maintenance as Grand Duchesses and it seems that the costs of your clothing, medical expenses, education, and other miscellaneous items exceed the sum of 45,000 rubles each year. Obviously that is a substantial amount of money and it will be difficult to maintain you in similar circumstances once you leave the palace and are on your own. Nevertheless, I have tried to anticipate your needs and have decided that each of you is to have the equivalent of that amount each year to provide for yourselves. Now clearly you cannot be walking around with vast sums of currency in your bags; it would be much too dangerous. You will have a substantial amount with you when you depart but that is to be used to cover unexpected expenses during your journey. Be frugal and be careful and never let anyone see what you have. And remember that initially, you will not need much money, as you will all be in convents. Anyway, when the catastrophe strikes the nation our currency will probably become worthless and you will need something to fall back on. That is why bank accounts were established for you years ago in Japan, in the United States and at the Vatican and why I have been drilling you individually on your account numbers and on banking procedures. But even then there is always the possibility that you may not be in a position to access those accounts, so you will need another alternative. I have done some research and have talked to Carl Faberge about this. It seems that precious jewels are a very stable form of exchange and their intrinsic value are universally recognized. No matter where you end up you will probably be able to sell a jewel or precious stone for cash, but you must always try and do business with someone reputable. I recently read a book on pearls and although I am sure you know how valuable they are, did you know that different types fetch much more than others? I have purchased a large amount of pearls for each of you, as well as additional gem stones. It seems that dealers sometimes hide diamonds and the like to safeguard them when they are traveling. They sew the stones into the lining of their clothes, gloves, and inside of shoes they pack in their cases. We will do the same," the Tsar announced.

"I want you to start on this project immediately and when you do so, refer to the jewels as "medicines." Just a precaution, of course, like so many others we are taking to preserve our secret. Alix please have your maids assist the Grand Duchesses in getting all the necessities together and sewing the jewels into their clothes. They must be sewn into your under garments so that no matter what you are wearing when you depart you will carry the valuables on your person. Remember, these clothes will be heavy so you will have to learn to adjust to the weight and this means you will have to launder your underwear yourselves in order to protect your resources. Ella has sent nun's habits from her convent for all of you, so you will just need to pack a few other items. Nicholas looked over at Isa and said, "Countess, will you take this page and throw it into the fire for me? I have discussed every thing on it."

"Yes, your Imperial Highness," said Isa as she took the paper from his hand, crumpled it up and walked over to the stove. She opened the door and threw it into the flames and waited until it was burned to ash before she returned to the table. Nicholas looked down at the next page and then continued.

"Now let us skip ahead to the day of your departure, which I foresee will be towards the end of March. I will return home from headquarters for a short visit and when I go back, Olga and Maria will travel with me in the first group, as far as Likhoslavl. There they will leave my car, purchase tickets, and board the regular train to Moscow. Ella will be informed of your imminent arrival and will arrange to have Sister Barbara board at Tver and accompany you the rest of the way.

Now the tricky part is getting you out of the palace and onto the train without arousing suspicion. You will each have one bag and Count Beckendorff will arrange for them to be placed in my private car on the Imperial train before you arrive. Your under things with the jewels sewn into them will be in these bags and you will put them on later when you don your habits. Now this is how I envision we will pull it off."

"Isa will drive to the hospital with the four of you, ostensibly to visit the patients, but in reality to ensure that Olga and Maria are seen by a number of people and their presence at Tsarskoe Selo noted. When Isa returns to the palace she will be accompanied by Tatiana and Anastasia. Olga, you and Maria will remain at the hospital, as you often do, until shortly after dark, at which time Isa will come back to pick you up. She will have the Count with her in the car, but instead of returning to the palace she will drive you to the train station where Valia will meet you. The Imperial cars will have been shunted onto their own siding and the area should be deserted except for one or two guards. Valia will be in uniform, and will gather the guards together at the front of the train and inform them that I have decided to return to headquarters that night. As you know, my train has a secret access installed in the floor of one of the cars. While Valia is addressing the guards, Count Beckendorff will enter the train as if to inspect it. He will open the secret door and the girls will slip out of the automobile, climb under the train and up into the coach. Once the Count has assisted you into the train, he will help you close the door and then return to the palace with Isa and Valia. Both doors to this car will be locked, so no one should come in. It is critical that you keep the blinds drawn and remain absolutely quiet with no moving around. If for some reason you feel as if you might be discovered, then lift up the seat of my couch and climb into that space. It is large enough to hold both of you and I have cleared everything out of it except for a few blankets in case you need to hide in there. Shortly thereafter I will board the train, and as soon as steam is up, we will be off to Likhoslavl. All of your goodbyes must be completed before you leave for the hospital and I beg you to be empty of tears because the parting will be difficult enough without an emotional scene. As soon as Isa reports that Olga and Maria are concealed on the train their doubles will move into their rooms and the *Masquerade* will have begun. In the morning your mother will let it be known that Olga and Maria have come down with something and are confined to their beds under the care of Dr. Botkin. Since a diagnosis is pending no one will be allowed to see them until the nature of their illness is categorized. I will continue on to Mogilev and remain for at least a week so suspicions will not be aroused. I will then return to Tsarskoe Selo to move Tatiana and Anastasia. Later, after everyone is in place, your mother will travel to the Crimea with Alexei and your doubles." At this point, the second and third pages of his notes went into the fire.

"Now, you may be wondering why Olga and Maria are going to Moscow when their ultimate destination is the convent in Warsaw. Because of the unrest in Petrograd I have determined that the safest route to their refuge is from Moscow directly to Warsaw. I want you as far away from Petrograd and Tsarskoe Selo as possible. I did have some concerns that it might be unsafe to travel through the German lines, but the Mother Superior assures us that thus far the Germans have respected the religious and left them free to do their work. The convent is still a safe haven and you will be left alone. Also, remember that here are many refugees moving back and forth across the lines with various religious orders ministering to them so you will not arouse suspicion. You will be dressed in the habit of the Catholic convent and Ella will have your papers and your Polish identity cards. Mother Superior will be sending two Russian speaking nuns to Ella's convent in April. They will escort you back to Warsaw."

"Tatiana and Anastasia, if all goes according to plan, about two weeks later, after I have returned from Mogilev and spent a few days here at the palace, we will use almost the same plan to set you on your way. The only difference is that when you leave Ella's convent you will be going east to Vladivostok where Prince Kanin has arranged for you to be met and taken to Japan. When you arrive in the city you will go immediately to the Japanese consulate. Prince Kanin has a representative there who will know your identity and will advise you as to the travel arrangements for the final leg of the trip. Initially you will both journey to Yokohama. There is a convent there with a school and an orphanage. Anastasia will continue the final years of her schooling and Tatiana you will be ministering to the children. You have had so much experience working with the war orphans in our country, and have such a calling for this type of work, that you should be very comfortable."

"Olga, Tatiana and Maria your formal education is at an end," said the Tsar. The three older Grand Duchesses sat there with expressionless faces due to the seriousness of the occasion, but inside they were delighted to know that they would no longer be required to sit daily for the mundane tasks their tutors gave them in the Imperial classroom. Tatiana was especially happy to know that she would be able to carry on her work with orphans. At one time she had been the President of the Society to Aid Widows and Orphans of the War. She was very disappointed when she had been forced to resign her position due to the demands of the *Masquerade.*

Nicholas took a moment to catch his breath and then for the first time brought up the possibility that everything might not go according to plan. "As I have explained to you before, we have a solid, well thought-out plan, but there is always the possibility that we might have overlooked something. For that reason, and wherever it could be done, we have created alternatives to provide more flexibility. The first, and as I see it, the most critical challenges, are your trips out of Russia and the Japanese have come forward once again to assist us in this effort. A Japanese presence on the Trans-Siberian railway seemed a necessity so we entered into an agreement to establish a fur trading mission at Omsk and it has been operating successfully for a number of years. The Siberian trappers bring their pelts to the mission and trade for cash or various commodities. It is located in an abandoned monastery on the edge of the city and is easy to find. If anything should go awry, you must make your way to Omsk and then to the trade mission. The staff is rotated periodically but always consists of a platoon of Imperial marines, dressed in civilian clothes, and commanded by an officer hand-picked by Prince Kanin. The commandant has instructions and will arrange to get you on to Vladivostok. We picked Omsk because it is a major transportation hub and it will be relatively easy to get you out of there, unnoticed. But remember this is only an alternative plan. I feel quite confident you will leave the country without incident. No one will know who you are and with the impostors in place no one will even know that you are missing. Your trips should go smoothly, but always remind each other that you must stay in character and do not under any circumstances reveal your true identity."

"Once you reach your destinations you will probably remain in hiding for at least a year. Olga and Maria you will be staying at the convent in Warsaw until the Mother Superior there decides it is safe for you to leave. Tatiana the situation will be the same for you but it will be Prince Kanin who decides when to move you and Anastasia. I have arranged for homes with everything you could possibly need to live comfortably. Much of the furniture has come from our palaces and we tried to include some pieces which will be familiar to you. In Poland, the house is in Zakopane, a beautiful mountain village. In Japan, the estate is in Nagasaki. These homes are very secluded and well protected by high walls but you still must remain secluded until events have unfolded. Of course, only a few know that these are the homes of Russian Grand Duchesses. And so you will begin a new life outside of Russia. I pray fervently that the time you are in your self-imposed exile will not seem too long and that you will be able to eventually come home to your Motherland. How will you know when time is right? Well, you must educate yourselves as to the facts and then make an informed decision. You must never take anything lightly and must think long and hard before coming to a conclusion. You must maintain a constant watch and read the newspapers so you are well informed about what is happening here, as well as in Europe and the rest of the world. If the situation in Russia does not improve you will have some decisions to make. For example, if an extended period of time goes by you and you see no signs that things are getting better, you may want to relocate to America . You will have to pray hard about it and look for signs that it might be the right thing to do. You will be older and wiser then."

"The one element of all this that I have been unable to explain comes from St. Serafim's letter. It is his reference to the man in white who travels the world. You must constantly be on the lookout for signs that will indicate who this is. Pray often for inspiration and God will help lead you. I cannot prepare you for this other than to caution you against chasing phantoms."

Nicholas looked at his wife and daughters, and glanced at Isa and the Count. "I know this is tiring but we are nearly finished for today. The time may come when you wish to be married and have children. The information and knowledge that you have should not be divulged too quickly. At some point it may be necessary for you to share all this information with your families. After all, if the chosen one is from your lineage, then you will have to prepare your children just as I have prepared you."

"When the time comes for us to leave and when we are on the train, I will be giving each of you a special ring. I will give you the details and discuss its purpose at that time. You were all very brave when you received your tattoos and in the future they may become very important. No one but a few family members, such as your grandmother, Aunt Olga and your uncles George and Sandro, will know about these identifying marks. This is the only way a true Grand Duchess can be identified. If someone ever comes forward and falsely states that she is my daughter,she can be unmasked immediately."

"I am so terribly sorry that you will not all be together, but in time you will be able to visit each other, as long as you use caution. Now that is enough for today but do not think that we are finished. In the next weeks we will be going over everything again and again." He stood up and threw the last of his notes into the fire.

"Girls, I hope you will live your lives to the fullest and never have a day of regret. Your future is bright and you must never forget who you are. You are Romanovs, and daughters of the Tsar of Russia!"

Nicholas smiled at them and said, "now why not get started on your 'medicines'."

Chapter 40

March 1917 – Tsarskoe Selo. Despite the palpable aura of impending doom that seemed to blanket the country in those early weeks of the new year, the Imperial family had experienced a period of contentment that it had not felt for a long while. The change in Alexandra's emotional state had been startling and had been partially responsible for the new atmosphere at Alexander Palace. But a more likely reason was the fact that the family was facing the onrushing crisis not with resignation, but rather with determination. They acted together as a close-knit unit and drew emotional sustenance, as it were, from each other's individual strengths. There was no foolishness or excessive gaiety because the situation just did not allow for it, but neither were there complaints, bickering or short tempers. Everyone pulled together and it was well that they established this rapport for February had rushed in like a raging bull. The winter was exceedingly harsh and contributed to the hardships the people of Petrograd were already experiencing. Food was in short supply due to the inefficiencies of the Russian rail system. The shortage of engines and repair parts caused by the war, as well as the priority given to military traffic, had greatly reduced the number of trains available to transport needed supplies to the general populace. Wages had not kept up with the increase in the price of food and bread lines were common. Hungry citizens were understandably susceptible to manipulation and throughout the month riots occurred as desperate people looked for solutions. Orators stood on the street corners exhorting the people to action but there was no action to be taken; except surrender or revolution, two options that were inedible and fed no one. It was a volatile situation; a gas leak just waiting for a spark to set it off.

At the beginning of March, as the events in Petrograd grew more worrisome Nicholas called Alix into his study so they could speak in private. "Sunny, I have just finished reviewing the latest reports from the city and I find in them cause for concern. I think we should consider starting the *Masquerade* at once."

"But Nicky, St. Serafim promised you fifteen years and we have almost ten months until 1918 begins, so I really do not think a few weeks will make much difference. Must we rush into this? We will never see our daughters again and I wish to spend as much time with them as possible."

"I sympathize with you entirely, darling, but I am overwhelmed by this premonition that something unexpected is about to happen. It is nagging at me and I feel we must act now."

"What do you propose we do?"

"I will leave for the Stavka in three days and take Olga and Maria with me. We will execute the plan exactly as we have rehearsed. After the girls leave the train at Likoslavl I will continue on to Mogilev and spend a week there before returning to the palace to repeat the process with Tatiana and Anastasia."

"Oh Nicky, in three days?"

"Yes. Three days. Sunny, I know how very difficult it will be to say good-bye but maybe a quick break will make it easier than dragging it out for another three weeks."

"Its just that we have all become so close these past two months. Think of the years lost because of my refusal to accept what was obvious to so many. You know I have not had a headache in the weeks since Father Grigory's death. I just hope I am strong enough to face the children."

"You will be Sunny. We are all depending on you," replied her husband.

"Oh Nicholas, I thought I would be prepared for this when the time came but nothing, nothing can prepare you for the loss of your children."

The Tsar gathered Alix in his arms and gently kissed her cheek. "We will get through this together my darling Sunny. You are my strength and without you I would be lost."

Alix smiled at him through her tears and gently stroked his cheek. "Very well then, my dear, what would you have me do?"

"The plan calls for Ekaterina and Dalida to replace the girls as soon as they are safely on the train. I have talked to Dr. Botkin at some length and he has advised me that it would probably be best to have them run fevers for a day or two and then come down with the measles. That means they would be isolated so I want you to take care of the necessary arrangements. Now when I return to the palace I will remain for a week and then leave with Tatiana and Anastasia. As soon as I have departed, Helena and Franny will assume our daughter's identities and then also come down with the measles which, it will be rumored, they caught from exposure to their "sisters." As soon as practical you will leave for the Crimea to rest and recuperate. Nothing has really changed except that we will start a few weeks earlier than originally planned."

The decision made, Nicholas and Alexandra parted to begin preparations for the imminent departure of Olga and Maria. First Nicholas dispatched a wire to Ella, in Moscow, to alert her to the early arrival of some "medical supplies." Next he sent a telegram to Kanin so the prince could alert his operatives along the route. Finally, he informed Isa and Benckendorff that the timetable had been advanced and then gathered all the children together to inform them of the change in plan. The Grand Duchesses were surprised by the announcement but also somewhat excited that the day they had so diligently prepared for had arrived at last.

The next two days passed quickly and the hustle and bustle of preparation prevented anyone from dwelling too much on the rapidly approaching separation. The night before they were scheduled to leave Olga and Tatiana were alone together in their bedroom while Olga finished her last bit of packing. She was not taking any mementos but only practical things which she would need on her journey and as she looked around the room at familiar items she wondered what would happen to everything once they were gone. She glanced at her sister and tears gathered in the corners of her eyes as she realized that this would be their last night together. Who would she have to share her confidences with now? Oh, what sorrow! Just then, when she was about to lose control, a knock sounded on the door and Anastasia peered in. "May we come in sisters," she asked.

"Yes, of course," replied Tatiana. Olga removed a blanket from the bed and spread it on the floor for the four to sit on. Tonight was the last night that OTMA would be together. The next evening their lives would change irrevocably and an adventure would begin that would take them to far away lands.

"I cannot believe that Olga and I leave tomorrow," said Maria. "Papa told us it would be the end of March before we left for Aunt Ella's."

"I am sure something must have happened to make him change his mind like this. I know Papa would not have you leave early unless it was absolutely necessary," answered Tatiana.

"I have to admit I have noticed increased tensions lately," said Olga. "There has been talk in the hospital about some of these revolutionaries causing trouble in Petrograd. The thing that is so disconcerting is that the minute anyone realizes I am about or listening, they change the subject. It is so frustrating. We live in a different world here at the palace and Petrograd could drop off the face of the earth in a day and we would know nothing of it. Of course, that will all change tomorrow. But Tatiana, do you not sense a change in the Russia we know?"

"Yes, I do, but remember, that is why Papa has developed such elaborate plans. He has prepared for all of this."

"I do not think he was fully prepared," interrupted Maria. "If I remember correctly, when he read to us the letter from St. Serafim, there was a mention of fifteen years to prepare. I think he has always believed we had until 1918. It is why I am surprised we are leaving so soon."

"It is true," said Olga. "The letter did state that, but I think papa is being practical. Every day the imposters are here they risk discovery and I think he has decided that our departure is better too soon than too late."

"Why are you worrying about it?" asked Anastasia. "What is done, is done. You are so wrapped up in all this that you forget that after tomorrow we may never be together again. I do not know about you but I am saddened and frightened." Unable to continue, she began to cry. Her three sisters hugged and comforted her just as they had done on that night so long ago when Anastasia had almost drowned on the *Standart*.

"Anastasia is right. We must stop trying to make sense of this and enjoy our last night together," said Tatiana.

"Well, there must be some way that we can see each other again. Although with Maria and I in Poland and you two across the world in Japan, I admit it seems unlikely" said Olga.

"I have to say that I have prayed something would happen so we could all be in Japan together. Wouldn't that be grand," said Tatiana.

"Yes, if you don't mind the absence of a father, mother and brother," Maria blurted out.

"Maria you know what I meant. Under normal conditions you would be happy anywhere, as long as there was a handsome man around," her sister teased. The three girls laughed and Maria soon joined in. She had to admit that she enjoyed flirting.

"What shall I ever do locked away in a convent?"

"Oh you will be fine Maria," said Olga. "I truly believe we will see each other again and why not? Father says that we will control our own destinies. Certainly we could set a date several years in the future and meet when things have settled down. We will have new identities and papers."

"I do not see any harm in it especially if we wait long enough," said Tatiana. "There must be a place we could meet which has large crowds of people where we could blend in."

"Maybe we could meet on a ship and take a cruise," said Anastasia. "We always enjoyed our trips on the *Standart* so much."

"No, I think we would need a much larger crowd," said Olga.

"What about some sort of festival or celebration?" suggested Maria.

"I think you are on to something Maria. There must be something that is held every few years," said Olga. "Something like the Olympics."

"What about the World's Fair," said Tatiana.

"Yes, that is it," shouted all three girls in unison.

"That is a splendid idea," said Olga. "Wait, I believe I have a book on the last World's Fair. Maybe it will mention future events." She went over to her bookcase and quickly found the book she was looking for. She came back over to the blanket and they all looked through it. "I think there is a list in the back." Olga flipped the pages to the correct section. "Well, it says here that there will be one in America in 1923 but nothing is listed after that."

"No, I think that would be too soon," said Tatiana, and her sisters nodded in agreement.

"I seem to remember France often hosts the World's Fair. Let's meet at the first World's Fair in France during the 1930s. That should be enough time to wait," said Maria.

"What if there isn't one in France in those years?" asked Anastasia.

Olga took her book and thumbed through it. "Well it indicates here that there has been a Worlds Fair in France every decade since 1830.

"Let me see your book please," asked Maria. "Look at this picture. It looks like the entrance where they take your ticket. We can meet here to the left of the entrance."

"I am not sure. The theme changes from fair to fair and it is unlikely the entrance will look like this; and anyway how would we recognize each other in the crowds," said Tatiana.

"Let me think. If we each carried something that no one else would probably have. A red flower; perhaps a rose," said Maria.

"Yes, that would work. Sisters, I think we have a plan," said Olga.

"Let us make a solemn promise right now that we will meet," said Anastasia.

"Everyone form a circle and join hands," said Tatiana. The four girls got to their knees and clasped hands.

"Repeat after me," said Olga. "I promise that I will make every effort to meet my sisters at the first World's Fair of the 1930s, that is held in France. We will meet on the second day of the fair at noon by the left side of the main entrance and each of us will carry a red rose." The other three repeated her words and then they sat back down.

"It still seems so unreal that we are leaving Russia," said Anastasia. "I wonder what will happen to our look-alikes."

"Well, papa says that they will be sick in bed until we are out of the country and then they will travel with Mama and Alexei to Livadia," said Olga.

"What do you suppose will happen there?" Maria asked.

"I do not know the details but I assume Papa will arrange for them to appear to die from their illnesses, or stage some type of accident. Once someone dies from a contagious disease their coffin is rarely opened and the funerals would probably take place at Livadia, which is a long way from where the revolutionaries are active.

"But what if someone did open the coffins?" asked Maria.

"So many people die everyday at the tuberculosis hospitals in the area it would not be difficult to find an unclaimed body. Those that have no family are buried with little fanfare. Papa could easily find bodies to fill the coffins," Olga answered.

"Oh stop this morbid talk," Tatiana cried out. "You are making me quite depressed."

"Tatiana, you work nearly everyday in the hospital and are accustomed to seeing people die. How can you be so squeamish?" asked Anastasia.

"I am not squeamish," said Tatiana, "but I can certainly find better things to talk about."

"Well then, go ahead," said Olga.

"I cannot stop thinking about these girls who are taking our places. They are risking so much to help us," said Tatiana.

"They will be richly rewarded once they leave Russia," said Olga.

"But what if something should happen and they never make it out of the country. I feel guilty that our lives are considered more important then theirs."

"Tatiana, we all feel the same way but you must remember what the bible says. There is no greater love than to lay down your life for another," said Maria. "I believe God will adequately reward someone filled with so much love."

"Yes, but we are not the one's making the sacrifice. I cannot help being distressed by the whole affair. I do not think our doubles really know how much we appreciate what they are doing for us," said Tatiana. "Did we ever even thank them?"

"Not in so many words," said Olga. "But I think they know, and Father has expressed his gratitude and explained how important they are in all of this. He has said he would do everything in his power to keep them safe."

"Yes, but we have never told them ourselves and now it is too late," said Tatiana glumly.

"Why is it too late? Toodles is just across the hall. Why not have her take us up," suggested Maria.

"Yes, let us get her to take us up," said Olga. "It is late and no one will be the wiser. Let us take turns slipping into the dining room and once you are all there and we are sure no one has seen us I will get Toodles. I am sure Papa will not mind." The three girls did as Olga suggested and quickly slipped through the interconnecting rooms until they were in the dining room. Olga went and explained their request to Toodles and soon she and the four girls were up in the common room in the secret attic space. They took seats at the table while Toodles roused the doubles. A few moments later four drowsy girls in nightgowns and robes wandered into the room to find four Grand Duchesses dressed in identical nightgowns and robes, waiting to greet them.

"What is wrong," asked Ekaterina rather sleepily. "Are we replacing you now?"

"Oh no, not until later tomorrow, as planned," said Olga. "Please come and sit down, we must speak with you."

"Yes," said Tatiana. "We are sorry for waking you up but we had to speak with you. Tomorrow will be a busy day and we will not be able to see you. We wanted to say good-bye, but more importantly we wanted to thank you from the bottom of our hearts for offering to take our places."

"We realized we had never thanked you personally," explained Maria.

"Of course you have. Everyday has been filled with kindness and you have showered us with gifts and treated us as if we were really your sisters. I never thought a grand duchess would even speak to me much less become my friend," said Dalida. "This has been a wonderful experience for us and if it were to end tomorrow we would have no regrets. I think I speak for us all when I say we have come to love you and would do anything to keep you safe. We have been well thanked so do not worry yourselves."

"Well, we just had to tell you ourselves," said Anastasia smiling over at Franny, her double.

"You are very welcome," said the four doubles in unison. The two groups of Grand Duchesses spoke together for a while longer and then, when the Tsar's daughters rose to go back downstairs, hugs were exchanged and a few tears shed. The hour was late so the Grand Duchesses quickly retired for the night but there would be very little sleep as they were all anxious about tomorrow's events.

The next morning, after breakfast, final preparations were completed. Olga and Maria's bags were ready and Count Benckendorff had given them both their new identity and travel documents. They were familiar with their new names and had practiced enough that they felt comfortable with them. The four daughters spent the rest of the last day pretending outwardly that everything was normal but beneath their glacial expressions, their hearts were breaking.

The late lunch they consumed that afternoon was the last meal they would share together and everyone was quite aware of the fact. There was little conversation and everyone seemed content to be alone with their thoughts. They separated after lunch and agreed to get together later for the final briefing. Everything was on schedule and the time was drawing near for final good-byes. When the Grand Duchesses had a busy schedule and could not get to the hospital during the day they would often go in the late afternoon to make rounds and attempt to cheer the soldiers. They were always welcome, no matter what the hour, because one thing soldiers craved was feminine companionship, and the four vivacious girls certainly provided it. This evening, however, they would have to work very hard to keep smiles on their lovely faces, for the *Masquerade* was about to begin and it started with their visit to the hospital.

Alix rested in the Mauve Boudoir while Nicky took care of some last minute packing in the bedroom next door. The Tsar then joined his wife, who by now was in a dreadful state. Tears flowed down her cheeks and, as hard as she tried, she could not gain control of her emotions. Empress or not, she was still a mother and the realization that she would never see Olga and Maria again was a crushing burden to carry. Her only consolation was that they would soon be with her sister in Moscow and out of harm's way. She was thankful that through a series of letters and telephone calls she had made peace with her sister.

"Oh Nicky, my heart aches so badly I feel as if I cannot breathe," sobbed Alix. The Tsar moved quickly to her chaise, sat beside her, and took her into his arms in a tender embrace. "My children are leaving me. I do not know if I can do this," she said as she clutched at his shirt with her clenched fists. "It is as if they will be dead to me."

"Oh my poor Sunny. I know it is difficult but you must calm yourself for the sake of the children. If they see you like this it will only make them more anxious."

"I know, I know," she said sadly. "I contained my emotions all morning when I was with the girls but when I came in here and remembered all the happy times we have spent in this room I lost control. I have been so busy that it was easy not to think about this day, but now it is upon us. I did not know it could be so heart wrenching to do God's will."

"Sunny, you are looking at this in the wrong way. Instead of thinking that your children will seem dead to you, it would be better to focus on the fact that through your sacrifice you are saving their lives. One day you will surely be reunited with them, if not in this world than in the next."

Alix sighed plaintively. "You are right as usual Nicky, and I truly think I have cried my last tear. There are none left. Please excuse me, I must freshen up. I do not want the children to see me in such a state and have their last memory of me be of a tear stained, disheveled woman." Alix went into her dressing room and adjoining bathroom where she washed her face, fixed her hair and straightened up her clothes.

Promptly at half past two the Tsar and Tsarina were joined in the Mauve boudoir by Alexei, their daughters, Isa, Count Benckendorff, Doctor Botkin, Count Tatishchev, and Valia. The four Grand Duchesses could immediately see in their mother's eyes the terrible sadness she felt and they knew, in spite of her best efforts to hide it, that she had been weeping. All four rushed to her side and she embraced them in turn. Nicholas greeted the rest of the group and they all settled down before he began to review the evening's activities.

"As soon as we are ready, about five o'clock, Isa will drive the four girls to the hospital to visit the sick. From that point on, everything will go as we have discussed before and gone over time and time again. Isa, I suggest you and Count Benckendorff pick Olga and Maria up from the hospital around seven o'clock. Valia, you should arrive at the station just before Isa and the Count. Once the girls are safely on the train you will all return to the palace. I will depart for the station at eight and as soon as the cars are shunted off the siding and coupled to the engine I will depart. I know there will be a lot of speculation when it is known that I left for the Stavka in the middle of the night especially when there is so much turmoil in Petrograd. But let the rumors float. They will divert attention from the real reason for my departure."

"How long will you remain at Mogilev, sir?" asked Valia.

"About a week and then I will return to the palace and we will use the same formula to bring out the other two Grand Duchesses. Alix, are the doubles ready to assume their roles?"

"Yes, everything is prepared. Later tonight, when I am sure you are on your way, Ekaterina and Dalida will slip down from the attic. I have set up Anastasia's and Maria's room as the sick room. Anastasia will stay with Tatiana while her "sisters" are ill. I will have all the curtains drawn in the sick room and give word out that the girls are not to be disturbed. Dr. Botkin is now a member of our *Masquerade* and he has suggested we use measles as the cause of the sickness. I will work with him to make the illness a plausible one, red spots included."

"I am honored to be allowed to provide this service to your family. I would give my life to save Russia," said the humble doctor.

"Well, everyone, that is it for now," announced the Tsar. "We will begin at five. Now if you will excuse me, I would like to spend these last two hours with just the family." The rest of the participants filed out, leaving the Imperial family alone. Alix ordered tea and they all sat to enjoy the refreshments while reminiscing about the wonderful times they had shared together. The photo albums were taken out and they laughed over some of the more silly pictures. They talked about the trips to Livadia and the summer cruises on the *Standart* and as is so often the case, the trying times were overlooked and only the fond memories recounted. Unfortunately the time raced by and before they realized it the two hours were gone and it was time to say good-bye. Each member of the family took a moment to hug Maria and Olga and tell the two how much they loved them.

Alix was the last to say good-bye to her girls. She hugged them both tightly in her arms. "If not on this earth, then in heaven we will be together again".

"Oh, Mama, Papa, we will miss you dearly," said Olga. Maria smiled bravely but her lips were quivering and she was fighting back a tear.

"Come now girls," said Nicholas. "It is time to go. Isa will take you to the hospital and it is important that you be seen by the staff. Olga and Maria, if anyone asks you why your spirits seem low just tell them you are not feeling well. That will fit in with our plan to spread the word in the morning that you are ill. I will see you both in about three hours, so be brave and play your role."

"Wait," shouted Alexei as he hurried over to his sisters. He reached into his pocket and removed two of his toy soldiers and gave one to Maria and one to Olga. "These soldiers will guard you and keep you safe on your journey."

"Thank-you, Alexei," said Maria and she gave him another hug.

"You must take good care of everyone while we are gone," said Olga as she hugged him one last time. And with that the girls followed Isa out to the waiting automobile. All the Tsar and his wife and son could do now was sit and wait for the return of the Count and Isa with the word that everything had gone according to plan.

And it did. Isa and the Count picked the girls up on schedule and when they reached the train Valia ordered an inspection of the guards. With their backs to the train the sentries could not see the Count slip the Grand Duchesses into the coach. Once inside the compartment, the two bid farewell to the Count. "Thank-you so much for your loyalty to my father," said Olga.

Count Benckendorff had been with them their whole lives and watched them grow from little babies into these impressive young women. He knew this would be the last time he would ever see them and his heart was heavy. "It has been my pleasure to serve your family all these years," he replied. He walked to the door to the compartment and turned to look back at the two young ladies sitting so quietly. "Your father will be here soon," he said gruffly, but unable to hide a tear.

"Thank-you again," cried Maria, as she ran up and kissed him on the cheek.

As soon as Benckendorff had disembarked the train and locked the door, Valia approached. "Is the baggage safely aboard?" he asked in a low voice.

"Yes. Every thing is in place and Isa is waiting to drive us back to the palace. I know the Emperor and Empress will be anxious for news."

When the Tsar was notified that all had gone smoothly he made the announcement that he was returning to the Stavka. Benckendorff alerted the Tsar's staff of the decision and with little delay the Imperial train departed Tsarskoe Selo later that evening.

After Nicholas left for Mogilev, Alix brought down the two impostors, Ekaterina and Dalida who were to fill in for Olga and Maria. They lay down in the beds in the sickroom and Dr. Botkin took their temperatures shaking his head worriedly as he read the results. In the morning Alix would apply a few "measles" to their faces. These would get progressively worse over the next few days. The room was very dark and tomorrow, even with the sun up, the darkened shades would keep the room dim and shadowy. Alix bid the two girls goodnight and she sat in a chair in the room, as she often did with her own children, keeping watch. Her thoughts though were miles away with Nicholas and her daughters as their train roared through the Russian night.

❦

The rhythmic clicking of the iron wheels on the rails had acted like a lullaby to the Tsar's tired daughters. They had tried in vain to stay awake, realizing these precious moments would be the last they had with their father, but like the disciples in the garden of Gethsemane, they just could not keep their eyes open. Nicholas looked at their sleeping figures well aware that in much too short a time he would leave them at a train station, never to see them again. Sometimes, in moments such as this, he was beset by doubts and wondered if he was really doing the right thing sending his innocent daughters off into a harsh world they had never experienced. He felt he had planned well and prepared them to the best of his ability but he acknowledged that the future was so uncertain. How many people had committed themselves to this *Masquerade* solely on his assurance that letters and dreams were reason enough to take action? It seemed to Nicholas that their faith in God must be greater than his and the realization humbled him. Whenever he was confused and unsure he took the only action which gave him any comfort and that was to bow his head in prayer. For a few minutes Nicholas lifted his soul to God, begging Him to protect his precious children and then, exhausted by the events of the past few days, he too dozed off. He was awakened several hours later by Valia who had entered his compartment to let him know the next stop was Likhoslavl.

The Tsar stood up, stretched, and then gently woke his two daughters. "The next station is Likhoslavl, so it is time to put on the shifts containing your" medicine" and change into your nun's habits. But before you do I have something to give you and some last minute instructions. Nicholas reached into his pocket, took out the small leather boat, and showed it to them. The girls looked at the case and were intrigued by its design but despite their curiosity they waited patiently for their father to explain its significance.

"When I first laid out the details of the plan, back in January, you will recall that I mentioned I would be giving you special rings once we were on the train. Well, the time has come to take care of that final detail and in a moment I will have you each choose one, but first I want to make clear to you the importance of these rings. As you are well aware by now, I have established bank accounts for you in Japan, the Vatican, and New York City. You have memorized the account numbers for all three but because the funds in the United State consist of a significant amount we have added extra safeguards. To withdraw funds in Japan or from the Vatican Bank you need only present your identification papers and account number. The account in New York is different. To access your funds there you will need your account number, a password, and a special seal. Documents with instructions for the bank president as well as a facsimile of your seal are already in place. Concealed in these rings are the signets which will be used to identify you. They are the same in all four rings but of course your account numbers are obviously different. When the time comes and it is safe for you to come out of hiding, you may travel to the United States and retrieve your money. You will need to make an appointment with the president of the bank and ask to speak with him in private. Tell him what you need and he will ask you for your account number and an impression from your signet, rendered on a wax pad in his presence. When he has established that the seal and account number are in order he will ask for the password. The password is *Serafim*; not Saint Serafim or any other variation, just *Serafim*. Once your credentials have been verified you will have access to the funds I deposited for you. If by chance you do not wish to live in the United States you may transfer funds to another country. Just do not make any hasty decisions and remember large sums of money arouse scrutiny. Be careful and gradually move your money if you need too. I know you have studied about banking in the United States and have an understanding of how the system works. Remember, when you access your accounts no names are involved, only the signet impression, account number and password. Now you may wonder what would happen if you were to lose the ring. That is why all the seals are the same. You may use your sister's ring if necessary, to retrieve your funds, because you will know your account number and the password." The Tsar loosened the ties on the case and held it out in front of Olga. "Take one," he said.

"But I cannot see inside the bag, Papa."

"I know," said Nicholas. "Just reach inside the bag, feel for a ring, and take it out."

"Yes, Papa," said Olga. The opening was small and it was only possible to fit two fingers into it. Olga reached in and picked out the first ring she felt. When she held it out, and could see it clearly, she was surprised at its simple elegance; she had been expecting a heavy, ornate piecewith many precious stones. Nicholas then placed the case in front of Maria. She reached in and could feel nothing. The rings had all slipped to the other end of the boat and could not be retrieved from the opening.

"Papa, I cannot reach one," said Maria. The Tsar realized what had happened and tipped the case so the rings would tumble back to the other end. Again, he placed it in front of Maria. She reached back in and could feel all three of the remaining rings. Maria removed one and looked at it. "Can we wear them now?" she asked.

"No, for now you must wear them on chains around your neck and under your clothes. Now let me show you how the rings work." Nicholas took Olga's ring and demonstrated how to open it. By pressing the second of the small diamonds circling the center stone two times an ingenious system of springs was activated. The center stone, which had been fashioned from a brilliant sapphire, could then be pivoted out of the way to reveal the tiny signet which could then be removed to make an impression. "You see the way these rings have been made. No one, unless they knew what to look for, would realize that they could be opened." The Tsar handed the ring back to Olga. "Now both of you try." He watched as the two carefully opened the rings and took out the signets. When they had practiced a few times Nicholas took out his watch, looked at it and sighed.

"We will be at the station soon," he said. "You need to change into your disguises now." The Tsar re-tied the boat and slipped it into his pocket. "While you are dressing I will go out on the platform for a cigarette." The girls took their bags, set them on the table, and began to take out the items they would need. Nicholas left them and walked to the end of the car. When he opened the door he was met by a blast of cold air but he found it invigorating and stepped on out. Shielding his lighter with the palm of his hand he managed to get his cigarette lit. He stood there staring into the darkness and wondered if either of the two girls had picked out the one ring that was different from the others or whether it was still in the case. He could check later, of course, but that would seem almost sacrilegious, as if he were betraying a trust. This way only God knew the answer and that was as it should be. Certainly if he were supposed to know, it would have been revealed to him, just as other things had. He suddenly lost control and wept bitterly as he thought of his precious girls, soon to be gone forever, and his family torn apart. Nicholas was beside himself, but he knew he must compose himself for his daughters sake. He would have been surprised if had been able to hear what Olga was saying.

The girls had finished putting on their nuns' costumes and their clear spectacles. "I know this is very serious business," said Olga, "but I cannot stop thinking how exciting it all is. We are going to be free. Our whole royal identity will be wiped away and we can live how we want, without having to be told what to wear, what to eat, where to go, and what to do. It is something Tatiana and I often talked about, a fantasy, of course, but one that now seems to be real. Do not think me ungrateful, for I do appreciate all that I have had, but I always hated the idea that I could not marry whom I wanted."

"Olga," Maria cried out, " our family may never be together again. Are you forgetting that father thinks he will be killed and we have no idea what will happen to mother and Alexei?"

"I am not making light of all of this," explained Olga. "I am just trying to see the situation in practical terms. And we will see each other again. Remember our pact to meet in France."

"But maybe that will not work out," said Maria and she began to weep. "It is quite possible that we might never see Tatiana and Anastasia again."

Olga put her arms around her sister. "Maria, you must stop crying. We must be brave for father. This must be so hard for him."

"You are right," said Maria as she pulled back and wiped the tears from her face. "We must be brave for Papa." At that moment their father rejoined them and they sat together around the table. He was calm, but the girls could sense that he was quite upset.

"Girls," said Nicholas, "is there anything else we need to discuss?"

"Papa, I am still unsure of a few things," said Olga. "I recall that when you read St. Serafim's letter to us there was mention of a great saint being raised up from your royal line. You have implied that it was one of us, or at least one of our children, who would lead Russia to a new future. But if this is so, how will we know who it is? If I were the one, for instance, how would I know it? And how would I possibly know what to do," questioned Olga.

"Olga, whoever it is, she will know," said Maria with a quiet confidence and wisdom beyond her years.

"I too, am confident that when the time comes the appointed one will know," said the Tsar. "It will be revealed to her. How, I cannot say, but you must have faith. Right now my biggest concern is to see to it that all four of you get safely out of the country. Now when we arrive at the station in Likhoslavl I will debark the train from one of the cars forward of this one to divert attention. Since the car we are in now is the last one I see no need to use the secret exit. You will be waiting by the door to the rear platform and as soon as the train stops Valia will help you get safely down. Make your way around the back of the train and go immediately into the station. Buy two one-way tickets to Moscow. While you are waiting for your train, try not to draw any attention to yourselves and be on your guard. On the other hand if someone engages you in innocent conversation it would look suspicious if you ignored them so use your common sense. Your first stop is Tver. When you arrive there, step down, as if to stretch your legs. This will allow Aunt Ella's nuns to easily find you, if it is crowded. When you re-board they will come with you and take you to the convent in Moscow where Ella will be waiting to fill you in on all the arrangements she has made."

"Yes, Papa, we understand," responded the Grand Duchesses. The two girls sat quietly, aware that their great adventure was about to begin. As the train began to slow they experienced a whole range of emotions, but the dominating one, overriding excitement and fear, was profound sadness. The Tsar opened the shade on the window slightly to peer out, and he could see that they had arrived in Likhoslavl. The train moved slowly on to a siding so it could be shunted on to the spur line running down to Mogilev. The Tsar stood to embrace his daughters one last time. As he took each of them into his arms he squeezed them tightly. "May God protect you both and keep you safe," he said, "until we meet again in the after life. Now it is time to go. Valia is waiting."

Later, after he had boarded the train and it had pulled out of the station, the Tsar thought about Olga and Maria waiting so disconsolately in the Likhoslavl train station. Although everything had gone smoothly now that he was alone, he felt what could only be described as total desolation and he struggled with it the remainder of the journey. Of all those on the train only Valia had an understanding of what Nicholas was suffering. When he finally arrived at the Stavka the Tsar sent a coded telegram to his wife indicating the initial phase of the plan had been successful.

⋘⋙

Ella sat at her desk looking at the third in a series of telegrams she had received from her brother-in-law. The first had informed her that the timetable was being advanced. The second wire had given a tentative arrival time and now this one gave her the information she needed most. *The medical supplies for your hospital will arrive on March 9 on the first train.* The telegram said nothing else and was not signed but that was unnecessary as Ella knew what it meant. It gave her just enough time to position Sister Barbara and a companion at Tver to meet her nieces. She wondered what had happened to induce Nicky to move everything forward three weeks. He was probably aware that the unrest which was plaguing Petrograd had not yet disturbed the transportation system in and around Moscow, so perhaps he had decided to be extremely cautious and move earlier than planned. Ella made the necessary arrangements and to her great relief Olga and Maria were joined on the platform at Tver by Sister Barbara and her companion and accompanied by them for the remainder of their journey. The disguises were very effective and even if someone were looking for the Grand Duchesses they would never have made the connection between the two nuns and the Imperial family.

When the girls arrived at the convent, they were immediately escorted to Ella's office where she had been anxiously awaited their arrival. She embraced her two nieces. "I cannot believe it is you; your spectacles make you virtually unrecognizable. If you were wearing these outfits and I saw you in a crowd, I would be unable to pick you out as a member of the family," she said.

"Mama and Isa helped us to prepare our disguises and I for one felt anonymous and completely at ease," replied Olga.

"You must be very tired from your journey," said Ella. "You will be spending time with the Polish nuns, who are here to escort you back to Warsaw. I want you to be as comfortable with them as possible since you have such a long journey together. I have found them to be quite efficient and they have been a tremendous help in the hospital. They speak fluent Russian and their habits are so like ours that they appear to be members of our order. You will meet them in a little while. They will be surprised that you are here already, but they are flexible, and are probably anxious to return home. I will hate to see them leave. Now remember, they do not know your true identity so do not make a slip-up."

"When will we be leaving for Warsaw," asked Olga.

"Probably near the end of the month," responded Ella. The Mother superior sent word that they were flexible and could take you in at any time. Now did your father send me any instructions?"

"Yes, he did," Olga replied. "He will spend one week at the Stavka and then return to Alexander Palace. Our sisters will leave the palace as soon as possible thereafter and arrive here exactly as we have. We thought we had said our final good-byes, but if Maria and I do not leave until the end of March, we may see the others one last time."

"It all seems so unreal," said Maria. "It was very difficult to leave father on the train. He was strong, but I knew his heart was breaking, as were ours. To see you like this has made me realize how important members of a family are to each other. Father understood this when he arranged for two of us to be together."

"Just before we departed Count Benckendorff gave us completely new identity and travel papers," explained Olga. She reached into her bag and took out a brown leather billfold and handed it to her aunt. Ella looked at the papers and saw a picture of Olga dressed just as she was now, wearing her spectacles. There was also another set of papers with her dressed as a peasant in case they did not travel as nuns, and Ella could see how completely effective the disguises were. She looked at the name on the two sets of papers; it read Minka Sawicka.

"And what is your name, Maria," asked Ella?

"My name is Zyta Kowalska," answered Maria. "Father said both of our new names mean 'strong' in Polish and we are actually becoming quite accustomed to them."

"What fitting names. So Olga will be Sister Minka and Maria, you will be Sister Zyta," said Ella. "Now let me call Sister Barbara. She will take you to the refectory for something to eat and then show you to your rooms. She has been a *Masquerader* for some time and helped teach the imposters, so you can trust her implicitly."

"Thank you, Aunt Ella," said the girls.

"Oh no! You must call me Mother Elizabeth from now on," said Ella.

"Yes, Mother Elizabeth," replied the girls, flustered that they had made such a serious error so soon. If they had been outside of Ella's office, and someone had overheard them, the mistake could have been disastrous. Both girls vowed to themselves to be much more vigilant in the future.

As soon as the girls departed, Ella arranged to send a telegram to Nicholas thanking him for the medical supplies, which had arrived as promised. It was her intention to have the Grand Duchesses live the discipline of the convent rule until the time came for them to leave for Poland and so they were awakened early the next morning to participate in the recitation of the Divine Office. They would be assigned chores and treated as if they were members of the community, but Ella made sure Sister Barbara kept them so busy that there was little time for idle conversation with the other nuns in the convent.

While Olga and Maria were getting settled in, events at the palace in Tsarskoe Selo proceeded according to plan. Those involved in the charade were nervous at first, but when no unexpected obstacles appeared, everyone began to relax. No one doubted that the two sick Grand Duchesses were anyone but Olga and Maria and thus far Alix had been able to keep visitors away, especially since Dr. Botkin had rendered his diagnosis. It was definitely measles.

There was one fly in the ointment, however, and that was the presence of Anya Vyrubova at the palace. After Rasputin's death the need for a conduit to the staret was no longer necessary and Alix did not want to leave her friend alone in a cottage outside the walls. Anya's quarters were in the other wing of the palace but oftentimes she would spend her evenings in the family wing. Alix had not yet confided in Anya and she would not do so until Nicholas gave his permission, so the impostors were always hidden away when Anya was in the Mauve Boudoir. Alix had worried that when the two girls became "ill" her friend would insist on visiting them but ironically the person who could most easily unmask the *Masquerade* was now herself, down with the measles. Alix looked in on her once a day and she alternated sending Tatiana and Anastasia to see her as well. She was not sure yet how she was going to handle the situation when Anya recovered because at that point she would have four sick impostors instead of just the two. She knew Anya would want to help with the nursing, so all the Empress could do was pray, and hope the state of affairs would resolve itself. As soon as Nicholas returned she would talk to him about the situation. As it turned out, though, Alix need not have worried for Anya Vyrubova was loyal to the Imperial family to the very end.

With Alix, Isa, and the Count competently handling affairs in Tsarskoe Selo and two of his daughters safely settled at Ella's convent in Moscow, the Tsar was able to breathe a little easier when he arrived at Mogilev the afternoon of March 9th. The first phase was completed but now he must wait impatiently at the Stavka for about a week before returning to Alexander Palace. He continued to receive more and more urgent messages and reports on the tense developments in Petrograd. The situation in the capital was continuing to deteriorate as the strikes escalated and breadlines grew longer. The succeeding days brought news of riots, but with his plans already made he stubbornly refused to recognize that he had miscalculated the speed with which events would unfold. The revolution was at hand and he was not prepared for it, so he stayed on in Mogilev, sticking to his schedule, and apparently unaware of the danger facing his family and himself.

Chapter 41

March 11, 1917 – Moscow. It was only two days after her nieces arrived that Ella thought her world had collapsed around her. She was sitting at her desk, working her way through several stacks of bills and invoices. Her charity work was expensive business but as of yet she had not been forced to touch the principal of her private fortune. The interest from her various accounts subsidized her work but the increase in prices due to the war was making commodities scarce and prices high. She struggled with the figures, trying to come up with a way to make some cutbacks. Her thin shoulders were bent from fatigue and she was weary, although the day had barely started. The four hours of sleep she allotted herself each night was not really enough and it was beginning to catch up with her. She closed her eyes momentarily and was about to doze off when the quiet of her office was suddenly interrupted by a loud knock at the door. Before she could respond, Sister Barbara rushed into the room and shut the door behind her.

"Mother Elizabeth, you must come quickly; some men have come into the front of the convent and are calling out for you," exclaimed the frightened nun. "They are a dreadful lot; dirty, smelly and with all sorts of vulgarities coming from their mouths." Ella was shocked, but she knew she must keep her composure, for the sake of Sister Barbara, and her other nuns, as well. She slowly arose from her desk and walked around to Sister Barbara.

"Sister," began Ella calmly, "go and gather all of the nuns who are not on duty at the hospital and have them gather in the chapel. Instruct them to begin Morning Prayer, even if they have already completed it privately. I suspect we are dealing with vodka courage here and these brutes are less likely to intrude if formal prayer is going on. When you have organized everything come and join me wherever I may be. I will confront them but I want someone with me for support and I prefer it to be you, my dear friend."

"What about the Grand Duchesses," Sister Barbara cried, forgetting in her distress that she was never to use those words.

"Sister, get control of yourself. Think what you are saying. Would you risk everything with such talk?" she admonished. Ella gently led Barbara to the door. "You must relax and act as if we have nothing to hide. I have confidence in you, so get on with it. Have the two new nuns go to the chapel with the others. They will blend right in so do not be faint of heart. You must set an example for our young guests and the rest of the community as well."

"You are right of course," said Sister Barbara. "I apologize for my lack of control. I will do as you have directed but please promise me you will not let them take you from this convent."

"I do not plan on going anywhere with them," said Ella emphatically. When her friend left the room Ella got down on her knees. "Lord," she prayed, "please watch over this convent and all who dwell here. If my life must be sacrificed for your will to be carried out, then I freely accept." She got to her feet and quickly walked to the front of the convent where she arrived in time to find the chaplain, Father Mitrophan, trying to reason with the men. One of the sisters had advised him of what was going on and he was attempting to convince the men to leave the convent, but the more he remonstrated with them, the more determined they became. There were nearly a dozen of them and Ella could see they were wearing remnants of Imperial Russian Army uniforms, but with the Tsar's crest removed. These men were obviously deserters or mutineers. They did not seem to have a leader, and were completely intoxicated. It was mob rule at its worst but fortunately it was a small group, and Ella knew from experience that if you gave drunken men what they wanted without showing fear the situation would sometimes defuse itself.

"Bring us the German traitor," one of them shouted at the priest!

At that moment Ella walked forward and nodded at the men. "Gentleman, I am Mother Elizabeth, the foundress of this convent, how may I help you?" she asked in a gentle yet firm voice.

"It is her, the German," whispered one of the men.

"Yes, I am the former Grand Duchess Sergei Alexandrovich," said Ella calmly. "You all know me and know the work I do here and in the countryside. I do not understand why you are here with weapons. We are all loyal Russians and pose you no threat."

"We know you are hiding someone here," said one of the revolutionaries.

Ella's heart nearly stopped when she heard his words. She knew that it was absolutely impossible for these men to suspect that the Grand Duchesses were hidden at her convent, but who else could they be speaking of. "Gentlemen, you must certainly know we have nothing to hide here," said Ella.

"Then you won't mind if we take a look around," snarled one of the men.

"Of course not," Ella responded, "but first, if you will allow it, we will go to the chapel and I will say a short prayer for you all. Then, when we have finished, I will take you to any area of the convent or hospital you wish to see."

"Very well, we will follow you to the chapel," said the man who, by consensus, seemed to be the spokesman. Ella was disappointed that he acquiesced because she had been sure this ragged bunch would have no desire to go into an area where religious activities were taking place.

However, she had miscalculated and instead of leading these ruffians away from the Grand Duchesses she was taking them to the very place where they were hiding.

Meanwhile Olga and Maria knelt in the chapel among the other nuns chanting Morning Prayer as Mother Elizabeth had directed. Sister Barbara had told them only that some drunken ruffians had come into the convent and then she had rushed off to gather the rest of the sisters. Maria leaned over and whispered to Olga, "I have a real bad feeling about this. What If those men are looking for us?"

"Maria you are not thinking clearly. Certainly if our absence was discovered, Papa would have sent word and even if he did not alert Mother Elisabeth, I doubt that an organized search could have begun here in Moscow so quickly. No, this has nothing to do with us."

"I think we should leave the chapel and find some place to hide," said Maria.

"Absolutely not," ordered Olga, her voice rising slightly. "We will do as Mother Superior has directed us, and remain here with the others. Maria you are forgetting that the best defense against discovery is the anonymity that our habits provide."

Sister Mary looked over at them and held a finger to her lips. This was no time for a lengthy conversation and they were disturbing the routine of prayer. Her intervention was timely for at that moment Ella and Sister Barbara walked in with the group of men. The two entered the last pew, knelt down, and began to pray. Ella was relieved to see that the men remained in the back of the chapel and that several had even removed their hats. All the nuns were praying and did not turn around but each one of them could feel and smell the presence of the intruders and sense their hostility.

When she completed her short prayer Ella rose, and accompanied by Sister Barbara, walked out of the chapel with the group of revolutionaries close behind. Normally she would have rejected any effort to violate the sanctity of the cloister but all the community was up and about and she made a calculated decision not to antagonize these dangerous men by resisting their search. She knew that the Grand Duchesses were safe for the present and since she was not hiding anyone else she felt comfortable letting the men look around the convent, hospital, and grounds. Ella personally escorted them throughout the compound and then led them back to the convent and through the various rooms. "Maybe we will find what we are looking for in here," one said as they entered a large storage room."

Ella could not imagine what they were looking for and every time she questioned them the spokesman gave vague answers. Ella leaned over and whispered to Sister Barbara, "Go, and tell the two Grand Duchesses to stay in the chapel until I come and get them and then meet me at the hospital." Sister Barbara disappeared down the hallway.

When the men came out of the room, they noticed she was gone. "Where did the other one go?" they asked.

"Gentlemen, you must understand how busy we are here. We have a hospital, with many, many sick, to tend to," she said. "Sister Barbara had to go and check on one of my patients. She will rejoin us shortly." When the search of the convent was completed Ella led the men over to the hospital. They entered and looked through the wards. They searched under beds, in the operating room facilities, the storage closets and still Ella was not sure what they were looking for.

Ella turned to the men coming out of the ward. "Well, you have seen everything," she said. "I will escort you to the door."

"Wait a minute," said one of the drunken men, "what about that room over there," he said as he pointed across the hall.

"We have not been in there," said another. One of the men placed his hand on the door and attempted to open it. The door was stuck and the knob jammed. He vigorously wiggled the knob. Suddenly the door flew opened as one of the revolutionaries kicked it in.

"Wait," called Ella, "do not go in there. That is the isolation room for typhoid fever." The men all jumped back.

"Well, we must inspect the room," said one of the men boldly.

"Of course," answered Ella, "but typhoid is highly contagious and you would certainly need to be quarantined, especially if the health officials found that you had been exposed. I will wait out here while you search." The men looked into the dimly lit room and their courage quickly deserted them. There appeared to be a patient in the bed but in reality it was a stack of bedding covered by a blanket. Imagination did the rest.

"Go on in," said one of the men to the other. "All the alcohol in you will keep you from getting any disease."

"Then you go in, "said the other man, "you are drunker than I am."

"No, we are finished here," said another. "No one would be stupid enough to hide in a room with a typhoid victim." The men walked away from the room and Sister Barbara, who had rejoined them, quickly closed the door. The episode showed what a cowardly lot they were and Ella took advantage of the situation to end the encounter.

"Shall I escort you out," asked Ella..

"No, we can leave on our own," said the man, "but we know you are hiding your brother, a known German spy, and we will be back to find him."

Another of the men walked up to her and she almost flinched. She could smell the alcohol on his breath and the stench coming from him was nearly unbearable. He glared at Ella and said, "You may look like a nun and act like a nun," he said, his words slurred, "but I know you are a German spy."

"I am sorry, but you are mistaken. I work for God and no one else," said Ella as she escorted the men to the portal. When they had gone she asked the priest to lock the gates. "No more will these gates remain open," said Ella, "we must keep them locked at all times. It is becoming unsafe." Ella returned to the chapel and instructed her nuns to resume their normal duties. She whispered to Sister Barbara to bring Olga and Marie to her office and when they arrived she embraced them.

"Oh thank God they didn't find us," Maria exclaimed. "I did not think we would be in danger like this. My heart was pounding so loudly I thought those men would hear it. Papa said this would be very simple and that no one would be looking for us."

"Everything will be alright," said Ella gently, even though her own heart was racing. "They were not looking for you, they were looking for your Uncle Ernie."

"What would they want with Uncle Ernie?" asked Olga, who had managed to remain calm through the entire incident.

"They hate him because he is a German and we are at war with Germany," explained Ella. "They have a strange notion that he is hiding in the convent. It makes me realize that you are not safe here any longer. I am certain we will see these men again and even though they are not looking for you, I do not want to take any chances. Now, I must give this all some thought, but first I want to pray for guidance. Return to your duties and when I have come up with something I will call you."

Ella struggled the remainder of the day to find a solution to the dilemma. There were just so many variables. If it was not safe for Olga and Maria to be in Moscow then it was just as dangerous to allow Tatiana and Anastasia to continue with their part in the plan. She would have to try and contact Alix and warn her not to send the other girls until the situation in Moscow was resolved. First, though, she had to decide where to hide the two nieces that were with her and there did not seem to be a viable resolution to that predicament. Finally, exhausted by the challenges she faced, Ella called everyone in, laid out the problems, and asked for advice.

"Mother," said Sister Mary, "why not let them come to my parents dacha near Sergiyev Posad. It is a little village north of here, only an hour or so away. My parents winter there and come back to Moscow in the spring," explained the nun.

"That is very generous of you sister but the presence of two strangers in a small town might create more problems than solutions. We know the Grand Duchesses are not scheduled to leave until the end of the month so we are talking about nearly three weeks. That assumes that rail passage to Warsaw will still be available and I have a feeling it may not be. "

"There is another option," said Olga. "Just before we left Tsarskoe Selo our father called us all together and outlined a somewhat daring alternative plan to be used in the event any of us had problems. He told us that if anything happened we were to make our way to the Japanese trade mission in Omsk and identify ourselves to the person in charge. Arrangements have already been made and he would see to it that we were taken to Japan."

"But you are supposed to be going west, not east. How does this apply to you?" Ella asked. "Certainly Prince Kanin would not be expecting you."

"My father made it quite clear that this alternative plan applied to all four of us. He also confided to me that Prince Kanin had originally offered to take us all to Japan but for security purposes it was decided to divide us into two groups. I have met the Prince and I am positive he would welcome any of the daughters if we sought asylum."

"Then what is it that you are proposing to do, Olga?" asked her aunt.

"Since you think it is too dangerous for us to remain here and you are worried about us getting safely to Warsaw I suggest you send someone to the station and purchase two tickets for Omsk on the first train in the morning. We will travel as nuns and use our Polish identity papers. If asked, we will reply that we have a new assignment and are on our way to Omsk to begin our work."

"Oh no, Olga, I could never send you off alone, on such a perilous journey," Ella exclaimed.

"Dearest aunt, have you forgotten that this is exactly the plan for Tatiana and Anastasia. They were going on from Moscow to Vladivostok by themselves, a much longer and more arduous journey. We are certainly up to the same challenge as our sisters."

At that moment Sister Barbara interrupted. "I have a proposal, if you will allow me."

"Of course, dear friend, any suggestions are most welcome," the Mother Superior replied.

"Well, Sisters Catherine and Irene have been involved in the training of the impostors from the beginning and are close friends. It so happens that Irene is originally from Omsk and has relatives there. Why not have the two of them accompany the Grand Duchesses? Sister Irene can see them to the trade mission and then wait and see if all goes well. She and Catherine can visit Irene's relatives for a few days and then return to Moscow. Let me call them in and we can discuss it," said Sister Barbara.

While she went to look for the other nuns, Ella asked the girls what they thought of the idea. Maria had little to say for she was confused by the sudden turn of events; but Olga was very enthusiastic about it. When Sister Barbara returned with the other nuns Mother Elizabeth told them about Olga's suggestion.

"I know the old monastery well," exclaimed Sister Irene. "It was abandoned long before the Japanese leased it and when I was a child we sometimes walked out there to play. It will not be a problem getting there. The only difficulty I foresee is that none of us speak Japanese."

"I have been assured that the manager speaks English and Russian and one or more of his agents also speak our language," Olga interjected. "I also speak and read a little Japanese so It should not be a problem."

"Very well," said Ella, "it is settled. I want you all to pack and then get some rest. I will have Sister Mary take care of the tickets immediately and I will get you up in time to have some breakfast before you leave for the station. Our chaplain, Father Mitrophan, will drive you." Father Mitrophan was Ella's confessor and she had confided in him on several occasions. She wanted to ensure that everything she did was morally correct and she found the priest's guidance very helpful. He would now play a small role in the plan.

"Mother Elizabeth," said Maria, "before we go I want to ask about the original plan. Tatiana and Anastasia are supposed to be coming here. What is to become of them? It seems as though everything is falling apart."

"No, it is not," said Ella. "You must have trust in our Lord. Anyway, as insensitive as it may seem, they are not your concern. Your main responsibility is saving yourselves. When you are finally on your way I will get in touch with your parents and we will determine what we should do next, but for you the decision is made."

"Do you not think we should wait and see if the Polish nuns can escort them to Warsaw?" asked Sister Catherine.

"I really do not see that happening now," said Ella. "The situation is becoming much more unstable than I realized and I think it would be dangerous to send them to the west. I am sure things will only get worse here and we cannot risk using the convent. No, I think we must go ahead with the plan we have just outlined. As for getting to Poland, that can be worked out later. Everything will be fine and I do not want any of you to be concerned. Now go and get ready. The four of you will depart together on the first train leaving for the east."

CS&O

In Petrograd the political situation continued to deteriorate. Members of government and various bureaucrats sent the Tsar frantic telegrams urging him to appoint a Ministry responsible to the Duma. They sincerely believed it was the only solution which would calm the emotions of the people, who were by now spilling out into the boulevards and byways. But it was much too late and though no one realized it yet, the monarchy was doomed. Massive strikes added to the number of protesters in the streets and looting, especially for bread, became commonplace. To make matters worse fiery orators stood on nearly every street corner and inflamed the passions of the already angry masses. It was a situation out of control and Nicholas, who did not understand the gravity of the events taking place in the capital, reacted in the only manner he knew. Instead of attempting to placate the people he sent word to the Military Governor of

Petrograd to quell the disturbances by whatever means necessary. This could only translate to military force and thus the die was cast. The rule of the Romanovs was about to come to an end.

೦ಕ೪೨

Ella had spent a restless night worrying that she might have over-stepped her authority in arranging to send the Grand Duchesses to Omsk. She hoped that her decision to follow Olga's suggestion would not undermine any action Nicholas or Alix were contemplating. It seemed to her, in retrospect, that sending the girls to the east was the best way to guarantee that they could be brought safely out of Russia. She would have been relieved to know that her assessment was the correct one. Rumors had begun to filter in about the chaos in Petrograd but here, in Moscow, things remained relatively quiet. But she knew instability could develop momentarily and she was anxious to get everyone off to the station. Sister Mary had been able to secure four of the last few tickets available on the 7:00 AM train and shortly before daybreak on the morning of the 12th of March, Ella woke everyone up for breakfast and a final good-bye When they were alone together in her office the tears of the aunt and her two nieces flowed freely for they knew this was more than likely the last time they would see each other.

"Never forget that you are a Grand Duchess of Russia," Ella reminded them. "Your father was anointed by God to rule this country and you are his legacy. Through the words of our blessed St. Serafim we know that one of you has been chosen for a special and sacred mission. No matter what happens, always hold this in your heart and live your lives so as to reflect favorably on your family and your country. Remain loyal to your Church even though you may not be able to practice your faith publicly. Now I bless you in the name of the Father, and the Son, and the Holy Ghost. May God watch over you my dear nieces and know that you will always be in my prayers." Olga and Maria hugged their Aunt Ella for the last time and rejoined the others. Sister Barbara led them to the rear exit of the convent where a sled awaited them. The four nuns climbed in and Father Mitrophan set off for the train station, arriving about fifteen minutes before the train for Vladivostok was due to depart. Sisters Catherine, Irene, Minka and Zyta boarded the coach, found their seats and settled in for the long journey. After a short delay the locomotive and its string of cars pulled out of Moscow station and headed east into the vast interior of Russia. For Olga and Maria it was but the second stage of what was turning out to be a great adventure.

When the chaplain returned from the station and informed Mother Elizabeth that all had gone well, she went quickly to the chapel to offer a prayer of thanksgiving and to also pray that a solution to the problem of notifying Nicky and Alix would present itself. About an hour later, as if in answer to her prayers, she had an unexpected visitor. Mr. Bruce

Lockhart had been sent by the British Embassy to look in on Ella, because she was a grandchild of Queen Victoria and cousin to King George V. He stopped by to see her whenever he was in Moscow. "Mr. Lockhart," said Ella as she greeted him, "it is so good to see you again, but quite unexpected."

"Yes, well, I apologize for calling at such an early hour, Mother Elizabeth, but I am catching an early train to Petrograd. It is an express so I should be there by early this evening. I wanted to stop by before I left to see how you are doing and ask if you are in need of anything," responded Lockhart.

"I am quite well and in need of nothing unless, of course, you have a carload of bandages and other such necessities," answered Ella, with a smile. "Please join me for tea."

"No, I am afraid I have just a few moments. I have a message for the Ambassador which requires his urgent attention."

"If I may inquire, what means do you use to safeguard private correspondence when you are delivering it?"

"Why I have a diplomatic bag," said Lockhart. "Why do you ask?"

"Then there is something you can do for me after all," said Ella. "I have an urgent message for the Empress and I am concerned that with all the turmoil, conventional methods might not work."

"Say no more," said Lockhart. "I will be glad to deliver it for you personally."

"Thank you so much," said Ella. "Let me get it together. I will only be a moment." Ella rushed to her office and took out a sheet of stationery. She thought for a few minutes about the information she wanted to convey and decided to keep it simple. In her clear hand she wrote,

Alix, the medical supplies which you sent were immediately forwarded to Omsk. Do not send the remaining medical supplies to me.

She signed it, *Ella.* She hoped the meaning was clear enough for Alix or Count Benckendorff to decipher. Ella then sealed the letter and returned to the parlor where guests at the convent were entertained. She handed the note to Mr. Lockhart and asked him if it would be possible to deliver it that very night. "Certainly, Mother. As soon as I have finished at the Embassy I will take your note down to the palace. Leave it to me, and if there is nothing else, I must be off." Ella saw him out and then sent a messenger to the telegraph office with a wire for the Tsar. In it she used the same phrase as in her note to Alix. She anticipated that Nicholas would soon return to Tsarskoe Selo and make a decision about what to do next.

C3⬥80

Later that same morning, as events unfolded in Moscow, the Tsar sat in his study at the Stavka reading a coded telegram he had just received from Count Benckendorff. It was the Count's daily update on the political climate and contained ominous and frightening news. It appeared that the situation in Petrograd had deteriorated into anarchy and when the Military Governor had attempted to put down the disturbances by force, the Petrograd garrison had mutinied and turned on its officers. The revolution had begun. The rapidity with which this had evolved stunned Nicholas and he knew he had to make some difficult decisions and make them quickly. One action he must take was readily apparent. He needed to get back to the palace as quickly as possible and somehow get Tatiana and Anastasia on their way to Ella's convent. Unfortunately Ella's telegram never reached him and it would be another full day before he was made aware of the situation in Moscow. He came to the conclusion that he should proceed as they had planned originally, with some minor variations. Alix must immediately move the two Grand Duchesses to the attic and replace them with Helena and Franny. As soon as the substitutions were made Alix was to leave for the Crimea with Alexei and the four impostors. His two daughters would stay in the attic until he arrived at Tsarskoe Selo to take them on to Ella's. At this point the Tsar was under the impression that the eastern route was still available and consequently he went with the most current information he had. Satisfied that this was the best course of action, under the circumstances, he encoded a rather lengthy telegram to Beckendorff and then called Valia into the study.

"Valia, I have just received an alarming wire from Count Beckendorff. He advises that the situation in Petrograd is chaotic and getting worse by the minute. I have decided that we will depart immediately for Tsarskoe Selo and I am directing the Count to prepare for the departure of the Tsarina, Alexei, and the doubles. When all is ready he is to send them to Livadia."

"Sir, if the Empress leaves the palace, who will look after the grand Duchesses," asked Valia.

"I will have Count Benckendorff stay, and Isa as well," said Nicholas. "We should be there in a few days time and hopefully the situation will stabilize enough that we can transport Tatiana and Anastasia to Moscow. I still believe we will be able to continue as planned. The Count has asked for instructions and I have them here in this telegram. After you direct the engineers to get steam up please take care to see that this is sent and receipted for."

The initial tasks taken care of, he then informed his staff that he would depart the Stavka that evening and return to Tsarskoe Selo where he would direct efforts to quell the unrest in the capital city. It was wishful thinking, however. Throughout the day more and more units turned away from the government and joined forces with the rebels and as the day wore on the situation continued to worsen. By the time evening fell and Nicholas departed Mogilev for the last time, Petrograd was in complete and utter chaos. .

ೞೲ

It was late in the evening of the same day when Count Benckendorff entered the Tsarina's drawing room to find the Empress completely distraught and weeping.

"Imperial Highness, what has happened?"

She held up her hand and he could see a letter in it. "This is what is the matter," said Alexandra. "Everything is falling apart and I just do not know what to do." The Count put formality behind him and pulled a chair next to hers. "Something has happened at Mother Elizabeth's convent," Alix continued. "It must be serious because she sent the girls on to Omsk, but she doesn't say exactly what has happened. Here, see for yourself." Beckendorff took the note and read it.

"If I may your highness," said Beckendorff, "I agree that something has occurred in Moscow, but I see this in a positive light. It seems that your sister and daughters, for whatever reason, have fallen back on the Tsar's secondary plan and the Grand Duchesses are on their way out of the country. It is exactly the kind of flexibility and initiative that we hoped for when we put the *Masquerade* together."

"You are probably right," Alix sniffed, "but what will become of Tatiana and Anastasia if we do not send them to Ella?"

"That is an entirely separate matter that we will have to take up with the Tsar.

"Yes, I see," said Alix. "The Emperor will know what to do."

"Your Majesty, may I now address my reason for coming at such a late hour?"

"What is it, Count Beckendorff?" asked the Empress, alarm apparent in her voice.

"As I informed you earlier, the garrison in the capital has mutinied and now groups of deserters are roaming the countryside looting and harassing the landowners. If your personal guard does not stand fast, you all may be in danger here," he replied..

"Then we must get word to the Tsar immediately," said the Empress. "He must decide what should be done with the two Grand Duchesses here at the palace since they will obviously not be going to Moscow."

"I will prepare a letter explaining what we know and have one of the Tsars Aides-de-camp hand carry it to him."

"Yes, I agree, but please emphasize to him that we are waiting anxiously for instructions," said the Tsarina. "Inform me as soon as you receive some word."

Benckendorff left to take care of this most important communication and within the hour, the message, in the personal code that he and

Nicholas had devised for such situations, was on its way to the Tsar. Meanwhile the Imperial train rushed northward, from Mogilev, carrying Tsar Nicholas II to his final destiny.

Chapter 42

March 13, 1917 – Tsarskoe Selo. Count Benckendorff studied the most recent telegram from the Tsar and was somewhat confused by its content. It had evidently been sent just before the Tsar left Mogilev to return to Tsarskoe Selo and directed him to send Alix, Alexei and the doubles to the Crimea immediately. The Count and Isa were to remain at the palace and manage affairs until he arrived to take Tatiana and Anastasia to Ella's convent. What puzzled him was the fact that the Tsar seemed totally unaware that Olga and Marie had left for Omsk and that the deteriorating situation in Moscow precluded sending Tatiana and Anastasia there. It was too soon for the Aide-de-camp to have reached the Tsar with the letter explaining the changed circumstances but certainly Ella would have notified Nicholas of what had occurred. Benckendorff hesitated momentarily and then decided his only course of action was to carry out the last order he had received. His immediate task was to complete the arrangements to send the Empress to the Crimea but before doing so he decided to speak to the Tsarina. The Count had been with the family for a long time and he could almost guarantee what Alexandra's reaction to the Tsar's request would be. So before starting the complicated process of moving the family he decided to first discuss the matter with her. He went immediately to the Empress' quarters to show her the telegram.

"Have you any word from him?" inquired the Empress, as he entered the Boudoir.

"Yes, your Majesty," replied Benckendorff, "that is why I have come. I have just finished decoding this telegram, which was sent by your husband yesterday afternoon. For some reason delivery was delayed and it only just arrived." He handed it to her and said, "as you can see he has requested that I have your personal belongings packed, as well as those of Alexei and the doubles, and arrange for you to leave for the Crimea, immediately," explained the Count. "Isa and I will remain here until he arrives and then we will decide what must be done, considering this new information.

"Count, you are a dear friend and I have no desire to make things more difficult than they already are, but under no circumstances will I agree to leave before the Tsar arrives," said the Empress. "How could anyone expect me to leave with two of my daughters trapped here at the palace and the other two, alone on a train, somewhere in the Urals. It is too much to ask and I will not leave without the Emperor."

"Your Imperial Highness, the Tsar's instructions were most explicit. It is imperative that you follow his orders. Every hour the situation is becoming more and more dangerous and if you are still here when he arrives it will make things even more complicated," said the Count. "No one knows that two Grand Duchesses are still here at the palace. They will be safe, I assure you. Please, your Imperial Highness, do as the Emperor has requested."

"No," said Alix emphatically. "I cannot leave when everything is in such turmoil. It seems obvious that the Tsar does not know the Grand Duchesses have left Ella's convent. This changes things dramatically for he must still think Moscow is a safe exit point. I will wait for the Tsar to arrive and after we decide what should be done with Tatiana and her sister, then, and only then, will I agree to leave."

"Very well, your Highness," said Benckendorff, with resignation in his voice. He knew from experience that further argument was futile. When Alexandra set her mind to something she was extremely stubborn and no amount of reasoning would change her decision. The Tsar was right in ordering her to leave but she could not see it, and her obstinacy on this occasion could only make matters worse. Every hour they delayed would make it more and more difficult to get everyone safely out of Alexander Palace.

Later that morning the weather took a turn for the worse but in a way it was fortuitous because the claps of thunder, the lighting and the icy rain kept everyone indoors and hid the presence of a lone figure struggling to reach the entrance to the palace. He presented a bedraggled appearance and it was only the authority in his voice and the inexperience of the sentries that influenced them to call Count Benckendorff for instructions. After a quick conversation on the phone, the stranger, his cloths soaking wet and his body chilled to the bone, was directed into the relative warmth of the palace. He was greeted there by the Count who whispered to him, "I told you never to come here. Now your cover is blown."

"Sir, the information I bring is of the utmost urgency, so much so, that retaining my anonymity seemed unimportant. Now, where can we speak in private," he choked out, almost overcome by violent trembling.

Benckendorff opened the door to his office and the two stepped into a room heated by a roaring fire. "Warm yourself while I send for hot tea. When it had arrived and the agent could speak more coherently he broke the alarming news. "There is a rumor that the Duma is sending troops to arrest the Empress."

"What, you cannot be serious? Give me the details!"

"I believe they plan to keep her under house arrest here in the palace but I cannot be certain. Some members of the Duma would only be too glad to hang her or lock her up in the fortress but I do not think any action will be taken until tomorrow. This awful weather will work in our favor."

"What are conditions really like in Petrograd?"

"Sir, the city is in chaos. Drunken soldiers and sailors swarm the streets, waving their red hats and scarves and celebrating the revolution. All government services are at a stand still and the Duma is unable to gain control of the situation. I thought it would be calmer here in Tsarskoe Selo and although the atmosphere is less tense, there is still some unrest. I was lucky to make it here safely." Benckendorff thanked his trusted informant and sent him on his way with enough rubles to find accommodations in town. He then called the Empress on the house phone and asked to speak to her.

"I was just preparing to lie down for a while, so please tell me over the phone," said Alix.

"Your highness, what I have to say is for your ears only."

"Very well, then, I will see you in my Mauve Boudoir."

Count Benckendorff made his way to the Empress' rooms where she greeted him clad in her dressing gown with her hair caught back in a ribbon. The count had rarely seen her dressed so informally and he was somewhat uncomfortable. "Well, Count, what brings you here with such a grave look on your face," she inquired.

"Your Highness, I have just received word from one of my best agents that they are preparing to arrest you."

Alexandra was stunned by the news but she quickly recovered. "Who is going to arrest me and by what authority do they presume to attempt such a thing?" she demanded of the Count.

"Some radical elements in the Duma are evidently behind this. They have no real authority, but Petrograd has fallen to the revolution and, since no troops have arrived to defend the city, they are attempting to seize power. Word from around the country is equally disturbing. I do not think this is an isolated incident, so we must act accordingly."

Alix was alarmed by the prospect of arrest because such action might separate her from her daughters, and the imposters, and make the introduction of the last two doubles very difficult, if not impossible. "When will this arrest be attempted and where are they likely to take me?"

"I do not know for sure, but I believe we have at least until sometime tomorrow. This storm will delay them from coming out today and even if they do come, there is a good chance they will allow you to remain here under house arrest. Much depends on how your personal guard reacts. Your Highness we must make preparations without the benefit of the Tsar's guidance. Most importantly we will have to substitute Helena and Franny for your daughters, and do it tonight. The situation is worsening even as we speak."

"No, no, we must wait until the Tsar returns," she replied. When confronted with stressful situations Alexandra had a difficult time making decisions and today was no exception. She just did not want to face this on her own. In this case, however, Count Benckendorff was equal to the task. He was quite accustomed to Alexandra's obstinacy but today he was having none of it and for once he was unconcerned about his position in the hierarchy. He was going to act no matter what Alix decided.

"Your Highness I must insist . We have to do it now; otherwise it will be too late. You must face the facts. We do not know where the Tsar is or what his circumstances are. It could be days before he reaches the palace, if at all. He might well be under arrest, but regardless of his situation I know with certainty what he would expect of us. We must save your two daughters. It is what we have prepared for and, if you will pardon me, I have no intention of letting anything happen to the two Grand Duchesses in my charge"

The Empress was somewhat taken aback by the Count's curt response, but in her heart she knew he was right. "I know we are supposed to be flexible," she said "but the prospect of arrest has driven out any ability I might have to think clearly. What do you suggest?"

"Well, we still have contact with Gatchina where Grand Duke George is in residence. The area surrounding Gatchina is relatively calm and we have not received any information of revolutionary activity in the vicinity. I suggest we take advantage of this nasty weather and send Tatiana and Anastasia to Gatchina as soon as possible. Although there are risks, the Grand Duke's estate is rather isolated and sending them there will buy us some time. I truly believe it will be several days, maybe even weeks, before the rebels start to think about the other palaces."

"Very well. Notify everyone concerned and after lunch we shall meet to work out the details." Just then the telephone rang. "Yes, I understand," said the Tsarina. "Arrange the guards as you see fit." She hung up the phone. "The garrison in Tsarskoe Selo has gone over to the revolution, but the palace guard is still loyal, so far."

"Then we must act immediately, your Imperial Highness."

Alix stood up and began pacing up and down. "Yes, we must. Please tell the others then come back and let us begin."

When the Count returned he informed the Empress that the girls were somewhat shaken by the unexpected news, but had reacted maturely, and were already beginning to get things organized. For the next hour the Tsarina and her trusted advisor worked together, examining different options before finally coming up with a plausible scenario.

While they were working on the specifics, Alix called on Isa to help Tatiana and Anastasia prepare to depart. Time was of such critical importance she could not even spare a moment to tell her daughters why they were leaving so suddenly and also because she did not trust herself to remain calm.

The plan the two came up with was relatively simple. The doubles would come down and assume Tatiana and Anastasia's roles while the two Grand Duchesses went to the attic. There they would dress themselves in army uniforms, which Dr. Botkin would obtain from the storeroom at the hospital. With gangs of drunken and leaderless soldiers roaming about, looking for loot and women, the Count felt the Grand Duchesses would be safer if they looked like young men rather than peasant girls. Alix debated this issue with him but finally agreed to allow the girls hair to be cut. Once dressed in uniform, and wearing the Red Cross armbands of medical orderlies, they would slip downstairs into the basement and follow the tunnel all the way to Catherine Palace hospital. Dr. Botkin, wearing his Medical Officer's uniform would be waiting with an ambulance at the entrance where wounded were delivered for treatment. When Tatiana and her sister joined him in the requisitioned vehicle the doctor would depart immediately for Gatchina, ostensibly to pick up wounded and return them to the hospital.

When all the preparations had been made, Benckendorff sent a courier to Gatchina with a message to the Grand Duke explaining the change in plans and alerting him to expect a delivery. The Empress said her final tearful good-byes and the plan was put into motion. Hopefully, by the time Botkin arrived with the girls, George would be prepared to hide them. Despite the deplorable condition of the road, and the unavoidable delays, the late hour and bad weather worked in their favor and there was only one incident during the trip. Dr. Botkin and his two orderlies were accosted, after traveling a few miles, by three men seeking transportation to the capital. The doctor explained that he was going only a short distance but that he would let them ride in the back of the ambulance until they reached the next town, where they could find shelter. The men were grateful for the kindness and climbed in the back where they huddled together for warmth. When Botkin dropped them off they were profuse in their thanks. As for the girls, they held their breaths the whole time, petrified they might be discovered. But some smudges of dirt, strategically placed on their faces had successfully masked their femininity. Needless to say, they did not speak a word until the men were gone.

As soon as Alix was sure everything was going as planned she sent a trusted courier to try and locate the Tsar, whom she assumed was on his way north to Tsarskoe Selo. The message he carried informed Nicholas that Alexandra had sent the girls to Gatchina. It also repeated the news that Ella, because of the unrest in Moscow, had made the decision to send Olga and Maria on to Omsk. It was well that the Empress restated this important change in the plan because for some reason the Aide-de-camp dispatched earlier with that information had failed to reach the Tsar. Nicholas still assumed that two of his daughters were in Moscow and the other two at Alexander palace. And so, as Alix waited through the night for news from Dr. Botkin that he had completed his journey, the fate of the *Masquerade* rested in the capable but unknowing hands of a young officer working his way south to find his Tsar.

It appeared to Alix that one thing after another was going wrong but finally fortune smiled and the second courier was able to make his way south through the various rail stops, before they were taken over by revolutionary factions. It was common practice that when the Imperial train left one station word was passed ahead to the next that the Tsar was in route. When Alexandra's messenger arrived on the south bound train at Malaia Vishera, a town approximately one hundred miles south of Tsarskoe Selo, he was informed that the Tsar's train would be passing through without stopping. The young officer immediately presented his credentials to the station master and explained that he had important dispatches to hand deliver to the Tsar. The master was at first reluctant but finally, after some discussion, he agreed to display the appropriate signals to stop the Imperial train.

It was very late that night when the Tsar's train pulled into the station at Malaia Vishera. It was an unscheduled stop and Nicholas was irritated that someone had made the decision to delay his journey. He was anxious to get to the palace and whisk the girls away before things got too bad in Tsarskoe Selo. Normally he would be asleep by this hour but he was so intent on returning home that he had remained awake to work on an alternate plan to get the girls out if the situation changed. And, of course, it had changed and dramatically so. At this point he was still under the impression that Alix, Alexei and the doubles were on their way to the Crimea and so he was not concerned about their safety at the moment.

As the train came to a complete stop at the station, Nicholas could see a lone figure waiting anxiously on the platform. One of his staff members stepped down to inquire as to the delay and was approached by the young officer, who was apparently quite nervous. "I have an important message for the Emperor," said the courier. "It is from the Tsarina, and I have explicit instructions to deliver it to him in person."

"One moment," said the staff officer. He disappeared back onto the train and a minute later he returned to escort the messenger to the Tsar. The young man handed the letter to Nicholas and stood at attention while the Tsar broke the seal and read the correspondence from Alix. He paused, then looked up, and asked, "Are you the person responsible for stopping my train?"

The courier's knees were almost knocking together at the enormity of what he had done but he managed to choke out an answer. "Yes, your Imperial Highness, I ordered the station master to stop the train."

"Do you know what is in this letter?"

"No sir, my instructions were to guard it with my life, destroy it rather than have anyone but you receive it, and place it personally into your hand. I have done all these things."

"Yes, you most certainly have and I commend your initiative. My family will be forever in your debt for the service you have rendered this night. You are welcome to come with me to the palace where I can reward you properly but I must warn you we are proceeding into danger."

"Sir, my reward is to be able to serve you. As for the danger, I am a soldier."

"Very well then. Get yourself off to the dining car and get something hot to eat and drink. We will be leaving immediately." The young officer saluted and left the Tsar's presence. When he had gone, Nicholas reopened the letter and read again his wife's astounding news. The salient points jumped out at him. Tatiana and Anastasia were on their way to George at Gatchina. Ella had sent Olga and Maria on to Omsk, and apparently Alix had not yet departed for the Crimea nor did she seem inclined to do so. But with all four girls relatively safe he could not understand why she would further delay her departure. He tried to read between the lines but fatigue was beginning to overtake him and he found it hard to concentrate. At that moment Valia entered the compartment and announced to the Tsar that he had just received some disturbing information.

"What is it now?" questioned the Tsar. "I don't know if I can take any more bad news."

"I have just spoken with the staff at the train station and they said that the next two stops are in the hands of some revolutionaries and we might not be able to get through," Valia answered. "They suggest we divert to Pskov and proceed to Tsarskoe Selo that way."

"Very well," said Nicholas, "you can inform the engineer momentarily, but first I need some input from you," he said, as he showed Valia the message from Alix. "At this point I do not know exactly where Olga and Maria are. I can only assume that Ella has taken the appropriate course of action and that they are safe for the present. Tatiana and Anastasia are in Gatchina with George by now and we need to focus on them for the present. Obviously the route through Moscow and on to Japan is no longer available."

"Your Highness what of Sandro?" Valia asked. Perhaps you could use him to assist with the two Grand Duchesses in Gatchina."

"Valia, I think you are on to something. Sandro is in Kiev with my mother, and is working on arrangements to get her and my sisters out of the country if necessary. Sandro could take the girls with my mother. The question is, how do we transport them from Gatchina to Kiev?"

"Would it be possible for George to move them to Pskov?" asked Valia.

"I assume it is possible," said Nicholas. "What are you thinking?"

"Well, we will shortly be switching on to the track to Pskov. If George could meet us there with Tatiana and Anastasia we could slip the girls on to the train and then instead of proceeding on to Tsarskoe Selo we could return to Mogilev. The Empress Dowager could come up on her train, meet us in Mogilev, and take the two Grand Duchesses back to

Kiev," said Valia. "Then whatever plan Sandro has come up with can be adapted to include your daughters."

"I think you might have something here," said Nicholas. "But what excuse would I give to the staff for suddenly returning to Mogilev?"

"The troops at the Stavka are still loyal. When we arrive in Pskov the word coming from Petrograd will be so bad that you will decide to return to Mogilev to organize resistance to the anarchy. It will take a while to assemble enough rolling stock to transport an entire regiment to Petrograd and that will give you time to work out details with Sandro and your mother. Actually, it is not such a bad idea. Circumstances have become so bad we may have to fight our way back to Tsarskoe Selo.

"It sounds plausible enough," said Nicholas. "Anyway, we are so short on options right now that I think we should try this new plan."

"What about the Empress," asked Valia, "has she left for the Crimea yet."

"I pray to God that she has," said Nicholas, "but I really do not know. She mentioned nothing of it in her letter and now it seems communication with the palace has been cut off. Nevertheless I want you to try and get word to Benckendorff and insist that she leave immediately."

"Then we will go forward with this plan?" asked Valia.

"Yes," replied the Tsar. "Communications are unreliable but we must make the effort. Before we depart Malaia Vishera dispatch telegrams to George, my mother and Count Benckendorff. Be cryptic but make sure the essentials are clear. Things are in such a state that I doubt anyone is monitoring the telegraphy for content. I would even be willing to delay here for an hour or two in hopes that we at least hear from George. We must know if he will be able to meet us in Pskov." Valia left to carry out his instructions. He succeeded in reaching Gatchina and Kiev but the telegram to Benckendorff was never delivered. It would be some time before Alix and the Count were made aware of what had transpired.

They waited for what seemed like hours for some word from George and finally the Tsar, dejected by his inability to communicate, gave orders to get underway. In the early morning hours of the 14th of March, just as the Imperial train was creaking into motion, a telegrapher came running down from the wireless office towards the Tsar's compartment, waving a slip of paper over his head. Valia stepped down to receive the message and then hopped back on the train as it began to pick up speed. He glanced at the cable and made his way to the Tsar's compartment which he entered with a broad smile on his face. "It is from the Grand Duke," he announced. The Grand Duchesses had arrived safely at George's palace and the faithful Dr. Botkin was already on his way back to Alexander Palace to report. George, accompanied by his two military valets, would meet the Imperial train at Pskov that very night. Nicholas was elated and, although he still had much to think about, he was so exhausted he had to try and get some sleep. The last thing he remembered thinking about, before sleep took him, was whether Alix had done as he had asked and departed for the Crimea. At this point, that element of the *Masquerade* was something he had no control over, so it served no purpose to worry about it. When he awoke, several hours later, the train was arriving at the station at Pskov.

CRØ∂

Later that same morning a small group of disorganized revolutionaries presented themselves at the entrance to the Alexander Park demanding the gates be opened so they could arrest the Empress. The palace guard had no intention of being dictated to by this leaderless rabble and quickly mobilized. When the mob persisted the Officer of the Guard ordered them to disperse and threatened to fire on them. Frustrated by the loyalty of the household guard they satisfied themselves by making threats. "We will remember how you behaved when we return," one of them shouted. The Sergeant of the Guard strode out and struck the man in the face, knocking him to the ground. "Remember this. We take our orders from the Empress." The mob quickly dispersed and thus was Alexandra spared the humiliation of being hauled off to an undetermined fate.

As soon as the threat was over the commander of the guard reported the incident to Count Benckendorff. He in turn carried the news to the Empress and again urged her to depart for the Crimea, but she refused to agree. The Count then informed her that members of the Duma had banded together to form a provisional government and the next attempt to arrest her would be better organized.

"How can that be?" she asked. "The Tsar is the head of the government and no one has the right to supercede him. I must stay here, for the time being, to provide some continuity. I still have influence, you know."

Benckendorff shook his head in exasperation. "Your Imperial Highness, I do not wish to seem disrespectful but you evidently have no idea how much the situation has deteriorated. I am afraid any influence you have ends at the gates to the palace and even then there is no guarantee the guard will remain loyal." But try as he could, no amount of argument or pleading on his part could sway her. Alix was going to wait for her husband and that was that.

She now had all the doubles in sickbeds, where they would remain until Nicholas arrived. She would spend her days pretending to care for them during their bout with the "measles" while at the same time she worried about her real daughters and how they were faring. Alix wondered if in the end she would know that they had reached safety. It would mean so much if she at least had that to hold on to. Oh how she longed for Nicky to be at her side. His strength gave her such comfort at times like this.

CRØ∂

As events were hurtling toward an unexpected conclusion at Pskov, hundreds of miles to the east, things were going quite well. When the train from Moscow to Omsk made its scheduled stop at Perm, before starting through the mountains, some passengers had disembarked and the four nuns were able to move from the day coach to a compartment. Now the train was just beginning its laborious climb through the passes of the Ural Mountains with the next scheduled stop at Ekaterinburg. It was still winter here in the mountains and the train was slowed by the resistance of accumulated snow against the plow mounted at the front of the locomotive. But progress was steady and the scenery so spectacular that even the tedium of the long journey could not dampen the spirits of the nuns. For Sisters Catherine and Irene it was a welcome break from the strict routine of the convent and for the Grand Duchesses it was the third day of an adventure, but one they could not fully enjoy because of the circumstances under which it had begun. Their move to a second class compartment provided a measure of privacy and eventually they would have to discuss the arrival at Omsk. But for the time being they were all content to enjoy the harsh beauty of the deep gorges, the waterfalls, and the rushing streams.

As was the case on these long stretches, food and drink were at a premium and once travelers had consumed their personal supplies they had to rely on what they could purchase from locals when the train made a scheduled stop. Mother Elizabeth had seen to it that the four started out with a full hamper but the nuns had shared their supplies with some less fortunate companions, who were eager and most grateful for their generosity. The plan now was to replenish their necessities when the train reached Ekaterinburg. Until it did they would have to quell their hunger with the few scraps that remained.

By the time the train pulled into the station at Ekaterinburg everyone was famished and Olga and Maria insisted they be allowed to purchase food and tea for the whole group with their ample supply of rubles. The four nuns stepped down to stretch their legs and Olga said "let's go get something from that old woman over there. She is selling some sort of food items." When the two Grand Duchesses approached her, disguised as they were in their habits, she looked up at them with resignation. Olga indicated she wished to buy bread so the vendor took a piece of newspaper and placed it on the little table before her. She picked up a loaf of bread, cut a piece off the end, placed it on top of the newspaper, and handed it to Olga. "Oh, "I thought I was buying the whole loaf."

"Sister, the loaf would certainly cost more than a nun would have," said the woman, "and we are too poor to give it away." Olga smiled at the woman and said, " mother do not be concerned about the cost. A benefactor has provided for us on our journey and we have sufficient to pay what you ask." She proceeded to purchase four loaves, some sausages, cheese, and a quantity of bedraggled looking fruit. She also had their canteens filled with hot tea. The woman wrapped up their purchases in the newspaper and took their money and when she paid, Olga gave the woman a little extra. "Thank you so much, Sister. I wish I could be as generous."

"God bless you and keep you safe," Olga replied.

Maria deposited their provisions in the compartment and then she and her sister strolled the platform while awaiting the call to board. Ekaterinburg seemed a pleasant enough city, from what they could see of it at a distance. On one corner they could make out an imposing house, obviously the home of a wealthy businessman. The two stopped to read the notices on the station bulletin board and while they were doing so, two men, speaking rather loudly, came up behind them.

"We must get more of the peasants out this way to join our cause," said one man.

"Yes, but they seem to be much more loyal to the Tsar in the countryside than in Moscow and the larger cities," replied the other. "I think we need to be better organized if our party is to achieve dominance. Let us go back to Moscow where there is a stronger following."

"Yes, there is strength in numbers. You get the tickets while I find us another bottle."

As the two men moved away one of them thrust a flyer into Maria's hand and snarled, "here sister, why don't you pray that the Tsar is blown to pieces." Maria was horrified but said nothing. Olga, on the other hand could not restrain herself, and throwing caution to the wind asked the man why he felt that way about the Tsar. "You must be locked in a convent all the time," he shouted, "and I do not have time to educate you right now. But you will learn soon enough," he said as he weaved away. Maria grabbed Olga's arm and literally pulled her on to the train. "Sister, what are you thinking? This is no time or place to start a debate and bring attention to bear on us."

"I am sorry, I won't lose my composure again." Her promise lasted about twenty seconds, the time it took her to open the flyer in Maria's hand and look at it. It was a caricature of the Tsar and Tsarina, with collars and leashes around their necks, being walked like dogs by the Kaiser. The picture infuriated Olga and she ripped at the picture over and over until it was in small pieces which she threw in the trash receptacle.

"What is happening to Russia?" questioned Maria. "I feel as if it is dying a painful death."

"Yes, the things father discussed with us are starting to make more sense," whispered Olga. "Soon all will be in chaos. Maria, for the first time, I am afraid."

"Then we shall be afraid, together, my dear sister."

At that moment the last call was made and the locomotive lurched into motion. Sister Catherine opened the food parcels but the Grand Duchesses had both lost their appetite. As the train left the main station

Olga could see a spur line leading to what appeared to be some kind of secondary depot. She wondered for a moment what might be its purpose but as the train picked up speed and cleared the town, she leaned back and put it out of her mind.

Chapter 43

March 14, 1917 – Pskov. When the Imperial train arrived in Pskov, Nicholas was immediately briefed on the situation in Petrograd and for the first time made aware of the fact that a provisional government had been formed and that it was calling on him to abdicate. Members of the Duma hoped that if they could convince the Tsar to give up the throne, and then widely publicized the decision, the announcement of his abdication would, by itself, have a calming effect on the unrest in the capital. Nicholas knew that he must consider the political situation, and quickly, but it was difficult to do so when the safety of his daughters was in doubt. George had indicated in his telegram that he would arrive at Pskov after dark and sunset was still several hours away. Nicky arranged for the trusted Valia to go into town in the late afternoon to gauge the situation and when he had made contact with the Grand Duke to bring him directly to the train, along with his two "orderlies." A visit from the Grand Duke, to discuss the abdication issue, would not seem out of the ordinary since he and the Tsar were known to be close. As for Tatiana and Anastasia, there were so many military personnel about that their presence, dressed as they were, should go unnoticed. Once on the train they could lock themselves in an empty compartment and remain there until the train departed for Mogilev. Nicholas refused to even consider the notion that he might not be allowed to leave because if that occurred, and the girls were found out, the *Masquerade* was over.

Abdication would mean disgrace and scorn, but these he could deal with. What would be harder to face would be the disappointment of his wife, the Empress, and his mother, the Dowager Empress. Nicholas knew that if he decided to abandon the throne their humiliation would be the greater. He could admit to no one but himself that the dominant emotion he would experience would be one of relief. He had never wanted to be Tsar and he had never been properly prepared for the role. His idea of paradise was a place where he would never have to make another decision, but he was not quite there yet. He had to be sure in his own mind that if he did abdicate it would help and not hurt Russia. And so he asked for advice, not from his wife or mother, whom he knew would react emotionally but from those with whom he had served. He ordered one of his military aides to telegraph his generals in the field and obtain their assessment of the situation. As the day went on the answers arrived, one by one, from his senior military leaders across the nation. Overwhelmingly, they urged abdication, citing for the most part the mutinous attitude of many of their troops, who evidently supported the provisional government. Even Nikolasha, from his distant post, urged him to give up the throne. Nicholas had never deceived himself that the people loved him, but they would nevertheless be upset if he acquiesced to the advice he was receiving. They might not like him but they loved what he represented, a monarch chosen by God. This act of abdication would shake their convictions and he prayed silently that their faith was strong enough to withstand the disruption of sacred and long standing traditions.

Aides were in and out all afternoon reporting on the conditions in Petrograd and after examining the facts Nicholas realized he had run out of options. He bowed to the inevitable and made the decision to give up the throne, but before notifying the provisional government he called in Count Tatishchev to discuss the particulars.

"Ilia," said the Tsar, "you know what is going on and I wanted you to be the first to hear what I have decided. I will abdicate tomorrow morning but I will do so only under certain conditions. I intend to give the revolution what it wants, a document with my signature which they can publicize and claim validates their legitimacy. I want you to prepare the document, but do it in such a manner that it has no validity and can later be repudiated, if not by me, then someone from my lineage. Can you do this for me?"

"Of course, your Imperial Highness, if you are certain this is what you want to do. As you say, they are probably more interested in your signature and the word "abdicate" then anything else. If the document we give the government's representatives contains those two elements they are unlikely to challenge the rest of the contents. That is why they must come to you, on your home ground as it were, where they will be uncomfortable. I suspect they will arrive, witness your signature, and with the manifesto in hand race back to Petrograd with their trophy. They certainly will not be experts on rules of succession, so when you abdicate you should also abdicate for your son, which by law you cannot do. He must do it for himself and that will automatically invalidate the document. To make certain, though, you should name as your successor your brother Michael who is ineligible because of his illegal marriage to a woman who is not only a commoner but a divorcee."

"Excellent Ilia," said the Tsar. "I am going to leave it to you to have the draft prepared, if you will. Get Prince Vasily to help you; he is especially good at creating the appropriate flowery language. When it is ready, send word to the provisional government that I am prepared to abdicate. I want it to appear that it is my decision and not one that is being forced on me. Let us see how they react. In the meantime I need to consider alternatives for getting the Grand Duchesses out. I am not comfortable with the idea of having them with my mother and Sandro roaming the Crimea. No, I need a better option. At any rate, when you receive a reply from Petrograd do not hesitate to bring me the news. I will be anxious to know what they plan."

Later that evening Tatishchev brought word that the new government had already dispatched two members of the Duma to plead with him to give up the throne. Vasily Shulgin and Alexander Guchkov were on their way to speak to the Tsar and were scheduled to arrive sometime the next day. As it turned out, due to interminable delays, it was the next night before the two men reached Pskov.

When the sun finally set and it began to grow as dark as it would at that time of year, Nicholas started to worry. The telegram from George had not been specific as to what time he might arrive and Valia had not yet reported back. An hour passed and then another, and Nicholas began to imagine all sorts of catastrophes. Suddenly there was a knock at the door to his study. The Tsar made sure the curtains were tightly closed and then said, in a shaky voice, "Enter!" Valia walked in followed by George and two young soldiers. "George, thank God." Nicholas exclaimed! "I was beginning to become concerned that something had happened. Now tell me where you have hidden the girls." George looked over at Valia and shrugged his shoulders.

"What is going on," said the Tsar, "and tell me George, why are those undisciplined orderlies of yours grinning at their Tsar like a pair of friendly baboons?" George could hold back no longer and laughed aloud.

"Nicky, they are friendly, I assure you. Do you not recognize your own?"

Finally the Tsar caught on and realized that the two smiling soldiers were indeed his missing daughters, Tatiana and Anastasia. He nearly wept with relief, as he hugged them tightly. He nodded at Valia and George and acknowledged once again the wonderful service of these two men. Nicholas was overjoyed to see his daughters although he was shocked by their appearance and short hair. He obviously would not have recognized them on the street and certainly not known they were women. "Young gentlemen, we anticipate leaving for Mogilev some time tomorrow and we will have an opportunity then to acquaint you with all that has occurred. Valia will show you to your quarters now, as I know you must be exhausted. Keep the curtains closed and do not leave the compartment under any circumstances. I will come to you. Valia keep an eye on things and George please remain. I have something to discuss with you." When the others had gone Nicholas got right to the point. "George, when the representatives from the Duma arrive tomorrow I intend to abdicate."

"Oh Nicky, I am so sorry to hear this. Are you sure it is the best move?"

"Yes, my mind is quite made up and the paperwork is already completed. But I want to talk to you about the girls."

"What about them?"

"For some reason, and I do not know what it is, Ella sent Olga and Maria on to Omsk and advised us not to send the other two girls to her convent. I was going to leave for Likoslavl in a day or two and take the girls as we had originally planned but that is now out of the question."

"What do you propose?" George asked.

"When I realized that the way east was blocked I asked my mother to meet me at Mogilev with the intention of having her bring the girls to Kiev when she returned. Then Sandro could include them in whatever plans he had made to get my mother and sisters out of the country. However, I have decided against that. I want you to come with me to the Stavka and then accompany the girls to Kiev on my mother's train. In the city you can purchase whatever you need for a long journey."

"I don't understand," George replied, confusion evident on his face. "What long journey?"

"Dearest friend, I would like you to escort the Grand Duchesses from Kiev all the way to Omsk. Come, study this map with me." He paused while George joined him at the map. "You would leave Kiev and make your way southeast to Volograd. Then a turn to the northeast to Magnitogorsk and on to Omsk by rail or boat or a combination of the two. The girls will travel as nuns and when you reach the Japanese trade mission you can put them in the care of the Commandant. By then Olga and Maria should have passed through and when you are satisfied all is in order you can return by whatever route you choose. What say you to this plan, George?"

"It will work," the Grand Duke replied. "I will make it work."

"Good. As soon as I finish this abdication business we will depart for Mogilev. On the trip south we can work out the details and have all our preparations in place when we arrive."

The next day was one of nervous anticipation as the principal players waited impatiently for the Duma members to arrive. Hour after hour passed and as the tension grew the Tsar began to express his concern to George, Tatishchev, and the others. But finally, with the white winter night fully upon them, a car arrived at the station bearing the two representatives of the new government. They were treated with courtesy, ushered into the Tsar's study, and given seats at the table. Nicholas intended to conduct this interview on his own terms and although it was obvious Shulgin and Guchkov were ready to begin, the Tsar had refreshments brought in and deliberately made small talk for the better part of an hour. When he knew the politicians were about to have an attack of apoplexy, he relented and said softly, "very well gentlemen, let us begin. But before we get to the reason you are here I must have the answer to a simple question. Does the new government intend to continue the war if I give up the throne?"

"Yes, your Imperial Highness, it is our understanding that Russia will honor her alliances and continue the fight," Shulgin replied.

"Very well then, but before I sign anything, there are two conditions which you must agree to."

There was immediate consternation expressed by the delegates. "Sir, we were not authorized to grant any concessions," Guchkov exclaimed.

"Nevertheless, you will grant them or your journey will have been in vain. Relax gentlemen, these concessions, as you call them, are innocent enough. As my last official act I intend to recall Grand Duke Nicholai Nickolaevich and have him relieve me of my duties as Commander in Chief. To facilitate this transfer I intend to return to the Stavka this very night. There will be a formal ceremony in a few days and I will give my final good-bye to the troops. Do you agree?" Shulgin and his companion nodded their assent. The Tsar stood up and retrieved a document, an ink pen, and his seal from the desk and returned to the table. He looked at the instrument of abdication and, after a moment, carefully affixed his signature. He then placed his seal on the paper and became, at that instant, what he most longed to be, an ordinary citizen.

The two men across from him quickly read the manifesto and expressed their disappointment when they realized Nicholas had abdicated in favor of his brother Michael and not Alexei, his son. The young heir was well liked in the country and the provisional government had counted on his popularity and youth to soften the public reaction to the take over.

"Gentlemen this meeting is over. You have what you wanted, but if you are unhappy with the idea of Grand Duke Michael on the throne, talk to him. He will probably be easier to convince to step down than I was. I assume that we will read about these eventful few hours in the newspapers tomorrow evening. Good night to you and have a safe journey back to Petrograd." The two men were escorted to their car. Shortly after midnight the Imperial train lurched into motion, picked up speed and began the long run south to Mogilev. Before going to bed Nicholas struggled somewhat with the realization that he was leaving Alexandra and the four imposters behind at Tsarskoe Selo. But he really had no choice. This after all was what they had trained for and he had to get Tatiana and Anastasia on their way.

As it turned out Grand Duke Michael would refuse to accept the throne unless he was invited to do so by a body representative of the people. When such an invitation was not forthcoming the three hundred year old dynasty ended quietly, without an outcry or a whimper. As for the last Tsar, he was fast asleep, exhausted but relieved, and happy the nasty business was finally over. Tomorrow he would explain everything to the girls.

⋘⋙

The ex-Tsar's study was located in the sleeping-car of the Imperial train and after a light breakfast Nicholas had Valia bring the girls there to discuss the recent events and make plans for the future. Later he would gather the others, but for now he wanted to be alone with his daughters.

He looked at Tatiana and Anastasia sitting there and knew that he must tell them what had taken place late last night and it tore at his heart. Will they think their father a coward, he wondered. I always told them to be strong and to stand up for what is right, and now look what I have done.

"Girls," he began, "I need to speak to you about a number of things that have occurred since we last saw each other but before I do so, for my own peace of mind, I have to know if everything appeared to be in order when you left the palace and what influenced you to do so."

"Three events occurred, Papa, which prompted Mama and Count Benckendorff to send us to Gatchina," Tatiana replied. "First was a message from Aunt Ella telling us that Olga and Maria were unable to go to Warsaw as planned. Something happened, what it was we still do not know, but Aunt Ella sent them on to Omsk. She also advised Mama not to send us to Moscow. Next, there was an altercation at the gate to Alexander Park which was handled nicely by the household guard but which nevertheless worried the Count. Lastly, word arrived that the Tsarskoe Selo garrison had mutinied. At that point the decision was made and Helena and Franny moved down to take our places. We said good-bye to Mama, Dr. Botkin drove us to Gatchina, and here we are."

"Let me tell you right away then," said the Tsar, "that the plan for your departure remains basically the same; you will just be using a different route. Your grandmother intends to meet us at Mogilev and take you back to Kiev. Once you are ready to leave, cousin George will escort you all the way to Omsk. From that point on everything will be as before. I might add that there is a good possibility you will see your sisters again, although that depends on Prince Kanin. Do you understand what you must do?"

"Yes, Papa," they answered in unison.

"Well then, do you remember the letter from Saint Serafim which I read to you some time ago?" asked their father. The girls nodded. "In it he mentioned that Russia would be drowning in an abyss without hope of rescue. Late last night I helped push Russia into that abyss."

Tatiana and Anastasia looked at the Tsar with complete confusion. "What does that mean, Papa," asked Anastasia?

"It means that I had to abdicate, to give up the throne," said their father. "Russia is no longer under the rule of the Romanovs. Now it is controlled by the Duma, but soon it will be ruled by the devil himself." Anastasia was really too young to grasp what her father had just told her, but Tatiana knew exactly what he meant and her eyes filled with tears.

"Oh, papa," cried Tatiana. "I am so sorry for you."

"Do not weep for me, my child, but weep for Russia," said Nicholas. "Our land will suffer greatly. This is the beginning of what St. Serafim prophesied."

"If you are no longer the Tsar," asked Anastasia, "then who are you?"

"I am a common man now," answered Nicholas. "I am a citizen of Russia just like the peasant."

"No, Papa," said Tatiana. "This is not right. The Russian people love you, they will never accept this."

"It is done Tatiana. It is the Russian people who have sent representatives to the Duma and they in turn requested my abdication," explained Nicholas.

"It is just unbelievable," said Tatiana.

"Papa," asked Anastasia, "if you are no longer the Tsar and are just a commoner, you can leave the country with us now, and no one will care."

Nicholas looked at his daughter. His abdication had happened so quickly that he had never considered that. Maybe she was right. If the Romanovs were now the same as everyone else, would his sacrifice be meaningless? He quickly put the thought from his mind. He was still the Tsar and no piece of paper could change that. "My sweet child," said Nicholas, "I am only concerned about my daughters right now. You must not concern yourself with my well-being. I still have many friends who will help me if I need it. Now, to the other reason for calling you here. I must have you choose your rings." He retrieved the boat shaped pouch from his desk drawer and brought it over to his daughters. Tatiana chose her ring first, and Anastasia took the one that was left. Nicholas then gave them the same instructions that he had shared with Olga and Maria on the way to Likoslavl. When he was satisfied that they understood everything and had repeated back his directions several times he put the pouch away and they reminisced about the old days until the train arrived at Mogilev. The Grand Duchesses understood that until they were safely on Minnie's train and headed south for Kiev that they must remain hidden and therefore would see little of their father. Tatiana and her sister were to spend the day on the train, concealed from view, while Nicholas met with the military members of his former headquarters. The atmosphere at the Stavka was a somber one and the situation awkward for those who had loyally served their Tsar. No one was quite sure how to act around a former monarch. At this point Nicholas had no real position of power, but in the end everyone chose to ignore that fact and treated him with respect and kindness. This included all the foreign military observers and attaches as well.

Late the next morning, Minnie, accompanied by Sandro, arrived to meet with Nicholas and arrange to take the girls. Nicholas greeted her train when it pulled in and had her cars shunted to a siding next to the Imperial train. He immediately joined her in her drawing room and proceeded to update her on the situation and the events of the last few days. As expected she was devastated when she learned that her son had abdicated. It was beyond her understanding as to why he needed to make such a decision at this time but she believed that his action was most likely driven by the requirements of the *Masquerade*. She refused to acknowledge that the deteriorating political situation was really the reason, and that Nicholas was forced into it. Not wanting to cause her more hurt than she was experiencing already Nicky was content to let her believe what she wanted and did not press the issue. Minnie was also upset to learn her son did not know the exact whereabouts of Olga and Maria but, having met Prince Kanin, she was sure if they reached Omsk they would be safe.

"Mother, Tatiana and Anastasia are aboard my train, as is George. The three of them will return with you to Kiev and George will escort my daughters from your palace to Omsk. The girls are prepared to leave on short notice but George will need to purchase some things in Kiev before he can leave. That will free Sandro to work on arrangements for you, Olga and Xenia. Is that satisfactory, mother?"

"I have no intention of leaving Russia," said Minnie. "I will see this through to the end with you and Alix."

"No Mother, it is not possible. Remember the conspiracy I told you about. Your life would be in grave danger."

"I am an old woman, Nicholas. It matters not to me if I lose my life especially if I share martyrdom with my son."

"Mother, I appreciate your willingness to make such a sacrifice but it is not necessary or required. I have already explained that it is important for you to survive this revolution. You will be a symbol of hope to the Russian people during their times of trial. I beg you to please do as I ask and spare me any further worry." Minnie, when confronted with Nicholas' impassioned words, could only nod her head in agreement. "I will do as you ask, but it will break my heart to leave Russia. I wish there was another way."

"So do I mother," he said gently, "so do I."

"When do you want to bring my granddaughters aboard?"

"Tomorrow night. That will allow you enough time to make preparations. They are traveling in uniform as George's orderlies but they still should remain hidden their hair has been cut and I doubt you will recognize them. I certainly was fooled when I first saw them."

"Oh my dearest son, how difficult this all must be for you. I will do everything you have asked but I have one request of my own. I wish to remain here until you depart. This may be the last time we see each other," she said with a sob in her voice.

"Mother," said Nicholas enfolding her in a hug, "of course you may remain."

The 17th and 18th of March were busy days for Nicholas but he tried to spend as much time as possible with Minnie between his meetings. The troops at the Stavka were assembled so he could address them and say his good-byes. His aides established a schedule and he met personally with the military attachés from the various foreign missions as well as all his generals. Then rumors began to filter in that he might be placed under arrest and there was talk among his officers of resisting. Nicholas was afraid that any armed confrontation would endanger the girls so as soon as it became late enough on the 18th, George, accompanied by his two orderlies slipped across the short distance between tracks and boarded Minnie's train. Nicholas had decided that tomorrow, after he completed his good-byes, he would start for Tsarskoe Selo and attempt to rejoin his wife. It was a risky proposition but there was really no other option. After he went to bed for the night it took him quite a while to fall asleep. It was difficult to face the reality that the plan they had worked on for so many years seemed to be in difficulty. Yet he knew he could not succumb to the fatalism that threatened to overwhelm him. No, he must focus instead on overcoming the obstacles and making his plan succeed.

CREO

The seemingly endless journey was nearly over and the four nuns, who had been together for days, went over their final arrangements one last time. Omsk was on the horizon and before long they would disembark and see if the preparations made by the Tsar many years ago were still in place. If they were not, Olga and Maria had no idea what would become of them. Sister Irene had urged a cautious approach. "Sisters, if we hire transportation at the terminal and drive straight to the mission I can almost guarantee that within an hour the whole town will be gossiping about the two nuns who went to the trading post. Better if we go to my parent's house first and circulate the story we agreed on. You are two Polish nuns who Catherine and I met in Moscow, and shared a compartment with on the journey to Omsk. You have been granted permission to travel to Japan to work in a convent orphanage which your order maintains in Yokohama. To ensure your safety the Japanese will escort you the rest of the way, but not until you have rested for a day or two. It might be wise to suggest that there could be another group coming later, just in case your father decides to send Tatiana and Anastasia by another route. After we have visited with my parents and had some lunch I will ask my father to walk into town and hire a car. He will come back, pick you up, and accompany you to the trade mission, then return home. At that point you are on your own. Of course, Catherine and I will be here for a week but I am not sure what we could do if you are not received as expected. But I think all will be well and hopefully we will be able to see you off at the station when you leave for Japan. Have I forgotten anything?"

"No, Sister Irene, you have been very thorough," Olga replied. Although the Grand Duchesses were both nervous there was a sense of satisfaction that they had successfully completed the second stage of their journey.

Later that afternoon a car drove up to the gates of the Japanese trade mission and as it did the two passengers in the rear noticed that the compound still looked much like a monastery. There was a large stone wall surrounding the buildings with only one entrance which was guarded by two young men in uniform. When the car came to a stop the Grand Duchesses stepped out and the driver removed their bags from the boot. They said good-bye to Sister Irene's father and paid the driver who then, at Olga's insistence drove off, leaving the two nuns standing alone at the entry way. She had deliberately burned their bridges behind them and now there was no turning back. As the two nuns approached the gate the faces of the sentries remained impassive but when the taller nun addressed them in Japanese, they could not hide their surprise.

"I have been directed to speak only to your Commandant. Would you notify him we are here? Olga had rehearsed the line over and over and she evidently had it right for one of the guards turned and went into the compound. He returned a few moments later and, when it became evident that Olga had exhausted her conversational Japanese, signaled the two nuns to follow him. They were led into the walled area and then to what obviously was the old chapel. It had been converted into the commandant's office but some of the old frescoes still remained on the walls and ceiling. The girls were led to a large desk and the guard motioned for them to sit down. He then turned and departed, leaving them alone with the imposing figure seated at the desk. He stood up and greeted them in Russian. "Over the years a number of officers have commanded this post, always with the expectation that one day you might arrive. It seems that the privilege of welcoming you has been placed by fate in my unworthy hands. It is an honor to have you here," said the man. "My name is Colonel Akahito Fukumitsu. Prince Kanin alerted us that you might be coming when he passed through here on his way back to Japan."

"Sir, I do not wish to appear rude, but do you know who we are?" Olga asked in a trembling voice.

The Colonel smiled at them before answering. "I could make an educated guess as to who you are but I do not intend to speculate. Prince Kanin has given me orders and they do not require that I know your identity. I have been directed to deliver you safely to the Japanese consulate in Vladivostok where passage to Japan will be arranged. A trusted officer and a full squad of armed Imperial marines will be your escort and they are pledged to give their own lives in defense of yours, if necessary. You can leave whenever you are ready, but I recommend you rest here for a few days. We have an agreement with the railroad and one of the personal cars that are maintained here will be coupled on for you and my men. In the meantime I have arranged quarters for you that contain a private hot bath which I am sure you will enjoy. Laundry facilities are also available next to your rooms and I assume you will want to take care of your own things."

"Sir, this is most generous of you but we do not want to labor under false pretenses. We are not the ones you were expecting."

"I am not sure I understand," replied the Colonel.

"The two of us were supposed to leave Moscow and proceed to Warsaw but the situation made that impossible. Knowing that Prince Kanin had offered to take a number of us to Japan I elected to come to Omsk and request your assistance. Two more nuns may arrive later. Will this change things or cause you great inconvenience?"

"I think not. Prince Kanin made it clear to me that Japan was paying a debt of honor, so if I assist you how can I be wrong? Now we must maintain the fiction that you are nuns so what shall I tell my officers and men?"

"I am Sister Minka Sawicka," Olga explained. "My companion is Sister Zyta Kowalska. We are from eastern Poland and have received permission from the Japanese government to work in an orphanage which our order maintains in Yokohama. The two that may be coming later will probably use the same story."

"Very well then, that is how we shall proceed. I will, of course confide in my second in command. In the unlikely event something happens to me he will be able to carry on. Now let me have you shown to your quarters."

"Sir, before we go I have one last request. Would it be possible for you to send a wire to your military attaché at Mogilev and have him inform the Tsar that the two lost crates of medical supplies have turned up in Omsk and that they will be shipped on to Vladivostok in a few days? You might also ask if the whereabouts of the other two crates are known."

"Yes, of course," said the Colonel, "I will see to it immediately, but I must tell you our communications are not totally reliable. We do not always receive a confirmation."

"Then I must ask that we be allowed to stay here until we get some sort of response. It would be difficult to leave here without knowing."

"I completely understand," answered Colonel Fukumitsu. "It shall be as you desire but do not worry too much, we will keep trying until we get through. As for you, with the civil unrest in your country, I think you will be safer traveling first to Japan and then later on to Poland, if you still plan to go there."

"That remains to be seen," Olga replied. "So much depends on events inside Russia."

Maria was amazed at the transformation in her sister. The longer she was on her own the more confident Olga became. But just then the Colonel summoned an aide to escort them to their quarters. As tired as they were, the only thing either of them could think of at that point was a hot bath and a long nap. The rest could wait.

Chapter 44

March 19, 1917 – Mogilev. The morning of the 19th dawned clear and cold. Winter was evidently not quite ready to let go of its grip on the land. Nicholas dressed carefully, in a plain uniform, without insignia or badges of rank. Today, his final day at the Stavka, he intended to assume the character of Citizen Romanov, a role he would play until the end of his life. He had no meetings scheduled and had intended to spend as much time as possible with his mother and daughters but before he could join them Count Tatishchev came in and informed him that the Japanese military observer, General Takeo Nakajima was requesting to see him on a matter of some urgency.

"Well then, bring him in," said Citizen Romanov. The Count did as he was directed and showed the General into the study.

"Your Imperial Highness, thank you for seeing me on such short notice. Let me first express the regret that my staff and I experienced when we learned of your decision to abdicate."

"Good morning, General. I am afraid the title you addressed me by no longer applies but thank you for your kind sentiments."

"Sir, I assure you I will always look upon you as the Emperor of Russia. I know you are very busy so let me get to the purpose of my visit. I received a communiqué early this morning from the Colonel commanding our trade mission in Omsk. When I decoded it I found that it contained a cryptic message which I was asked to deliver to you personally. The General handed the decoded telegram to Nicholas. It read,

> *The two lost crates of medical supplies have turned up in Omsk.*
> *They will be shipped on to Vladivostok in a few days. Do you know the whereabouts of the other two crates ?*

The Tsar looked up with a broad smile on his face. "General this news is most welcome. I had hoped to receive it before I left for Alexander Palace and it seems that God has answered my prayer. Would it be possible for you to get off a reply?"

"Of course, your Highness. What would you like to communicate?"

"A simple line will do." Nicholas took a pad and wrote out a short message.

> *The other two crates are here and will be shipped to Omsk, in two or three days. All else is well*

Nicholas had no intention of worrying Olga with details of the recent events. He was sure she and Maria would learn in time. Perhaps even from their sisters. "General Nakajima, did Prince Kanin make you privy to his involvement with my family ?"

"He told me what I needed to know, so I understand what this is all about."

"Well, then. When Grand Duke Nicholai arrives from the Caucasus I will, of course, be gone. Would you please brief him on the situation as soon as he gets here? I suspect he will not hold the position of Commander in Chief for long. I cannot believe the new government will tolerate a Romanov in a position of power."

"Very well, your Highness. If I may be so bold, what are your personal plans?"

"I will travel to Tsarskoe Selo to rejoin my family and then we will proceed to the Crimea where I hope to become a gentleman farmer. General, I must go now but let me tell you how grateful I am for all you have done for us."

"It has been an honor to know you sir." General Nakajima bid him farewell and left the study. Nicholas tidied up his desk and burned any revealing or compromising papers that were lying about. Once his work was completed he joined Minnie, George, Sandro and the girls in the Empress' train where he gave them the electrifying news about Olga and Maria. They visited for a while but much too soon it was time to say farewell. The parting from his mother was more difficult than Nicholas had anticipated He would miss her frankness. She was the one person in this world that he could trust to always tell him the truth and to speak her mind. It was a quality he admired and would miss. Although they hoped to meet in the Crimea in a few weeks somehow they all sensed that this could well be the last time they saw each other.

೦೪೮

Later that day Colonel Fukumitsu called Olga and Maria into his office and informed them that their message had been received. The two girls were very relieved to hear that their whereabouts were now known by their father and they were elated to learn that the other two girls were coming, though via a different route.

"This must mean we are all to go on to Japan," Olga observed.

"I agree," the Colonel replied. "When I first read the wire I thought it might be well to wait for the others and have you go on together but on further consideration I decided it would be safer if you left as soon as you are rested. We can not be sure when the others will arrive and your continued presence here could arouse suspicion. I suggest you leave on the east bound train the day after tomorrow."

"Very well," replied Olga, "we will follow your advice. You are most kind."

"An honor, I assure you," the Colonel replied.

ᏣᏍᏝᎧ

There had been no word from Nicky in several days and Alix felt that she was living in a vacuum. Although events all around her were racing to a dramatic conclusion, at Alexander Palace it seemed as if time had stopped, and the days passed with excruciating slowness. If not for the time consuming charade of caring for her "sick children," which occupied most of her waking moments, the uncertainty of not knowing what had become of her husband might have overwhelmed her. But just when she thought she would lose her mind from worry, Count Benckendorff, who had refused to report unconfirmed rumors, came up with some solid information. He hurried to the sick rooms of the impostors where he knew he would find the Empress in one of them, sitting in a chair, and reading to the girls. "Your Imperial Highness," said Benckendorff, "I must speak with you at once. It is very urgent."

Alix could see from the look on the Count's face that he had information of importance so she excused herself and the two walked into the Grand Duchesses drawing room and sat down. "What is it?" inquired Alexandra.

"First of all I must tell you," said the Count, "that the rumors that have been circulating around the palace have been confirmed. The Tsar has abdicated. I am so sorry that I have to be the one to bring the news, your Imperial Highness."

"Better you than anyone else, my dear friend," said Alix. "But are you quite certain?"

"I am afraid so. It is now in all the newspapers and copies of the manifesto have been printed as flyers and are being circulated throughout the capital."

"If only I had been with him, maybe things would have gone differently."

"If I may say so, your Imperial Highness," said Benckendorff. "he must have thought it through long and hard before he came to the decision. It could not have been made lightly."

"Nonsense," said Alix. "You and I both know that he was pressured into this by those deceitful generals. But what is done, is done and there is no turning back. Anyway I cannot think about it now, it will drive me mad. Is there anything else? If not, I must get back to my sick children."

"Your Imperial Highness," said the Count with great care. "I beg you to leave immediately for the Crimea as your husband has asked you to do on numerous occasions."

"No," she replied, "that is out of the question. I will wait for the Tsar."

"This is your last opportunity," said the ever faithful Count. "They are coming to arrest you in three days."

"I was told they were coming for me before but it was just a band of drunks whom my guards handled with ease," said the Empress.

"This time is different, your Majesty," said the Count. "It is the new government which is sending a contingent to put you under arrest. What if they want to take you and the children away and incarcerate you in Peter and Paul Fortress?" he asked.

"We will be sure that if they actually come to arrest me, all my children will appear to be at death's door and, of course, the Tsarevich will have to be put in a sick bed immediately," she said. "Oh, I pray that Nicholas returns soon, then we can all go together. At any rate start preparations for the journey and we will leave as soon as he returns."

Count Benckendorff nodded his assent and bowed before departing to begin the packing, but he knew in his heart that they had waited too long. Alix sat quietly in the empty room before resuming her routine. She was devastated by the news but for once reacted stoically, an approach to bad news that she rarely displayed. She recognized, however, that it was up to her to hold things together until Nicholas returned and she could not allow herself to slip into melancholy.

The next few days were difficult and with her future, and that of her family growing more and more uncertain, the servants became nervous as well. Each day many of the palace employees, especially the younger ones, drifted away, unwilling to be associated with the disgraced monarchs and fearful for their lives. Alix immersed herself in caring for the impostors and she tried to imagine that it was actually her own children who were so very ill. It was not too difficult a task for she had become quite fond of the girls and it was easy for Alix to treat them as her own. Her ministrations kept her from thinking too much about her real daughters and where they might be. She treated their imaginary illnesses as if they were genuine and spent hours each day by their bedsides reading aloud to help relieve the boredom they must be feeling. No one except members of the *Masquerade* were allowed anywhere near them and Isa, Madeleine Zanotti and Toodles were able to maintain the fiction that there was a measles epidemic rampant in the royal wing of the palace.

Three days later, as Count Benckendorff had predicted, General Lavr Kornilov arrived at Alexander Palace and in the name of the provisional government placed the Empress in protective custody. He informed her that the former Tsar would join her the following day and although Alexandra was dismayed by the notion of arrest she at least had the comfort of knowing that for the time being her husband was safe. The household guard was replaced by a special detachment and a new Commander, loyal to the revolution, was installed. Before he could take any action he was approached by Dr. Botkin and informed that all four of the girls and their brother Alexei were suffering from severe cases of the measles and had to remain in quarantine. There was the potential of serious side effects such as heart problems, ear abscesses, and anything else the good doctor could associate with the measles. It was imperative that they remain in bed and not be moved. The guard commander was unconvinced until he was allowed to look into the sick rooms and see for himself the wretched condition of the children. Alix had used theatrical face paint to make dark circles around their eyes and the tell-tale red spots on their faces. Because hair loss was associated with the disease it was common practice to shave heads so the hair could grow back evenly. With their hair gone and the curtains drawn, they all looked quite ill. The ploy evidently convinced those in charge and the temporary house arrest became a more permanent one lasting about five months.

The confinement posed a new dilemma for Alix, however. Since they were evidently not going to the Crimea where they could stage the impostor's deaths, the girls would eventually have to recuperate and once they were up and about, discovery would be a possibility. There were still as many as a hundred servants, retainers, court functionaries, and advisors working in the palace but very few of them had contact with the royal family so Alix was not too worried that discovery would come from that quarter. But recently Anya Vyrubova had begun to recover from her illness and would soon want to see the children. She knew them too well to be fooled, but Alix hoped the bald heads would throw her off. Alix truly wished she could share their secret with Anya since she was such a dear friend but she agreed with Nicky's assessment. Her friend loved to talk and each day had received many visitors to her sickbed. She loved to be the one in the know and was incapable of keeping a secret or protecting a confidence. Whether by accident or design it was possible that she would reveal their plans, and therefore Nicky and Alix were sure she could not be trusted with the secrets of the *Masquerade*.

CQ℘

After Nicholas bid farewell to his mother, Sandro, George, and the girls, he boarded the Imperial train and departed for Tsarskoe Selo. Just before he left, four members of the Duma arrived to accompany him on his final journey north. The men were not heavily armed and received no resistance from the staff but Nicholas clearly understood that his movements were now restricted and he was essentially under arrest. That morning had been an extremely stressful one due to the fact his daughters and two grand Dukes were on the Dowager Empress' train, parked on the siding next to his. He had been unsure as to what the provisional government's attitude toward other members of the Imperial family might be and until he actually departed he had been filled with uncertainty and worry that his mother could be ordered to Petrograd.

That evening as the train rumbled north ex-Tsar Nicholas entered the dining car where he was forced to have his evening meal with his captors. The men sat around the large table laughing and drinking. Nicholas walked up to the table and stood before them. "Ah, Citizen Romanov, do join us," said one of the men casually, inviting the Tsar to his own table. A look of shock mixed with anger came over Nicholas's face and was not lost on the men at the table. This was the first time since he abdicated that someone had addressed him in that way. At the Stavka, although he was no longer Tsar, Nicholas' troops treated him with complete respect and continued to refer to him as "Your Imperial Highness". For the first time the reality of his position was made clear to him and he knew he was in for a difficult time.

"Friend, please sit down and share with us," said one of the others, trying to be civil to Nicholas. The man could see how affected the Tsar was and he actually felt sorry for his former sovereign. Nicholas sat down at the table, food and drink were passed to him, and he served himself. After satisfying his hunger he sat quietly for a long time, not really knowing how to act. He was used to having authority over every living thing in Russia, now he was reduced to asking permission from strangers. The men began to discuss what might become of Nicholas once he was taken back to the palace.

"Might I ask if it will be possible to join my family in the Crimea?" asked Nicholas.

"Your family is not in the Crimea," answered one of the men. "By the time we arrive they will be under arrest at Alexander Palace."

"What do you mean?" asked Nicholas in dismay. "I had sent word for them to go there some time ago."

"Well, Alexandra seems to have a mind of her own and she never left," said the man.

"How dare you speak of the Empress in that manner," said Nicholas.

"You must understand, comrade," answered the man, "that when you abdicated, she lost her title as well."

"Why are they under arrest?" asked Nicholas. "They are innocent of any crime."

"Your children may be, but your wife? Now that is another story," said the man. "She is accused of plotting with Rasputin to destroy Russia."

"That is absurd," cried Nicholas. "Rasputin is dead."

"True, but before he died, it was said that he was governing Russia."

"That is utter nonsense," said Nicholas. "If my wife is guilty of anything, it can only be that she loved Russia too much. As far as Rasputin is concerned, he was an illiterate peasant with no understanding of anything but the bottle." The men laughed at this comment.

"She will remain under arrest until she can be cleared of the charges. You should be concerned about yourself, Nicholas," one of the others chimed in.

"What of my daughters and the Tsarevich," asked Nicholas. "Certainly they could be sent to the Crimea."

"For now they will all remain under arrest at the palace and you will join them there," said one of his captors. "Now why don't you return to your sleeping car, you look rather tired." Not wanting to spend any more time then was necessary with his wardens, Nicholas returned to his compartment. He was exhausted and when he stretched out on his bunk, fully clothed, he immediately fell fast asleep. The next thing he knew, it was morning. Nicholas got up, removed his rumpled clothing, and donned a fresh uniform. He took his time as he was in no hurry to join his four guards.

It would be several days before the Tsar finally arrived in Tsarskoe Selo and during that period his thoughts were constantly on Alix and the imposters. A number of unanswered questions plagued him. Why had Alix remained at Alexander Palace? What must have happened to cause her to disregard his request that she leave? He wondered what effect her decision would have on the *Masquerade*. It saddened him to think that the refusal of Alix to leave for the Crimea had now placed the impostors in potential danger and he knew he must find a solution to this dilemma. Thank God his daughters appeared to be safe and on their way out of the country. George, he was certain, had started for Omsk with Tatiana and Anastasia by now and although Nicky had never planned for all four girls to live in Japan he was sure Prince Kanin would make allowances for the changing situation and respond accordingly. But because he had no way to communicate with the Prince, the fate of the four girls was in the hands of the Japanese.

His thoughts returned to the doubles. There must be some way he could free them from their captivity at Alexander Palace. The provisional government, which was in reality a committee composed of members of the Duma, was not riddled with radical revolutionaries. Alexander Kerensky, who had emerged as a principal voice for the new government, seemed to be reasonable if not sympathetic. Nicholas had met him once before and was sure he could convince him to free the "Grand Duchesses" and allow them to join his mother in the Crimea. He knew his new daughters were prepared to sacrifice their lives for their country but he was not yet prepared for them to do so, not if he could prevent it. The thought never entered his mind that their lives might be in danger, only that they might face some sort of imprisonment, although for what reason he could not imagine. The sketchy plans he had considered for their faked demise, in the Crimea, would never see fruition and with so much on his mind he was incapable of generating even a glimmer of a solution. He would just have to wait and see what the situation was when he arrived at Tsarskoe Selo. It might turn out that they were to be exiled but unfortunately that possibility did not adhere to St. Serafim's prophecy. Quite simply, they were all in God's hands. It was all very troubling, but fortunately Valia had been allowed to accompany the Tsar so he was not totally alone and had someone to discuss the situation with.

The rail trip from Mogilev took much longer than usual and Nicholas did not arrive at Tsarskoe Selo until the day after Alix was arrested. When the train finally reached Alexandrovsky station it was shunted onto the siding reserved for the Imperial train. The provisional government had previously made arrangements for a large touring car to transport the six men to Alexander Palace. When the Tsar disembarked, with Valia and the members of the Duma, he could immediately sense a change in the atmosphere of the town. Usually his arrival was a festive occasion, with the guard turned out and the band playing, but now it was a somber event made more so by the sullen looks on the faces of the curious onlookers. This change became even more apparent when the unmarked car pulled up to the gate of the park and was stopped by a sentry, who sat at his place of duty, half asleep and was obviously not a member of the crack Imperial Guard who normally walked this post. He got to his feet, stretched, and strolled over to the Tsar's car.

"Who goes there?" demanded the guard.

"It is Nicholas Romanov, Vasilly Dolgoruky and four members of the Duma," the driver responded in an insolent manner.

"Very well then, drive on," ordered the sentry. Nicholas sat in the back of the car, mortified at the disrespect shown him, and for just an instant, was very angry. But he caught himself before commenting on the situation, because it came to him that this was just the beginning of a long series of humiliations he would have to endure. He vowed to suffer any future embarrassment with studied indifference and he had no intention of letting his captors gain any satisfaction at seeing him react to their rudeness. The driver pulled through the gate and drove to the Imperial entrance to the palace. When the automobile came to a stop, Nicholas was ordered to exit the car and instructed to go directly into the private family quarters. He would be allowed to move freely throughout that wing of the palace only. The car drove on and the driver deposited Valia at the entrance to the service wing of the palace.

"What is expected of me?" he asked the members of the Duma as he stepped out. One of them answered, "you are on your own as far as we are concerned. Just stay out of trouble."

Desperate to see Alix, Nicholas had not delayed but hurried up the steps and through the doors opening into the vestibule of the Imperial apartments. He was appalled at what he saw for the once immaculate antechamber was filthy and was filled with foul mouthed soldiers slouching on the priceless furniture. They all looked up at him when he entered and Nicholas could hear disparaging remarks as he passed through. Some deliberately impeded his progress but although he was no longer Tsar of Russia, he maintained his dignity. He saluted the soldiers as he walked towards the double doors leading into his private quarters but sadly his salutes were not returned.

The doors into the Imperial family's quarters were opened by a pair of slovenly guards and Nicholas walked through the doorway into the corridor which led to the Tsar's private rooms. The doors slammed behind him and as he looked around, he could see that the hallway was bare and quiet and he felt utterly alone. It had been close to a week since he had left General Headquarters for the last time. No court members, no servants, not even his wife was aware that he had returned home. He started for his bedchamber, but stopped when he saw a lone figure hurrying down the long hall towards him and heard the familiar voice of Count Benckendorff. Nicholas remained silent as the elderly man approached. "Your Imperial Highness, we have all been ill with worry as to your whereabouts. I was just informed of your return," said the Count. "The Empress will be overjoyed to see you."

"Count Benckendorff," said Nicholas, "I gave specific orders for you to pack up the household and have everyone leave for the Crimea. Why did you disregard my orders?" he asked reproachfully.

"Your Highness, you must know that I did my best to carry out your wishes and insisted on a number of occasions that the Empress leave," answered the Count, "but she refused all my entreaties. Her Highness said she could not depart as long as the whereabouts of the girls were uncertain. She preferred to wait for you."

"She should have left," said the Tsar.

"I did my best to persuade her, but to no avail, and by the time she finally agreed, it was too late."

"I understand, dear friend. Do not think me ungrateful for all you have done. I know how obstinate she can be, so think no more of it. If it comes up when I speak to her we will put the issue to rest. What is done, is done. Now, did the palace receive word of the . . . ," Nicholas swallowed and then continued, "of my abdication?"

"Yes," said the Count with sadness in his voice. An uncomfortable silence ensued as the two men stood looking at each other. Benckendorff could see the exhaustion in the Tsar's face.

Nicholas looked down and shook his head, "I had to do it, I had to do it," he kept repeating.

"Your Imperial Highness, please," said the Count. "You must not reproach yourself. You were acting in the best interests of Russia."

"You need not refer to me any longer as Your Highness," said Nicholas. "I am now Nicholas Romanov."

"You are my sovereign, ordained by God to rule," said Benckendorff. "Because of all that you have done and the sacrifices you have made to save Russia, you have earned the right to be called Tsar."

In spite of himself, tears filled the Tsar's eyes. "You have been a loyal and trusted friend, Count Benckendorff," said Nicholas. "I do not know what we could have accomplished without you. I thank you from the bottom of my heart. But now I must see my wife and inform her of what has taken place. Would you have her join me in the Maple room?" asked Nicholas. "I wish to speak to her alone, but later I would like you to join us to discuss some other concerns."

"I do not know if you are aware of it," said the Count, "but the guards are supposedly for your protection. The reality is that the Imperial family is under arrest here at the palace. Fortunately, most of the staff is allowed to come and go as usual, but I do not know how long that will last."

"Yes, I was aware of my family situation. The news that we have some communication with the outside, however, is most welcome," said Nicholas. "Now if you would, please go and ask the Empress to join me." When Count Benckendorff left to find Alix, Nicholas walked wearily to his private quarters to freshen up and then went to the Maple room. He did not know what he would say to his beloved wife. He supposed that everyone would expect him to be humiliated at the disgrace his abdication brought on the family. After all, with the stroke of a pen he had ended three hundred years of Romanov rule and certainly that was reason enough to be ashamed. Yet despite all that had befallen him in the past week, it seemed that the only thing that truly mattered was the *Masquerade*. He needed but a few more weeks to ensure that his daughters were safe from the *great evil that would seek to destroy them*. This concern alone far outweighed any other considerations but still he wondered how Alix would react. Nicholas did not have to wait very long for an answer for the door flew open and Alix rushed into the room and into the arms of her husband. All the pent-up stress and emotion of the past several weeks sought an outlet and they both began to weep. Nicholas took his wife's face in his hands. "Sunny, why did you not leave when I asked you to? Did you not realize that you might have sealed the fate of the imposters?"

"Nicky, my heart was torn," said Alexandra. "I just could not leave my real daughters in jeopardy here at the palace and walk away. I was waiting for your return so that we could all travel together. I never anticipated what has come to pass and I still do not know where the girls are."

"Sunny, my dearest, let us speak no more of this. You did what you thought best and I can now relieve you of some of your anguish. All of the girls are safe and within a few more weeks will be out of the country. Before I left Mogilev the Japanese military attaché informed me that Olga and Maria had arrived safely in Omsk and would be escorted on to Japan. When Prince Kanin decides it is safe, they will travel to Poland as originally planned."

"Oh, thank God for His mercy," Alix exclaimed! "Please tell me everything, Nicky."

"Sunny, as we speak, George is accompanying Tatiana and Anastasia to Omsk by a different route. After they arrive there they too will travel on to Japan and George will probably return to Gatchina. I am confident that somehow Prince Kanin will get word to us when they arrive." Nicholas proceeded to tell Alix of the meeting at Mogilev with George, Sandro, and his mother. He then told her the complete story of the events surrounding his abdication and to his surprise she did not react negatively when he talked about it. Alix was so relieved that her daughters would soon be safely out of the country, that nothing else seemed to matter.

"Now, Sunny, it is your turn. Answer me truthfully. Is the *Masquerade* working?"

"Beyond our most hopeful expectations," Alix answered. "Dr. Botkin has engineered a measles epidemic and your son and four daughters have all been infected. They are, of course, quarantined and I am convinced that is why we are being left alone in this wing of the palace. As heartless as they are, I was sure they would not take me away from my sick children," she explained. "When a man, describing himself as the commandant of the palace, came to apprehend me, we took him in to see the children. They put on such a remarkable performance that he agreed to leave me under arrest here at the palace."

"How is Alexei," asked Nicholas.

"He is quite well since he spends the day in bed. Doctor Botkin has obtained ample supplies of herbs and such to make his special tea in the event he has a real episode. They will all have to recover eventually and when they do, we will enter the most dangerous period. If the girls can get through the first week without being discovered, I think we will be all right. The main problem is Anya. When she is fully recovered I do not see any way we can keep her from visiting the girls. And if we do let her come over she knows the girls too well to be fooled by shaven heads and some make-up. I am sure she would pledge her silence but she is such a gossip I am afraid to chance it."

"How much time do we have?" Nicky asked.

"A few days at most."

"Well, let me sleep on it. But in the end we may, through necessity, have to confide in her."

Just then they heard a knock at the door. "That must be Count Benckendorff. I asked him to join us for a moment," Nicky explained. At the Tsar's invitation the Count came into the room, followed by Valia who, upon entering the palace, had gone in search of his step-father.

"I am glad you came Valia. I wanted to talk to you and the Count about the impostors. As you know, the plan to get all of us to the Crimea has fallen through." As the Tsar continued no one noticed the pained expression that came over Alix's face; they were too intent on what the

Tsar had to say. "It is imperative that the doubles remain in place for the time being and I pray they will be convincing. What I ask from you is that in the coming weeks you consider every possibility and share with me every probable scenario that will provide safety for the girls. If we are exiled it will not be a problem, but if we are forced to remain in the country who knows what may develop. I am literally drained of ideas so I hope you will apply your considerable intellects to the problem and come up with a plan we can use. And now, gentlemen, if you will excuse us, I have not seen my wife in some time, and we have much to discuss. I must also see how my daughters are doing," he said with a smile. "Good night to you, my dear friends."

The problem of Anya was solved a few days later when Kerensky himself, accompanied by members of the Duma, arrived to place Anya under arrest. She was to be interrogated as to her relationship with one Grigory Rasputin. Anya was terrified and refused to leave her bed, insisting she was too ill to be moved, even though this very morning she had announced she was ready to see the dear children and help with their nursing.

Finally Kerensky asked Nicholas to have Dr. Botkin examine Anya and see if she was fit to leave. Nicholas was able to speak to the doctor privately and asked him to give Anya a clean bill of health. It was a devious way to handle the problem, but Kerensky had assured the Tsar that Anya would not be mistreated and would be released once the investigation was completed. After the examination she was cleared to depart and Alix joined her to help gather her things. There were tears when she was escorted out of the palace, a simple woman whose only crime was her friendship with the Imperial family. Anya was eventually released and worked behind the scenes to free the family but she was never allowed to rejoin her friends. As always the *Masquerade* had priority.

The next few weeks passed slowly for Nicholas but he gradually adjusted to the routine of his captivity. He spent as much time as possible outside, in strenuous exercise, initially building snow towers and shoveling snow. As the weather warmed he helped plan a large kitchen garden and as his girls gradually came out of the sick rooms, they joined him working in the garden. Their hair was still very short and they wore hats and scarves but their resemblance to the real Grand Duchesses had completely duped everyone who was not involved in the plan. The guards had forbidden conversation in any other language but Russian but this did not pose a problem as the three oldest girls were Russian and Franny had become so fluent that her slight Polish accent was no longer distinguishable.

During this time of captivity they still lived a comfortable life, a life which they recorded faithfully with their cameras. They photographed every activity and ensured that their faces appeared in most of the shots.

Once they were developed, these prints, along with the ones they had taken months earlier, were mixed in with photographs of the real Grand Duchesses. In the evening Alix supervised the girls as they put together the photo albums that documented their existence. She gave them suggestions as to what her daughters would have done and thus artwork and dried flowers were added to their pages As the girls worked, they all thought, but never voiced, the question they most wanted to be answered. Would anyone in the future look at these albums closely enough to see their faces there?

CREO

As the train turned south from Komsomolsk and began the final leg of the long passage to Vladivostok, Olga and Maria were finally able to relax a little. Although the officer in charge of the detail of marines had been a perfect gentleman and solicitous of their comfort, nevertheless the journey had been very trying. There were, of course, the obvious cultural differences, the contrast between the nun's habit and the uniforms of their escorts, for instance. Then there was the unusual food which was prepared for them each day by one of the detachment. Maria hoped she might never see a bowl of rice and fish again though she knew that was wistful thinking. But there was something else and the two sisters discussed it when they were alone. It was not just the suspicion of the marines, for when it was a question of duty their faces always showed an impassive determination. No, there was more to it than that. Olga thought it was a general disdain for women and for foreign women in particular. And yet on one occasion when the train made a scheduled stop, a mob, desperate for transportation, tried to board their car. The escort had fixed bayonets and almost eagerly interposed themselves between the girls and the ruffians who backed down quickly when they saw the opposition. It was a strange land they were going to and perhaps, they agreed, it was better that they were going to a convent for awhile.

When the train arrived at Vladivostok the girls were introduced to the teeming, strategic and vitally important terminus of the Trans Siberian Railway. There was so much activity in the city that two nuns escorted by a squad of marines hardly raised an eyebrow but when they arrived at the Japanese consulate they still heaved a sigh of relief. They were able to thank their escort in Japanese, for there had been daily lessons on the way over. The Consul then welcomed the two young women to the consulate and informed them they would be leaving for Japan in two days and would be his guests until they departed.

Four days later their ship arrived in Yokohama where they were met on the pier by a beaming Prince Kanin. All their apprehension dissipated when they received his warm greeting. For Olga and Maria the long journey was over.

CREO

George reached Omsk with Tatiana and Anastasia about the same time their sisters were arriving in Yokohama. The journey from Kiev to Magnitogorsk and then onward had involved a number of changes since there was no direct line. George was traveling in civilian clothes but he still worried that during one of the many transfers someone might recognize the distinctive features of the Romanov family. So before leaving Kiev he made the ultimate sacrifice and shaved off his beard. The change was dramatic but even so he decided that when they reached their destination he would remain at the station and send the girls on to the trade mission by means of a hired conveyance.

This time, when two nuns arrived at the entrance to the old monastery, the guards acted as if they were expected and immediately ushered them into Colonel Fukumitsu's office. The Commandant greeted them warmly and asked if their trip had been uneventful. "Sir," Tatiana replied, "we were, of course, somewhat apprehensive during the journey but except for unexpected delays there were no problems."

"I had thought you might have an escort for the first part of your journey," the Colonel observed. "The other two nuns who arrived here earlier appeared to have traveling companions."

"A friend did accompany us and is waiting at the station for news of our safe arrival here at the mission. His name is George Konstantine and he is traveling as a businessman. Would it be possible to send a message to him that all is well? He intends to start the return journey as soon as possible."

"Of course. I will see to it immediately," replied the Colonel. "And I expect you would like to know that the other nuns who came through Omsk earlier should be arriving at their final destination just about now."

"Oh sir," Anastasia cried out, "that is indeed wonderful news. Would it be correct to ask what arrangements have been made for us?"

"Certainly, my child," replied the Commandant who proceeded to tell them what they might expect.

Two days later Tatiana and Anastasia were on a train bound for Vladivostok, accompanied by a detachment of Imperial marines. Their passage would mirror that of their sisters in nearly every aspect except one. When the journey finally ended there would be a joyous, if only temporary, reunion of the Grand Duchesses at a Catholic convent in, of all places, the teeming city of Yokohama, Japan.

Nicholas and Alexandra were justifiably worried about the odyssey their daughters had embarked upon but they had absolutely no control of the situation. They could only pray that God would keep the girls safe and that somehow they would learn that their efforts to spirit the children to safety had succeeded. Their prayers were answered several weeks later when Count Benckendorff informed them that he had been contacted by the Japanese Embassy. "Your Highnesses, I have wonderful news. All four of the Grand Duchesses have arrived in Japan and are in the care of

Prince Kanin." Despite her best efforts Alix broke down and began to weep and when the Count withdrew he left the two relieved parents enveloped in each other's arms. They did not know at the time that this was the last word they would have of their beloved daughters.

Chapter 45

August 1917 – Tobolsk. In the middle of August, Alexander Kerensky directed that the Imperial family be relocated, "for their safety and protection," to the town of Tobolsk on the eastern slopes of the Urals. After a long and arduous trip by train and boat, they arrived in the town and learned that the governor's house would serve as their new place of confinement. Across the street from the mansion, another home was requisitioned to house the retainers and friends who had voluntarily accepted the fate of their sovereign. Initially few restrictions were placed on their activities but nevertheless the long months of captivity were beginning to take their toll and even the change of scenery did not lessen the boredom.

One summer morning, shortly after the move to Tobolsk, the Tsar stood alone, staring pensively out the window of his bedroom. Alix was still asleep and Nicky used the uninterrupted quiet to consider the events that had brought them on the long journey to this exile in Siberia. Some incidents had occurred as predicted but he was bewildered that others had never come to pass. For instance, years ago he had been promised an unmistakable sign that would indicate to him the fate of his beloved Russia. It seemed like yesterday that Sergei and Ella, dining with him at the Winter Ball, had relayed a cryptic message from the Pope. Now, despite the thirteen years that had intervened since that lovely affair, he remembered with clarity the words of the Holy Father. *"When the sun falls from the sky you will know the fate of Russia."* What could that puzzling sentence possibly mean? Surely, after so many years he should have received some revelation that would indicate the timing, if not the meaning of it all. Nicholas was a man of faith but he was subject to doubts, just like everyone else, and he desperately needed this sign to energize his belief in what he was doing and what he had already done. He knew that the sign, whatever it might be, would have special meaning for him, but it could only happen in God's time and according to St. Serafim's letter, time was running out.

He thought back to the vivid nightmare he had so long ago, the dream in which his finger had been severed, and how the sign promised in that dream had occurred just a few months later. Nicky began to toy with the possibility that the failure to cut off his finger, as bizarre as it seemed, was somehow connected to the unfulfilled prophecy. Perhaps he needed to first carry on with the amputation in order to place events in their proper sequence and thus provide the atmosphere for the promised sign. When the tissue samples were removed from his toe for preservation by Dr. Botkin, it had not turned out to be a major ordeal and perhaps this could be done in such a way as to avoid causing too much distress. Nicholas realized, as he stood there staring into space, that he had come to the decision, after all these years, to go ahead and do it. Of course, it must be accomplished without any publicity and in such a manner that it appeared to be an accident.

Unaccountably, the Tsar began to tremble and he was overcome by a sense of impending doom. Nicholas had convinced himself that once he removed his finger the next step would be his martyrdom. He had no way of knowing that he still had much to suffer and that the time for his ultimate sacrifice was not yet at hand. But in this trance-like state his mind began to wander and he tried to envision how he might be put to death. Beads of perspiration began to trickle down his face and he shuddered at the thought of some grotesque end to his relatively short life. As his body shook, he felt his knees give way and he fell to the floor. "Oh, God," he prayed aloud, "I am afraid, so afraid. Please protect my family from the fate that awaits me and do not allow those entrusted to my care to suffer for my mistakes. Give me strength, Lord, for only you really know what I am going through."

Alix awoke at that moment and was shocked to find her precious Nicky in such a terrible state. Never before had she seen him like this and it alarmed her. She made her way over to him as quickly as her worn body would allow, took him in her arms, and embraced him. "Oh Nicky, darling, my heart breaks to see you like this," said Alix as she tried to calm him. "What is it that has you so troubled?"

The Tsar, realizing her concern, regained his composure and stood up. He removed a handkerchief from his pocket, wiped his face, and then straightened his clothes. As he helped his wife to her feet he noticed tears welling up in her eyes. He gently wiped them away and led her to a chair. "I am so sorry to distress you but I have just had an unusual experience." He explained what had happened and the decision he had come to. "I am convinced that my fate is finally decided," he told her.

Alix looked puzzled. "What do you mean Nicky?"

"I must drink from the cup," he said.

"I do not understand. What cup? I see no cup here," she said.

"It is not an earthly cup, but a spiritual one prepared by God for martyrs."

"But Nicky, I have to tell you that there is talk of a group of loyal soldiers who are planning to help us escape," said Alix. "Are you telling me that no matter what happens you will not leave Russia?"

"What are you asking Sunny? You know very well that it has always been my intention, from the very beginning, to remain in the country. When we first discussed this years ago you insisted you would remain at my side and share my fate and it was understood to mean in Russia. Then Dalek was killed and Alexei came forward to stand with us. I cannot predict what will happen to you and our son or our new set of daughters but I am convinced my future is tied inextricably to the Motherland. How else could St. Serafim's prophecy be fulfilled? No, the only way I would leave Russia is if I were taken out against my will or somehow, without my knowledge," said Nicholas. "I will take no part in planning an escape, but there is no reason for you and the children to forgo an opportunity to flee. All I can do is ask God to give me the courage and strength to carry this heavy cross."

"But you have carried this cross for Russia since the day you became Tsar."

"Yes, but people have always spoken badly about me and said I was not fit to be the Tsar. They believe I led Russia into ruin willfully, without any concern for the future," he said, with sorrow in his voice. "They blamed me for the loss of the war with Japan, they chastised me for my supposed involvement with Grigory Rasputin, and they believed I stood by and deliberately let the nation slide into chaos. They could not imagine the pain I felt when those innocent people were killed at the coronation or shot down on that bloody Sunday years ago. They believed that I was indifferent to the suffering and blamed me for every injustice that occurred during my reign. And rightly so because who else should bear the responsibility for such tragedies, if not I."

The Tsar paused and stared off in the distance. "You know Alix, not much has changed in my lifetime. The soil is rich and food plentiful but my people are starving and they believe their Tsar has abandoned them. What good is this bounty if our antiquated transportation system cannot deliver it to the population centers? I should have done more. I took our great wealth for granted and had I been more observant much could have been accomplished. I think that one day, be it a decade from now or a century, the world will learn about all that has transpired here," said Nicholas. "People will have read all the things written about us, and then make new judgments. I hope they realize that I did not seek sympathy, for I do not deserve it. And yet I have the hope that history will not judge me too harshly as an individual, for I have loved this great country and its people without reservation. I believe a new and better Russia will emerge as a result of the *Masquerade*. And that, Alix, is why I am ready to 'drink from the cup,' and the best gift you can give me at his point, is your understanding."

"You shall have it, my dearest. But let us not forget our daughter's role in all of this," reminded Alix. "The future evidently depends upon one of them and she must be open to the will of God, as you have been."

"I believe that through my sacrifice…"

"Our sacrifice," interrupted Alix. "I would never leave you, for without your comforting presence there could be no life for me. My place is by your side and if you are to drink from the martyr's cup then so will I.

"Oh, my precious Sunny, you have always been by my side, through the calm, and the storm," he said. "I never thought for a moment that you would abandon me. My faith tells me our sacrifices will enable the chosen daughter to carry out her destiny. I have been thinking further about the sign and I am convinced it will be some sort of announcement that the great and calamitous evil Serafim spoke of is about to occur and Russia is to enter the final stage of her torment. I look at the sun everyday and have noticed nothing but a strong brilliance that burns my eyes and causes me to see black spots. So to complete my part in this I believe I must now sever my finger and have it preserved," said Nicholas.

"Must you do it, Nicky? An open wound can be dangerous and easily become infected. Oh darling, this is all very distressing. It has been years since you first told me of your dream and I had quite forgotten about it."

"You know I must do this, Alix," he answered.

"But how will you accomplish it? We are watched constantly."

"It would be very easy to fake an accident when I am splitting wood. That is one of the few times the guards pay little attention to me. I could have Doctor Botkin bring whatever he needs in his pocket and join Gilliard and me at the wood pile. After I worked for a few minutes he could remove the finger at the chopping block, and then together with Pierre help me into the house where he could retrieve his bag and treat the wound. Botkin would, in effect, have become the faceless man of my dream and by acquiescing to the act I would certainly be satisfying St. Serafim's request to sacrifice my finger. Once the stump is bandaged I will wear a dark sock over my hand to hide it until I can wear some gloves and hopefully, none of the guards will notice. But even if someone does report to the commandant that I have suffered a minor accident, it should not matter because the significance of my wound would never be understood by anyone but you and a few others. I will speak with Botkin tonight when he comes to check on Alexei. I want to get this finger off and preserved as soon as possible," he said.

"What will Botkin do with it then?" questioned Alix.

"He can give it to Doctor Derevenko to safeguard and hold until it can somehow be delivered to Nikolasha. It will, of course, be in a sealed reliquary of some sort."

"But Derevenko knows nothing about the *Masquerade*, does he?

"No, but he can be told enough to take care of the matter," said Nicholas. "I know that he is as trustworthy as Botkin. Many wished to join us when we were brought to Tobolsk but the government limited the number who could accompany us. The men and women who willingly sacrificed their own safety and possibly their lives to come here with us, can be trusted completely. I do not have reservations about any of them, for they have proven their loyalty."

"Yes, I must agree," said Alix.

That evening Nicholas spoke with Doctor Botkin and they devised a plan to remove the finger. Pierre Gilliard, the French tutor joined them and was also included in the planning. He had traveled with the family to Tobolsk to continue the children's lessons and resided in the house across the street. For the most part he sat silently, appalled at what he was hearing, but unwilling to interrupt. The discussion was very clinical and Pierre felt as if he were in a doctor's office discussing the removal of an appendix. He did not really understand what was happening but it was obvious that he was expected to participate. The Tsar had anticipated they would just slice his finger off with an ax but Botkin convinced him that they had to avoid shattering bone and that using an ax was too imprecise. The doctor felt that a scalpel would be the best way to remove the finger; the cut could be made at the joint with great pressure and the skin pulled down and sutured. Nicholas was aware that he could take nothing in advance to ease the pain but afterward, the doctor had sufficient pain-killers to ease Nicholas's discomfort. Because Botkin was allowed to come and go in town and visit the Imperial family as well, he would be able to take the finger to the house across the street, and give it to Doctor Derevenko. The doctor would preserve the finger and ensure that it was delivered to Nikolasha with instructions to prepare appropriate authenticating documents and deliver the whole package to the Russian Orthodox Church. Alix had convinced Nicky that the Church would be elated to have a relic of the last Tsar of Imperial Russia.

Two days later, after all the arrangements were in place, Nicholas went outside into the fenced yard of the compound which the family had virtually unlimited access to. He had directed Alix to remain inside with the younger children as he did not want them involved in what was coming. The three older girls were enlisted to distract the guards at the gate; an easy task since lonely soldiers, far from home, liked nothing more than the chance to talk to a pretty girl. Nicholas had noted the mild flirtation that went on and counted on it to hold the guards interest while events developed at the other end of the yard. Firewood was not needed at this time of the year but the kitchen used its share and splitting wood was an almost daily affair. Nicholas was soon joined by Doctor Botkin and Gilliard who had walked over from the Kornilov house across the street. Together they began sawing and splitting wood with an ax. Previously two saw horses had been set up with a plank of wood placed across them to provide a flat surface. As soon as the Tsar was sure the two sentries were fully occupied he turned his back to them and laid his left hand on the plank, his fingers spread apart. Doctor Botkin stood facing the Tsar and Gilliard stood next to Nicholas to catch him should he faint from shock. Botkin had wrapped gauze around the finger, so that when it was severed, the blood would not splatter everywhere and Nicholas had put a sock on his hand to hide the lightly colored gauze. Although Doctor Botkin had removed more limbs than he cared to recall, this was the last Tsar of Russia and the faithful doctor felt a twinge of nervousness as he prepared to make the cut.

"It is time, gentlemen," said Nicholas gruffly. "Let's get on with it."

"You give the word when you are ready your Highness and Pierre, you must be prepared to catch the Emperor if he falters," said the Doctor.

"Yes, I am ready," said Gilliard. He spoke bravely but he had never experienced anything like this before and he was afraid he might be the one to falter. His knees felt as if they would give way underneath him. He took a deep breath and regained his composure.

"Do it," Nicholas ordered.

Botkin took the razor-sharp scalpel from his pocket and slipped off the protective cover. Nicholas closed his eyes and immediately envisioned Saint Seraphim and the Pope standing next to Botkin with encouraging smiles on their faces. Nicholas felt utter contentment and it seemed as if his heart would burst with joy. It was but a temporary euphoria, however, and ended abruptly when he felt a sudden and excruciating pain in his hand. He opened his eyes to discover blood seeping through the gauze; Botkin quickly took a cord out of his pocket and applied it as a tourniquet. Nicholas left the severed finger in the gauze and put the sock back over his hand to hide everything.

"Come, Pierre, it is finished. Let us get the Tsar into the house so I can get to work on this." Nicholas was very pale but he walked unaided as Gilliard and the Doctor escorted him back into the house.

One of the guards noticed the Tsar going inside and asked, "is your father unwell? He usually stays out longer then this."

"Dr. Botkin thinks it could be the beginning of influenza but my father insisted on coming outside and getting some fresh air. I am sure the good doctor is ordering him to bed," Ekaterina answered.

"It may just be something he ate that disagreed with him," Helena added. "But then again it could be contagious. If you are at this post tomorrow perhaps we could continue our conversation, but now we must go back inside." The girls bid farewell and slowly walked back to the house. They had planted the seed and the Tsar's contrived illness would allow him a few uninterrupted days to fight off the fever and recover from the effects of the loss of his finger. Contagious diseases were killers and not even the Commandant would enter his room. As long as the doctor was in attendance and kept him informed he was content to stay away. After a few days Dr. Botkin reported that it had been a milder form of the flu and the Tsar would soon be back on his feet. Still, some of the guards were suspicious and would not come too close to Nicholas for quite a while. The Tsar wore gloves with cotton pressed into the finger to conceal the missing portion and once it was completely healed it was difficult to see a difference. He doubted anyone would even notice but he still was careful. He had completed his part of the bargain, now the rest was up to the Lord and St. Serafim.

As the short summer days fled and the chill of autumn began to be felt in the air Nicholas became more and more despondent. He had anticipated that by now he would have received the long awaited sign, whatever it might be, but as yet nothing unusual had occurred. But one day in late October, as he prepared to go for a walk, he overheard two guards outside his room discussing an article in a two week old newspaper that one of them had managed to obtain.

"Listen to this nonsense," one of the soldiers observed. "According to his account the reporter traveled to some place called Portugal and said that one day while he was there he witnessed the sun spinning around the sky and it looked like it was falling to the earth."

"They just make up those stories to sell more papers," said the other guard.

The Tsar, who had been listening from his room, was astonished. The sentry seemed to be describing an event much like that promised by the Pope. He had to get that newspaper; even if it meant swallowing his pride and appealing to the guards. A new set of wardens had been put in place recently and they seemed much more insolent and rarely passed up an opportunity to humiliate their former sovereign. Nicholas prepared himself for a confrontation then walked to the doorway and asked," When you are finished with the newspaper, do you mind if I look at it?" Both guards turned him in pretended amazement

"Did you hear that, Romanov wants my paper," said the one.

"Step back into your room," said the other, motioning with his hand. The Tsar did as he was directed and stepped dejectedly back into the room.

"Wait Romanov! I have something for you to read," said the one holding the newspaper. He ripped a page from the paper and handed it to the other guard. "Here, he can read about dancing suns falling from the sky," he said sarcastically. The soldier took the paper, crumpled it into a ball, and threw it at the feet of the Tsar.

Nicholas could not believe his good fortune. The one bit of news he was interested in had literally been placed at his feet. He reached down, picked up the crumpled piece of paper, and walked over to the table. He began smoothing out the wrinkles and when it was clear enough to read he could see that the article was dated October 14, 1917, nearly two weeks earlier. He began to read the reporter's account of a strange series of events which had taken place over the past six months in the remote Portuguese hamlet of Aljustrel, in the parish of Fatima. Apparently three young children from the village claimed that on the 13th of each month, beginning in May, a woman, dressed all in white had appeared to them and appealed for prayers, penance and acts of sacrifice. Having just removed his finger Nicholas could certainly identify with the last of the lady's requests. There was, of course, skepticism, curiosity, and outright ridicule but people of faith were convinced some spiritual episode was occurring. Consequently, the report went on, a crowd numbering nearly 70,000 had gathered on the 13th of October to see what might happen. It was at this juncture that the sun rotated unnaturally for about ten minutes and then seemed to fall towards earth before returning to its normal place in the heavens. What gave the incident credence was that prior to the sun's antics it had been pouring rain and the crowd was soaking wet. But when the sun returned to its usual place everyone was bone dry. So many people attested to the occurrence that Nicholas was convinced it was the sign he had been waiting for and he anticipated before much longer he would learn the fate of Russia.

Just then he heard Alix outside the door. The guards were harassing her, but she kept silent and managed to enter the room without a major confrontation. The sentry slammed the door behind her and she shook her head in frustration. "It gets a little worse each day," she commented to her husband. "Yes," he replied, " but we must not let them see how much it hurts."

"What is it you are reading, Nicky?" she asked.

Nicholas passed the newspaper to her. "I managed to convince one of the guards to let me have it. See for yourself. I believe this is the sign I have been waiting for but I would like to have your opinion.'

Alix read the article and when she had finished she sat quietly, her face pale with emotion. Finally she spoke. "Nicky this must be the sign Ella told you of so long ago. Even though the article has nothing to say about Russia I think we must read between the lines. This is not a mere coincidence."

"What do you mean? You have me totally confused."

"Nicky, it is my mother trying to signal us from above."

"I still do not understand," he replied

"This parish where this took place is called Fatima," she said. "Few people know that my mother's nickname as a child was Fatima. What are the chances of such a twist of fate? This makes the connection to Russia obvious as far as I am concerned"

"I see, but still, what about the fate of Russia?"

"Nicky we have had to wait before, just be patient. The new year is upon us and it is our final year. Soon things will begin to happen at a pace we could never have envisioned. You will have your answer in good time. We must just be patient and have faith."

Nine days later, when Leon Trotsky engineered the takeover of the government and Russia fell into the hands of the Bolsheviks, the Tsar thought he had received the answer to the question of Russia's fate. But he was mistaken. Russia had indeed fallen into the abyss and would remain there for many years, but there was one final piece of the puzzle to be put in place and that piece became Nicky's Christmas gift from the ever faithful Dr. Botkin.

As the Christmas season approached Alix busied herself with the girls knitting socks and making various other gifts to send across the street to the loyal servants. The family was still allowed to receive packages and letters, but first they had to be opened and read by the commandant. Doctor Botkin usually brought in the items they received because he had nearly unfettered access to the family. He could also go to the pharmacy for medical supplies, on walks through the town, and to church. A day earlier, when he was attending services something unexpected happened. A man in a business suit approached and asked if he was Dr. Eugene Botkin, the Tsar's personal physician.

"Who are you and why do you want to know?" Botkin asked him warily.

"My name is Father Walsh and I was sent by the Pope to ascertain the condition of the Imperial family and deliver a letter to the Tsar. You were pointed out to me in the town." Botkin was immediately suspicious because he was aware that the revolutionaries had sent forged messages to the Tsar trying to bait him into making an attempt to escape.

"I can tell by your expression that you have concerns about this," said the priest. "I have met the Tsar privately and he knows me to be a man of integrity. I know because of the situation that I cannot approach him directly and that is why I am appealing to you. But to ease your concerns let me give you my hotel and room number. You can speak to the Tsar and if he approves I will put the letter in your hands. I assure you he will be most anxious to receive it."

Botkin nodded curtly and walked off. Later that day he had the opportunity to speak to Nicholas and was surprised at his enthusiastic response to the news of Father Walsh's presence in Tobolsk . "Eugene I think I have misinterpreted recent events and I expect that the information in this letter will make everything clear at last. Please contact Father Walsh first thing in the morning and bring me the letter. Botkin did as the Tsar directed and the next morning met with Father Walsh at his hotel. The priest gave him an envelope which the doctor concealed in his coat. The two men exchanged pleasantries and then shook hands. The doctor did not want his absence to be noticed so he made a quick stop at the pharmacy, as he often did, and then returned to the compound.

When he arrived back at the mansion Botkin went immediately to Tsar's room and knocked on the door. "Your Imperial Highness, I am here for your check-up." The guard standing nearby scowled at him and then reluctantly opened the door.

"Remember Doctor he is merely Nicholas Romanov, enemy of the people and nothing more," said the sentry. Botkin walked into the room and the guard slammed the door behind him. The guards were inconsistent; some closed doors others left them opened, so the family never felt as if they had any privacy. Botkin quickly explained what had happened at the hotel and gave Nicholas the note.

"Maybe you should wait to read it," suggested Doctor Botkin. "That guard may burst in here any moment and make off with it."

"I do not believe I have the patience to wait," said Nicholas. "And what if something happens and I am unable to read it later. I will have to take my chances and look at it now. And by the way, from this moment on you are no longer to address me by any of my old titles."

Botkin started to object but Nicholas cut him off.

"No, you must not risk using these titles. All it does is antagonize the guards and we have enough problems with them as it is," said Nicholas

"You are right, of course," Botkin acknowledged. He turned and walked out of the room and closed the door. He intended to engage the guard in conversation in the hope that a short respite would give Nicholas the time he needed. Back in the room, Nicholas had quickly and excitedly opened the plain envelope. There was no letterhead or signature, but Nicholas knew who it was from. It consisted of only a few words, but they were the words he had been longing to see. It read,

This is your nation's fate. In the end, Russia will be converted and there will be a time of peace."

Nicholas bowed his head and he held the paper to his heart. "Thank you God, thank you," he whispered. In his mind the future success of the *Masquerade* was confirmed. He opened the paper one more time to look at the words and a profound sense of peace came over him. He walked over to the fireplace and threw the envelope and paper in and watched until the fire had consumed it all. Strangely, as if God had intervened, the last word to disappear from the page was "peace."

Everything he could do had been accomplished and Nicholas became resigned to his situation. Through the long winter months he was a rock who gave his family the strength and courage they needed to survive their ordeal. Finally the long days of darkness gave way to the beginnings of spring and almost before they knew it April was upon them. Alexei spent a good part of his days with his new sisters for he had come to look upon them as family and enjoyed their company. One day he was playing a card game with the three older girls, and Franny walked into the room. "I have just overheard some disturbing news," she said.

"What is it?" Alexei asked with concern.

"The soldiers are planning to take papa away," she replied. "There is talk that they will move him in a day or so to Moscow for trial."

"Then I will accompany him," said Alexei.

"No, they said they will take only him," said Franny.

"We have to do something," said Dalida. If they change their mind and allow someone to go with him, I will volunteer. Remember, I may be a Grand Duchess on the outside, but inside I am still a loyal soldier."

"Yes, I think that is a good idea," said Franny. "You are also very strong and that may come in handy."

"It is better if they do not take my father at all," said Alexei. "I think I have a way to prevent it."

"What is it," asked the girls?

"I cannot say, because it must seem a surprise to everyone," he said.

That evening the boy brought his sled from outside and placed it at the top of the stairs leading to the second story. He sat on it and pushed himself off and the sled went hurtling down the stairs. When the front tip of the left runner caught on a step the sled flipped forward and Alexei went tumbling to the bottom. The girls came running out of their room and Franny screamed when she saw Alexei's motionless body lying at the bottom of the stairs. The commotion caused Nicholas and Alexandra to come out of their room and when Alix saw her son she nearly fainted. She gasped and hurried down the stairs behind Nicholas. The Tsar picked Alexei up in his arms and Alix took a handkerchief out of her pocket. She wiped the blood from his mouth and nose and kissed his forehead. Alexei stirred.

"Why did you do such a foolish thing?" asked Nicholas, as he shook his head.

Alexei opened his eyes and whispered; "Now papa they will not be able to take you away from here, when your son is so ill." With that he lost consciousness. The distraught parents, with tears streaming down their faces brought Alexei to his room and placed him on the bed. Doctors Botkin and Derevenko were called for and the Commandant of the guard was informed. The three arrived at the same time and were shocked at the condition of the boy. The Commandant walked over to Nicholas. "We will delay your leaving until the day after tomorrow, and when the time comes you may bring whom you wish with you. Let me know who you want so I can arrange transportation," he said and left the room. The Doctors immediately tended to Alexei but he was in a terrible state. "Botkin, don't we still have the ingredients to make his special tea?" Nicholas asked.

"No sir," said Botkin. "Without my knowledge, the soldiers confiscated my bag with the ingredients. It is possible that I can find some of them here in town. The sassafras is readily available, but some of the more exotic herbs may not be."

"Do you remember the formula," asked Nicholas?

"I do," said Alix. "I will write it down." Botkin turned to Doctor Derevenko.

"You stay with the Tsarevitch and I will go into town for the ingredients. I will explain later about this tea." Botkin went into town but as hard as he looked he could find only a few of the necessary items, the sassafras and some of the herbs. He could not find opium in the town and he had to substitute for some of the other items. When he got back to the house, he prepared the tea and prayed that this new mixture would work. Whenever Alexei regained consciousness the two doctors, working in shifts fed the potion to the young boy and although he still writhed in pain, the bleeding and swelling slowly disappeared. Through a process of elimination, the Doctor deduced that it was the sassafras that caused the improvement in the hemophilia but he would never be able to perform the necessary experiments to verify this medical breakthrough. The secret would go with him to the grave.

The next day in spite of Alexei's illness, the Tsar was informed by his captors that he was being removed to Moscow to stand trial and would be leaving later that day. He appealed to the commandant to allow him to remain until Alexei had fully recovered, but to no avail. Alexandra talked over the situation with Nicky and after much discussion made the choice to travel with her husband and leave her precious sunbeam in the care of Dr. Derevenko and his new sisters. She had promised Nicholas that she would stay by his side and die by his side, if that was to be, and she knew she must go. Nevertheless, she suffered the pain only a mother can truly understand when she had to leave her son behind. Valia, Dalida, and Dr. Botkin accompanied the royal couple along with a few of their faithful friends. Those remaining would follow when Alexei was well enough to travel.

C3&O

Nicholas, and those traveling with the former Tsar, never reached Moscow. The Bolshevik groups in the Urals were among the most independent in all of soviet Russia and the competition to control the fate of the Imperial family was fierce. Vladimir Lenin had placed the disposition of the Tsar and his family in the hands of his henchman, Jacob Sverdlov, who proceeded to play a devious game with the competing groups.

And so it was, that after a journey of nearly two hundred miles in horse-drawn carts Nicholas and his party reached the railhead at Tyumen, supposedly to board the train to Moscow. But the final destination had been changed and after much confusion their captors delivered Nicholas and his companions into the hands of the Ural soviet in Ekaterinburg. When the train pulled into a secondary depot a few miles from the main station, in order to avoid an angry mob, the Tsar, his wife and daughter were receipted for like cattle and then, along with the others, were whisked away to the Ipatiev house which had been requisitioned to serve as their new prison. It was the same imposing home that Olga and Maria had noticed when they passed through the town months earlier, on their way to Omsk. The noble and ever faithful Valia was detained at the station when it was determined he was carrying a large sum of money. He was murdered by the Bolsheviks a few days later, the first of many to die for his loyalty to the Tsar. Nicky and Alix never learned of his fate and were spared the sorrow of his loss.

Three weeks later, amidst much joy and exhilaration, the rest of the "family" arrived and were reunited with Nicholas, Alix, and Dalida. The excitement wore off soon enough, however, because the conditions of their confinement were much harsher than those they had experienced up to now. For one thing there was less room for the family and retainers in the house and not much more in the way of an exercise yard. Here there would be no long walks through the town to church. The fence was so high they could not see over the top and the townspeople were prohibited from peeking at the famous family. Now they were truly prisoners.

A day or two after the happy reunion the two oldest girls were out walking in what they referred to as the garden. The melting winter snows had turned it into a muddy quagmire but after days of traveling they were glad of the opportunity to stretch their legs, breathe some fresh air and relieve the boredom of the house. Except for the short periods allowed daily for exercise they were locked into the second floor of the house with all the windows nailed shut and the glass painted over. The two girls strolled arm in arm and smiled pleasantly at the guards as they passed by. They had gone only a few paces past the guard post when one of the sentries spoke up.

"Ekaterina, is that you?"

Instinctively the young woman stiffened when she heard her real name spoken aloud for the first time in many months. However, she quickly recovered and continued to walk on with her companion. She prayed that her reaction had gone unnoticed but both she and Helena were extremely worried that somehow they had been exposed. They finished their walk and returned to the house as calmly as they could, but their stomachs were churning with suppressed emotion.

The guard, whose name was Ivan Petrov, continued staring after the young women for some time, confusion evident on his face. His companion was amused and made light of the encounter. "Are you insane?" he asked. "Who is this Ekaterina of whom you speak? All I see is two of our prisoners out for a stroll although I admit I do not know which one is which. What were you thinking?"

"You are correct Paul; of course it is the Tsar's daughters. It is that just for a moment, maybe it was the light or something, the oldest girl looked like someone I knew a long time ago. I know it sounds crazy."

"Crazy is an understatement. How could it be anybody but the Tsar's daughter? They have been under arrest for over a year."

Ivan nodded in agreement but he could not shake the thought that somehow he knew the young woman who had just passed by. Many years ago, before the war, he had been in love with a young girl named Ekaterina but her family died from influenza and she moved from their village. He had never seen her again but this woman looked so familiar that the memories flooded back. The incident continued to plague him but he had to admit there was no logical explanation for what must be a simple coincidence.

The Grand Duchesses returned to the second floor and as soon as possible Ekaterina reported what had happened to Nicholas. He understood her concern but assured her that as long as she did not slip out of her role, no one would doubt she was his daughter. The Tsar and his family were unaware that rumors had surfaced that the prisoners in the Ipatiev house were all impostors and not the real Imperial family. The whole notion was preposterous and it was just as well Nicholas and the family did not know of them for it might have affected their ability to act normally. But a rumor repeated often enough takes on a life of its own and before long the authorities in Moscow heard of it. Soon strident voices wishing to know what was going on became more numerous. Lenin knew there was no validity to these rumors. He received weekly reports on the status of the Imperial family and he knew they had been under arrest since the Tsar abdicated. It was an absurd situation but he knew he must take action to dispel these rumors once and for all. He therefore decided to send to Ekaterinburg the only man in his administration who could put an end to these insane theories once and for all. Two days later, Ivan Rakyovich, the only Bolshevik who had ever interacted personally with the Tsar's family, was on his way east to the Urals. He was to investigate the rumors, make a determination, and report personally to Lenin upon his return. A report would be filed and a public statement issued.

About a week after the incident in the garden, the guards were called to a meeting by the Commandant, Alexander Avdayev. He informed them that Moscow was sending an inspector to verify the identity of the Imperial Family. "Apparently the leadership is reacting to the ridiculous rumors that have been circulating about our prisoners. I advise you to treat this visit seriously because, as you well know, everything this inspector sees will be reported back to Lenin, himself."

"Hey Ivan, maybe you are on to something after all," joked Paul.

"I told you it was nothing, a mistake," said Ivan.

"You two in the back, what are you mumbling about?" Avdayev asked.

"Ivan thinks he knows one of the Grand Duchesses," Paul Kotlov replied. Ivan just shook his head at his friend's finger pointing.

"Well, it is no matter, the expert will be here tomorrow, and we will know for certain at that point. Do not discuss this among the townspeople. Is that clear?"

"Yes sir," shouted the detachment which was then dismissed.

The next day the guards ordered the Imperial family to gather in the drawing room but refused to answer any questions as to the reason for this break in the routine of their confinement. When they were all assembled the guard left to inform the Commandant the family was ready. The Tsar and his wife sat quietly with Alexei and the Grand Duchesses and after what seemed an interminable wait, Commandant Avdayev entered the room followed by Ivan Rakyovich. Alix gasped when she saw him but quickly recovered. The reason they were all together in this room was now obvious but before Avdayev could make an introduction the irrepressible Franny jumped up, ran over to Rakyovich and asked, "Are you here to instruct us again Monsieur? I so loved your classes." The tense atmosphere was instantly dispelled and the other girls went over to greet him. Avdayev ordered everyone back to their seats. Rakyovich walked around the room and examined each of the girls in turn without speaking a word. He nodded at Avdayev and the two turned and walked out of the room.

"Well that was very odd," said Ekaterina.

"I agree but we will not talk of this. They are evidently confirming our identities, so the *Masquerade* must be working, but as you know these walls have ears and we would not want to make a slip," said the Tsar. The group dispersed and went back to what they were doing.

The Commandant's office was located on the second floor of the house, opposite the family quarters, and Avdayev and Rakyovich immediately retired there. "Well, out with it man. What do you think?"

"This is ridiculous. There can be no question that these women are anyone other than the Grand Duchesses. I spent several hours a day with them over a two week period and I assure you I could not be easily misled. I absolutely confirm that the young women who I just observed were the ones I taught in Tsarskoe Selo. I can also attest that Alexandra is the former empress although I must say she has aged somewhat. There can be no doubt. I am sure of their identity," said Rakyovich. "I cannot vouch for the former Tsar and his son since they were not at the palace when I was there, but as far as I am concerned it is beyond belief to suggest anyone in that room was an impostor."

"It is as I expected," said Avdayev. "I hope your report will put an end to these silly rumors."

"My reports only contain the truth. You will receive a copy in several weeks but I have no objection if you wish to publicize my findings." The two men shook hands and Rakyovich left to catch his train. His report squelched the rumors and no more was said about the identity of the Imperial family. Everyone was satisfied with the results except Ivan Petrov. The more he saw of the Grand Duchess Olga, the more he was convinced she was his lost love, but he knew there was no way to prove his theory. And even if he could; to what purpose. It would only put Ekaterina in danger, which was something he would never do.

The summer heat intensified as June came and went and conditions at the Ipatiev house became almost unbearable. With the windows sealed the family's small suite of rooms were sweltering and everyone was on edge. The constant presence of the guards and the requirement that all doors remain open made it impossible to discuss anything that might relate to their situation. They received no news and were kept in the dark about the war, the revolution and anything else that was occurring outside the fence of their prison. It was only late at night that Nicky and Alix could risk discussing anything and they had to whisper quietly in the dark, in French. Their main concern had been to somehow devise an escape plan for the girls but they had lost hope after the move to Ekaterinburg; the security was just too tight. This night, as they lay in bed, Nicky wondered aloud whether he should somehow alert the impostors to the fact they might have to share his martyrdom.

"I just do not know darling. I think we should leave it be for now. I am sure they already know and dwelling on it will just make it worse."

"Maybe you are correct but I just want to do what is right. It was never my intention that anything would happen to these girls."

"I know that and so do they. They honor and respect you and, like us, are willing to give their lives for Russia."

Nicky kissed his beloved wife goodnight and they fell asleep in one another's arms. The one consolation of the Tsar's captivity was his beloved Sunny. Her spirituality now gave comfort to them all and in spite of her infirmity she inspired them to remain strong. She insisted they stick to a schedule and the younger ones continued their lessons while she and the older girls worked industriously on various handicrafts. They participated in daily prayers and each night, for their entertainment Nicholas would read from a novel.

The month of July brought new changes with it. Commandant Avdayev was abruptly removed and replaced by Yakov Yurovsky. He seemed to the family to be a hardened Bolshevik of the worst kind. The slackest of the sentries were replaced and the guard unit began to act in a more professional manner. The Imperial family was concerned by these changes but by now they knew better than to express objections. The tension mounted each day as more and more changes took place. Alexei's companion, Seaman Nagorny, who had cared for him ever since they left Tsarskoe Selo and had willingly followed them into captivity, was removed from the Ipatiev house. Once away from the house he was stood against a wall and shot. Yurovsky met often with the family and although he was polite there was no deference in his manner and he seemed to take delight in refusing the Tsar's requests for better conditions.

Very late on the night of July 16th, a commotion started on the second floor as guards pounded on the doors and barked out commands. "Wake up, wake up," they shouted into the family quarters. "You must be downstairs in thirty minutes. Do not bring anything with you." In spite of the entreaties of the Tsar they gave no reason for this rude awakening. Not withstanding the guards urging, the group moved slowly as it struggled to come awake and get dressed. "Maybe we are being moved to a new location," whispered Alix. The Tsar nodded but he really believed something more sinister was planned. However, he had heard rumors from the guards that forces from what had become known as the White army were approaching the area. If they were almost to Ekaterinburg then that could explain the need to hurry. Once they were all dressed and assembled in the drawing room they were directed to go down the stairs to the basement.

Nicky lifted Alexei into his arms in order to carry him down the stairs. The weight of the young boy in the Tsar's arms forced him to move carefully as he made his way down the dimly lit stairway. Alix followed with the four girls and though their faces were obscured in the dim light Nicholas was aware of the identity of each of them. Dr. Botkin and the remaining three retainers, the cook, the maid, and the footman, Alexei Trupp, followed in single file. As they entered the room a sense of foreboding overwhelmed the Tsar. Except for two chairs at the far end, the room was empty. Like a magnet he was inexorably drawn to one of the chairs and as he sat down in it the boy in his arms woke up. The child looked around sleepily and said "Papa, please let me stand at your side." The Tsar acquiesced reluctantly. The Empress sat in the other chair and the girls stood behind with the servants and Dr. Botkin. They waited patiently in the unnerving silence. Was this to be their moment of martyrdom Nicholas wondered? He reached out and clasped his wife's hand and gently squeezed it. He looked at her with all the love he had in his heart and hoped that his eyes conveyed what words could not, at this moment, adequately express. She smiled back, the sweet gentle smile that he had fallen in love with and for a brief moment they were transported to the day they had first met.

He then turned in his chair to face the young women that had become like daughters to him. In spite of all the hardships they had endured not once did they express the wish to give up. He raised his hand and blessed them. One by one they took his hand and kissed it. Again no one spoke but their expressions all spoke volumes.

Outside the basement, in the guard's day room, Yurovsky had gathered a contingent of men for his special purpose. Each was handed a revolver or pistol and given their instructions. Ivan Petrov realized at this moment that he had come to a fateful decision. He walked forward, laid his pistol on the table, and spoke loudly and clearly, "I will have no part in this." Much to his surprise his friend Paul Kotlov laid his weapon down as well. As they turned to leave Yurovsky ordered them to stop and remain in the room. "I will talk to you about this later."

For the group in the room next door, the wait was interminable but eventually the sound of boots could be heard and the double doors burst open to admit a group of unwashed, foul-smelling men who filed in and stood before them. Yurovsky walked forward, bent over the Tsar, and whispered into his ear, "these are not your daughters."

"What? What?" said Nicholas as he tried to stand up, but Yurovsky drew his revolver and struck the Tsar on the side of the head. The room closed in upon the former sovereign and he lost consciousness and fell to the floor.

෴

It was nearly 3:00 A.M. when the Fiat truck cleared the suburbs of Ekaterinburg and headed out the road that led into the Koptyaki Forest. The old truck had not been designed to carry such a heavy load and it really was not up to the task. There were continuous delays when the engine overheated and had to be cooled down. The condition of the road deteriorated and the men had to get out frequently and push the truck clear of ruts and holes. Several hours passed before it finally turned north onto a seldom used track that led to some abandoned mines. In a matter of minutes the vehicle became completely bogged down, the engine hopelessly overheated. The driver of the truck was ordered to remain behind while the others went ahead to search for a grave site. A damp fog swirled around the vehicle and like most superstitious men the driver felt a shiver of fear as he considered the dead bodies lying in the truck bed behind him. As the wait grew longer he became more and more apprehensive until finally the unnerving silence became unbearable and he climbed out of the cab. He walked to the front of the Fiat in hopes of seeing the others returning, but there was only silence. The fog became thicker and he could barely see five feet. He was so wrapped up in his own fears he was oblivious to the fact that in the back of the truck there was something going on. A ghostly figure struggled to free itself from the entangling arms and legs and finally succeeding, slipped over the open tailgate and staggered off into the forest. A minute later a second figure followed and disappeared into the mist.

A few days later, the White Army broke through and captured Ekaterinburg. The Commanding General and his officers had hoped to find the Tsar and his family when the city was taken. Instead they found a bloodstained room in the basement of the Ipatiev house and in the abandoned guard room next door the bodies of two young men, each shot in the back of the head. It would be years before "The House of Special Purpose" would give up its secrets.

Chapter 46

June 1922 - Yokohama, Japan. In the months following the events at Ekaterinburg, Russia slid rapidly into the chaos of civil war. In 1918 the Americans, British, and Japanese occupied the port city of Vladivostok in order to guarantee access to the terminus of the Trans-Siberian Railway. Refugees from all over Russia began to make their way eastward in the hope of escaping the fighting and reaching safety in the city, and its population soon took on an international flavor. Prince Kanin could look back over the past five years with a sense of gratification, satisfied in the knowledge that all their preparation had yielded the desired results. The unplanned arrival of Olga and Maria was fortuitous because it allowed the prince to make arrangements for their safety long before the flood of refugees ensued. It was the solution that he had initially recommended to the Tsar and some higher power had evidently intervened to make it all come together.

Although he allowed them to put aside their disguises as nuns the prince felt it necessary to keep all four women somewhat isolated, at least initially. The original plan had called for Olga and Maria to go to Moscow and then to the convent in Warsaw but that fell apart when Ella changed the arrangements and sent them to Omsk, and ultimately, Japan. When they arrived in Yokohama, Kanin had them put up in a home belonging to one of his most loyal retainers and there they began to sharpen their language skills and submerge themselves in the local culture. The prince had attempted to get them to Poland in the past, but with that newly created nation involved in border disputes and wars with a number of countries, including Soviet Russia, he decided to wait until things were more settled, before sending Olga and Maria there.

Tatiana and Anastasia, had reached their destination a few weeks later and continued with the original plan. They took up residence in the convent and orphanage complex where Tatiana's nursing skills were much appreciated. Tatiana had dyed her hair jet black and because of her oriental looks, she often passed for a Japanese. Of all the girls, Anastasia had the most difficult time adjusting to her new surroundings. She longed for the independence fluency in Japanese would give her so she concentrated on learning the language as quickly as possible. She also helped out by teaching English to the nuns and lay staff at the orphanage. Prince Kanin had insisted that the four sisters not get together in public and that they use discretion when they gathered for one of their infrequent private meetings. Olga and Maria occasionally came to the orphanage to play with the children and bring them treats and toys and it was during these visits that they were able to steal some time together.

But for the most part they saw little of each other and it saddened the two pairs of sisters that they could not be together more often. They were living so close to one another and yet it was as if they were separated by many miles. Prince Kanin maintained that their father had never wanted them all together and though the change in plan had put them in the same city he was determined to adhere as much as possible to the Tsar's wishes.

In the five years they resided in Yokohama all four Grand Duchesses mastered the language and eventually felt less like strangers in a foreign land. They did not stand out in a crowd particularly, because the city was teeming with people of many different nationalities. At this time many Polish exiles had made the trek across Siberia and on to Japan, hoping one day to finally return to their country. The new Polish government had established a consulate in Tokyo and Prince Kanin had been able to get authentic documents for Olga and Maria so they were able to retain their original Polish names and identities. When the time came, the two girls would have the documents they needed to make their way to Poland as legitimate citizens.

The Port of Yokohama had been opened to trade in the middle of the last century and in 1920 the Japanese began to commemorate the event with a yearly celebration. And so, in the fifth year of their sojourn in Japan, Olga and Maria could be found strolling through the streets of the city, taking in the sights and generally enjoying the revelry of this, the third annual festival. Brightly colored streamers decorated the stalls of the various vendors who were selling everything from kimonos and fans to traditionally dressed dolls and all types of lacquer ware. Many food stalls were set up as well, and customers could sample food from all over Japan. Boat races were scheduled for later in the day and that evening there was to be a fireworks display that promised to be breathtaking. The two young women walked along examining with curiosity the wide variety of items being offered for sale. They eventually stopped at one of the food vendors to sample some delicacies. Living in a Japanese home, as they were, they had by necessity come to enjoy the food, and were always willing to try new dishes. .

Maria stopped at a food stall. "Olga, have you tried sashimi?"

"No, not yet. What is it?"

"It is raw seafood dipped in a special sauce," answered Maria. "It is quite delicious."

"I will try a taste of yours," said Olga. Maria ordered a serving and paid the vendor. By now she was quite proficient with chop sticks and deftly removed a morsel which she placed on Olga's tongue.

She chewed it slowly and savored the delicate taste. "It is quite good," said Olga.

The two continued to walk, nibbling on their snack and looking at the various booths. Flags fluttered and each vendor tried to outdo the others with elaborate displays to draw in the buyer. It was a wonderful feeling to be able to walk freely through the streets, but it had not always been so. An inherent suspicion of foreigners was a cultural phenomena and Prince Kanin was hesitant at first to expose them to a prejudicial environment. But the Prince was quick to learn, as were the four Grand Duchesses, that the fastest way to break down hostility was to be able to communicate and as they became more fluent in the native language he slowly removed restrictions on their movements. Nevertheless, they were always aware that they lived a precarious existence and would be in mortal danger if anyone discovered their true identity. The Prince's theory, which so far had been effective, was that the best place to hide was in plain sight. But now, as the two "Polish refugees" continued their enjoyment of the festivities Olga had the distinct feeling that they were being scrutinized by someone. She stopped and scanned the throng around her, trying to pick out the source of her unease and at the same time alerting Maria of her concern. Finally her glance settled on a man who appeared to be an official of some sort. She had noticed him earlier near the sashimi stand and realized that he must have been following them. When she caught his eye he smiled and began to approach them. For a minute Olga almost panicked but the man did not appear to be especially sinister and she knew that it was unlikely anyone attempting to harm them would do so in such a public forum. Anyway, if it came to that she had in her bag, the small, two-shot derringer the Prince allowed her to carry and she knew how to use it. They waited nervously as the gentleman drew near and seeing this he immediately apologized. "I am sorry if I alarmed you, but I was sent by Prince Kanin. I have been looking for you all morning but just caught sight of you when you stopped at the vendor's booth. I had to be sure I had the right women," he said.

"How did you know we were here and how did you identify us?" asked Olga.

"I went to your residence and was told that you had come to the festival," said the man. "The Prince had provided me with photographs of you and the rest you know. Here is a note from him." Olga opened it and read: *I need to meet with you. The bearer of this message is to be trusted.* It was in Russian and Olga recognized the Prince's seal.

"Would you please come with me now? My car is just over there," the messenger said and pointed to his vehicle.

"Very well, we will accompany you," said Olga. The two women went with him to the car and soon were on their way to a secluded estate outside the city. When they arrived they were escorted to the room where Prince Kanin was waiting. It had been over a year since they had seen him and Olga and Maria greeted him with obvious affection. Their contact had been deliberately curtailed because the Prince was quite well-known and he had not wanted to draw undo attention to the girls by making frequent visits to their lodgings. Nevertheless, he was very involved in their lives and received regular reports on their well-being. As for the Grand Duchesses, they looked upon him as a surrogate father and trusted him implicitly. Anastasia was particularly fond of this kind, efficient man who had such an enormous impact on their lives. The Prince, for his part, had always looked upon the girls as his special responsibility and he took his task very seriously, especially now that so many of the Romanov family had been murdered by the Bolsheviks. But by some mysterious, unspoken agreement the fate of their father, mother and brother was never discussed and the girls had come to accept what they believed was the inevitable outcome of the Tsar's decision to abdicate.

"It is so good to see you again," said Olga.

"Indeed," said the Prince.

"So why have you called us here?" asked Maria.

"Right to the point, as always," said Kanin with a smile. "I have brought you here to inform you that you will be leaving soon for Poland," he said.

"I thought we would be staying in Japan indefinitely," exclaimed Maria, disappointment evident in her voice. "Why do we need to leave? We are safe here."

"Yes, she is right, Prince Kanin" said Olga. "What is the point of us leaving now? We have come to love your country and have adapted to the culture."

"I am sorry this is so sudden but you both know this was always your father's wish," explained Kanin. "I do not know why Poland was the place he chose or why it seemed so important for you two to go there, but that is what he wanted. I have always carried out the Tsar's instructions, just as my Emperor directed me to do, and I am sure you would not want me to go against his wishes now."

"No, of course not," said Olga in dismay, "but it just seems pointless now."

"I would have sent you to Poland much sooner had it not been for the war with Russia," said the prince. "But a peace treaty was signed last March and I have been working on arrangements ever since. Poland is now an independent state and we will be able to carry on with your father's original plan. I have been in communication with the authorities in Poland, specifically a man named Joseph Pilsudski," he said. "We have been negotiating the return of Polish refugees here in Japan and have come to an agreement to begin sending small groups back to Poland.

"Have you informed him of the *Masquerade*?" asked Maria.

"It seemed dangerous to include anyone else, especially someone I did not know personally, and since your father left it to my discretion, I decided against it. You and the others we are sending back will all have authentic documents issued by the Polish consulate in Tokyo so I do not foresee your identity being revealed. I think I made the right decision," he said.

Olga smiled at Prince Kanin. "Sir, when everyone abandoned the Tsar, you came to his aid," she said. "My father trusted you, and my sisters and I trust you as well. Now what is the plan for getting us to Poland?" she asked.

"I believe your sister Tatiana told you about the children from Siberia that she is caring for," said Kanin.

"Yes," said Maria. "We have spoiled them terribly with gifts and candy."

"They are actually Polish orphans," said the Prince

"How sad," said Maria. "Some of them were just babies."

"But what does this have to do with us?" Olga inquired.

"The Japanese government has decided to participate in the actual transportation of refugees, as a humanitarian measure. We have several ships being readied. Some of the orphans will be included in the first group returning to Poland," said Kanin. "There will be several missionaries accompanying them as well as some nurses and doctors and you will travel with them disguised once again as nuns. I understand that this is unexpected, but it is the perfect opportunity and we must take advantage of it."

"What is to become of us when we get to Poland?" asked Maria.

"Initially you will go to the convent in Warsaw at which your father made arrangements so long ago," said Kanin. "You may receive new identities once you arrive but that is something you and the Mother Superior will have to decide together. I have made contact with her through our intermediaries and she is expecting you although it is impossible at this time to know exactly when that will be. I anticipate the trip will take six to eight weeks. When the ship's arrival time is established she will arrange for you to be met and escorted to Warsaw."

"How long must we stay at the convent?" Maria asked.

"Not too long, I would imagine," answered the prince. "Your true identities have been hidden for a long time and that will make it easier for you to move about. You know, of course, that my involvement in your lives is almost at an end and from the day you arrive in Poland you will, by necessity, begin to make your own decisions. I have watched you grow-up and I am convinced you have the maturity to do so, but I must say that I will miss you both very much."

"When are we to leave?" asked Olga.

"In about a week," said Prince Kanin.

"So soon," said Olga. "How are we to pack up our things and be ready in time?"

"I suggest that you depart from here much as you arrived, with one or two pieces of luggage. You do not want to stand out from the other refugees who have so little and I think people would find it odd for a nun to have as many belongings as you both have managed to accumulate. Those items will be packed and delivered to the estate in Nagasaki where your sisters will eventually reside. By the way, I have arranged for you to meet with them one last time. In three days a car will pick you up and bring you here. I have planned a private luncheon for the four of you and you can have the whole afternoon together."

"Thank you so much Prince Kanin for being our faithful protector and taking care of all these details for us. Please do thank the Emperor for us," said Olga.

"I will see him soon and pass along your regards," said the Prince. "Now I suggest that you go right home and prepare for your trip." Prince Kanin opened the door and called for his driver to take the girls back to their residence.

Apparently the family with which they were staying was aware that someday their guests would leave, so it came as no surprise when the girls arrived home and began to pack. They spent the evening cutting jewels from their undergarments and sewing them into new ones. The habits they would wear were being prepared for them at the convent and they would don them shortly before they departed. The next day two men arrived to pack and move the larger items.

A few days later, as the Prince had promised, a car arrived to take them to the luncheon with their sisters. Olga and Maria were the first to be delivered to the estate and were escorted by Prince Kanin to the special room that had been prepared for them. It was filled with fragrant flowers arranged with typical Japanese artistry. Olga walked over to the table and looked at the plates of elegantly displayed delicacies. Tears filled her eyes as she realized that many of the dishes contained traditional Russian foods that she had not eaten since she left Tsarskoe Selo.

"Come see," Olga called to her sister. Maria came over and was moved to tears as well.

"It is like a little taste of the past," she said.

"Prince Kanin is so kind," said Olga. Just then the door slid back and Tatiana and Anastasia were ushered in by the prince. The four girls welcomed each other with love and obvious affection. When the greetings were concluded the prince turned to Olga and asked "Is everything to your satisfaction?"

"Oh, yes," said Olga. "It was so thoughtful of you to do this for us."

"Then I will leave you for now," said Prince Kanin. "You will have complete privacy and perhaps it would be better Olga, if you tell your sisters the news."

"What news?" asked Anastasia.

"Your sister will explain everything," said Prince Kanin. "I have instructed the staff not to disturb you and I will be back after you have had a long visit."

When the prince departed Olga proceeded to tell her sisters about the imminent departure of herself and Maria for Poland.

"I knew the time would come," said Tatiana. "It was always father's wish."

"I wish I could go with you," said Anastasia. "I dislike it here."

"Do not complain Anastasia, it just makes the parting more difficult," said Olga. "This is how it must be."

"Well, I will be twenty-one years old in a few days and it is about time for me to start making some decisions on my own. I have thought about going on to America," said Anastasia. "Papa did say we might eventually go there. Why not now? I could go on the ship with the two of you and just stay in the United States."

"I support you Anastasia, at least about making decisions," said Olga. "I just do not think this is the right time to strike out on your own. It would undermine the prince's careful planning and dishonor our father's wishes."

"I think we need to do as we were told by father," said Tatiana.

"Yes, I concur," said Maria.

"Please everyone. Let us not spend this time second-guessing a plan that has served us so well," interjected Olga. "Let us enjoy our meal together. It may be the last one for a long time." They all nodded in agreement and knelt around the table and for a while all that could be heard were sighs of delight and satisfaction. After they had sampled small portions of every dish Tatiana got up and retrieved a plate with cookies from a side table. Each of the girls helped themselves. As Maria was eating a cookie, Olga looked over at her and began to laugh.

"What is so funny?" asked Maria.

"Watching you eat that cookie reminded me of the time when you were little and we were having tea with mama and papa," explained Olga. "You asked for a cookie and they refused, so you ran up to the table, snatched one and pushed the whole thing in your mouth. Then you announced defiantly, 'there I ate it all up'. It was so funny but mama was very upset and father had to save you from her wrath." The others laughed as they remembered the incident. They continued to reminisce about days gone by until Anastasia brought them back to the present.

"Do you all remember the pact we made before we left Russia?" she asked.

"Yes, of course," said Olga.

"We will meet at the first World Fair held in France in the decade of the 1930's," said Maria.

"Yes, and we will carry a red rose and meet near the admission gate at noon of the second day of the fair," added Tatiana.

Olga poured heated saki into tiny cups and handed one to each sister. Taking up her own she proposed a toast. "A safe journey to Poland, a happy sojourn in Japan, and a wonderful reunion for all of us, in Paris." They continued to visit until Prince Kanin entered the room about an hour later and announced that it was time to go. The four Grand Duchesses, eyes filled with tears, embraced for the last time. Prince Kanin remained quietly in the background until they were finished. When Tatiana and Anastasia departed, Olga and Maria remained behind to discuss with the prince, the final details of their trip.

A few days later they joined the other expatriates and boarded the ship that was to take them to San Francisco. If they thought their journey from Tsarskoe Selo to Yokohama had been a grand odyssey they were soon to learn what a truly arduous trip entailed. The voyage across the vast Pacific took sixteen days and was miserable from the start. The vessel was crowded and rough weather brought on seasickness. It was days before the inexperienced travelers were able to cope with the rolling motion of the ship. In the meantime the stench from the overworked heads was enough to overcome all but the hardiest sailors. When the ship finally reached San Francisco the refugees were faced with a six day railway crossing of the vast United States. Fortunately arrangements had been made for Polish-American groups to assist along the way and the refugees received an especially warm welcome in Chicago. From there it was on to New York where a ship was waiting to take them on the final stage of their journey. This time the weather co-operated and the voyage across the Atlantic was more comfortable. Still it took nearly twenty days to cross the ocean, transit the North Sea and reach the port of Gdynia on the Baltic coast. Various groups were waiting to take the refugees in hand but the two Grand Duchesses were met by nuns from the convent who immediately escorted them to the station where they all entrained for Warsaw. Two days later they were safely hidden away in the convent and their long journey was over.

Coming as it did on the heels of a truly tiring journey the solitude and peace of the convent seemed, to the young women, like an oasis in the desert. But after a few months Olga began to chaff at the restrictions the monastic life placed on her. Ever since the incident with Dalek, so long ago, she had become a woman of action and the long periods of quiet and prayer went against the grain. She tried to compensate by devoting herself to nursing in the hospital and orphanage but she still felt imprisoned by the convent walls and longed for the day she would be free to leave. Maria on the other hand embraced the religious life. She found great comfort and peace praying in the chapel or participating in the simple chores assigned to her by the Mother Superior.

CRECO

On September 1, 1923, as Tatiana and Anastasia went about their duties at the orphanage in Yokohama, disaster struck the nation of Japan. Tatiana was in the medical ward looking after some children and Anastasia was in her classroom preparing her English lessons for a class later that day when suddenly the ground started to shake violently. The windows in Anastasia's classroom shattered, sending shards of glass across the room and several pieces hit her in the head as she tried to make her way out. Blood began to trickle down her face and into her eyes, making them sting but she managed to retrieve a handkerchief from her pocket and wiped the blood from her eyes. She made it into the hallway just as a huge crack opened up behind her. It was all she could do to maintain her balance and keep from falling into the opening. Earthquakes were a fairly frequent phenomenon in the Far East but Anastasia had never experienced one of this magnitude and she was terrified. As she made her way down the hallway that led to the medical wing, she could hear horrible screams and it seemed to her that this might be the end of the world. The roof was caving in and pieces of the ceiling fell on her, knocking her down several times. In many rooms beams had fallen on the patients and staff and the injured and dying were moaning piteously. "God have mercy on us, please God have mercy on us," Anastasia cried out. And for a moment the tremor ceased, just long enough for her to get all the way to the medical ward where she prayed she would find her sister alive. She entered the ward but was unable to see anything because the plaster from the walls and ceilings had crashed to the floor, causing a thick cloud of dust. The ward was a wreck. Beds that were once neatly lined along either wall were now scattered everywhere. She heard cries for help, but all she could think about was her sister. Anastasia was in such a state that when she called out to her, she forgot herself and used her sister's real name. "Tatiana," she cried out over and over again. She heard a noise just ahead of her and through the haze noticed an overturned bed. Lifting it aside she found a young boy covered in blood. The young woman knelt beside him, carefully lifted his head, and cradled it on her lap, not knowing what else to do. Anastasia tried to ease his pain but could tell by his labored breathing that the poor child was dying. She cried out several times for help, but there was no answer. Everything was in shambles and most people were either badly injured or already dead. She looked back down at the child and realized he had died. Anastasia rose, covered the body with a sheet, and as the dust settled, made her way further into the ward. A hand protruded from under a pile of debris and Anastasia gasped as she recognized the special ring their father had given them years ago. Since arriving in Japan, Tatiana had always worn her ring on her hand. "No, no, it cannot be," Anastasia cried out. Using all her strength she lifted up the heaviest pieces and threw them off to the side, away from her sister's seemingly lifeless body. She shook her sister by the shoulders and said to her. "Please wake up! Do not leave me alone in this strange country," she cried. She sat her sister up and held her in her arms. "Tatiana," begged Anastasia, as she rocked back and forth "this cannot be your destiny, you must not die." After several moments Tatiana's eyelids began to flutter and she regained consciousness. "What has happened here?" asked the older sister in a tired voice, as she surveyed the damage in the hospital. Suddenly she remembered her patients and staggered to her feet but she was dizzy from the blow to her head and nearly fell.

"Please sit down for a moment and let us make sure you are not injured. You were unconscious when I found you," said Anastasia. "The little boy over there has passed away. How many more patients were there?"

"Only two more," said Tatiana wearily. She remained sitting on the floor while Anastasia searched the room for the other two children. Unfortunately they were also among the dead. Tatiana shook her head sadly. "Why did this have to happen? I do not even know where to begin."

"I think we should try to find Mother Superior," suggested Anastasia, "she will know what to do."

"Very well," said Tatiana, "but we must help anyone we meet along the way as best we can. Let us gather as many medical supplies as we can carry and make our way to the convent." The convent was separated from the hospital and orphanage by covered walkways. As the two girls walked out through the doors, they looked around and saw that most of the buildings had sustained serious damage. The convent was damaged, as was the corridor that led to the chapel, but miraculously the church itself was completely intact. Tatiana and Anastasia carefully made their way there and when they went inside, they found it filled with injured men, women, and children. The nuns who had not been seriously hurt were tending to the people. The two Grand Duchesses found Mother Superior among the uninjured and tending one of the victims.

"Thank God, you two were not harmed," said the nun.

"I fear I have a slight concussion but my sister got through it with just a few scratches. We brought some medical supplies from the clinic," she said, as she began to unload the bag.

"Excellent," said the Mother Superior, "we are in great need. I will send some of these men over to retrieve more. The convent gardener and handyman have been bringing the injured into the church since it sustained the least damage. And there is the possibility of another shock.," she explained. "The dead, we will have to tend to later."

"I think my sister and I should go and help find the injured," said Tatiana.

"No," said the Mother Superior, "you must stay here in the church where it is relatively safe, and we can certainly use your help."

"As you wish, Mother," said Tatiana. The two women immediately began to tend to patients. Although Anastasia had sponsored her own hospital in Russia during the war, and had spent many hours visiting wounded soldiers, she had no formal nurse's training and had to rely on Tatiana to tell her what to do. Food was salvaged from the kitchen and brought over to the church as well as blankets and any other items that could be useful. There continued to be slight tremors that frightened everyone but as the hours passed it seemed the worst was over.

Two days later an automobile carrying Prince Kanin arrived at the entrance to the courtyard of the convent. He had driven through the city to survey the damage so he could give an assessment to the Emperor. The devastation was overwhelming but the Japanese, in their typically stoic fashion, were already hard at work digging out from under the effects of the catastrophe. However, despite his concern for the plight of his countrymen, his primary mission was to ascertain the whereabouts and condition of the Grand Duchesses. He stepped down from the car and made his way to the chapel which seemed to be the center of activity. He was quite worried because after all, he had given his word to the Tsar of Russia, on behalf of the Emperor, that he would look after any of his children who came to Japan. He knew that logically he could not be held responsible if they were killed in an earthquake, but the Japanese did not think that way, and the debt that the Emperor felt Japan owed the Tsar would still be unpaid if anything had happened to them. He was, therefore, greatly relieved to find the girls in the church alive and, for the most part, unscathed. He approached Tatiana and touched her on the shoulder. She turned around to see the familiar face of the prince.

"Prince Kanin," said Tatiana, "what are you doing here in Yokohama? You were not here during the earthquake were you?"

"No, I was fortunate in that respect," he replied. "I was sent by the Emperor for two reasons. One was to survey the damage and the other to verify you were both safe. He motioned to Anastasia to join them. "I realize this is bad timing but the moment has come to bring you away from Yokohama and send you to Nagasaki. I was there insuring everything is ready for your arrival, when I received word from the Emperor about the quake. He was quite worried that something might have happened to the two of you," said the Prince.

"I appreciate his concern, as well as yours," said Tatiana, "but I cannot just leave this place with all these poor souls suffering and dying, while I go live in luxury."

"You are as stubborn as your other two sisters," answered Kanin with a smile on his face. "As you know they did not want to leave Japan. I had to convince them that it was your father's wish and it must be carried out."

"I understand that," responded Tatiana, "but could we not postpone leaving for a few days?"

"What difference will a few days make? It will take months, if not years to repair the damage. I can appreciate your desire to help, but the devastation is beyond belief. The sooner I get the two of you to Nagasaki, the sooner I can come back here and work on the relief effort. So any hesitation on your part will cause a delay in bringing assistance to these people."

Tatiana reluctantly conceded that the prince was right. "Most of our things have been destroyed but we were able to retrieve our valuables."

"That is all you will need. Everything you could possibly want is ready for you in Nagasaki, but we will stop on the way to purchase any essentials you might need on the trip."

"When do we leave?" asked Anastasia.

"As soon as you can pack your things," said the Prince. "I will drive you to the train station in Nagoya, which is just a few hours away by car. The train will take you to Hiroshima where you will board the ferry to Nagasaki," he said. "All the arrangements are made. I have brought the couple who are in charge of maintaining your new home with me and they will escort you to the estate. And of course my security people will be in the background if there should be a need. Now, may I suggest you get your things together and let us be off. While you are getting ready I will explain everything to Mother Superior."

"Very well, dear friend," said Tatiana, "but may we please have a few moments to say goodbye. After all this has been our home for many years now." Prince Kanin nodded and Tatiana and Anastasia went to gather their things and bid farewell to the community. As she looked at the faces of those she had lived and worked with for so many years Tatiana felt an overwhelming sense of guilt triggered by the notion that she was deserting them in a time of need. Grand Duchess Tatiana was one of those rare persons of high station who genuinely feel a strong love and affection for those less fortunate than themselves. In this sense she had much in common with her sister Maria who was also quick to show compassion to the less fortunate. Anastasia, of course, felt differently and although she felt sorry for the residents of Yokohama, she was happy to be leaving. After the last of the farewells they joined Prince Kanin and his people in the car and set off.

The trip itself was uneventful and they reached the estate in Nagasaki with no difficulty or delay. Tatiana immediately fell in love with her new home but it was not so for Anastasia. The walled estate was too far outside the city for them to walk into town and experience the vitality and international flavor of the port. And with their nursing and teaching skills no longer being utilized the days, at least for Anastasia, seemed protracted and boring. She longed for parties, adventures and dare she think of it, love, and marriage. But how was she ever to find it in this beautiful, quiet oasis devoid of any young people her own age?

About a week later, the two sisters were in the garden of their estate, hidden from prying eyes by the wall that surrounded the compound. Tatiana stood at an easel working conscientiously on a watercolor landscape while Anastasia sat by her attempting to compose a haiku. "Tatiana, is this what our life is to be, a life of seclusion and boredom?"

"Oh Anastasia, how can you be so unhappy in such a beautiful place? We should be grateful we are alive and safe."

"You misunderstand me. I am not ungrateful. I recognize the sacrifices that have been made by so many to bring us to this point in our lives. It is just that sometimes I miss what our lives might have been like had the revolution not occurred."

Tatiana leaned down and kissed her forehead and said wistfully, "I do too, but our lives here have many consolations." Both women turned back to their work. A gentle breeze ruffled their hair bringing with it the scent of flowers from the garden. Their thoughts turned, as they often did, to their sisters, thousands of miles away, and they both wondered if the weather in Poland could match the beauty of this autumn day in southern Japan.

CRYO

And so the four Grand Duchesses settled in to their new way of life, waiting for the day when they would be free to resume a normal existence. For Maria and Tatiana, a feeling of contentment filled them and they embraced their new surroundings. Olga and Anastasia on the other hand were filled with a sense of adventure and they chaffed at the limitations their seclusion forced on them. The sisters coped with their isolation in different ways, but they were all conscious that this was just a new stage in their lives. The one thing they all had in common was the desire to be together one day in Paris.

But they were unaware that the *Masquerade* would continue to affect them in ways they could not foresee.

Epilogue

It all began with a prophecy contained in a short letter, on a paper yellowed with age and like all prophecy it required the basic elements of belief and then acceptance. It is a fact of life that not everyone is blessed with the faith to recognize the truth of such a phenomenon but often times individuals are willing to act on someone else's faith even if they, themselves, remain somewhat skeptical. The power of such faith cannot and should not be underestimated for it is surely a powerful force even for those who do not understand its impact on other persons. This collective trust, based on one individual's spiritual experience, was what made the *Masquerade* a viable plan.

So when Saint Serafim of Sarov put his pen to paper so many years earlier he foresaw that his message would ultimately be accepted by the man to whom it was addressed. It did not matter if others were cynical or disbelieving, it only mattered that Nicholas II, Tsar of Russia, had the strength and will to convince others to support him regardless of their occasional lack of faith. It appeared that he was successful.

Of course, much depended on the ability of the messenger to deliver the message and in selecting Elena Motivilov, Serafim had picked the best possible agent for the task. Elena was not only a woman of faith, but was a visionary in her own right as her prediction of Sergei's murder would bear out. Nicholas accepted her intervention without question.

Nevertheless, there were several perplexing elements in all of this which, as the *Masquerade* had unfolded, remained puzzling. For instance, what was the significance of the seals marked OTMA and why was the fifth seal blank? And who was the mysterious man in white who traveled the world? Perhaps only time would tell and it was possible that in the overall context of the plan that the answers to these questions might never be revealed.

As for the influence of dreams on the Tsar's behavior; they were easy enough to explain. The human race has long accepted the reality of dream motivated action. Had not an angel appeared to Joseph in a dream, warning him of danger? And as a result had he not fled to safety in Egypt? The literature of mankind is filled with such episodes and although Nicholas was by no means a mystic, his deep spirituality certainly made him susceptible to such experiences. It was no surprise to those close to him that the Tsar was willing to act on the guidance he received through this medium.

Thus was the intricate plan conceived, developed, and matured, in some instances at great loss, but always for a noble purpose. And as long as one of the Grand Duchesses remained alive, the guiding hand of Nicholas could be felt, directing in person, *The Tsar's Masquerade.*

CPSIA information can be obtained at www.ICGtesting.com
Printed in the USA
LVOW010216160213

320280LV00001B/25/P